SHORT STO

MONTREAL, CANADA

Copyright by Ben Sperer, Montréal, Québec

All characters, events, names and dates mentioned in these stories are fictitious. Any resemblance with real people or places is purely coincidental and not intended.

Any reproduction or use of these stories in any shape or form is strictly prohibited.

To the three angels in my life:
My Mother, Daisy and Rosette.

PROLOGUE

Given the time and opportunity, I guess most of us like to reflect on events that either happened to us, or could have. We then resolve to commit these products of our memory or imagination to paper "one of these days". Of course "these days" become increasingly elusive during the course of a busy life. And so, we usually enter our mature years with stories and events stashed away in the remote corners of our mind. Sometimes we hit upon them by chance or in association with related circumstances, and if faced with an interested audience, we will bring them to life with the introductory "this reminds me of a story…"

Well, after all these years, I have finally decided to put pen to paper (an obvious metaphor in this computer age) and drag some of these stories from the confines of my mind to the front of your eyes.

I do hope you will enjoy them.

Ben Sperer
Montreal, Winter 2018

TAXI! - 8

THE PEARL - 23

A TRUE STORY - 32

IN MEMORIAM - 35

THE KEY - 42

DIAL "M" FOR ROBBERY - 46

REVENGE - 51

MY BROTHER JERRY - 55

A FRIEND'S ADVICE - 79

THE CONTESSA - (A True Story) - 83

THE COIN - 101

MUSIC, MAESTRO, PLEASE - 124

THE FOOTBALL POOL - 135

LET SLEEPING DOGS LIE - 150

LE PANAMA - 171

BLANCHE - Part I - 178

BLANCHE - Part II - 203

A CANCELLED MEETING - 248

FATHER KNOWS BEST - 258

THE BLIND DATE - 272

PREVENTIVE MEDICINE - 279

AND LIFE GOES ON - 284

THE INHERITANCE - 315

THE VERMONT VACATION - 326

PARTNERS - 338

WHAT A DIFFERENCE A NIGHT MADE - 354

THE SECRET LIFE OF ARCHIE BENSON - 376

A LIFE IN COURT - 390

KARL - 409

THE TWINS - 419

THE FAMILY SECRET - 429

YOLANDA - 465

A PERFECT CRIME? - 499

A STORY OF ART - 514

HAPPY BIRTHDAY - 537

THE ROBBERY - 549

FATHER AND SON - 573

THE EXECUTIVE - 631

TAXI!

This is the amazing story of Michel Galieni, a story revealed in a neatly typewritten manuscript. Its author, my best friend for as long as I can remember, asked me to publish it by submitting it to a leading news service, but only the day after his death. In fact, he kept the manuscript in a safety deposit box of a Paris bank and gave me the key to it.

It is with tears in my eyes and a very heavy heart indeed that I have to report the death of my childhood friend Michel just two days ago. I went to the bank, opened the box and found the manuscript he had mentioned to me.

It is a truly unbelievable story and what is even more amazing is that although throughout the years we shared so many, if not all our innermost feelings and thoughts, he never even uttered a word about the core of all this to me. Thinking of him, now that he is gone, I find it quite amazing that a human being can keep a secret from his closest friend for so many years. But then, I came to realize that a secret is not a secret unless you take it to your grave without sharing it with anyone on earth, and that is what he did.

Here is Michel's story, word for word.

* * *

"Dear Reader,

By the time your eyes come to rest on these lines, mine will be closed forever. I will be dead. "Morto per sempre" as we say in my native land. You see, I am from Corsica, the beautiful island that is inhabited by Italians but belongs to France. In fact, it gave France some of its most famous sons, like Napoleon Bonaparte, President François Coty, and the unforgettable singer Tino Rossi, to name just a few.

My name is Michel Galieni and I am about to tell you the story of my life, or rather a part of it, the part that really matters. As you will read what follows, you will see why you and many others had to wait so long to hear the truth about what happened some thirty-two years before I penned this letter in Paris.

For thirty-two years the Préfecture de Police de Paris, a venerable institution that prides itself as being a world leader in crime detection did not know what really happened on that fateful morning of the 22nd of November 1979 on the rue Gambetta and continued to unfold in later years. Would you believe, dear reader that the Parisian Police still don't know what happened that day, that is, of course, until they read these lines.

So, without further ado, let me lift the curtain, let me turn on the lights - or whatever you prefer to call it – on the amazing story of my life.

* * *

At the time this chain of events started to unfold in 1979 I was a cabdriver in Paris. I drove my own Peugeot which I traded in every three years because, as you can imagine, the wear and tear on taxis is punishing, to say the least.

In fact I had been driving cabs for many years and I made a reasonable, yet far from extravagant living. I was divorced, after I had caught my wife cheating on me not once but twice. "That's it", I told her. "Let's go our different ways. We're just not meant for each other". There were no children, so the separation proceeded smoothly. I left her the flat and most of its contents and moved out. I even agreed to pay her some alimony. In time I learned to adapt to a bachelor's life and coped quite well. Mind you, I had some nice lady friends with whom I spent my free evenings and went on summer vacations, mostly to my native Corsica.

On the morning of the 22nd of November 1979, I left my flat as usual at seven in the morning, walked across the street to take my car from the garage and started work, picking up fares and sometimes joining a line of cabs at taxi stands. By eight o'clock I had already picked up three fares, all for relatively short distances. I had deposited my last customer in front of a shop on the rue Gambetta, and, driving slowly on account of heavy morning traffic, I noticed a middle-aged man running out of a small apartment house. He looked a mess. A real mess. His hair was unkempt, his shirt unbuttoned, his coat was open despite the bitter cold that late November morning. In his hand he held some objects such as a small case, and a bunch of papers which he also clutched tightly under his arm. But what really caught my attention was the man's panicky look and behaviour.
I could notice all this in detail because traffic was almost at a standstill. As I passed this man he frantically waved at me. I stopped immediately and let him in. He literally fell into the backseat and with a highly agitated voice said: "Take me to Saint François hospital as fast as you can. I need to go to the emergency entrance. I am not feeling well at all. Please hurry!" I replied, "Of course, Monsieur, but traffic is very heavy. It may take me at least fifteen minutes to get there. Why didn't you call an ambulance?" "I did", said the man, "but they told me that it would take them fifteen minutes just to get to my place, so I took my chance and grabbed a cab." "Okay", I said. "I will try to take less congested streets." I really tried very hard because the man in the back was moaning and talking to himself, as though being in agony.

We finally reached the hospital. As I stopped in front of the emergency and prepared to help the man out, he tossed a few bills at me, opened the door and ran out into the hospital entrance without even closing the car door. My God, I said to myself, I hope he gets help fast.

Traffic was still heavy so I decided to join the rank of cabs in the hospital yard, where I was fourth in line.

Before looking at the morning paper, I took a glance at the back seat to check that the place was clean, when I noticed a leather pouch or case, about ten by twenty centimetres in size lying on the floor of the car. I figured that the sick man had dropped it. I picked it up and instinctively opened it. What I saw inside were contents that not only took my breath away but that were to have a profound and lasting impact on the rest of my living days.

First of all, there was a French passport made out in the name of Claude Bertholet, then there was an identity card that every French citizen has and also two bank books; each from a different bank. There were also some business cards all indicating the name Bertholet, his address and phone numbers, showing his profession as that of a real estate agent. I was stunned and took a closer look at what I was holding in my hands, when another cab drove onto the line just behind me. The driver stepped out and motioned to me to do the same. "I just dropped off a woman at the emergency entrance right after you", he said. "As I helped her into the lobby I saw the man you had brought, take a few steps and then collapse to the floor like an empty sack. People tried to help him up but he seemed to be motionless. I saw hospital workers rushing to the scene, but I think the man was dead. Well what can you expect in a hospital emergency!"

I said I was sorry to hear that, immediately got back into my seat and drove off because I needed time and quiet to think about what I should do next. I could of course drive back to the hospital and try to return the object to the man, but the words "I think the man is dead" stopped me. I looked again at the documents in front of me.

There were two checking account books from two big banks in Paris. I was amazed at the frequency of transactions during the last two years. Large amounts, like hundreds of thousands of Euros went into or came out of the accounts all the time. This man was obviously a major real estate agent who constantly bought and sold properties, making his payments or receiving them in cash. The balance in one bank account was 2.7 million Euros and 1.8 million Euros in the other.

Then I flipped through his passport. As I did I noticed that the face on the photograph bore a more than casual resemblance to myself. I kept looking into my sunshade mirror and saw that we both had bushy eyebrows, similar face contours and, most importantly, similarly recessed hairlines. With a bit of imagination I really could pass for the man in the photo. Even our ages were similar; both in our early forties.

Then there was his French identity card, the "Carte Nationale d'Indentité Securisée or "CNIS" as it was commonly called bearing a similar photo as in the passport. The signature in both documents was practically the same. A sweeping "C" underlining the name Bertholet in distinct characters.

I looked again at the four documents in front of me and a crazy thought entered my mind. Really crazy. What if I drove home, changed into a business suit; complete with tie and hat? Then I would drive to branches of the two banks other than those that held the accounts just to avoid some employee who might have known Claude Bertholet, I would appear very casual, as though in an often repeated occurrence, sort of utter "here I am again", and withdraw half a million Euros from each bank. I would identify myself with the two documents in hand, sign "C. Bertholet" as per the sample in front of me, say "merci et à la prochaine," and walk out of the banks.

Since Monsieur Bertholet was in a coma only half an hour ago, there was little chance that he has already become aware of the loss of his papers. In fact, he may even be dead by now, going by the cabdriver's observations in the hospital lobby.

But, what if I am caught, my conscience interjected. Well, that is the risk I am taking. I could be arrested in the banks for attempted theft and impersonation. That could well happen, but, I interrupted myself: will any similar opportunity ever come again in the life of Michel Galieni - célèbre inconnu – one of the 15,000 cabdrivers in Paris? No, I answered my own question. This is definitely the once in a lifetime opportunity to lay my hands on a cool million Euros and change my life from A to Z. "Michel", I said aloud, "no", I yelled at myself, "go and do it. If you don't, you will regret it for the rest of your living days."

And I did, exactly as I had planned. Believe it or not, it worked almost perfectly well. One bank paid me out the half million Euros after a detailed scrutiny of all the documents I presented and after one employee said he remembered paying me a similar amount a couple of years ago when I was buying a property in his neighborhood.

The other bank wanted me to talk to the manager who also asked me all sorts of questions for which I fabricated answers on the spur of a moment. But after a few uneasy moments he appeared satisfied and authorized the withdrawal slip.

I stuffed the loot, all in bundled one thousand Euro bills into the attaché case I had taken with me and majestically walked out, flagged a cab and drove to my humble home, one million Euros richer then when I had left it one hour earlier. It was now just about one o'clock in the afternoon.

All this sounds like a fairy-tale, but it's true. Absolutely true. Oh, I almost forgot. Before entering my apartment I stepped into a public phone booth and called the St. François hospital.

"Bonjour", I said to the operator. "I was in the emergency lobby this morning when I saw a man fall to the floor and attendants tried to revive him. He looked like someone I know. Could you tell me how he is doing?" "One minute" answered the girl. Then she came back and said: "I am sorry to inform you that this patient, whose identity we are still trying to determine, died about an hour ago of cardiac arrest." "Oh, I'm sorry, thank you very much, mademoiselle", I said, and hung up.

* * *

When the doctors of the emergency department of St. François hospital confirmed the death of the man who had earlier collapsed in the entrance lobby, they started to fill in the required forms, but to their surprise they were unable to find any identity papers or documents on him that showed his name or address. He had some cash on him, some receipts or stubs, but nothing, absolutely nothing about his identity. The hospital doctors were at a loss and informed the police of this bizarre situation.

"How did the patient arrive at the hospital?" the police asked. No one had any answers other than: presumably by taxi, which then drove off.

The police decided to place an ad in the next morning's papers, requesting anyone who could supply some information about the deceased "inconnu" to come forward.

Well, they were lucky. During the course of the next few hours they received help not from one but from three different sources.

First, there was a call from some people residing in a small apartment house on the rue Gambetta who called the local police station to report an endlessly barking dog in the flat below their own. "A single man named Monsieur Bertholet lives there. He has a dog but we have not seen M. Bertholet since yesterday morning and the dog is probably barking because he is not being taken care of. Please come to investigate", was the message.

Within a short time two policemen arrived at the flat, tried to enter but found the door locked. They forced their way into the flat and found a famished dog barking furiously in a beautifully furnished apartment in utter disarray. They saw some pictures on the wall, sent copies of them to the hospital, which compared them with the deceased man and in short order confirmed that the dead man was indeed one Claude Bertholet.

The second clue came the next day, after the police published a notice in the Paris papers requesting anyone who had information regarding a certain Claude Bertholet to come forward.

The two banks reported that M. Bertholet had visited their branches to withdraw some money. The third response came from a cabdriver who said that while waiting at a taxi stand in front of St. François hospital, he briefly talked to the driver of the cab who had delivered the unfortunate patient to the emergency department. However, he could neither remember the face of the cabdriver, nor his car, or his license number. Their conversation lasted a minute, he told the police, and then the taxi drove off.

The last clue in the case came from a Dr. Jean-Paul Bertholet in Lyon, who told the police that the deceased man was his father and that he was on his way to Paris to take care of the funeral arrangements.

As for the banks, the police asked them when the withdrawals had taken place. When they answered between twelve noon and one o'clock pm, the police asked the hospital about the time of Bertholet's death, which was around eleven in the morning of the 22nd of November.

Thus the police knew that the million Euros were taken by an imposter who had either stolen or found the identity papers of Claude Bertholet. Most probably, they were withdrawn by the taxi driver who drove the patient to the hospital, a supposition that gained credibility by the report from the cabdriver who had briefly spoken to the man who brought Bertholet to the emergency department, but could not remember anything that could shed light on that cabdriver's identity.

Based on all these snippets of information, the police opened a file of this criminal case and assigned an officer to lead the investigation into finding the thief of the million Euro heist. That file bears the date of 22nd November 1979.

Dear Reader, would you believe that thirty years later that file was still open and unchanged because the thief was never caught, thus joining the host of the other dust-gathering "unsolved crime" dossiers in the Paris Préfecture de Police.

*   *   *

To tell you the truth, it took me quite a while to get used to the thought that inside the heavy Chinese vase I had inherited from my parents, lay ten one hundred bill bundles of a thousand Euros each, all neatly wrapped in plastic kitchen pouches. I placed a bunch of artificial flowers on top of the old vase which stood in a corner of my living room. That was to be the secret cache of my heist. I thought that since that vase had always been there it would not attract attention.

For a couple of months I followed the news about the police frantically looking for the thief of the million Euros. They interviewed dozens of people, from neighbours of the dead man to his close friends, to people who were in the emergency hall of the hospital at the time of Bertholet's arrival. They talked to the bank employees who handed over the money to the imposter. They solemnly declared that Monsieur Bertholet presented all required documents to satisfy them of his identity.

But nothing, no clue, no possible lead, absolutely nothing came to light that could help them in their investigation. After several months of fruitless efforts the file of "L'Affaire Bertholet", as some papers had entitled this mystery, was taken out of active circulation and relegated to the semi-graveyard of unsolved crimes.

During the first few months following the incident, I felt very uneasy whenever I saw a policeman which was several times a day what with my crisscrossing the streets of Paris in my cab. I also checked my phone messages, just in case I heard the ominous "Monsieur Michel Galieni, you are wanted at the local police station". But I never heard or saw anything of the sort.

I began to relax and started making plans about how to put the money to good use and how to spend it in a way not likely to attract undue attention.

To be sure, I had already decided to get out of the taxi cab business and buy a shop where cars are serviced and repaired. I knew this trade well enough and was sure that I could be successful. By word of mouth I heard that a small service station in central Paris was up for sale. It did not take long for me to contact the owner who wanted to retire and I bought the shop, which had room for a dozen cars. Of course, I paid in installments spread over time in order not to attract attention with big lump sum payments.

The company I bought was called SERAP, an acronym for "Service, Evaluation, Reparation d'Autos à Paris" and it had established a strong reputation for rapidity, reliability and honesty in the automobile trade.

Well, I worked very hard to maintain and expand that reputation. Over the next three years I enlarged the shop to accommodate sixty cars and I added a great deal of modern equipment as well as highly qualified mechanics. Business was very good and I helped it along by constantly delving into the cache in the Chinese vase to invest in more equipment and staff.

In fact, as I passed the fifth year of my entry into the business, I not only had two repair centres now taking care of some one hundred vehicles but I had also built up a solid reputation for good car maintenance in Paris. SERAP had become a household name.

It was about that time when I received a phone call one day from the office of the Préfet de Police de Paris, the Chief of the Parisian Constabulary. A secretary told me that le Commandant de Castillon would like to see me in his office two days later at nine in the morning. My immediate reaction was "That's it, they found out about my robbery and goodbye to everything!" After a second of panic I managed to say: "Could you tell me why the Préfet wants to see me?" "Of course," she replied with the sweetest of voices: "the Commandant wants to discuss your possible role in taking care of our police vehicles." I heaved a sigh that reverberated throughout my body and said: "Well, Mademoiselle, that is very good news indeed. I shall be there at nine o'clock, and thank you very much."

That conversation with Commandant de Castillon turned out to contain not only a most interesting proposal, but was indeed a turning point in my professional life. What the Chief proposed was for me to head a service centre exclusively dealing with some one thousand of the three thousand or so police cars of Paris. We would start out with my own two shops and gradually add more existing facilities already owned by the police. As well as buying and creating new shops until, within the next two years we would complete the service centre and make it an integral part of the Préfecture de Police. All this under my direction and management, of course, with generous remuneration commensurate with that important position.

I could not believe what I heard, especially when the Chief repeatedly told me that he had considered four other candidates for this high post but what tipped the scale in my favour was my personal reputation of integrity and reliability as evidenced by the many satisfied SERAP customers the police had talked to.

Completely swept off my feet, awed and happy beyond words, I mustered a wide smile and said: "Mon Commandant, I consider this a profound honour. I am sure we will be able to work out a mutually satisfactory agreement. In principle, I am interested, and would like to meet with the responsible department heads as soon as possible to put together the whole project, which, I need not tell you, will become the key centre of my professional life. Mon Commandant, you can count on me!" He got up from his desk, shook hands with me and said: "Monsieur Galieni, permit me to welcome you to the distinguished family of directors in the Police of Paris, the finest in the world, we would like to believe. Congratulations and good luck. My secretary will be in touch with you shortly. Au revoir, Monsieur."

*   *   *

Within days I started chairing meetings at police headquarters with all kinds of officials to prepare the project, lay out the plans and proceed step by step towards the implementation of a service station network for a thousand police cars. A truly grandiose undertaking. But, you know what the most emotional time during these hectic days was: when the Paris police bought my own company as part of the network and paid me handsomely for the acquisition. A business I had created with stolen money and they were still looking for the thief! Believe me, I had the strangest feeling the day the Chief of Police personally handed me the cheque. "Well", I said to myself: "don't they say that life is stranger than fiction?" It is indeed. And this strange feeling which is called "Ironie du Sort" or the "irony of fate" really never left me.

The next years were filled with strenuous days of putting together and managing the huge project. I worked very hard, surrounding myself with the most competent people I could find.

Eventually, I headed, what I was told, was a department that functioned like a giant Swiss watch movement.

The Paris police establishment is a very close-knit group and I soon became a member of the Directorate's inner circle, participating in many policy and administrative meetings which went beyond my own field of interest. In fact, after some eleven years of service, I was appointed a sous-Préfet, an assistant to the Chief of Police, one of three that were part of the Préfecture's top echelon. Of course, with a salary to match the appointment. But what was much more important to me was the smart salute I received from the honour guard in front of the police headquarters every time I entered the building.

* * *

The years went by like a whirlwind. There were hectic times but mostly followed by normal routine days when everything ran according to plan.

Shortly before my sixty-fifth birthday, the Chief called me to his office to say that I had now been in the department for twenty years and it was time for me to retire. In fact, his office had already prepared a big gala party for me which was to include my investiture into the National Police Hall of Fame.

Need I tell you how I felt when the new Chief of Police who had replaced my old friend de Castillon told me all this. I tried to hide the tears that were slowly coming into my eyes.

"Do you agree with all these preparations to honour your well-deserved retirement?" asked the Chief.

"Yes and no", I replied. "What do you mean?" he said. "Well, I agree with celebrating my 65th birthday, but I don't agree with my retirement. If it pleases you, I would like to stay on for another five years. I am in perfect health and I enjoy my work beyond words, and, there are always new projects that need development and attention. In other words, I don't consider my mandate fully accomplished."

The Chief laughed and said: "You must be kidding, but who am I to refuse a good offer? Alright", he replied. "You are on for another five years, but no more. And that is final!" We had a good laugh and parted with a handshake and a hug.

The twenty years of service party was a celebration I will never forget. I sat at the head table right next to the new Chief of Police and the mayor of Paris. Speeches were made describing my accomplishments and dedication to the police administration in general and police car maintenance in particular. I was honoured by the police choir with songs and readings of poetry. It was truly a spectacular event which ended with my own speech thanking everyone and announcing that I would stay on for another five years, which met with applause that I thought would never end.

*   *   *

The next five years passed with much of the same, except that I was appointed Principal Assistant to the Chief of Police. On my uniform and cap there was just one star less than the one worn by the Préfet de Police.

But the real blockbuster came when I finally retired on the anniversary of my twenty-fifth years of service and the Minister of the Interior pinned the Honour Medal of the National Police on my jacket, embraced me and shook hands with the words: "Monsieur Galieni, vous l'avez mérité." This time I let the tears flow freely, especially when the entire attendance rose from their seats and shouted: "Vive Galieni!" In my wildest dreams I could not have imagined a more beautiful ending of a lifelong career at or near the very top of government.

*   *   *

My dear Reader,

Here you have it. The story of my life, and what a life it has been. I wrote this biography in Cannes, on the French Riviera, where the authorities gave me a beautiful and elegant flat overlooking the azure blue Mediterranean Sea, to enjoy for as long as I pleased. A sort of retirement home, for it is part of a larger complex housing retired senior officials and personalities.

To sum it all up: I am a man who started out as a criminal, who, by the way, is still on the loose, and ended up as a decorated and honoured law enforcement personality, finally in pampered retirement.

"Go figure", as they say.

And this, my friends, is the true story of my life.

*   *   *

Well, I read the story not once but twice and I even kept going back to some pages. I could not put it down. But when I finally placed it on the table in front of me, I went over the records of the Paris Préfecture to make sure that none of the officials mentioned in Michel's narrative were still on active duty. I wanted to spare them any embarrassment the publication of Michel's story could cause them.

Only after I found out that they had either passed away or had retired a long time ago, did I fulfill Michel's request by sending the manuscript to a news service, accompanied by a note explaining its origin.

An amazing story, indeed.

*   *   *

THE PEARL

Istanbul in the mid-nineteen-twenties was, beyond any doubt, one of the most exciting places on the European continent. Its magnificent setting across winding waterways had recently provided the background for the historic and convulsive changes brought about by the collapse of the moribund Ottoman Empire and its rapid replacement by the brand new republic forged against all odds by Kemal Atatürk. No wonder that an air of invigorating anticipation and hope lay heavily over the city, causing new businesses and buildings to surface everywhere like sprouting mushrooms.

But another and totally unexpected windfall was also to descend upon the city on the Bosphorus. Almost overnight it became a haven to thousands of Russian emigrés fleeing the establishment of a new order in their country in which there seemed to be no place for them anymore.

In fact, an entire society which had practically dominated every facet of life in Russia had laid down their arms in defeat after a bitter struggle with power-hungry masses emerging from every corner of the country. It was nothing short of the poor taking over from the rich in a violent confrontation in which the latter were left with no choice but to leave or face ruin and even death at the hands of their erstwhile subjects.
And so, running away, some with little more than the clothes on their backs, others holding on to incredible jewels and treasures hidden among their personal belongings, streams of Russians arrived in Istanbul, at the time, still known by its old name of Constantinople.

A short crossing on the Black Sea provided the perfect escape route into an albeit uncertain future, not only because of the very different ethnic and cultural environment they were now facing but because the rest of Europe was also in the throes of severe political upheavals in the aftermath of the First World War.

However, thanks largely to their worldly sophistication and rescued remnants of their former riches, many of the emigrés soon began to open restaurants, private schools and small businesses, often bringing to them the elegance and allure of their bygone lifestyles. Of course there were also those less fortunate who had to provide for themselves and their families by waiting on tables or cleaning homes or tutoring children. Suffice it to say that despite their initial apprehensions and fears no Russian émigrés could be seen panhandling on street corners. Within a few years the vast majority had managed either to integrate into Turkish life or had chosen to travel on further to destinations such as Paris.

* * * * *

Aram Terzian was an Armenian jeweller whose family had owned the same shop in the Grand Bazaar for almost a hundred years. In fact that small store had become their second home. Many a baby had been nursed there by mothers helping out when their husbands were ill or away, while Aram's grandfather had actually died in the store at the ripe old age of ninety-three.

The Grand Bazaar is really one of the largest shopping centers in the world. Opened to the public in 1461, a mere six years after the conquest of the city by the Ottomans, it houses over 3,000 shops and hosts some 400,000 visitors each day.

Aram was busy rearranging the many gold bracelets in the display case in front of him, when a customer entered his store. Aram had never seen this man before, and with his customary smile, asked how he could help him.

"Yes, I hope you can help me" said the stranger, adding: "I have been told that you are an honest and reliable man, Mr. Terzian." "Thank you Sir", replied Aram. "We have been in this business for generations and always try to satisfy the wishes of our customers."

"Well," continued the stranger, "let us see if you can satisfy my wishes, but first let me introduce myself. I am Igor Yousoupov, to be precise, Prince Igor Yousoupov". "Oh", interrupted Aram, "What an honour indeed to welcome you to my humble store. Please sit down and tell me what you need, Prince Igor. I am at your service."

The visitor smiled benignly and proceeded to take out of his pocket a small box which he opened very gently. In it, on a black velvet cushion, lay a pearl. But it was not an ordinary one. It was two perfectly shaped pearls linked or fused together like a figure-eight, about four centimeters in size. Aram had never seen anything of that kind. Noticing his wide-eyed expression, the visitor took the pearl out and handed it to Aram. "Please inspect it carefully," he said. Aram took out his loupe, and, moving under a strong light, started to look at the object with professional scrutiny. After a few minutes he turned to the visitor and said: "Well, Prince, all I can say is that this jewel is one hundred percent genuine; two absolutely perfect pearls naturally fused to look like the curves of a beautiful lady, if I may say so, and to be honest I have never seen a likeness of it, never. Therefore, I cannot estimate its value."

"Oh, no…no", interjected the visitor amid a burst of laughter. I am not here to sell it. On the contrary, Mr. Aram, I am here to ask you to find me an exact match, a duplicate, in other words, an identical second pearl because I want you to make me a pair of earrings which I intend to give to my wife on our upcoming twenty-fifth wedding anniversary."

"How nice of you sir", said Aram. "And what a beautiful gift it will be. Not only beautiful, but unique and extremely precious, for sure. But, as I said before, I do not have a match for your pearl, sir."

"I know", said the visitor, "and I did not expect you to carry one in your inventory, but I want you to help me find the match. Can you?"

"Well," said Aram, "I can try. After all, many beautiful pearls are coming all the time from Japan so we should be able to find one. How do you think we should go about it?"

"I will tell you," replied the visitor calmly, "First you will take a photograph of my pearl, then you will note all its technical details, such as colour, surface, shape, size, weight and so on. Then you will place an ad in two of the most read newspapers in which you will fully and accurately describe the pearl, adding that one of your customers is looking for a perfect match and is offering seventy-thousand dollars for it. Finally, you will give the name of your store, phone number and address and then we will both sit back and wait. It's as simple as that."

"Seventy-thousand dollars?" exclaimed Aram. "That does not make sense. Admittedly I cannot give you a price for your rare gem but if you want to buy the two pearls as separate entities I can sell them to you for fifteen thousand each."

"Yes, shot back the customer "that is for separate pearls, not for the natural combination or fusion you are holding in your hand. This is a priceless rarity. And besides, what seems to be the problem? You are not paying the finder, I am. All you have to do is inform the public of this opportunity and if someone comes forward with the matching item, you will make sure that it is the right one and then you will phone me. I will come and consummate the deal. In other words, I will pay the person seventy-thousand dollars and you will make a beautiful pair of earrings for me. C'est tout" concluded the visitor with an elegant gesture of his hand.

Aram had listened very carefully to the calmly delivered, almost professional speech. Then he thought to himself: There is no risk for me. I am merely acting as middleman. If a matching pearl is found I will make a handsome profit from the earrings. And I am getting publicity in the papers.

After a few moments he said: "Alright, Prince. Let's do it exactly as you suggested but I warn you, it may take a long time before we find your match. Such rarities don't grow on trees", he added with a resounding laugh. He took out his camera from a drawer, shot a few pictures of the pearl, wrote down all the details and measurements and led the visitor to the door, thanking him for the opportunity and expressing the hope that a finder would soon come forward. Aram went back to his chair behind the counter, taking a deep breath after what had been a rather unusual morning.

* * * * *

The next few weeks were business as usual at Aram's jewellery store, except for regular phone calls from the prince enquiring whether he had received any offers.

A month or so went by, but then one late afternoon, Aram had a phone call from a woman who asked if the deal of the rare pearl was still on. "Of course, madam", replied Aram. "Why are you asking? Do you have one?" "I might, replied the caller. "I would like to come to your store and show it to you. Is tomorrow morning agreeable?" "By all means" said Aram. "It will be a pleasure to welcome you to my shop. You have the address?" "Yes, I do," replied the woman. "See you then, tomorrow morning." "Good day, madam."

The next day, shortly after nine, a middle-aged woman, well-dressed and refined in her comportment, entered Aram's store. Without much ado, she took out a pearl wrapped in a white silk handkerchief. "Please tell me if this is what you are looking for. Take your time to inspect it carefully", she added, before sitting down on the chair offered to her.

Aram took out his loupe and went over the pearl like only a professional jeweller can. He measured and weighed it and then, turning to the lady, with a bright grin on his face, he said: "Congratulations, madam, it is precisely the very pearl we are looking for. What extraordinary luck." The lady took back the pearl and said: "And your customer will pay seventy-thousand dollars for it?" "He will indeed, madam. Hardly a day goes by without him calling me to repeat the offer. Do you want me to give him the good news?" "Yes, please", replied the lady. "Tell him to come and pick up the item and to bring with him seventy-thousand dollars either in cash or as a certified cheque. I will not accept a personal cheque, you understand?" "I certainly do, madam", said Aram. "I will call him right away, make an appointment and inform you accordingly. Please leave me your phone number and thank you very much."

He immediately called the prince, who was absolutely elated. He kept repeating: "What wonderful news. Do you know how happy you made me? God Bless you, Mr. Aram. Please tell the lady to come to your shop on Friday afternoon around three o'clock and I will be there with a certified cheque for seventy-thousand. I am so anxious to complete the transaction. See you Friday afternoon. Goodbye."

Aram phoned the lady who said she would be there on time. And so she was. Beaming with expectation and elegantly attired, she came ten minutes ahead of time and sat down while Aram offered her a cup of coffee. Well, it turned out to be not only, a long, but also fruitless wait because the prince did not show up. Repeated phone calls from Aram remained unanswered. Frustrated and tense, they both concluded that the buyer must have had an accident or some other unexpected mishap preventing him from keeping an appointment he himself so anxiously wanted.

The next day the prince phoned, profoundly apologizing and saying that he had indeed suffered an accident and could the seller please come back the following day. She did, of course, but, alas the prince did not. Again, the lady, by now visibly angry and very tense, waited together with Mr. Aram for over an hour without any sign of life from the prince. Aram called several times but there was no answer.

It was at this point that Aram began to smell a rat, as the saying goes. Following a sudden impulse, he asked the lady to show him the pearl again. He looked at it, this time with minute attention, and he suddenly realized that the pearl the lady was offering for sale was actually the very same pearl the prince had shown him when he first came into the store. There was no doubt; it was one and the same.

Greatly disturbed by his discovery, he approached the lady and said: "Madam, I don't mean to pry but could you tell me where you obtained this item?"

A very apprehensive woman said: "Oh, I have had it for a long time. It is sort of a family heirloom."

Aram was aware that the lady was lying. She was fidgety and did not sound convincing, which made Aram come back to her: "Please, madam, tell me the truth. I think we are dealing with a clever crook who duped both of us. Please tell the truth."
When he uttered these words, the lady gave out a sudden scream and slumped back into her chair. She started to cry. Perhaps sobbing would be a more appropriate description of her lamentable condition.

"I don't believe this", she finally said. "I can't believe it", and between sobs, she told Aram: "A few weeks ago, at a party in one of my friend's homes, I met a good looking man who introduced himself as a former general in the Czar's army and close confident of the imperial Romanov family. Given the abundance of titled emigrés we have in town these days I was not surprised. During our conversation between frequently drained vodkas, he showed me a notice in one of the daily newspapers placed by you, a very reputable jeweller, if I may say so, saying that you were looking for a certain pearl and that someone is paying seventy-thousand dollars for it.

Then this man tells me that, by coincidence he happens to have the very same pearl you are looking for, but given his high position in émigré circles, he feels uncomfortable publicly offering his family jewels for sale. So, he says to me since they are paying seventy-thousand for it, I am offering it to you for fifty-thousand and you go to Aram Terzian and get your seventy-thousand. In other words you make twenty-thousand dollars right there and then. Now, he adds, don't take my word for it. Check it out completely before you say yes. First, I am giving you my pearl. Take it to the jeweller and ask him to verify that it is the exact match they are looking for. Be sure he examines it very carefully. Then verify that the buyer is indeed offering seventy-thousand dollars and then, only then you buy it from me and take it to Terzian. "Madam", says the general, "I don't think you have ever made money so easily in your whole life. Think it over and if you are interested you will find me right next to the bar over there. Where else would you find an old soldier?" With this, he leaves me pondering. Should I do it or shouldn't I? I have the money. I am not a wealthy woman to be sure but I have the money and who doesn't want to make a fast twenty-thousand dollars these days? I know that Aram Terzian is a very reputable jeweller and would never lend his name to a shady deal. The general came across as a sincere person and, moreover, he is confident enough to entrust me with the pearl. Then I say to myself: Nothing ventured, nothing gained. So, why not? Next thing you know I walk over to the bar and shake hands with him. That's the whole story, Mr. Aram."

The lady's speech was frequently interrupted by tears. At times she stopped as if she were unable to continue. But when she had finished she held her embroidered handkerchief close to her face and cried her heart out.

Aram was deeply moved and felt very sorry for the poor woman. He told her that if she wanted, he could try to sell the pearl for her, but even if he found a buyer, which he was not sure he could, the item would fetch a mere fraction of what she had paid for it.

"What a fool I was", the lady said, "but don't you think anybody would have fallen into the trap?" Anxious not to hurt her even more than she had already endured during the past few days, Aram said: "No, madam you did not act like a fool, you just happened to meet a clever crook, that's all." "What would you have done in my place", she retorted. "Well, I would have told the "general" alright, I agree to this deal but I will pay you the fifty-thousand after I receive the seventy-thousand from the buyer. And, madam, this would have been the last you ever saw of this 'general' and his pearl."

"My God", exclaimed the lady, "why did I not think of that?" You are absolutely right. How stupid of me. I am so ashamed of myself." "Don't be, madam, Aram said, "You are just more trusting in people than I am."

"Do you think I should report this to the police and lay charges against this man?" the lady said. "Madam", replied Aram, "that would be a real waste of time and money, if you ask me. First, our prince cum general has long disappeared into thin air, but even more important you would have a hard time laying charges, because come to think of it, he may not have broken any laws at all. Our elusive friend may well have committed one of those perfect crimes. There is such a thing, you know."

"The perfect crime," he repeated to himself, as he led the lady out of his store.

A TRUE STORY

Sometimes things happen in our lives that are strange and unexpected to the point that they are actually hard to believe.

I was reminded of this just the other night at my son's home when the completion of dinner gradually turned to small talk and one of the guests talked about an encounter with a person he had not seen since he last sat with him on the same school bench in Vienna fifty years ago. It was the mention of Vienna, where my late father had grown up that made me bring this true story into the foreground of my mind. I thought that it deserved a repeat performance.

In the early years of the last century my father lived in Vienna. He was in his early twenties, worked for a large textile company and fully enjoyed the carefree and frivolous pre-World War I years of operettas and waltzes, of dazzling military parades, of rich pastries and wiener schnitzels. The French called it "La Belle Époque".

Being a bachelor, my father spent a good part of his free time in the home of his best friend who was married. Well, it so happened that one day, this friend while riding in a horse-drawn carriage became the victim of a severe accident when the carriage collided with a motorcar. The frightened horses started to run amok and my father's friend ended up in the hospital with multiple fractures, some of them severe.

What followed was a lengthy stay in hospital with surgeries trying to mend the badly injured body. Among the doctors tending to the patient was also an elderly physician who had been a resident there for many years. He had not left the side of the patient since the moment of his admission to the hospital.

It so happened that the day before his fateful accident, my father's friend had bought a ticket in the Austrian State Lottery and, believe it or not, this ticket won the jackpot which was several million shillings, a huge fortune at that time or indeed at any time.

When the wife found out that they had won this large amount of money and after overcoming her own delirious reaction, she did not know what to do next. In other words, she was scared to tell her hospitalized husband who was conscious but still fighting for his life, fearing that the excitement of the news may actually kill him. So she decided to consult the faithful doctor. She did and he said: "Leave it to me. I will give him the news in a way that will avoid any excessive or dangerous reaction."

A few days later, while visiting the patient with his wife in the room, the doctor, after some general comments, said: "This morning's paper is reporting that someone won the jackpot in the National Lottery, apparently a huge sum." To which the patient responded: "I bought a ticket, but as usual it is a complete waste of money.
I have never won anything." "Well, said the doctor, if you did, what would you do with the loot?" "I am sure I will find a way to spend half of it, because the other half I would give to you for the simple reason that if I get well and can walk again it is mostly thanks to you and all the personal care you are giving me. I would not enjoy a penny unless I knew that you shared it with us." They all had a good laugh and then the conversation turned to other matters.

That same evening, when the doctor went home he had a phone call from his patient's wife. She said: "Of course I agree with my husband. You are saving his life. You deserve it.

In fact, the surgeon told me today that my husband is well on his way to a complete recovery and you are without any doubt the main architect of this miracle.

Tomorrow morning on my way to the hospital I am stopping at the bank. If you meet me there I will transfer fifty percent of the jackpot into your account. Okay?" She hung up.

The doctor was immensely agitated. He did not expect all this to happen so suddenly. He took a couple of drinks to help him calm down but he could not go to sleep. He tossed and turned but an hour later he felt increasingly stronger chest pains. He phoned an ambulance, was rushed to the hospital and hours later, despite all efforts, died of a massive heart attack, most probably brought on by the excitement and shock. He obviously could not cope with the sudden realization that he had become a multi-millionaire.

Only a few days later, the wife told her husband what had happened. There were tears of sorrow over the doctor's death and tears of joy over the win. A couple of weeks later the patient left the hospital, all injuries healed and his health restored.

The couple lived a long and happy and, needless to say, very affluent life. Every year they left flowers on the grave of the unfortunate victim, feeling the heavy burden of having caused his death, albeit most unintentionally.

IN MEMORIAM

People walking through Badenerstrasse, a quiet side street lined with townhouses and some professional buildings, mostly housing doctors and lawyers in downtown Cologne, sometimes stop in front of a red brick edifice with a rather large brass plate on the entrance's left side bearing the inscription: KRANSFELD INSTITUT der KRIMINALOGY. Visitors please ring bell to enter.

This is the story behind the intriguing Criminology Institute.

***

Franz Mühlmann is, for all intents and purposes, a household name in Cologne, Germany, and this for good reasons. There are six large furniture stores bearing his logo in Cologne and another four in Aachen, not far from the Belgian border. They all sell sensible, affordable and stylish quality merchandise. No wonder that over the years the company grew to its present size on account of a solid base of satisfied customers.

Mr. Mühlmann, now in his early seventies was ably assisted by his son Hans, a trained interior decorator and designer. The family, that is both father and son and their families, lived in the same large house on Römerstrasse at the outskirts of Cologne. They had bought the newly built home sometime in the mid-fifties. At the time it was one of the many developments rebuilt on the debris of homes destroyed during allied bomb raids in World War II.

The two families had been living in the four-story home for almost half of a century when one day in February during an exceptionally cold spell they discovered that the basement had been flooded due to a broken pipe filled with frozen water. Needless to say that a hastily summoned repair crew soon arrived to dry, repair and replace the damaged plumbing.

It was on the third day after they had started work that the foreman of the crew summoned Mrs. Mühlmann to show her a metal box they had discovered during their digging.

The metal container was dug out from the dark earth and Mrs. Mühlmann took it up to her flat. Placing it on the kitchen floor she managed to pry it open. It contained a neatly packed and well-preserved collection of type-written pages in separate files, each labelled with the title of its contents. She counted twenty-four files.

Surprised and amazed by her find she phoned her husband who told her that he would be coming home shortly to have a look at this strange discovery.

Needless to say, the rest of that evening was dominated by this most interesting event as the entire family unpacked and looked at each of the twenty-four files. What they had in front of them was a collection of crime stories or episodes written for serialized radio or television programs. Each file contained a different episode, all showing Joseph Kransfeld as author and all dated 1937. They had been buried for over seventy years.

None of the Mühlmanns had any idea where these manuscripts could have come from but they decided to find out. First of all, they started reading the texts and found them to be very well written and perfectly suited for dramatization. In fact, they could fill a successful TV broadcast season.

"What do we do with this and who is Joseph Kransfeld?" was the question on all of their minds. "Obviously" said Mr. Mühlmann senior, "we have to involve the Cologne City Registry." They did and soon found out by going through the archives that Joseph Kransfeld was a highly respected lawyer in pre-Nazi Germany who lived with his family in a large house exactly where the Mühlmanns now resided. It had been completely destroyed by allied bombs in 1943. The city archives also revealed that Joseph and Magda Kransfeld were deported to Dachau concentration camp where they unfortunately perished. The couple had one son, Erich, who never came forward to claim the property of his parents and this, despite many attempts by the German government to locate him. After many years of futile searches it was assumed that he died during or after the war without leaving any trace. Finally the unclaimed land on which the Kransfeld home once stood was declared city property and sold to a construction company which built the house bought in turn by the Mühlmanns.

After some deliberations, the Mühlmanns decided to show these stories to a literary agent, especially after they found out that they were all based on actual cases the author had handled in court, which might also give them some historical value. The agent found the material perfectly suitable for use in a current popular TV crime series entitled "Call Inspector Meissner". When the agent offered the texts to the TV station they immediately fell in love with them and offered to pay an amount of 200,000 Euros for exclusive rights to all twenty-four episodes.

The Mühlmanns agreed but said that they would like to clear the legality of the transaction with their lawyer before signing up with the prospective buyer.

While the lawyer was busy going through the files in an effort to come up with an opinion, Mr. Mühlmann received an unexpected letter by registered mail from a Mr. Eberle, one of the city's numerous intellectual property agents.

The letter said:

"It has come to our attention that you are trying to sell a collection of twenty-four manuscripts suitable for use in the production of serialized broadcasts, all of them authored by a certain Joseph Kransfeld.

We must inform you that the said literary material and all the rights pertaining to and deriving from it were purchased from Mr. Kransfeld by a company later acquired by us and are therefore our legitimate property.

Taking into consideration that you have offered the above-mentioned object for sale to a third party, we have referred the matter to the appropriate legal authorities to demand that you immediately cease and desist this fraudulent attempt or face legal action within the full scope of the law. You will receive official notification to this effect from a Court of Justice. Govern yourself accordingly."

And indeed two days later the Mühlmanns received a summons to appear before a local court. When the family lawyer stood in front of the judge he was told that following a plea received from a party claiming legal rights to the material they had offered for sale, the Court herewith asked them to stop any further negotiations with the prospective buyer pending an investigation into the legal ownership of these twenty-four manuscripts. This may take several months, after which an official report will be issued clarifying all legal aspects of this matter. The lawyer was asked to sign a notification which he did on behalf of the Mühlmanns.

It did, indeed, take several months, four to be precise, before the family heard anything further about this case.

The notice came in the form of a registered letter, identical copies of which were addressed to the Mühlmanns as well as to Hans Eberle, the plaintiff, also residing in Cologne.

This is what the letter said:

In the matter of the twenty-four manuscripts authored by a certain Joseph Kransfeld and claimed as property by Mr. Hans Eberle, the undersigned judge in conformity with the powers vested in him by the German Civil Code has reached the following final and binding decision:

A thorough investigation of all circumstances pertaining to the case was launched and duly completed with cooperation of all available archives and databases dating from the beginning of the aforementioned case to the present. As a result of this investigation, the following actual chain of events could be reconstructed and is herewith entered as official record of the case:

Mr. Joseph Kransfeld was a prominent and highly respected criminal lawyer residing with his family in Cologne during the nineteen-thirties. He also taught law at Bonn University. With the advent of the Nazi regime and being Jewish he was dismissed from both the university and the bar association, preventing him from continuing in his law profession. For a while he tried to earn a living by assisting non-Jewish lawyers but this was also terminated. The Nazis also confiscated all his bank accounts. Thus, Mr. Kransfeld was soon left without any source of income.

Adding to these woes, Magda, Joseph's wife was diagnosed with incurable cancer, requiring palliative treatment which prevented the couple from leaving the country.

Desperately in need of money, Mr. Kransfeld decided to author some criminal stories based on his professional life in the courts after a friend who headed a local radio station told him that he would buy such episodes from him for use in the station's programming. However, by the time Mr. Kransfeld completed twenty-four of these episodes, the radio station had been taken over by the Nazi government and placed under the control of Dr. Goebbels' Propaganda Ministry. This automatically precluded them from buying any material from a Jew. The only alternative left to Kransfeld was to find a non-Jewish person who would pretend to be the author and share the proceeds of the sale with him.

A certain Kurt Brahm agreed to become the fictitious author and signed an agreement to this effect with Kransfeld, pledging to share half of the proceeds of the sale with him. However, despite this written agreement, Mr. Brahm sold the manuscripts but did not pay Kransfeld anything, pretending that the Nazi authorities would punish him if they found out about the fictitious deal. But when Mr. Kransfeld insisted on payment of his share, Brahm did not hesitate to report him to the authorities as a Jew trying to do some illegal deals. In short order, Joseph and Magda Kransfeld were arrested and taken to Dachau concentration camp where they both perished shortly afterwards according to official records.

It has also been established that the twenty-four manuscripts purchased by the station were never used because of the outbreak of the war.

In view of all of the above information this Court declares the claim to ownership of the twenty-four manuscripts by the now-deceased Kurt Brahm, as well as by his apparent successor, Hans Eberle, as null and void being based on a defrauded agreement signed under Nazi government rules and conditions. Without any doubt, the ownership of these twenty-four manuscripts belong to Joseph Kransfeld and his legal heirs or descendants.

Furthermore, this Court declares that since no heir to the Kransfelds could be located and since Mr. Franz Mühlmann found the above-mentioned manuscripts on premises owned by him, he is herewith considered their legitimate owner.

This letter is entered as an official Court document dated as above.

***

The reaction of the Mühlmann family to this decision was swift and predictable. They sold the twenty-four manuscripts for 200,000 Euros then added another equal amount to this and founded the Kransfeld Institute of Criminology to honour the memory of the unfortunate author.

They also created a painstakingly documented and illustrated life story of the Kransfelds which is prominently displayed in the lobby of the Institute.

During the years since its foundation the Kransfeld Institute has become an internationally recognized and fully accredited school for aspiring writers and aficionados of crime stories. It also offers lectures and panel discussions on the subject. In addition, it sponsors an annual contest for the best crime story in which the winner receives a prize of 10,000 Euros.

***

Nothing could atone for the incredible suffering that Joseph Kransfeld and his wife went through in the latter part of their lives. Nothing. But at least their memory was preserved by honouring Kransfeld for his lifelong contribution to the practice of law and by dire necessity, to the dramatic arts – his last hurrah.

THE KEY

Fred Timmins was a young promising litigation lawyer. At thirty-two years of age he was already a junior partner of Bergman Couture LLC, one of Canada's most successful law firms. He was married to Janet, a strikingly beautiful brunette three years his junior. Although they had tied the knot some three years ago, the couple was still childless since they had decided not to raise a family until the fifth year after the wedding in order to give them time to adapt to each other, travel and enjoy undisturbed time together before plunging headlong into the real world of changing diapers and burping crying babies.

Fred and Janet were a well-adjusted couple, but since both pursued hectic and consuming careers, she being a financial analyst, their marriage, after three years was still more of a working relationship or a bond based on mutual love and respect. Romance was on the menu only when and where possible. Mind you, the two were genuinely in love with each other and enjoyed spirited and fulfilling sex.

Because litigation was not the main thrust of Fred's law firm, the principals had decided that one lawyer could handle the caseload of both the Montreal and Toronto branches. That is why Fred was obliged to divide his time between the two offices. Hence his frequent absences from his Montreal home.

*   *   *

One cool and breezy spring evening, Fred had offered one of his colleagues a lift to his home which was located just a block away from his own house.

As he dropped off his colleague, an unmarried young lawyer, he noticed that his house door was wide open and a lady waved to the stopped car, shouting: "Come quick, your sister from Australia is on the phone", causing Fred's friend to jump out of the car and run, waving a speedy "bye, thanks" to the driver.

Fred waved back and drove home but when he parked the car in his driveway he noticed a key on the floor in front of the seat beside him. Obviously his friend had dropped it while rushing out of the car.

He picked up the key and saw that it looked very much like the one to his own house, but then, he thought, many keys look alike.

However, intrigued by the similarity, he tried to use it to open his own door, and lo and behold, to his great surprise, the lock opened with ease.

Fred did not say a word to Janet about this as she greeted him on entering the house, but he was shocked by the discovery.

How come a colleague had a key to his house? The thought immediately grabbed his mind and dominated it throughout the evening. He tried to hide it from Janet who first served dinner and later cuddled up to him in front of the TV. They chatted and talked about their day and the day's events but the discovery of the key was on the backburner all the time. In fact, the thought about it kept intensifying as the evening wore on.

Could it be that Janet had a lover? Theoretically it was quite possible what with his frequent absences from home. And his colleague Eric, was a very good looking and fetching young man.

Could it be?

All kinds of thoughts began crossing his mind. Little remarks from Janet, unanswered phone calls he had made from Toronto, followed by what now sounded to him like lame excuses:

"Oh, I was out shopping" or "I went to the supermarket."

Could it be?

Fred went to bed with a heavy cloud of doubt over his head. He had never thought of the possibility of Janet being unfaithful to him. But the proof of the pudding was right there. In his trouser pocket was another man's key to his house.

It was a restless night for Fred as he went again and again over his marriage, over his role as a husband, as a lover and as a companion. While he found himself perhaps not the perfect hubby, he could not really blame himself for having driven his wife to adultery.

After the usual hearty breakfast and goodbye kiss and hug, Fred drove to the office, torn by doubts which by now had turned into certainty. He was a cuckold husband with two big horns on his head. "Cornuto" as he had heard an Italian friend describe the league of betrayed husbands.

"What now?" He asked himself as he sat down in his office chair.

But when his secretary brought him his usual morning coffee and he took a few sips, a thought suddenly occurred to him.

What if the two houses had the same key and the same lock? "Highly improbable", he said to himself.

How to find out?

He searched in his file and found the receipt of his lock installation and phoned the company. "Is it possible for two houses in the same neighborhood to have the same lock?"

A company manager to whom his call was referred answered: "No, Sir, no two identical locks and keys are ever sold in the same neighborhood, not even in the same city." But then the manager asked Fred for the number of his contract and said he would call back shortly.

Two minutes later, the call came through. "Sir, we found the contract of your lock and key. We also found that an identical lock and key were sold to a hardware store in Halifax. As I said, added the manager, we may sell identical combinations in different cities."

Fred was still trying to put his thoughts in order, when there was a knock on his door. It was Eric, the suspect from last night.

"Hey Fred, thanks for the lift," intoned his colleague lightheartedly. "Guess what? I lost my key somewhere. Don't ask me where and when. It was a very good lock that I had bought a couple of years ago at a hardware store in Halifax and had it installed in my Montreal home when I moved here. So to be on the safe side, this morning, I bought a new lock which they installed right away. You know, these things cost a fortune. Anyways, thanks again for driving me home last night, see you!"

With that final remark, Eric left his office.

*   *   *

"Wow", shouted Janet as Fred came home that evening with a big bunch of red roses in his hand. "What's the occasion for this celebration? They are gorgeous." She said with a smile that lit up her beautiful face.

"Oh, nothing special," replied Fred, "As I drove home the thought occurred to me how lucky I am to have you. So I stopped at the florist to get you these."

That was the most passionate night the two had enjoyed in a long time.

DIAL "M" FOR ROBBERY

They were four, all from Montreal and all friends for many years. What started out as a threesome, soon evolved into a four-man team on account of the growing complexity and sophistication of their job. They were bank robbers.

Call it luck or meticulous planning but they had successfully despoiled several banks in and around the city as well as a credit union, a supermarket and even a hockey stadium. Once or twice they came pretty close to being nabbed but in the end they managed to get away with it.

While they all performed specialized tasks in each heist, their uncontested leader was Mickey Leblanc. It was he who did all the preparatory work, who spent a long time at each prospective target to study and research all the details, then to prepare the plan of action, including not only the individual assignments but also the precise instructions on how to carry them out. That is why they did not only call him "The Boss" but also had no objections about his pocketing twice as much as they did. Mickey took 40% while the others got 20% of every heist. If they pulled off three to four good jobs a year, they all made pretty good money. Of course they knew that their capers would not go on forever, but they were eagerly looking forward to Mickey's call for yet another planning meeting.

It was great while the going was good!

It was a gray November morning when they were summoned to a meeting at Mickey's home in Montréal's East End. This time the target was a Caisse branch in Ahuntsic, one of the city's less populated districts. As usual, the boss had meticulously worked out all the facets of the heist down to the finest hair-splitting details.

Mickey, accompanied by Pierre and Joe, was to arrive at the site at three in the morning in his van, disengage all the alarms, break into the building, then, in order to lessen exposure, fifteen minutes later, Jacques, the fourth man would arrive in a separate car to join them. By three fifty-five the job would be completed, they would all carry the loot to their cars and disappear from sight. The rest, as the saying goes, would be history. In fact, Mickey estimated the total take to be worth some six to seven million dollars.

After all the accomplices had been thoroughly briefed and rebriefed, Mickey turned to Jacques: "You arrive at three o'clock. You bring the get-away bags and the black facemasks but you don't come to the site yet. Instead you wait in your car at the corner of Dumont and Brocard streets, the cellphone in your hand. That is two blocks east from where we are. As soon as you get my call at 3:15, you drive to the end of Dumont Street and you will be facing us. You will walk over and join us. Is all this perfectly clear?" "Yes, it is" replied Jacques.

Jacques did, of course, as he was told. As of three o'clock he sat in his car at the designated corner, waiting. At three fifteen he nervously looked at his phone but there was no call. He waited another three minutes, but when he still did not hear from the boss, he assumed that either it took them longer to penetrate into the building or something may have gone wrong.
He decided to drive to the end of Dumont Street. He saw Mickey's car parked right in front of the bank. He grabbed the bags and ran over, entered the building and found the team feverishly breaking into safes behind the counters and stuffing wads of money bundles into their pockets. Mickey shouted to him: "Quickly, you empty the first three broken safes while I am breaking into the ATM machines." One of the guys came up from the back with money bundles stuffed in his pockets and emptied them into the bags that Jacques had brought.

The mad rush of breaking into drawers and safes and stuffing money into pockets went on for a little while, but then Mickey shouted: "Okay guys, that's it. We are already ten minutes over our timeframe. Run to the car with the bags. You did a great job, I think we grabbed more than I expected. Get some sleep and be at my place around noon."

They all got out of the building but they did not get very far because as they emerged, they were blinded by a dozen powerful flashlights beamed at them by policemen, all with drawn revolvers. A voice from an amplifier speaker shouted: "Freeze. Do not move an inch further. Drop everything in your hand and lift your arms over your head. You are surrounded by police."

The four men were in shock and breathless. What had happened? The voice from the speaker came back: "Now, drop everything and stay where you are. You are all under arrest. You will be taken to the station where your rights will be read to you." All four men were handcuffed, placed in different police cruisers and taken to the headquarters downtown.

The next twenty-four hours were a very painful experience for the robbers. Processing them took hours. By the time they were lead back into their cells, a whole day had passed. They were exhausted. After a simple fast food meal, they were locked up in separate cells. It was there that Mickey, sitting on a hard cot, had an opportunity to review the events of the last day. He asked himself: What happened? How come the police apprehended them? How did they know exactly where they were? The more he asked himself these questions, the more certain he became of the answer.

They were betrayed and only one person could have done that. Jacques. To be sure he never really liked the guy. It was he who sat in the car waiting for his call. It was he who had the time to tell the police exactly where they were located. It was Jacques who arrived at the scene not three minutes but a full ten minutes late, the time he needed to tip off the police. He was now certain of this. It was Jacques, but why did he do it? It must have been because he was paid off by a rival gang who wanted to get rid of them. He would receive a fat payment from his arch rival who surely also offered him a job with a bigger stake in the loot and, most importantly, his rival would have ensured that Mickey was eliminated from the business for a number of years. All these thoughts kept racing in Mickey's mind for hours. Needless to say he resolved to put a bullet between Jacques eyes, either himself or by proxy, as soon as he could.

The next morning, still kept separate from the other guys, Mickey was taken to a large bathroom where he could shave and wash up. On the way back to his cell, he saw the morning newspapers on a table. He asked for a copy and was given one. Back in his cell, he started to read the paper. Of course, the botched robbery made banner headlines. Prominently featured was an interview with a man by the name of Claude Trepannier whose photo was also shown above the column.

"I still cannot believe what happened last night" reported Mr. Trepannier. "My wife and I were sound asleep when the telephone rang. I looked at my watch. It was three fifteen in the morning. I picked up the receiver and heard a loud voice almost shouting into the phone: 'Everything went well. We are now inside the building. Pierre and Joe are beginning to crack the cash dispensers.

You will empty them one after the other. Don't forget the bags. Park your car at the corner of Dumont Street facing the Caisse. You'll see my car parked in front. Hurry. You should be here in three to four minutes.' Then the person hung up. I didn't know what this was all about. My first thought was it must either be a hoax or a real robbery with someone having dialed the wrong number. I went back to the bedroom and found my wife sitting up in bed. I told her about the strange call. She immediately said: 'call 911. It's a robbery in progress. They will tell the police.' You know, my wife is pretty smart and she reads a lot of crime novels. So I did as she told me. Now I know that she was right. It was a robbery and someone had dialed the wrong number."

Mickey put down the paper. He felt like wanting to disappear from the face of the earth.

"Oh my God" he shouted out loud. Then he said to himself: "On second thought, that bullet between Jacques' eyes belongs to me. Not a bullet, but a cannonball is what I need right now!"

REVENGE

Mildred Robinson was the assistant manager of a savings and loan association in a Detroit shopping mall, a job she had held for almost twenty years. At sixty-three years of age, she was a widow since her husband, Michael, had lost his life in a car accident some five years ago. She had one son who lived in New Jersey.

Although Mildred had a number of friends, some of them intimate and dedicated, it can be said that for all intents and purposes, she was alone in the world and lived an uneventful, simple life divided between her nine to five job and her daily housekeeping chores.

Feeling the need to somewhat break the monotony permeating her existence, she decided to fulfil a dream she had nurtured for many years, which was to take a trip to Las Vegas and taste the excitement of sitting at one of the roulette tables, fingering a pile of slippery chips in front of her.

Using a week left over in her annual vacation, she booked herself a seat on an airline as well as a room in a medium-priced hotel and set forth to the glittering gambling mecca of the world. She was awed and excited and full of anticipation as she entered the hotel's large roulette hall, taking her place at one of the many busy tables.

In her purse she had two thousand dollars which she had saved for a long time in anticipation of this trip.

She bought some chips and started to place small amounts on different numbers, needless to say without a single win. She recalled that she always considered seven as her lucky number and started repeatedly placing chips on seven, again without any success. She watched woefully as the croupier kept sweeping her chips away like worthless debris.

Mildred had now been sitting at the table for two hours, presiding over the shellacking not only of her dwindling pile of chips, but also of her hopes to hit the jackpot. She was now very frustrated, coming to the conclusion that the number seven was definitely not her lucky star.

It was now getting close to lunch time. She was hungry and decided to leave the table in order to grab a bite in the restaurant on the first floor.

Mildred was just about to leave the roulette table when a man who had been sitting right next to her said: "No luck with seven, eh? Why don't you try another number like twenty-two?" He laughed at his own remark and got up from the table just as Mildred was gathering her few remaining chips. She had lost several hundred dollars.

Many of the other gamblers around the table were also getting up. Suddenly an idea occurred to her. Perhaps the man sitting next to her was right? Perhaps he had a hunch? What if twenty-two *was* her lucky number? She started to think and ideas got mixed up with feelings and omens, until a sudden urge dominated her entire mind.

"Play the twenty-two."
She quickly left the table, bought a thousand dollars' worth of chips from the cashier, hurried back and without a further thought, placed the entire pile of chips on number twenty-two.

Like in a trance she watched the wheel seemingly endlessly spin and spin until it finally came to a rest, and you guessed it, the little white ball landed neatly in the groove of number twenty-two.

Mildred was dumbfounded. She did not believe her eyes. The croupier pushed back the pile of chips in front of her and with a big grin handed her a little note to be exchanged at the cashier for a cool thirty-six-thousand dollars – the jackpot. Thirty-six times her stake.

"Congratulations, Madame" uttered the croupier as she hurried away to claim her loot.

Not in her wildest dreams had she expected that she would win. She stuffed the crisp dollar bills into her purse and went up to the restaurant. She had just realized how hungry she was.

Unbeknownst to her, the man who had given her the lucky advice was also sitting at a table in the same restaurant. He was having a sandwich and was joined by a couple who had been at the roulette table when Mildred won the jackpot.

Unaware of their friend's advice to Mildred, they said to him: "You missed a great spectacle. The lady that was sitting next to you throughout the morning won the jackpot after you left." "Oh," said the man, looking up from his sandwich. "Yes, she won $36,000 on number twenty-two."

The man almost choked upon hearing this. "Are you sure of that?" he asked. "Of course" replied his friends. "We can still hear the croupier's voice: 'Number twenty-two takes all!' She had bet a thousand dollars. I think I saw her in the restaurant a few minutes ago."

The man got up and said to his friends: "I must congratulate that woman". He started looking around and quickly spotted her sitting all by herself at a nearby table. Approaching her with a smile from ear to ear, he shouted: "Well, congratulations. I hear you won the jackpot, and," he stopped for a brief second, "with the number I gave you. I am so happy for you, I really am!"

He was still standing since Mildred had not asked him to sit down and there was a good reason for that. In her racing mind, she was sure that he would now claim a cut, or a finder's fee or some sort of recompense for having given her what turned out to be the winning number.

Without any hesitation and keeping a stone face, Mildred said: "I don't remember you having given me any number, Sir. The number I used happens to be my Mother's birthday and that's why I put my money on it."

Having said that, she turned her face away from the man and continued eating to indicate that she considered the conversation terminated.

The man, still standing, was flabbergasted. What a cheap, mean and dishonest woman. He felt like calling her ugly names which she deserved. He was disgusted and hated the sight of her.

But he did not display any sign of his feelings. Nodding his head he also started thinking fast.

How to teach this woman a lesson she will not forget?

"Well," he said to Mildred, looking her straight in the face. "Never mind where the lucky number came from. The main point is that you won. And, you know, of course, what to do when Lady Luck smiles at you, don't you Madam?"

Mildred now looked at him.

"You go back to the table, sit at exactly the same spot and continue gambling because once you are on the lucky streak, there is definitely more to come. Don't abandon your good fortune. That would be foolish. Go get the rest of the winnings before the day is out. Goodbye Madam." With that he smiled broadly and left the table.

Needless to say, Mildred followed the advice of this "guru" to the last, the very last crisp thousand dollar bill in her now empty purse.

MY BROTHER JERRY

My name is David Balinski and this is the story of my older brother Jerry.

To be sure I never intended to write this biography but something extraordinary happened two days after his recent death. While cleaning up his home and going through his papers, I came across a neatly typed manuscript which bore the laconic heading "My Mother's Story".

Intrigued by this discovery I sat down and read the document from start to finish. It is an amazing story of which I had not the slightest idea, none whatsoever.

When I put the last page down, I had made up my mind to set its contents into proper perspective by preceding my mother's story with an account of Jerry's life as I and the world around us saw or rather perceived him. Needless to say that by so doing, I also created the record of our family.

We are all creatures of circumstance so to speak. In other words our lives are shaped to a certain extent by events unfolding around us, but in Jerry's case these events not only came to bear on him, they dominated, harassed and finally molded him into the person he became.

May he find in death, the peace that eluded him for so long.
*   *   *

My parents, Simon and Alicia Balinski, accompanied by their two children, Jerry, aged five and myself, aged three, arrived in Montreal in mid-1946 from Palestine. My dad had obtained a Canadian immigrant visa on account of his two-year war service in the British Army.

After some months of hardship both my parents found steady jobs in Montreal and with the financial support of the Jewish Community Service, we moved into a small house in Cote St. Luc, where we lived for some fifteen years.

I distinctly remember our first winter, my years in elementary school, our summer camps and our friends with whom we played street hockey even on bitter cold winter days.

It was a happy childhood. While my dad was more reserved and not given to showing much affection, my mother was a truly dedicated woman who took care of her family in an exemplary way.

On High Holydays, we went to the synagogue with my parents. Over the years my dad had become a respected member of the congregation to which we belonged.

In time, my mother gave up her job because my father had now progressed to sales agent in a large real estate company and was making good money.

In short, I can say that my older brother and I grew up in a normal middle class family very much akin to all the other kids on the block. We loved our parents and there was peace and understanding at home.

After high school, Jerry and I entered university which we both left with degrees; Jerry in Economics and I, in Law.

It didn't take long for both my brother and I to find jobs, he as a financial analyst in an investment company and I in a well-known law firm. We were both set on long-lasting careers that should take us through productive professional, and of course, family lives.

But in December of 1968, a terrible thing happened that shook the foundations of our little family. My mom had developed a bad cough that did not respond to any treatment. When she finally went to St. Mary's Hospital for x-rays, she was diagnosed with lung cancer. The news came out of the blue sky and hit us very hard.

The next six months were hell, both for my poor mother and for the rest of us. She was in and out of the hospital, chemotherapy and radiation, but nothing helped. By the end of the year, she passed away, leaving an irreplaceable void.

That sad event left profound marks on all of us, but especially on my older brother. In fact, thinking back to those days, I believe my mother's death transformed him in many ways. He became sometimes introverted, not talking to us at home, while at times he was nervous and bellicose, picking fights with me and our father, often for no reason at all.

I was told that this aggressivity also spread to his professional life, even though one of his superiors saw it as a sign of self-assurance, when he forcefully delivered arguments at board meetings.

This rather confrontational attitude also spilled over into Jerry's social life as he started to stake out his place in society.

Hidden behind a broad smile and a polished demeanor, he relished picking arguments on any given subject, hammering home his views which were invariably at odds with those of his partners, with merciless vehemence that only abated when his exhausted victims failed to rise at the count of ten.

However, while this demeanor often won him more foes than friends, this was not necessarily the case with his girlfriends, who were clearly impressed by this young man who seemed to know where he was going, but more importantly, knew how to get there.

And so it was that at one of the dinner parties in a friend's home he met Lillian, or Lill for short. She was pretty, with long blond hair, had a pleasing figure, had obtained a B.A. in literature and enjoyed her job as a copywriter. Lill possessed a keen mind, knew what was going on in the world and expressed her opinions with logic and a tempered approach that did not fail to impress the young men around her, but in particular, Jerry.

He engaged in long conversations with her and found her also physically attractive.

That first encounter was followed by invitations to dinner and before long, Jerry thought that he had found the right person to share a life with. In fact, Lill's sobering and down-to-earth approach to daily life had helped to disarm Jerry and perhaps even mollify his natural aggressivity.

As for Lill, she was smart enough to sense that behind the courteous, and, at times even effusive suitor, there may lie some more aggressive traits, but she figured that love as well as an orderly and happy life together would go a long way in turning him into a loving husband, albeit one with somewhat more assertive traits than the run-of-the-mill variety.

The two were married in a spectacular wedding attended by family and friends. Both partners looked resplendent in their formal attire.

After a brief honeymoon in the Caribbean, Lill and Jerry settled down in a beautiful home in Hampstead, which the couple had received with the loving compliments of the bride's parents. All seemed set for a long and happy life.

In line with current fashion, the couple decided to delay the creation of a family for some three years to give them time to adjust to each other, and, even more importantly, to travel to places in the world they had never seen, sort of creating a memory bank of experiences and adventures before they settled down to the more mundane experience of tending to babies and toddlers.

Lill continued to work, but despite her professional preoccupations, she managed to provide her husband with an exemplary home life replete with all the trimmings and even extravagances of an above average modern household.

However, despite the exciting atmosphere prevailing during the early days, there were some not so positive undercurrents that had begun to surface as early as a few months into their marriage.

For instance, Jerry's growing habit of bringing work home and disappearing for hours into his small study right after dinner, often until bedtime, leaving Lill alone to clean up and then either watch TV or find company in the paper's crossword page.

At first Lill thought of this peculiar behavior as an exception but she soon found out that it was one of her husband's standard habits.

To make matters worse, he never apologized for leaving her alone in the living room after dinner at a time when most working couples find relaxation in sharing thoughts and experiences of the day. In fact it soon became clear to Lill that the weekend was the only time she could talk or listen to her husband.

Then there was Jerry's refusal to accompany her on any of her shopping trips for clothes and accessories. "I don't know anything about women's dresses" he would tell her. "So, why don't you go and buy what you want for yourself and I will pick out my own ties and suits during lunch break from work." This left Lill with the clear impression that her husband had little if any interest in her appearance.

Another problem Lill faced was Jerry's frequent hostile attitude towards suggestions and thoughts she expressed both when they were alone, or in company. No sooner did she express an opinion on any subject at hand, that Jerry cut her off with remarks such as "No, no, no, you don't understand" or "you're wrong" or "why on earth do you say that?" or any other words to rebuff her. When he did this in company, some of their friends often had to step in to defend her in spite of her husband's negative approach.

These and many other unpleasant gestures by her husband finally began to take a toll on Lill's expectations and dreams of a happy marriage as she had seen not only in her parent's home but also in the harmonious relationships of their friends.

By the middle of their second year, Lill had reached the inevitable conclusion that the two were not meant for each other.

In fact, she had already talked about her predicament to her parents who were in favour of a divorce now, before the problem would be aggravated by the arrival of children.

It was at about this juncture that, one evening, I phoned my brother on a personal matter. It was Lill who picked up the phone, unfortunately, at the very moment of another harangue with her husband. I could clearly hear my brother's shouting voice as well as Lill's tearful tone as she answered the call with an "Oh, hi Dave, how are you? Hold on, I am passing the phone on to Jerry."

The conversation with my brother lasted only a few minutes but when he had hung up, it was amply clear to me that I had inadvertently been exposed to a family feud between a shouting husband and a crying wife. I was deeply shocked by this discovery. Why would a gentle and pleasant person like Lill be sobbing during a conversation with her husband?

The next morning, I phoned Lill at the office. "Hi, this is David" I started. "I could not help becoming party to your repartee with my brother last night. I heard him shouting, which did not surprise me. This is how he is. But what I could not stomach was your sobbing. You two obviously have a problem and I wondered if I could help in any possible way. Listen, how about meeting me for lunch later on? Please don't refuse my offer to help. I consider it my duty towards both of you. I will be at the restaurant "Chez Paul" right around the corner of your office at 12 noon. Meet me there, please. Bye now!"

When we met a few hours later, I could clearly see deep lines under Lill's beautiful eyes, and despite her broad smile, I was aware that my sister-in-law was definitely under some emotional stress.

After a few generalities, I came right to the point. "Are you unhappy Lill?" I started. "You don't have to tell me about my brother. I know he sometimes loses control over his voice and even his behavior. Tell me if you want me to talk to him to try and smooth things out between the two of you. I can always say that I heard you crying on the phone and want to offer my help in making peace, that is, if we are dealing with an isolated incident that caused the spat. What do you think, Lill?"

Lill had listened to my monologue with a smile, which however faded as I went on. She started to talk, looking straight at me, first hesitantly, but then the words came out of her mouth like water spilling over a retaining wall.

She gave me a fairly succinct account of what her marital life had been like during the past eighteen months. After telling me that she had talked to no one about her problem except her parents, I said: "Why did you two not go and see a family counsellor? These professionals can solve a lot of marriage problems." To which Lill replied with a helpless shrug: "I did suggest it, not once but many times. But your brother categorically refused, even telling me not to bring it up again."

Not wanting to belabour the subject any longer especially since Lill was on her lunch break, I said: "Please promise to let me know whenever you feel that I can be of any help whatsoever."

"I promise", she replied as she hurried back to work.

Hardly a fortnight had passed since that lunch "Chez Paul" when I found a message on my phone when I came home from work. It was Lill who asked if she could meet me again for lunch later that week.

As I had anticipated, this time it was Lill who started relating a number of incidents that had occurred since our last lunch meeting which made her realize that far from abating, Jerry's behavior had worsened to the point that she looked forward with relief when he disappeared into his study every evening. Lill appeared genuinely desperate and asked me to talk to my brother. "Maybe there is something wrong with me and I am the cause of his temper tantrums", she said. "Please talk to him and try to understand him. I can't. I've given up."

A few days later I asked my brother to meet me for lunch without giving him any details.

I had reserved a table in a secluded corner of the restaurant and that turned out to be a wise decision, indeed.

I came right to the point by telling him that in a recent phone call, I had overheard his shouting voice and Lill crying.

"I believe you two have a problem and I want to help in bringing you together again", I said. "I am your brother, I love you and if I don't offer to help in a difficult situation, who will?" I added.

Jerry had been fidgeting with his fork while listening to me, obviously irritated by what he heard. As soon as I had finished talking, he shot back: "Look Dave, I appreciate your offer but we don't need it. You do things your way and I do things my way. Okay? I don't intend to change. This is how I am, take it or leave it. The one who has to change is Lill. She has to get used to my ways which make more sense than her preconceived ideas of marital bliss and puppy love and the 'Yes dear, no dear' she saw in her parent's home. She just has to adapt to a different lifestyle and the sooner the better."

I tried to offer suggestions of him being more mindful of her upbringing and thus make the adaptation process smoother and less confrontational, but he kept interrupting me with angry retorts. Finally before leaving me, Jerry said: "Look Dave, do me a favour. Keep out of this and I mean keep out of my private life. I don't need your help or advice. You follow me?"

With a cursory "Bye and thanks for lunch", Jerry left the table without looking back once.

A few days later I sat down with Lill at "Chez Paul" and told her about the outcome of the conversation with her husband. After listening intently to my words, she started to cry. Silently and almost unobtrusively, tears were running from her eyes. She kept wiping them as she bravely continued our conversation.

"I will try", she said. "I will try to leave the room when he has his shouting bouts and I will try to discuss only what is strictly necessary when he comes home from work. Maybe that conciliatory approach will help in taming the violence in him. I will do my best." She said, adding: "I hope he will appreciate my understanding and cooperation."

That evening, after dinner in my home, I stayed up thinking. Two things were uppermost in my mind. The first was an immense wave of compassion for Lill, that gentle and beautiful woman who was trying to save her marriage by both adapting to and appeasing her husband.

The second thing that made me think was that Jerry had not always been that aggressive or bellicose a person. What had brought about this change in him? I asked myself and I really could not find a reason for his obvious transformation.

A few days later, I phoned Jerry intending to relate to him Lill's accommodating intentions, but he refused to meet me for lunch. All I could do was to give him a brief outline of her cooperative intentions in the hope that normal relations could eventually be reinstated between them.

"Okay, Dave", was Jerry's reply. "I heard you. Let's see if she will change. I doubt if she can but let's wait and see. Thanks, Dave." He ended the conversation with a cursory "Bye".

*   *   *

These unsuccessful attempts to save my brother's marriage were actually the beginning of a long drawn-out effort during which I not only repeatedly tried to mollify my brother's attitude, but also sought to provide support and solace to Lill, who was trying to cope in one way or another with her husband's behavior.

But while my peacemaking efforts were a complete failure, another development started to take place.

As might have been foreseen, my repeated meetings with Lill, which were originally solely motivated by compassion and wanting to help, gradually turned into some deeper feelings and ended up with both of us falling in love with each other.

It came naturally. She was very unhappy to the point of having decided to divorce Jerry and I had no binding relationship at the time.

Jerry and Lill had now been married for two years. During one of our lunch meetings we decided that as soon as the divorce formalities were completed, the two of us would tie the knot.

We were both very excited about this and I noticed that Lill's pretty face which had developed premature lines during the last year, began to regain its beauty.

The next two months were a real nightmare for all three of us.

While the divorce formalities were on-going, Jerry's behavior began to worsen. He accused his wife of having come under my influence and he accused me of having turned her against him. The divorce, itself, was an ugly episode with the two lawyers frequently at odds with each other but in the end the court pronounced the separation in view of the obvious and very real incompatibility of the two sides.

As was to be predicted, the real storm broke out when, after all the divorce formalities were completed, I informed my brother that Lill and I would get married.

We were so happy and excited at starting a new life together that we ignored Jerry's unpleasant comments, trusting that in time both sides would forget the marriage that was not meant to be and go on with their lives.

*   *   *

More than twenty-five years have passed since my brother's divorce and my marriage.

Twenty-five years during which many things happened in the Balinski family.

Let me start with my dear dad who passed away in 1990 at the age of eighty-five. I am sure that the awareness of the strained relations between his sons, Jerry's early divorce but most importantly, my mother's premature death did not help his heart condition he had been living with for many years.

He never remarried. Dad spent his last years in retirement from a profitable real estate business. In fact, he amassed a small fortune but gave away most of it either to charities or to local museums. He also left Jerry and myself, as well as my children some money in his will.

Dad died as a respected member of the congregation. Several highly placed community leaders delivered very laudable eulogies at his funeral.

I was heartbroken because I had loved my father, even more so after my mother' death, which hit me far too early in my life.

*   *   *

Lill and I were both maturing into middle age after twenty-five blissful years. Ours was an exemplary family life. We had two beautiful children, actually two beautiful daughters who had inherited much of their mother's looks and gracefulness. Both were professionals, one in business management and the other in healthcare.

I had become a senior partner in my law firm.

The family enjoyed trips abroad, a very comfortable second home in the Laurentians and we even managed to spend every year some time together, in Florida, where many of our other friends were also vacationing.

All in all, it had been a very pleasant twenty-five years I could look back on.

*   *   *

The story of my brother's life, however, was a very different kettle of fish. He never remarried after his divorce, preferring to spend long stretches of time with alternating lady friends, some of them divorcees or widows.

Professionally he was doing well. After a number of years with the same investment company, he joined a bank as asset manager. He also travelled often and lived in the same house all these years.

Although we did not meet too often, I tried to keep in touch with him, especially on his birthday, on the graduation of our daughters and I always invited him to my home on the High Holydays. On most of these occasions, he came, usually with a gift and accompanied by his lady friend. He did not talk too much and left with a reserved: "Thank you Dave. It was very nice."

But this routine relationship underwent an abrupt change when, one afternoon, I received a phone call from one of his lady friends, informing me that my brother was in the hospital after having suffered a heart attack.

I immediately rushed to his side, but was told that he was in intensive care. The next day Lill and I, together with my daughter Jodi and a bouquet of flowers, went to the hospital where he was recovering from a serious and almost fatal coronary thrombosis. Outside his room, the doctor told me that he would need a while to recuperate, and afterwards should lead a measured and quiet life, keeping away from stress.

After Jerry was sent home. I went to visit him and told him: "Jerry, the house adjacent to our duplex has been vacated and is up for sale. I strongly suggest, no I insist that you sell your house and move right next to us. In fact, I will have a passage built between the basement walls. You should not live alone. I will help you with the move. I want you to consider our home as if it was your own. You can have your meals with us if you wish. We want to keep an eye on you just in case you don't feel well. That's all."

To my surprise, Jerry flashed a smile and said: "Thanks Dave. Okay, I'll do that. I appreciate this very much. I'll try not to bother anyone."

"No bother, Jerry", I replied. "You take it easy and you'll be just fine. Lots of people have heart attacks these days."

Well, everything went as planned and after a few week of hard work by all concerned, Jerry was comfortably ensconced in the house right next to ours.

I don't know whether it was the heart attack or the passing of time, but by the time Jerry became our next door neighbor, he was a far cry from what I had known him to be. He was mostly quiet, read a lot, watched TV and went for regular walks, even in the winter. He often sat down to dinner with us, acting for all intents and purposes, like a regular member of the family. Gone was the aggressivity that had been his hallmark for so many years.

This peaceful coexistence lasted a good many years. Not once during this time was there a problem between us. He led his life and we did ours and although I cannot say that there was an excessive or exuberant show of love between us, we all got along just fine.

But this pleasant routine came to a sudden end one night when Jerry fell from his chair while sitting down to dinner with us. We immediately phoned for an ambulance which arrived within minutes.

That night at about three in the morning, my brother Jerry passed away after another heart attack, despite frantic resuscitation efforts.

There was a short but dignified funeral. Not too many people attended and most of those who did were actually friends of mine and Lill's. One of my daughters and I read eulogies briefly describing his life. The Rabbi spoke some eloquent words and we proceeded to the cemetery for the burial.

We were all genuinely sad, especially since we had grown used to the presence of a quiet and undemanding elderly man near us.

It was a few days after the funeral that I discovered Jerry's hidden manuscript entitled: "My Mother's Story".

I think the time has now come to reveal it. So here it is, word for word, exactly as I found it.

*   *   *

**My Mother's Story
By Jerry Balinski**

This is the story my mother told me a few days before her death. It was a rainy afternoon and there was no one else in the house at the time. She was lying in bed and I sat near her doing some homework while keeping her company. She was at the end of a long but unfortunately unsuccessful battle with lung cancer.

I was twenty years old, attending university.

I must tell you that I loved my mother very much and this for a number of reasons. First and foremost she took very good care of me and my younger brother David as well as of my father. Everything we needed was there and it was done with a smile and a kiss or a hug. Secondly, she taught us not only what is right or wrong but she spent long hours reading stories to us. She even watched us when we went skating or playing baseball. And, of course, she was always there when we were sick or fell or hurt ourselves as we grew up.

That's why I was so sad, so terribly sad when our dad told us that mom was suffering from an incurable disease and she may soon be no longer with us. I cried my heart out when I heard this and thought that the whole world around me had collapsed. Why, why must she leave us, I kept asking myself.

That afternoon, in her room, sitting up in bed, she suddenly said to me: "Put away your book. I want you to listen to my story, to our story, but I want you to promise me to keep every word I am going to tell you for yourself. Just for yourself. Remember that this is a promise to your dying mother. Don't cry, she added when she saw me reaching for my handkerchief. I've done enough crying during the last few weeks for all of us put together. Don't cry. Just listen and remember all I am going to tell you. Alright, my love?" "Okay, Mom", I said.

"When the Germans entered Poland in 1939," she started, "I was a young Polish woman living in Warsaw and I was a prostitute. Yes, a prostitute, working in a high class, very elegant bordello together with a number of other girls. Why was I doing that is a long story but let me just tell you that I came from a broken home. My father was an alcoholic and my mother was a poor, chronically depressed woman. I grew up in poverty and neglect. The need to survive made me drift to the whorehouse before I was twenty. I had many customers, most of them rich and famous, who looked for pleasures that they could not find in their homes.

Among my steady customers was a very wealthy Polish businessman, a widower who fell in love with me and promised to marry me. He was good-looking and very kind to me, bringing gifts and flowers every time he came to be with me, which was very often. I liked him very much and genuinely looked forward to starting a new and normal life with him.

One day, he came with a bunch of roses and told me that he wanted me to say goodbye to what I was doing, move into a nearby small hotel until he could prepare the place where we would live together, somewhere in the Warsaw suburbs. Needless to say, I was delighted and could not wait for that day. He also told me that he had made all arrangements for my leaving, with the owner of the place I was working. And, he had already paid a month's rent in advance to the hotel where I would stay.

He also gave me some money to tide me over until we got married. He visited me at the hotel, always telling me that our marriage would take place in a matter of weeks or even days. Of course, life in Warsaw was severely disturbed by the raging war.

Well, I had been waiting in the hotel for about three weeks when I discovered that I was pregnant. My future husband was delighted, brought me more flowers and paid the hotel for another month's stay. 'Please be patient, we are almost there', were his parting words.

But, believe it or not these words turned out to be the last ones I ever heard from him. He disappeared. He never came back. Gone. I tried very hard to reach him by phone or messenger but, to no avail. He had vanished. I must tell you that because of the German invasion, the bombardments and fighting around Warsaw, I could only assume that he had either been killed or else arrested for some reason.

Need I tell you that I was now getting desperate? Really desperate.

While still waiting in the hotel, I had a surprise visit one day from a man by the name of Simon Lebovitz. He had gone to the brothel to see me and was told of my present address.

Simon was one of my regular clients whom I had not seen in a long time and there was ample reason for his disappearance.

Simon was actually a convicted criminal who had been sentenced some two years ago to serve fifteen years in prison because he had been found guilty of a number of crimes.

In fact, the Lebovitz case was all in the Warsaw papers at the time.

Simon had embezzled large amounts from unsuspecting retirees and widows under the pretext of investing their money and giving them big returns. But he used all this money for himself and paid interest from the amounts he continued to take from people. He had done this for a number of years but when the fraudulent scheme was discovered, the unfortunate victims tried to get their money back but in vain. He had either spent or hidden it away. But this was not all.

One elderly couple, from whom he stole all their life savings, committed suicide when they realized that their only nest egg was gone.

Another fleeced investor went to Simon's home one night to demand the return of his money. A fight broke out between the two during which Simon shot and killed the man. However, Simon's lawyer pleaded self-defence because the victim was, apparently, reaching for his gun, as Simon shot him. In fact, a loaded gun was found in the dead man's pocket.

At the end of the trial, which was widely featured in the media, Simon was sentenced to fifteen years in prison for tax fraud, embezzlement and having caused the death of three people.

He had been in jail for two years, when, in late 1939 the war started and the Germans bombarded Warsaw with their dreaded screaming, diving planes, disrupting the life of everyone. They also scored a direct hit on a penitentiary right outside Warsaw, where Simon was. In the confusion and chaos following the air attack, a number of inmates managed to escape, and among them was Simon. And now he was in my hotel room telling me about his escape.

'Alicia', he said: 'As you can imagine, I cannot stay in Warsaw for too long now. Both the Polish police and the Germans will soon start to look for the escapees, including myself. In other words, I need to get out of Poland as soon as possible. You once told me that you knew someone who forged documents, passes and I.D. cards. Can you put me in touch with him? I need forged papers now to leave the country. I will pay what he demands and you, as well, for your help.'

As I listened to him, an idea entered my mind. You must understand that I was about to give up hope of ever seeing my runaway friend again. I was pregnant and dreading the rapidly expanding German occupation and all the atrocities and problems it involved. In other words, I was quite desperate.

So, I told Simon: 'I will take you to the forger right away, but on one condition; you will take me with you as your pregnant wife when you leave the country.'

If it took me a few seconds to come up with this "quid pro quo", it took Simon less than a second to say: 'Okay, Alicia, you've got a deal. Let's get the hell out of this place, like yesterday!'

We went to this forger, and believe it or not, within three days, during which Simon was hiding in my room, we had perfectly legitimate-looking Swiss I.D. cards of Mr. and Mrs. Bruno Egli, residents of the Canton of Basel.

Within hours we packed a few belongings and headed for the Central Railway Station in downtown Warsaw. Imagine our joy when we found out that one of the last trains to leave Warsaw for neutral Switzerland was due to depart in a few hours. Well, on board of this train were also the Eglis returning home just in time.

After a long and frequently interrupted journey, we finally arrived in Basel. Dead tired but overjoyed of having made the incredible escape. We headed for a small hotel which was to be our first shelter until we could decide on our next moves.

Well, it turned out that the next moves were not entirely up to us, but rather up to the Swiss police to decide.

When entering Switzerland, the Border Police had made photocopies of our papers and sure enough found out that they were fakes. However, when we told them that we were a Jewish couple from Poland, fleeing certain death by the Nazis, and that I was pregnant, they informed us that the Swiss government had just enacted a law admitting pregnant Jewish women fleeing from Nazi-occupied countries, allowing them and their immediate families to stay in Switzerland until the end of hostilities in Europe or until they could leave for other destinations.

Can you imagine our joy when we heard this? Especially my joy, considering that I was a Catholic posing as Simon's Jewish wife.

Well, from then on everything went almost according to plan. You were born in 1940 in the Basler Kantonsspital while your father worked as part of a construction crew, building new airports all over Switzerland.

We received monthly cheques from the government and had free medical care.

After all that the two of us had gone through in Poland, Switzerland was like living on another planet. We loved it.

In 1942, we received a letter from the Swiss branch of the Jewish Agency telling us that a convoy of Jewish migrants would leave for Palestine and we were part of it.

We were issued temporary papers identifying us as Sam and Alicia Balinski, names we had given the Agency, pretending that our Polish papers were lost. By the way, I almost forgot. I converted to Judaism in a beautiful, small synagogue in Basel.

And so, by the end of 1942, the three of us arrived in Haifa on a Turkish boat we had boarded in Istanbul after our journey from Switzerland. It was a long and tiring train ride especially with a two year old baby, because the Germans had already occupied much of Europe and we had to stop frequently for controls and inspections.

Needless to say, we were very excited to set foot on the soil of the Holy Land. We were sent to a Kibbutz and lived together with a spirited group of residents who had been in the country for many years as well as newcomers like us. We all worked on farms and loved the communal lifestyle.

Shortly after our arrival at the Kibbutz, I became pregnant again. Your father and I as well as all the Kibbutzniks around us were delighted when we told them of the happy event.

At the beginning of 1944, that is after two years at the Kibbutz, your father joined the Jewish Brigade, which was an integral part of the British Eighth Army stationed in Egypt.

Sam, as he was now called, served in the Brigade, at first as a soldier, but later on as a Staff Sargent until his demobilization in early 1946. He saw action in Europe and fought in France and The Netherlands.

On his return to the Kibbutz, he was told that on account of his war service in the British Army, he qualified for an immigration visa to Canada or Australia. Well, Australia seemed too far away to us but Canada looked like a promising destination in North America, offering a brighter future for our children. Remember all this was before the establishment of the State of Israel. Palestine was still under British Mandate and there was a lot of unrest in the Middle East at the time. So we opted for Canada, and the rest, my dear Jerry, is history.

On a final note, my mother ended her story, "I want you to know that I never regretted that moment in my hotel room in Warsaw, when I told Simon "I'll take you to the forger provided you take me with you." It was the best decision I ever took in my life.

I had to get this story off of my chest while I can. Remember your promise my dear, beloved Jerry, to keep it for yourself. You have a right to know the truth. I love you very much."

Her last words were drowned in not tears, but sobs. I sat up next to her in bed and held her in my arms for a very long time.

I silently left her bedroom with a feeling that I had just lived through the most touching, most significant and also the saddest hours of my young life.

Less than a week after this experience, my poor mother passed away just hours after we rushed her to the hospital.

I had lost much more than a mother. I had lost part of my young life.

*   *   *

This is my mother's "Story of My Life", faithfully written down by my brother Jerry that I found among his personal belongings.

When I had finished reading it, I sat down, in his now empty living room, and thought about what it all meant.

In fact, it was a revelation of my parent's background that was completely unknown to me.

Never in a million years would I have guessed that my late father, the respected and honoured member of our congregation, devoted husband of my mother, was in reality a convicted murderer with blood on his hands, a thief, a criminal who ruined so many lives, who escaped from a fifteen year prison sentence and my beloved mother, my guardian angel was once a Polish prostitute in a whorehouse.

I relived the afternoon that my brother Jerry, had spent in our dying mother's bedroom and tried to experience the feelings all these unexpected revelations evoked in him.

Especially when he became aware that he was not even my dad's real son, neither my natural brother, but the illegitimate child of an unknown Polish man who disappeared from view.

While all these revelations shocked me profoundly, as I went on reading my mother's story, I also realized that I learned about them at a mature age, as an established and successful professional, whereas my late brother faced these unexpected and shocking truths as an adolescent, at an age when young people are most vulnerable to external influences impacting on the formation of their personalities and their place in the society they are a part of.

All these thoughts amply provided me with an explanation as to why Jerry had become a different person after he had learned the truth about his real background. I now understood why he had turned into a confused and embittered man who felt that he did not belong to this righteous, conformist and respected life his parents projected to the world around them.

Jerry just could not handle the shock his mother's revelations created in him and, what aggravated the turmoil in his mind was the knowledge that he was not allowed to share this burden with anyone around him, neither with me nor with my father, who was not really his dad.

As all these thoughts went through my mind, I suddenly started to cry because I came to realize that Jerry had forfeited a good part of his adult life because of his emotional problems and only reverted to a balanced and normal individual in his later life, when it was too late for him to enjoy family and friends.

I cannot describe the sorrow and sadness I felt that evening in Jerry's empty house.

I decided to honour my brother's and my parent's memory as well as his promise to my mother by simply taking the manuscript with me and locking it up with my other personal papers, safely away from anyone's reach for as long as I lived.

A short while later, I was back in my own home, surrounded by my loving family to enjoy another day in our lives.

That night I went to bed with a smile on my face. A warm feeling had suddenly come over me.

A feeling of intense love and bittersweet compassion, of nostalgia but most of all, regret for not having been able to help my brother Jerry, by sharing the onus he carried for the best part of his life.

A FRIEND'S ADVICE

They say that life is stranger than fiction. But sometimes life can be even more than that. It can be more interesting or indeed more heartwarming than fiction. I think that the following true story may lend credence to that statement.

It all started sixty-five years ago in Istanbul, Turkey. I was in my twenties and had a very close friend with whom we enjoyed the premarital bliss of doing everything young people have always been doing to make life interesting, amusing and even naughty. We were part of a small group of youngsters who shared similar values and interests in life.

It so happens that this friend of mine had met a young girl, who was both attractive and intelligent. They started dating, obviously with the thought in mind of eventually ending up at the altar. But, while both began to develop strong feelings for each other, my friend confided in me that he found her too serious, too reserved and perhaps too shy to share a life with him. "She hardly says a word and only responds when talked to, while I am outgoing and participate in whatever goes on around me, she sits there like a beautiful wallflower. I realize she has a great deal of qualities, but because of this difference between us, a marriage will just not work." He kept telling me.

Just at that time, I received an offer from one of my father's friends who owned a textile factory in Yorkshire, England. The offer said: "Why don't you come and work in our mill for a year or so. If you like it you may want to stay here and if you don't you can always return to Turkey. It will be an experience for you and I happen to have a vacancy in my management team."

Needless to say, I jumped at the opportunity and within a couple of weeks I was on my way to Liversedge, a small community in Yorkshire, halfway between Leeds and Huddersfield.

Barely two weeks had passed since I had plunged into a very different and yet very exciting world, when I found, one evening upon returning to my room on the second floor of a local pub, a letter on my pillow. It was from my friend in Istanbul. I ripped it open and was stunned by its contents.

"I gave my relationship with Edda a great deal of thought after you left for England", the letter began. "And I came to the conclusion that this will not be a good marriage because neither will I make her happy nor will she make me happy. We are just on opposite poles. She is presently away with her parents in Paris, but on her return next week I will break off our relationship and tell her to make other plans. Let's go our own ways. Goodbye and the best of luck to you. I am sorry."

This, or words to that effect was what my friend intended to tell the girl on her return to Istanbul.

I read this letter twice and then sat down behind a little desk beside my bed to pen a reply.

On three closely scribbled pages, I told my friend that he would be very wrong in severing this relationship on account of her shyness and timidity. I reminded him of the fact that this girl had not been brought up in cosmopolitan Istanbul but in a small Turkish town by parents who had espoused local customs that relegated women to a more reserved role in society and that it was up to him to bring out her real personality by making her feel important and needed, indeed as part of his life. "Bring out the best in her." I wrote.

"Let her make the decision as to how to spend a weekend or what movie or restaurant to go to. Don't be the leader in your relationship. Ask for her advice and counsel and let her feel important and even depended on and you will see how she will come out of her cocoon and rise to challenges."

I also reminded my friend of her qualities, especially of her honesty, her good judgement, her intellect and her kindness.

In short, I hammered away on these three pages my advice to give the girl a chance.

It was late at night when I finished the letter and dropped it into the nearest red circular container with the crown and the words "Royal Mail" on it. When I went to bed, I felt that I had done my best to help a friend take a step back and ponder before making a decision that could not be revoked.

For a few weeks there was silence, but then, one day I had a phone call from my friend and his girlfriend, shouting: "Ben, too bad you will miss the most important party in our lives. We are celebrating our engagement in two weeks. You can raise your glass of beer or whatever you drink in an English pub to the health and good luck of the three of us. And thanks for everything, Ben", both shouted happily before hanging up.

Well, the rest is history, as they say. They got married while I was still in England. When I returned to Turkey, I saw them a few times, then I got married and eventually emigrated to Canada. My friend and I lost contact with each other. He settled down to become a dentist in Istanbul and I started a new life in Montreal.

*   *   *

The next chapter in this heartwarming story started a few months ago or a good sixty-five years after I had written that fateful letter in Yorkshire.

I received, one day, an e-mail from a person who wrote: "Dear Ben, you don't know me and I don't know you but I must meet you at the earliest possible date.

You see, I am the son of your one-time closest friend in Istanbul. I am now sixty years old, happily married with two grown children and I live in England.

My father died a few years ago and my mother just passed away recently. But when I cleared up her belongings I found a roll, tied up with a red ribbon in a locked drawer. I opened it and read a letter written to my father by a certain Ben Sperer in 1951. I read it again and again and could not believe my eyes. Here was an advice from a man I never met and this man was the reason for my parent's marriage and consequently for my presence in this world. Obviously my mom had kept your letter as a precious souvenir. So, I decided to meet this Ben Sperer, but where is he and is he still around after all these years?

Well, I made enquiries in Istanbul, found someone who told me that this man now lives in Canada, I asked some more people and finally located you.

Do you understand why I must meet you, Ben? I decided to come and see you in two weeks. For a few days I want to talk and listen to you in an effort to bring back part of my parent's life and my life. For me it will be a journey into the past to revive a story that started in a Yorkshire pub and led to sixty-five years of happiness, shared by two adoring parents and one son, whom you are now about to meet."

Well, meet we did. For four days we travelled in and around Montreal, I introduced him to my family and friends and then he invited me to visit him in London. In fact, I spent three memorable days with him and his family and one evening he asked his closest London friends to spend "An Evening with Ben Sperer" during which I related the preceding story in all its details.

A story which had remained dormant for so many years.

*   *   *

THE CONTESSA - (A True Story)

There are times in everyone's life that are marked by change, sometimes even convulsive change, brought on by extraordinary events that fall out of a perfectly blue sky, like an unexpected blizzard or thunderstorm.

The early nineteen-eighties were one of these watershed times in my life.

I had been married for twenty blissful years to Daisy, the love of my life and we had a son, who had graduated from high school and was trying to orient himself towards a career or profession. I had an interesting and well-paid position in a large pharmaceutical company and looked forward to steady ascension to senior management. We were all in perfect health and had surrounded ourselves with caring and interesting friends, with whom we shared our leisure time, which included regular vacations abroad.

In short, we were a happy well-adjusted family, living the life like so many others in our upwardly moving world.

But then, most, if not all of this changed by rapidly succeeding events that began to unfold in the early days of 1980.

It all started with a phone call from a well-known Swiss publisher who asked me to join his company as head of a medical literature division. I was in my late fifties at the time and looked forward to a regular retirement ushered in by the proverbial set of golf clubs accompanied by a "thank you and goodbye" letter signed by the board chairman.

After much soul-searching, and some encouragement from my wife who rightly held that a chance like that was not likely to recur in my life, I accepted and embarked on a completely new career starting with the creation of a new business and all that this involved.

To celebrate this promising phase in our lives, my wife and I went on a short vacation to Mexico from where Daisy returned with a bad chest cold. That was what we thought it was. But the day following our arrival in Montreal and after a visit to our family physician at St. Mary's hospital, we were given the devastating news that Daisy did not have a cold but advanced lung cancer. And this without any foreboding symptoms except the recent cough.

This utterly terrifying revelation was followed by months of chemotherapy and surgery, but all of it to no avail. By the end of 1980, the true love of my life was laid to rest in an early grave. She had attained the ripe age of fifty-four.

Needless to say that the year that followed was beyond any doubt, the most somber and most trying time of my entire existence.

Trying to cope with this irreplaceable loss and the absence of my son who had suddenly decided to move to a kibbutz in Israel, and on top of all this, my attempts to crank up a new business, was indeed a horribly trying experience as I approached middle age.
Little wonder that I developed symptoms of a depression and had to contact one of my doctor friends whom I had known from my previous life in the pharmaceutical field. He recommended a two to three week vacation, away from my present surroundings.

I followed his advice and ended up a short while later at a Club Med resort in Southern Turkey. It was a newly opened luxurious spa offering all sorts of diversions and activities, and of course, beautiful beaches on the Mediterranean.

I checked in one evening at the Club and made myself comfortable in the small bungalow assigned to me. Shortly afterwards, I went to the dining room and sat down at a table for two in anticipation of a well-deserved dinner, following the lengthy journey. While gazing at the menu, I suddenly noticed a lady approaching my table and politely asking if she could join me. I said, "Yes, of course", and helped her to sit down.

A conversation immediately started and continued in an animated way throughout the lengthy dinner.

Anna Maria Fiorini was an Italian lady married to an Austrian government official. She was very attractive, in fact, I would say that she was beautiful, in her late forties, very elegant and well-groomed. She spoke several languages fluently and told me that she was a Contessa, her father being Count Fiorini, who was for many years the legal advisor to the Vatican and a close friend of the Pope. She not only told me a great deal about herself, but she also asked me endless questions regarding my personal life.

I can safely say that during the two hours of dinner and later on a terrace overlooking the beach where coffee was being served, my new acquaintance and I had talked non-stop about ourselves, our lives and about our worlds.

It had been an interesting evening indeed when we parted close to midnight, promising each other to meet again the next day on the beach.

When I finally crawled into bed, I felt I had related to Anna Maria, a good portion of my life and, in exchange had listened to a great deal of herself and her background.

We met at the beach the next day and between dips in the azure blue Mediterranean, and lunch, continued to talk about anything under the sun.

It turned out that Anna Maria and her husband had been married for some twenty-three years, had a married daughter and, except for the first five years of their marriage, had lived separate lives. She found her husband to be extremely boring, and getting on her nerves, a typical bureaucrat, albeit one with a PhD in political science.

So, after five years of an unpleasant relationship both decided by common accord to live their own lives. They could not divorce since they were Catholics, and had been married in the Vatican by her uncle, a Cardinal. Anna Maria had inherited a sizeable fortune from her late father which enabled her to constantly travel around the world, staying for weeks or even months in the most expensive five-star hotels. She was, however, always home in Vienna for Christmas, for her husband's birthday and when he was ill, but the rest of the time she followed the jet-set, in other words wherever it was sunny and elegant and exciting, like Dubai, Las Vegas, Hawaii, Paris or New York. The world was her playground.

This arrangement also suited her husband since, he, first of all, found her to be frivolous and tiring, furthermore, he was completely immersed in his political life which required him to travel and attend meetings abroad, and, besides, he had adequate domestic help which saw to it that he was always impeccably attired and fed.

So, for both, this was a perfect arrangement. Their union was based on common interests, and friendship without the elements of passion, romance or even physical nearness.

All this, together with countless other details and anecdotes, Anna Maria told me during the first few days of our encounter in exchange for my report which appeared rather modest and straight-forward. The story of a happy marriage, the raising of a family and a busy professional life just like many other young Canadian couples, unfortunately cut brutally short by the unexpected loss of my wife.

When I came back to my room in the afternoon of the first day at the beach, I found several pieces of luggage inside my bungalow. I had the answer to this intrusion served to me during dinner. "I decided to join you in your place", Anna Maria said with an impish smile on her pretty face. "I hope you don't mind. I think we make good company, don't you think?" she added. "What a splendid idea", I replied. "I hope you will not be awakened by my snoring." I joked. "The walls in the bungalow don't seem to be soundproof." "Who said anything about walls?" She burst out laughing.

I realized that I had not just found a conversation partner but more, indeed much more than that. I had actually swallowed a bait, albeit a very pleasant and tasty bait, but, a bait all the same. I had been gently drawn into a new world which was completely different from my hitherto parochial existence.

In fact, this two-week vacation turned out to be a honeymoon, an extravaganza, an incredibly passionate experience many a man could only dream of.

Anna Maria and I became inseparable lovers and I must say that she was the most pleasant company one could imagine.

She regaled me with intimate stories of her friends which included European aristocracy and even the ruling family of Monaco.

About a week had passed since our encounter, when one evening after dinner, Anna Maria opened up with her plans for the future:

"This is what you and I will be doing as soon as we leave this place by the end of next week. Listen carefully", she added. "I decided that I want to spend the rest of my life with you", she continued. "We will be a couple, just like married people. I will be the only woman in your life and you will be the only man in mine. And this is how we will live from now on.

As I told you", she went on, "I cannot divorce, not only for religious reasons, but also because Peter is an official government figure and I want to spare him any embarrassment. So, we will keep our relationship secret from him. He knows that I travel all the time and, of course meet people, so, as far as he is concerned, you, my darling, will be just another vacation acquaintance. Leave it to me, I will manage it very nicely.

Now, you and I will meet many times during the year. Both in your residence, which will be our home, and, in vacation spots anywhere you would like in the world. You name the place and I will be there for as long as you can stay. I realize that you have a business to run. And, speaking of business, you can either continue with your new career in publishing or you can own a nice and very elegant men's wear boutique on Bond Street. You see my best friend's husband owned a well-known men's shop in London. He just died two weeks ago and my friend has asked me if I either want to join her as a partner or buy the entire store from her. So, you see, we have a ready-made, very efficiently run business that I can buy tomorrow, and you and I can own it, lock, stock and barrel. I am sure you will soon learn how to manage it. This way, you will leave Montreal and move to London, where I own a flat on Sloane Street in Belgravia; one of the best places to live in London.

You will resign from your new job with the Swiss publishers, and will move to England. My lawyer will take care of all necessary formalities. I am sure there will be no problem. As for your son, he will either stay in Israel or he can join you in your London flat. It has two bedrooms and is beautifully furnished.

I will stay at the flat with you from time to time and we will continue to meet anywhere you wish for short encounters, if necessary even for weekends because you will be busy with your shop on Bond Street."

Anna Maria had been talking uninterruptedly with an emotionally enhanced voice and full of enthusiasm. She seemed very sure and assertive. Obviously, she had given her proposal a lot of thought before revealing it to me.

I was sitting with my scotch in my hand, facing and listening to her as though in an unreal setting.

Then she moved very close to me and, looking straight into my eyes, she said, "You realize, of course, that I am madly in love with you. You are my dream come true and you are the first man in my life to hear these words from me. You have everything I have ever looked for in a man – elegance and brains." And then she said, "Tell me that you love me too. From your behaviour during the last week I think I have the answer to my question. I know you love me and I know that we will be very happy together."

She came closer to me and we kissed passionately.

It's very difficult for me to describe my state of mind at that moment and my reaction to these sincerely uttered words. She looked into my eyes seeking a reciprocal declaration of love. But I was actually at a loss for words. Of course I had immensely enjoyed every moment of our being together. How could I not have? Here was a beautiful woman, intelligent to the point of being bubbly and effervescent, elegant in her demeanour, a dream come true you might say.
And yet I had not fallen in love with her. Was it the too precipitous cascade of events of the past few days, was it the vast divide between our backgrounds or perhaps that here was a married woman who offered me a lifelong relationship based on keeping it secret from her husband? Or even my subconscious rejection of suddenly becoming a man kept in style by a rich woman. Most probably a combination of all of the above that prevented me from honestly saying to her: "I love you too Anna Maria and I want to spend the rest of my life with you!" I just could not say these words to her. Neither could I lie or pretend, especially not in the face of her sincerity and her determination.

She kept looking into my eyes seeking an answer. And all I could say to her was "I love everything about you Anna Maria, you are a man's dream come true. But I cannot tell you that I want to spend the rest of my life with you under the conditions you mentioned before. I don't want to spend a life in secrecy, hiding from your husband and your family. I am just getting over not one but two traumatic events in my life: the loss of my wife and the change in my profession. I need a home, I need peace and quiet to cope and function. I need the warmth of a family, not the constant displacements and the unfamiliarity of hotel rooms even if they are in five-star palaces."

"You don't need to travel all the time to see me", she interjected. "You will live in London in a beautiful flat in Belgravia, with a housekeeper to take care of everything."

"Look", I said, "I have an idea. How about we try this relationship out for one year. Let me go back to Montreal, let me get my new job going and let us meet as often as possible in your favourite spots. Let me also consider the thought of living in London. Let's see if it works for both of us. I am willing to give it a try."

"Okay", she said, somewhat disappointed, "but I am still convinced that we will both achieve a modus vivendi and end up with a happy relationship albeit in a 'Flying Dutchman' jet-set style."

Making every minute of our last days at the Club Med resort count, we enjoyed our togetherness and then left each other for our respective destinations. She went back to Vienna and I to Montreal. Our goodbye at the airport was heart-wrenching to say the least. She cried like a child and did not want to let go of my hand. Never in my life had I gone through an emotional parting scene like that.

Back in Montreal, I plunged headlong into my new job which involved the thousand and one details of setting up the branch office of an international company.

I had moved to a new flat on Nuns Island. On many evenings, when I came home after a busy day and a restaurant dinner, Anna Maria phoned to chat and tell me when and where we would next meet.

And meet we did over the following months. From Geneva to Greece and from Copenhagen to the Balearic Islands. She, that is her travel agent, made all hotel reservations. All I had to do was to show up at the chosen place. It was a tiring but also exciting life, because in addition to these perambulations, I also had to travel repeatedly to Switzerland to coordinate all arrangements with my new company.

It was now 1983 and it was beyond any doubt the year I spent more time sitting in airports and planes than in all the years of my life before.

And then, towards the latter part of that year Anna Maria surprised me one evening. When I arrived home at my flat on Nuns Island, she was sitting in the lobby of the building, jumping up to hug me as I came in.

"Surprise, surprise," she yelled. "I arrived earlier today, I am staying at the Ritz Carlton and I brought a lawyer from my solicitors in Paris. He knows Montreal well and has already compiled a list of beautiful properties in Westmount, one of which I will buy so that we can have a 'pied-a-terre' in Montreal. You see", she added, "since I know that you want to start this new company of yours, I thought that if we have a house right here in Montreal, you can stay here and I will come from time to time, of course, without arousing the suspicion of my husband. I am sure that I can manage it during my frequent trips. I did not think you liked the idea of the shop on Bond Street too much. What do you think? Tomorrow we will meet with my lawyer. Together we will look at some of the Westmount properties. Okay?"

I was beginning to feel like a trapped animal. Or even like a puppet being manipulated by a person holding the strings.

In contrast to my uneasy feelings, Anna Maria was reigning supreme like a maestro who is in full control of his orchestra and enjoys every moment of running the show.

After dinner with my unexpected guest, I went back to my flat and spent a good part of the night reviewing the turn my private life had taken and the direction in which it was going at a fast clip. Frankly, I felt I had lost control.

The next morning, I told Anna Maria that contrary to our agreement, we had only gone through half of the year we had set aside as a trial period. "Why precipitate things?" To which she answered, "Because I cannot wait for the moment we will belong to each other! But, she added, "You are right, let us see how the next few months will allow you to get used to a different kind of life, to my kind of life, the one that is spent in the fast lane. Life is short, you know! Hah-ha!"

A day later, we both flew to New York where she had booked tickets for "Evita", the play that was raking in rave reviews at that time. Two days later, she flew to Hawaii and I was back in Montreal.

Shortly, after that visit, I was invited to dinner by some friends in Montreal where I happened to meet a very nice lady I had never seen before. She was a recently widowed mother of three grown children. We started a conversation which lead to another invitation to dinner by the same friends.

Jeanette was very attractive, very smart and well-read. She was born in Paris to Polish émigrés, had spent the German occupation of France, during the Second World War, in Switzerland, and ended up with her parents in Canada where they all joined other friends and relatives from France. She had been married to a man who died of a sudden and fatal heart attack.

During our subsequent get-togethers, we discovered that we had a good deal of common interests and shared similar values and family traditions.

What had started as a casual meeting at a dinner table soon developed into a relationship in which I was beginning to compare the two women as life companions. And this comparison lead me to some important realities.

To be sure both Anna Maria and Jeanette possessed all the physical and mental attributes that made them very desirable companions indeed. But the big, and to my mind, insurmountable difference was that Anna Maria offered a life of excitement, of constant change, of thrills, and even of suspense, since our relationship had to be kept secret, and, also the somewhat unpalatable feeling of becoming a ward in the life of a wealthy woman. Jeanette, on the other hand, offered stability, a comfortable home life, a family and traditions and values that were very much akin to my own upbringing and background.

I must say that both prospects were immensely attractive to a man who had been torn away from a serene and routine life by the death of his wife while also going through a professional change. However, the prospect of landing in a safe haven of tranquility and order, instead of embarking on an adventurous journey on the uncharted high seas, was much more attractive and desirable. Needless to say, I opted for the first choice.

I continued to meet Jeanette and after a few more get-togethers, fell in love with her. Given her obvious qualities and attributes, this was bound to happen. And when I found reciprocal feelings arising in her, I successfully proposed. We decided to live together "until death do us part."

Within days of this decision I arranged to meet Anna Maria in Cannes in order to tell her about my decision.

To this very day, I find it difficult to relate the effect, my sincere and perfectly honest explanation delivered in carefully chosen words, had on her. She was devastated and kept crying like a child that lost her mother. I felt like the meanest low-life in the world while talking to her on a bench in the park. She did not even let me say goodbye to her or touch her. She just got up and walked away, leaving me to lick the wounds of my aching soul.

I went back to the hotel, checked out and flew back to Montreal feeling sick to my heart. She had not deserved that ending.

Although I tried to convince myself on the flight that I had really acted in the best interest of my life and that given her wealth, she would soon find solace or replacement in other places and with other people, I still hated myself for having broken a gentle heart.

That, for all intents and purposes, was the very last time in my life, I saw Anna Maria. The sight of a sobbing woman walking away from me became the terminal seal of a closed chapter in my life.

I returned to Montreal, trying to forget the whole affair and shortly after that plunged head first into my new relationship with Jeanette as well as into my new job.

I told Jeanette that I had had a romantic involvement with a lady I met during a recent vacation but that I had put a definite end to that relationship. She understood and did not pry into the details. She just said: "Listen, at sixty years old I did not expect you to have lived like a monk!"

My new life continued to develop like any well-intended and well-planned endeavour. Soon I had replaced my previous life with a comfortable home, a loving family I had inherited from Jeanette's previous marriage, and a steadily growing publishing business. It all seemed to fall into place. I began to enjoy the regular life of anyone fortunate enough to mesh a fulfilling professional life into an equally exciting and endearing home life.

But I was soon to find out that the heartbroken lady that walked away in Cannes had not really closed the book on this episode, as I had done.

In fact, several months later, I received a phone call from my sister who lived with her husband in Cologne, Germany, telling me that she had heard from Anna Maria. The Italian lady told my sister that she was a former friend of her brother and since she had heard many nice things about her, she would like to meet my sister and her husband. Perhaps during a vacation or on a weekend, somewhere in Germany or Italy.

My sister, who knew, of course, the background of my past affair found the request odd, but agreed to spend an upcoming summer vacation on the Italian Riviera with Anna Maria.

Those two weeks my sister and brother-in-law spent with Anna Maria in the seaside resort of Camogli were actually the beginning of a long and close relationship between the three. They not only met regularly in different spots in Europe, but they also talked on the phone, exchanging opinions and experiences. My sister, with whom I used to communicate at least once a week, kept telling me about their friend's endless questions regarding me and Jeanette. Whether I was a happy man, how I did professionally and so on. In fact, my sister always told me that Anna Maria used her ties with her as a bridge to myself. I also heard that Anna Maria was still very much in love with me and that apparently she was not interested in close relations with any other men. Although she kept travelling all over the world, she still lived with the memories from our encounter in Southern Turkey.

This state of affairs continued for many years, except that in 2005 I received a letter from Anna Maria in which she told me that following a heart-to-heart conversation with my sister, she had decided to finally close the chapter of her love affair and that she now accepted the fact that we would never meet again. Her last sentence was: "It was a beautiful dream, but, alas, most dreams do not come true! Adieu."

I did not reply to that letter, but a short while later my sister told me that Anna Maria still kept on talking and asking questions about me. "For heaven's sake, doesn't she understand that this is a lost cause?" my sister said to me over the phone.

*   *   *

For thirty years I lived my life with Jeanette like a married couple does. We were a happily united, perfect twosome. I pursued my business career, travelling often, sometimes with Jeanette. We spent memorable vacations in Europe and North America. I became part of her family and she became part of mine.

My son married and had two lovely children and Jeanette adopted them like her own, just as I became a surrogate dad to Jeanette's children.

I never told Jeanette anything about Anna Maria because I felt that there was nothing to say. I had no personal attachment whatsoever with that lady I had left for good so many years ago. So why bring it up? Why cause unnecessary doubts in Jeanette's mind, when there was absolutely no reason for it.

*   *   *

During the winter of 2009 my idyllic life with Jeanette came to a completely unexpected and dramatic jolt. Following a bad cold and a lingering cough, Jeanette went to a hospital for a chest x-ray, only to be given the horrible news that she actually had lung cancer. And it was in an advanced stage.

What followed were almost three years of alternating treatments, surgeries, hospital stays and long periods at home while undergoing therapy.

For three years I never left the side of my beloved Jeanette. In fact, I learned to read and even to do crossword puzzles with one hand while holding Jeanette's hand with the other. I suffered through these three years watching that beautiful lady withering away and eventually abandoning our world despite the frantic efforts of attending doctors and nurses. I was a broken man, especially since this was the second time in my life I had lost my most precious companion.

*   *   *

Shortly after Jeanette's cancer diagnosis, I received a surprise letter from Anna Maria, in which she said that she had heard about the illness from my sister. She wished Jeanette a return to good health. Just a few comforting words. I replied, thanking her. Nothing more.

Throughout Jeanette's illness I never heard again from Anna Maria, until a few weeks after Jeanette's tragic death in early 2012, when I received a phone-call from her expressing condolences and saying that she wished to leave me alone with my grief for a while and that she would contact me again sometime later, when "your wound has somewhat healed.".

I was very touched by this phone-call and thanked her sincerely. I thought that it was a very elegant and respectful way to participate in my grief.

Jeanette's death was a terrible shock to me and not only because I had grown very fond of her and she had become an indispensable part of my life, but also because in the meantime I had passed middle age and was indeed facing, all by myself, the bitter snows of life's winter.

Anna Maria was as good as her word. Just over a year after Jeanette's death she called again, expressing the wish to meet me after more than 30 years. "Just as old friends", she added.

I thought it was a very good idea. She went on: "You know what I have been thinking of? How about we meet again in Cannes, where I saw you for the last time. How about you rent a small apartment for a month, say in January, and we enjoy each other's company, talking about our lives during the past thirty years. Just like old friends who meet again." Her voice was full of emotional expectation.

"An excellent idea." I said. "I really look forward to it." "Imagine", she continued. "You are now in your nineties and I am in my eighties. I've had heart surgery two years ago after a mild heart attack, but this reunion will give me a new hold on life. My husband is still the old bore he always was but I learned to live with him like you live with a physical problem. You just get used to it and that's it. I will tell him that after the summer I want to take a vacation just by myself in Cannes to relax and read all the books I always wanted to read!"

I told her that I would rent the apartment as of the first of January and she could arrive one day later to join me. She laughed, and, full of excitement, shouted: "Yes...yes. I'll be there on the second of January. Come and pick me up at Nice airport."

I agreed and told her that as soon as I arrived I would call her to get her flight information. I even asked her what she would like for breakfast so that I could prepare it for her. She laughed and joked like a teenager, and she made me laugh too in expectation of our meeting. "Just one thing," she said. "When you call to ask for my flight number and my husband answers the phone, introduce yourself as Mr. Winter, someone I told my husband I met in Greece two years ago while on vacation. Just say you wanted to know how I am doing following my heart problems. Then, I will call you back on your cellular phone to give you the information. Okay?"

"That's fine." I said. "Oh, I am so excited, she kept repeating. I love you. See you in a few weeks. The line is not broken! Ha-ha", she laughed as she put down the phone.

Through the internet I found a delightful little flat in a small garden at five minutes walking distance from the sea, and, as agreed, phoned Anna Maria on the morning of January 1st in preparation of meeting her at the airport. I was really looking forward to meeting that lady who had not taken me off of her mind for 30 years.

Her husband answered the phone. I said: "Good morning, Sir. My name is Franz Winter. My wife and I met your wife in Greece and she was complaining of some heart problems. We would very much like to know how she is doing and also wish her a Happy New Year."

There was silence at the other end of the line. I thought the line had gone dead and ventured a "Hello?" A shaky voice came back: "Mr. Winter, I regret to tell you that my wife passed away last week. She had another heart attack, this time a really bad one, and was pronounced dead on arrival at the hospital. Thank God she did not have to suffer. It came unexpectedly and my daughter and I are still under the shock."

I was at a loss for words. I really felt terrible. "I'm so sorry", I finally managed to say. "I am so terribly sorry. She was such an outgoing and charming lady. We loved being in her company."

"Yes", her husband went on. "She was a charming lady. I lost a precious companion. But you know what really broke my heart? Before the end of the year, my wife told me that she intended to take a vacation by herself in Cannes, in the South of France. She said that she had been there many years ago and found it to be a relaxing spot that would help her recover and recuperate from her heart problems. I was very happy to see her so excited about that vacation. I watched her throwing a few books into her suitcase. 'I will sit on the beach, watch the waves and the seagulls and just enjoy the Mediterranean sunshine.' Those were her words. I am really heartbroken that she was not destined to enjoy that vacation she so ardently looked forward to. C'est la vie!" he concluded.

"Yes indeed, Sir, C'est la vie! How tragic." I replied. "Please accept our most sincere condolences. Our thoughts are with you."

"Thank you, Mr. Winter," he replied and hung up the phone.

I suddenly felt like I was looking into a deep, dark abyss. Like a part of me had been taken away, cut off. I was shaken beyond description. I still am.

THE COIN

If ever there was a dreary and never-ending day, this had to be it. Sir William Hartley, chairman of the company bearing his name, sat at his desk, wishing the silver-framed clock, a gift from his wife on his sixtieth birthday, would soon point to five. He could then get up from his leather seat, relieved that the day was over and done with. He would reach for his hat and coat and head for his waiting Bentley, which would take him through the heavy London traffic to the nearby Criterion, his club, beloved watering hole and refuge from this mundane world.

At precisely twenty minutes past four, Betty, his secretary for the last twenty-one years and, except for his wife, the only person from whom he could hide nothing, called on the intercom. Her voice was crisp and youthful, not at all betraying her past-retirement age. "Mister von Brüning from Hamburg for you, sir. Do you wish to take the call?"

Sir William immediately recognized an old business friend whom he had repeatedly met during export negotiations in London and Hamburg. Over the years, he had developed a liking for this silver-haired German aristocrat, who, in many ways, thought and behaved more like an Englishman of good breeding than did some of Sir William's very own friends in London.

He wondered why von Brüning would call him so late in the afternoon.

"Yes, I'll take it, Betty." He picked up the phone.

"Hello, Bill. Please don't tell me it's pouring in London. We've been drenched in Hamburg since last week. How are you?" There was a warm intonation in the caller's voice.

"Oh, I'm fine, Rudy, apart from the usual little aches and pains that come with getting older."

"Nothing serious, I hope."

"No, Rudy, nothing serious at all, thank you. I guess I'll be around for a few more years, at least long enough to attend the opening of our new mill in Yorkshire," replied Sir William. He added quickly: "But what can I do for you, Rudy? I do hope you're calling to tell me that you and Leni are coming to visit us in the near future. It's about time we picked up the conversation, or should I say debate, about numismatics where we left it off on that lovely cruise in your sailboat last summer."

"Well," came the somewhat hesitating answer, "You're partly right. I do want to come to London but, well, it's a long story. Frankly, Bill, I don't know how to word it, how to put it to you."

"What do you mean?" interjected Sir William.

"What I mean, Bill, is I want to ask you for a favour. A big, very big, favour. As a matter of fact, a favour you may rightly decline, and, if you did, I assure you I would understand perfectly."

"All right, Rudy, let's hear it," interrupted Sir William, somewhat impatiently.

After a deep breath, von Brüning forged ahead, some of his usual self-assurance returning.

"Bill, you are on the Board of the Royal Numismatic Society, aren't you?"

"Yes," replied Sir William, "I have that honour. My grandfather was one of the founding members, you know. Do you have in mind to apply for membership? If you do, I'm afraid there's no chance in hell; the rules limit membership to one hundred only. We already have applications from some forty people, all of whom are kept in abeyance."

"I know your rules," said von Brüning; "You told me about them years ago. No, applying for membership was not what I had in mind, Bill. What I really wanted to ask you was to allow me to attend your next meeting as a visitor."

A brief silence was followed by a very uncomfortable sigh at the other end of the line. After a long moment, Sir William came up with words to the effect that such a request was unprecedented, at least to his knowledge. Furthermore, it was very irregular since this was a very private club that generally did not admit visitors. He tried to choose his words as carefully and as gently as he could, making it very clear to his German friend that there was nothing personal in this, and that although occasional visitors had been admitted to some social functions of the Society, known as 'Open Evenings', no non-member had ever been allowed to attend a regular business meeting.

Hoping that his rather verbose reply would close the matter, Sir William was just about to change the subject when von Brüning repeated his request with much more emphasis and even some pressure. He reminded Sir William that he had in the past taken him, not once but three times, to meetings of the Hanseatic Numismatic Club, Germany's most exclusive and closed circle of coin collectors and dealers as an official representative of the Royal Numismatic Society. Would it not be fair, and just, for the British to reciprocate in kind, he questioned, especially since the Hansa Club had invited Sir William to sign its Golden Book as an honorary member.

By now Sir William was genuinely lost for words. In an effort to cut this uncomfortable conversation short, he told von Brüning that he would discuss his request in the morning with Lord Keene, Chairman of the Society, and he promised that he would support the request and recommend that it be granted exceptionally.

Von Brüning seemed relieved and thanked Sir William profusely and repeatedly for his cooperation and support, using words such as "I'm counting on you" and "Please try not to disappoint me" before finally hanging up.

At this point, Sir William was ready not to drive to the Criterion, but to fly to it. He thought he needed his Glenfiddich and water more than anything else in the whole world. Without further ado, he grabbed his coat, hat and umbrella and was 'gone for the day'.

The following morning, at the civilised hour of 10 A.M., Sir William phoned Lord Keene. As he had expected, the objections to von Brüning's request came not in words, but in cascades and avalanches. Sir William was treated to a recital of the Society's standing rules and bylaws, all of which added up to one word: NO. Only after Sir William related the event of his own invitations to the Hansa Club as an official representative of the Royal Numismatic Society, and repeatedly vouched for his German friend's high credentials and social standing, did Lord Keene appear to relent. A final salvo, in which Sir William accepted any and all responsibility for the smooth and uneventful comportment of the visitor, did the trick. Lord Keene agreed with the proviso that it would not set a precedent and that Sir William inform the Secretary of the Society of Brüning's visit well in advance.

Sir William leaned back in his comfortable seat, happy to have achieved victory on two fronts: his word still carried some weight with Lord Keene, and he was glad to have spared his friend Brüning the obvious humiliation of a refusal, and himself the embarrassment of delivering it.

Without further ado, he called Hamburg and let von Brüning have the good news. And good news it certainly appeared to be, judging by the German's excited and even elated reaction. The thank yous continued well after what Sir William considered the conversation ended.

* * * * *

Rudolf von Brüning hustled quickly through airport immigration and grabbed a taxi for Central London and the Royal Oak Hotel, where he had reserved a room for the night. Sir William would meet him at six at the hotel bar and, after a drink or two, they were to drive to the Royal Numismatic Society on Carnarvon Street. As the cab whisked him through the London traffic on this unusually sunny November afternoon, he could not help but admire the orderly flow of vehicles on the road and pedestrians on the sidewalks. There was a sense of sedate dignity, accentuated by venerable buildings lining the streets. There was no doubt in his mind that, despite wars and a crumbling empire, despite the Beatles and the Punk generation, London was still – and in all probability would always be – the 'Grande Dame' of European cities, unsurpassed even by his beloved Hamburg.

He checked in, took a quick shower and decided to relax for the next hour in preparation for the long evening ahead.

At precisely five minutes to six, he entered the elegant bar of the hotel, Mecca of generations of travellers and celebrities from the four corners of the world. Sir William was already sitting at a table and seemed genuinely delighted as he noticed his German friend entering the bar. The two shook hands for an extended time, patting each other on the shoulder and enjoying every moment of their reunion. They ordered drinks and canapés and after the usual banter about weather, family and business (in that order), Sir William made it a point to emphasize to his friend the importance of the exceptional invitation extended to him by Lord Keene. Sir William wanted to be sure that von Brüning was not only fully aware of the uniqueness of the invitation, but that he would also rise to the occasion by attending the proceedings with reserved discretion, which was tradition in so many English institutions. What Sir William really wanted to convey to his German friend, but could of course not say in so many words, was that he hoped von Brüning would be seen, rather than heard, during his visit to the Society. Von Brüning listened attentively and, except for frequent nods and smiles, did not have much to contribute to what Sir William was saying between frequent sips of his single malt.

At about seven, after repeated glances at their watches, the two rose and proceeded through the Royal Oak's magnificent lobby to Sir William's waiting Bentley. A short drive through the darkened streets brought them to No. 42 Carnarvon Street, home of the Royal Numismatic Society since its foundation in 1857.

Those who would expect No. 42 Carnarvon Street to be a place of plush opulence with maroon velvet curtains, crystal chandeliers hanging from the ceiling and multicoloured marble staircases, exuding a somewhat musty glory of bygone days, would be pleasantly surprised. As a result of many redecorating efforts over the past 150 years, the interior was simple, yet very elegant and even luxurious. Harmonising hues of beiges and browns on ceilings and walls, accented by beautiful antique furniture and precious carpets, helped to create an atmosphere of discreet and relaxed elegance. Perhaps the only true reminders of the past were the many paintings on the walls depicting either landscapes of different parts of the world, people of whom the Society was particularly proud, or animals, predominantly horses.

Upon entering the Society's lobby, Sir William inscribed both his and von Brüning's names in the leather-bound Register. Since there was no section provided for 'Guests', he wrote von Brüning's name under his own, adding 'Guest of above'. He turned around to find von Brüning standing in front of a large board on an easel bearing the announcement: "Tonight: LECTURE OF THE YEAR. Speaker: Lord Walston".

Sir William, flashing his usual broad smile, shook hands and waved to friends as if he were at the racetrack in Ascot. He took care to introduce von Brüning to as many members as possible, muttering the usual: "I would like you to meet my friend Rudolph von Brüning, from Hamburg. He is my special guest tonight." To some of his closer friends, he added: "We have known each other for many years and I have attended many meetings of the German Numismatic Society. That is why Lord Keene was happy to reciprocate the honour. I'm sure we'll all make Mr. von Brüning's visit both pleasant and memorable." Most members of the Society appeared genuinely pleased to meet the visitor, and some confided that they had already been informed by the Secretary of the expected visit. Obviously, the Secretary had done his job diligently.

At precisely 7:30 P.M., the doors to the main auditorium opened and all members filed in. Of considerable size and oblong in shape, the auditorium contained about hundred comfortable leather seats, all facing the elevated podium, which was at one end of the hall. Some of the seats were positioned at slight angles so as to avoid the regimented appearance of a theatre hall. Small end tables rested between clusters of seats. The walls were beautifully panelled with rosewood, and heavy red and blue oriental carpets covered most of the oak parquetry floor. In the centre of the room was a heavy and large round table, on which an equally heavy silver tray was resting. The concealed lighting completed the soft and pleasing atmosphere.

Von Brüning seemed very impressed and took in all the sights like a first-time visitor to a museum or an art gallery. He was surprised to see the contemporary and even modern design of the Society rooms, which contrasted strongly with the rather patrician and very conservative decor of his Hamburg Clubhouse.

All members took their seats and continued to chat, sometimes laughing, sometimes waving at friends and acquaintances. Soon, the huge room was almost full. Sir William had seated himself and his friend close to the lectern, partly because his hearing was not as good as it used to be and partly because he wanted his German friend to get a closer look at Lord Walston, the 'Speaker of the Year'.

In fact, this was indeed a very special event in the annals of the Society, because, although it was called the Lecture of the Year, many a year had gone by without such a special lecture. Only if the chairman of the Society considered the subject of outstanding importance would he allow it to be presented as a 'Lecture of the Year'. Everyone was therefore excited and intrigued, expecting to hear an oration of above average significance. To be sure, Lord Walston, the speaker, was a highly respected art collector, well known for his frequent travels and participation in foreign expeditions, searching for lost or rare treasures.

Slowly, the noise in the hall subsided to the level of a hum, ceasing altogether upon the entrance of the speaker striding to the lectern. He was accompanied by the Secretary of the Society, who approached the microphone ahead of the speaker. With a few words, he thanked the members for coming and introduced Lord Walston as a gentleman who needs no introduction.

Lord Walston was a tall, slender man in his late fifties, with bushy grey hair and a long aquiline nose. Although he wore frameless glasses, it was impossible not to notice his very lively eyes, constantly scanning his surroundings as if he was afraid of missing something of interest. He carried with him a small slide tray, as well as a white folder, obviously containing the text of his lecture. He placed everything gently in front of him and inserted the tray into a small slide projector on the lectern. Removing the pages from the folder, he waited for the last whisper and hum to cease. The main lights dimmed and the lectern light was lit, illuminating not only his papers, but by reflection also his face. His features and sparkling glasses were clear even to those people seated at the far end.

After some shuffling of papers, adjusting of glasses and fiddling with the slide projector. Lord Walston began to speak, sometimes glancing at his voluminous notes, sometimes looking straight into the audience:

"Mr. Chairman, my honourable numismatic friends! Tonight's lecture has been entitled 'Lecture of the Year' by your Board. If I may say so, I humbly agree, for what I am going to talk about this evening is, in fact, an almost unbelievable story. Put in other words, it is the result of a lifetime's work actually began by my father and carried on by me. But let me get to the point.

You are all familiar with the ancient coins of Croesus. This king, who lived in the third century before Christ, ruled over an enlightened and prosperous people on the island of Crete. Croesus was not only a powerful and visionary monarch, he was also a great patron of the arts. He commissioned hundreds of shrines and temples, busts and statues, mosaic-decorated houses and amphitheatres, some of which have survived to this day and are on display in various museums, including the British Museum here in London."

At this point, Lord Walston flipped on the projector, and on the wall behind him appeared a series of antique edifices and artifacts, some well preserved, but many others in ruins. Some slides showed mosaic floors of outstanding beauty, others depicted marble busts and Cretan gold jewellery. Lord Walston continued, after having turned off the projector.

"But, gentlemen, I am sure you will agree that the greatest achievement of King Croesus, and indeed his legacy to the world, were his coins, known as the 'Coins of Croesus'. Let me show you what they looked like."

Lord Walston again flipped on the projector and showed the obverse and reverse of an incredibly beautiful gold coin.

He went on: "As you can see, this coin is of rare beauty and detail, and there is good reason for this. Although gold coins have been minted since the days of the Pharaohs, and later on in Greece, Croesus's coins were the first to be sculpted by hand. Legend has it that these coins were cast from a mould and then crafted one by one by a team of artisans to bring out every detail in lifelike relief. Each of these coins measured slightly over two inches in diameter and had a thickness of about 3/16 of an inch."

Lord Walston turned off the projector and proceeded to explain how the Croesus coins eventually disappeared from the face of the earth, or almost."

Apparently, immediately following the death of King Croesus at the hand of his arch rival and eventual successor Medeas, the latter ordered all Croesus coins collected and melted down to be replaced by a new coinage bearing his own effigy. This operation was so ruthlessly efficient that Medeas succeeded in recovering all but three coins, which he reluctantly and publicly accepted as 'missing'.

"The first detailed reference to the three Croesus coins in modern times appears in 1573 in the Court annals of the Maharaja of Jaipur. There, one can read that one of these coins was found and purchased for the Maharaja's Collection. This very purchase turned out to be a judicious one, because this coin is still in India and can be viewed at the National Museum of Antique Treasures in New Delhi."

"So, there you have it," he said. "Two missing coins are what the world of numismatics has inherited. And here, gentlemen, I must take a breather."

Stopping as if to let his words sink in, he took a sip of water from the shiny crystal glass in front of him. The almost completely silent audience sat spellbound, awaiting his next words.

Lord Walston resumed. "Given this background, it is only natural that many collectors and coin enthusiasts have searched the world for the missing Croesus coins. In fact, the British Museum organized an expedition to Egypt in the 1850s after someone reported having seen one of the Croesus coins in a Cairo antique dealer's collection. Unfortunately, this turned out to be a wrong bit of information, for despite frantic searches all over Egypt, no trace of any Croesus coins could be found. Several of our monarchs commissioned art dealers in various parts of the world to search for one of these coins, but they all eventually gave up their searches empty handed, to the evident disappointment of the royal family.

"And this, gentlemen, is where I must refer to my own involvement and to the point of this lecture. Alerted to the challenge of finding these missing treasures by my late father, I dedicated any spare time I could to the search for a Croesus coin. I can say without exaggeration that the coin you saw on the screen here had actually cast a spell over me. To the dismay of my family, many a summer vacation turned out to be an excuse for my visiting innumerable antique shops and dealers, numismatic societies, art collectors and what have you. Needless to say, it all lead to nothing. I have carried on this search throughout my entire life. Many times I felt as if my beloved and patient wife was about to tell me: 'Listen, you dunderhead, it is either me and the family or that confounded gold coin of yours'. She never did, but if she had, I would not have blamed her in the least."

He paused dramatically, surveying his now totally rapt audience. "Well, gentlemen, the French, who have a word for everything, say, '*Cherchez et vous allez trouver*', without, of course, adding any time limit to this adage. I stand tonight in front of you, and with immense pride and joy, I can tell you '*J'ai trouvé*', or perhaps in a more fitting analogy, *EUREKA!*"

Immediately following this clarion call, the entire hall broke out in thunderous applause. In fact, a standing ovation faced Lord Walston, who had produced the coin and was holding it with his two hands above his head, for all to see. He kept turning from side to side to make sure that everybody caught a good look at his prized treasure.

When the applause died away and all were seated again, the first shouts from the audience of "How did you find it? Where was it?" could be heard. The speaker raised his hands in an effort to stem the flow of more questions and calmly said, "I was coming to that, gentlemen." Adding, with a smile, "Please bear with me, will you?"

By now, complete silence had been restored in the hall, and Lord Walston started to describe the fascinating events that led to his discovery of the coin. He had been told by an Egyptian friend that in the late 1800s, the Khedive of Egypt, who ruled the country at the time as a dependency of the Ottoman Empire, had decided to sell some non-Egyptian treasures of the Cairo Museum. This was done in an effort to raise money for the museum's upkeep and to buy up original Egyptian treasures, which were rapidly disappearing, as they were being acquired by European governments for display in their own national museums. In fact, many of the Egyptian treasures acquired at that time are still the pride of museums in London, Paris and New York.

Among the items earmarked by the Khedive for sale to the highest bidder was one of the original Croesus coins, which for some reason was stashed away in one of the museum vaults. According to Egyptian records traced by Lord Walston, this particular coin had been acquired at one of the auctions by an Austrian nobleman. The next step for Lord Walston was to locate the descendants of this nobleman and to find out if the coin was still in their possession. This search lead to further chases, mostly of the wild goose variety. Many descendants remembered hearing about the coin in their childhood, but no one knew where it could be and, indeed, whether it had survived more than a hundred years since its original purchase.

The breakthrough came when an elderly member of the family seemed to remember that he was baptized in, and later, as a boy, attended a small church in Hungary. There, he remembered, the altar was decorated with an elaborate silver sculpture depicting the crucifixion and other events surrounding the life of Christ. In the centre of this particular altar ornament was embedded a Greek gold coin, which the former Austrian nobleman remembered was always referred to as 'of great value and a gift to the church by his family'. Lord Walston immediately travelled to Hungary, located the little church and, lo and behold, found the silver altar decorations intact and beautifully maintained, having been kept in a safe place during and after two world wars. It took Lord Walston just a few minutes to recognize the Croesus coin resting in the centre of the silver sculpture.

The rest of the story involved prolonged negotiations with the local church authorities, with some surviving members of the original family that had donated the altar monstrance, including the coin, to the local church and, of course, with representatives of the current Hungarian government, who kept refusing to release the coin. Lord Walston and his attorney had to use two means of persuasion: a hefty amount of hard cash and the fact that the coveted coin should not be considered a national treasure, being neither Hungarian nor Austrian, in fact, not even Christian in origin.

At this point, Lord Walston produced the coin again and said, "And here it is, after all these centuries and after setting me personally back for a good part of my old age sustenance. I have had it authenticated, following its removal from the surrounding silverwork, by both the Louvre in Paris and the British Museum, and I have the official certificates here with me. I propose to lend it to the British Museum, for permanent display, where it will be encased in a pilfer-proof lead crystal box in the Hellenistic Section on the second floor."

Closing the folder in front of him, removing his glasses, and taking another sip of water, he concluded, "And now, before consigning this rare treasure to the cavernous halls of the museum, I would like you gentlemen to take a good look at it. I will pass it on to the first person on my right in front of me, the Earl of Cranmore, I believe, and I shall be most obliged if he would pass it on to anyone wishing to view it. Asking you to handle it very gently and indeed lovingly seems superfluous, I am sure."

The Earl of Cranmore received the coin with both of his hands, as if being entrusted with the most delicate and precious jewel on earth.

The entire hall broke out in loud applause and ovation, frequently interrupted with exclamations of "Hear, hear", "Unbelievable", "Good man", "What a story" and the like. Lord Walston gathered all his papers and stepped down into the hall to talk to members of the audience. There was no doubt that Lord Walston was indeed living his finest hour, for it is well known that our triumphs are meaningless unless we can share them with others, and, hopefully, bask in the warm glory of their appreciation.

The very animated atmosphere on the floor was interrupted only by the occasional exclamation of members who held the coin in their hands and could not hide their excitement. This fluid and at times noisy atmosphere, rather different from the discreetly conservative tone of normal proceedings, continued for about half an hour. Suddenly and very unexpectedly the lights went out in the hall, including emergency and red exit signs. There was total and complete darkness.

To describe the next minutes as panic would perhaps be an exaggeration, but it was certainly a very unpleasant and even scary situation. Some members tried to shuffle toward the exits, bumping into chairs, tables and each other, while others tried to flick on lighters and matches, soon realising the futility of their endeavours. At one point, there was an anguished cry from one member who had fallen to the floor and was asking for help to get up. The total darkness and shuffling became increasingly ominous and oppressive as the seemingly endless minutes went by. In perhaps ten minutes, as suddenly as the darkness had descended, all the lights came back on again, temporarily blinding everybody. The incident was attributed to a power failure caused by the construction that was underway in an adjoining building.

As the general conversation in the hall resumed, Lord Walston asked the last person to have looked at the coin to please return it to him. Nobody came forward. Lord Walston repeated his request. Twice he raised his voice so that it could be heard by all, but again nobody came forward to return the coin. By now, all conversation on the floor had ceased and in icy silence members looked at each other, some expressing disbelief and even utter amazement at the situation.

Obviously concerned, Lord Walston was about to make one more request, when he was held back by the Secretary of the Society, who said to him, "Let me handle this, please." In a few quick steps he reached the elevated platform, where he spoke into the microphone: "Gentlemen, despite several requests by Lord Walston, his coin has not been returned to him. May I ask your cooperation in this matter? Who held the coin in his hands, please?"

Immediately, one member shouted, "I did. I received it from Sir Oliver on my right, looked at it and passed it on to Lord Kenmore." The latter jumped to his feet and declared with a strong voice, "I indeed received the coin, admired it and gave it to either Sir Alexander Grey or his companion, I can't remember." It was the companion who rose next and said he had had the coin but had passed it on. And so it went for what seemed to be an endless repetition by members who had held the coin but had passed it on. Still, the coin was nowhere to be found.

An air of helplessness, anger and stunned disbelief descended on the gathering. The Secretary grabbed the microphone again and, in an obviously shaken and trembling voice, said, "Gentlemen, permit me to ask one last time for the return of the coin to its rightful owner. Perhaps I should ask you to look on and under your seats and even examine your suits, as the coin may have slipped into folds or creases during the blackout. Please also examine the floor area around you, as it may have fallen onto the carpet."

For the next few minutes, members looked around their seats, got up and sat down again, shrugging their shoulders. No coin was returned to the Secretary.

In brisk strides, the Secretary ascended the platform again, and, visibly frustrated and annoyed, he said, "Gentlemen, this is indeed a very grave situation. One I would have never expected to witness in these hallowed halls. I am afraid I now have to say to you things that will not be very pleasant, but what has to be done has to be done. Let us face it, the Croesus coin was here right in this hall, and still is here right in this hall. Since Lord Walston started his lecture no one has entered or left the room. Let me be blunt: one of us must have the coin. There is no magic in all this. I will therefore ask you to authorize me to call in an inspector from Scotland Yard, to help us in this matter. We will have to give him the authority to question and, if need be, to search us, beginning of course with myself. But before picking up the telephone, I would like you to give me your consent for this very serious measure by a show of hands."

Several hands started to rise, joined by more and more signs of approval, until practically everybody had raised his hand. Suddenly, the heavy silence on the floor was interrupted by the accented voice of Herr von Brüning.

Ashen faced and groping for words, he stood to address the Secretary, saying very clearly, "Sir, I refuse to be interrogated and searched by the police." He looked around him, avoiding eye contact with his host, Sir William Hartley, and repeated very firmly, "Sir, I am sorry, but I must refuse to be searched by police or anyone else." With this, he sat down, staring straight ahead of him.

Sir William immediately jumped up and approached his German guest, whispering excitedly and emotionally into his ears. Von Brüning gravely shook his head and waved his hand 'no way'.

The silence in the hall gave way to animated conversation. Why did this person, who was not even a member, refuse to be questioned or searched? At this point, most members were getting up and moving about, talking to each other about what to do. The Secretary, amazed at the unexpected turn of events, stepped down from the platform to consult with Lord Keene and some members. The whole gathering seemed to talk to each other, obviously debating the question: "Where do we go from here?"

Suddenly, an ear shattering outcry erupted from the very centre of the Hall. Near the big round table, one member and then others shouted, "We found it! Here it is. The coin, the coin!"

The noise in the hall came to an abrupt end, as if cut by a sharp knife. The total silence did not last long. Shouts of "Are you sure", "Let's see it", "What happened" were heard from all corners of the room. One of the two men who had spotted the coin on the floor picked it up and held it as high as he could for all to see. He then almost ran over to Lord Walston and handed him the lost and found *corpus delicti*. The recipient turned it over and over and, with a sigh of visible relief, said, "Thank you. This is it. Why was it lost?"

During the power failure, the coin had slipped from someone's hand or from a seat onto the floor, where it rolled near the huge brass paw of one of the round table's massive oaken legs. In the shuffling and commotion in the darkness, someone inadvertently pushed the table enough to bring the lion's paw to rest right over the coin where it disappeared from view. An accidental jolt to the table by another member moved the piece of furniture sufficiently to reveal its concealed booty.

The almost unbearable tension that had prevailed ever since the lights had gone out now gave place to small talk and laughter. The sense of relief could be read on the faces of everyone. A nightmare had ended with the realisation that it had just been that: a freak accident, unrelated to the normal course of events.

However, not everyone was part of this general relief and loosening of spirits. Quite apart from the groups now chatting, joking and laughing stood Sir William Hartley and his German guest. Both were pale, continuing to go through the ordeal and unable to talk to or even face each other.

The Honorary Secretary approached the two men, looking first at his old friend Hartley and then at von Brüning. In a calm but firm voice, he said, "Sir, I believe we all deserve an explanation. You refused to be interrogated or searched by an inspector when I proposed this admittedly very unpleasant procedure, which had become necessary as a last resort. Here we were, some seventy upstanding people and one missing coin, and I mean 'missing', since we all tried to find it and it was nowhere to be seen. What else could I do than to call for a drastic solution?

"Everyone agreed with my way of thinking, except you, sir. I am sure that by acting the way you did, you realised that you would be thought of as having appropriated the coin. What other explanation could there be? I am sorry to say it so bluntly, but for a good moment, you, sir, in the eyes of some of this country's most important people, including two members of the Royal Family who are among us tonight, were believed to be a thief. Why, may I ask, may we all ask, did you act the way you did?"

The Secretary removed a handkerchief from his pocket and repeatedly wiped his forehead, obviously very shaken and very nervous. The effort to make this address had taken a lot out of him, for he now looked drained and tired, all colour gone from his usually rosy face.

Von Brüning shifted from one foot to the other and was visibly tense. However, the tension was much more evident on the face of Sir William Hartley. He looked as if the weight of the whole world was resting on his shoulders. Well aware of the fact that he had brought the German to this gathering, he looked at von Brüning and said, " Rudy, do tell us why on earth you acted the way you did, won't you, please." He strongly emphasized the "please".

By now, all the members had gathered in a wide circle around the three men. They had followed the Secretary's somewhat emotional address in silence and were eager to hear an explanation from the German visitor.

Von Brüning looked around him and, with a slight trembling in his voice betraying his obvious emotion, he said, "Gentlemen, and particularly my dear friend Sir William, when I asked you some time ago to make it possible for me to attend a meeting of the Royal Numismatic Society, it was for a very good reason. I wanted you gentlemen to be the first to know about a very important discovery I had made. You see, and Sir William is well aware of this, I am a dedicated coin collector and in my time I have often chased, and sometimes found, what I was looking for. But no other coin in the world ever received more of my attention than one in particular about which I had read and studied since my early adulthood. In fact, I can safely say that I have dedicated my life to finding one of these rare coins. I travelled to dozens of countries, following leads, paying dealers fortunes for what usually turned out to be nothing more than promises.

"But my lifelong search finally paid off. By a stroke of luck, and setting me back a fortune, I found the object of my lifelong perambulations after years and years of unbelievable efforts."

He reached into his pocket and took out…a Croesus coin!

"Here it is, gentlemen, the third and the last of the famous Croesus Coins."

He stepped forward and handed it to the Secretary to examine. There was utter amazement among the members.

"Yes, Sir William, my good friend, that is why I wanted to be here among this gathering tonight. I wanted it to be a surprise. Here in my pocket is the speech that I had prepared to tell you about the history of this coin, a task which Lord Walston so admirably accomplished for me, in a manner of speaking. Everything he said tonight about the coin were words almost taken right out of my mouth."

He continued that he had wanted to relate the amazing story of the search for the coin and, finally, by a mix of perseverance, money and unbelievable luck finding it in a place no one would have expected it to be.
"But all this will remain untold for now, I am afraid."

Continuing to look at his very attentive and speechless audience, he said, "I am sure, by now, you know exactly why I acted the way I did. As a matter of fact, I had no choice. First of all, I need not tell you of my immense disappointment when I realised the subject of Lord Walston's presentation. Of course, I decided immediately not to say anything about my own discovery. How could I? As I believe you gentlemen would say, I would have stolen his thunder and would have greatly diminished the genuine importance of his amazing discovery.

"As for my refusal to be searched by the police, honestly, what else do you think I could have done? What would you gentlemen have believed if a Croesus coin was discovered in my pocket? I would have walked out of this room in disgrace and perhaps even in handcuffs. My only recourse was to refuse the search in the hope that sooner or later, Lord Walston's coin would be found. Not for a single moment did I think that any one among you had appropriated the coin. I was completely sure that it was only a matter of minutes before the coin would be found on a chair or on the floor or somewhere in this room. I myself looked frantically all around me on the carpet, as did many others in the room. I wanted to gain time and, as you all saw, my strategy paid off. That is all, gentlemen."

Tired to the point of exhaustion, von Brüning slumped on one of the leather seats behind him, pulling his handkerchief from his pocket and wiping his very emotional face.

The silence that followed von Brüning's lengthy explanation was soon superseded by a round of applause led by Sir William and the Secretary. Lord Keene, both of his hands deeply implanted in his pockets, after exchanging a final glance with the Secretary, stepped toward von Brüning and said in his deep baritone voice, "Sir, this is indeed an amazing story. On behalf of all the members, I want to express regret at the way this evening's meeting affected you personally. I am now well aware of the disappointment and frustration you endured.

"When I welcomed you to our midst earlier this evening, I had no idea what the next few hours would portend, but then, we never do, do we? Our meetings are usually very sedate and certainly very uneventful.

"If Lord Walston's story is an amazing one, which it certainly is, yours is every bit as amazing. In fact, tonight we were treated to not one but two outstanding events in the history of numismatics, and we are all very grateful to you, Mr. von Brüning, for having chosen our Society as a forum to tell the world about your discovery. May I add my personal appreciation to that of our members."

He was interrupted by "Hear, hears" from throughout the room.

"However," he continued, "I believe that the last chapter of the Croesus story should not be told as a painful explanation and indeed as a postscript to a meeting, but as a triumphant tale at the core of one of our forthcoming sessions. Mr. von Brüning, will you accept our official invitation to come back and tell us about your coin and how you came upon it at one of our next meetings, and this time not as a visitor but as a specially invited guest of honour? Our secretary will be pleased to inform you of the timing. Admittedly, the element of surprise will be missing from your presentation, but we will try to make up for it by extending to you a very warm reception in our midst and, of course, by double-checking all of our electric wiring beforehand."

The subsequent laughter and applause did not seem to end. Lord Keene's words had made von Brüning feel like a hero. He was happy to the point of constantly wiping tears from his eyes, but it was Sir William who had the last word. At the top of his voice and pointing with both hands to von Brüning, he said, "Gentlemen, I have yet to sing *For He's a Jolly Good Fellow* without a decent drink in my hand. Let's proceed to the bar, and by the way, this round is on me. I think we all have quite an evening behind us."

MUSIC, MAESTRO, PLEASE

Peggy Monroe stood in front of her stateroom mirror, putting final touches to her impeccable appearance. She liked what she saw and sat down, waiting for a knock on her cabin door from her parents. It was dinnertime aboard the super luxurious *Royal Ocean Breeze,* a floating palace catering to the real upper crust and those who wanted to be perceived as a part of it.

Peggy had just turned nineteen and was not only beautiful and gracefully sexy, but she exuded a contagious *joie de vivre,* which drew looks of admiration from everybody. She had a way of showing interest in people and responding vivaciously, making her very desirable company anywhere. Small wonder that her parents were very proud of their only child.

There was actually a very important reason for the Monroes to have booked two staterooms on the *Breeze*'s Caribbean cruise. To be sure, Phil needed a respite from his lucrative but exhausting law practice in New York's financial district, but there was more to it. The real reason was Peggy. About a year ago, during an after-hour birthday party for one of her friends, she had met a tall and bearded musician from the band providing the night's rather noisy entertainment. They had danced a few times that night and on many following nights. Peggy had taken a serious liking to Ken Marino, the band's pianist. In fact, the two had fallen in love with each other.

If Peggy was immaculately dressed and groomed, Ken was the very opposite. His clothes looked as if they had been retrieved from the municipal garbage dump, which they probably were. His shoes were beyond repair and provided minimal protection, especially on cold and rainy nights when he walked Peggy home. His face was mostly hidden behind a hirsute jungle, mingling beard, moustache and hair into one dark brown mess. As if this scruffy appearance did not suffice, Ken was also heavily into most, if not all, psychedelic drugs.

People who saw Ken and Peggy could not help but wonder what on earth had brought these two different people together. Could it be that opposite poles attract each other or that both needed an escape from their environment? She from her orderly and proper family background, he from the wild life in which he was plunged to the hilt.

Needless to say, Peggy's association with Ken met with severe disapproval from her parents. Time and time again, they asked her to break it up and to return to the life generally prescribed for the daughter of a well-to-do New York lawyer and a society-conscious mother. Peggy was well aware of the difficult situation she had gotten herself into, but she was in love and nothing else mattered.

One day she noticed a missed period and immediately told Ken about her ominous discovery. His reaction was predictable: "What do you want me to do? I can't marry you. You'll be in the shithouse with your parents for the rest of your life, and you know as well as I do that I'm neither fit to be a father nor a husband. My advice is to get rid of it. Now! Before it's too late."

Although Peggy had anticipated Ken's reaction, she was deeply hurt by his detached and matter-of-fact attitude. Peggy ran home with tears in her eyes, which turned to sobs as she fell on her bed. This is how her mother found her.

Peggy did not say a word to her mother when the latter tried to comfort her. She did not need to. Although her mother knew nothing about the missed period, and even less about her daughter's conversation with Ken, she sensed correctly that she had broken off her relationship. It did not take long for Mrs. Monroe to phone the travel agent asking her to book two luxury cabins on the first available Caribbean cruise ship. Hence the Monroe's presence on the *Royal Ocean Breeze*.

The first two days into the voyage passed uneventfully. Contrary to her usually outgoing behaviour, Peggy was quiet and seemed sad and immersed in her thoughts. Her parents were caring as always, but they realized that their daughter was going through a difficult time, and they let her cope with her problem without once mentioning Ken. Yet, they knew, as only loving parents can, that it was all over between the two.

Day three was billed as "Las Vegas Afloat". The whole ship was transformed into a monumental gambling palace, replete with everything Las Vegas and Reno can offer. In the evening and late into the night there was a black tie dinner, ballroom dancing and a spectacular show put on by none other than the famous *Cirque du Soleil*.

It was at one of the roulette tables that Peggy happened to sit near a handsome and well-mannered young man of twenty-six or so. A conversation soon started, which continued after they had left the table to have a drink at one of the numerous bars. The conversation was animated and reflected their desire to get to know each other. Peggy spoke about her school years and her family; Richard told her, among other things, about his recent graduation from medical school, an event followed in short order by his discovery of a small red box on his bed pillow containing a cheque for $5 000, a Rolex watch and a ticket for a Caribbean cruise on the *Royal Ocean Breeze*. His parents had sneaked up to his room, gently pushing the door open at the very moment he opened the red box. The sight of the proud and happy parents hugging their son "The Doctor" was something to behold. Richard's face was still smiling as he described the scene to Peggy.

That evening turned out to be a long night for both. They kept walking along the deserted promenade decks, breathing in the balmy sea air and talking. Call it love at first sight or "chemistry". The next few days Peggy and Richard were inseparable. She introduced her new friend to her parents, who seemed impressed by his self-assured demeanour. They were also elated that their daughter had found company aboard the ship.

The relationship between the two continued after their return to New York, blossoming rapidly into an intense love affair. In fact, on one of their nights out in a Manhattan restaurant, Richard proposed. The answer from Peggy was neither a yes nor a no, but a frantic search for a handkerchief to contain the tears which suddenly gushed from her beautiful eyes. It took a little while for Peggy to regain her composure before she started telling Richard about the part of her life she had kept from him. She spoke about her infatuation with Ken, about the end of their relationship and about the souvenir of a romantic night at Ken's place she was carrying. She apologized for not having told him earlier and explained that she had only recently received positive confirmation from her gynaecologist.

Richard held her hand throughout her speech and grabbed both of them when she had finished. He squeezed them gently and both fell silent for a long time. He kept his eyes on her while she managed a faint smile. Finally, Richard let go of her hands and looking straight at her, said, "Peggy, I must admit I didn't expect to hear this. But, listen, what's past is past.

"I also want to make a confession. During one of my medical courses on sexual function and dysfunction we tested our own sperm counts. Several tests repeatedly showed that I'm infertile. Of course, this may be a temporary condition, but the fact is that my sperm failed the tests at the time. Peggy, I think we may have a trade-off here. I want you to know that I love you and I am with you all the way."

When he said this, Peggy put her hand around his neck to draw him closer and kissed him. They were oblivious to the world around them. Luckily the waiter had seated them at a corner table.

After a few minutes, Richard asked, "Do your parents know about the baby?"

Peggy shook her head, adding a quiet, "No, no one does except my doctor."

"That's fine, Peg," continued Richard. "And no one needs to know either. Let's get
married soon, but on condition that your musician friend never claims he's the father. Never ever. He must get out of your life and mine and stay out for the rest of our lives. Do you think you can get him to solemnly pledge this? He didn't want to accept parenthood and that's that…life moves on. Can you talk to him?"

Peggy was beginning to regain her usually outgoing and peppy composure.

"Sure, I'll talk to him."

The rest of the evening was spent quietly. A lot of ground had been covered over dinner and when they kissed goodnight, both felt a sense of relief and expectation of better things to come.

A few days later Peggy met Ken and told him about Richard. She told him everything and asked for his solemn commitment to keep away from her and her family-to-be, and to take the secret of his paternity to his grave. Peggy was surprised at Ken's reaction. Unlike his earlier declaration to "get rid of it," he became emotional, now that he realized that, together with his child, he was also losing Peggy. He even tried some
"can't we…" and "what if we…" approaches, but when his attempts met with Peggy's polite but very firm refusals, he soon realized that this was the last time he would ever see her.

The separation took a heavy toll on Peggy. They left each other without a word. Peggy felt drained, especially when she had spotted tears in Ken's eyes as she gently withdrew her hand from his.

* * * * *

Richard and Peggy looked like movie stars on their wedding day. All the guests were unanimous in commenting that they had never seen such a beautiful couple. They soon settled down to a busy life. Richard took up residency in a New York hospital, and Peggy started enjoying domestic bliss, caring for a loving and considerate husband and coping with her advancing pregnancy. Her father liked to tell friends that it was not his wife but destiny that had arranged for the cruise on the *Royal Ocean Breeze*.

Jamie arrived a few days late, but in time for jubilation by parents and family. All went well, except for Peggy's strange feeling every time somebody said "Now who does he look like, his dad or his mom?" But soon, Peggy got over this, and, in time, completely forgot Jamie's roots. Nature has a wonderful way of making us blot out what we don't need or want to know. For Richard, this was his beloved wife's baby and, therefore, also his own.

In time, the little family lived their lives just as any other well-off folks. Richard attained increasingly responsible positions in the clinical and academic world; Peggy developed an interest in political history and attended several lectures each week. Jamie grew up a handsome and smart kid, the pride of his grandparents and his mom and dad, in that order.

When Jamie turned four, his parents noticed that he often sat on the stairs leading to his bedroom, listening to classical music from the stereo CD player in the den. Realizing that the boy loved music, his parents hired a tutor who came twice a week to teach Jamie the basics of music. Jamie enjoyed it immensely. When he was at grade school, he would run home not to watch TV, but to play the piano. And so it went throughout his school years. He was an average student, but a gifted pianist.

Even before his graduation from college, Jamie, now appearing under the name James Gaynor, gave numerous solo performances at charity affairs, social events and parties. He continued to take lessons from concert pianists and spent hours practicing and memorizing scores.

At twenty, James started playing at international music festivals, often bringing home trophies, medals and prizes. He was the pride of his family and friends, who thought of him as a rising star in the world of classical music.

* * * * *

Ken's decisive and sad meeting with Peggy had not only terminated his relationship with his girlfriend, but it had also been an occasion for long and deep reflection. He was acutely aware that he lost his lover and his child because of his debauched lifestyle. He was now twenty-four, reasonably good as a disco pianist, but what did he really have to show for himself? Drug addiction? Long nights at the bar, waking up with splitting headaches? Sure, he enjoyed the crowds and the music and the pay, but where did it all lead?

Ken soon made up his mind. One evening, after a busy night at the disco, he told the manager he was quitting, he needed a change in his life. The manager tried to dissuade him, offering better pay and shorter hours, but Ken had made up his mind. He left the club and, two weeks later, he was busy rearranging his life. He stopped using drugs and enrolled in the conservatory, after having successfully passed a piano audition. He took a job playing background music on the grand piano every evening in an elegant downtown hotel lobby, where his greatest problem was having to wear a black suit, shirt and tie.

He took his studies very seriously, graduating from every class with honours. Eventually, after five years, he left the conservatory with a well-deserved diploma in orchestration and conducting. Together with the diploma came the school's highest distinction for musical accomplishment, and a job as conductor of a newly formed symphony orchestra in a medium-sized city.

Ken never married and he sometimes wondered why. He often met young women and asked them out for dinner or to the theatre, but he was so deeply immersed in the world of music that he seemed to have no time left for anything else. There were the almost daily rehearsals with the symphony orchestra, recordings, teaching at the local music academy and, to round out his busy life, he practiced his beloved piano at least two hours every day. No wonder his friends kept telling him that he couldn't get married because he was already married to his music.

From conducting, he rose to musical director of his orchestra and then was offered the coveted position of conductor of a major European orchestra. He accepted on condition that he could continue as roving guest conductor to enrich his experience and versatility.

Now in his late forties, Kenneth Marino was an established and respected name in the world of classical music. Financially, he was very well off. In fact, he employed an accountant and a financial advisor, to keep track of his multi-source income and growing investments.

One day he received an invitation to guest conduct The London Philharmonic Orchestra at the Royal Albert Hall. On the program was also Rachmaninoff's Piano Concerto N° II, featuring as pianist, James Gaynor. He was stunned by the coincidence. To be sure, he had from time to time heard about Jamie's successful recitals, but he had never come into contact with him. He was very much aware of his promise to Peggy to take the secret to his grave. He could, of course, refuse the offer, but something inside made him send a letter of acceptance to conduct Rachmaninoff, one of his favourite composers.

The performance at the Royal Albert Hall turned out to be memorable, to say the least. The London Philharmonic and James Gaynor combined to give a brilliant performance. The delighted audience called conductor and pianist repeatedly back to the stage for a standing ovation.

That night turned out to be the start of a musical relationship that was to significantly further Jamie's career as well as the fame of Ken Marino. The two appeared together often, either with Ken's own orchestra or as guests of famous symphonic ensembles around the world.

Without ever betraying his real feelings towards Jamie, and without Jamie ever suspecting anything else than purely professional interest Ken became his protector, guide and mentor, constantly making sure that Jamie played his favourite concertos with the best orchestras and under the most renowned batons. This relationship was to last for many years. Audiences all over the world eagerly awaited programs in which Ken Marino conducted, with James Gaynor at the piano. From Tchaikovsky to Liszt to Beethoven to Rachmaninoff, the two covered the world of orchestral music to the absolute delight of their audiences.

The relationship continued after Jamie's marriage, his becoming a father and other benchmarks in his life. In fact, the two interacted so perfectly during their performances that they did not even need to rehearse together. They just went on playing beautiful music, until one evening when, after a concert in Paris, Ken took the applause, only to collapse in his dressing room minutes later. He was immediately rushed to the hospital, having suffered a massive heart attack.

The next few days, radio, TV and the press kept informing the public about Ken's condition, and the news was not good. Despite all the efforts of a team of cardiologists, Ken's condition kept declining. Five days after having entered the hospital, a special bulletin announced that the famous conductor Kenneth Marino had succumbed to a severe coronary thrombosis. Ken was dead at the age of sixty-four. He had never complained about his health during years of a gruelling professional life that took him from concert hall to concert hall and from city to city. The doctors at the hospital ascribed his inability to recover from the attack to protracted over-exertion, lack of rest and exercise and a relentless dedication to his profession.

It came as no surprise to anyone when the management of Ken's orchestra, reflecting the wish of all its musicians and fans, asked Jamie to deliver the eulogy at the funeral service. Jamie immediately accepted and prepared a brief speech, which he delivered in front of a crowd of mourners filling every square inch of the church.

Fighting back tears, Jamie spoke about the life of Ken the musician, from his humble beginnings as a disco pianist to a career spanning over forty years, which brought him to the pinnacle of musical accomplishment. After having outlined the major appointments and honours conferred on Ken, he turned to his own relationship with the conductor.

Starting with their first meeting at the Royal Albert Hall, he talked about the years they worked together planning concerts and refining renditions of complicated piano recitals. He described Ken Marino as the best mentor and teacher he could have ever dreamed of having. "In fact," Jamie concluded, "not even a father could have been as caring and as supportive as Ken Marino had been to me. I always felt his loving hand over me when I sat at the piano."

As he said these words, a woman's cry was heard. It was more than a cry, it was a sob, coming from someone who obviously could not contain her emotions. People turned to notice a lady dressed in black with a lace scarf over her head, hiding most of her face, clutching a handkerchief.

Jamie finished the eulogy, and the coffin and pall bearers started leaving the church, followed by the attending crowd. As Jamie walked towards the exit, he passed by the lady in the black dress and veil, still holding her handkerchief to her eyes.

Jamie stopped to offer condolences and to comfort the crying lady. When she turned to face him, he could not believe his eyes. There was his mother, gently reaching for his hand.

Surprised at her presence there, Jamie said, "What are you doing here, Mom? Why did you come here?"

Wiping the last of the tears from her face, she said calmly, "I came to say goodbye to the man, who, as you put it so well, held his loving hand over you as if he was your father."

THE FOOTBALL POOL

I was in my early twenties and, like so many other young men of my time, trying to find a professional direction in which to proceed and hopefully succeed following the tumultuous years of the Second World War and its aftermath. After talking to a family friend who happened to own a small textile mill in Yorkshire, England, I was offered a junior position in his company as well as "digs" in a nearby pub cum Bed & Breakfast.

I grabbed the opportunity in the hope of learning both the commercial side of the textile business as well as the technical aspects of what appeared to me as an interesting and indeed venerable industry.

And so it was that I arrived one grey and drizzly afternoon in Heckmondwike, a small Yorkshire town situated halfway between Leeds and Huddersfield. I had taken the train up from London and then the bus to my destination. To say that the long bus ride on winding country roads was anything but exciting would no doubt be an understatement. In fact, it was achingly boring, primarily because we kept driving past endless rows of identical small houses, their only distinguishing feature being the different color of the entrance doors. The streets and little gardens were spotlessly clean, but I had the distinct feeling of a heavy cloud of unexciting and depressing uniformity lying over these suburban neighbourhoods.

When we finally arrived at the "Boar's Head", one of the two local pubs serving Heckmondwike, I was surprised to hear the bus driver shout after me, "Good night, lad," as I stepped off the double-decker, grasping my suitcase.

If the long ride from Leeds was unexciting, the reception I received at the *Boar's Head* was certainly not. Mr. Dalton and his wife, Lena, both in their mid-fifties and publicans for all of their adult lives, grabbed my bag and, after having waved the bus driver goodbye, led me into the house, past the pub rooms and up into my bedroom on the floor above. Then they made me sit down in the empty taproom and welcomed me in the most charming and caring manner, asking questions and listening carefully to what I told them about myself and my family.

I will never forget those first hours of my arrival at what was to be my residence for the next few months.

The Daltons immediately took me not only into their home, but right into their hearts. They made me feel comfortable and at ease, like I was part of their family. It did not take long to find out one good reason for their behaviour. They had lost a twenty-year-old son, their only child, on the second day of the Allied landing in Normandy, and sometime during our conversation, the Daltons confided that I reminded them very much of their late Eric.

I soon settled down to a routine life of very early wake-ups, fast breakfasts and rickety bus rides to the mill, all at the crack of dawn. Then came full days at the Century Textile Company doing all sorts of odd jobs: at first in the weaving rooms, then helping the pattern designers, then working in the accounting office, until finally graduating to the sales department.

It was there that I came into my own. Being a natural extrovert and good communicator, I loved accompanying the salesmen on their weekly rounds to neighbouring districts. Eventually I graduated to a territory of my own in London, a substantial promotion. Every two weeks or so I traveled to London with a bulging bag of upholstery fabric samples, intent on soliciting orders from the London Transport Authority and other prospective clients. Our products were of high quality, reasonably priced and they came in a great array of colours and patterns. No wonder that I usually returned to the head office on Monday morning with a full order book and a great feeling of accomplishment to boot.

My usual routine was to call on my accounts on Thursday and Friday, then on Saturday enjoy some sightseeing, of which one can never have enough in London, go to a play in the evening and then return to Heckmondwike on Sunday. My regular trips to London became not only meaningful contributions to the company's balance sheet, but they were also welcome breaks from the cozy, yet utterly dull and uneventful life in parochial Heckmondwike.

The Daltons continued to spare no effort in making me comfortable and happy. They introduced me to some of their regular pub patrons and saw to it that I was never lonely.

Unlike her husband, who often indulged in card games with his friends or simply dozed off in his favourite armchair, the sport pages of the Manchester Guardian folded over his chest, Lena Dalton was a hard working woman. She single-handedly did everything there was to be done to keep the *Boar's Head* in tiptop shape.

Apart from all the ordinary housekeeping chores, she also managed the business side of the pub, ordering and receiving supplies, keeping accounts and, when most busy housewives slump into an armchair at the end of a long day, Lena took up position behind the counter and helped her husband dispense the familiar ales and stouts and lagers that delighted their thirsty patrons. In so doing she also had a friendly word here and a joke there for all her regular customers.

I could not help but admire this truly outstanding woman for her efficiency in doing so many things so well.

I soon found out that Lena had but one weakness. She was a passionate player of the weekly football pools. In those days there were two prominent lottery companies, each vying for and exploiting the innate desire of UK residents to gamble a few shillings or even pounds every week in the hope of hitting the jackpot at least once in their lifetime.

The idea was simply to guess the scores of matches played over the weekend in the British Football League. If all your guesses turned out to be correct, you would win a huge amount of money, all of it paid out immediately after the weekend games, and free of tax to boot.

While "playing the pools" was definitely the most popular indoor sport in the UK, it was nothing short of a passion for Lena. During the week she read all about the teams, the matches they played and even the individual players, in order to fill in the forms with intelligent guesses as to what the final scores would be. She talked football with anybody in the pub she thought could contribute a meaningful opinion to her weekly guessing game. Then, when she thought she had heard and read enough, she would quietly disappear into her bedroom and diligently fill in the form provided by the lottery company.

This ritual of filling in the forms every week was considered sacrosanct by the Daltons and all their friends and customers. Whenever someone would ask "Where's Lena," her husband would put a finger to his lips and, with a whimsical smile, say: "Not so loud, please. Lena is upstairs guessing about goalkeepers, centre forwards and the like. You think it's easy, to predict what these clowns will be up to on the weekend?"

Everybody would laugh until Lena came down from her solitary confinement. They would then observe a sealed and stamped envelope in her hand, which she would promptly drop into the enormous red mail box that stood right outside the pub entrance, like an ever present sentinel. Then, having accomplished her duty, she would return to the pub, ignoring any lingering remarks by patrons about her gambling ritual. She would simply say: "We all have our weaknesses, don't we? One of these days I'll wipe off those smiles from your faces with a fat cheque from the lottery company, trust me!"

With that, she would turn to the sink behind the counter and start washing and drying glasses. It was very clear that Lena did not consider her weakness a subject for general discussion, let alone light-hearted banter. To her this was a private and serious matter.

This weekly procedure took place on Thursday evenings. All lottery entries had to be mailed to the company by Thursday before midnight, if one resided anywhere outside London, and by Friday before midnight for residents in the London area. Entries received after this cut off date would not be honoured. Since the League matches were played on weekends throughout the English Isles, all results would be in on Sunday evening. By Monday morning the lucky winners would be promptly notified by the company.

The system worked perfectly. No complaints of impropriety were ever received from the gambling public.

*****

A few months into my stay at the *Boar's Head*, I was about to leave one Thursday afternoon for London in order to call on my growing list of clients, when Lena Dalton intercepted me just before I left. She held a sealed and stamped envelope in her hand. She asked me to mail it before Friday night, stressing the word "before", adding that sometimes she wondered whether the local mailboxes were emptied as regularly as they were supposed to be. Since I was on my way to London anyway, could I drop off the envelope in any mailbox in the city?

I agreed, of course, stuck the envelope into my pocket and left.

A few hours later I checked into my usual home away from home, a comfortable little Bed & Breakfast place on London's Edgeware Road.

The next two days were hectic. All of my time was spent with calls on existing as well as new accounts, telephone calls to the company back in Heckmondwike, some new orders and a great deal of travelling within the city, all the while carrying a sample bag that seemed to get heavier and heavier as the days wore on. Finally, utterly exhausted but grateful to have opened some new accounts, I made my way back to Edgeware Road. I sat up in my room for a long time, committing the fruit of my extensive labours to paper.

On Saturday morning I was awakened far too early by a telephone call from one of my clients with whom I had become quite friendly. He invited me to spend the day with his family at his Hampton Court home, not far from London. Never having been there, I eagerly accepted and enjoyed a truly memorable day, admiring Tudor architecture at its very best, as well as appreciating the company of friendly and interesting people. After supper, my client drove me back to my hotel room in London.

The next morning I checked out and made my way to the railway station and a mid-day train back to Leeds. I picked a comfortable window seat in one of those old-fashioned and rattling railway carriages. I was just about to go over the newspaper, when I suddenly realized with a terrible shock that I had forgotten to mail Lena's football pool entry. For a moment my blood literally froze in my veins.

What to do?

The train had not left the station yet and I could easily jump out, but for what purpose? The deadline for mailing in all entries had long passed since midnight two days before.

I was utterly devastated. How could I have been so negligent and careless? I had disappointed Lena, who had trusted me and for whom participating in the weekly lottery meant so much.

I put the newspaper aside and felt miserable to the point of wanting to cry. Then I realized that nothing would be gained by losing control of myself, so I started thinking what my next steps should be.

I had two choices.

Tell Lena that I forgot to mail her entry and ride out the storm that was bound to follow this revelation. In any case, the storm would end on Monday morning when the results would be announced on the radio. I was sure, or at least I hoped, that Lena's guesses would not be the correct ones. After all, she had been playing at this game for many years and had never submitted a winning combination. Never.

This choice had two important disadvantages: first, I would cause Lena unspeakable anguish, and second, I would be branded an unreliable person in Lena's eyes. I did not cherish this thought at all, given the mutual respect that had developed between us since my arrival at the *Boar's Head* and her frequent references to the late Eric in conversations with me.

My second choice was to lie. I could pretend I had mailed the envelope on time. Again, the chance of winning appeared so remote in my judgement that I truly thought I could get away with this treachery. Lena would thank me for having dropped off the envelope, and the following day she would simply say "Well, better luck next time," as she usually did.

This second choice would clearly spare Lena any suffering whatsoever, but it had its disadvantages too: it made me a rotten liar. I did not like that prospect either.

I sat out the rest of the train ride, agonizing over which way I should go. Finally, just as the train was pulling into the cavernous Leeds Central Station, I had made up my mind. I would save Lena from spending a sleepless night. I would blatantly lie to her:

"Oh yes, Lena, I mailed it on time with my wishes of good luck." This is exactly what I did, flashing a broad smile to Lena on my return to the pub on Sunday night.

I avoided lunch at the company canteen next day. The flock of butterflies in my stomach had left no space for any food intake, and I remained in my office, reading the local paper.

At three o'clock my phone rang. I picked it up and to my great surprise I heard Lena's voice at the other end of the line. Her words were spoken in haste and without any preamble: "Ben, find some excuse and come home immediately, please. Take the next bus. OK? See you soon!"

I ventured a "What happened?" to which she replied, "Never mind, Ben, I'll tell you when you're here. Please hurry!"

I cannot describe my panic. I figured that she had compared her entry with the results she had just read in the morning's paper and had discovered that she was a winner; otherwise, why would she want to see me now? What to do? How to tell her the truth? I was helpless and felt like a doomed man going to the gallows.

In a trance, I left the office and took the bus home. I did not even try to figure out what to tell Lena. I was caught in a trap I had set myself.

Ten minutes later I stepped off the bus. I walked towards the *Boar's Head*, more dead than alive. I noticed that the door of the house was wide open. Music, mixed with laughter and loud shouts, was pouring out the entrance.

My worst fears were confirmed.

A cheering Lena moved among friends and neighbours she had hastily summoned, laughing and handing out drinks to everyone. As soon as she saw me, she ran towards me, grabbed my hand and, at the top of her voice, announced, "Here he is, the man who brought me luck! My lucky angel. For twenty-eight years I sent in my forms and never won a red penny. And then I asked Ben to mail my form and 'boom' I won. You brought me luck, boy!" She kissed me on both cheeks and pressed a glass of booze into my hands. To top it all, I hear a cheerful "For he's a jolly good fellow" with glasses raised to me.

I stood there like a perfect idiot, not knowing whether to smile and cheer like everyone else, to cry or, better still, drop dead. Oh how I wished I was dead right there and then.

Finally I managed a weak smile. I asked Lena," How do you know that you hit the jackpot?" She replied elatedly, "How do I know? I compared the copy of my entry with the result published in the paper."

Standing there in shock, I suddenly hear the vroom of a motorcycle driving up the hill. The driver steps off and says: "I have a special delivery for Lena Dalton." "You are looking at her." Lena shouts back. "Sign here." Says the messenger and drives off.

To the shouts of "open, open", Lena takes out a cheque which she flashes for all to see.

I stared at a very legitimate and business-like cheque from the lottery company made out in the name of Lena Dalton for a cool amount of 250,000 pounds, the figure mentioned twice, once in letters and then in digits.

Lena left me, off to celebrate some more, and I went up to my room. I did not know whether I was coming or going. The excitement had given me no time to reflect on what on earth had happened. I sat down on my bed and tried to put some order in my thoughts. I had definitely not mailed Lena's entry. Of this I was painfully certain.

I tried to recall all my moves in London. This was easier said than done. I had met so many people during my business calls, had changed so many means of transportation and had reached into my pockets so many times that events seemed to blend and blur.

But then a sudden thought occurred to me. Could it have been the chambermaid at the Primrose Lodge in London, who found the envelope in the room, realized that I may have forgotten to mail it before the midnight deadline and then threw it into the mailbox on her way home from work. I immediately called the hotel and asked to talk to the chambermaid. A few minutes later, a crisp voice said: "Can I help you Sir?" "Yes", I said. "I am the guest who stayed in room 216 yesterday. Did you find an envelope in my room?" "Oh", she interrupted me. Of course I found your lottery entry on the floor and mailed it on my way home. I hope I did the right thing Sir." "You sure did", I replied. "Thank you ever so much." "Sure", she said. "I'm glad I could be of service."

I listened to her and tried to hide any sign that could betray my emotional reaction to her words.

"You know," she added, "I've been playing the lottery for as long as I remember and I've never won anything. I'm beginning to think it's all a big hoax. They take your money and nobody wins anything. Bunch of crooks, if you ask me."

"You're right, nobody wins anything. Thanks anyway."

Why didn't I tell this poor woman the truth? I figured that if I did, she would ask for, and indeed deserve, a substantial reward. After all, she had made it all come true.

* * * * *

Within the next few months, Lena and Doug Dalton sold their tobacco and stale beer smelling pub in Heckmondwike and moved to a beautiful small house with a lovely garden on the outskirts of Bath, fulfilling a dream Lena had cherished all her life. She shed no tears when she gave one last look at the *Boar's Head* where she had toiled and scrubbed and served and cooked for so many years, all just to eke out a living and to put a meagre pension away for their old age. Now, after all these tiresome years, she was determined to enjoy life with Doug and a golden retriever puppy they bought shortly after they moved to their new home.

I left Heckmondwike shortly afterwards and moved to London, having been appointed Sales Manager, Southern Region, for the Century Textile Company. I enjoyed my work very much and continued to contribute to the company's growth.

* * * * *

And one middle-aged chambermaid, the real heroine of this story, continued to make up the rooms of the second and third floors of the Primrose Lodge on Edgeware Road, just as she had done for so many years.

Nothing exciting or unusual ever happened in her dull life. She had long ago given up hope of ever changing things for the better for her sick husband and herself.

"Some people are plain lucky, and some are not" she used to say with a resigned shrug. She never knew how close she had come to the real meaning of these few words.

LET SLEEPING DOGS LIE

Al Borowsky was not born with a silver spoon in his mouth; far from it. The only child of an alcoholic father on New York's skid row and a recurrently depressed mother, he grew up in utter poverty. With the help of local social services and benevolent neighbours, he made it through school, eked out a living as a teenager and finally ended up in the U.S. Army. After many years in uniform, never rising above the rank of platoon sergeant, he called it quits and returned to civilian life with a few dollars and a meagre army pension to his credit. For years he made do with odd jobs here and there until arthritis prevented him from undertaking anything too physical. Now, in his late sixties, he mostly hung around New York's Central Station, either sweeping floors or guarding idled construction equipment. The pay was not great, but then he lived very frugally and simply and the army pension certainly helped. He had no relatives and few friends.

Al was now on his way to one of the station's souvenir shops that had asked him to help in re-arranging the store's shelves. He was just about to enter the shop, when he walked by an empty phone booth and noticed an envelope lying on the floor. He picked it up and opened it. To his surprise, he found inside an unused airline ticket for a flight two days later from New York to Las Vegas and return. The ticket was made out in the name of Edward Cahill, who must have dropped it while using the public phone.

Al put the envelope in his pocket and proceeded to the souvenir shop, where he put in a day's work. Back home, in the evening, he took the airline ticket out and started to toy with the idea of using it. He would take out some four hundred dollars he kept under his mattress, fly to Las Vegas and try to sleep over either in the cheapest roadside motel he could find, or better still, in a YMCA or shelter for the poor. After all, except for the clean barracks during his army days, Al had never enjoyed what you may call comfortable living.

Finding this ticket was actually a stroke of fate. Al had always dreamt of going to Las Vegas, not to gamble, because he couldn't afford it, but to see the incredibly beautiful hotels and casinos he had so often admired on posters in Central Station.

And so it was, on the day of the flight, Al went to LaGuardia Airport and checked into flight 335 departing for Las Vegas. He had no luggage except an old tote bag into which he had stuffed a few pieces of clothing and some personal items. He was full of excitement and thought that maybe God made him find this ticket in order to grant him some measure of happiness before his final departure from this unkind world.

* * * * *

Edward Cahill, "Eddy" to his many friends, sat in his office, pondering what had gone wrong with his once flourishing business. Eddy was a building contractor who had built a small one-man operation into a ten-employee enterprise during a hectic ten-year span. His job was to locate people or companies wanting to have something built or decorated and then contact companies and suppliers that could execute the work according to the client's specifications and at the right price. For years Eddy enjoyed a steady flow of business, which made it possible for him and for his wife, Eileen, to live a very comfortable life indeed.

Despite their many attempts, Eddy and Eileen did not have any children and, over the years, they had accepted that perhaps they were not meant to. They had a good, solid and uneventful marriage. Every year they took two vacations, one on the North American Continent and the other in Europe or Asia. Both of them were outgoing, sociable types and they had many friends who shared their interest in the arts and in travelling. In short, Eddy and Eileen, though childless, were a well-adjusted upper middle-class couple, living in a high-rise building overlooking the East River on Manhattan's Seventy Second Street.

But then, things in Eddy's business started to change. Individuals or companies looking for contractors did the locating and selecting process themselves, thus avoiding the commissions and fees they had to pay Eddy's company. What started as an isolated case soon spread to the entire construction business, and Eddy's company was bidding less and less for fewer and fewer projects. To make matters worse, a very important construction company from the West Coast decided to muscle into the New York area, underbidding everyone else in an effort to corner the market, which they successfully did.

Eddy's woes had now lasted for over two years. Eddy and his staff at first tried to run harder after each prospect, then they cut their fees to a bare minimum, but neither of these measures helped reverse the decline of their business. Eventually, Eddy fired his staff one by one, leaving him almost alone, with only a young receptionist. He spent his days calling both former clients and new prospects, but the general reaction seemed to be the dreaded "Don't call us, we'll call you."

All his financial reserves were now used up and since practically no new funds were coming in, Eddy soon had to sell off some minor investments he had made in New York's lively real estate market during his company's better days. Then he started to borrow from banks and even from some former clients, all of which he approached under the false pretence that he needed the money to finance projects that would soon yield substantial earnings. Eddy and his wife continued to entertain and travel, and Eddy continued to keep all his business woes to himself; Eileen knew nothing about his growing problems. She had never really been part of his professional life and she was not part of it now. He often lied to her as well as to their friends, answering the question " how's business?" with a noncommittal "fine, fine."

Drained of all possible sources of income despite his feverish attempts to broker even minor restoration and repair jobs, Eddy sat at his desk one day, realising that he had finally reached the end of the road. His debts, which included sums owed to harassing loan sharks, had mushroomed into large amounts he could not possibly pay off. He could not think of a living soul who could lend him another nickel. Furthermore, he had long passed the point at which he could just close shop and start fresh in another field, including seeking employment.

Eddy Cahill was desperate and deeply depressed. The idea of jumping off the fortieth floor of his apartment building appeared much more reasonable and even beckoning than carrying on with his present life. He was immensely sorry about abandoning Eileen, but there was still some money in their joint account, which he had not touched, and which would allow her to continue for a short while until she could somehow rearrange her life. She was well educated, still young and could easily find a job. To be sure, he knew the pain his death would cause Eileen, but he also knew that he had no other alternative. Or had he?

He took a pencil and started to jot down some figures on a pad on his desk. An idea had suddenly entered his desperate mind, trying to replace his acceptance of suicide as the only possible way out of his predicament.

What if he appropriated all the money in the joint account, used up all the last lines remaining on his credit cards, drained the money in his and Eileen's old-age pension funds, asked his wealthy brother, a prominent upper Manhattan psychiatrist, to lend him a sum of money for just one week, took all this money and flew to Las Vegas? He would gamble all of it on the blackjack and roulette tables. If he won and won big, he could return to New York, pay a fair amount of debts off and make a fresh start by taking a job somewhere. If he lost, he would then jump off the roof of his apartment building, but this time, he would know that he really had tried everything to save himself.

This desperate idea immediately grabbed his mind as a plausible solution. In fact, it dominated his thinking and his plans as he raced to the banks, to his brother's office and finally to a travel agent from whom he bought a return ticket to Las Vegas with a turn around of five days. He made a few more phone calls, went home and told Eileen that he would be leaving the following day for Las Vegas to attend a Builders' Convention and would be back by the end of the week. Next day, he packed his suitcase, went to his office to take all the money he had gathered the day before, stuffed it into a tote bag and headed for La Guardia Airport.

Approaching the airline check-in counter, he noticed to his dismay a crowd of passengers, all waiting to be processed. Eddy reached into his pocket to have the airline ticket ready, but there was no ticket inside. Eddy went through all his pockets. No ticket was to be found. He tried to trace his movements during the last days, but it was impossible to know where he could have lost the ticket. He had been to so many places and had made so many telephone calls. He would tell the airline agent that he had lost the ticket he had bought days before and would request a replacement.

Eddy looked around, aware that the line in which he stood was hardly moving. He suddenly became very impatient and nervous. Losing the ticket may have be an omen, a portent from God to force him to think twice before embarking on this truly desperate course, this last stand. He suddenly felt very tired and very confused, hesitating between remaining in line to take the Las Vegas flight, come what may, or perhaps to think the whole thing over.

Eddy stepped out of the lethargic line of waiting passengers and strolled over to the nearby bar. He ordered a drink, and then another.

He was still clutching the empty tumbler when Flight 335 to Las Vegas left La Guardia without him.

Even more confused than before, Eddy stepped outside the airport concourse, breathing in the fresh evening air. Holding the garment bag in one hand and the tote slung over his shoulder, he walked aimlessly across the bridge over the expressway and found himself in front of one of the airport motels. He went in and checked into a room under an assumed name, intent on coming up with a plan of action. He felt utterly lost and depressed.

He entered his room and stretched out on the bed. He turned on the TV but was so tired that minutes later, he fell into a heavy but restless sleep. He must have been sleeping for several hours when he woke with a splitting headache and an empty stomach. He suddenly realised that he had not eaten since breakfast at home the day before.

He looked at the TV where a news program was just being aired. The first item was the extensive coverage of an airline crash. A plane with a full load of passengers and a malfunctioning landing gear had slammed into a building and immediately burst into flames. All 186 passengers and crew were killed. It was the worst disaster that had ever occurred in a U.S. Airport. The ill-fated flight was 335 out of La Guardia.

Eddy Cahill was stunned. This was the flight he was supposed to have boarded. He picked up the phone and called the airline asking for confirmation. Yes, he was told, Flight 335 had crashed in Las Vegas. There were no survivors, and most, if not all of the bodies were burned and charred beyond the possibility of identification. Eddy asked if an Edward Cahill was on the list of passengers. He was told that yes, Edward Cahill had indeed been a passenger on the ill-fated flight. Eddy thanked the airline representative and hung up. Someone must have found his ticket and used it.

Eddy Cahill was legally and officially dead. For all intents and purposes, Eddy had freed himself of all his debts and obligations. His "death", which would be made public before long, had drawn a definitive and conclusive line not only under his life but also under all his commitments. As for Eileen, she would receive a handsome survivor's compensation from the airline, amply replacing the money he had withdrawn from their joint account.

From whatever angle he looked at it, he was now a free man, ready and able to start a new life. Provided, of course, that he acquired a new legal identity.

Eddy was genuinely heart broken about "losing" his wife. Over the years they had grown very attached to each other, and he shuddered at the thought of not having her beside him. However, the feeling of release from all his financial woes, from a thousand Damocles' swords hanging over his head, dominated his mind so strongly that he relegated everything else to the back burner.

At the crack of dawn, Eddy checked out of the airport motel and took a taxi to the Port Authority on 42nd street. There, he boarded the first Greyhound bus leaving for Burlington, Vermont. He chose that destination for two reasons: first, he knew no one there and did not expect anyone to recognize him and, second, Vermont had always beckoned to him as a rural place of relative peace and quiet, and this is what he now needed most in order to plan his next move.

After a smooth three-hour ride, he arrived in Burlington and checked into what looked like a quiet resort motel surrounded by beautiful maples and firs, using the name S. Smith. He had a light meal and spent most of the evening and night catching up on sleep, for by now, he was close to exhaustion. Next morning, his first move was to buy several morning newspapers. As was to be expected, the terrible crash in Las Vegas dominated all front pages. There were pictures of utter destruction: the plane had literally disintegrated after hitting one of the airport hangars and exploded in a fiery blast. The press coverage confirmed that none of the bodies could be recovered for identification since the explosion had reduced the plane to rubble and ash. The official reason given for the disaster was that only one set of wheels in the landing gear assembly had deployed and that although the captain had managed to put the aircraft safely onto the ground, he was unable to slow it down and to control its direction. This is why the disabled aircraft slammed into the empty hangar at the end of the runway.

The local Vermont papers also reported another accident, this one on Route 89 which starts in Concord, New Hampshire, and ends at the Vermont-Quebec border. A passenger bus on its way to Burlington had collided with a truck, trying to overtake it. The driver of the bus was forced off the highway, landed in a ditch and he and one passenger in the front seat were injured. Everybody else escaped with some minor cuts and bruises. Since the accident had occurred near a ramp leading into Burlington, uninjured passengers were able to walk to their homes, while the injured ones were taken to a nearby hospital.

Eddy read this news item twice. What if he went to a local psychiatrist to tell him that he had been a passenger on the bus, but that was all he could recall. In fact, he would tell the psychiatrist that he couldn't remember his name, his address, his family, nothing. He would therefore request the psychiatrist's help in acquiring an identity and identification papers.

Through the yellow pages, he located a psychiatrist, made an appointment and went to see him. He told him about his traumatic accident, insisting that he was desperate because he couldn't remember anything that had taken place in his life prior to the event. He said that in the confusion and shock following the accident, he had lost his wallet containing all his IDs and credit cards, but that he had found a scrap of paper in his pocket with the name of S. Smith. He therefore assumed that this might have been his name. S. Smith, that's all.

The psychiatrist was very intrigued by what he heard. He asked Eddy to repeat his story over and over. He frequently interrupted him with questions that Eddy pretended he could not answer. Eddy clung to his story with steadfast and stubborn monotony. He just could not remember anything about himself.

After the session, which had lasted over two hours, the psychiatrist advised Eddy to return to his motel and to come back to him in a week's time. By then, the good doctor predicted, he should have recovered from the shock to the point of knowing who he was and is. Eddy paid him his fee and went back to his motel room, spending the next few days mostly relaxing and going for walks in the evenings.

A week later he went back to the clinic and repeated his story, word for word. This time, the psychiatrist, after another fruitless question and answer session, told Eddy to come to the hospital, where he would like him to meet the head of his department and some of his colleagues.

At this session, many more questions were hurled at Eddy, some to confuse him, others to perhaps jog his memory, but it was all in vain. Eddy clung to his amnesia story with iron clad persistence. There were some more sessions with other doctors, consultants and residents, but in the end, they had to concede that their patient, tentatively named "S. Smith", had indeed suffered post-concussion global amnesia and there was no telling if and when he would recover his lost memory. The doctors also concluded from the patient's accent and his general deportment that he must be American-born or at least someone who had lived in the United States for a long time.

Reaching the conclusion that nobody can exist indefinitely without a legal identity, the hospital doctors filled in some forms and applications, which included Eddy's fingerprints, signed and sealed everything before sending the file to the Department of Justice in Washington. There it was established that since identical fingerprints could not be located anywhere (Eddy had never been fingerprinted) and since the hospital not only endorsed the diagnosis of amnesia but also vouched for Eddy's bona fide account of events, there were no objections in allowing the patient to assume the legal personality of Stephen Smith. The return envelope from Washington contained application forms for Social Security, US Citizenship and all other papers that would grant Stephen Smith full legal status.

It took a few more weeks for the various Washington departments to verify and process all the information, but finally, one day, Eddy received a registered manila envelope containing all the documentation.

Eddy was elated. He thanked the doctors in the hospital for their help and immediately applied for a credit card, after having explained his case to the local bank manager. He also opened an account into which he deposited part of the amount he still carried around with him.

When all this was completed, Eddy placed himself in front of the mirror in his motel room, and with a grin on his face, told himself: "Goodbye, Edward Cahill, also known as Eddy, goodbye for good! And welcome Stephen Smith, Steve, for short." He was so happy, he continued talking to himself: "Hello, Mr Smith! Hi Stephen! Nice to meet you, Steve." Satisfied, he packed all his belongings, checked out of the small motel and checked into the best hotel in Burlington, proudly filling in and signing the form at the reception desk as Stephen Smith.

That evening he went to the most expensive restaurant in town, ordered the best steak dinner and drained a full bottle of the best French champagne, all in honour and to the future life of Stephen Smith. Mr. Smith was now ready for action.

His first move was to go to a hair stylist and have his hair dyed from the greying black nature had provided him with, to a much younger looking light brown. For weeks, he had also started growing a moustache. For obvious reasons he wanted to look different.

His next move was to leave the confinement of Vermont for the big city, where he could start a new business and hopefully a new life. After all, he was only in his late forties and he still had a sizeable amount of cash left over from his earlier life.

After some thought, Stephen Smith chose Chicago as his new home. Three days after his arrival in the windy city, he had found a nicely furnished apartment in a residential neighbourhood near the lakeshore. After some enquiries and meetings with a bank manager and a lawyer he had located through the yellow pages, he decided to go into the wholesale shoe business. The bank manager had alerted him to an opportunity in this field. One of the bank's clients, a major importer of shoes from Italy and Spain, had suddenly died and his widow was looking for someone to buy the business lock, stock and barrel. After some due diligence which confirmed what the bank manager had told him, Stephen eventually signed the agreement with the widow and became the designated owner of *Comfort Shoe Inc*. Needless to say, Stephen not only had to fork out most of the cash he still retained, but he also had to borrow money from the bank.

Stephen quickly learned the business and began to enjoy it.

A few months after having acquired *Comfort Shoe Inc.*, Stephen, while having breakfast, read an item in a Chicago daily that made him put down his coffee cup with a jolt, almost breaking it. On the obituary page was a photo of an elderly lady. She was his aunt, a cousin of his late father, to be precise, who had recently passed away. The item read that since she had no other direct relatives left, she had willed her entire fortune, valued at two million dollars, to her nephew Edward Cahill, the New York businessman who had tragically died in the Las Vegas plane crash. Obviously, his aunt had made out the will many years earlier and had never changed it. She had left him her sizeable estate in Connecticut, her money and even her jewellery, but she had left it to Edward Cahill, not to Stephen Smith. And since Edward Cahill's widow, Eileen, was Edward's only legal heir, the whole package would go to her.

Stephen spent quite a few dinnerless evenings and sleepless nights after that, mulling over his options and alternatives. He finally concluded that returning to New York as the resurrected Eddy Cahill, cured of his amnesia and ready to claim the inheritance that was rightfully his, would open so many Pandora's boxes that he could never hope to lead the normal life he had just started to enjoy.

To begin with, the debts he would have to pay back, the lawsuits for fraud, tax evasion and embezzlement he would have to cope with, the angry loan sharks, the shame of a social outcast he would have to live with, not to mention the puzzle of his official death, all these were insurmountable obstacles of immense proportions. No inheritance from his late aunt could compensate for them. He was much better off to stay where he was, run his shoe business and within a few short years, he could pay off all his debts, thus becoming its full owner. Let Eileen enjoy his dead aunt's worldly belongings. It was God's way, perhaps, to reward her for all the heartbreak she had gone through and to punish him for having caused it in the first place.

A few months later, at a Christmas party given by one of his suppliers, Stephen met Norah, an attractive and bright divorcee in her early forties. Strangely enough, what attracted Stephen most, was Norah's resemblance to Eileen. They both had dark, almost black, hair, a roundish face and big, expressive brown eyes. They both were tall and slim and wore their clothes with elegance. It did not take long for the two to strike up a close relationship, which both seemed to enjoy very much. Norah had two grown children and they got on famously with Stephen.

From the first day of their encounter, Stephen told Norah that he had lost his memory as a result of the trauma he had suffered in a bus accident and that for all intents and purposes he was a single man without familial attachments of any kind. At first Norah found it difficult to believe the story. As time went by and she began to appreciate and value the humane and open character of Stephen, she became convinced of his amnesia and that Stephen had indeed lost the memory of his life prior to the fateful bus accident in Vermont.

Almost two years after they had met, Norah and Stephen were married in a simple, yet emotional ceremony in a small church on the outskirts of Chicago. Stephen's side was represented by his sales manager and some of his senior staff as well as by friends and business associates. Norah's whole family was there to help give the couple a warm send-off. It was a beautiful wedding and everyone wished the couple well on their second attempt at matrimony, for it was tacitly assumed by all that Stephen must have had a family life prior to his memory loss.

The next few years brought few problems and many successes, both in their professional as well as their personal lives. Stephen developed the business and even opened a branch office in Los Angeles, run by his trusted sales manager. Within a relatively short time, he had repaid the bank loans, becoming the proud owner of the *Comfort Shoe Co. Inc.* He cashed in on the growing demand for stylish Italian footwear and soon became the most important importer of ladies' and men's shoes in the Chicago area.

* * * * *

It is hard to describe the shock, the thunderbolt that hit Eileen when she first heard the news of the disaster at the Las Vegas airport. She immediately called the airline, hoping that by some miracle Eddy had missed the plane, but no, the airline confirmed with great regret that he had indeed been on the flight and that he had perished along with the rest of the passengers and crew. Eileen was told that the airline would keep in touch with her for further announcements, but since all bodies had practically disintegrated in the explosion that followed the fiery crash, there would be no individual identification process. At best, a symbolic interfaith mass burial ceremony was planned for some time later.

As she was trying to cope with the news of Eddy's sudden death, however, she came upon some more bad news. When she went to the bank to withdraw money from their joint account, she was told that her husband had completely emptied it just before he left New York. The only money she had access to was in her personal small savings account. Eileen was surprised and shocked that Eddy would do a thing like that even if he needed the money for some gambling. This was not like him.

The cascading news and events during the days following the airline disaster, the immense pain caused by Eddy's death and the frequent communications from the airline, relegated Eddy's unexpected cash withdrawal from their account to second place. She did not even have time to think about it.

Sooner than she thought, the airline came through with a substantial cash settlement, which her lawyer found adequate and advised her to accept. The amount she received more than made up for the loss of her joint account.

Shortly after the crash, however, rumours began to reach Eileen that Eddy had accumulated immense debts. These rumours were soon confirmed by Eddy's lawyer, who pieced together for her the widespread calamity Eddy had created over recent months by borrowing large sums from multiple sources: banks, insurance companies, suppliers, even friends.

It took Eddy's lawyer months to clean up the mess. Unfortunately for the horde of creditors, there were no assets left to compensate them for their losses, and even Eileen was officially listed as an unsecured creditor because of her loss of the joint account. When all was said and done, Eddy's creditors were left licking their wounds.

* * * * *

For fourteen years Stephen Smith had not gone near New York. Although he had altered his appearance by colouring his hair and growing a moustache (nature had also contributed its share by adding a few wrinkles to his face and a few inches to his waistline), he avoided setting foot near his former home state. Several times, Norah had suggested trips to the Lincoln Centre or the Metropolitan, but Stephen always came up with an excuse and a substitute evening at the Civic Theatre in Chicago or even a weekend in San Francisco. Norah never questioned Stephen about his refusal to go to New York. In her eyes, Stephen was a perfectly honest and straightforward individual whose only aim in life seemed to be his and her pursuit of happiness.

But then one day Stephen received an invitation to attend the International Shoe Fair, which this year had chosen New York City as its venue. Stephen debated a long time with himself whether he should chance an appearance in Manhattan. He ought to go because the International Shoe Fair was indeed the most important trade event in his business, but prudence made him think otherwise. He was trying to come up with a plausible excuse for not attending the event, when Norah came home one evening with a surprise: she had purchased two airline tickets to New York and had made reservations at the St. Regis Hotel for the entire week of the Shoe Fair. She had even reserved seats for a Broadway show. Stephen feigned joy at hearing Norah unveil her surprise travel arrangements; he couldn't do anything else but express his thanks and his anticipation of a great week together in New York. He had no other choice.

Two weeks after Norah's surprise announcement, she and Stephen flew to New York. They checked into the St. Regis, where Norah had reserved a beautiful suite on one of the upper floors. She was very excited about the forthcoming events she fully intended to enjoy together with her husband. Stephen took great pains not to show his apprehension at going back to the city from which he had taken leave under such painful circumstances. He was clearly hopeful that the past fourteen years had erased any serious risk of being recognized.

Norah and Stephen spent an hour in their suite, freshening up and getting dressed for dinner, then they headed towards one of the beautifully decorated salons off the lobby.

Norah was still chatting about the plans she had made for their stay in New York when Stephen was suddenly struck by a lightning bolt. Entering the hall by an adjoining door, was Eileen, holding the arm of a handsome middle-aged man. There was nowhere to hide; the two couples were going to walk right past each other. For a brief moment, Stephen hoped Eileen would not notice him. But then she and her escort turned toward him and Norah. As they passed each other, Eileen's eyes widened, though the rest of her face betrayed nothing. Stephen followed the couple with his eyes for a brief moment, then, in utter shock, continued to walk towards the other side of the hall, sitting down on a leather couch with Norah. He took a brochure and pretended to read it, thinking quickly what his next move should be. He looked in Eileen's direction and saw that she and the man she was with had also taken a seat at the other end of the hall. Obviously, Eileen also needed time to cope with her shock.

Should he walk over and talk to Eileen? If he did, he would not only have to account for his past but risk losing his present and future life, including his marriage, a dreadful prospect, indeed.

Eileen, sitting at the opposite end of the hall, had very similar thoughts racing through her mind. First of all, she asked herself, what was this dead man doing here? He had obviously tricked everybody into thinking he had perished in the crash. Now that he was alive, should she ask for an explanation? If she did that and everybody had a good laugh over the resurrection of Eddy Cahill, what next? She would have to return not only the substantial settlement from the airline, but also the inheritance she had received from Eddy's aunt. But above all, her marriage would be the first victim of the resurrection of her former husband.

Minutes had gone by since they first set eyes upon each other in the hall of the hotel lobby. Minutes that seemed to last forever. Then they both got up, holding on to their spouses, and started walking slowly towards each other.

When their paths crossed, Eileen and Eddy, for a brief moment, and almost unnoticed by their partners, looked into each other's eyes, smiled and nodded.

Then, they continued their stride towards the hall's opposing exits, each into their own orbits.

LE PANAMA

Commuting by train can be, and usually is, a boring and monotonous experience, especially for people who have to repeat the same forty-five minute ride from their suburban railway station to the city and vice versa, day in day out. Some commuters take refuge in the newspaper, others try their hands at crossword puzzles and still others start or conclude their business days with office work. But the fact remains that the daily commute is mostly considered an unavoidable but necessary evil, like paying taxes or walking the dog on dark and windy nights.

Not so for a group of six people who every work day took the train from Versailles to the Gare St. Lazare in downtown Paris. Although these six had been living in the same neighbourhood for many years, they did not usually interact socially with each other, except every morning on the 8:03 to Paris and every evening on the 6:33 back home. It is here that they all occupied the same compartment day in day out.

Over the years they had worked out a routine strategy of having the conductor put a sign of "RESERVE" on one of the compartments or they took turns in arriving a few minutes early to sit down and see to it that nobody else occupied the other seats. It worked out perfectly well, especially with the cooperation of friendly and properly tipped conductors.

The group of six co-travellers was made up by a husband and wife, he a general practitioner and she his receptionist, an overweight and constantly smiling accountant, a tall and greying shoe store manager, a real estate agent and a man owning a wine and liquor store on rue de la Galette.

Obviously a diverse group, but they all shared a few very important traits: they were all keenly interested in French politics and always ready to debate issues of the day. They also had a more or less pronounced sense of humour and a voracious appetite for telling and listening to funny stories. There was one exception, however. Armand Boileau, the real estate agent, did not have a funny bone in his tall and almost ascetic body. He was very knowledgeable on anything political or military, but he gave the general impression of preferring root canal surgery over venturing a laugh. A smile, often resembling a nervous twitch, was all that could be extracted from him. As a result, Armand was often obliged to tolerate the teasing remarks of the others who delighted in his inability to see the humorous side of everyday life. There was another aspect to Armand that set him apart from the others. He was very wealthy and, you guessed it, at the same time very stingy. Although they all knew he owned buildings and land in many parts of Paris, he constantly complained about having to spend money to the point that they often good-humouredly called him *"le pingre"*, the tightwad.

By contrast, Pierre Dulac, the rotund accountant, was no doubt the funniest, the most outgoing and the most entertaining member of the group. He was a practical joker by nature and could describe a simple ride in the Paris metro or buying a baguette from the local bakery in such a way that his listeners would crack up laughing to the point of wiping tears from their eyes. Pierre was the natural *"bout d'entrain"*, the "life of the party".

Doctor Petit, known as *"le toubib"* (Arabic for doctor), was also endowed with a remarkable sense of humour. In fact, when Pierre told one of his stories he mostly eyed *le toubib* because he was certain of a resonant reception.

Over the years this group had become close friends. They shared among themselves many personal experiences and observations that they withheld even from their own families.

And so it was that one warm June day, the group assembled on the 6:33 looking forward to some chit-chat aboard the train and, later, to a relaxing evening with their families. As they took their seats, they noticed that Armand was absent. A few minutes later, as the train pulled out of the Gare St. Lazare, Pierre said to the others: "Listen to this. I just saw Armand board the train so he must have gone to the toilet. I noticed that he was wearing a white Panama straw hat, one we have never seen before on him. He must have bought it today. How about asking him to show us his new hat? We'll pass it on and mess it up as each of us handles it roughly. Then, when it reaches *le toubib* in the window seat, he'll say "This is a ridiculous hat. You can't wear this thing. Your wife and kids will make fun of you when you walk into the house. With this, he'll open the window and throw out the hat! What do you think of this joke on *"le pingre?"*

The others were listening intently to the accountant's proposal. Some laughed out loud and thought it was a hilarious idea, others, especially the doctor's wife, disagreed
"No, you can't do this," she said. "Armand must have paid a lot of money for that hat. Panamas are not inexpensive, you know."

Le toubib agreed.

"It's true that we will all get a chuckle looking at *le pingre's* face when his hat flies out the window, but we should not make him pay for our practical jokes."

"Wait a minute," said Pierre. "How about we all chip in to buy him a new hat? How much could he have spent for the Panama? I am sure no more than one hundred Francs; we'll each pay twenty. After we throw out his hat and have all a good laugh, we'll give him the money to buy himself another one."

They all agreed that the spectacle was well worth the expense. Pierre quickly collected the money and put it in his pocket.

A few minutes later Armand arrived. He greeted his friends cordially and was about to take off his hat to place it on the overhead rack, when they all exclaimed, "Oh, a new hat! It's beautiful! You must have bought it today!" "Yes," said Armand proudly, "I bought it today and it cost me a fortune. I'm glad you all like it. I never wore a white hat, but apparently it is the latest fashion. Besides, you should not walk in the sun without protecting your head."

As Armand sat down, Jacques, the wine merchant sitting next to him, said, "Let me have a look at this beauty. Show it to me."

"I'd rather not, if you don't mind. It is white and very delicate. I myself am handling it like a raw egg."

"Come on," said Jacques, "I'll be careful. I just want to look at it, please."

Very reluctantly and carefully, Armand lifted the hat from the rack and handed it to Jacques. That move sealed the fate of the unfortunate import from Panama. Watching helplessly as the hat started its fateful journey, Armand was in a frenzy, jumping up and shouting, "Please, for heaven's sake, be careful! What are you doing to my hat? Don't touch it, you are ruining it". The headgear passed from one to the other, each of them fingering it clumsily and wiping off presumed stains and marks left by the preceding tormentor, until it finally reached *le toubib*. By now Armand was frantic with anger. He was close to tears as he repeatedly tried to retrieve his prized possession from the posse gone wild.

Under the watchful eyes of the others, *le toubib* looked at the mangled hat and said to Armand, "Don't tell me that you're going to wear this dirty thing? It's filthy and lost its shape. Surely you don't want to be seen with this contraption on your head. You, a well dressed man? Never!" With these words, he tossed the Panama out into the passing countryside, shouting, "Good riddance and adieu."

The next few minutes were pandemonium pure and simple. Armand's complexion had turned purple as he furiously shouted, "You are crazy and cruel, all of you! You had no right to do this to me. I buy myself the most expensive hat I have ever worn and you behave like crazed children. I'm furious and I don't want to talk to any of you anymore."

He collected his newspaper with a crisp snap and was about to walk out of the compartment when Pierre held him back.

"Calm down, Armand, what's the big deal? It is only a hat after all. But listen, perhaps we went a bit too far. I don't know what you paid for it, but here's a hundred Francs. Go and get yourself another one tomorrow. OK?" He took out the money and stuffed it into Armand's pocket. "Now calm down and stop behaving like a child who lost his favourite toy."

Armand glared at everybody before sitting down.

"*Eh bien*. I'm still mad, but I forgive you." A round of applause followed by some friendly pats on Armand's back brought a faint smile to his face. After a few minutes, normal conversation resumed. The incident was closed.

* * * * *

Well, for all intents and purposes this little story could end here. But it does not; in fact, it cannot. For, like so many other events in life, there is always another, often unsuspected side to it.

That same day, around noon, Armand ran into Pierre at a bistro on the *rue François*. They both happened to be in the area and spotted each other in the crowd. As they sat down at a table, Armand removed a brand new Panama hat from his head and hung it up. Pierre sensed that something was not quite right with Armand. He asked him if he was alright.

"Listen to this", said Armand. "This morning I walked past Chauvet, the men's store, and in the window I saw a beautiful Panama hat. Believe it or not, I fell in love with it and entered the store, asking the salesman if I could try on a Panama. I try on a few and ask for the price. A fortune. A small fortune. People could live a month on that. I am about to walk out, but the sales clerk keeps telling me that it is the latest fashion and that I look like the Prince of Wales in it.

'You'll be incredibly elegant wearing it with any outfit, Monsieur,' he says. I keep looking in the mirror, and you know what? He is right! The hat really looks good on me. I never had a white Panama, so I tell myself, 'What the hell. It's better to spend on garments than on doctors, no? So, I tell the beaming clerk, 'I'll take it. Don't put it in a box, I'll wear it.' I pay and walk out, feeling a bit guilty for having spent one hundred Francs but also proud of my new acquisition.

"Since I spent the rest of the day mostly walking, I wore the hat, until I ran into a sudden gust of wind, which blew it off my head. I picked it up and walked into a nearby hotel lobby to look at myself in a mirror. I noticed that the hat is really too small for me. It sits on top of my head, not at all fitting properly. I check the size tag and, indeed, it is a five and a half. I always wear a five and three quarters. How stupid of me. How come I did not notice it? Anyway, I decide to go back to Chauvet and ask for a larger size. I ran my other errands and went back to the store, but the clerk looked at the hat and said, 'I am sorry, *Monsieur*, but I cannot take it back. You have worn it on a hot day and the inside is sweaty. Look,' he says, 'the leather rim is stained.' I say, 'But I bought it only a few hours earlier from you.' 'I know,' says the clerk, 'I sold it to you, but I am sorry.' So I ask to talk to the manager and get the same story: 'Would *you* buy a worn hat from us, *Monsieur*? We are sorry.'

"There you are. I paid a fortune for a beautiful hat one size too small. I am furious at myself. I am heartbroken. Believe me, I don't even feel like eating."

After a few reflective moments, the accountant said, "You know what, Armand? I have an idea. How good are you at acting?"

"Why?" said Armand.

"Because, if my idea works, I will get you the money to buy a new hat."

"What do you mean," said Armand.

"Listen carefully to what I am going to tell you. But it will only work if you play your part really well, like a member of the *Comedie Française*. If you act well, you may end up with a new Panama, this time size five and three quarters."

BLANCHE - Part I

Based on a True Story

The summer of 1891 was a particularly hot one in Constantinople, the glittering capital of the Ottoman Empire. Most people who could afford it, and even those who could not, had left the city for the cooler hills and islands in the nearby Sea of Marmara, a meandering waterway surrounding the city.

The Ottoman Empire was beset by rebellion and insurrection from its many ethnic constituents trying to rid themselves of the shackles fierce Turkish warriors and greedy Sultans clamped on them ever since the Ottoman Turks had made their fateful entry into Europe in the middle of the fifteenth century. Yet, despite these constant uprisings in the far-flung empire, the Sublime Gate, as the official seat of the Ottoman rulers was called, still inspired awesome respect and even fear, not only in Turkey, but also in the four corners of the world.

Constantinople, renamed Istanbul by the Turks, with its 500 mosques and over a thousand graceful minarets, its teaming bazaars and elegant shops and its truly multinational inhabitants, personified the splendour and glory, the wealth and tradition of the Ottoman Empire. In the narrow streets of the capital, you could see officers of the Sultan's Army in their resplendent uniforms, European ladies in their finest turn-of-the-century attire, deeply veiled Turkish ladies and businessmen of all ethnic backgrounds rubbing shoulders in a colourful mosaic of people.

Max Gutmann, the general manager of the local Singer Sewing Machine Company, and his pretty wife, Lina, had not left the sweltering city for a very good reason. Lina was in her ninth month of pregnancy and the baby was due any moment. Naturally, Max wanted his wife to be within easy reach of a good hospital.

Max was a self-centred and over-assertive man, two features he abundantly shared with his wife. In keeping with their social standing, they appeared to live an orderly and conservative life, but in reality, their efforts to keep up with the rest of the world, mostly its upper crust, often caused tension and arguments between them. Among their friends they were known as argumentative, egotistical and snobbish.

Blanche was born late one evening in August and immediately became the focal point of Lina and Max's life. The baby had her mother's clean and beautiful features and a very light complexion, hence the parent's decision to name her Blanche.

From the beginning, nothing but nothing was good enough for Blanche. She received the best baby care, including a wet nurse to fill the gaps when Lina did not have enough milk. Blanche always wore the cutest and most expensive clothes, and on Sundays was paraded by her doting parents in the finest English perambulator in the city's parks and streets. As a toddler, she was only allowed to play with children of the wealthiest and most notable people in town.

Blanche was an exceptionally beautiful child. Her round face was lit up by her large dark eyes, which contrasted very pleasingly with her peachy and immaculate complexion. She had a small stubby nose and full lips. Her roundish face was framed by abundant silky hair of an almost black hue.

The best school in Constantinople, at the time, was the *Bürgerschule*, a German school, heavily subsidized by Imperial Berlin with the object of disseminating Germanic culture. It was hoped that German-educated Turks would grow up to become national leaders with a friendly disposition towards Germany. Needless to say, the *Bürgerschule* was an exemplary institution of advanced learning and progressive thinking. It was there that the Gutmanns decided to send Blanche. She eventually graduated from what the Germans call *Oberrealschule*, or College. She was, by now, a beautiful seventeen-year-old.

Blanche's thirteen years at school were not entirely uneventful. Her spoiled upbringing at home often made it difficult for her to conform to the school's Teutonic discipline, and more than once did her teachers have to send her home with a reprimand for insubordination and stubbornness. But by and large, Blanche proved to be a good student, more interested in putting the whole scholastic experience behind her than in allowing herself to get involved in flirtatious escapades and other extracurricular activities. Perhaps her upbringing and her self-consciousness moulded her into a natural snob who gave of herself just enough to be superficially involved, without being a true participant in the adolescent world around her.

On graduation day, a very extravagant event attended by students' parents, as well as Turkish and German dignitaries, Blanche looked to the future with hope, dreams and excitement, albeit without a specific intention in mind as to what she wanted to do next. These vague expectations were, however, in direct contrast to her parents' plans. In fact, they had for some time carried on a correspondence with several "finishing schools", where upper bourgeois parents sent their daughters to help them accomplish the smooth transition from teenage girls to young ladies. They had singled out in Switzerland a school that taught the art of being the perfect housewife, from baby care to home decoration, in Vienna, a school for gourmet cooking and baking, and in England the best institution to teach social grace and impeccable manners. Six months in each location, they thought, should turn their beloved daughter into a most eligible bride, ready to satisfy even the most demanding of suitors. Further, they had already lined up some private tutors for piano lessons, ballet and art classes, after completion of her European finishing courses.

Blanche threw herself into her pre-arranged education with resignation, but nevertheless a keen resolve to succeed. Not only did she want to please her parents, but she also believed that if she added all the knowledge she acquired to her personal beauty, of which she was very much aware, she could conquer the most eligible bachelor in the entire world.

On her twentieth birthday, her parents resolved to devote every conceivable effort to help their daughter find the most suitable husband in the world, the true *Prince Charming*. Nothing but the best would do.

All these years of fine-tuned education had indeed created a very accomplished young lady. Mentally astute and physically beautiful, Blanche was made to believe that the world was hers for the asking. However, her talents and her appearance drastically clashed with her egoistic and harsh character. She was the centre of the world and nobody and nothing else mattered to her. With the exception of her parents, she had not nurtured any close relationships, primarily because she thought that they had nothing to offer her.

And so, Blanche faced an adult world, not intent on participating in it, but on benefiting from it. Rather than eating the cake, she wanted to pick the raisins from it, and only those she fancied, throwing the rest carelessly away.

* * * * *

In 1911, Bulgaria was still constitutionally linked to the Ottoman Empire. Because of its almost entirely agricultural and rural economy, it was a major supplier of everything the earth brought forth. From wheat to rose oil, from dairy products to wines and meats, an abundant flow of Bulgarian produce had created an affluent society of local farmers and landowners. Although rich and powerful, many of them lacked, however, sophistication and polish, of which they were fully aware. Theatres, concert halls and other cultural centres were practically non-existent; any artistic activity that occurred was confined to private homes or clubs. Accordingly, wealthy Bulgarian parents often sent their daughters and sons to nearby Constantinople, the glittering metropolis where art and culture abounded, to find suitable brides and husbands. As part of this tradition, Mark Levy arrived one September day in Constantinople, at the age of twenty-six, looking for the girl of his dreams to marry and take back to his homestead in Plovdiv, Bulgaria.

Mark was by no means a stranger to Constantinople. He had repeatedly visited his two uncles, who owned the largest company of stevedores and chandlers in Turkey. From spacious warehouses near the waterfront, the two Levy brothers supplied ships, trains and hotels with everything from table linen and cutlery to fresh local produce and the finest imported delicacies and spirits. Business was good and steadily growing. Young Mark now stayed at the home of one of his uncles, who almost immediately laid down plans to introduce the eligible bachelor to family, friends and neighbours, with particular emphasis on those who had pretty and unmarried daughters.

Tall and muscular, Mark had blue eyes and dark blond hair. His gait was energetic and vibrant. He was highly intelligent, kind and considerate and had a sizeable family fortune behind him. He had spent most of his formative years in Sofia, Bulgaria's capital, and his looks showed that he spent most of his life in the open air, rather than inside an office. He preferred loose-fitting and sporty clothes to more formal attire, but he wore everything with a natural grace and even elegance. To say that Mark Levy was a perfect catch for any eligible girl was truly an understatement.

Spotting a stunningly beautiful girl at a charity ball, Mark wasted no time in strolling over to the table where Blanche Gutmann sat between her proud parents. He introduced himself and asked for the favour of a dance, which was granted. The two took to the floor, obviously unaware of the fact that this was to be the beginning of a relationship that would eventually culminate in a resplendent wedding such as even the blasé Constantinople society had rarely seen. Most people called it the wedding of the decade. Presided over by a full complement of Levy families and their Bulgarian friends on one side and the Gutmanns and their many Turkish friends and business associates as well as by some official dignitaries on the other side, Mark and Blanche were given a royal send-off into marital life.

After a tearful farewell from her parents, Blanche and Mark climbed the steps to the special carriage that had been added to the Orient Express in order to accommodate the returning Levy clan and all the wedding gifts and personal belongings. Amid shouts and kisses and tear-soaked handkerchief waving, the overnight train journey would bring Blanche to a completely new life in Plovdiv, and Mark back to his rural hometown.

Blanche was radiantly happy and very much in love with Mark. Throughout their short courtship, the wedding and now their trip to Bulgaria, Blanche and Mark looked like the happiest and most beautiful couple on earth. They had every reason to look forward to a long and comfortable life of marital bliss, surrounded by loving parents and friends.

Plovdiv, once known as Philippopolis, was a small provincial town, nestled halfway between the capital Sofia and the Black Sea port of Varna, Bulgaria's celebrated resort area. Founded by the Romans on the banks of the Maritsa River, Plovdiv enjoyed all the benefits of a fertile valley flanked in the north by the Siredna Gora and in the south by the Rodop Mountains. Because of its geographically protected location and abundantly irrigated soil, the Plovdiv valley had supplied the entire country for centuries with wheat, corn, rose oil, tobacco, all kinds of fruits and vegetables and even a rich array of dairy products.

It is in this valley that the Levys had established their sprawling homestead. Fleeing anti-Semitic persecution in the wake of the Spanish Inquisition, they arrived in 1492 in Constantinople. As their traditional occupation in Spain had been the exploitation of olive tree plantations, they soon discovered the agricultural opportunities offered by Bulgaria, at the time an Ottoman province. In time, they moved, together with a number of other Jewish families to Plovdiv. Over the centuries, they had contributed to their Bulgarian and Turkish hosts not only valuable products and considerable taxes, but also human resources such as doctors, administrators and even a few high ranking officials at the Sultan's Court. They were very much part of the Bulgarian national fibre and its ethnic elite. Although they had jealously preserved their Jewish heritage, they looked upon themselves as Bulgarians first and foremost.

By the end of the 19th century, the Levy families controlled several dynamic enterprises, both inside and outside Bulgaria, all related to agricultural products and their derivatives. Efficiently administered like any large corporation, different business activities were controlled by different family members, all of whom had received prior training and all department heads, some of them outsiders, reported to an administrative board chaired by the titular head of the Levy families.

Mark had attended business school and agricultural college in Sofia and then studied economics in Vienna before being appointed head of a new family venture into cosmetics. In fact, his first task was to establish soap factories in Bulgaria, Austria, Germany and France. He was determined to shape the family's cosmetic business into yet another successful venture in the string of prospering Levy enterprises.

* * * * *

Blanche and Mark and their voluminous luggage were picked up at the train station and taken to a beautiful house Mark's parents had purchased for them during the young couple's courtship in Constantinople. It was situated on a tree-sheltered street in the best part of Plovdiv, near the homes of other family members and local notables.

The fact that she had moved from a glittering and eminently cosmopolitan Constantinople to rural and provincial Plovdiv hit Blanche very hard the very day after her arrival in Bulgaria during a stroll through town. Schools, a synagogue and food shops were nearby, but there were very few clothing stores in the area. Those stores certainly did not carry the designer dresses to which Blanche was accustomed.

She suddenly felt cut off and banished from her beloved hometown on the Bosphorus, from her many friends, but most of all from her doting parents who had been so much the focal point of her life. However, the fact that she was very much in love with Mark and thrilled by his mature personality and the attention with which he surrounded her helped to overcome her fears and apprehensions. Indeed, she looked forward to the excitement of decorating her new home, of meeting new friends and of being Mrs. Mark Levy.

The house Mark's parents had given them was spacious, well laid-out and surrounded by beautifully kept grounds. There was even a small stream flowing in and out of a large pond in the back of the property. Mr. and Mrs. Levy, not wanting to interfere with the young couple's taste, had furnished the house with only basic necessities, such as beds, tables, chairs and kitchen utensils, leaving it up to Blanche and Mark to turn the house into their own home.

Summoning a well-known decorator from Sofia, they proceeded to plan and design every room, from the basement to the attic. After Mark had allocated a budget, the decorator immediately left for Vienna and Florence, where she was to make selections and purchases. During the next few months, Blanche's home echoed with the noise and clatter of arriving crates and boxes and with the shuffling of artisans putting everything into place, painting walls and arranging furniture, drapes and carpets to suit the very meticulous demands of the mistress of the house. Mark left all decorating arrangements to her; his only meaningful contribution was to approve the constant additions to the original budget with a smile, not once questioning Blanche's decisions.

When everything was in place, Blanche and the decorator went back to Vienna and Florence to purchase some paintings and other artwork. They came back, placed everything in their proper places, and the decorator was sent home to Sofia, where she could have easily gone into early retirement. The whole operation had taken five months, but the house had indeed become a home. It was not only beautiful to look at but also comfortable and even cozy.

The young couple settled down to an elegant lifestyle. They gave several parties, first to entertain Mark's parents and other family members, and subsequently to meet their neighbours, friends and business associates. Thus, the radiant young Levys made their debut into Plovdiv's society with grace and elegance.

Mark proved to be the ideal husband. Although he was a consummate businessman, leaving the house at the crack of dawn and coming home in the late evening, he often sent Blanche messages during the day and never missed an opportunity to bring her flowers and little gifts. On special occasions such as her birthday, or on religious holidays, he traveled with Blanche to Sofia to buy her expensive jewellery and whatever else she asked for.

A year and a half into their marital life, Blanche became pregnant. The family doctor's news caused an outburst of joy. Led by Mark's mother, all female members of the family began to treat Blanche like a precious princess, or rather like an invalid. Very much against her will, they made her lie down frequently and rest and they constantly visited her, making sure that she was "comfortable". These well-meaning but grossly exaggerated manifestations soon began to irritate Blanche to the point that she felt like a trapped animal, deprived of her freedom of movement and other decisions.

Although she faced motherhood with natural excitement, her pregnancy began to weigh on her like an unbearable burden, because of what appeared to her as the inane behaviour of the family and especially her mother-in-law. Blanche began to cry a great deal and for the first time since her departure from Constantinople, she told her mother of her unhappiness. Mrs. Gutmann tried to calm her and recommended patience and understanding for the rather archaic and rural lifestyle and behaviour of her in-laws, a lifestyle which was very different from the westernized and modern mentality of the Gutmanns.

Blanche suffered through her pregnancy. On one hand, she did not want to hurt Mark's feelings. Mark found his mother's overbearing behaviour somewhat natural and, at worst, annoying. He kept urging Blanche to be tolerant and to accept it as an expression of his mother's love rather than interference into her life. Blanche was glad when it was all over and she became the mother of a beautiful baby boy. Although she could count on plenty of household help, the young mother devoted every minute of her waking hours and very often even her nights to the baby. By caring for her newborn so intensely she also succeeded in shaking off the interference from other family members. Bringing up Charles became Blanche's main occupation, and she relished every moment of it. Mark proved to be a loving, albeit somewhat distant, father, leaving the chores of diaper changing and burping entirely to Blanche.

For the next year and a half, Charles became the focal point of the young family. All social and other activities were subordinated to the time and attention reserved for him. But then, almost eighteen months to the day after Charles' birth, Dr. Aronof confirmed to Blanche that she was to be a mother for a second time. Again, everybody was elated and jubilant, including Blanche and Mark.

A month after Dr. Aronof had given Blanche the good news, she sat down with Mark one evening after having put Charles to bed and had a long talk with her husband. She had braced and prepared herself for this conversation for some time. Blanche told Mark that after almost three years of life in Plovdiv, she had come to the conclusion that she did not really like it. Mark listened to her with alternating surprise and consternation. She told him how much she had suffered during her previous pregnancy and even later, when his mother tried to run her life for her, how domineering and even oppressive some family members had been and still were.

"But you're used to people doing things for you or taking care of you, aren't you?" said Mark.

"Yes, but most of the time when my parents told me what to do, I sort of agreed with them because it made sense to me. Your mother wants me to bring up the baby like her grandparents did, and I can't stand it.".

Blanche could not bear the idea of going through this agony again with her second child. She also told Mark that in her three years in Plovdiv, she had met many loving and caring people, but she had not made one single friend in whom she could confide and to whom she could relate.

"You are my only friend and, indeed, my whole world in Plovdiv," she said, adding that in two years, with a few rare exceptions, they had not gone to any art galleries or concerts or the theatre, simply because there were none in Plovdiv. She went on and on, decrying her isolation in Bulgaria, often wiping tears from her eyes.

Realizing the gravity of Blanche's words, Mark kept his silence, only looking from time to time into his wife's eyes and holding her hand.

And then, Blanche asked Mark to request from his father a relocation to Constantinople, where his two uncles were running the family's stevedoring business. At this point, Mark interrupted her and said this was impossible. He pointed out that his responsibility was to create and develop the family's cosmetic business and not the stevedoring. Also, there were already two family members in Constantinople and there was no need for a third one. He was needed at the head office and nowhere else. Blanche did not take these objections seriously. She reminded him that his uncles in Constantinople were getting older and their children were not considered capable successors, as Mark himself had repeatedly told her. In any case, Blanche was adamant and made it clear to Mark that her unwillingness to bring up the children in the restrictive and family-dominated environment of Plovdiv was not negotiable. Mark tried very hard to dissuade her, offering Blanche the prospect of more frequent trips to anywhere she wanted, but in view of her second pregnancy, even he had to concede that nothing much could change in their lifestyle for at least another two years.

In the end, a reluctant and visibly disappointed Mark told Blanche: "Look, I promise to discuss the matter with my father in the morning". The two went to bed hugging each other as they had been doing since the day they fell in love in Constantinople.

For Mark, this discussion was a rather painful revelation. Although he continued to be deeply in love with Blanche, he realized that despite all his efforts to make his wife as happy as any doting husband can, she really placed her personal desires above her duties to him and to her family. He fully appreciated the difference in their backgrounds, but he had hoped that a few years of life in Bulgaria would prepare Blanche for a life with her husband, wherever his profession might take him, rather than wanting to hang on to her rather frivolous and selfish way of life as a young girl.

Mark spared his wife the details of his long and, at times, very painful discussion with his father and the other members of the Advisory Board. All he told Blanche, two days later, was that she could start making preparations for their move to Constantinople. Blanche was elated, and, in a slightly lesser way, so was Mark, when he saw how her face lit up like a blossom burgeoning into a beautiful flower. On one hand, he had sensed all along that Blanche never really adapted to the Bulgarian lifestyle and was unhappy, but on the other hand, he was sad to leave his parents and friends and start a new life in Constantinople, both professionally and socially. He also asked for and received permission to continue to lead the soap project, in addition to his involvement with the Constantinople branch.

The next six weeks were marked by a great deal of moving and packing. When the Plovdiv house had been completely emptied of its contents and everything was either on its way to Constantinople or already piled up in the new house Mark and Blanche had purchased during one of their frequent trips to Turkey, the entire Plovdiv establishment, parents, family and friends gave the couple a rousing farewell party. Many eyes were filled with tears, but Blanche's obvious happiness brought out smiles on everybody's face. Though they all agreed that life is short and one might as well enjoy it when one can, some family members resented Blanche's selfishness in uprooting her family from a place they all had come to regard as an ancestral home. Mark's mother was openly upset about the young couple's departure and told her husband that she believed Blanche was more of a burden than a helping partner to her son.

It was one of those cool spring mornings when the overnight train from Sofia pulled into Constantinople's *Sirkeci* station. Blanche and Mark, accompanied by little Charles and his nurse, stepped off the train into a waiting limousine, which rattled through the crowded downtown streets and finally reached their new house on a hill overlooking the Bosphorus Straits. It was a beautiful mansion surrounded by a well-kept garden, which would henceforth be the home of the growing young family.

While Blanche was busy arranging and decorating the new home, Mark joined the family's stevedoring business. As in every new job, there was a period of learning and getting acquainted not only with an unfamiliar occupation, but also with unfamiliar people, as well as a completely different environment. However, given his natural intelligence and his familiarity with the family's way of doing things, it did not take too long for him to assert himself as an efficient manager, set on running the day-to-day business and also expanding it by venturing into new product lines and services.

Within a few short months, Blanche had completed the decoration of the house, trying not to exhaust herself on account of her pregnancy. She was overjoyed at not having to cope with the constant intrusions of her mother-in-law, which had turned her first pregnancy into such a nightmare. By the time Laura was born, everything in the new home was in place. Blanche had made ample use of the talents of the best decorators and painters to be found in Constantinople. She spent a fortune to adapt and add to the things she had brought over from Plovdiv, making sure that the new decor reflected the refined taste of current and past Ottoman eras. A small army of Turkish and Armenian artisans saw to it that the house looked every bit like a small seraglio.

Mark continued to be a devoted husband and father. Blanche was very happy with her beloved parents and her old friends close by, two beautiful children and plenty of servants and helpers that read every wish from her lips. In addition to all of these blessings, she had escaped the backward and oppressive environment of Plovdiv and could now enjoy the very colourful and sophisticated social life lead by Constantinople's upper crust. Blanche had indeed achieved every wish and dream of her childhood and adolescence, and it seemed as if this blissful life would go on forever and ever.

*****

Shortly after Laura's third birthday, Blanche became suddenly aware that Mark traveled to Europe more often than before. To be sure, his occasional trips to Vienna, always of short duration, were made for good apparent reasons. Mark had retained his responsibility for the cosmetic business, and the Levys were building a large soap and cosmetic products factory on the outskirts of Vienna. The construction of the building had been completed, and now they were installing the most up-to-date machinery, in order to manufacture a high quality product line. This crucial phase of the project required Mark's supervision.

What drew Blanche's attention was that Mark's trips to Vienna now took place every three weeks or so. No sooner had he returned from a four to five days' absence, than he started preparing for his next trip. Blanche asked him whether all these frequent trips were really necessary, and could he not delegate an assistant to supervise the plant installations. Mark told her that the project was in its final stages, that almost all was already in place and as soon as the first product batches were manufactured, he would leave everything to the newly appointed plant manager. That would be the end of his trips to Vienna. When Blanche asked him when this would happen, he simply said "in a month or so."

Although Mark's explanations sounded very plausible, Blanche began to feel uneasy every time Mark kissed her goodbye, and especially every time he returned a few days later, laden with gifts and toys for the children and yet another piece of valuable jewellery for her. She did not tell anybody, not even her beloved mother, but deep inside, Blanche began to suspect that Mark was having an affair with another woman in Vienna. As time went on and Mark's trips continued with almost monotonous repetitiveness, her suspicions grew into certainty. There was another woman in his life.

Blanche was shattered. She asked herself how this was possible. She had given Mark all and everything a man could ask for: her youth, her beauty, her body and her love. She had given him two lovely children and a comfortable home. Why on earth would he become a philanderer? She spent sleepless hours searching for a reasonable answer.

Finally, during one of her sleepless nights, she decided to find out exactly who this other woman was and why Mark had strayed. Early the next morning, as soon as Mark had left for the office, she located a private detective agency and went to see them. She told the two men who ran this company of her suspicions and asked them to secretly follow her husband during his forthcoming trip to Vienna. They were to come to the train station, where she would point out Mark to them and from then on they would travel with him to Vienna. From a safe distance, they were to follow him everywhere he went, observing everybody he met and reporting to her all of their findings in great detail. She offered to pay them generously as long as she received complete information about Mark's movements and contacts from arrival to departure.

One week later, the unsuspecting Mark and his incognito observers were on their way to Vienna, and another week later they were all back in Constantinople. Blanche, with a heavy heart and emotions she could not hide, went to the private eye office on the agreed day and waited impatiently for the two agents to make their report.

They told Blanche how they had not left Mark out of their sight for one single moment throughout his entire stay in Vienna, day and night. Then they came to their findings.

"Mrs. Levy," they said, "we have good news and bad news." Blanche was listening to them as if mesmerized.

"The good news, Mrs. Levy, is that your husband does not have another woman in Vienna," They continued with great hesitation. "The bad news is that your husband has venereal disease."

Blanche stared at the men for a few seconds.

"He has what?" she asked, in utter disbelief.

"He has syphilis," they repeated.

"How do you know that?" she asked, holding back a gush of tears that were rushing to her eyes like a sea wave.

They told her how, the morning after his arrival in Vienna, Mark had gone to the city's huge general hospital, where they followed him to the Department of Venereal Diseases, and they saw him enter the clinic of Professor Schlesinger, one of the city's top venereologists. They waited for two hours outside the clinic and then they saw Mark leaving the dispensary. While one of the agents followed Mark out of the hospital, the other went into the waiting room of the clinic and talked to the receptionist, making sure that there was no one else around. He told the nurse that he was an agent hired by a life insurance company and that he would like her to help him complete his file on Mark Levy, who had just applied for a huge increase in coverage.

At first, she did not believe the agent and refused to continue the conversation. But when the agent told her that his interest in Mark's health was nothing personal but a legitimate business action by the insurance company and he slipped a substantial amount of money into her drawer to lend support to his business-like approach, she relented. She left Mark's file, which the professor had returned to her for filing, on her desk while she stepped out briefly.

The voluminous file had many entries, some with recent dates three to four weeks apart, and many reports, which the agent had no time to read. One thing, though, became abundantly clear to him: on several sheets the name of Mark Levy and "Syphilis" were unmistakably mentioned. Mark had been undergoing treatment for a prolonged length of time, and Professor Schlesinger was the treating physician.

As the agents wrapped up their briefing, all colour disappeared from Blanche's face. She had aged in a few minutes. Her eyes were staring out of two recessed holes in her ashen face. She thanked the agents, without even knowing what she was saying, and mumbled that she would send them a cheque immediately. She had braced herself to hear that Mark may have had an affair, but she was unprepared for what she had just heard. She could not believe it. In a trance, she arrived home and, without seeing the children, ran up to her bedroom, slammed the door and broke out in tears. She paused only to consider her next move. Obviously, she had to confront Mark and find out all about his horrible and unspeakable betrayal and crime against her and his two innocent children.

Hours went by until Mark finally came home, expecting to hug and kiss his wife in the living room, but she was not there. Thinking she had a headache, he rushed up to the bedroom. Upon entering, he found Blanche sitting on the bed with a handkerchief in her hand. Her swollen eyes and disorderly appearance shocked him. He quickly moved towards her in an effort to take her into his arms, but she screamed at him.

"Don't touch me, you murderer!"

He stopped in his tracks. "What are you talking about? What's going on here?"

"What's going on? I'll tell you what's going on. You married me and you made two children and you have venereal disease! You are a murderer and a criminal."

She burst into fresh tears.
Mark slumped into a chair as if felled by a gunshot.

He started to ask "Who told you this?" but immediately realized that this was a senseless question. He tried to say. "It's not true," but he knew that he had to tell Blanche the truth, if she would let him.

Blanche was shouting at him in a fury, repeating that he had infected her and the children and that he was an irresponsible murderer.

After many attempts to interrupt her, Mark finally started to tell her that, yes, he had contracted syphilis some fifteen years ago and that he had undergone treatment in Vienna, in Paris and in London.

"Three years before I met you, I had been pronounced completely and totally cured, free to marry and to have children," he cried.

He ran to his desk, unlocked a drawer and took out a file from which he produced reports signed by Professor Pichot in Paris, Professor Atkins in London and his own doctor, Professor Schlesinger, asserting that there was no trace whatsoever left of the disease in his body and that he could be a husband and father without the slightest shadow of a doubt or risk to anyone.

"I waited another three years after these reports were issued before marrying you," he said.

Unwilling to back down, Blanche shouted again,"If you're cured, why are you seeing Professor Schlesinger now?"

"Because after all these years, I wanted to have a three-month follow-up course, which required periodic blood tests," he explained. "I've just completed the second month and all the tests are completely clean. There are two final tests left and after that I planned to tell you everything, showing you the three-month test results ten years after being declared completely cured."

He added that he wanted to take her to Vienna so that she could hear from the world's greatest specialist that he was as healthy as if he had never had the disease, and had been healthy for over ten years.

Blanche frequently interrupted Mark, telling him between her sobs, "I don't believe you. You're a liar. You should have told me about this problem before we got married."

"There was nothing to tell. People don't talk about diseases they don't have. If I had told you, I might have lost you and I was too much in love with you to take that risk."

Mark continued to plead and kept showing the reports and letters, all attesting to his complete cure, but Blanche had worked herself into an emotional frenzy that rejected anything Mark said. After hours of endless shouts and screams, she drew herself up and demanded a divorce. Breaking into tears, Mark tried to take Blanche into his arms, but she stepped back.

"Don't touch me. I never want to see you again and don't you ever go near the children. Who knows what the future holds for them? You have infected them and they will either die or grow up as cripples. And who knows what fate is awaiting me, who lived with you without knowing what terrible disease you withheld from me."

She ran to their bed, grabbed his pillow and threw it into the adjoining dressing room. She also ripped the blanket from the bed and threw it after the pillow.

"I don't want to see you, go away."

Exhausted beyond imagination, she then fell on her bed like a lifeless sack.

Mark sat on the couch, his face buried between his two hands. He too was absolutely drained after hours of this fight, their first in all their years of blissful marriage. When Blanche fell limply on the bed, he got up, picked up his pillow and the blanket from the floor and left the bedroom, softly closing the door behind him.

Fully dressed and without even loosening his tie, as was his habit as soon as he came home, he spread the blanket onto the small sofa in the dressing room, threw the pillow on the sofa and tried to stretch out, but could not. He started pacing the room. Silence had now returned to the upper floor after the hours of screaming outbursts.

The scene had lasted well into the night. Since the children's room was on the other side of the staircase, they were spared the clamour of the confrontation. But two of the servants, the cook and a young maid, had been sitting up in Mark's darkened small office, alarmed and terrified by the quarrel. When the shouting finally ended, they went back to their own rooms. Hours later they heard the garage door open and a car leaving.

* * * * *

Every morning at precisely six o'clock, a team of maintenance workers descended on the sprawling offices, meeting rooms and corridors of the Levy's stevedoring company to sweep, clean, scrub and shine every corner of the building. It took them precisely one hour and a half to finish the job.

This particular morning, one of the maintenance workers reported to his supervisor that he could not open the door of room 22A, the office of Mr. Mark Levy. The two men then tried together, but the door seemed to be blocked or bolted from inside.

Assuming that the door had jammed, they pushed together and the door flung open. Slumped over his desk, his head surrounded by a pool of blood, was a motionless Mark Levy. In his right hand, partly open, he held a small calibre revolver. In front of the lifeless face was a hand-written note, a corner of which was soaked by the oozing blood.

Mark Levy was obviously dead. The note read:
"*My beloved Blanche,*

I can understand why you were so upset last night. Those were the worst hours of my life, and I am sure the same applied to you.

Perhaps I should have told you of my past problem a long time ago, but my parents agreed with me that it would not serve any purpose to tell you of what was long gone and completely cured. I wanted to take you to Vienna to meet Professor Schlesinger, with whom we were to celebrate ten years after he completely and radically cured me. The idea of a three-month follow-up ten years later was entirely mine and all tests showed that nothing, not even a trace or a scar, had remained. I did not infect you or the children, so help me God.

Blanche, forgive me for having made you unhappy. When the children grow up, I want you to tell them what happened and that they are as healthy as anybody else.

Blanche, I can do many things, but one thing I can't: I cannot live without your love and the love of my wonderful children.

Goodbye, Blanche. Forgive me."

Mark's funeral was attended by hundreds. Not only family and friends, but business associates and government officials from both Turkey and Bulgaria came to pay their last respect to the man clearly slated to be the future head of the Levy family. Blanche talked to no one, not even to her parents. Throughout the funeral, her eyes had an empty and dull look. Nobody saw her cry. She moved about like a lost stranger.

The entire family had come from Plovdiv. When Mrs. Levy arrived at her son's home, some of the servants who had overheard the entire episode, told her what had happened in the hours preceding her son's death. She was speechless and communicated with Blanche only in short sentences, mostly relating to the funeral arrangements. Mark's parents agreed for the funeral to take place in Constantinople, but when they returned two days later to Plovdiv, they took the body of their beloved son with them. He was buried in a simple ceremony in the family gravesite among his many cousins and uncles and aunts.

Mark's parents maintained the most perfunctory ties with Blanche, restricting their contacts to occasional letters and cards on special occasions. They clearly blamed Blanche's selfish and unforgiving nature for their son's death.

During the next few days, Blanche received a seemingly endless stream of letters and cables from near and far expressing compassion and condolences. Blanche never imagined that her husband had so many friends. She read all the messages and prepared thank-you notes. Among the many envelopes she opened was one, bearing the crest of the General Hospital in Vienna. She opened it hastily. It was a letter to her from Professor Leo Schlesinger, written the day before Mark's death. It read:

"*Dear Mrs. Levy,*

As your husband's doctor and friend of many years, I am taking the liberty to write you this letter. I am motivated to do so for two reasons: first, Mark told me recently that he would tell you about his past health problem and that is why I can now talk, or rather write, freely to you about this matter. Second, your husband also told me that as soon as the three-month's tests are completed, he intended to come to Vienna with you next month so that the three of us would celebrate the tenth anniversary of his cure.

I have already told Mark and I am telling you that he need not complete these tests, which were his idea in the first place. Your husband has been completely free of any trace of the disease for ten years now and that is why several of my colleagues in Paris and London as well as myself pronounced him healthy and fit to marry and have children.

I would also like to repeat to you the invitation my wife and I already extended to Mark to stay in our house. The top floor of our home, which used to be occupied by our now grown children, is empty and should be as comfortable as any hotel in downtown Vienna.

I am sure I need not tell you that the only real reward a doctor ever receives is in healing his patients. The one reward I cherished most in my long career as a physician was to know that Mark is a happy husband and father, for there is no other joy in life than good health, especially if you have had to fight for it.

Have a happy family life for many years to come! Mrs. Schlesinger and I are anxiously looking forward to meeting you and the children.

With kindest regards,

Dr. Leo Schlesinger
Professor and Physician in Chief, General Hospital of Vienna.

* * * * *

Blanche Levy never fully recovered from this tragedy. She never remarried but managed to raise her children with love and compassion. Years later, when she thought they had reached maturity she told them the truth about their father, albeit without any expressed feelings of remorse or guilt. But deep down and for a long time she felt the full weight of what her impetuous and rash behaviour had brought about during that fateful night.

As the years went by and memories faded away she told herself that while some people may be lucky enough to repair the damage caused by their blind and hasty emotional reactions, others may not. That's life.

And life must go on.

BLANCHE - Part II

Based on a True Story

Many a great city derives fame from its magnificent buildings or monuments or elegant avenues, all of them man-made creations, reflecting its history and past glory. Not so Istanbul, which owes its unforgettable beauty primarily to its natural location, straddling two continents and only secondarily to its architecture.

Residents and visitors alike can spend endless hours admiring the wooded hills rising from either side of the meandering Bosporus, an azure-blue waterway entering the city from the Black Sea in the north and exiting it at its southern tip near the legendary Topkapi Palace, once the convergence of an empire that ruled and inspired awe and respect from Europe and Asia to Africa.

By the mid-1920s, Istanbul, after its occupation by the victorious allies following Turkey's humiliating defeat in World War I was struggling to get back on its feet, if not any more as the capital of Turkey, but as its economic and cultural center. The political and administrative base had now been moved to Ankara, the brand-new capital of the Turkish Republic created in 1923 by its visionary leader, Kemal Ataturk.

Like a phoenix rising from the ashes, Istanbul wasted no time in regaining its stature of an international metropolis. The new government actively promoted the establishment of business and entertainment centers, social services and all the other components of civilized life. So much so, that by the 1930s, Istanbul was once again the "must" stop for roving foreigners including politicians and artists, tourists and investors, all seeking opportunities or excitement of which there was plenty to be found in the pulsating city.

It is in this sophisticated and lively environment that Blanche decided to raise her two children after the disastrous and sudden demise of her marriage to Mark Levy. For weeks, Mark's suicide continued to be the favourite subject of conversation, not only in the upper classes, but also in all strata of Istanbul's bourgeois society. But then, as attention drifted to other topics of the day, Blanche was left with the stark reality of her single motherhood, albeit financially cushioned by stipends from Mark's family in Bulgaria.

True to their word, the Levy's, who still clung to the unshaken belief that their son's death at his own hands had been brought about by his wife's irrational behaviour, continued to send Blanche monthly cheques. In fact, their lawyer had informed the widow that she would receive regular payments until the day she remarried and until the children completed their education.

Devoid of any monetary worries, Blanche set out to live henceforth for her children and for herself, very much akin to a life of leisure. One thing was firmly established in her mind, though: she did not want to remarry. And this for a number of reasons. First, she already had a secure source of income which she would forfeit if she remarried. Secondly, the traumatic collapse of her marriage to Mark had left her with deep emotional scars. She felt that she had her fill with conjugal life. And, furthermore, if she needed companionship, she could always dart in and out of relationships, frivolous or serious or even sensual, without the encumbrance of marital ties. Besides, a second husband may not turn out to be the most desirable father for her beloved children.

Compared to many other widows left with two infants, Blanche was indeed a very lucky lady. She was still very beautiful and elegantly attired. People who saw her in the street or at functions used to say that she looked like "someone out of the pages of Harper's Bazaar".

Little Laura and Charles, whom she now called "Carlo" were the focal points of all her attention and love. When they were ready for school she registered them in a private institution reserved for the city's affluent. In line with her own upbringing in exclusive European finishing schools, she taught her children poise and manners without delving too deeply into the need to imbue them with ethical or moral principles. What mattered most to Blanche was that her children should be able to navigate through life with social grace as full members of the upper crust, rather than as honest citizens who pay their bills on time. Such attributes she believed the children would surely acquire in time through their exposure to everyday life.

Appearance and façade before substance and essence was obviously Blanche's credo. And judging by the fact that while still a young woman she had fashioned for herself a life of plenty and even of opulence, simply relying on her appearance and style seemed to lend support to the validity of her concept of life.

As time went by and the children continued to provide Blanche with the tempered excitement of good grades in class, plays and outings, and finally graduation from high school, Blanche began to feel the need to spread her wings.

She had given years to their upbringing and apart from vacations and school trips, she had confined her social life to her home, her close friends and her parents.

Blanche decided to look for an occupation as a social assistant to a chief executive or prominent personality, who needed someone to manage his non-business obligations such as charitable donations, family celebrations, vacations and all other activities not handled by an office secretary. She figured that landing such a position would not only expose her to wealthy and important people but would also fit well into her savoir-faire for organizing, planning and managing things with flair.

Through her friends she spread the word about her availability. She did not have to wait too long for an opportunity and indeed an offer she could not refuse.

Peter Lambros was a local businessman of Greek descent who had managed to expand a family enterprise created by his grandfather into an international holding company that comprised a variety of successful corporations, mainly in shipping and transportation but also in supporting domains such as insurance and food. Operating under different trade names, Lambros controlled, from his Istanbul headquarters a global empire rivalling some of the largest conglomerates.

He was in his early fifties, had two married children and four grandchildren. Elena, Peter's wife, had once been a celebrated beauty but years of living in the fast lane and trying to keep pace with a relentless dynamo had aged her prematurely. She was tired and looked the part. She had another problem: despite constant attempts to get rid of excess weight, she had put on pounds around her waist that made her plump and unattractive. Her doctor said that it was all due to hormonal dysfunction and that short of starving herself to death, there was little she or he could do to reverse the bulging process.

Peter, on the other hand, was tall, good looking and although an abundance of grey streaks now pervaded his curly hair, his tanned and youthful appearance belied the fact that he was pushing middle age. A resident trainer who supervised his daily workouts also saw to it that Peter maintained a bouncy and athletic gait. Thus, judging by purely physical appearances, Peter and Elena were an unequal pair, a fact the latter was painfully aware of.

* * * * *

When Blanche reported for work she was welcomed into her private office by Nina, a colleague, who was to share with her the considerable workload created by administrating the social lives of not only the Lambros couple but also those of their immediate family. These included their children, grandchildren, siblings and even in-laws. In close emulation of his business dealings, Peter Lambros had created a family clan or group that enjoyed together anything and everything imagination, sophistication and, not to forget, deep pockets could conjure up. Perhaps inspired by his Mediterranean heritage, Peter had created a "family" in the true sense of the word. They shared their joys and sorrows, they celebrated and mourned together and they all believed that it was this sense of belonging that gave strength and indeed a purpose to their lives.

To further his goal, Peter had over the years amassed an array of facilities which all family members had free access to, preferably in affinity groups. There was a large flat in Paris, as well as a town house in London. There was a beautiful penthouse in a high-rise on Manhattan's upper Park Avenue as well as a villa in Cannes on the French Riviera.

Then there were seasonal subscriptions to operas and concert halls as well as theatres. In addition to these regular features available to all there were also impromptu events they could partake of such as vacations or leisure cruises.

Naturally this rich social program called for full-time organization and management which now required the services of not one but two people, hence the opportunity which arose for Blanche.

For two weeks after starting her job, Blanche was briefed by her colleague in great detail, letting her take notes and ask questions in order to familiarize herself not only with the facilities and events but also with the individual family members, their relative importance in the hierarchy and, of course, their personal relationships with Peter Lambros himself, or "the boss" as Nina kept calling him.

Nina Olinsky was an attractive and vivacious blonde with a warm, outgoing personality that almost immediately accessed and even stirred Blanche's feelings. After two weeks of background briefings, Blanche just knew that she would work smoothly with Nina, who in turn reciprocated by telling her "Glad to have you here Blanche. Welcome to the firm." These two women appeared to have built a bridge between them that would bode well for the cooperation and reliance on each other.

A few weeks after her debut in the job, Nina took Blanche to the head office in order to have her meet the boss. Peter Lambros was charming and spent half an hour with them, asking Blanche questions about her family and herself. While he treated both women with great courtesy, offering them coffee and chocolates, Blanche noticed a certain familiarity and ease between the boss and Nina, an observation which she ascribed to her colleague having been in the job for a long time.

At the conclusion of Blanche's introduction to the boss, she was convinced that she would enjoy her work as well as her new environment.

A few days later, while sorting out her files, Nina came into her office, closed the door behind her and sat down in the seat facing Blanche's desk, motioning her to do the same in the other seat next to hers. She crossed her elegant legs and said to Blanche: "I must tell you something before you find it out from others. It's a long story and it's for your ears only. Please use your discretion when the subject comes up in conversation with your friends. It's not the greatest secret in the world, but for years we have kept it sort of dormant and discreet as far as outsiders are concerned. Of course the family knows all about it and so do some of our friends, but it is certainly not common knowledge, if you know what I mean. Can I trust you, Blanche?"

"Of course you can," she replied. "We all have our secrets and some we even take to our graves. You can trust me, Nina." She repeated.

"Well," said Nina, with a broad smile, "After this big introduction you will really wonder what this is all about, won't you?"

"Yes, indeed," admitted Blanche, "I'm all ears."

"Alright," resumed Nina. "This is the story of my life." She underscored the last few words with a burst of laughter.

"I met Peter Lambros about ten years ago at the 'Flamingo', an exclusive night club in Istanbul. Very exclusive, to be sure. Only members of the social elite could afford the annual membership fees. There was nightly entertainment and members used to come either alone or often with their wives to spend a few relaxing hours, sip drinks and dance to the tunes of an excellent band. The idea was to be among friends and enjoy conviviality in a beautifully decorated locale. There was, of course, also a circular bar at one end of the place serviced by three girls, one of them being me. We were required to wear a black evening dress, to look our best and to tend to our clientele sitting around the bar. The standing order was: be polite, and friendly, but no folksiness and certainly no 'hanky-panky'. So, we used to listen to all kinds of happy or sad stories from patrons we expected to tell us "Good Night, my dear" after a few refills of the best whiskeys or gins available anywhere. It was pleasant work, the tips were great and I was in my late twenties. What more do you want?"

Well, one evening Peter Lambros came to the Flamingo, sat down and ordered a single-malt scotch. I remember him looking tense and tired, but soon, the smoothness of the drink appeared to have a similar effect on his composure, for he loosened his tie and started asking questions about me and my life. He definitely needed someone to talk to and I happened to be the audience. So, what else is new, I thought to myself. But as he went on talking, I realized that this was a very sensitive and intelligent man actually going through a marital crisis. He did not say too much at first but I got the picture loud and clear. He was obviously very successful in business but at the same time saddled with an unhappy marriage. I also gained the impression that he respected his wife enough not to cheat on her with one-night flings. He had children, seemed to be attached to his family, but after a day's hard work he could not come home to the warmth and intimacy of a loving wife, simply because for years, she had been nursing one depression after another. She had apparently not only become fat and unattractive as a result of an incurable condition but also edgy and moody.

All this Peter managed to tell me during that night between sips of whiskey.

When he finally left just as we were closing up for the night, I felt not only very sorry for the man but I also had the feeling that just by listening and showing genuine concern, I had given him some form of relief and that he would come back to me for more of the same.

I was not wrong. A few nights later he did. When he returned for the third time he asked if he could meet me for lunch. We did and enjoyed it, talking about ourselves and exchanging views on life and the world around us. Needless to tell you that I was flattered to be seen in the company of 'the' Peter Lambros.

There were more lunches and phone calls and flowers and believe it or not, we fell in love. We began to meet on a regular basis and derived immense pleasure from being together. You know, I have a good head for business and he often told me about his projects and deals. Sometimes he even asked for my opinion.

That, my dear, is how it all started some ten years ago," said Nina, getting up from her seat. "And now, I am going to let you get on with your work. Interesting story, eh?" she added. "As they say, the rest is history. I will tell you about it tomorrow afternoon. See you then, bye."

Blanche was amazed by what she had heard and needed a little while to let it all sink in. It was quite a story. Admittedly she had heard years ago that Peter Lambros had a mistress, but she had no idea that it was Nina who had conquered the tycoon's heart. Very interesting, she kept ruminating. She could not wait to hear the rest of Nina's story, for there seemed to be more to what she had told her.

And indeed there was more.

The following day, after having taken care of the mail and yet another orientation session with Blanche, Nina walked into her office with two cups of coffee, one of which she handed to Blanche. She sat down and said: "Are you ready to hear what happened next? Sort of part two of my story. Sit down and don't be shocked by what you will hear.

Well, for a while Peter and I continued to meet, mostly at odd times, whenever his busy schedule and my work at the bar permitted. We usually enjoyed the intimacy of my little flat and yes, we became ardent lovers. Peter told me that he had no other girlfriend except me, that I made him happy, that I helped him relax and 'recharge his batteries' as he put it. He always brought me little gifts or flowers and I often cooked meals for him which he appeared to enjoy immensely."

"Can I interrupt?" asked Blanche. "What about Elena? Did she not suspect him of cheating?"

"Aha," said Nina, with a broad smile. "I was just coming to that."

"Yes, what about Elena?"

"Well, Peter told her. He told her everything. You know, this man does not beat around the bush. Shortly after our relationship began, he told Elena that he had a mistress and that he had no intention of giving her up. But, he also told her: 'You are Mrs. Lambros, my wife and the mother of our children and you will always be. I promise you that I will never disgrace you by promenading with my girlfriend in public. I will keep my relationship private and discreet as much as humanly possible. Of course people will talk. So what? Let them talk. As far as the family and our friends are concerned you are my wife and nothing will ever change that. But what I do outside our home is my business and you don't need to ask me where I spent last night, because I am telling you right now. I was with my girlfriend.'

He said to Elena 'Look, what I am asking you to accept is not easy and I am sorry. I really am. But life is short and I want to live it as I see fit. Now, if you want to tell me that you cannot accept it, that you prefer to leave me or want a divorce – that is your decision. I don't want you to leave me. Think it over. It's not so bad, you know. Marriages sometimes go through different phases and who knows, one day I may even come back to the fold.'

"Do I need to tell you what Elena's reaction was, Blanche? For a few days she cried and moped, and avoided talking to her husband. But then, when she looked in the mirror and saw that her glamour days were way behind her and when she realized that she was surrounded by loving children and family and," intoned Nina, "last but not least when she thought of the access to her husband's checking account, she knew on which side of the bread the butter was. When Peter came home a few days later she simply said 'Have it your way, Peter', and that was that. In time she swallowed her pride and learned to live playing second fiddle. She still carries on with resigned dignity. She is still Madame Lambros and what goes on in her bedroom is nobody's business.

You know, Blanche, Americans have a saying that if you must cry, it is so much easier to cry in a Cadillac."

Nina looked at Blanche, who was listening spellbound to the story. "Do you want to hear more?", she said. "Of course," replied Blanche. Please go on. Your story sounds like a novel or a movie.'

"It does," said Nina, "but wait until you hear the rest."

"Well," she continued, "as I said before, Peter and I kept seeing each other, sometimes during the day, sometimes late at night after I left the bar, sometimes even on weekends. Peter was not only perfect company but a wonderful lover. We could not wait to jump into bed. But then, one day, our routine was unexpectedly upset. Although I was always very careful, I found out that I was pregnant. As soon as the doctor confirmed it, I told Peter, fully expecting to hear reproaches and even being scolded for my carelessness. But no, Peter calmly said 'If you want to have the baby, I am with you. We will find a way to handle it. Don't worry!'

Of course, like any woman who is in love with the father, I wanted to have the baby, our baby. I must admit though, that my unexpected pregnancy brought apprehension and even fear to my mind. Here I was, an unmarried woman, the mistress of a prominent man, living sort of in the shadow of society, walking around with a fat belly for all the world to see. What I mean to say is, what was to be my future, even if Peter put some money in my bank account. Up to my getting pregnant I had received nothing from Peter except generous gifts, flowers and bottles of champagne. But now, I was to become the mother of his child. Believe me, Blanche, I was scared and confused.

But leave it to Peter Lambros. He is really something else. A week or so after I had broken the news to him, he came to my little flat, our love nest, armed not only with flowers and a bottle of wine, but also with a plan. A plan that will take your breath away, Blanche. Just as it took mine away when he calmly exposed it to me that evening.

Well, enough said for today my dear. You must be getting tired of listening to my story," said Nina.

"Tired?" replied Blanche. "Are you kidding? I am sitting here, anxious not to miss a single word of what you're telling me. Nina, it is a fascinating tale. Please continue tomorrow afternoon. You must, Nina, I want to know the end of the story."

"There is no end," interjected Nina, "God forbid! It goes on, like life itself. See you tomorrow."

When Nina came back the following day, Blanche fetched two cups of freshly brewed coffee and a tray of cookies, which she placed in front of Nina.

"OK," said Nina. "Ready to hear the rest?"

"Sure." Said Blanche with a smile. You have my undivided attention."

"So, Peter came loaded with goodies and we had a beautiful Greek dinner which I had prepared just for him. After the last sip of wine, we sat side by side on the sofa, very relaxed and very comfortable and Peter unfolded his plan. 'Listen carefully,' he said. 'I have given this a lot of thought and I also discussed it with Alex, my lawyer.

First, you will leave your job at the Flamingo. You have to anyway. Whoever heard of pregnant women serving drinks at a bar? Secondly, you will move to a larger flat in a building of your choice and furnish it to your taste. Of course I will take care of the rent and your other expenses from now on. But, all these are details. Here is the core of the plan.

In our head office we have a young Russian accountant. His name is Ivan Olinsky. He is single and a reliable person. He has agreed to marry you, a sham marriage, of course. I made him an offer he could not refuse, not if he knows what's good, I mean very good for him. Don't worry, he will not touch you, not even hold your hand. The marriage can take place any day. The sooner the better.

You will then stay in your new flat just by yourself. About six months or so after you have given birth my lawyer will draw up divorce papers and Ivan will disappear from the scene, but you, my dear, will not be a single mother, but Madame Olinsky, the baby will have a "father" and a legitimate name, and I will avoid a lot of silly questions and stares from people. I am sorry', Peter added. 'But I cannot marry you for reasons I am certain you know, but listen, I'll take care of you, of that you can be sure. Why don't you think the whole thing over and let me know tomorrow if you go along with my plan.'

I don't know what you would have done in my place, Blanche, but I really did not have to think for too long. Here I was, a poor girl making a living as a barmaid. I was pregnant and I loved Peter. I put all this on one side of the scale and on the other side I put leaving him and trying to find a man that would marry me. Come on, Blanche, did I have a choice? Of course I accepted Peter's offer, knowing full well that I would always live in the shadow as his mistress or concubine or friend, call it what you want. Not a nice thought for sure but I would always live well. It was really up to me to give my life meaning and purpose by rising above my status. And by embracing a profession or a career if I wanted. I was not at all ashamed of my position or my way of life and decided to make the best of it.

Next day, I phoned Peter to tell him that I accepted his offer and that we would work out the details together. I also told him that I loved him to the point that I was prepared to share him with his wife. When I told him that half or even a quarter of Peter Lambros was far better than none of him, he laughed out loudly and told me that he loved me too. We were both relieved and I started to tie up all loose ends as planned.

"Well," said Nina, "I think I need another coffee. Let me get it. Do you want one too?" Blanche said "Yes, please." A few minutes later, Nina was back with the two cups.

"All this, Blanche, took place about nine years ago. Nine long years which I am sure were the most exciting ones in my life. Of course there were good things and bad things that happened, but overall I enjoyed my life as it is and I still do so.

And now, let me give you a brief update. Of course, my baby is now an eight-year-old princess. She is beautiful, has long blond hair and she is the apple of my eye. Her name is Vera.

Oh, let me tell you about my pseudo-husband Ivan. He turned out to be a very nice guy. He went along with all the arrangements prepared by the lawyer and was at all times polite and helpful. Of course, I told Vera that Ivan is her father and we divorced because we could not get along. I even made Vera visit him in the hospital when he was sick, even asking the child to respect and care for him. Unfortunately Ivan became an alcoholic or perhaps he already was a boozer before I met him. Then he developed all kinds of liver problems that lead to his death. It was a very sad story. Little Vera cried her heart out. Then after the funeral, Peter told me that he would legally adopt the "orphan." He did, and believe it or not, to this day, Vera believes that Ivan was her father who passed away and that Peter is her adopted father. I never told Vera the truth. Maybe one day I will.

By the way, Vera is now in third grade of a local French-language school.

As for Peter, he never changed and I pray to God that he never does. We still love each other and see each other regularly; in fact, my flat is his second home. He even has an office with all his communication gadgets in one room.

Elena grew into her role with a certain elegance or at least that is the impression she is giving. She is not well and already had several operations, but she is still running her household with authority. She is still Madame Lambros and people respect her for her discretion. She certainly does not go around bitching about her role as number two. You know, the French, who have a word for everything call it a *'ménage à trois'*. And this is what it is. Sometimes I think that the old Turks knew a thing or two about life when they kept a harem. It's just that some men need more than one woman, of course, if they can afford it, and Peter certainly can.

You know, what makes me very happy, above anything else? The fact that after Ivan's death, Peter could "adopt" his daughter and heap love and attention on her. Today Vera thinks of Peter as the man who replaced her father and I see no reason why I should tell her otherwise. Why expose the child to an emotional trauma, when there is no need for it. Don't you agree?" Nina said to Blanche.

"Of course," Blanche replied. "I think it worked out very well for all concerned and I can only admire those involved, that is Peter, Elena and also your daughter for having turned a situation that, I am sure, would have destroyed many other families into a successful "ménage" as you called it of reasonably happy people. My compliments to you, I really mean it."

Nina left Blanche's office, obviously tired after her lengthy narrative.
Blanche went home that evening thinking about all the things Nina had told her during the last few days. She mulled over the different events and she kept thinking that Nina must indeed be a remarkable woman for a number of reasons. She managed to make one of the city's most eligible men her lifelong companion, she did not destroy the life of his wife, or at least she did not think she did, judging by the fact that Elena was still Madame Lambros which in itself was certainly an enviable position to be in. And, most importantly, she enjoyed motherhood. In addition to all of this, she had an interesting and well-paid job that kept her busy on an almost daily basis.

Blanche thought that Nina was one of the rare people she knew who had her cake and ate it too.

The more she thought about Nina, the more Blanche not only admired her, but she decided that this woman would henceforth be her role model. She would closely work with her and learn how to make the most of every situation, how to take advantage of every opportunity and come up a winner. She knew that her new job would offer her the chance not only to excel and shine, bur also to turn her accomplishments into benefits for her and her children. She was determined to disregard convention and even propriety in an effort to reap the good life for herself, for Carlo and especially for Laura, whom she now called "Lulu". If Nina could do it so could she.

However, there was a difference between the two women. Nina saw her role in life as a giver of herself while Blanche intended to take out of it as much as she could.

Blanche was so excited about her future that she spent the best part of the night approving of herself for having planned her career so well. She finally fell asleep happy and fulfilled.

A few days after Nina had confided the story of her life to Blanche, she introduced the newcomer to family members not as her assistant but as her partner. "From now on the two of us will take care of all the things I bungled up so far," she told them. "Now you can blame not one but two girls if things go wrong." This was of course a joke, because no one had ever found fault with anything Nina did. In fact, without exception they all adored her.

Nina arranged their vacations, travels and events with utmost attention to detail. But she also performed many other functions for them. She gave interested family members bridge lessons, she taught the teenagers how to dance and she single-handedly catered for family celebrations with such expertise that everyone besieged her afterwards with questions of 'How did you cook the roast' and 'how on earth did you bake that delicious cake?' Over the years, Nina had become a "Jack-of-all-trades" for the family. That is why they just adored her. And that is also why they welcomed Blanche so warmly into their midst, perhaps as Nina's alter ego.

Blanche soon settled down to the routine office work which was considerable. For starters, Nina assigned her the task of administering the Lambros private properties abroad.

There was the flat in Paris, the one in London, the penthouse in New York and the villa in the South of France. All of them required constant attention. There were rents or taxes to be paid, there was maintenance and there were repairs to be made. Then, there were the staffs needed to keep all properties in tip top condition, ready to be used at short notice. Blanche immediately established the contacts and took control of all the files.

Then, Nina asked her to familiarize herself with the list of memorable dates of all family members, such as birthdays, weddings and other anniversaries, graduations and everything else requiring action, usually well in advance of the event.

It took some time, but before long, Blanche began to know more about some members than they themselves did.

Blanche also learned to issue a monthly newsletter for the family, outlining art exhibits, theatre, opera and concert performances and other activities abroad that may be of interest to individuals or groups.

After a few months the two women were working like a perfect team, so much so that all concerned, including Peter Lambros himself, often wondered aloud how Nina could have handled it all unaided for so long.

Blanche's life now evolved around the Lambros family. Just like Nina, she had become an integral part of it. It was therefore natural that as her children reached their teens she brought them into the family to meet and become friendly with other youngsters their age.

Carlo was an intelligent, though mostly street smart kid with good looks and an abundant mane of dark brown hair. He was sociable, had an easy smile and he had no problem to fit into the somewhat uppity atmosphere of the Lambros clan. After all, his mother had often enough taught him how to comport himself in the company of "nice" people.

Lulu, once an adorable little girl, was growing into a real beauty. She had inherited her mother's fair complexion, black hair and expressive eyes as well as her roundish face with the soft, regular features. The day her mother brought her to meet the family during a summer picnic, the 'ahs' and 'ohs' would not end when Blanche made her shake hands and say hello to everyone. Several family members jokingly said: "Why did you hide this beautiful girl from us? She is gorgeous".

As for Blanche, she soon had an opportunity to expand her role as Peter Lambros' social secretary, albeit in an extra-curricular manner. While attending one of Peter's dinner parties he gave in honour of a newly appointed bank president, she met a prominent local businessman. The two then got together after dinner and that started a relationship, mostly accented by spirited sexual encounters enjoyed by both participants, but not so by the man's wife when she hit upon the amorous conspiracy almost a year after its inception. In short order, she told Blanche to stay away from her husband or face exposure which would entail losing her job. The duped wife thus regained control over her philandering husband by letting him get away with a stern warning: "If I ever catch you again having an affair I will make a scandal", a prospect the well-known executive could ill afford.

For Blanche, this affair had been an interesting episode. She knew that it could not last too long, but long enough to have fun and to receive some valuable gifts as tokens of her lover's appreciation. In fact, she had added two beautiful fur coats to her wardrobe and a bevy of expensive jewellery.

This short-lived escapade served to get Blanche's feet wet in the *demi-monde* of extra-marital affairs. Over the years she was to have several of these. All of self-limiting duration. They always involved married men, they were all carried on in utter secrecy until found out and, most importantly, they never included Lambros family members. Through her frequent presence at Peter's official functions she had many opportunities to meet not only interesting but also wealthy men who could not resist the graceful and innocently provocative gyrations of Blanche's curves, not to mention her impeccable legs she was rightfully proud of.

To her credit it must be said that Blanche never allowed these relationships to turn ugly through dramatic exposures or scandals. She knew exactly when to call it quits and ready herself for another opportunity. She never told her children about her affairs, although it stands to reason that as they grew older they put two and two together when their mother came home late at night sporting a benign smile and a glittering necklace they had not seen before.

Nina, because of her physical and professional closeness to Blanche, knew of these trysts but she chose never to question or even discuss them with her colleague. Perhaps she thought that it was all a part or consequence of their profession, sort of all in a day's work.

* * * * *

Blanche who had entered her job as an eager amateur was now an accomplished expert in whatever she did at work. Together with Nina, the two had become an indispensable component of Peter Lambros' still growing establishment.

And yet, despite their consuming daily work, both women were still very much devoted to the upbringing of their children, of course, each in their own particular way.

Nina's daughter Vera was almost ready to graduate from school where she had been a rather mediocre student. She had inherited some of her mother's beauty and grace, but certainly not her high intelligence and wit. In keeping with her fearfulness not to embarrass Peter Lambros publicly, Nina had deliberately prevented her daughter from having too many friends, lest one or the other should ask questions about her origin. She often took Vera to family functions, where she was known as the girl Peter had adopted after her father's death.

* * * * *

Carlo had been an average student, usually bringing home passing rather than above average marks. When he graduated from ninth grade of his gymnasium, his mother thought that he had had enough knowledge crammed into his head. She wanted him to get an early grip on life by starting to earn money while at the same time learning a trade. It so happened that at the time of Carlo's graduation, Blanche was having an affair with a very wealthy local businessman. Talking about her children, she said to him one day: "Why don't you take my boy into your company and let him learn the business from the bottom up? You will find him intelligent and eager to get ahead. The man agreed and no sooner had Carlo left high school that he started working as a junior clerk in the import department of one of the city's largest companies. Soon Carlo became an assistant to the manager in charge of office equipment. Young and keen to learn, he took a liking to his job. Under the protective aegis of his mother's boyfriend, he embarked on a specialized professional career.

*****

As for Lulu, the cute little girl with the big dreamy eyes and the silky black hair her mother was so proud of, she became a very popular teenager and then grew into adulthood with a joie de vivre and light-heartedness unmatched by her mother's rather cool and calculating character. At school Lulu was every boy's dream girl and when she left at the age of sixteen quite a few teachers kept ogling her slender figure and beautiful features with wishful thoughts.

Not given to serious pensiveness and erudition, Lulu, in step with other pretty girls her age was out to have a good time while she could. She was often asked out by admirers and had a circle of friends composed of girls her age and young men a few years older, most of whom were studying to become professionals. One of them, Robert, in his mid-twenties and about to wind up his training at the local technical school, became Lulu's favourite beaux. He was tall, muscular and exuded an air of self-assurance which deeply impressed her. He was handsome to the point that his curly blond hair made him look like one of those Greek Gods in antiquity. Together the two were an incredibly beautiful couple.

Other than the occasional chit chat about her boyfriend, Lulu never told her mother that she had fallen in love with the handsome mechanic. But the day Blanche found out about it she had a long heart-to-heart talk with her daughter, urging her not to be foolish in firming up a relationship with what she called 'a repairman' when she could have the chance of meeting one of several eligible young men from the Lambros family. At first Lulu objected to the idea of being told whom to fall in love with, but after several discussions with her mother and, after Blanche arranged for a Gala reception to celebrate Lulu's twenty first birthday at the Lambros family circle, Lulu began to agree with her mother that it may be a better idea to associate with young men of wealthy appendage than with a fledgling technician.

Lulu's twenty-first turned out to be a memorable event for a number of reasons. First because she was gorgeous to look at and soon became the darling of the party. Secondly Peter and his wife spent the whole evening with the family and delighted Lulu to the point of making her cry when he handed her a little red-coloured key holder which opened the door to a brand new Buick convertible. It was this gift that really made Lulu realize that one is far better off associating with princes than with paupers.

After that party, Lulu became an integral part of the family. Prodded and constantly encouraged by her mother, she was often the life of the party at many get-togethers, adding a breath of fresh air to any event she attended.

It did not take long, however, for the inevitable to happen. One of Peter's sons-in-law, a forty-two year old father of three one day proposed Lulu to become his mistress. John was very blunt and went straight to the point when he met the young girl one afternoon at a coffee shop on the outskirts of the city.

"Look," he said to her, "my proposal should make a lot of sense to you. I think you are an absolutely delightful young lady and I want to ask you if you want to spend the occasional evening with me. I want to make it clear that neither you nor I will be exposed to the public in this, call it "affair, or liaison". It is strictly between you and me. I have a flat in one of the downtown office buildings and that is where we will meet. I will conform as much as possible to your availability and our get-togethers will not be long, out drawn affairs. I am sorry if I sound so blunt and unromantic, but, look, this is a proposal.

If your answer is 'no', please say so now or next time we meet and this conversation will never have taken place. If your answer is 'yes', there will be no embarrassing fur coats or jewellery changing hands, just gifts into your bank account to show my appreciation."

John was the first to leave the coffee shop. He took Lulu's hand and said: "Please say 'yes'. I can't wait to hear the word."

Lulu was stunned. She was certainly not prepared for that conversation. To be sure, her immediate reaction to his offer was indignation and revolt. She wanted to get up and leave the place. But John was so sincere and matter-of-fact that she suddenly felt transposed into another world. Perhaps into the real world of personal relationships, not as your grandmother or school teacher would see them but as they were in the real world which was beginning to open up in front of her.

That day she came home and sat up on her bed. She closed the door to her room and let thoughts freely roam in her head. She started weighing the pros and cons. What was she to lose? This was not a permanent or even long lasting thing. She could call it off any time if she did not like it. Mind you, John was not bad looking. In fact he was quite handsome and she liked his 'no beating-around-the-bush' approach.

If she accepted the offer she would neither tell her mother nor her brother. It would be a secret between her and John, just as he said it would be. And she would make money, a commodity you can always use.

She was not worried about her reputation because nobody except her prospective lover would know about this. So, she came to the conclusion: "Why not?"

But as she was getting out of her bed, brooding about the whole matter, she came to realize something else. The offer she had just received really did not shock her. After all, here was a man who asked her to become his mistress and he offered to pay for her favours. Not exactly a very honourable thing or something to be proud of. And yet, she was not offended beyond words or terribly shocked. She asked herself why? She thought of several possible reasons.

She knew full well that her mother was having affairs with married men. Not all the time, mind you but occasionally. She also knew that Nina had centered her entire life on living at the periphery of what you may call conformity or propriety. Could it be that growing up in this *demi-monde* had made John's proposal acceptable, even normal to her?

It was not Lulu who took the first step. It was John, who a few days later, phoned her to say hello. She was actually prepared for the call. After some unrelated banter, she told him: "John, I think we can work out something along the lines you mentioned the other day." His immediate response was: "Oh, great, that's wonderful news. Thank you my dear. I'll be in touch."

Thus started a relationship which was to last for a number of years. True to his word, John who managed one of his father-in-law's companies, kept Lulu's bank account well stocked, in fact, very well. They often met in his private flat in a downtown building which housed mostly offices and a bank but also some residences on the upper floors. It was a convenient hide-away because both he and she could separately enter and leave the premises without attracting any attention whatsoever.

Although the two were never seen in public together, rumours surfaced from time to time that there was something afoot between them, but lacking any tangible evidence, their relationship remained just a subject of gossip and conjecture in some after-dinner chatter, starting with: "They say that these two are having an affair. I wouldn't be surprised if it's true."

Lulu never discussed her private life with her mother or her brother. Perhaps she did not need to. Blanche had long ago drawn her conclusions but she pretended not to know anything.

Some five years into this discreet liaison, Lulu met a very good looking athlete, in fact the captain of the national swimming team, at a charity function. Alex had a wall full of trophies and cups in his home since he had lead his group to many victories, except, of course, the Olympics, although he himself had managed to bring home one silver medal from the last games. This feat alone had elevated him to the rank of a national hero. It was during the course of a function that his eyes fell on the beautiful Lulu and he fell for her, like the proverbial ton of bricks. He was an unsophisticated, down-to-earth individual from a rather modest background and held a job as a junior clerk in one of the city's banks. However, he was a personality and the uncontested idol of a generation.

The attraction between the two was spontaneous. They started dating and only a month or two after their first encounter, Alex asked Lulu to marry him. When she agreed, Alex was the happiest man in the world. He kept telling everyone that he was going to marry the most beautiful and most sophisticated girl on God's earth. She on the other hand found Alex to be a kind and considerate man, and besides, she was going to marry a national sports idol.

The announcement of their engagement made front line news not only in sports magazines, but also in the daily press.

Six months later Lulu and Alex were married in a spectacular ceremony and follow-up reception attended by hundreds of well-wishers. Everyone in town wanted to see the beautiful couple embark on a life of bliss and happiness. After a honeymoon in one of the country's chic Mediterranean resorts offered to them by the hotel management, they returned to Istanbul and moved into a small but comfortable house in one of the city's newly developing suburbs overlooking the Bosporus.

Lulu had never told Alex anything about her relationship with John. All he knew was that she was helping her mother run Peter Lambros' social affairs. This, she told Alex often required her presence at odd hours in different locations. She also told him that until they had children, she would keep her job because the pay was good and there was nothing unusual for married women to earn a living in support of the family kitty. Alex welcomed the additional source of income since his own earnings as a bank clerk were not spectacular, to say the least.

With John, however, Lulu was very frank. She told him that as the years went by she realized that she wanted to have a family, that she had met an honest and decent man whom she loved and with whom she decided to have children. She added, however, that since her extra-marital affair was a relationship of convenience, she did not want to terminate it, at least not for the time being, if this was acceptable to him.

John was pleasantly surprised to hear Lulu's reasoning. He had actually expected her to call it quits after her marriage. "Sure," he said. "I am all for continuing our get-togethers. Why not? If you feel comfortable juggling two balls in the air, welcome to the club. I have been doing it for years!"

And so, Lulu started to live a double life. She kept telling herself that after all, she was in complete control of her relationship with John and could end it anytime she chose to. Furthermore she reasoned, her bank account had by now grown into considerable proportions. John had indeed been a very generous bed partner. So why end a good thing?

Her love for Alex though, was sincere. She even thought of telling him the truth one day, after she would leave John. In her mind her course of life was neither sinful nor even dramatic. It was a reflection of the real world she lived in, rather than the make-believe world of fairy tales.

Devoid of any real guilt feelings, Lulu enjoyed her life including the thrill of her duplicity. She looked radiant, especially, when at the arm of Alex, the two went to sport events or social functions, mingling with the city's beautiful people.

But, as the saying goes, nothing is forever. Some two years into their marriage Lulu became pregnant, which for her, heralded not only the advent of motherhood but also the end of her frivolous life and the inevitable refuge into the traditional haven of conjugal life. Alex was elated, not only because he was to become a father, but also because he welcomed the thought of Lulu leaving her job of social assistant in favour of becoming the mainstay of his home. Besides, during the last year he had been promoted and was now department supervisor with a matching salary that, he thought would no more necessitate his wife's contributions to the household budget.

Ending her affair with John was easy enough, especially since there had never been more than a minimal emotional involvement between the two, but telling Alex about it as she had intended to do, was another matter. She thought long and hard and came to the conclusion that it would be better for all concerned not to reveal the truth to her husband. Why hurt his feelings now that the affair has ended? And what if he raised doubts about the baby's true father? "What you don't know, don't hurt you!" she said to herself and let it stay that way.

But as fate would have it, it did not stay that way. In a moment of carelessness, Lulu had left behind on the kitchen table a bank statement and when Alex casually looked at it, he saw not only a sizeable balance but also a recent considerable deposit. It was John's very generous parting gift of appreciation.

Alex wondered where that money came from. Lulu had never mentioned anything to him except that she was drawing a relatively good salary but nothing remotely approaching the amount he had just seen. When she came home from work Alex asked her whether she had recently won the jackpot in the national lottery. At first she did not know what that meant, but then, when she saw him holding the statement, she was struck by the proverbial lightning bolt. She thought she would die right there. Lost for words, she at first thought of making something up, but she quickly realized that she had been caught red-handed and there was no way out but telling him the truth.

She did exactly that, though in her own way. She used charm and tears and every possible manoeuvre to explain this as an old and now dead affair, she swore never ever to look at other men, but halfway through her *mea culpa*, Alex turned away and left the house without a word. He spent the next few days at his mother's home. It took several visits by Lulu and a great deal of crying on Alex's mother's shoulder to finally start the healing process. Alex finally forgave Lulu and came home. A few months later the baby was born and for all intents and purposes the marriage was saved from disintegration. But it was a patched-up union to be sure. Although the couple had a second child three years later and Lulu never resumed extramarital activities, the marriage had been dented. Somehow it lacked a component of passion and deep attachment which Alex thought he had found in matrimony. The two lived the uneventful life of so many other couples who take each other for granted and go through a lifetime of ho-hum normalcy.

* * * * *

Carlo took to his job at the Office Supply Company with gusto. He learned fast and soon received regular promotions. Not only was Blanche delighted to see her boy bring home letters of praise from his supervisor, but the company owner gave him a special bonus at year-end for his extraordinary contribution to the balance sheet.

Carlo was also successful in another area. He had met and had fallen in love with a girl who reciprocated his feelings. The two were happy beyond words and vowed to unite in marriage as soon as possible, which meant as soon as Carlo had saved enough money to rent and furnish a home. They spent many an evening dreaming of the family they intended to raise and about their life together.

Naomi was a truly remarkable girl. Medium-sized, well-built and attractive without being beautiful, she had an aura of warmth about her the outward sign of which was an almost constant smile. She was very smart, had managed to earn a Batchelor's degree in economics and was well-read to the point of being able to discuss most current subjects with eloquent authority.

Carlo did not tell his mother about the intensity of his relationship with Naomi. All that Blanche knew was that Carlo had a girlfriend and he was seeing a lot of her.

There was a good reason why Carlo kept his marriage plans secret. Naomi came from a modest, even poor family. Her father was a sales clerk in a local clothing store and eked out a living which was supported by Naomi's salary as an economist in a large insurance company. Fully aware of his mother's snobbish aspirations he rightly surmised that she would vehemently object to his marrying below what she considered his class. Hence Carlo waited until the wedding date was set to break the news to his mother. He hoped that by then it would be too late for her to utter anything but a grudging acceptance of the fait accompli.

*****

Nina and Blanche had become very close friends over the years. They worked very well in unison, sharing assignments, planning their activities together and taking care of Peter Lambros' numerous social commitments and involvements both at home and abroad. The two women, always impeccably attired and groomed, ran everything with fine tuned flair and competence.

In their private lives, Nina continued to be the shadow companion or the "Number Two" of Peter Lambros. Over the years, the very fact that Peter had a mistress had ceased to be a whispered rumour and had become an accepted fact. For all intents and purposes this was a *ménage à trois*, since Elena continued to play the role of Madame Lambros with dignity and almost imperceptible resignation.

As for Blanche, she had over the years opted for a lifestyle vaguely akin to that of Nina, albeit on a much more modest scale. She continued to have occasional flings with men from her boss' entourage. Taking advantage of her fluency in several languages, she was often asked by Peter to accompany high placed business associates to meetings as "girl Friday" or interpreter cum social assistant.

Peter was glad to help his powerful friends by occasionally loaning Blanche for short periods. If Blanches' role included also some more intimate or discreet assistance this was nobody's business. Over the years Blanche had developed her job into a pleasant, interesting and often lucrative occupation, which made her and her colleague Nina sort of birds of the same feather.

* * * * *

One evening, as the two were relaxing at the legendary Karagoz Bar of the Istanbul Hilton after a strenuous day at one of Peter's frequent company meetings, their conversation turned to their children. Nina's daughter Vera and Blanche's Carlo, in particular.

Vera was now in her late teens and had grown into an attractive blonde. Perhaps because both her parents had preferred to refrain from too much exposure to the bubbly social life of Istanbul society, lest some people should whisper to each other: "Do you know who this blonde girl is?" the young girl led a somewhat sheltered life. Like other teenagers she had, of course, her circle of friends, but her mother saw to it that Vera was not too prominent or popular. As a result of this protected existence, Very was a bit shy by nature and perhaps more attached to her mother than other girls brought up more independently or more freely.

Comfortably ensconced in the Bar's red leather seat, Nina said: "Blanche, I have been meaning to talk to you about this for some time. You told me that Carlo has a good job in an office supply company and that he is a bright and good looking young man. I am sure I don't need to tell you anything about my Vera. I think you know her as well as I do. How about getting the two together. I mean how about making a match? What do you think? I don't need to tell you that Peter will not be miserly when leading Vera down the aisle. She would certainly make a very good and loving wife and make Carlo happy. And, although Peter cannot appear as Vera's real father, you can rest assured that he will treat Carlo like a son-in-law."

The more Nina went on talking, the more Blanche became captivated by the idea. When Nina finally drained her dry martini and asked for the cheque, she had left Blanche not only with food but with a royal meal for thought.

She pondered about it that night and the next couple of days. And she came to the conclusion that it would be an excellent match. A logical follow-through to her many years of dedicated work. A one-in-a-lifetime opportunity for Carlo to marry not only a lovely girl, but into one of the city's wealthiest families. Going over it again and again in her mind she convinced herself that this was the best thing ever to come Carlo's way.

She could not wait to talk to her son. A few days later, after dinner, she casually broached the subject and said: "Carlo, I know you have lots of friends and you are having a good time, as indeed you should. But don't you think time has come for you to start a family? I mean to get married? I have been thinking, Carlo, that Vera would be an excellent choice for you. I don't need to tell you about her, you have met her often enough. She is certainly very pretty and bright and will make, I am sure, a perfect wife. And, my dear Carlo, she is a Lambros. Need I say more? Peter will not hesitate to give her away in a manner befitting his style and position. I don't think you would have to worry about your future.

Think about it, Carlo. It really makes a lot of sense. Why don't you ask her out, start dating her, and, who knows, you may fall in love so badly that you will end up proposing to her. How about it, Carlo?"

There was a long silence after Blanche had finished her well-rehearsed plea. In fact, it seemed the silence would never end. Finally, Carlo looked at his mother and said: "Thank you, Mom. I appreciate your concern very much and I know that Vera is a nice girl but I have other plans."

"What do you mean by 'other plans'?" asked Blanche.

"Well, I am already tied up and I plan to marry a girl you don't know. Her name is Naomi, I love her and we have decided to get married." Carlo saw his mother face turn into a mask of open-mouthed disbelief. So, to avoid what he expected to be an unpleasant harangue, he continued: "Yes, Mother, I know I should have told you, but I thought you would not approve of my choice. That is why I kept it to myself until Naomi and I were ready to make wedding plans and then, I wanted to introduce her to you.
Blanche appeared very disturbed by her son's surprise announcement. "And why do you think I might not approve of her?" she said.

"Because she comes from a poor family. Her father is a sales clerk in a downtown store and they live modestly in a small apartment. But Naomi is a gem. She is bright and beautiful. She has a wonderful disposition and we are very much in love with each other. So much so that we decided to get married and, believe me, Mom, I was impatiently waiting to break the news to you. I can even tell you that on weekends we're looking for locations where to live. I have a good job and she is working. Together, we have everything to start out in life. That's the truth, Mother, and now you understand why I am not interested in Vera."

Blanche realized that her son was really determined to pursue his plans and that turning the conversation into an argument or worse, a shouting match, would lead nowhere. She calmed down and edged closer to Carlo on the sofa before continuing to make her case. She had counted with the possibility that Carlo would not be interested in Vera because he may not have liked her or perhaps because he was not ready to get married, but she was certainly not expecting to hear that he had decided to marry another girl, and a store clerk's daughter, no less.

Blanche looked Carlo straight into his eyes and said: "I am sure that your Naomi is a nice girl. You would not have been interested in her if she wasn't. But, Carlo, my dear Carlo, how can you pass the opportunity to marry Peter Lambros' daughter? How can you compare a life of financial security and ease with a life with a poor man's daughter? It will take you years to buy a home or travel in style and here, you have it already presented to you on a silver platter.

Blanche went on and on painting scenarios of opulence versus modest living, applying them to his future life with Naomi. From time to time, Carlo interrupted her with words such as: "Mother, life is not only money" and "we love each other" and "I'm sorry, I am sure Vera is a very nice person, but I am in love with another girl. I am not the first who starts from the bottom and works his way up, especially if he has a loving and helping wife at this side." But, whatever he said was countered by his mother's strong arguments. "You are throwing away an opportunity that will never ever come back and I am sure you will regret it. With these words she left the room, leaving Carlo to think about the agitated conversation he had tried to avoid for months.

During the next few days and weeks, Blanche wisely did not revert to the subject, assuming that she had said enough to make Carlo come round to her way of thinking to make him reconsider his plans for the future. She was somehow convinced that sooner or later Carlo would grab a good thing when he saw it.

Life went on, as usual, but she knew, just by observing her son that in his mind and in his heart he was struggling, weighing one option against the other. She knew it because after that long conversation, Carlo never reverted to the subject. Had he decided against Vera, she thought he would have already told her so. He is silent because he has to convince himself and he has to prepare for the confrontation with his girl when he will tell her that he changed his mind. It's not easy, she admitted to herself. So, let me help him by leaving him alone to sort out things in his mind.

Like most mothers, Blanche was, of course, right in her assumptions. Carlo was indeed caught in a dilemma involving himself and two other people. Any decision he now took would have a far-reaching, nay, conclusive impact on the lives of three people. He had never faced a similar situation before and he was fully aware of the implication of his decisions.

The two most crucial thoughts on his mind were firstly the beckoning attraction of entering a life of financial security and all that it implied and secondly the heart-wrenching problem of telling Naomi that it was all over. He kept asking himself if his love for Naomi was really so strong as to make him turn his back on all that becoming Peter Lambros' son-in-law meant, not only from a financial, but also from a social and family standpoint.

For three weeks he pondered and mulled over the same subject. He kept seeing Naomi, albeit with a little less passion than before.

But then he asked himself: "What if Vera is not the right girl for me?" He had met her often at family functions and had found her attractive, but their conversations were usually confined to polite banter and generalities. He really did not know her. So, he decided that if he was to change horses in the middle of the stream, he had better take the horse out for a ride. He phoned Vera and asked if he could have dinner with her. He said that he had heard about her recent birthday and wouldn't it be nice if they drank a glass of wine together.

Vera thought it was a great idea and they went out for dinner in a small restaurant, choosing a corner table. Carlo told her that he had meant to ask her out for some time and that celebrating her birthday was a pleasant opportunity to keep closer ties with members of the family. Vera smiled and said that any reason was good enough to spend a nice evening in good company. It was a long drawnout meal mostly marked by animated talk about each other. Carlo asked many questions and answered as many. He found Vera to be a fairly intelligent, well educated but most of all a very pleasant person with an easy and loud laugh. In all, Carlo was impressed enough to ask Vera out for a second "look-see". This time they went to a cabaret and danced well into the night. When Carlo took her home, he kissed Vera goodnight and liked her closeness and the feel of her skin. He was impressed and decided to refrain from further meetings in order to give himself more time for thought.

That night he did a great deal of thinking in bed. He compared Naomi to Vera. There was no doubt in his mind that Naomi had more depth of personality and of character. She was more mature and, despite her youth more of a woman. She was also more educated and because she had a responsible job she was much more self-assured. In short, he concluded, Naomi was a young woman, whereas Vera was a young girl and this despite their similar age. Perhaps, he reasoned, it was because Vera had been sheltered by her mother, preventing her from being part of mainstream society. This, he reasoned had made her appear somewhat shy and naive. But, Carlo, said to himself, if Naomi is a flower in full bloom, Vera maybe a bud, that given time and encouragement will also blossom into maturity. She is a smart girl, after all.

When they went out for a third time, Carlo had definitely convinced himself that he could fall in love with Vera. That was the verdict of his heart and his feelings. But what his reasoning kept reminding him of were the Lambros millions looming in the background, and the good life and the security awaiting him. He told himself that it is so much easier and much more pleasant to start at the top rather than having to work one's way up during years of hard work, provided of course that one reached the top, which is not always certain.

However, now he faced the dreadful problem of terminating his relationship with Naomi.

Having to confront her appeared to him as the greatest challenge of his entire life. How do you tell a girl that loves you to the point of wanting to share the rest of her life with you and whose love you reciprocated, a girl with whom you spent several years of intimacy and sharing, of practically living together that it is all over and what do you give her as the reason for dumping her?

Carlo thought of all sorts of explanations and arguments but he realized that there was nothing he could invoke, no pretext he could give that would make any sense, especially to as smart a girl as Naomi. It would not take her long to find out that he really left her for Vera.

Carlo felt trapped like a caged animal. He briefly considered telling Naomi the naked truth and suffer the inevitable cataclysmic reaction, but he abandoned that idea simply because he could not muster the necessary courage.

A thought entered his mind: "How about asking Mother to discuss my dilemma with Peter Lambros. After all, his own daughter is at the center of the event, and besides, Carlo thought, people on the periphery of a problem, often come up with solution that those in the midst of it fail to see.

For the first time since the evening his mother had brought up the subject of Vera, Carlo now reverted to it. He told his mother that he had decided to leave Naomi in favour of Vera. He also told her of his problem and asked if she could discuss it with Vera's father. "Perhaps he has an idea how to get me out of the predicament," he added.

Blanche feigned surprise and delight, hearing Carlo's change of heart. She jumped up form her seat and hugged her son. It was, however, a show, because Nina had already given her the news about the three "discreet" meetings between the two children. She agreed with Carlo's suggestion and promised to go and see her boss the following day together with Nina. "I am sure he will come up with some suggestions that can help you. He is a brilliant man, you know," she added.

She was right. Peter did come up not only with an idea, but with a full battle plan.

He was, of course, delighted about Carlo's decision and told the two ladies that in view of the problems arising from his having to break off existing ties, he offered Carlo what he considered to be a different approach to the whole question.

"I think Carlo should move to New York," said Peter, "I will arrange for him to be given a good position in our American Shipping company. I will, of course, also arrange for financial resources Carlo could access upon his arrival. He would then find a flat, furnish it and prepare for Vera's arrival. Some six or eight months later she would join him not only in the apartment, but also on the altar. And we will all fly to New York to give the couple a roaring send off into happiness. How about it?" Peter added, obviously enjoying himself while talking to the ladies.

"This way," continued Peter, Carlo can tell his girlfriend that he is leaving the country because he decided to start a new life in America and not because of another girl. And, by the time the children get married, Carlo's girlfriend will have gotten over the episode. She may even have found another man. And, last but not least, Vera will have had time to prepare for her marriage."

"Blanche", Peter added, "If your son agrees with all this, I think he should leave at the earliest possible time and I will immediately ask my New York manager to prepare everything. He is a very good man and a friend of mine. You can reassure Carlo. Please let me know one way or the other." With that, the ladies left his office.

* * * * *

Carlo listened to his mother without interrupting her. He was once again reminded of the awesome power of the Lambros establishment that had just shaped the lives of two of its members with such attention to detail. Carlo was sure that everything would be ready on his arrival in New York. He smiled with excitement over the opening of new horizons and with relief over having been offered a better solution to extricating himself from his doomed relationship.

Carlo had rehearsed his oration before confronting Naomi. He had also wisely gulped down a few shots of Vodka, his favourite companion for stormy days. He knew, of course, that there would not be a: "Oh-I-see-well-goodbye-then" reaction. In fact he was fully prepared to face violence and invective. He told himself that everything in life comes at a price. So, pay it now and be done with it.

For a few short moments he felt guilty when he met Naomi in his small flat and she came towards him with outstretched arms. But Carlo soon brushed his feelings aside and went straight to the core.

He told Naomi that he had decided to leave Turkey and start a new life in the USA, because he had found an exceptionally good job there. He said that since he faced so many unknowns and risks he did not want to assume the responsibility of dragging her into his adventure and that therefore he wanted to end their relationship. He added the usual regrets and "I am sure you will understand," concluding with good wishes for her future. And then he braced himself for the onslaught and that it certainly was.

It started with disbelief in what he said to anger over the fact that he had made up his mind without involving her and making her accept a fait accompli. It then turned into insults over breaking up a relationship that was already at the steps of the altar and of making a fool of her before her parents and her friends. He had never seen her shouting and crying like that.

But then, after the sobbing ebbed and her dignity and reasoning returned, she literally threw Carlo out of her life. "Get out you bastard," she said calmly, "and stay out. I never want to see you again as long as I live." She grabbed her coat and was out before Carlo could say another word.

That was the end of the Carlo-Naomi love affair.

It was a bitter end, for sure. Naomi suffered a depression in the wake of that tumultuous evening and it took her months to recover. Perhaps she never really recovered because that episode left her with the reminder that you cannot and should not trust anyone who professes feelings for you, passionate and honest as they may be at the time they were expressed. People change their minds to suit their own interests, no matter how much they hurt others.

Carlo had actually destroyed a dream, a concept she had built based on her own beliefs and her own character. She vowed never to fall into that trap again as long as she lived.

* * * * *

Carlo arrived at New York's International Airport on a typically hot and muggy day in late August. He was met by a young employee from Intramar, Peter's shipping company. After a few days in a hotel he moved into a flat on uptown Madison Avenue, where he was handed an envelope containing the keys as well as a bank book with a sizeable balance in his checking account. He obviously started out at Intramar not as Carlo Levy, but as the boss' son-in-law.

With the help of a decorator, he soon furnished the flat with contemporary furniture in preparation for Vera's arrival.

Carlo adapted easily to the American way of life. He liked his job and his new home. The view from the living room, especially at night, was spectacular. He had heard that Paris was called the city of lights, but he thought that nothing in the world could compare to the awesome view of Manhattan's starlit skyline as it beckoned to him when he stepped out onto his penthouse balcony.

Carlo and Vera frequently phoned each other, discussing not only their daily lives but all the arrangements in preparation of their forthcoming wedding.

Carlo was so occupied with the many aspects of his new life that he hardly thought back to his years with Naomi and to the bitter ending of their relationship. Only when looking at some old photographs he had brought with him was he reminded of the girl that had once meant so much to him. But as his daily life evolved, he brushed aside all memories and was determined to build a successful and happy marriage. After all, the material prerequisites had already been provided by the tireless Peter Lambros.

Some eight months later, on a warm day in early April a fleet of black limos waited at New York's airport for the arrival of the Lambros group. There was Peter, Nina, Blanche and Lulu with her family and of course the star of the show, Vera. They all drove to the family's residence, not far form where Carlo lived.

Three days later they all gathered in a private room at the Waldorf Towers to celebrate the wedding. Needless to say, champagne flowed and caviar abounded while a small combo provided entertainment for the participants and two dozen guests. Vera wore a beautiful azure blue gown which she had brought with her. Everyone had a good time. The next day Peter returned home with Nina. Blanche spent two more weeks in New York, mostly shopping on Fifth Avenue.

*****

Carlo and Vera entered married life with a measure of trepidation. After all they had really not known each other for too long before becoming husband and wife. They soon found each other to be compatible and accommodating partners and they settled into a life of mutual respect and affection. Yet, a far cry from the passionate and all-embracing closeness Carlo had enjoyed with Naomi.

It is said that true and all-out love can only develop between people who are drawn to each other by desire and passion often referred to as "the right chemistry" or "love at first sight."

But when unions are arranged and manipulated by outsiders, as well-meaning as they may be, something natural is taken out from this bond, leaving stereotyped conformity and normalcy in its place. Perhaps Vera never possessed the emotional and intellectual depth that is needed to elevate marriage into the lofty heights of "one body and soul."

Another factor that shaped their marriage was Carlo's reluctance to have children. He had grown up with his mother's assumption that his father's venereal disease had never been cured, a totally wrong belief, as all the doctors who treated him repeatedly asserted. Although Blanche had never told her children not to procreate, Carlo was scared of becoming the father of a contaminated child.

Suffice it to say that Carlo and Vera spent an unexciting but elegant life among their upscale friends and neighbours. Nothing more, nothing less.

Of course Carlo ended up in a well-renumerated managerial position in his father-in-law's shipping company which often required him to take not only short out-of-town business trips but also offered him the opportunity to dabble in fleeting romantic encounters, all of course without ever arousing Vera's suspicion. For Carlo these perks were perceived as normal diversions from what had become a rather routine marriage.

* * * * *

Blanche continued to work with Nina as Peter's social secretary for many years. Despite the passage of time and their progression into middle age, both women kept dispensing with their duties at a steady pace that would put many a younger person to shame. Together or singly they continued to travel with Peter on business or with the family whenever called upon, all to the utmost satisfaction of all concerned including themselves.

Until, one day, during a routine medical check-up, Blanche was given the devastating news that she had pancreatic cancer. She underwent treatment but to no avail. A few short months following the diagnosis she passed away peacefully, with her children as well as Vera and Nina at her bedside.

After a week of mourning and responding to innumerable expressions of grief and condolence, Carlo and Vera returned to their home in New York, while Lulu settled back into her everyday family life in Turkey.

* * * * *

A life had ended.

It had been an agitated and, at times even tumultuous journey. Far from the conventional sailing through charted waters for which her doting parents had so lovingly prepared her, it had turned out to be a stormy passage indeed. And yet, it had also brought Blanche happiness and fulfillment beyond her wildest dreams.

Blanche never strayed form her belief that one must at all times display an appearance to the world, a *bella figura*. What created or what was behind that façade was not important. In fact, it could often skirt the fringes of ethics and convention, even morality. So convincing was her philosophy of life that her children not only followed her advice but also emulated her intuitively. They never thought twice when it came to disregarding a given promise or a vow. Not even when it involved those who loved them or relied on them.

From her early childhood on, Blanche had learned to be calculating and manipulative and to arrange everything and everyone around her to ultimately serve her interests and ambitions. And yet, although she often hurt or bruised other people's feelings, she invariable emerged from all her conflicts and encounters with aplomb. She was even admired and feted by her entourage including associates and friends for whom she always remained the *grande dame*.

She even managed to put the devastating experience of her ill-fated marriage behind her with nary a thought other than 'what's passed is past, life must go on'.

Her children mourned her, not only as a mother, but also as an inspiration and ever-present mentor who helped them live lives of plenty and elegance just as she herself did. They never realized or admitted to themselves that there is more to life than all that money can buy and more to substance than there is to appearance, more to morals than to panache.

* * * * *

Perhaps the most meaningful tribute to Blanche's life came from her son who, reflecting the spirit he had inherited from his mother insisted that her black marble tombstone be inscribed with her name, followed by the words:

"SIC TRANSIT GLORIA MUNDI."

Thus passes the glory of the world.

A CANCELLED MEETING

One of the perks in Tom Bentley's job was to attend the meetings of the company's Action Committee in Bristol. Started several years ago by the former chairman of Miles Electronics plc, these get-togethers usually lasted one full day and were meant to coordinate all marketing activities of the firm. They also served as boosters of morale and builders of esprit de corps. Managers of all the nine company stores across the UK got together six times a year to discuss and decide the course of Miles Electronics, an increasingly successful importer and retailer of electronic appliances. These periodic meetings started in the evening in one of nearby Bath's most elegant hotels. Everybody had as many drinks as he could safely cope with in the presence of the chairman, followed by dinner with the board members, after-dinner drinks and entertainment, usually a cabaret show. The atmosphere was relaxed and spiced with witty remarks and pleasant banter. The next morning, all attendees convened in Bristol, participated in the general discussions and presented their reports and recommendations. In the evening, they all returned to their homes, pleased to have accomplished a great deal and eager to turn their decisions into action, hence the name 'Action Committee'.

Tom Bentley was the Manager of Miles Electronics' London branch, the largest in the chain. He was in his early forties and married to Louise, also known as 'Lou', a former fashion model now in her late-thirties. To say that Lou was a beautiful woman would definitely be an understatement, for she was radiant. Tall, with long blond hair, blue eyes and a figure to die for, she attracted attention and stood out in any crowd. The two had a reasonably successful but childless marriage. Both were too busy to settle down and raise a family. He with the increasingly towering responsibility of managing a company branch and she with her absorbing work as fashion editor for one of Britain's leading ladies' journals.

Looking eagerly forward to the current Action Committee meeting, Tom had left the office early in order to catch the 4:22 express to Bristol out of Paddington Station. He was really looking forward to the pleasure of a couple of days 'with the boys'.

Boarding the crowded train, he found a seat and started to read the paper. One hour and 15 minutes later, he arrived in Bristol. He walked quickly to the taxi stand to get to the hotel. Standing in front of the reception desk a few minutes later, he was surprised to be handed a phoned-in message, awaiting his arrival.

It read: "Please call your office".

It was six o'clock by now. He immediately called and spoke with his secretary, who had been waiting for his call. She told him that earlier that afternoon, the Company Chairman had been involved in a car accident. Nothing serious, just a few bruises, but enough to keep him out of circulation for the next two or three days. Consequently, the Bristol meeting had been postponed for two weeks. Tom's secretary had already informed everybody else.

Her parting words were "See you in the morning, Sir".

Annoyed by the needless trip and the missed opportunity to spend a few pleasant hours away from his desk, he enquired about the next train back to London. There was a fast one, which would get him into Paddington by 7:45 PM.

Back in London, Tom decided to salvage what was left of the evening by taking Lou out to a nice dinner in an elegant restaurant, a treat he had promised her a long time ago, but kept putting off because of late business hours. He also decided not to phone her, in order to make it a pleasant surprise. Although it was almost eight he knew that Lou had an aversion to early dinners and she usually came home late from work anyway. He decided to make it a really special event by buying her some long overdue flowers. He would surprise her with a "Ta Da! Here are some flowers for the flower of my life" and "Get yourself into your best dress, while I make reservations at the Chancery Restaurant in Aldwich", her favourite. "The Bristol meeting is off, as you can see".

He jumped into the first cab in the line and gave the driver instructions to take him first to his florist and then home.

It is well known that successful marriages are not made in heaven. They are the result of tireless efforts on both sides to make them successful. Attention to each other's needs, even frivolous ones, as well as true love and understanding are certainly more important prerequisites than the occasional manifestation of physical attraction. But continuous care and attention are time-consuming and time for each other was indeed in short supply in the Bentley household.

What had started out as a perfect fit began to deteriorate a few years after their marriage, perhaps not perceptibly for Tom, but certainly for Lou. Tom continued to spend most of his waking hours in his business, relegating marital sentimentality and even to some extent sex, to a secondary tier in his marriage. The fact is that he was often just too exhausted to do anything else than to have dinner, chat a little with Lou, watch the news on the telly and go to sleep. Weekends were often spent with friends, not really providing adequate opportunities for Tom and Lou to restore their erstwhile intimacy.

Over the years, Lou had tried to remind Tom repeatedly that life is short and that there are also other subjects than the Miles Electronic Company to devote his attention to, like, for instance, herself. On such occasions, Tom apologized and promised to change things around, but he never did, perhaps because he did not realize that his wife was slowly but surely drifting away from him.

And so it happened about a year ago that Lou, in search of a dentist to take care of a cavity, thought of Arnold, an old acquaintance. Initially, a purely professional visit soon turned into frequent encounters and a spirited sex life. However, neither partner intended to break up their marriage, at least not for the time being, limiting their occasional capers to a fling, like the traditional tasting of the forbidden fruit, enjoying their secret rendez-vous immensely. They were both aware of the fact that they were potentially playing with fire, but they tacitly agreed that their trysts were indeed well worth the risk.

Like on many previous occasions, the Bristol meetings served not only the rather mundane needs of the Miles Electronic Company, but also the much more personal ones of Lou and her lover. In fact, Arnold, having told his wife that he had to attend a one-night dentist's congress somewhere in the Midlands, arrived at the Bentley's flat shortly after Tom's departure for Paddington Station. As usual, Arnie carried a basket containing not only a complete gourmet dinner for two, but an ample stock of Champagne, Vintage Beaujolais and Cognac to help set the stage for another cozy evening of intimate dining, pleasant chatter and above all, glorious sex.

For obvious reasons, dinner was quickly dispensed with, all of its possibly incriminating vestiges were safely made to disappear in the garbage chute and without further ado, the lovers turned their attention to more carnal gratifications. Between sips of Cognac, they kissed and headed for the freshly laid out bed, letting nature and their pent-up passions take their course. It was sex at its glorious, seemingly endless best.

Exhausted, they both took a breather before working up to more of the same, gently caressing each other, when suddenly, like having been hit by a lightening bolt, Lou stopped every movement and gestured to Arnie to do the same. She had heard Tom's voice on the lobby intercom, asking her to press the button, in order to unlock the building's door.

Lou was clearly terrified, jumping out of bed and running to the flat's intercom box. While motioning to Arnie to gather his clothes and to disappear together with every trace of his presence into the bathroom, she tried to appear calm when she spoke into the intercom, asking Tom what had happened. He briefly told her about the cancelled meeting and his invitation for dinner. She replied that she had a splitting headache and had chosen to spend the evening in bed, nursing her misery. Tom quickly retorted that she would feel much better if she changed venue and had a few drinks under her belt, but, "please press the button", he added and I will tell you all about the cancelled meeting. Lou did as told and rushed back into the bedroom, watching Arnie disappear with his clothes in his hands into the bathroom. He was horrified and tried to think fast. He noticed an open window and when he looked out he saw the dark sky and a ledge in front, like a small terrace. He was obviously in a penthouse apartment.

Lou threw some tell-tale bits and pieces into her cupboard and jumped into bed. Seconds later, Tom unlocked the door of the flat and stepped into the bedroom, which by now was messy but devoid of any incriminating evidence of what had really taken place in its confines during the past few hours.

Sitting on the edge of her side of the bed, Tom told Lou about the chairman's accident, about the cancellation and his unexpected return to London. Then, he picked up the flowers he had brought for Lou and presented them with the words: "Flowers for the flower of my life" and kissed Lou. At that point, she reasoned quickly that her only salvation was to leave the flat as soon as possible with Tom, allowing Arnie to make his exit in their wake. She told Tom that on second thought, going out would be a splendid idea and that he should immediately go down to the garage to pick up the car and wait for her in front of the building, where she would meet him in 10 minutes or less.

Tom was elated. What looked like a dismal afternoon had actually turned into a promising evening and he was happy to be able to take his beautiful wife to a classy restaurant. As Lou was hurriedly getting dressed simply jumping into clothes, Tom took off his jacket, saying that he felt like freshening up before leaving the flat. Lou immediately interrupted him, saying that he looked just fine and would he please go down right away to the garage to fetch the car, because otherwise they would be too late for any decent service at the Chancery. Tom insisted that he would only be a few minutes in the bathroom. At that point, Lou realised that she could not really prevent her husband from washing up. Any further attempt to get him out of the house would certainly arouse his anger and indeed suspicion. So, with a silent prayer and expecting the world around her to collapse and explode into a thousand pieces before disintegrating with a big bang, she turned around and simply said: "Alright, darling, use the bathroom, but don't be late".

Tom briskly walked towards the bathroom and opened the door. To his utter amazement, he saw a stranger, partly dressed and clutching pieces of clothing in his hand. Before he could open his mouth, Tom was grabbed by the stranger, pulled inside the bathroom and the stranger shut the door.

In a low voice, he asked a bewildered Tom: "Are you alone in this apartment?"

Tom mumbled "No, my wife is in the bedroom, but who the hell are you?"

The stranger told Tom to be quiet and please listen to what had happened. He told him that he was having an ongoing love affair with the lady in the apartment next door. When her husband suddenly and unexpectedly showed up, he just had time to put on his pants and to climb out of the bedroom window into the first open window he could find, which happened to be the adjacent one in Tom's bathroom.

He added that he could have broken his neck in the process, but, pointing to the open window in Tom's bathroom, he said: "This hole in the wall saved my life in more ways than one".

Tom listened to the story in disbelief, but then he broke out in loud laughter. He patted the stranger on the back and told him that he was indeed lucky, adding that as a man he could sympathize with him, but didn't he live a bit too dangerously? They both introduced each other, and Tom asked if he could help the stranger in any way. The stranger said yes, he needed a pair of shoes and a shirt, having rescued only his pants and underwear during the escapade.

Tom said: "I will get you shoes and a shirt and you can return them anytime to the doorman downstairs."

By now, the two had become buddies and Tom asked if he could get him a drink along with the shirt.

The stranger said: "Yes, please, but you said your wife is in the bedroom, what the hell are you going to tell her about my presence here?"

"You leave that to me", replied Tom.

He rushed out of the bathroom and saw Lou, who, in a terrified voice asked: "What is going on in the bathroom? Please tell me", to which Tom put his index finger on his lips and told Lou: "I will tell you everything as soon as we leave the house, darling, a most amazing and crazy story, indeed, ha ha".

With this, he took out a shirt and a pair of shoes from his clothes cabinet, filled two tumblers with his best Scotch and rushed back to the bathroom, leaving Lou bewildered and speechless. A few minutes later, the two men emerged from the bathroom and the stranger profusely thanked Tom for having saved his life.

Tom slapped him on the back and said light-heartedly: "Not to worry, old man, these things have been going on since Romeo and Juliet and probably even before. Glad I could help out this time, but if I were you, I would choose less risky lovemaking. You could have slipped off the ledge, you know".

The stranger agreed, apologized for the inconvenience and thanked Tom again. Then he was gone.

Tom saw Lou standing with her mouth wide open and said: "Come on, darling, let's get out of here. I have a story to tell you, you will not believe. Quite amazing, actually. Right out of a thriller on TV, you know".

Without a word, Lou quickly put on her make-up, adjusted her dress and followed Tom into the elevator. She was tense and completely bewildered. Within minutes, they were in the car, heading for the Chancery.

While driving, Tom kept mumbling to himself: "Unbelievable, quite amazing."

Then he turned to Lou, saying: "Darling, as soon as we sit down and have ordered our drinks, I am going to tell you a story you will not believe, you simply will not. You know, they say life is stranger than fiction, well I can now vouch for that. Wait until I tell you all about it".

By now, they had almost reached their destination. Tom looked sideways in Lou's direction and noticed that she was stone-faced, as if in a continuing state of shock.

The Maitre D. gave them a beautiful table in the corner, somewhat away from the noisy center of the dinning room. They sat down, ordered their drinks and after a few sips, Tom noticed that life was returning to Lou's face. In fact, she started to relax and smile, letting her beautiful features light up her face.

Tom was all excitement and, taking Lou's hand gently into his own, he said: "Now, hear this, darling. Let me tell you what went on in our bathroom this evening."

"As I opened the door, I saw a perfect stranger barefoot and half dressed, standing underneath the open window. Before I had time to ask him what the hell he was doing there, he tells me the craziest story I ever heard. Believe it or not, this man was caught by surprise while in his lover's bed. They were apparently having a good time when the lady's husband unexpectedly came home. Seeing there was no place to hide, the man looked out of the window and noticed another window right next to his. With only his pants on, he climbed out and, risking slipping and and a broken neck, he crawled on the sill into our bathroom window, which happened to be open. So, he is now in our flat and is shaking with fear, not knowing what to do next, when the door to the bathroom opens and I stand in front of him. Can you imagine his surprise and mine. Don't you think this is the funniest story in the world?"

By now, Lou started to utter a silent prayer of thanks to her guardian angel. She had fully regained her composure and joined Tom in laughing out loud. In fact, they both shook with laughter.

But then, Tom suddenly stopped laughing. As if cut by a sharp knife, his laughter ceased, as all color seemed to disappear from his face. He looked at Lou intensely and slowly put down his glass on the table. Then he said, more to himself:

"Wait a minute, aren't we the only penthouse flat on the top floor of the building?"

FATHER KNOWS BEST

Tom Bailey lazily stretched out in his favourite armchair, the sport section of the *Times* spread over his chest. It was Saturday afternoon on a drizzly and grey London day and the perfect setting for an after-lunch nap. At sixty-two Tom had every reason to be satisfied with himself, but he really was not. Although he had single-handedly developed a small real-estate agency into a very prosperous company, owning and managing a considerable number of choice properties in London and the Midlands, he was too ambitious and outright greedy to be able to sit back and enjoy life, or smell the roses as the saying goes. Tom and his fifty-six-year-old wife, Alice, had been married for too many years to remember and they had one son, Philipp, a doctor of thirty-two.

The Baileys were actually an odd couple. While he was an aggressive, no-nonsense go-getter for whom money and power mattered more than anything else, she was soft-spoken, mild mannered, caring and compassionate. All these attributes were easily discernible on Alice's face, which radiated warmth and love, two features very much absent from Tom's facial expression and demeanour. It was largely due to Alice's wisdom and dexterity that their marriage had survived many a marital crisis that would have easily wrecked other, more fragile unions. No wonder many of their friends openly referred to Alice as "the lion tamer".

Philipp was a doctor, specialising in cardiac surgery. Although genuinely loved by his parents, their love differed substantially. His dad wanted Philipp to become rich and famous, while his mother only cared about his happiness, both in his private life and at work. The fact that at thirty-two he was not yet married naturally preoccupied both his parents, but certainly not Philipp himself.

Philipp's father strongly believed that if his son was to follow the prestigious progression of his trade, he would need years and years to become a prominent Harley Street cardiologist. In fact, he may never attain the position of tending to the rich and famous, thus making a lot of money, unless he married into a wealthy and socially significant family which would open doors normally closed to the average commoner.

In this vein, Tom Bailey kept urging his son to attend upper class charity
functions and other social events frequented by the aristocracy. Whenever he read about social events in London, he would cut out the article and hand it over to his son always with the same words: "Get in touch with the organisers of this do, get yourself an invitation and mingle with the lords and ladies. You're bound to meet some pretty girls and then you take it from there."

Philipp's usual response was "Thanks, Dad. Please let me run my life as I see fit."

There was another, more important reason for Philipp to ignore his dad's persistent urgings: he had fallen in love with a pretty lab technician in his hospital. Of course he kept this liaison from his father, fully aware that if he knew about it, Philipp would never hear the end of it. However, Philipp had confided about his affair to his mother who had simply reacted by saying, "Whatever makes you happy is all right with me, son."

Pam Hatfield was not only pretty, but she brought sound judgment and good taste to whatever she approached: from music and the arts to ethics and personal relationships. Philipp was constantly amazed by how much she enriched his life, and this is why it did not take him long to fall deeply in love with the prim and perky Pam. She, in turn, fully reciprocated Philipp's feelings. He was her Prince Charming who had swept her off her feet since their first evening out.

They both knew that their relationship would eventually lead to marriage. Yet, although their personalities were so evenly matched, their backgrounds were certainly not. Philipp came from a well-to-do family who appreciated and could afford the better things in life. Pam on the other hand was one of three children born to very simple and modest people. Her father was a doorman at the Concordia Hotel on Victoria Road, and her mother was a chambermaid in the same establishment. Apart from his stint in the army during the war, Pam's dad had never travelled abroad; a few summer vacations at a Lancashire holiday camp when he was freshly married was all he could muster in the way of "good times". And yet, the hardworking Hatfields had put their children through decent schools, providing them with a fair chance to make a go of whatever they chose to become in life. Not only this, but the Hatfields had instilled in them a sense decency, of duty and of respect for others, not by telling them, but by setting the example themselves.

* * * * *

One beautiful and cloudless day when they were enjoying lunch in the hospital's outdoor cafeteria, Philipp told Pam that the head of the department of cardiology had asked him and two other doctors to spend ten days in a Paris hospital, where a well-known French cardiac surgeon was using a new technique of valve replacement. Philipp and his two colleagues were to assist the French surgeon during a number of open-heart operations and then report on their experiences to the cardiology staff in London. Philipp was obviously excited to be among the chosen specialists, and Pam shared his pride by lovingly holding his hands.

That evening, over dinner, Philipp told his parents about his forthcoming assignment in Paris. While his father grumbled warnings, "beware of pickpockets in the Paris metro," his mother quietly wiped a few tears of joy and pride from her eyes.

When the Baileys were alone in their living room, Tom once again harped on his favourite subject: how to get Philipp to cozy up to London's aristocracy by meeting girls from upper class families.

"I cannot understand why he doesn't want to make the effort," he shouted.

After listening to him for a while, Alice thought the moment had come to tell her husband the truth. After all, he had to hear it sooner or later.

"Tom," she said calmly," stop bringing up this subject. I think you ought to know that Philipp is going steady with a lovely girl and they fully intend to get married."

Tom looked as though he was about to explode.

"What? Getting married without telling me? What are you talking about? And how come you know it and I don't, eh?"

"Because children confide in their mothers."

"Nonsense," grumbled Tom. "So, can you tell me who this lucky maiden is?"

"Of course I can," she said. "Her name is Pamela Hatfield and she's a lab technician in Philipp's hospital."

"And who is this Pamela? Do we know her family?"

"No, Tom," said Alice calmly, "we don't. She's a lovely young woman, and that's what counts, not her dad's bank account."

"Wait a minute," he said. "I'm beginning to smell a rat here. Who are her
parents?"

"Well, if you must know, her father is a doorman at the Concordia Hotel and her mother is a chambermaid in the same place."

Tom's face was flushed with anger.

"What!" he shouted at the top of his voice. "A doorman and a chambermaid? My future in-laws? Are you out of your mind? That's ridiculous. I will not stand for this. I will not allow it, you hear me? And that's final."

He put on his jacket and shouted again "I need some fresh air. I think I'm getting sick over this conversation!"

He slammed the door shut and walked out into the cool evening air.

* * * * *

Pam Hatfield was late for work because she had driven Philipp to Heathrow airport for his early morning flight to Paris. It was the first time they were to be separated for more than a couple of days and they hugged each other, well after the familiar announcement: "This is the final call. All passengers must now be on board."

As Pam turned on the lab computer, in her office the telephone rang. A deep voice said "Miss Hatfield? This is Tom Bailey, Philipp's father."

She held her breath and said, "Hello sir, how are you?"
"Listen, I wonder if I can have a word with you," he said.

Not knowing what else to say, she managed, "Of course".

"What time is good for you?" He didn't wait for an answer. "How about five or five-thirty today?"

"Five-thirty is fine," she said, "as long as it's within walking distance of the hospital."

"No problem," he said. " Do you know the *Rendezvous,* a small restaurant just around the corner from where you are?"

"I do indeed," she answered.

"Well then, five-thirty, at the *Rendezvous*." He paused. By the way, I'll be wearing a brown tweed jacket and a red tie. Don't look for hair on my pate. There isn't any. You can't miss me."

"All right," she said with a chuckle. "Goodbye."

Pam went through the day with apprehension. At times she felt like she was harbouring a swarm of butterflies in her stomach. Why would Philipp's father want to talk to her? She knew that he was not aware of the relationship. Who had told him? Was he a harbinger of good or bad news? Well, I'll have the answers later, she thought to herself.

At precisely five-thirty she sat down at a table in the dimly lit *Rendezvous* and ordered a cup of tea. A few minutes later Philipp's father walked in. She could not have missed him. His balding head practically shone. His short body was topped by a round face and his restless eyes were constantly moving. He did not look at all like Philipp. Pam waved him over. He sat down, his pudgy hands on the table. After ordering coffee, he got straight to the point.

"Miss Hatfield," he started, avoiding the more intimate *Pamela*, "let me be frank. What I have to tell you is not pleasant, but it has to be said. I don't believe in beating around the bush, and I'm sure you don't either. I know that you have a relationship with Philipp, and I want you to put an end to it. Let me tell you why."

Pamela was not prepared for these words and certainly not for their blunt delivery. She was shocked, confused and deeply offended.

Tom, like an actor reading his lines, continued without interruption.

"Look," he said, "this is not because I think you're not good enough for my son. But you must admit that you are different. You come from a different background, you have a different upbringing and you have a different outlook on life. These, and many other differences, will prevent you, yes, prevent you, from sharing a happy and fulfilling life with Philipp. And happiness is what life is all about, isn't it?"

Without realising that Pam's face had turned ashen and that she was fidgeting with the teaspoon, Tom went on with his tirade.

"Miss Hatfield, please listen to me. God knows there are more than enough obstacles to surmount in any marriage. Don't you think that you would be much better off if you married a man of your background, of your milieu, and let Philipp find himself a girl that shares his lifestyle and values? Please, Miss Hatfield, listen to me. I know what I'm talking about. You will regret marrying my son, and now is the time to do something about it, not later."

Pamela's face was a mask. Pain and disbelief had distorted her beautiful features into a hollow grimace. Tears that she had been holding back burst forth like floods breaking a dam. She was sobbing, holding the restaurant napkin to her face in an attempt to hide her tears. For a few moments she was silent, then she said, "Does Philipp know of this conversation?"

"Yes," lied Tom, "he does."

This was the final blow for Pamela. She grabbed her purse and prepared to leave this nightmarish meeting. Tom held her back.

"Wait," he said, "don't go. I know very well that I'm asking a great deal of you. I also know that you're a hard-working girl. Can I put an amount into your bank account to make it easier for you to get on with your life without Philipp? Just tell me how much and I'll take care of it."

This was one thing he definitely should not have said, for it made Pamela jump up and run towards the exit, not before hissing "Keep your money. I don't want your lousy money."

Tom also jumped up, holding her by her arm.

"OK, forget the money. I own a lot of property in London. I'm prepared to give you a flat of your choice in a nice London neighbourhood. Two bedrooms, living room, garden, garage and all the rest, ready to move in. You pick the location and I'll give you the freehold. The flat will be yours forever."

As if to close the deal, Tom added, "Remember, you will stop seeing Philipp as of tomorrow, even if he wants to continue the relationship. You have to be the one to put an end to it. OK? You let me know by tomorrow which way you want to go."

He walked straight out of the restaurant without a goodbye and without another look at Pamela.

It is difficult, even impossible, to describe Pamela's condition after Tom left the restaurant. She was shaking with feverish intensity, turning from hot to cold. She had never felt like this before and she was scared of losing consciousness. As in a dream, she walked out of the place, jumped into the first taxi that came along and headed for home. She could not believe what had just happened to her. Her first reaction was to phone Philipp in France to ask for an explanation. Why had he kept all this from her?

She was lucky to find Philipp in his hotel room. He had just checked in and was delighted to hear Pam's voice. "How nice of you to call" were the only words he managed to speak before he heard sobbing and crying.

"What happened?" he asked. "For God's sake, tell me what happened. Did you have an accident? Speak to me, darling, please!"

She had by now regained a small measure of composure and started to talk to him. She told him everything. From his father's phone call to his final offer of a flat if she left him.

Philipp listened all through her monologue, only interjecting with an occasional
"My God", "I don't believe this" or "Go on, sweetheart."

When she had finished, there was silence on both ends of the line. He was mulling over his fiancée's words, and she needed to catch her breath.

A few seconds later, Philipp said, "Are you still there, Pam?" He heard her shaky voice say "Yes, I am." He told her that he had never talked to his father about her, that his dad did not even know about their relationship. His mother must have spilled the beans.

"Knowing mother, I'm sure there must have been a damn good reason to tell Dad about us." And then, he went on to tell Pam that what she had just heard was entirely his father's doing. It had nothing, absolutely nothing, to do with his feelings towards her and most of all with his desire and hope to marry her as soon as possible. As a matter of fact, he added, if his dad's approach achieved anything at all, it would precipitate their wedding day.

"I wish I could walk down the aisle with you tomorrow morning," he said.

Philipp's soothing words had breathed life into Pamela. She was now beginning to recover from the traumatic last hours.

Having reassured Pam, Philipp added," I hate to say this, but my father has broken every rule in the book, even for a concerned father. I'll never forgive him for lying to you, saying that I was aware of all this nonsense. It's unforgivable."

By now both were exhausted from their long telephone conversation. Philipp told Pam to hang up and stretch out on her bed.

"Let me do some thinking on how to handle this," he said. "Go get some rest, I'll call you back in about an hour."

It took less than an hour for his call to wake up Pam from an uneasy nap. By now Philipp had regained his usual calm as he told Pam about the plan he had formed in his mind. He told her that he wanted her to phone his father in the morning and tell him that she had thought things over and she was prepared to sever the relationship on condition that she receives a flat in Knightsbridge as promised.

"And," added Philipp, "you will tell him that you want all freehold formalities to be completed within seven days."

"Are you sure?" Pam asked.

"I want to teach my father a lesson. We're going to make him pay for our family home. How about that!"

Both started to laugh, but Pam raised some questions.

"You're asking your dad for a very expensive gift, and we'll both have to lie about our real intentions," she said.

Philipp interrupted her. "Yes, it is expensive, but he can afford it. He owns several good properties in that area. I think he's actually getting off easy, if you ask me. So, are you ready for action tomorrow morning? As soon as I'm back we'll plan the next steps. For now, let's get the flat, OK?"

They wished each other a good night and both went to sleep with the distinct satisfaction of having dealt successfully with a difficult situation, just as a general would feel when planning a decisive battle.

Pamela called Tom Bailey early the next morning. She played her role perfectly. Tom agreed to give her a beautiful flat in Knightsbridge, two bedrooms, living room, garden, garage and all. It was a dream home. By the end of the week, all ownership formalities were completed. Tom handed her the keys with a smile.

"I'm glad you saw it my way. I know it won't be easy for you, but, hey, a free flat in Knightsbridge soothes a lot of pain, doesn't it?"

*****

For the next three weeks, Philipp avoided contact with his father as if to show his anger and pain over the breaking up with Pam.

But almost to the day three months later, Pam and Philipp were married in a beautiful ceremony attended by family members, friends and many colleagues from Guys and St. Thomas Hospital. Everybody wanted to give the handsome couple a royal send off. The proudest people were the bride's parents beaming with joy. They still could not believe that their daughter would henceforth be a successful surgeon's wife. They kept very close to Philipp's mother, who was alone and constantly wiping tears of joy from her eyes. Tom had steadfastly refused to attend the wedding. When his wife told him of Philipp's decision to marry Pam, he was so furious that he disinherited his son on the spot and swore to never talk to him again as long as he lived. And he meant every word of it.

Philipp and Pam settled down to family life in their beautiful Knightsbridge flat. Two years after the marriage, little John was born and, another eighteen months later, he was joined by little Cynthia. Taking after their parents, the two kids were beautiful and a constant source of pride and joy for their parents and grandparents. Philipp's mother could not get enough of them. She was an almost daily visitor and helped Pam in every possible way to bring up the two children. John and Cynthia were very fond of their granny, but they had never met their paternal grandfather. Despite the passing years and many opportunities and attempts to mend the fences, he refused to have anything to do with his son and his family.

The past eight years had been very good for Philipp. He had received constant promotions, eventually earning a professorship and shortly thereafter became head of the department of cardiac surgery. He also kept a busy private practice and was making a very handsome living indeed.

Philipp's ascending career contrasted sharply with that of his father. Tom had heavily invested in overpriced real estate both in London and in other parts of the country, and when prices began to slide downwards, he had to sell at a loss. On numerous occasions he had to sell real estate just to cover mounting debts, until, one day, he had to part with the last of his properties. After some thirty years in business he was practically back to where he had started from. Tom had indeed fallen on very hard times. At close to seventy years of age, he had neither the physical nor the mental stamina to start afresh. His own two-story house on Lyall street was really the only property he still owned, and he was determined to hold on to it come what may. But then, one day he was faced with some more bad news. A London court ruled against him in an old tax claim objection he had filed years earlier. When the substantial payment became due he had no other choice than to mortgage his own house. At first, he paid the decreed instalments, but it soon became apparent to him that he had to put up the house for sale in order to pay off the debt as decreed by the court. He would be left with the balance of proceeds of the sale, but that was all.

And so, one bright and sunny day in May, when most people were enjoying the long awaited sunshine breaking through cloudy skies, Tom Bailey looked out of the window as two workers put up a sign in front of his house with the bold lettering "FOR SALE BY COURT ORDER".

Tom felt sick to his stomach. He sat down heavily on the bed, his face buried between his hands. He had tried everything to save the house. He and Alice had put so much into it. Money, time and love to make this their castle; and now it was going to pay off debts. Tom reflected on his shattered life and how all this could have happened to him. He who thought he had all the answers, who thought he had really made it. How could all this have happened to him?

He was overcome by an immense feeling of loss and desperation. He started to cry. At first he wiped the tears from his eyes, but then the sobbing took over. His whole body was shaking. He didn't notice Alice entering the room. She put her arms around him.

Without looking at her, he said, "We lost everything. Everything I ever lived and toiled for. Everything!"

There was a pause and then Alice said to him, "No, dear, we did not lose everything." She opened the door. "Come on in, children." And in they walked. Six-year-old John and four-and-a-half-year-old Cynthia.

"Hello Grandpa. This is for you."

They handed Tom a bulging envelope.

Tom took it and said, "What is this?"

"Please open it, Grandpa, it's for you."

Tom did as told.
The envelope contained the copy of a cheque made out the day before by Philipp to the court in full payment of the tax owed by Tom Bailey, as well as a letter from the court confirming that ownership had been restored to Tom as a result of the settlement.

There was also a note from Philipp. It read:

Hello, Dad,

It took a long time, but better late than never. Continue to enjoy your home.

Tom looked at the two smiling children in front of him and reached out, pressing them against his chest. He realized that he had indeed gained a great deal more than a roof over his head.

THE BLIND DATE

Doug Simpson, trader in one of the city's very successful investment banks, had one more phone call to make before the day was over. He had a hot tip, which he reserved for his best clients. He had already passed it on to four accounts and this was to be the last one. He dialled the number, expecting to hear the familiar voice of Jack Williams, one of his key accounts. Instead, his call was answered by a very melodious female voice. He asked for Mr. Williams, but after a hesitant "who?", he was told that he must have dialled the wrong number. There was no Mr. Williams there. He quickly apologized, hung up and, after a brief reflection to make sure that his memory served him right, he redialled Jack's number.

To his surprise, the same pleasant voice answered. This time she recognized him and said, "Don't tell me you're still looking for Mr. Williams?"

"I am indeed," Doug replied, somewhat embarrassed about his unreliable memory.

He started to say how sorry he was about the error, when the girl at the other end interrupted him. She laughed, telling him not to worry; it may not have been his fault at all, but simply a malfunction of the telephone system. She added that with all the millions of calls being made in New York, it really is surprising how very few miss their target.

Doug was pleasantly surprised and felt like continuing the conversation with that engaging voice. He said he hoped his calls had not interrupted something she was doing.

"Oh no, I was just reading a very good book."

Doug's question about what she was reading started a lively conversation between the two, which lead him to say that he liked her voice and was enjoying the conversation. She started to laugh, which prompted Doug to ask her for a date. After a brief hesitation, she accepted and they agreed to meet the following Saturday morning at eleven in the little square in front of the Plaza Hotel adjacent to Central Park. They also agreed to hold under their left arm the first page of the New York Times' Entertainment Section, folded, with the heading clearly visible. They both found this cloak and dagger routine reminiscent of spy stories and joked about it before they finally hung up.

The little square in front of the Plaza Hotel on Manhattan's Fifth Avenue can be a busy spot on summer days. Apart from serving as a favourite meeting place for people from all walks of life, its benches also provide welcome relief for tired feet. If you add the ever present New York Times crossword addicts and Manhattan's ubiquitous pigeons, you have, especially on warm days, all the combined elements of a little oasis right in the middle of bustling traffic between Fifth Avenue and Sixtieth Street.

It was indeed a very pleasant morning when Doug and his mystery date converged on the agreed meeting place. Although both were full of excitement and expectation about the encounter, especially since it was a first in their lives, they were also wary of the risks of a disappointing confrontation. What if he or she turned out to be fat and ugly? Hence, both, outsmarting each other, hid the newspaper in their coat pocket until seeing the counterpart displaying the signal.

For thirty minutes they walked up and down the square, mingling among people, trying to espy a folded newspaper under a left arm, but to no avail. Suddenly, Doug spotted a rather attractive young woman taking out a newspaper from her bag and opening it up to the Entertainment section. Thinking he finally hit pay dirt and, greatly impressed by the beauty of the lady, Doug immediately ran over and introduced himself with a broad smile, producing the folded page he had been hiding in his pocket. The young woman looked at him as if he had just landed from Mars. As she was about to walk away, he realized his mistake.

Trying to keep her from leaving the scene, Doug quickly told her why he had approached her. She retorted that she was looking up the show time of a play she intended to go to later that afternoon. Assuming by now that his real partner had not shown up and that the girl he just met might be a welcome and exciting substitute for starting a relationship, he asked her if she cared to join him for a coffee in a nearby pastry shop. To his surprise, she agreed, and a few minutes later, over coffee and cakes, they had an opportunity to discuss the details of their unusual encounter and also to talk about themselves.

They quickly discovered that they were both in the investment banking business, she working as a financial analyst in a well-known private bank. The long coffee break eventually turned into an evening on Broadway and a late dinner. Two complete strangers had met under very unusual circumstances. After a few more meetings, their relationship grew into a bond for life. Two years after the impromptu meeting in front of the Plaza Hotel, Doug and Cindy Simpson were married amid a cheering crowd of family and friends.

*****

Suzan, Doug's original blind date, was very, very disappointed. It was now almost an hour since she had arrived at the little square, full of excitement and anticipation about a very unusual encounter. She had started out by standing in the middle of the square, hoping that her partner would walk by with the folded newspaper under his arm. She started to walk among the small crowd, keenly looking for her target, but in vain. For a while, she sat down on one of the benches, watching everybody who passed by.

Finally, not thinking that he might have used the same ruse, she came to the conclusion that her presumed partner had chickened out, or perhaps something unexpected had happened to prevent him from keeping the appointment. She was making one last search among the people in the little square, when a young man suddenly approached her. In a very pleasant voice, he told her that he had observed her for some time as she walked around looking at people.

"Have you lost anything or are you looking for something?" he said, adding, "Can I help you, miss? You seem rather disconcerted. Perhaps I can help."

At first, she did not know what to say to the young man, but she was near tears and was glad to have been offered an opportunity to talk about her misfortune.

"Oh, thank you," she replied. "No, I didn't lose anything, but I am looking for someone, or I was looking for someone."

With this, she extracted the folded newspaper from her purse, tore it up and threw it into the nearest garbage bin. Noticing the puzzled expression on the young man's face, she told him how the blind date had started.

"Believe me," she said, "I will never do this again. I can't tell you how convincing he sounded over the phone. He made me come all the way here and he didn't even show up. Why did he do it?" She paused. "Perhaps I was naïve, or better still, plain stupid."

She took a tissue from her purse to wipe the tears which were beginning to accompany her last words.

The young man listened to her story, at first somewhat amused, but as she went on, he was seized by a strong sense of compassion. He felt like taking her into his arms to ease her obvious distress. He did the next best thing: he put his arm on her shoulder and said, "Calm down, it's surely not the end of the world. We all get clobbered by someone at one point or another. So what else is new? Come, let me take you home."

He gently coaxed her out of the crowd in the square.

They stood in front of the Plaza Hotel and she said to her unknown rescuer, "I don't even know your name."

The young man quickly introduced himself and so did Suzan, who was beginning to regain her composure. She apologized for having made a fool of herself, which led the young man to ask her if she would join him for a bite at the hotel.

Perhaps because she really needed a rest or because he seemed like a really nice person, she readily agreed. It was a long lunch. They talked about themselves, about the world around them and about a hundred different things. They discovered that they shared a lot of common interests. From music to sports and from ethics to everyday living, they seemed to have very similar views and concepts. They came from different backgrounds: she from a large middle-class family, he the only son of a well-to-do surgeon, but somehow the proverbial chemistry had kicked in. When they finally left the restaurant, they agreed to meet again, sooner rather than later. They did meet again just a week later and then met again and again. They fell in love and eventually exchanged vows in a beautiful wedding ceremony, long remembered by all those who attended it.

* * * * *

Like every fall, New York's social events season was in full swing as fashion shows, charity balls, art exhibitions and receptions of all kinds vied for editorial and pictorial exposure in the city's leading news media. One of these coveted events was the annual New York Fashion Show and Dinner at the Waldorf Astoria in Manhattan. Following the usual parade of stern-faced and underweight models, several rooms of the hotel were thrown open for cocktails and delicious tidbits before sitting down to a hundred dollar a plate dinner in the main ballroom.

In one of the cocktail rooms stood Dr. Andrew Latimer and his wife, Suzan, both clutching cool drinks in their left hands, ready to extend the other hand to people they expected to meet. Hoping to strike up a conversation with anybody that looked interesting, they strolled through the room and noticed another young couple also surveying the crowd. The Latimers casually approached them and, after a few remarks about the fashion show, exchanged introductions with Douglas Simpson and his wife, Cindy. Since physicians often wonder if they made the right investment decisions, and Doug Simpson seemed to be very knowledgeable in matters of the stock market, the two soon engaged in an animated repartee. Suzan and Cindy, both busy mothers of young children also discovered a great deal of mutual interest. The two couples were so much absorbed in their conversations that they almost missed the call for dinner in the adjacent ballroom.

Following the usual conveyor belt three-course dinner, the couples decided to go down to the hotel bar for a cognac before heading home. The conversation now turned to more personal matters. Andrew Latimer casually asked the Simpsons how they had met. At this question, both Doug and Cindy burst out laughing.

"You wouldn't believe how we met, it's an amazing story," Doug said.

He proceeded to tell the Latimers of their encounter on the little square in front of the Plaza Hotel some ten years earlier. He recalled every detail and was frequently interrupted by Cindy, who filled in little tidbits, making sure that her husband did not leave anything out.

Susan and Andrew listened very attentively to the Simpsons. From time to time, they exchanged looks and smiled.

"And that's how we met," concluded Doug, reaching out to Cindy to draw her closer to him.

"Didn't you ever wonder what happened to the girl you were supposed to meet?" asked Andrew.

"Well, she never showed up, as far as I could tell. I looked all over the square on that sunny Saturday morning, but she wasn't there. Yes, I often wondered what happened to her. Did she show up but hid the paper like I did, or did she just stand me up? I guess I'll never know."

Andrew seemed to have been waiting for his cue. With the brightest grin he could muster, he said, "Well, Doug, wonder no more. That girl did show up, but when she couldn't find you in the little square, she got so desperate that she settled for second best. I've been waiting ten years to thank you for hiding the newspaper that morning, buddy!"

PREVENTIVE MEDICINE

In most dictionaries *Hypochondria* is defined as an exaggerated fear of falling ill, but to Hubert and Janice Kozlovski it was the dominant feature of their lives. In fact they were constantly preoccupied with reading, talking and thinking about the risks of getting sick and what to do about it.

The two had met at one of the health courses on preventive medicine offered by a well-known medical school, and immediately discovered their common fear of falling ill. One word led to another, and before long the two were meeting after work to exchange information and advice. To be sure, their relationship was not marked by passion or carnal love as is often the case when young people fall for each other. Rather, they both felt a growing bond between them fed by their quest for ways and means to protect themselves from all kinds of diseases.

Hubert Kozlovski was an accountant by profession. Although in his early thirties, he looked older on account of his balding head, frail features and his tendency to dress very conservatively. He shunned bright shades and sporty clothes, even on weekends. All this, accentuated by rimless glasses on his pointed nose, combined to create a very distinct appearance of sober propriety and, yes, lack of flair and daring-do.

No better proof of the old adage "birds of the same feather flock together" could be found than in the personality of Janice Webster, a lab technician in a major hospital. She too preferred grays and greens to yellows and reds, and most of her dresses were combinations of skirts, blouses and blazers worn with flat shoes. She was pretty without being flashy, mostly because she wore no make-up and her hair was neatly combed and tied in an unobtrusive knot at the back of her head.

Their meetings led to a deeper relationship, and Janice was not surprised when Hubert asked her to marry him. The wedding came and passed like any other event in their lives. They soon settled down to a routine life, which actually differed little from what they were doing when they were single.

While planning and accounting were often subjects of their daily conversations, health issues of all kinds remained the main topic of their frequent repartees over dinner, and even in the intimacy of their bedroom.

A few months into their married life, Janice became pregnant. After an ascetic nine months, during which she avoided any possible contaminant or wrong move, she gave birth to a healthy boy they named Arthur, or Artie for short.

Raising a newborn is, of course, a labour of love and dedicated care for any parent, but for the Kozlovskis it became a sacred mission of doing everything right and proper for the baby. In addition to punctually breastfeeding and exercising the baby, they made sure that the air Artie inhaled was at all times pure and free of contaminants. They had air purifiers installed in the tot's bedroom and, when outdoors, filters in the baby's carriage saw to it that Artie breathed nothing but unadulterated air.

In constant consultation with their paediatrician, the boy was given all the necessary immunization shots, including those for rare and uncommon diseases,
"Just in case".

And so, Artie grew up not only sheltered and protected from contact with disease but also immunized against it. At the age when other kids start going to school and run around on the playgrounds, Artie was educated at home by a tutor who was made to wear a protective face mask in Artie's presence.

In time Artie grew up to be a very concerned boy, concerned about his health and the avoidance of disease. Obviously, his parents had passed on their deep fear of "catching something" to their son. He avoided crowds, and if he was exposed to them by necessity, he made sure that he held a medicated handkerchief in front of his mouth at all times. Then, on coming home, he would go straight to the bathroom, carefully wash his hands with disinfectant soap, brush his teeth and hang his clothes in a special closet containing germ killers and antiseptics.

By the time Artie entered high school he was an expert in all measures that can possibly be taken to protect himself from contamination, and he applied them all meticulously. In fact, he went much further than what his parents had taught him. If this phobia was his parents' constant preoccupation, it became a passion for him. He was determined to live a life free of any and all risks of falling ill.

Naturally, his educational interests gravitated towards health and medicine. He assigned a cursory place to all the other subjects at school and avidly followed the developments in the medical world from newspapers, radio and T.V. Whenever he visited the family doctor for much too frequent check-ups, he engaged the physician in interminable question periods about preventing and avoiding disease.

Artie Kozlovski entered college with the intention of choosing the medical profession, not, as many other young people, motivated by a desire to heal their fellow men, but in order to maintain his own health above all.

Artie drew up a list of all the organs in his body and began preparing plans of protecting the vulnerable areas. He followed special regimens and diets for his heart, his lungs, his liver, his kidneys and made sure that all parts of his body benefited from stringent protective care.

One preoccupation which loomed foremost in his mind was the need to be vaccinated and immunized by injection or by medication against all known and emerging pathogens. Alarmed by reports about rare diseases coming into his world from underdeveloped and unclean countries, he established running communication channels with Tropical Disease Control Centers all over the world. He asked to be shipped antibodies and sera for all uncommon infections as soon as they could be isolated so that immunization medications could be prepared for him. Then he had them tested by specialized laboratories and administered to him, sometimes orally but more often by injection.

Considering that one day he may have to travel, he turned his interest to bites: by snakes, reptiles and insects. He had their venoms shipped to him in order to prepare protective immunization programs, all of which he followed to a tee. It can be said that he was indeed one step ahead of protecting himself against any and all known, and even some not yet known, affliction besetting mankind.

And so it was that Arthur Kozlovski, now a twenty-four-year-old student of medicine, stepped out of the laboratory one rainy evening, having received yet another round of shots of the latest sera against emerging and potentially dangerous pathogens. Despite the hard-hitting rain and blowing wind, he stood in front of the building and reflected on his efforts over the years to protect himself against falling ill. He stood there and was very proud of himself. In fact, he gloated because he was overwhelmed by a sense of physical security, of having been able to prepare for any and all assaults on his health, for having cheated death caused by disease.

He looked around. Since there was nobody in sight, he shouted at the top of his voice as if wanting to communicate with God himself: "Nothing, nothing can happen to me now! I am immunized against everything, you hear me!, EVERYTHING."

He closed his eyes in a moment of ecstasy. He could not see the object that had been pried loose by the gale-strength wind from the roof of the building behind him.

It struck him right at the back of his head with a shattering blow, killing him instantly. His lifeless body fell to the ground like an empty sack.

He was obviously not protected from *all* kinds of shingles.

AND LIFE GOES ON

Burials in Montreal's Cote-des-Neiges Cemetery are common, daily affairs. Sometimes several processions wind their way through rows of well-kept gravesites to reach their allotted destinations in different sections of the vast grounds. Stately trees and benches contribute to create an air of serene dignity, befitting its role as the final resting place for many Montrealers, including some of its favourite sons and daughters.

It is here that Marie-Louise Lagassé was put to rest on a cool but cloudless November morning. After a brief bout with pneumonia she had suddenly passed away at the age of seventy-nine surrounded by her beloved son André, his wife Julie and their two teenage daughters.

The funeral was attended by all members of Marie-Louise's family as well as by André Lagassé's friends and business associates of whom there were many, given his prominent position in social and professional circles.

No one who came to mourn the passing of Marie-Louise will forget the serenity, the sadness and true sorrow permeating the burial. But the most visible expression of grief came from her son, André. He was standing at the open grave, his face buried in a handkerchief to contain his sobbing. His whole body shook as he lifted his right arm to wave a final goodbye to the woman who had not only been his adoring mother but his confidante, his role model, his idol throughout his fifty-six years.

Slowly and lovingly, Julie and her oldest daughter led André away from the grave and let him regain his composure during the long walk back to the waiting limos at the cemetery's main gate.

Some of his closest friends patted him on the back or briefly shook his hands. As he made his way to the gate he was suddenly approached by a man he had never met before. The man shook his hand, expressed his sympathy and said: 'Mr. Lagassé, I am sorry to bother you at this time. My name is Henri Duval. I am a notary and I was entrusted some years ago by your mother with a box containing some papers. She instructed me to deliver it to you upon her death. Please tell me when I can do so.' André, still clutching his handkerchief said, 'Anytime, Mr. Duval. I am sure you will find my home or office address in the telephone book. On second thought, please let me have it as early as possible. Thank you very much.'

André wondered what this was all about, but the overwhelming impact of the day's events soon occupied his mind to an extent that he forgot about the brief encounter at the cemetery gate. He was only reminded of it two days later, when Mr. Duval phoned to say that he would drop off the box later in the evening. This he did and after depositing a small wrapped-up package on a table near the entrance, Mr. Duval said to André who stood in the doorway, 'This sealed box was given to us by Mme. Lagassé many years ago with the written instructions to hand it over to you personally immediately after her death. She said it contained some family papers. If you want to see her instructions, we have them in our office. Here is my card.' André asked Mr. Duval to come in and have a coffee, but he thanked him saying he was expected home. He said goodbye and left.

* * * * *

It was not until early next morning that André went to his study to open the parcel left by Mr. Duval. It contained a bundle of handwritten sheets neatly tied together with a red ribbon. He immediately recognized his mother's very clear and upright style. André closed the door to his study, sat down and pulled the first page from the pile.

"To my one and only son, my dearly beloved André.

By the time you read this I will no more be among you and my wonderful family. My family that I loved so much, not only because of the warmth and love it gave me but also because of the great pain I went through to create it, to bring it to life and to keep it alive. Believe me, André, it was not an easy task and what's more I had no one to confide in all these years, no one except my diary, which I kept hidden in a secret drawer no one had access to except myself.

It was after your father's death three years ago that I decided "enough is enough". I must tell the truth. I must come clean with myself and especially with you, Julie and the children. I just cannot take this burden to my grave as if it never took place. This is why I am now telling you what really happened. My dearest boy, this is an amazing and frightening story, a story you may find difficult to believe, and yet it is the truth. A truth I myself often found very hard to accept.

* * * * *

I was nineteen years old when I met Pierre Lagassé at a friend's wedding party. We danced a few times and I fell for him like a ton of bricks. He was seven years older than myself, he was the most handsome man I had ever seen and he danced like Fred Astaire. That night he literally swept me off my feet. I was madly in love with him and wanted nothing else than to spend the rest of my life in his arms. He took me home and when he kissed me goodnight I knew deep down that this handsome dancer would be my partner for the rest of my life. I just knew it.

The next day, over dinner, I told my parents that I had fallen in love with a very handsome young man who had an engineering degree. My mother was elated and wanted to know everything about him. My father, a well-known pediatrician simply said, 'I don't believe in true love at first sight. Let's see if he will reciprocate your feelings. Having a good time at a party is one thing and turning it into a lasting relationship is another.'

Well, I proved my dad wrong. Within days Pierre started to ask me out to dinner and within a few more days he became my lover. We went on a short vacation together and began enjoying each other's company very much. Pierre was a wonderful companion. He was well-read, came from a well-to-do family in Outremont and, at 26 not only had a good job in a construction company, but also had many friends who all welcomed me warmly into their midst.

My parents also found Pierre charming. My father especially was impressed by Pierre's sophistication and elegant mannerism.

Believe it or not but three months after we had first set eyes upon each other Pierre asked me to marry him. The day he proposed was a Sunday and we were having dinner in a restaurant on St. Lawrence Boulevard. It was the happiest day of my life. It still is. I will never forget how a gush of warmth and desire came over me as he spoke holding my hand. I wanted so much to make him happy. I wanted to be the best wife in the world. I loved him beyond reason and convention, beyond everything I had read about and seen in the movies.

The next six months or so were filled with preparations for the wedding which was to be celebrated in his favourite church. Pierre was a devout Catholic and wanted to conform to all the rites and traditions of his faith, mainly for his parents' sake.

I gave up my classes at nursing school where I was in my second year because I was too busy with the forthcoming wedding and also because I thought that since Pierre had a well-paid job I would not need to work for a living after we were married. Besides, my father had told me that he had left a sizeable amount of money for me in his will.

Our wedding was the talk of the town. Everybody who was anybody came. Between his parent's guests and ours, we filled all the pews. Following the church service, my mom and dad threw a beautiful party at the Ritz hotel. As they say "a good time was had by all."

After the party we hardly had time to change into street clothes and rushed to the airport. Two blissful weeks in Puerto Rico. It was heaven on earth. We came back suntanned, relaxed and happy. Very happy.

What followed was the routine life of newlyweds. Setting up and furnishing our home, starting a small social circle of friends, keeping in close contact with our parents. We did and enjoyed everything together.

Very early in our marriage Pierre told me that he was eagerly looking forward to his role of paternal educator and guide. He often talked to me about the sanctity of parenthood in which he strongly believed. He used to say: "We must pass on the torch to our children so that they can continue the family line."

Consequently I became very much aware of the need to become pregnant early on. Not that I myself considered it of great urgency. I thought we could have a few years just by ourselves to travel and to enjoy life to the fullest before settling down to the routine of changing diapers. But Pierre was all for starting a family at the earliest possible time. To be sure, Pierre was a wonderful sex partner and we spent long hours making love. However after several months there were no signs of my becoming pregnant. At first I talked to my mom who gave me some advice but when it did no lead to any results we went to see a specialist. He examined both of us and found no reason for us not to have a baby. 'Just keep on doing the good work and be patient. Sooner or later you will join my flock of expectant mothers', he said as he led us out of his office.

Unfortunately his prediction did not materialize. Months and months went by but although I was still diligently trying to conceive I waited in vain for the familiar prenatal signs and symptoms.

The pressure created by this ongoing situation began to affect both of us. It affected me because I felt unfit to bear children and fulfill my part in raising a family. It affected Pierre because he was denied the satisfaction of being a procreator.

Mind you, we were deeply in love and throughout this childless period, Pierre was very close and very caring at all times. He even came up with ideas of taking short vacations more often or changing our diet or me taking afternoon naps as possible remedies for my infertility.

Almost two years had passed since we had tied the knot. Pierre continued to enjoy his job in the construction company and I could look back with pride on the creation of a beautiful home and a very nice circle of friends.

One evening after a candle-lit dinner at home, I brought up the subject of adoption. I should not have done that, because Pierre suddenly burst out as if letting steam out of a kettle. 'Do you mean to say you gave up? Are you telling me that we will never have a child of our own? No, I don't want any adopted babies,' he said emphatically.

I had never seen him act like this before and I realized that my inability to bear him a child had become a very serious matter in his life, perhaps more serious than I had realized.

Months went by. The familiar problem hung over me like a dark cloud. We were approaching our third year of marriage. We were still very much in love with each other. Perhaps my inability to have a baby made me love Pierre even more. I felt guilty and wanted nothing more in life than to give him the good news he desperately longed for.

One evening he came home with some flowers although he had brought me flowers a couple of days earlier. I sensed that he wanted to say something special to me. I was right.

Swirling a glass of cognac in his hand, he said 'Sweetheart, let me first tell you that I love you as deeply as on the day we got married. You are the loving and caring wife I always dreamt of and I know exactly what you are going through and have been going through during the past three years. I feel very much for you and admire your patience for putting up with the pressure I have created for you. I am sure you also understand my position which is sincere and honest. Darling, I don't want to beat around the bush. I have given this a lot of thought and I want to make you a proposal. Believe me it hurts my soul and my heart but I have to tell you this. Let us give ourselves another year or so. If by the end of next year we still don't have a baby we will part company. Now let me add immediately that you will not suffer financially. I will take care of you. You can trust me. But we will separate so that you can find a man who will either not want children or agree to have adopted ones. I will try to find another woman who may help me raise a family. Sweetheart, I know you realize how much this decision and my talking about it is taking out of me. For weeks, I have struggled with my conscience but I think my proposal to you is honest and fair. I cannot ignore my beliefs, my upbringing and my background. I must do what I think is right.' With that, he put down his glass and came over to me. We clung to each other for a long time. I cried my heart out.

To be sure, I was anticipating something of the sort to happen, but when it actually did, I was devastated. That evening I felt as though the ground on which I stood had suddenly given way, as though my whole world had fallen apart. After a while, Pierre said he felt like taking a brisk walk around the block. I took a sleeping pill and went to bed. An era in my life had suddenly collapsed that very evening.

The following months went by as usual. Pierre stopped bringing up the subject of pregnancy. We lived a normal life caring for and even doting on each other as we had always done. We met our parents and friends regularly. I did not mention a word of my marital problems to my mother for fear that it would make her very unhappy. I still had "a year or so" ahead of me and I strongly believed that God would create a miracle to help me. I was right.

* * * * *

A few months later, two things happened in quick succession that were to bring about an unexpected and fateful change in our life.

The first was the evening when Pierre came home with a bottle of champagne under his arm. He was smiling and looked very happy. That afternoon, the president of his company and his own boss, the vice-president of Overseas Projects had come to his office to tell him that they had good news for him. 'You know about our project in Central Africa, don't you, Pierre?' said the president after he had sat down. 'It comprises the construction and turn-key delivery of an airport, a hotel, a shopping mall and an office tower all to be completed within the next three years. Thanks in great part to Jean-Luc here, all financial and legal arrangements were completed last week. This is the most important project we have ever contracted and we want you to be in charge of Phase One. This phase will run slightly over one year and will involve the hiring of local contractors, obtaining all permits, setting up our local cost accounting, financial and personnel operations as well as ensuring the cooperation and goodwill of the government and the local authorities. As you can see, Pierre, it is a big job and we think that you can handle it very well.' A that point, Jean-Luc, his immediate boss, took over and said 'You will, of course be assisted by four people from head office, each of them already familiar with the project and reporting directly to you. You have a week to go through the most important aspects of the job and then, it's off to Africa for some 14 months. Don't forget to pack your suntan lotion.'

The president interrupted, 'It's not so bad, Pierre, you can come back to your wife for Christmas. But we want you to be on the spot during Phase One. You will have to be everywhere and survey all activities closely. And now, let me give you the good news, Pierre. If the company is satisfied with your performance and I bet my bottom dollar that we will be, you will come back to Montreal next year as chief engineer and as a vice-president. So, what say you? Do we have an African Project Director or not?'

Pierre was slowly recovering from his initial shock. He was elated and speechless. In his confusion, he said 'I thank you both for the fantastic opportunity and for your confidence in me. I am sure I will make you proud. May I discuss it with Marie-Louise before giving you my answer tomorrow?'

'Of course you may', said the president. "By the way, you will be staying at the Hilton, the best local hotel, but we do not recommend that you take your wife with you. She will be more comfortable right here.'

The next morning, Pierre stood in front of the president and with a broad grin on his handsome face accepted the tremendous challenge offered to him.

*****

This was the first event that happened shortly after the crucial evening at home. The second event came a couple of weeks later from a completely different and unexpected direction.

I had been using a manicurist for a number of years. Anna was not only very good at taking care of my nails but she was also a very pleasant girl in her early thirties. Every time she came to our house to do my nails I kept admiring her lovely face, her rich dark hair and her gorgeous figure. I often asked her why on earth she was wasting her time trimming nails when she could be a fashion model. Over the years we had become friendly and we often exchanged news and views relating to our private lives. One day, as she sat in front of me, I noticed a certain tension and nervousness in her movements. I asked her if she had a problem and in response she started to cry. She finally pulled herself together and told me all about it. Among her regular clients was a well-known actor who had seduced her and they had made love. Believe it or not, a few weeks later she realized that she was pregnant. When she confronted her lover with the news, he said 'I cannot let you have the baby. I am married, I have a family and I am a prominent actor, something like a role model. Here is a nice cheque. Please have an abortion and let's forget the whole thing.' Well, that was easy for him to say. I told him: 'I do not want to have an abortion. I had one, two years ago, and I almost died. Never again will I have this done to me.' Now you know why I am so nervous," she added. "I am scared stiff and I don't know what to do."

As the poor girl was talking, constantly wiping tears from her eyes, a fiendish idea entered my mind. An idea which, if properly turned into reality, could solve the problem of not one, but four people. Here is what I proposed to her right there and then.

'Look,' I said to her, 'Would you be prepared to put your baby up for something like an adoption?'

'Yes.' She said. 'I know all about single mothers but I have neither the means nor the place to care for a baby and bring up a child. Taking care of a baby is a fulltime job and I have to earn a living. But, how can I be sure that my baby will find a good home with good people who will make it part of their family?'

'Would you consider me and my husband good people to bring up your baby?' I asked her.

'Of course I would.' She replied.

'Well, here is my plan.' I said to her. 'First of all, I want your solemn assurance that what I am going to tell you and what we are going to do will remain a secret between you and me. A secret we will both take to our graves. Can you swear this on the holiest thing in your life?'

'Yes.' She said. 'I swear on the grave of my dear mother that I will never ever say anything to anyone about this.'

'Okay then.' I said. 'I will pay you immediately an amount on account. You will carry the baby until your condition starts to become obvious. At that point you and I will disappear to a remote motel in Vermont. We will stay there until you have the child in a local clinic. Then we will complete all adoption formalities and when we will return to Montreal, I will be the official mother of the child, pretending that I gave birth to the baby. As befits a woman giving up a baby, you will be out of the picture. You will vanish as far as the child is concerned and you will never lay claim to it or even want to see it. Needless to say I will pay you handsomely for this and for your sealed lips. I will of course take care of the stay in Vermont and all the rest. Do we have a deal?'

Anna's tears of despair had, within an hour, turned to tears of relief. She jumped up and embraced me. She was truly happy and showered all kinds of celestial blessings upon me. 'I'll do anything you want,' she said, 'as long as my baby, sorry "your baby", is in good hands.'

My next step was to see Leo, my first cousin and a lawyer, who was also a very trustworthy friend. I told him the whole story and he readily agreed to take care of all the legal formalities.

*****

I was elated. Mind you, plenty apprehensive of how the whole thing would proceed, but elated. In my mind I went over the course of events. The more I thought about it, the more excited I became.

Pierre was to leave for Africa in a week's time. Before his departure I would make sure we made love to our heart's content, like wow! Then, as soon as possible, I would send Pierre a jubilant message with the "good news". 'Guess what? We finally made it. I am pregnant.' Then I would follow Anna's prenatal experience to a tee and keep Pierre informed about all "my" aches and pains, until Anna's blissful condition would begin to be visibly evident. At that point, I would tell Pierre that I wanted to have the baby in a quiet place, away from snoopy friends and crowds. 'I waited so long for this event and I want to be perfectly relaxed when the time comes. I don't want to take any chances.' I would tell him. From the place in Vermont where Anna and I would stay, Pierre would continue to receive messages about my developing condition and then, one day I would phone him, 'Bonjour Papa', with the baby and myself blaring into the phone.

A short while later, Anna and I would return to Montreal. Anna would disappear from the scene, all papers sealed and signed and I would wait for Pierre the "proud father" to come home. How about that for perfect mimicry? I was really proud of my mise en scène.

Oh, one more thing, Christmas was to come in about two months after my "pregnancy" announcement so when Pierre would come home for his year-end vacation I could easily fake an early prenatal condition.

I was convinced that God in his infinite wisdom had brought all these coincidences and events together in a divine configuration in order to save my marriage. That it also solved Anna's and her impromptu lover's problem was the icing on the cake. But most important of all, it would make Pierre a happily fulfilled father and this to me was the crowning of the whole exercise. I cannot tell you, André, how much I loved your father. My life would have come to nothing had he decided to leave me.

* * * * *

By the way, I also told my parents who had just retired to Florida exactly the same story I told Pierre. Needless to say my mom was elated and wanted me to keep her constantly informed about my condition. Of course I promised to do so, and I did.

* * * * *

Well, everything went according to plan. Shortly after Pierre's arrival in Africa, I phoned him with the "good news". I cannot tell you his joy, his elation. He actually
cried. He kept sending me kisses over the phone and wanted to come back immediately. 'Nonsense,' I told him, 'you do your job and I will be just fine.'

Before Anna and I left for Vermont, I told Pierre that I had decided to ask my manicurist Anna to come with me as a helper and companion, 'You see,' I told him, 'I am doing everything to set your mind at ease. I will not be alone.' Pierre was very happy about this.

Several months into her pregnancy, Anna and I left for a lovely little place in rural Vermont and I made the necessary arrangements with a local doctor at a nearby clinic.

In my phone calls, I continued to feed Pierre all "my" aches and pains Anna was actually going through.

Just one day later than expected, Anna gave birth to a beautiful baby boy. We finalized all legal papers. I paid Anna the agreed sum and two weeks later we returned to Montreal. She to her home and I to a beautifully redecorated house complete with baby room, toys and colourful dangling ducks and Disney mobiles.

Needless to say, the first few days and weeks were a real challenge for me. I had to learn a lot of things, but let me tell you, women don't have to learn how to care for a baby. It comes naturally. It is like an instinct. Look at animals. They do everything perfectly well and so did I. Our friends thought that I was the ideal mother and I began to love not only my surrogate role but that little bundle of joy. I could not put it out of my arms.

Fourteen months after he had left Montreal, Pierre came home. He was the happiest person in the world and so was I. He for two reasons: First he enjoyed the fatherhood that had eluded him for so long and second, because true to his word, the company president appointed him Chief Engineer and Corporate Vice President, all during a beautiful dinner party at the Ritz Hotel.

This, my dearest André, concludes the first part of my story. It is the story of how you became part and parcel of the Lagassé family. Exciting, eh?

* * * * *

I don't need to tell you that you soon became the hub around which everything else evolved. From weekly photographic sessions posing with your parents to the ritual of putting you to sleep, to phone calls from his office, 'How's the baby doing?', your father soon became the most doting and adoring parent I could imagine. I just basked in the warmth of his happiness.

You were such a handsome baby! Your big dark eyes dominated your face and when your dad and I conjured up your first smile we were so elated that your dad phoned the florist right there and then to order a dozen roses for my bedside.

As the weeks and the months went by, I kept silently praying to God, thanking him for the miracle he had created in bringing so many seemingly unrelated events together in such a masterly way. It may be true that every baby brings joy and happiness, but you, André, brought more than that. You brought a "raison d'être", a meaning and a purpose into our lives, you gave us a family.

*****

True to her promise, Anna completely disappeared from my world. Through some friends I later learned that she had married a bank clerk and had moved to Toronto. At first I caught myself thinking of her, hoping that you had inherited the right genes, but as time went by, her image faded from my mind and you, André, became a true part of me. I began to develop physical, almost biological ties with you which totally bypassed and even excluded your real mother. It was as if Anna had never existed and you were my natural child.

Perhaps the only time I was jolted back to reality, was when people told us 'My, he looks just like you', or 'He definitely has his father's eyes.' When I heard such remarks, I used to involuntarily look at Pierre, but when I saw his happily contented smile, I soon learned to accept these remarks like any normal banter.

Your childhood came and went like that of most other kids. Actually you were brought up under two guiding principles. That of your father, teaching you all the virtues and ethics he had learned from his parents. This included duty, loyalty and hard work inspired by a disciplined and unwavering belief in the Catholic dogma. He wanted you to stand out among your friends, your colleagues and society at large as a role model of propriety.

As for me, I wanted the very same things for you, but I also believed in teaching you the importance of love and compassion, of tolerance and above all of a sense of humour.

I now know, my dearest André that we both succeeded beyond our wildest dreams. Throughout your school years, throughout your studies, throughout your professional and family life, you not only absorbed all the virtues your father and I wanted to instill in you, but you firmly believed in them. From the day you brought home your first high school diploma, to your professional achievements, to your role as a family man, your father and I never ceased to be proud of you. We both loved you deeply, very deeply. I still do my dearest André.

Then came your marriage to Julie. Do you have any idea how elated your father was as we led you to the altar? You continued to make us very happy when your lovely little girls were born and whenever we saw you as a successful and fulfilled man adored by his wife and his children.

Your father often used to tell me that when looking at you, he saw himself, he saw an unbroken chain of Lagassés who for generations had believed in their faith and had given their best to make this a better world.

This my dear son, concludes the second part of my or should I call it your story. To put it into a few words, you grew up, reached adulthood and maturity as any normal child in a close-knit, loving family would.

* * * * *

But then, one day, something happened that was to change my life forever. Believe me, I am still shuddering when I go back in my mind over the events that unfolded when you were just over twenty years old, twenty-three to be precise. We were all coming back from a vacation in the Caribbean. I checked my phone calls and as I did, I suddenly felt as if someone had hit me over the head. There was a message from Anna, asking me to call her back. Why on earth would she want to talk to me, more than twenty years after she had vanished from my life? I thought she lived in Toronto. I had not heard from her in all these years. So, why this call? I did not like this at all. I debated whether I should ignore it, but my reasoning urged me not to.

The next morning I called the number. I hardly recognized her voice, but it was Anna. I managed a 'How are you. Why are you calling me?'

'I need to talk to you.' She replied 'I am in Montreal for a few days. Can we meet tomorrow?' My answer came before she had finished her question. 'No.' I said. 'No, Anna, I am not going to meet you tomorrow or any other time. You have no right to call me and you know it. Please leave me alone. I am sorry, Anna,' I said 'but I cannot talk to you.' I was about to put an end to our conversation, but she cut me off.

'Listen, my dear,' she said, 'you and I are no strangers, you know. I would not be so gruff if I were you. I have an important reason for asking you to meet me. You better come. That's all I can tell you over the phone. There is a small pizza place on the Main, corner of Roy and St. Lawrence. It is called "Luigi's". How about 2 o'clock tomorrow afternoon? Of course this is just between you and me. You come alone, eh?' She hung up.

I was speechless and scared. Not only did I not expect to hear from her, but her voice was very unfriendly, even menacing. Why would she want to talk to me after all these years? No need to tell you that I spent a sleepless night going over different scenarios, all of them scary and ominous. To Pierre, I feigned a sudden headache.

Anna was already sitting at a table in the back of Luigi's when I walked into the seedy and smelly pizza parlour. She had put on a lot of weight since I last saw her and looked a far cry from the pretty girl I had known.

We both ordered coffee. Anna started the conversation with a cursory 'Hi, Marie-Louise.', which I countered with an equally cursory 'Hi, Anna, what's up?'

'OK.' She said, 'Here's the story.' As she began talking it seemed to me that she was reciting a well-rehearsed monologue. She was not nervous and her words were to the point.

'Jack and I were married for almost twenty years. He died about a year ago from a massive heart attack right at his desk at work. Shortly after his passing, the manager of the bank he worked for called me to his office and told me that they had just discovered that Jack had systematically defrauded the bank for many years. He placed a pile of files on the table in front of him. Looking at me he said "Mrs. Miller, your husband stole about a million from his clients' accounts over the years and here is all the evidence that the audits we just finished have brought to light.
Of course the bank will reimburse its defrauded customers. Out of respect for a dead man and for other reasons we will not press charges, but, I am sure you will understand that you will not be eligible for any pension, except for his government old-age security. Were you aware of all this?" I was not and said so. Well, the bank manager said "You can inspect all the audit findings and all his records if you wish. I am sorry, but consider yourself lucky that he escaped many years in jail."

Anna continued talking while I listened silently. From what I had heard so far, it was beginning to dawn on me what this meeting was all about.

'Of course,' Anna went on, 'I soon found out that Jack had left nothing in the way of deposits or cash. He must have either gambled the money away or made bad investments. By the way, we had no children. Jack did not want any. It was just him and me. The long and the short of it is that, I am left with practically nothing to pay my bills.'

Anna took a deep breath. "And this is where you come in. I need money, my dear." Needless to say that this "my dear" was far from a term of endearment. It was pure irony mixed with a dash of sarcasm.

My premonition was right. I also knew that Anna was so cocky because she knew full well the catastrophic consequences any divulgence of our secret would entail for me.

I felt very sick, very scared and above all very helpless. Anna was now looking straight into my eyes, waiting for a reaction. I did not know what to say, except the obvious, 'How much do you need?'

'A hundred thousand.' She said calmly. At that point I realized that when I had paid her of for the adoption years ago, I had inadvertently mentioned "Thank God my father left me some money". She had obviously not forgotten that careless remark of mine.

'A hundred thousand.' I said, 'Are you out of your mind?'

'No,' she said, 'I'm not. Considering what you are buying, it's a good deal. So, say we meet in three days at the drugstore right across the street at the same hour, that is 2:00 p.m. and you bring a bag with a hundred thousand dollars in cash. Any denomination will do. Of course you come alone and tell no one anything about this, or the deal is off. You know what I mean, don't you?' Anna got up and walked straight out without another word. I paid for the coffees and left the place a minute later.

To tell you the truth, I had suspected something of the sort after her curt phone call, but I never thought that Anna would blackmail me. I had been living in a fool's paradise all these years. I could not believe it, but there it was. One hundred thousand dollars or else. This in addition to the fifty thousand I had already given her at the time of the adoption. What I really dreaded as I drove home from the seedy pizza parlour was that Anna would be encouraged by my ready compliance to ask for more.

What was I to do? Of course, I could not go to the police. In fact I could not discuss this with anyone in the world. Even the lawyer who had helped me had meanwhile passed away.

After a sleepless night during which I kept mulling over all kinds of possible alternatives I came to the bitter conclusion that I really had no choice. I just could not opt for the disclosure of what had happened so many years ago in the Vermont clinic. I just could not bear the sight of you looking at me "is it true, Mom? Am I not who I thought I was?" Or your father looking at me with bewildered eyes. I just could not bear the consequences of Anna revealing the truth.

I paid up, André. I dipped into my dad's inheritance and paid Anna one hundred thousand dollars, all in cash, as she had demanded. However, when I gave her the money I told her very clearly "that was it". No more. Not a penny more. She looked at me silently and nodded gravely which I took for some sign of understanding or agreement.

As you can imagine, this unexpected confrontation with a past I had pushed back into the remotest corner of my memory profoundly changed my life. Not outwardly, but inside me. I kept ruminating on all sorts of "what if?" I conjured up all kinds of ominous scenarios, all of which made me feel sick.

Of course, neither your father nor you were aware of the trauma I was going through. I did my best to hide it all from you and I am sure I succeeded. Only once did your father catch me crying during a sleepless night. I came up with some silly explanation and promised him that "all would be fine in the morning".

A few months went by and I did not hear anything from Anna. I was beginning to forget the whole episode like you do with a bad dream. Life went on, you continued to make your dad and myself very happy with your excellent marks at University. Your father too did very well at his construction firm. He was now General Manager of the company and what's more, he sat on the board of three major Quebec corporations. We took vacations more frequently and as you know your father bought a beautiful home in Palm Beach, Florida. Everything seemed to be going our way.

But then, whammo. The proverbial lightning struck. Again. This time it came in the form of a phone call one day around noon. With the same terse intonation, Anna asked me to meet her in the same seedy pizza parlour on St. Lawrence Boulevard. I tried to shake her off, saying I was going away and in any case, I had no more money to pay her. To this she replied, "That's fine Marie-Louise. I am sure your husband will not want to see this episode spill into the public domain. Not now that he has just become the top dog of his company. Perhaps I should involve him too? Listen, Marie-Louise," she said, before hanging up, 'be there tomorrow at two.'

Of course I was there in the same seedy, smelly place. Even sipping coffee from the stained cup was revolting. Anna came immediately to the point. 'I want another hundred thousand from you. This time, I cannot give you three days, but only two. I have to return to Toronto by Friday. So, you have tomorrow and the next day to get the cash together and give it to me, like last time.'

I could not hold back tears and started to cry. I tried hard not to attract attention in the restaurant. Luckily we were sitting in a dark corner and there was no one around except a sloppily dressed waitress.

'I cannot give you that money.' I said, 'I don't have it.'

'How come?' she said. 'When we were in Vermont you spoke about an inheritance from your father. Don't tell me you spent it all on fancy clothes?' How stupid of me to have mentioned my father's money to her, but then, twenty odd years ago Anna was a frightened innocent-looking young woman who looked to me as the angel from heaven who had saved her baby and indeed her life. This was now a totally different person. Tough, mean and merciless. Her only concession before she got up was 'You pay this money and I will not bother you again. I promise. Does it make you feel any better? Get me the money and I'll be out of your hair.' Like last time, she got up and without looking back walked out of the place.

*****

André, I guess I should tell you at this point that my dear father had left me three hundred thousand dollars. With the ups and downs of the markets, this sum had of course swollen to more but not too much more. If I gave Anna another hundred thousand, I dipped deeply into the kitty. My nest egg would be mostly gone. I need not tell you that although your father was earning good money, every person wants and indeed needs a little nest egg, stashed away in a safety deposit box, just in case. You never know in life.

What was I to do? Again, I had not a living soul to discuss the mess I was in. No one!

Of all the pain and agony I went through, the hardest was to hide it all from your father and to pretend that all was fine and dandy in our little world. It was terribly difficult to carry on as if nothing unusual had happened.

Well, you guessed it, two days later I was there with two bulging shopping bags stuffed with the loot. Without a word, not even a "thank you", Anna took the two bags and briskly walked away. I just had time to tell her 'No more. That's it, goodbye!' To which she nodded and mumbled a 'Yap. Goodbye.'

My dearest André, I wish I could tell you that that was the end of the story and that Anna had sucked enough out of me to let me and all of us live in peace. But, it was not to be. Anna came back, less than a year later.

André, what I am now going to tell you will shock you. It will make your world stand on its head. You will not believe what you read and yet, you better believe it. Your mother accomplished it all with her own manicured and elegant hands.

It was a few days after your graduation from McGill's engineering school when I found a small envelope marked "Private" among the mail. It was a note from Anna. "Marie-Louise, I just read about my boy's graduation. I am so proud of him. He looks wonderful. I feel I should congratulate him and I have a strong urge to tell him who is who. You can't deny this to a mother, can you? You can avoid all this by bumping up the sum with another fifty thousand. If you make it a round figure, say two hundred and fifty thousand, I solemnly swear I will let you off the hook, for good. I swear. Phone the number on this page and tell me where and when. Make it fast."

Well, this little note did it! Now I knew that I had fallen prey to a criminal who would stop at nothing to blackmail me and go on blackmailing me. Of course I did not believe a word about stopping at the "round figure". And of course I did not doubt for a second that she would not hesitate to contact you and even your father and reveal a past that would put an end to my world and to our world, as we knew it.

Oh, André, I was lost and desperate. My mind raced to come up with a plan to face the doom, the catastrophe about to hit me.

André, almost thirty years have gone by since these events took place.

For thirty years I carried a horrible secret in my bosom. I sheltered you and your father from the truth, but now that your dad has passed away, I will tell you everything. Your father lived his life out without knowing the truth, but you must know.

This, André, my dearest André is what happened on that October evening in our penthouse in the Sherbrooke street apartment.

I was scared and desperate. I decided that the only way I could save our lives as we had been living them for all these years was to somehow get rid of Anna. Once this idea was firmly established in my mind, I proceeded to implement it without delay. There was no other way.

I knew that your father would be away in Toronto on an important company meeting lasting three days. I picked those three days for my undertaking. I knew that your father had many years ago brought back a stun gun, some kind of Taser from one of his African business trips. The company had given him the device for self-defence purposes. I took this gun from its box and reading the instructions, loaded and charged it. It works by delivering a powerful electric shock that can temporarily knock out the victim. It is used by police to subdue dangerous people.

Next, I called the number in Anna's note and asked her to come to our apartment where I would give her the fifty thousand dollars, definitely "the last she would ever get from me". I asked her to come in the evening, around 8 p.m. and told her that I would be alone at home, Pierre being away on a business trip.

Then I composed and wrote in block letters a brief suicide note. Something like "I cannot take it any longer. I want to die. Life has no meaning for me anymore since my husband died" and so on. I made it sound very realistic.

Pierre was in Toronto, I was all alone when the bell to our apartment rang. I held the stun gun in my right hand in my pocket. As soon as Anna appeared in the door I pointed the gun at her face and fired the charge. Anna immediately collapsed, in fact, she slumped down like an empty bag. I immediately slipped the suicide note into her pocket and dialled 911. I gave my name and address and shouted into the phone that I had a visitor, an old acquaintance of mine, who keeps going to our balcony as if she wants to jump over the railing. 'I am trying to hold her back, but I need help. Please come immediately to prevent a suicide. She is going again to the balcony as I am talking to you. Hurry, before it is too late!' I shouted into the phone.

Then I dragged the still unconscious Anna by her feet to the balcony and in the dark pushed her against and over the railing into the gaping void in front of me.

I rushed back into the apartment, tidied up everything and phoned 911 again. 'Where are you?' I yelled. No sooner had I put down the receiver than I heard police sirens from the street below, then I saw an ambulance and within minutes two paramedics rang my bell. I shouted at them 'Why did you come so late? We lost her. I had a hard time to talk her out of it and then to hold her back, but her mind was made up. She jumped right in front of my eyes. How terrible.'

Ten minutes later the police came and looked around the apartment. They listened to and noted my account of the suicide. Then they told me that I would have to come to the station the next morning. They asked a few more questions and left. Anna had been taken to a hospital, where she was pronounced dead.

I immediately called your father. He was just having a late night drink with some business friends. I sounded scared and cried. He asked me why my old manicurist would visit me after all these years and why she would choose our apartment to commit suicide. I told him that I had run into her the day before in a Montreal store and had invited her to come up for a coffee or a drink. Your father said that he would take the first plane out of Toronto and that we should go together to the police enquiry. 'Calm down,' he said, 'what a horrible story. Are you alright?' He also told me to call our lawyer immediately.

The next morning your father came back. He had in the meantime talked to the lawyer and we went to the police together. The police had already compiled a dossier. I learned that since her husband's death, Anna lived alone in Toronto, that apart from a sister in Calgary she had no relatives and no children. They found the "suicide note" in her pocket. The police asked me for a statement of what had happened in my apartment that led to Anna's suicide. I told them that Anna was my manicurist many years ago and that I had not seen or heard from her since. However, the day before her suicide I had unexpectedly met her in a Montreal store. We started to talk and Anna told me that she was very depressed because her husband had died without leaving her any money. She also told me that she was desperate because she had arthritis in her hands which prevented her from going back to her profession as a manicurist. In fact, Anna was crying and seemed lost. I told her to come visit me in our apartment and relax over a cup of coffee. I thought that just talking her problems over with me could provide some relief. Well, the following day Anna came, she was agitated and nervous. I asked her to sit down, but she kept walking out to the open balcony, continuing to tell me about her problems. At one point, she stood near the balcony railing and said to me things like "I am lost, I don't know how to cope" and so on. I tried to get her back into the living room but when she kept returning to the balcony, I got scared she might do something crazy. So I ran into the next room to call the police or 911 for help. Then I ran back into the living room. She was holding the railing. I again called 911. This time in front of her, but it was too late. She jumped as I tried to hold on to her jacket.

Since no one claimed the body or laid any charges, the police labelled it an unfortunate suicide. Your father arranged for a funeral, which we attended together with a priest. There was no one else, not even her sister, who claimed to be sick when notified by the undertakers.

One more thing. Nobody ever found the two hundred thousand dollars she had taken from me. She never deposited them in a bank, or it would have been reported following her death. I assumed that she invested the money in some shady business and lost it.

Needless to tell you that your father and I kept talking about this tragic event in which we had been "unwillingly involved, sort of like strangers witnessing a personal tragedy." We talked about it for a while and then forgot about it.

*****

My dearest André, I am telling you about this horrible episode which happened so many years ago as if it was something that happened to someone else. But it did not. It happened to me or rather I made it happen. I, the loving, gentle Marie-Louise Lagassé turned into a cunning murderer and what is more, I got away with it, or so I like to think. No, André, I did not get away with it. To this day it weighs heavily on my conscience. Very heavily.

Why did I do it? Why did I commit this horrible crime? Well, what choice did I have, André? Destroy the life of your father? Destroy his confidence and trust in me? Hit him with the truth that his one and only beloved son was really not his son at all, but that of a blackmailer and an irresponsible lover, furtively conceived out of wedlock. And what about you my dearest boy? What about you? Could I tear you away from your studies, your upcoming career, the position your father was grooming you for with so much pride and love and expose you as an illegitimate offspring?

No, my dear André. I had no choice. I did what I had to do. I made sure that the Lagassé family continued to sail undeterred through all these storms with nary a jolt. "Ignorance is bliss", they say.

I remember when your father was lying in the hospital, knowing full well that the end had come. Dr. Bellefeuille took his hand and looked at him with sad and helpless eyes. In those final moments he looked at me and at you. I saw a faint smile hush over his face. He was happy to have left a Lagassé moulded in his image, in the image of the clan. His life had not been in vain. No one can ask for more from the good Lord when the moment comes to heed the final call.

I feel pride and satisfaction as well as guilt when I look at your pictures on my night table. I see you as a baby, as a cocky hockey player, at graduation and with Julie and the girls. I see you throughout your happy and fulfilled life and I realize that although I did not give you life at birth, I gave you life after birth if you can call it that. But I did it at a very heavy price. I deceived your father and yes, I killed your mother. Make no mistake, André, I killed your mother in cold blood.

What a strange story of a family. A happy father, a happy son and a sinful mother. I still cannot believe that I managed to play such an outwardly serene and normal role when there was so much turmoil in and around me.

And now that your father is gone, that you have grown into maturity and middle age, I know that you can and will cope with the truth.

I brought happiness to your father and to you. And I basked in the warmth of this happiness. But I also took someone's life and that is the cross no one can help me bear.

All I can hope and wish for is that you, my beloved André will forgive me. Please do, my darling son. I could not rest in peace if I knew that you did not forgive me.

*****

André put away the last page. He had read the entire document almost without stopping. Only once or twice did Julie knock on the door to bring him a cup of coffee. He was hardly aware of her brief interruptions.

André sat there in a trance. He felt as though he had been watching a movie that took him into a different world, only it was not a different world. It was his own childhood, his growing up and his adulthood he had just watched come to life again.

Not in a million years would he have suspected what he just read. His mother was obviously not only an extraordinary person but also an extraordinary actress. She never let the slightest sign betray what went on inside her. Her struggles, her pains, her hopes and indeed her agony. To all around her she was a paragon of serenity, of righteousness and of self-confidence. She was Madame Lagassé.

He looked at the pile of handwritten pages. What a story. What an amazing story. He was stunned beyond words.

Gently, as if not wanting to disturb the memories she had brought to life so vividly in her elegant hand-written style, he picked up all the pages and placed them in the fireplace facing his desk. He then took out a small can of lighter fluid, doused the whole pile and lit a match. The flames licked away hungrily at the loose pages. He was fascinated by the sight of the consuming flames. There goes the tale of my life, of my father's and of my mother's lives and of all those whose life my mother touched. What an amazing lady, you were Marie-Louise Lagassé, he said almost audibly.

The flames had died down. He took an empty box and carefully placed all the ashes, scrap by scrap, cinder by cinder into the container. He did not leave the tiniest piece behind, not even the charred remains of the ribbon that had held the bundle together. As he sealed the box, the said to himself, 'Mom, you took your secret to your grave and so will I. I promise you.'

He got into his car and drove to a florist where he bought a dozen red roses, his mom's favourites. Then he drove to the cemetery and asked one of the attendants for a shovel. 'Can we help you?' said the man. 'No, thank you.' André replied. "I'll return it to you shortly.'

He stood in front of the gravesite. He felt as if she stretched her arms out to hold him close to her chest. With the shovel he dug away a few loads of fresh moist earth until he had created enough of a hole to hold the box of ashes. He placed it in the depression and heaped as much earth as he could on top of it. When all of it was done, he evened the surface and placed the bouquet of roses diagonally over the grave, as if to pay tribute to a person whose life had been unusual and out-of-the-ordinary.

He stepped back and could not contain his tears. Just a few days ago he had come to bury his mother's body. Now he had come to bury her very soul. He felt her spirit all around him. A spirit of love and sacrifice, of determination and strength.

He was so proud to have been Marie-Louise's son.

THE INHERITANCE

David F. McLear had every reason to be proud of himself. At the age of twenty-one, he had inherited a small kitchen furniture store from his father and had turned it into a major kitchen supplier during a hectic forty-two year span. There were McLear Kitchen Centres in most major US cities, including Honolulu, offering kitchen furniture as well as complete installations, all at affordable and very competitive prices.

David McLear ran his company with a strong hand matched only by his ego. Nobody but nobody told David what to do. He was the boss of the enterprise. No wonder that his son Robert found it extremely difficult to integrate into and then to manage his father's company. At every step he had to suffer criticism and violent outbursts, until one day he called it quits and told his father that he had had enough of being treated like a schoolboy. Robert left his father's company and, since selling kitchens was the only business he knew, he set up his own company specializing in kitchen cabinetry. Needless to say that this competitive course of action earned Robert unmitigated disdain and even hatred from his father, who promptly disinherited him and swore never to talk to him again as long as he lived.

This turn of events was sad indeed, especially since Robert was the only child of Bettina and David McLear. If David ran his business like an autocrat, he did not do much better in managing his family. His wife had long ago given up any hope of reforming or domesticating her husband. Over the years, she adapted to the situation by participating in a hectic social life of her own. Except for her occasional bouts with migraine, she would leave the house around 11 AM and not return much before dinnertime. A dedicated housekeeper took care of practically all the household chores. For all intents and purposes Bettina and David lead separate lives, especially after their son had reached his late teens.

But then one day, shortly after her forty-ninth birthday, Bettina noticed a lump in her back. She had it checked out, only to receive the devastating news that it was a malignant tumour. It had already spread to other parts of her body. Bettina was not fifty when she succumbed to metastatic cancer after months of alternating hope and despair.

David took his wife's death with resignation, as if it was the inevitable outcome of bad fortune. Nobody saw him cry, but then he was not given to emotionality anyway. About a year after her death, David, now in his early sixties, met a stunning forty-one-year-old divorced lady at a friend's dinner party. Janet had everything to make any man take a second, third and fourth look. She had a beautiful face framed by long blond hair, bright blue eyes and full lips with sparkling white teeth brightening up her face every time she laughed, which was very often. Her figure was stunning, and she wore her clothes with casual elegance.

David did not waste any time in asking Janet out and sending her flowers. He hadn't done that for Bettina since the early years of their marriage. Within the next few months their relationship became more intimate. Despite the difference in age, Janet found David to be a spirited lover and she was impressed by his very assertive and no-nonsense attitude towards life.

When reflecting on the wisdom of her relationship with a much older man, she reasoned, what do I have to lose? He provides abundant gifts, sex, entertainment, travel and whatever makes the difference between watching TV at home and an active and interesting lifestyle. One thing was sure though, she was definitely not in love with David. Yet, she did not see a reason for not carrying on this relationship for as long as it would last.

About a year later, David proposed marriage, but Janet politely dodged an immediate answer, saying she needed time to think it over. In the meantime, their relationship continued as before.

One evening, while Janet was waiting for David to pick her up for dinner at her favourite restaurant, she received a phone call from his housekeeper, informing her that Mr. McLear had suffered a heart attack earlier that afternoon and was now in hospital. Janet immediately rushed over to the Intensive Care Unit, where she briefly saw David and talked to his doctors.

Apparently David had had a massive heart attack. His chances of survival were reasonably good, but since the infarcted area on the myocardium was unusually large, his recovery would be slow. The doctors warned her that he would have to lead a somewhat restricted life, at least for the foreseeable future. Janet took a keen interest in everything the doctors were telling her.

Three weeks later, David was back home, pampered and tended by his housekeeper as well as by Dr. Peter Drummond, his personal physician of long standing. Under their watchful eye and tender care, David made remarkable progress and started to enjoy many aspects of day-to-day living.

David's cardiac accident had provoked a great deal of cold-blooded reflection in Janet's mind. What if she accepted his proposal? After all, he was a very wealthy man and he was also a very sick man. If she managed to be in his will, it probably wouldn't take too long before she could be a very wealthy widow. A few days later she said "Yes" to David over dinner and a glass of wine.

David was elated. He kissed his bride-to-be, and together they made plans for a quiet and simple wedding. Janet moved into David's elegant and spacious home, giving up her own apartment.

One sunny weekend shortly afterwards, David and Janet were married in a simple ceremony at a downtown hotel. A few people attended, but David's son was not among them. The day after the wedding, David asked his wife to come with him to his notary, where he drew up a new will in which he left the sum of forty-five million dollars in cash and assets to his wife, Janet.

Outwardly, Janet took it all in with relaxed dignity and a few kisses. Inwardly, Janet felt she had accomplished the greatest coup of her life. She had made it!

The McLears settled down to a comfortable and elegant lifestyle, somewhat restricted by David's occasional pains, discomfort and constant need for medication. Dr. Drummond became a quasi-permanent fixture of the household since he often supervised his patient's physiotherapy and cardiac monitoring to make sure that the recovery was uneventful and smooth.

A few months after the wedding, Janet went to Dr. Drummond's office, telling him she wanted to discuss her husband's progress. The doctor told her that her husband had made a remarkable recovery from near death. Although he was still a very sick man because of the extensive scarring of his heart, he could easily live another ten years or more, if properly cared for and if lucky enough to avoid another heart attack. As he said this, Dr. Drummond noticed a visible change in Janet's expression. She was fidgety and seemed to be at a loss for words.

"What's on your mind, Janet?" he asked.

After a pause, she said, "Peter, if David is such a sick man as you say, and if he risks suffering another heart attack any time, what is the reason for prolonging the agony for him and me?" She looked the doctor straight into his eyes and awaited an answer.

There was none. Dr. Drummond immediately realised the reason for her visit and the implications of the words he had just heard.

Janet continued. "You know, of course, that I am the sole heir to some forty-five million dollars. In view of what you just told me, would it not be sad if I had to stand by for ten years or more watching my husband's declining health until the inevitable and merciful end came?

Dr. Drummond continued to listen silently.

"Let me be clear," she continued. "If you, his doctor, can provide an end to his suffering in such a way that it comes completely naturally and is undetectable by any forensic investigation, I am prepared to give you one third of the inheritance, fifteen million."

Dr. Drummond was flabbergasted by what he had just heard. But as Janet unfolded her plan in a very businesslike manner, he began to realize that he was witnessing her true personality. She had obviously married David with his money in mind, and for no other reason. Once he accepted this fact, he was no longer amazed or disturbed by her words.

Without any sign of emotion, he looked at her and managed a "Hum, that is some proposal, Janet. I was not prepared for this."

"So," she said, "do we have an agreement?"
"Well" he replied, "You are talking about a very grave and risky course of action. You have obviously given this a lot of thought and you expect me to agree immediately? I want to think it over very carefully before I decide to stick my neck out."

Janet was obviously disappointed.

"This must be the most profitable risk you have ever taken in your life. I am sure you will accept my offer. Call me within the next twenty-four hours", she said.

She grabbed her purse and breezed out of the room before Dr. Drummond could show her out.

It did not take long for Dr. Drummond to collect his thoughts. Many conflicting ideas entered his mind. He was a middle-aged G.P., long past the age when doctors climb the ladder to academic success and wealth. Apart from a few savings, he had not much to show for his many years in practice. Fifteen Million Dollars was one hell of a lure. And yet, there was no doubt in his mind that he would never participate in any attempt whatsoever on David's life.

He reflected long what he should do next. Two things were clear to him: He had to somehow warn David about his wife's sinister schemes and he had to help Robert to receive some of the inheritance money he had been deprived of by his irrational father.

Two days after his conversation with Janet, Dr. Drummond called on David McLear. After a routine medical examination he told his patient: "David, I am your doctor and not your family counselor, but if I was in your place I would reconsider my earlier decision and reinstate Robert as a rightful heir. He is your son, isn't he? Everybody knows that you left everything to Janet. Why? What do you really know about her? She'll be laughing all the way to the bank when you're gone. Think it over, David."

As Dr. Drummond was talking, he noticed that his patient was shaking his head and was getting very upset.

"Janet is the most caring and most devoted person I have ever met. She deserves every penny of my money. As for my son, he's a good-for-nothing bum, and my decision to disinherit him stands as firm as it did years ago."

Dr. Drummond tried to make more derogatory remarks about Janet, including an insinuation that she may even try to get rid of him. David became very furious. He slapped his open hand on the table and shouted:

" I've had enough of this. I don't want to hear another word. I know that my good-for-nothing son is behind all this. I'm surprised and furious that you became his tool. I resent your interference in my family affairs."

He wrote a cheque for Dr. Drummond.

"Thank you for your services. As of now you're released. I'll get myself another doctor. Thank you and goodbye."

He handed the cheque to Dr. Drummond and got up to open the door for the hurriedly departing doctor.

A few days later, David told Janet that he desperately wanted to take a nice long vacation with her, perhaps a boat cruise, combined with a leisurely stay in the south of France. He asked her to make the travel arrangements. Two weeks later the McLears left for what you might call a dream vacation. A two-week cruise on a super luxurious liner visiting Mediterranean ports and another week on the French Riviera. The travel agent chose the best ship and the most elegant hotels in Cannes and Monte Carlo.

David was happy like a child. He felt that this change of venue would improve his health problems.

During the next two weeks the couple visited Spain, Italy, Greece, Turkey, Egypt and Morocco. When they finally landed in Marseilles to board the train to Cannes, they were both convinced they had spent the two most beautiful weeks in their entire life. On the train ride they talked endlessly about the various places they had visited. They were now looking forward to a restful week among elegant people, walks on the promenades and perhaps some gambling in the casino. But, it was not to be. On the second night of their arrival at the Negresco Hotel, David was suddenly taken by violent chest pains. He was rushed to a nearby hospital. With Janet at his side, he was pronounced dead of cardiac arrest as a result of a second massive coronary thrombosis.

As soon as the formalities were completed, Janet flew back to the U.S.A with her husband's body. A funeral was arranged a few days later. It was attended by a large crowd of family and friends. To Janet's surprise, her husband's son and Dr. Drummond attended.

Without wasting any time, Janet called her husband's lawyer, asking him to execute the will and to transfer the inherited amount of cash and securities into her bank account. The lawyer replied that he would need a little time for the probate and other formalities, but that everything should go very smoothly. He added that Janet could look forward to a very comfortable life indeed.

While the lawyer was tending to the formalities, Janet received a phone call from Robert. He inquired if he and Dr. Drummond could meet with her to discuss a matter of "common interest." Janet immediately replied that she was not aware of any "common interests" between them and that she had no intention of meeting them.

Robert told her: "Oh really. I wouldn't be so sure, if I were you! We do have some common interests and unless you prefer to be faced with some unpleasant surprises, I suggest we meet tomorrow afternoon in Dr. Drummond's private office."

Robert's voice was firm. He was waiting for an answer.

Janet thought fast. She realized that evading this meeting would only delay and not eliminate whatever Robert had in mind.

"Okay, I'll be there at 3 PM." Without waiting for an answer, she hung up.

Punctually, at three the next day, she entered Dr. Drummond's office. Both he and Robert were already there. Janet was the first to talk.

"I really don't know why I'm here," she said "If you're referring to the inheritance, you better forget that subject altogether. My husband died of natural causes, and his will will be executed according to the laws of the land. Is there anything else you wanted to discuss? I have to be somewhere in half an hour. I don't like to be late."

Robert looked at her and at Dr. Drummond. "Yes, Janet, there is something we want to discuss. My father left an amount of some forty-five million dollars. Both I, his legitimate and only son, and Dr. Drummond, who treated him for many years, want a part of the inheritance. Let me be very clear: we want you to share the forty-five million three ways: Twenty for you, twenty for me and five for Dr. Drummond."

Janet's face turned a deep red.

"What!" she screamed. "You want to share? You should have behaved differently towards your father if you wanted to inherit money from him. He disinherited you, and that's that! As for you, Dr. Drummond, how dare you claim anything! You were paid for your services and you know that David died of natural causes following a second heart attack. I refuse to continue this conversation. Besides, you have nothing to support any claim. Nothing!"

Janet grabbed her bag and was about to get up, when Dr. Drummond said, "Not so fast, Mrs. McLear! Not so fast!"

He opened his drawer and took out a cassette tape.

"This, Janet," he said, "is the account of your statement in this office when you asked me to murder your husband. Let me be precise: I had your voice electronically verified by a court-approved expert as being yours and nobody else's. This tape leaves absolutely no doubt of your request to me to kill your husband in order to put your hands on the inheritance. Do you want to listen to your words? As for David's death in a hospital on the French Riviera, you have no coroner's report, no autopsy. Just a form they filled in giving your husband's name and age, his address, the cause of death and the date. Any court will have no difficulty in establishing a possible relationship between David's death and your recorded intention to kill him.

"Janet, between the tape in my hand and the simple note issued by a local French hospital, not to mention that the will in your favour was signed by a severely depressed patient recuperating from a massive heart attack, there is enough incriminating evidence for David to contest the will. In my files, I have several reports from psychiatrists treating David during his post-infarction depressive state. Janet, you will have one hell of a time trying to hang on to anything your husband left you! I mean anything."

Janet had listened to Dr. Drummond intensely. At first, she seemed defiant, ready to fight her way out of this situation. But when she saw the tape and remembered her incriminating proposal, she turned very pale and slumped back into the seat. Her hands were shaking. She clutched a handkerchief to wipe the sweat from her beautiful face, which suddenly seemed to have lost all its glamour. She looked around the room without saying a word.

Dr. Drummond thought that he had made his point.

"You have no choice, Janet," he said. "You really don't! We strongly suggest that you avoid discussing this conversation with your lawyer or anyone else. I'm sure you'll come up with a suitable explanation for sharing your inheritance."

Janet had difficulty getting up from her seat. After a long silence, she said dryly, "Yeah, I'm sure I'll come up with a suitable explanation."

*****

Readers of the Los Angeles Times could not miss it: there, in a column on the first page, was a news item that was also picked up by several national TV and radio stations and even made it to the pages of the international press. Under the heading: HONESTY AND GENEROSITY ALIVE AND WELL, it said: "WIDOW AND SOLE HEIR TO THE MCLEAR FORTUNE SHARES MILLIONS WITH DISINHERITED SON AND DEVOTED DOCTOR." The item described how Mrs. Janet McLear, legitimate heiress to her husband's fortune of forty-five million dollars, decided to voluntarily give up part of this amount to the disinherited son and another part to Dr. Peter Drummond, who had diligently attended her sick husband for many years. The article concluded by praising the outstanding generosity and selfless magnanimity of Mrs. Janet McLear, calling her a rare "angel" in an otherwise greedy world.

THE VERMONT VACATION

Funerals, by definition, are sombre and moving events honouring the departed and providing family and friends with an opportunity to pay their last respects.

Lillian Malevski's was no different, or perhaps not entirely so.

After the customary prayers and the rabbi's solemn dedication, her son Alan delivered a short but very poignant eulogy, extolling the virtues and contributions of his beloved mother. He chose his words carefully and frequently wiped a tear from his eyes, but when he came to the end of his oration, he said:

"As some of you may know, my mother was an avid reader of crime and suspense stories and often told us the outcome of the plot halfway through the story. In all the years I cannot recall a single case where she erred. She was always dead right in identifying the culprit well before any of us would even begin to speculate. I guess she was a born detective, who in another world and in another life would have ranked with the likes of Sherlock Holmes and Hercule Poirot.

True, she always enjoyed our applause and 'bravos' whenever she rightly predicted the outcome of a case, but what she really craved for was standing in the public limelight for having solved yet another crime. Oh how she would have loved the accolade!

Well, all I can say is better late than never, Mom!"

The ceremony ended with some more prayers, including the cantor's moving incantation of the mourner's lament. And then the procession slowly left the parlour for burial at the nearby cemetery.

As the crowd filed out behind the casket, many asked each other what Lilly's son had meant by his last words: "better late than never", but no one seemed to really know. Some said that they heard rumors, but were not sure.

They were all to have their curiosity rewarded when, a few days later, the Montreal daily newspaper published a lengthy report under the ominous heading *"Bizarre Death of Montreal Woman"*.

This is a rendition of the story, bizarre indeed!

* * * * *

It all started with a conversation at the Malevski family's kitchen table in their Hampstead home. While dessert was being served, Alan, the father of the two teenage girls said "I have a surprise for you. I made reservations today for a two week vacation at a brand new luxury hotel and spa in Charlotte, south of Burlington, Vermont , right on Lake Champlain. I have the brochures here. It is a beautiful place. They have everything: beaches, swimming pools, tennis courts, bicycle trails, there is sailing on the lake and all the entertainment you want. And this is just the hotel. Then there is a spa with all the facilities. Something for every one of us, including for mom. In addition, the place is just minutes away from the county hospital, just in case mom is not feeling well, but I am sure we will not need any hospital. Just knowing it's there is enough.

So, what say all of you? Do I get advance kisses? Everyone at the table shouted approvals. The dates were set for the first two weeks of July. They were all very excited and planted noisy kisses on Alan's cheeks.

* * * * *

Alan Malevski was a busy fifty-two year old physician with a family practice in three different locations: a hospital, a private clinic, and a community medical center. His wife, Sarah, now in her late forties was a one-time social worker who had married Alan twenty-two years ago. They had two pretty and intelligent daughters: Julie, sixteen and Lynn, fourteen. They were all very close and devoted to each other, in fact, the Malevskis could easily be described as a well-adjusted family.

Rounding out the group was Alan's mother Lillian, better known as Lilly. Now in her early eighties, she had lost her husband many years ago. She was still very active and very much attuned to whatever went on around her. The two girls loved her. Over the years Nanny had become sort of a confidante to them.

But Nanny had a problem and a serious one at that. She had a bad heart. For years she was being treated for cardiac dysfunction, but then it worsened to the point that during the past year she had to undergo not only by-pass but also valve replacement surgery.

She went through all these woes with courage and hope for better days. She was now in her third month after the operations and was beginning to feel well enough to lead an almost normal life which included walks, work at home and of course baking the best marble cakes this side of Vienna, as vouched by all those who were fortunate enough to bite into them.

But baking was not her only hobby. She was also an avowed fiend of crime and suspense stories, in fact she devoured them, often stopping in the midst of a whodunit to guess and write down who done it. And, believe it or not she was never wrong.

* * * * *

Time went by very quickly in anticipation of the planned vacation, until finally, one afternoon. Shortly after Alan had come home from his clinic everyone climbed into the brand new white BMW for its maiden trip to Vermont.

In the front seat, next to the driver, sat Sarah, right behind her, loaded with electronic gadgets and earphones sat Julie and Lynn. In the back was Nanny who could either sit or lie down comfortably between two cushions and a blanket.

Everyone was in high spirits, and although Sarah had run back to the house at least three times to make sure all the water taps were closed, the alarms were set and all the lights were off except those that could deter prospective burglars, Alan hit the road, heading east and then south to the U.S. which they reached after about two hours on account of his overly careful driving.

In fact, he constantly shouted: "You're O.K. Mom?"

Which was answered with: "I'm fine dear, just fine."

They arrived in Burlington, where Alan left the Interstate 89 and turned into Route 7 which follows the lake in an almost straight southern direction.

Alan must have driven half an hour or so when his mother suddenly started moaning and then shouted: "I can't breathe, stop the car."

Alan immediately pulled to the side of the road and ran out to get to his mother on the rear seat. She was very pale and had difficulty breathing. Alan quickly grabbed the oxygen bottle and the defibrillator he had wisely brought with him without telling anyone.

Stretching his mother out on the back seat he immediately applied all the resuscitation procedures prescribed in case of a cardiac arrest. Calmly and professionally he went through cardiac massage, defibrillation, oxygen and injections. He also closely monitored her heart function and other vital signs.

Alan must have worked for almost one hour and sweat was now running from his front.

Finally, he got up and said in a sombre voice. "she didn't make it, we lost her. It was a massive attack and she had no chance, sorry, I'm so sorry."

He started to cry and so did the rest of the family which was standing outside the car under a street lamp. Darkness had by now fallen.

It was a very sad sight. the whole family was crying and holding on to each other.

Finally Alan stepped aside and, pulling his cell phone from his pocket, dialled 911. He gave a brief report of what had happened and after a cursory conversation was told to proceed to the next exit and drive some eight miles to the county hospital in order to let the staff take out the body from the car and do what is necessary, including filling out all the reports and forms.

Noticing he was very low on gas, he said: "I need gas!" "that's O.K." the voice said "On your way to the hospital there is a gas station. you can fill up there, but proceed to the hospital right after filling up." "Thank you for your help" , said Alan. "I'm on my way."

They all got back into the car and Alan continued to drive South on Route 7. After some ten minutes he saw the gas station which also had an adjoining rest area. He stopped and asked the attendant to fill up the car with premium gas. As the attendant shouted: "yes sir", both Julie and Lynn said: "Daddy, we both have to go to the washroom. It's a must, daddy!" "O.K.," said Simon. Whereupon Sarah walked with the two girls to the rest room.

After a few minutes, the attendant said. "it's seventy-two dollars, sir." Alan gave him his credit card, and realized that he also had an urge to visit the men's room.

As soon as the attendant was back with the bill Alan said to him: "Can I park the car for a few minutes, we will all be back shortly."

"Sure" said the attendant. "Just drive around the wall here on your right and park the car behind it." Which Alan promptly did. He then ran out of the car in the direction of the men's room.

* * * * *

Pete, the gas station attendant who had just told Alan where to park, was actually part of a roaming gang of car thieves who had a considerable number of thefts to their credit. When he filled up the spanking new BMW he knew exactly what to do.

Not aware of Lillian Malevski's body lying on the backseat, he immediately phoned his accomplices, telling them where the BMW had just been parked.

Within minutes they were on the spot, lowered two ramps to the ground, jump started Alan's car and drove it straight inside the small truck. Then they pulled up the ramps closed the back doors and drove off as fast as they had come.

* * * * *

A few minutes later, the Malevskis emerged from the restrooms, heading for their parked car, but there was no car in sight.

Alan was stunned. He ran back to the gas station and shouted: "where is my car?" "It must be where you parked it, sir." was the answer. "No it is not there!" answered Alan. "Come see for yourself."

The attendant walked behind the wall with Alan and shouted: "my God, you are right. Its gone." "How could my car disappear!" shouted Alan.

" I don't know. I was busy at the pump. I guess it was stolen, sir." "But we were only away for ten minutes, or less." said Alan. " I know." replied the attendant "those guys work fast."

"What do I do now?" screamed Alan. "call the police, sir. I'll do it for you." Whereupon he took out his cell phone from his pocket and dialled.

Within minutes a police cruiser appeared and two troopers jumped out of the car.

Both Alan and the attendant told them what had happened and Alan also reported that in the back seat was the body of his mother who had just passed away and that they were on their way to the hospital to report the death. Alan also added that he had already notified 911 of what happened.

The two troopers looked around the gas pump and the area where Alan's car had been parked, but they could not see much in the dark.

They talked to the attendant who repeated he had not seen the car after it left the pump.

A few minutes later, the policemen told Alan: "Sir, there is little we can do tonight other than issue an APB for the stolen car. We will be here early tomorrow morning to continue our investigation. In the mean time let us take you and your family to a nearby motel so that you can all spend the night there. You, Sir, are required to give us a full report as to what happened while sitting down in the Motel lobby, O.K.?"

And that's exactly what happened. Sarah and the two girls went to their room and Alan sat up for about an hour relating the exact course of events to the two troopers, who took notes.

An hour later, an exhausted Alan found his wife and two girls in their room. They were all exhausted and after a light snack went to sleep.

* * * * *

Meanwhile the two car thieves drove their truck to the backyard of one of the accomplices and started to paint the BMW a dark crimson red. As they prepared their gear they looked into the back seat and to their surprise discovered Lillian's body. Horrified, they phoned their pal at the gas station to tell him of their discovery.

"I know" Pete said "Just heard about it from the driver, it came as a surprise to me too." "So what do we do now?" said his friend. "Get rid of it. What else!" was the reply, adding: "While Johnny starts the paint job you pull the body into your car, drive it to the wooded area behind the church and bury her underneath a tree, but make sure you pick an isolated spot, you know, away from the main road. O.K.? Do it now before any troopers start snooping around." "I'm on my way, Pete." replied the man.

While his friend started to paint, he pulled and lifted the body into his nearby car, drove to the small woods and buried the corpse in a secluded spot. Then, he covered the site with some branches and leaves he had gathered around him. Satisfied with his work, he drove back to help his friend put the final touches to the paintjob.

The two car thieves now looked at a shiny crimson BMW fitted with a Vermont license plate. After locking up their truck-*cum*-paint shop they both got into the stolen car and headed for Concorde, New Hampshire, where they would deliver it to the largest car theft ring on the east coast. Cash on the barrel and a bus back to Vermont ready for their next foray.

* * * * *

The next morning, shortly after eight, two troopers and detective inspector Garry Wilson from the state police headquarters in Montpellier arrived at the motel and took Alan back to the gas station. Inspector Wilson, a veteran officer, had been asked to lead the investigation on account of the dead woman.

The police started looking for clues that might help them. They questioned the attendant again only to hear him repeat: "I am as stunned as you are. I have no idea how the thieves could have driven away with the car, I never saw the van after it was parked behind that wall."

But the inspector did find some clues. He saw the tread marks left by the new BMW's tires in the moist soil and followed them for a few metres, after which they abruptly disappeared.

He concluded correctly that the car was driven up a ramp into a waiting truck after having being jumpstarted by the thieves.

He had no idea what the truck looked like and was convinced that the thieves had already seen to it that the external side panels had been altered to avoid recognition by any possible eyewitness at the gas station.

* * * * *

In the meantime, Alan had phoned his insurance company in Montreal to report the incident. They told him to make sure the local police had all the facts on records, including the details about his dead mother. They also advised him that they were making arrangements for a rental car to be delivered to his motel.

An hour later the family was on their way back to Canada.

What a sad ending to what they were all looking forward to as a great vacation.

* * * * *

Inspector Wilson was fully aware that finding the stolen car was going to be a tough nut to crack on account of hundreds similar BMW vehicles on the road. He therefore started by looking for the body of Lillian Malevski first.

He figured the thieves had to get rid of the body before using the car, either by dumping it into a river or a lake, which was a risky alternative because the body might surface, or by burying in a field or a forest near a main road, and not too far from the gas station.

He started by dispatching search teams to areas around the scene of the crime.

For two days squads of policemen searched the countryside with no success, but then, on the third day, the Charlotte police station received a call from a school teacher who reported that during an outing with her class in the nearby woods, some kids had noticed a pile of dead branches underneath a tree and below the branches there was freshly dug up earth.

Within minutes the police were on the spot and, yes, they found the remains of Lillian Malevski.

Inspector Wilson had the body taken to the hospital morgue but as he inspected it still wrapped in the blanket with which Alan had covered it, he noticed a tiny red stain on the hem of her skirt. A stain the size of a dime. It felt moist and smelled of fresh paint, he took out his pocket knife and cut out the cloth with the paint on it, which he placed in a small plastic bag.

The inspector then phoned Alan that they had found his mother's remains which were now resting at the hospital morgue. He asked him to come back to Charlotte to identify the body, complete the necessary paper work and make arrangements with the undertaker to have her transported to Montreal.

*****

Inspector Wilson then drove to a local paint shop where he had the sample in his plastic bag identified as car paint and he also obtained the details of the colour.

He now knew that the thieves had painted the white BMW a crimson red. He immediately posted a second APB with the correct colour and shade of the stolen car.

Within minutes tens of police cars in Vermont, New Hampshire and upstate New York started looking for a red BMW SUV. They did not have to look for too long. Two days after the APB had been released, a cruiser from Concord, New Hampshire reported a brightly shining red BMW parked outside a roadside motel on the outskirts of town.

The policemen checked the Vermont licence plate on it only to find out that the plates belonged to a black Ford sedan, also stolen.

They immediately located the drivers through the reception desk and, revolvers drawn, they pushed open the door. They found the two thieves watching TV with beer cans in their hands.

They had been apprehended so quickly that they did not have time to reach for their guns or escape. The two were handcuffed.

The policemen then phoned for reinforcements and within a matter of minutes the arrested men were on their way to the station followed by the recovered BMW driven by another policeman.

Ten minutes later Inspector Wilson phoned Alan to give him the news. "We found your mother and now we found your car. Come with the proper papers and pick it up."

* * * * *

The next morning, Inspector Wilson held a press briefing in which he told the hastily assembled media the whole story. From the unfortunate death of the Montreal lady, to her disappearance in a stolen car to the avalanche of arrests that the theft had already triggered. In fact within hours of finding the BMW a number of middle men and accomplices, all related to the East Coast stolen car syndicate, had been apprehended and were now in custody.

With Alan by his side, the inspector thanked all local and state law enforcement officers who had taken part in the hunt. He then turned to Alan and said "Sir, I want to conclude this conference with a special appreciation of the late Mrs. Lillian Malevski, the real heroine of this incredible story. Had she not carried that tiny spot of red paint on her skirt I would have never found out that the car we were looking for was red and not white. We would still be chasing an inexistent object.

It was she who helped me solve the case. We just followed through.

Frankly, Dr. Malevski, I have been a police officer for nearly 25 years and this is the first time a corpse helped me solve the case. May your mother rest in peace. Please accept our sincere condolences together with our sincere gratitude."

Alan thanked the inspector for his kind words regarding his mother, and all the police officers involved in the case. He then drove back to Montreal in his altered car. Despite his obvious grief there was a faint smile of serenity on his face.

Lilly Malevski's life long dream had finally come true. Sadly too late for her to enjoy.

PARTNERS

One of the most frequently encountered manifestations in the wide realm of personal relations is, no doubt, the twists and turns they undergo throughout a lifetime.

The causes of these changes are obvious: We all have to react and adapt to new and often unexpected situations, which, in turn change our attitudes towards each other, more often than not in a drastic way.

This is the story of one such relationship.

*   *   *

They met on a cold and wet November evening in a small hotel near the Central Railway Station of Basel, Switzerland.

Willy Goldin, the 18 year old son of a wealthy Jewish furrier in Leipzig, Germany and 19 year old Abraham Kozlowski, from Krakow, Poland, who was still wearing a black tie because he had just lost his 42 year old father after a long drawn-out illness.

The year was 1937 and Europe had been turned upside down by a muscle-flexing Nazi Germany goose-stepping to the tune of its leader or "Führer" as he preferred to be called.

Willy and Abe were actually part of some thirty Jewish youngsters who had been spirited out of their countries by tireless and often daring members of the American Jewish Joint Distribution Committee, better known as "The Joint". A relief organization, which ever since 1914, had been rescuing victims and prospective victims of European anti-Semitism, assembling them in neutral countries, and at the first opportunity, taking them to Palestine, which in 1937 was a British mandated territory in the Middle East.

This particular "Joint Meeting" was organized by two representatives in order to inform all thirty members of the group that they would board a train bound for Istanbul three days later and from there they were to travel to Haifa by a Turkish ship. They would be accompanied by one of the "Joint" agents until they reached their destination. Everyone was issued the necessary railway tickets and they were told that British entry visas to Palestine, as well as all other documents would be given to them upon arrival in Istanbul.

Needless to say, all this took place in a very festive mood since everyone was eager and excited to finally reach the safety and opportunities offered by the Holy Land, their future home.

After the meeting, Willy and Abe sat down in the hotel's small restaurant, and, over a glass of beer decided to become friends and to keep together, not only for the rest of their journey, but for good. Both thought that this was a wise decision. They exchanged addresses and details of the next of kin they were now leaving behind in Europe and vowed to help each other like friends do.
"Everything becomes much easier to accomplish, to endure and even to enjoy when it is shared by two people rather than going it alone." This pledge was sealed with a hearty handshake, clicking beer mugs and the exclamation in unison of the old French adage: "L'Union Fait La Force".

Thus, in this small Basel restaurant, filled with the whiff of tobacco smoke and stale beer, was formed the friendship of these two youngsters. A friendship which was to permeate their lives for a good many years.

*   *   *

To use the apt metaphor of the accurate Swiss watch movement, every phase of the group's trip was well-planned and executed.

The journey in the venerable Orient Express took them to Zagreb and Belgrade in Yugoslavia, from there to Sofia and finally into Istanbul's Sirkeci railway station, where they were lovingly welcomed by the resident "Joint" representative as well as by several members of the local Jewish community. Then they were taken to a small hotel.

It took about a week to assemble all the Turkish travel documents and the British visas, but thanks to the frequent interventions of the impatient Joint representatives, everything was finally set for their sea passage to Haifa.

They enjoyed their stay in Istanbul thanks to the care and affection of local Jews who took the group on sightseeing trips and a couple of movies.

In an emotionally charged and festive mood the group of thirty, accompanied by a new "Joint" agent, embarked on their short trip to Haifa, the last leg of their long odyssey from their beleaguered homes in Europe to what was to become their new home. They were all eager to sow their seeds in the biblical ancestral land of which they had only heard and read about in their prayer books.

Willy and Abe had kept in close contact throughout the long journey and felt as if they been good friends for many years, as they disembarked in Haifa. When they were told that they would all be accommodated in different kibbutzim, the two young men asked to be assigned to the same kibbutz.

And so it was that the two friends ended up in a very attractive commune called Beit Oren where the members immediately took them into their hearts.

They were allocated adjoining rooms in the same house. After meeting most of their fellow kibbutzniks, they soon settled down to the very busy, highly regulated daily routine of their agricultural settlement.

Adapting to a completely new life in a very different environment which included a different climate, a new language and the feeling of being part and parcel of a close-knit team, did not come automatically or spontaneously. It had to be developed gradually, but eventually everything fell into its place, primarily thanks to the open-hearted and outreaching attitude of the members around them.

Willy, who had always loved handling machinery, found his vocation as a mechanic, learning how to maintain and repair agricultural equipment, while Abe joined a class of accounting novices, who were learning how to manage the economic and financial affairs of the kibbutz.

For all intents and purposes, Willy Goldin and Abe Kozlowski had become devoted kibbutzniks going about their daily lives.

* * *

Almost seven years had passed since the two had arrived at the kibbutz. Willy was now not only a certified mechanic but also in charge of the tool shop tending to a variety of agricultural machines and devices.

Abe had found his place as one of the four accountants who worked in the finance department.

During these seven years the close, almost brotherly ties that had marked their erstwhile relationship had gradually cooled and this for a number of reasons.

First, Willy had met, in the kibbutz, Anna, a pretty and vivacious girl hailing from Vienna. What started as a flirtatious episode in his life eventually grew into a love affair. In fact, the two became inseparable and intended to get married "one day".

That day actually came in the summer of 1942, shortly after Willy's twenty-second birthday. The Kibbutz gave them a rousing send-off into marital bliss. They also allocated to them a small house on the grounds in the family section.

Thus, it looked as if Willy was set on a traditional and predictable course in his life. He was liked and admired by all the people around him, primarily because of his open and friendly personality.

Abe's place in the kibbutz on the other hand, bore none of these features. He was most of the time a loner, preferring to keep away from gatherings, reading books or listening to foreign broadcasts on his shortwave radio.

In fact, when the two met from time to time, they mostly exchanged generalities and banter rather than feelings and opinions.

In the spring of 1944, the kibbutz was visited by a group of British army personnel who informed them that their government had just authorized the formation of a Jewish Brigade to be drawn from Palestine and that applicants would have to fill in forms and present them in person to the draft board. If accepted, the kibbutz members would be sent to Cairo for training and their integration into the British Eight Army, at the time headquartered in Egypt. From there, they would be assigned to posts in the various theatres of war, which included Italy, Continental Europe and even North Africa.

That meeting with the British army officials immediately unleashed a wave of patriotic feelings since most if not all members of suitable age wanted to become part of the fighting force that would help spell the doom of the hated Nazis who had not only been the cause of their uprooting but had also caused the death of their families including their parents.

Both Willy and Abe enlisted and were sent by train to the British headquarters on Cairo's Sharia Al-Antikhana street. They were issued uniforms and army kits. As was to be expected, Willy was posted to a unit of the Royal Electromechanical Engineers (or REME for short), while Abe ended up in the Army's Pay Corp.

The two old friends met at the barrack's mess hall, where they looked at each other in their snappy uniforms. They shook hands, exchanged a few words such as: "You look smart" and "So do you", and "Good luck" and "Good luck to you too". After a "Let's keep in touch", a half-hearted promise neither of them were too sure they would be able to fulfill, the two saluted each other with a smile and went their separate ways.

Both were full of excitement and pride as well as a good measure of apprehension, knowing full well that they were now part and parcel of the deadliest war in human history.

*   *   *

Within days after his certification as a qualified army mechanic, Willy was assigned to a tank brigade fighting its way through Italy in pursuit of Field Marshal Kesselring's retreating German army. As Allied troops continued their advance, Willy participated in many battles with the Germans which took him and his unit through most of Italy. By the time the Germans surrendered to the Americans and British and thus put an end to the Italian campaign in early 1945, Willy had not only reached the rank of Captain, but he had a chest full of medals and citations for efficiency, leadership and even bravery under enemy fire.

After the end of hostilities in Italy, Willy was assigned to the Allied occupation army from where he was discharged with honourable mention in the fall of 1946.

Abe's military career had been much less spectacular and interesting. His was primarily a desk job in the Army Pay Corp, following the fighting units from a safe distance. He did receive some campaign ribbons and some promotions, the last of which was that of a Second Lieutenant. Abe also served with the Occupation Army in Germany and was demobilized in 1946 shortly before Willy was.

In fact the two returning officers were part of several demobilized kibbutzniks who were feted by their families and friends. The main reason for the celebration was that although two young men had been wounded, none of the group had lost their lives. This in itself was a reason to celebrate not only the return of the soldiers but also their reintegration into their families and their community.

*   *   *

As was to be expected, Willy and Abe had not been in touch with each other through their war service. Now they shook hands, hugged each other and exchanged a few memories from the eventful two years they had gone through.

However, although Willy and Abe kept exchanging their stories, Willy became aware of a certain distance and even coolness in Abe's attitude towards him, which he attributed to possible jealousy over the fact that he had returned from the war as a decorated officer, while Abe had only made it to the lowest army commission and had just a few campaign ribbons to show for.

Willy was now fully aware of the fact that the two had grown apart to the point of an unbridgeable cleft that separated them. They had nothing in common and were really not interested in each other any longer. Their war service and experience had just confirmed to them that they lived in different worlds.

And so, life in the kibbutz resumed its post-war normal course as if nothing had happened to interrupt it.

* * *

This state of affairs was to continue until 1947 when both Willy and Abe were informed by the new post-war governments of Germany and Poland that they were eligible for payments of money as reparation for the lives and properties lost during the Holocaust. Of course, there were many formalities to go through but they were assured that payment would soon come their way.

Willy immediately started to fill in the necessary forms, but also decided that as soon as he was to receive payments, he and his family, which now included a beautiful little boy, would leave the kibbutz to start a business of his own. He intended to create a company selling and servicing agricultural irrigation equipment of which there was a dire need in Israel. He knew that he was fully qualified to run such a company, both technically and business-wise.

With the help of his wife, Anna, Willy started to make enquiries about the setting up of an irrigation company. From the feedback he received from various sources, including kibbutzim and private agricultural companies, it looked as if there was indeed a need for these installations and, given the right products, the right prices and proper services, Willy's company should do very well.

The only problem now was to get the necessary initial capital to take the project off the ground. Taking everything into consideration, Willy came to the conclusion that he would need a starting capital of some 250,000 US dollars to cover stock, personnel, office, warehouse space and transportation.

Willy had informed the top people in the kibbutz of his intention to leave them as soon as he had completed his financial and logistic preparations such as talking to suppliers and finding a suitable business location. He had also told his closest friends about his plans but he had not said a word about all this to Abe.

That's why he was surprised to receive a phone call one evening from Abe asking him if they could meet since he wanted to discuss something with him. When Willy asked: "What about?" Abe simply said: "It's a long story and I prefer to talk to you over the weekend in a quiet corner. "Ok", said Willy.

They decided to meet on a Saturday morning.

After a few generalities, Willy came to the point and said: "So, what is it you want to discuss with me?"

Abe pulled his chair closer to Willy's, and, looking very much as if he had prepared his speech well in advance, he said:

"Ok, Willy. I've heard that you and your family intend to leave and set up an irrigation equipment company of your own. I think it's a great idea and I'm sure you will be successful. Hey, the desert is there and it's everywhere in this country and it needs water, doesn't it? Because of several reasons I want to ask you to take me into your company as a partner."

As Abe said this, he noticed Willy raising both hands in a rejecting gesture, signifying "No".

Abe also lifted his hand and, preventing Willy from talking, he blurted out: "Let me finish Willy, please let me finish. You see, I have recently heard from a lawyer in Poland that the government has agreed to compensate me and my brother, the only survivors from the Holocaust, with a substantial amount of money. My father owned a shirt factory in Krakow. When the Germans occupied the country, the Polish administration took away not only the factory but all of our possessions. Of course, they sold the factory to a local Pole. Now the new government of Poland is paying me reparation money for all our losses. I am to receive the funds shortly.

I am prepared to invest at least fifty thousand dollars in your company and make it 'our' company. In other words and to be precise, I want a 25% share of the business."

As he said this, he noticed an ironic smile on Willy's face, clearly rejecting the idea out of hand.

Abe continued: "I'm sure you will find it difficult to raise the initial capital of the company. Here is fifty thousand dollars cash and perhaps even more on the table. You're off to the races, Willy", he concluded, slamming his hand on the table next to him and leaning back in his chair.

Willy had listened, visibly impatiently to the long tirade. When Abe had finished, he calmly stood up and said: "Thank you Abe, but I don't need and I don't want a partner. My negotiations with the bank are going well, suppliers are willing to give me credit and with God's help, I am pretty confident that I can start a business in a matter of a few months. So, Abe, thanks again. I am sure something else will come your way to use your money."

With that, Willy considered the meeting over and was set to leave when Abe grabbed his arm and held him back.

"Wait," he said. "I'm not finished. If your refusal to accept my offer is motivated by financial or business reasons, how about our friendship which we sealed so many years ago in that smoky bar in Basel? Did that not mean anything to you? Does the fact that as an accountant I can be a vital controlling presence in your company not mean anything to you? You need me just as I need you to start a good business!"

As if driven by an obsession, Abe continued: "And how about our being members of a kibbutz, where we learned to share and help each other?"

A worked-up Abe had come to the end of his plea.

"Please don't say no to my offer", he concluded. You will see that we will both benefit by working together." He looked at Willy for a reaction and the reaction was delivered calmly.

"Thank you again, Abe. Look, what happened years ago between us in Switzerland has no bearing on the realities of today. We both went to war, we both have responsibilities towards ourselves and our families and we have to live our own lives as best as we can. I have chosen to go into this new business and I want to do it by myself. You are free to live your own life, make your own plans and bring them to fruition. In this I wish you the best of luck. I really do from the bottom of my heart. So, now I want to go back to my family to spend the rest of the weekend with them. I'm sure you also have plans of your own."

With that, Willy extended his hand to Abe and said: "Goodbye".

But Abe ignored the gesture and said: "Sit down Willy. You may be interested in this story."

"What story?" asked Willy. Instead of answering the question, Abe went on: "You know they say it's a small world. And sometimes that's so true. I'll tell you a strange story. When I was stationed in Germany I worked in a statistical department of the British Army of Occupation. There I met a sergeant who had just been transferred from Monte Cassino in Italy. When he saw that I was a member of the Jewish Brigade, he told me about the adventure of another Brigade member stationed in Monte Cassino who had just avoided a court martial and all sorts of serious consequences because he had a love affair with a local girl and she became pregnant.

When the girl's parents reported the case to the British Commander, he summoned the officer in question and told him that if the tests after the baby's birth would confirm that he was the father, he would have to either marry the girl or become legally responsible for his child, depending what a local court would decide. In other words, this captain was in deep trouble because, as you can imagine, he was already married in Palestine and had a child.

Imagine that captain's luck when shortly after the baby's birth and the confirmation that he was indeed the father, that girl met a local Italian suitor who consented to marry her, baby and all.

Apparently that girl was very beautiful and had no trouble finding a husband. When the marriage took place, the girl and her parents went back to the British Commander to tell him that all is forgiven, and that they will forget the wartime episode since their daughter's new husband had agreed to be the baby's legal father.

To end the story, the captain got off the hook, but he left a little boy in Monte Cassino as a souvenir. Interesting story, don't you think?" concluded Abe, who now took a short breather.

Willy had listened to this narrative with mixed expressions on his face. But now, looking his silent friend straight into his eyes, Abe said: "That officer from the Jewish Brigade was Captain Willy Goldin."

With these slowly spoken words, Abe got up, and without saying anything further, walked away, leaving his friend as if he wanted his words to slowly sink in.

"Bastard", was the only word Willy uttered as he left the place to rejoin his family. He told his wife that he had met Abe for a chat, that's all.

*   *   *

The meeting with Abe had taken place on Shabbat. Willy told his wife that he had a stomach ache and would like to spend the rest of the afternoon taking it easy. All he really wanted was to be left alone for a few hours.

His wife reminded him of his promise to take her and the boy to the beach on Sunday, the next day.

"Of course", said Willy. "I'm sure I'll be OK by tomorrow."

That Saturday afternoon and the night that followed it probably contained the most painful hours he had lived through in a long time.

To begin with, the memory of his love affair with Gina, the beautiful and warm-hearted girl. She was so different from any person he had ever been close to.

The guilt feeling of having betrayed his wife Anna, a feeling that now, long after the affair had ended, came back as an accusation making him feel ashamed of himself. The thought that somewhere, in another country lived a little boy who was his son, perhaps even looked like him and acted like him, albeit in a different language.

The terrifying idea that Anna, his unsuspecting and loving wife, could suddenly be exposed to a secret in a relationship in which there were not supposed to be any secrets between husband and wife.

Then he became aware of the deep hatred he had felt rising in his mind and heart as he listened to Abe's tirade, delivered with merciless glee. There was no doubt in Willy's mind that heavy-handed pressure and blackmail were behind Abe's attempt to become a partner in his new business. "What a bastard", Willy kept repeating to himself. "What a bastard."

All these and more thoughts kept coming back into Willy's mind throughout the evening and sleepless night until the early morning hours.

After breakfast, the family got into the car and Willy drove to the beach near Hayarkon Street, which was already full of people taking advantage of the beautiful day that was unfolding under a cloudless sky.

They found a vacant spot, unloaded all their belongings under the shade provided by two wide parasols. Willy started to play one of the popular card games with his five-year-old son, while Anna started reading a book she had picked up at the library the day before.

At about eleven o'clock, little Shlomo had enough of the game and wanted to listen to music on his pocket radio. Willy got up and said to Anna: "Anyone want to join me for a dip in the sea?" When the answer from Anna was "No, I want to finish this chapter! Why don't you go for a swim and when you return we will have lunch? I brought some nice things with me!"

Willy proceeded towards the sea. He was glad to be by himself for a little while, because his experience from the day before was still occupying his mind. "Perhaps the cool seawater will do me good", he reasoned as he stepped into the beckoning waters.

There were not too many people swimming as he started his favourite crawl and headed for the open sea.

He must have been swimming for some ten minutes when he stopped to catch his breath, looking around him. There was no one else in sight except one swimmer at a certain distance.

As he was resting in the sea he suddenly noticed that the other person started swimming towards him. He also noticed some very jerky movements, as if there was something wrong. Yet, the person kept swimming towards him as if trying to reach him at all costs. He was struggling and thrashing his arms and he kept making some gurgling sounds. Suddenly Willy recognized the swimmer. It was none other than Abe. He seemed to be exhausted and out of breath.

The very moment Willy recognized Abe, some thoughts flashed through his mind: Should I try to save him or just leave him to fend for himself? Another thought reminded him that desperate swimmers had often caused the drowning of their rescuers because of their irrational attempts to stay afloat by clinging to them at all costs.

Willy turned away and started swimming back to the beach. Without saying a word to anyone about what he had just gone through, he rejoined his family.

Anna unpacked lunch and they all had a hearty picnic spread out on towels and beach chairs.

About an hour had passed since Willy had come out of the water, when they heard an announcement that a swimmer had just been brought ashore by the lifeguard. His body was found floating at a distance. Revival attempts at the first aid station had failed and he was pronounced dead by drowning. His body had been transferred to a nearby hospital.

The next day announcements from the police and the kibbutz confirmed the identity of the drowned swimmer as Abraham Kozlowski, a kibbutz accountant, single and with no apparent family ties.

* * *

Willy Goldin never told anything about the whole story to anyone. He lived a long life, eventually becoming a wealthy Israeli industrialist presiding over a large family that adored him.

Willy took his secrets to his grave. Over the years he learned to live with his memories just like people learn to live with a physical problem.

He did not regret anything except the thought that kept coming back to his mind that somewhere in the world lived a man who was his son; his own flesh and blood. A son conceived in tender love he would never see.

* * *

WHAT A DIFFERENCE A NIGHT MADE

If you think that Murphy's Law has been repealed, you are greatly mistaken. The adage, "if anything can go wrong, it will" was alive and well in Jane Bowman's kitchen on that rainy April afternoon. First it was the oven that conked out, then the blender which expired with an ugly jarring sound as if to join the oven in solidarity.

Jane was halfway through preparing the evening meal as she stood helpless and disconsolate in her kitchen, feeling like "where do we go from here?" She definitely had to abandon her plans for homemade dinner and instead phoned her husband to tell him about her culinary mishaps, suggesting a visit to a nearby restaurant.

"Sure Janie" was the immediate reply. "Why don't you come to the office to pick me up around six?" "Great idea. See you soon!"

Lorne and Jane had been married for three years now. He was a litigation lawyer in a Montreal law firm, well-liked by the senior partners and his colleagues. Jane was the only daughter of a well-to-do couple living in one of Hampstead's tree-lined streets.

The young couple, she, in her late twenties and he in his mid-thirties lived in a nice home close by her parents. They had no children since they had decided to start a family only after the third or fourth year in order to give them time to enjoy their togetherness and before getting tied down with the more mundane chores of parenthood. In fact, they frequently travelled and had a spirited circle of friends, just like many other couples of their standing.

* * *

It was just about six when Jane entered her husband's office. He told her that the senior partner had just called him for a fifteen minute meeting to discuss the summer vacation plan. "Please make yourself comfortable, I won't be too long. Why don't you decide where you want to go for dinner. I am going to get coffee for myself. Would you like some too?" "No thanks", replied Jane. "Don't worry about me. I have today's crossword puzzle to keep me company." With that, Lorne left her.

Jane must have been sitting for some five minutes, when the phone on the desk clicked and a voice started talking on the intercom. "Hi big boy, it's Cathie. I just heard you're coming back to Toronto on Monday for the McDougall case. Good luck. It's a mess as you know. Listen, I booked the company suite for you as usual. That's where I will meet you after dinner. I can't wait for an encore. Yummy! Am I falling in love with you or what?

See you in the office. Bye love."

The crossword Jane was holding fell from her hands. She felt like she was struck by lightning. What, her Lorne had a lover or girlfriend or mistress at the Toronto office? That can't be true. But it sounded true, alright. Jane jumped up from her seat, grabbed her coat and breezed out of the office, down to the garage, into her car and drove straight home in utter shock.

Half an hour later, a tired Lorne came back to his desk and found his office empty. He walked over to the ladies' room and called out: "Janie are you there?" But there was no answer. Back in his office he called home. He did not know what else to do. Jane answered the phone with a terse "Yes".

"What happened? Why are you home? You're okay?" "Come home. I'll tell you what happened", was the answer and she hung up.

Lorne immediately sensed the gathering of a major storm. Putting one and one together, he correctly surmised that Cathie had called while he was out of the office, not aware of his absence and Jane's presence. Since their last get-together she had called him repeatedly with all sorts of amorous tidbits.

With a great deal of trepidation, Lorne unlocked his house door finding dark rooms throughout the first floor. There was an eerie silence around him as he climbed the stairs to the bedroom. He opened the door and saw Janie crying, sprawled on the bed with a box of Kleenex beside her.

He had guessed right. Janie had listened to a call from Cathie. He had no time to utter a word before the avalanche came thundering down. Janie's face was red and her eyes were full of tears.

"You dirty bastard, you scum, you cheat, you liar." She shouted at Lorne.

"You took advantage of a loving wife, of a cozy home and of all the goodies I and my family have heaped on you, to cheat on me. Didn't you realize that it was bound to come out sooner or later? I heard every word from your lover. Tell me, aren't you ashamed? Why, why? What is it that you lacked in our marriage? I gave you everything. All my love, I kept an impeccable home down to anything and everything you fancied. My parents took you into their hearts like a son, so what is it you do not have? Tell me, you bastard." With that Jane fell back onto the bed and kept on crying.

Lorne had not said a word since his arrival in the bedroom. He had just taken off his jacket and stood there with an empty expression on his face.

"Okay, I am sorry it came out this way." He finally started to say, lost for words.

"What does it mean I'm sorry? Tell me why you are fooling around? Why? Why?"

"Okay", he repeated. "You want an answer or a reason. There is no answer. All I can tell is that it was a one-time fling about a couple of weeks ago. After a long day of meetings and a dinner laced with a couple of martinis, we made love. That's all. A one-time fling. Don't ask me why or how, but it just happened. You can believe me or not, but that's God's own truth. That's why I said 'I'm sorry'. I didn't do it to start an affair and I'll put an end to it. Obviously that night together meant much more to her than it did to me."

"You're lying", Jane shot back. You have an affair with this woman." "No, no help me God, I am not having an affair."

Jane got up and went to the bathroom. A few minutes later she came out. She had washed her face, but her eyes were still red and swollen. She sat on the edge of the bed while Lorne was looking at some mail on the dresser.

There was a long silence between them. Then Jane said: "Okay. There's no need to belabour this any longer. I am prepared to take you by your word. I am prepared to draw a line under this stupid and irresponsible fling of yours in order to save our marriage. Let's say it was a foolish fling. Let's say it never happened, but on two conditions: First you will talk to her tonight, right now and tell her that whatever happened between the two of you is over, finito, for good. You will use the phone in the kitchen and I will listen in from the phone here. And secondly, we will go tomorrow to the cemetery to your father's grave site and there on sacred ground, you will swear never to repeat this kind of nonsense. You will promise me that in front of your dad's grave. And that will be the end of it. I want the whole episode to be behind us. Let's go on with our marriage. Okay?"

Lorne had listened to Jane's emotional delivery in utter silence, not even looking at her. In fact, there was not much he could say. He looked tired but otherwise there was no expression on his face. When Jane had finished, he slowly got up from his chair and went down the stairs.

A good ten minutes had passed since he had sat down at the kitchen table. All kinds of thoughts were racing through his mind like flashbacks of his married life, which by and large had been uneventful and fulfilling. It could not be called an unhappy marriage since nothing really unpleasant had marred their life together. He also thought of that evening at the Toronto office and the dinner laced with too many martinis. Cathie's sexy movements, one thing leading to another, ending up in bed with her at the company suite. Perhaps the excitement of tasting the "forbidden fruit" away from home.

With a lot of resolve and a swarm of butterflies in his stomach he dialed Cathie's number.

"Hi", he said: "This is Lorne" and before letting Cathie say anything to him, he continued: "Listen Cathie, I really don't know how to start. Well, how about: my wife heard your call this evening. She was in my office while I was in the boardroom with the rest of the guys. I am sure you will understand when I tell you that what happened between us that night must be for the first and last time. I promised Jane not to meet you again and I intend to keep that promise. I have no choice. Otherwise it is the end of my marriage.

I'm sorry Cathie, I'm deeply sorry for having seduced you, creating all kinds of ideas and expectations. Please forget the whole episode as if it never happened. I'm trying to do just that and please do it too. Again, forgive me. I shouldn't have done it."

There was no sound from the other end of the line throughout most of Lorne's speech, which prompted him to say "Hello? Are you there?"
"Yes, I am", came a sullen voice: "And I understand your remorse. I took our first night together for the beginning of something more serious. Okay, I was wrong. Of course you hurt me. No girl jumps into bed with a man unless she has strong feelings for him.

Go back to your wife and never put your hands on me again. Okay? You disappointed me Lorne. Bye." She hung up.

A minute later Jane came down the stairs and said: "I'll fix a light dinner with what I can find in the fridge." "That's okay with me", answered Lorne.

After a quiet dinner, they both went up to their bedroom. Lorne said: "If you don't mind I'll sleep tonight in the guest's bedroom."

"Sure", was Jane's laconic response. "I'll make up the bed for you. See you in the morning for breakfast." With a somewhat uneasy smile on their faces, they bid goodnight to each other, obviously in need of a breather after a rather agitated evening.

*   *   *

The second part of Jane's request took place just two days later. They went to the gravesite of Lorne's father and, true to form, he vowed never to stray again. He followed it up with a short prayer after which Jane placed some fresh flowers on the tombstone. With hands held firmly together they left the cemetery.

A chapter in the marital life of Jane and Lorne Bowman had come to an end and both were visibly relieved that it was all over. They could go on with their lives. After all, their erstwhile decision to start a family only after the third year of their marriage was still awaiting fulfillment.

*   *   *

Lorne's phone call from Montreal had come as a shock to Cathie. Although she realized that she was walking on thin ice when she spent the night with him, she was clearly under the impression that her lover was really a frustrated and unhappy husband who tried to find an alternative to his marital problems. In other words she thought that their night together heralded the beginning of a relationship that might eventually end in Lorne's divorce and then with her marrying him. After all, in her mind Lorne was not an irresponsible philanderer or frivolous girl-chaser but a respected lawyer who was supposed to be accountable for his actions.

However, his phone call was unmistakably clear. It was the beginning as well as the end of their relationship. Anticipating an uneasy night ahead, she took a sleeping pill and went to bed.

A few days after the telephone call, Cathie woke up with an uneasy feeling because she just realized that although it was the approximate time of her monthly period, she had felt no sign of it. When she phoned her doctor the next day, he recommended that she see a gynecologist, which she promptly did. But when she had undergone some tests and examinations, the good doctor told her that she was pregnant. Although he congratulated her on the "good" news, Cathie was stunned and really unpleasantly so. She knew of course that it could only have been the consequence of her intercourse with Lorne Bowman since she had not been with any other man.

Cathie was close to tears. She did not know what to do next. She went through the afternoon at the office but when she came home in the evening, she called her older sister Lill in Vancouver. Lill was also her best friend and trusted councillor on many previous family and even professional issues.

Married to Peter Stern a successful dentist in Vancouver, Lill was a happy and well-adjusted mother of two children.

"Hi Lill, it's me and I have a problem. A big one. Can you help?" "What's the problem?" asked her sister. Well, Cathie told her of the pregnancy after having spent a night with a very nice man she knew but she did not give her sister his name. All she said was: "He is or was a friend and I made a big mistake going to bed with him. I made an even bigger mistake by not being successful in the contraception. Moreover, I can't ask him to marry me. He is a married man. I really messed things up, Lill", she said while starting to cry over the phone.

"Oh my God", was the first reaction. Then after a minute, Lill asked: "When were you told you are pregnant?"

"Today. This morning." She answered.

Lill took a few moments to get her thoughts together and then she said: "Look, stop crying and let's see what options you have. Well, the first obvious one is to have an abortion as soon as possible and get the whole thing over with.

"No, I don't want to have an abortion," Cathie interrupted her impetuously. "I am scared and I hate the idea of any surgery killing a living thing in me."

"Well" continued Lill, "the only alternative is to have the baby and marry a man who will accept you as a single mom. Happens all the time nowadays." As she said this she stopped for a second and then continued: "Wait a minute a thought just occurred to me. Yes, I think it's an excellent idea."

Do you remember Josh, Peter's best friend? You met him several times in our home when you visited us." "Of course I remember Josh", said Cathie.

"Well, two things about Josh. To begin with he is a hell of a nice guy. Perfect gentleman and a very good dentist too. Both he and Peter graduated at the same time, and are very close buddies.

Josh broke up with his girlfriend recently and is sort of on the loose, or up for grabs, if you know what I mean.

The second thing is that every time you visited us, he made some very complimentary remarks to me about you. Your professionalism as a lawyer, your tasteful and elegant appearance, your looks etc.etc. In other words, he liked you very much. What if I talk to him tomorrow and tell him that you have had a one night fling with a married man and despite your efforts at contraception, you just found out that you got pregnant. "Is he prepared to marry you in your present condition and accept the baby as his own? Look, if you two get married now here in Vancouver and you have a baby eight months later, no one will ask any questions. Of course, the big 'if' is whether he is interested in a) marrying you and b) with a baby?

What do you think", asked Lill to a silent Cathie, who had listened to the long conversation without uttering a word. "I don't know." She finally replied. "I remember Josh, of course and found him good-looking and interesting, but I don't know the guy. And why would he want to marry someone bearing another man's child?" "I don't know either", Lill replied, but all I can do is ask him. Do you want me to? Look, under the circumstance it may be a perfect solution, of course, provided both you and he want to do it.

Cathie", her sister went on. You don't need to give me an answer now. Think it over and call me in the morning. Let it sink in and tell me which way you want to go. Okay? By the way, did you tell your lover of the pregnancy?" added Lill. "No, I did not and I don't intend to." Was the reply.

"Okay, I will think it over tonight." Said Cathie. "But one thing I can tell you already is that I don't fancy abortive surgery."

"Alright", Lill said: "Calm down, honey. I'm sure there is a solution to your problem and it may well be what I suggested. You have a good night's sleep. Stop crying. I love you. We'll talk in the morning."

It was not an easy night for Cathie. She kept mulling over the idea from all possible angles, and finally fell asleep. The next day she went to work. At noon during the lunch break, she called Lill with the simple words: "Call Josh!"

Three days had passed since Cathie and Lill had talked. She went to work but her mind was somewhere else. When she came home in the evening her phone rang. It was Lill. "Guess what?" She said. "He is willing to marry you as you are. Apparently he likes you very much and even told me that he had intended to phone you after he broke up with his girlfriend. How lucky can you get?

As for the expected baby, he was at first a bit hesitant and wanted to know who the father was. I told him the truth that I didn't know and that you don't want to tell. After much thinking, he finally said: "Okay, Lill. Given that Peter seems to be the happiest husband I know, given that your sister cannot be much different from you and given that I liked Cathie very much the moment I saw her, my answer is 'Si, si, si'. I am going to phone her tonight when she is home from the office. How's that?"

Lill added, "Needless to say, I could not stop crying after he hung up. I am so happy for you Cathie."

The rest of the telephone conversation, which was frequently interrupted by sometimes tearful and sometimes laughing banter was a reflection of the love and compassion that existed between two very close-knit sisters.

*   *   *

Josh did indeed call her and it was the strangest conversation Cathie ever had on the telephone. "Hello, this is Josh Cooper. I don't know if you remember me but we met several times at your sister's place here in Vancouver."

"Sure I remember you, Josh." Cathie interrupted. "I talked to your sister and I am sure she related our conversation or part of it to you." "Yes, she did", said Cathie.

"Well, if you are free this coming weekend, would you like to have dinner with me? I haven't been in Toronto in a while and if you are available we can go to a nice restaurant and pick up our conversation from where we left off when I last saw you a few months ago. Does that sound alright to you?"

"Yes it does." Replied Cathie. "Why don't you phone me on Saturday when you arrive and check in at the hotel? I can then pick you up and we can go out for dinner. There are several good restaurants in the downtown area. Would you want me to make a reservation?" "Sure", replied Josh; "Why don't you do that and I will phone you as soon as I arrive."

"Very good." Said Cathie.

"I look forward to seeing you again, goodbye," were Josh's parting words to which Cathie replied, "So do I Josh. Have a good trip."

Needless to say, Cathie spent the next few day with a great deal of mixed feelings which included trepidation, some excitement, and even uneasiness. But when they met on Saturday evening, most of the traditional butterflies in her stomach rapidly vanished because of Josh's jovial and light-hearted attitude which he displayed throughout that evening. In fact he managed to put Cathie at ease right from the start and he kept up that pleasant, almost natural aura throughout their meeting.

It was he who carried the bulk of the conversation, asking Cathie about her professional life, her hobbies and her recreational activities, thus creating a light-hearted and pleasant atmosphere spiced with humor and witty remarks throughout the dinner before broaching the subject at hand.

He told her about the demise of his relationship with his girlfriend, then he repeatedly mentioned that he had liked her right from the first time of their encounter in Vancouver and that he had told this to her sister some time ago. He then referred to his own disappointment over a discontinued relationship and followed up with the remark that they are both survivors from emotional mishaps. He then came out with the direct question as to whether she would consider dating him with a view of marriage that is, of course, provided she liked him and they both fell in love with each other. After all, he added with a broad smile, "it still takes two to tango."

Cathie had listened to his speech without once saying a word, but she was very impressed by his mature attitude and proper selection of words. In fact, she admired him for having put everything to her so succinctly and naturally.

Without waiting for a reaction, Josh went on: "If you accept my proposal, why don't you arrange for a transfer to your firm's Vancouver branch? Move to the West Coast, where you can stay with your sister. And you and I then can get together to discuss all the details, including what I understand from talking to Lill, is your pregnant condition which is not a problem for me. After all, I think I would have wanted to marry you even if you were divorced and brought a child into our marriage."

The next two weeks were very hectic for Cathie. After many long distance calls with Lill and her mind resolutely made up, Cathie managed to find a position in another law firm in Vancouver and resigned from her Toronto job. Then she packed all her belongings and had them shipped to her sister, bid goodbye to all her many friends in Toronto and finally, with a sigh of relief, she boarded the plane to Vancouver.

Things had developed so fast for her during the past weeks that it seemed like she was part of a movie running over the screen. Of course she had uneasy feelings of facing the unexpected, but her evening with Josh and his calm and logical approach to a difficult situation had convinced her that she was on the right track. In addition, under close observation across the dinner table she had found him to be pleasant-looking, impeccably dressed and most of all, exuding a personal charm that she felt could be the catalyst to falling in love with him.

*   *   *

Within days Cathie had moved into her sister's spacious house and had repeatedly met Josh, who arrived one evening with roses and champagne to propose formally. It was a beautiful and happy evening for all.

During the days preceding their decision to tie the knot, the couple had amply discussed the prevailing circumstances of their marriage.

Josh told Cathie that he will not adopt her child but take it as if it was his own. "Nobody needs to know" he assured Cathie, holding her hand. "And since I expect us to have some children of our own, they will all grow up as brothers and sisters, our children. You, Lill and I will be the only people in the world to know otherwise. Okay?"

They both embraced each other after this solemn vow. Cathie also told her future husband that for many reasons she will not reveal to anyone in the world including him and her sister the name of her baby's real father. Josh agreed with the words: "Okay, honey, what difference does it make in the future of our family whether it was Peter or Paul. The baby is our child and that's the end of it."

Within weeks, a simple but beautiful wedding became the beginning of their marital life. There was an elegant reception at one of Vancouver's downtown hotels. The couple looked radiant and happy beyond words.

Cathie had really fallen in love and the same could be said for Josh. In a short spell of time the traditional chemistry had spread its magic wings embracing both with warm and sincere feelings for a long and fulfilling union.

*   *   *

Jane and Lorne's "mending of fences" took less time than expected. Within a few weeks they seemed to have forgotten the whole unpleasant episode in their young marital life.

Lorne became increasingly involved in litigation cases and a few years later received the coveted reward of being appointed a senior partner in the firm. He now headed a department, with lawyers in Montreal, Toronto and Vancouver reporting to him.

On one of his trips to Toronto he was told that Cathie had been relocated to Vancouver.

The couple's home life evolved in the familiar routine of so many young people except that in spite of their usual and even very active sexual life, Jane did not become pregnant. They started wondering why. Well, after a number of tests and examinations, Jane's gynecologist had the answer. Jane had a tumor in her ovaries which prevented the natural process of insemination. "However", the doctor assured her, "it is not a malignant growth but something that can be removed surgically and that will allow you to have children."

Jane was both relieved at the news of the benign tumor but also apprehensive at the forthcoming surgery, which the doctor recommended should be performed "the sooner the better".

Less than a month after this diagnosis, Jane was recovering from the operation in the hospital, when the doctor came into her room with a grim face. He bore bad news. While the growth was indeed benign, it had actually penetrated into the ovaries to an extent that its excision necessitated the removal of a large ovarian section. "In other words", added the surgeon, "I had no choice. Either remove the growth completely before it could become cancerous, or remove only parts of it in the hope that what was left would be sufficient to enable you to become pregnant, but facing the risk that it could in time turn malignant. I naturally opted for the first alternative to save your life, albeit a childless life."

Jane broke out in tears as she listened to the doctor's sombre words and Lorne, who rushed to her side to hold her hand also reached for his handkerchief.

"I'm very sorry Mrs. Bowman, but our first duty is to save lives and that is what I did. Please let me know if you need anything. You should be able to leave hospital by the end of this week." With that the doctor was gone.

The next few weeks were not easy, especially for Jane who felt a sudden void like a dark abyss in her life, her role as a wife and as a mother badly marred. But, in time husband and wife learned to accept the facts of life and started considering adopting a child.

It did not take long to locate an adoption agency and discuss their wish to adopt a baby girl, which is what Jane desperately wanted. After a number of meetings and interviews, they finally found what they were looking for. A delightful baby whose mother had recently died in a car accident. The disconsolate father was desperately looking for a home for the little girl, since his next-of-kin lived in another province.

And so, after all the necessary and even unnecessary tests and examinations had been performed, Lorne and Jane brought their little bundle of joy from Winnipeg to Montreal. They were elated and immediately fell in love with the baby, a beautiful little girl with big blue eyes dominating a perfectly shaped round face, like a little doll, who soon became the focal point in the life of her adopted parents. In fact it did not take long for both Jane and Lorne to completely forget the baby's origins. The little girl became emotionally and almost physically their very own child.

* * *

Over twenty-six years had passed since the Bowmans in Montreal and the Coopers in Vancouver had started their respective family lives. As if they were living on different planets, they never communicated with each other, in fact they did not even know of each other's whereabouts.

Lorne had become a very respected litigation law expert who had not only amassed a bucketful of certificates, testimonials and honours, but had also been appointed a professor at the Law Faculty of McGill University. He was now head of his law firm, had made a lot of money and lived a happy life surrounded by his loving wife Jane and their beautiful daughter Peggy. That little beauty had in fact grown into a stunning young lady who combined good looks with a very pleasant personality and a strong attachment to her doting parents.

The Bowmans were for all intents and purposes a picture-perfect family.

* * *

Much the same could be said for the Coopers of Vancouver. In the twenty-six years of their marriage, Cathie had given birth to three children. David, their first born and two girls who joined him a few years later. The family still lived together in the same large house although David, who in emulation of his now retired mother, had studied law and had just been admitted to the B.C. Bar. He also had a small pad in an apartment overlooking the Pacific Ocean.

Cathie had left her law practice shortly after the birth of her third child because she was too busy tending to the growing family.

Josh continued his dental practice but because of creeping arthritis of his back, took occasional vacations with Cathie and sometimes with the girls to help him relax from a life spent not only standing up but also bending to the right angle of reaching all of his patient's molars.

The Coopers were a well-adjusted and smoothly functioning family, respecting and loving each other.

*   *   *

It was at this juncture in the lives of these two families that the Canadian Bar Association happened to hold its Annual Convention in Toronto. It was announced as a very special event to commemorate its founding one hundred and twenty years ago. On that occasion the new board of governors would also be introduced. And one of its proud members was Lorne Bowman from Montreal.

Naturally Jane and Peggy had been preparing for that event and were very excited in anticipation of the gala dinner at which the special honour was to be bestowed on Lorne. It was the crowning of his career.

*   *   *

It was Dr. Cooper who had picked up from the local newspaper, the news about the forthcoming Canadian Bar Association convention in Toronto.

That evening at the dinner table, he mentioned it and, turning to his son David, he casually said: "You know something, I think your mother and I should attend that event with you. For one thing, you need the professional exposure among your peers now that you have been called to the bar and secondly nothing in the world could deprive me from watching my son moving among his peers while attending the various functions, not to mention attending the gala dinner at which I can tell my table neighbors: 'This is my son, The Lawyer.' While they all laughed, David's face lit up like a lantern. "Do you really mean it Dad?" The words: "Of course I do." were seconded in harmony by his mother's laughing voice: "What a wonderful idea!" There was a great deal of talking and hugging around the table.

"What a better way to start a long and successful law practice than by celebrating it among your future peers and perhaps even a few opponents in the courtroom." added Josh, before they all drank toasts to each other.

*   *   *

The extraordinary meeting of the Canadian Bar Association in celebration of its foundation one hundred and twenty years ago turned out to be just that. A celebration replete with lectures, committee meetings, activity reports, city tours, and, of course, a gala reception in one of Toronto's most elegant hotels.

Literally thousands of lawyers from all over Canada, many accompanied by their spouses, had arrived to make this event a true celebration.

Some downtown stores and restaurants even featured special "CBA Convention Specials" which helped create a festive aura in the usually sedate and conservative city.

The proceedings had been going on for three days and the Gala Dinner was planned for the evening of the last day. It was at this black-tie venue that the nomination of Lorne Bowman to the National Board of Governors would be announced. It was the truly crowning event for Lorne, Jane and their daughter Peggy who arrived at the hotel dressed for the occasion.

Preceding dinner, an elaborate cocktail party was arranged in the hotel's lobby and several adjoining reception rooms to accommodate the large crowd.

For half an hour the Bowmans had been walking through some of the festively decorated rooms, greeting friends, politicians and dignitaries that were quick to congratulate Lorne on his forthcoming nomination.

Suddenly Lorne came face to face with another couple that crossed their path. Lorne looked again at the lady holding her husband's arm and at that moment the lady also looked at Lorne. After a split second of eye contact, Lorne shouted: "Cathie, is that you?" Cathie shouted back: "Yes, it is me!" "What are you doing here?" said a smiling Lorne, "I thought you left the law practice years ago?" "I did" replied an equally smiling Cathie "but my husband and I are here to give our son David a proper introduction to the profession, he has just been called to the B.C. Bar." With that she made an introductory gesture towards David. "How wonderful." said Lorne. "Welcome David to the world of law practice. I am sure you will find it most rewarding."

This repartee was followed by introducing all the members of the two families to each other and by Lorne and Cathie's "My God, you haven't changed" and "neither have you", followed by everyone talking to each other, like a typical unexpected reunion of friends after twenty-six years.

"You know what?" Said Lorne: "We must sit together at the same table to celebrate this surprise run-in. How about going into the dining room right now to find a table for six before the crowds come in." "Good idea." Making their way through the crowd, they entered the dining room and, were just lucky to find an empty table where they all sat down.

They talked about everything and anything while enjoying dinner, which was frequently interrupted by speeches from the head table, including the presentation of an award to Lorne to honour his appointment as a Governor of the CBA Board. Needless to say, all at the table rose to applaud. Lorne, looked radiant and proud, as did Jane and Peggy, who could not stop kissing and hugging her dad.

After dinner, some people strolled over to the nightclub where a band was providing soft dance music. It was Josh who suggested they all have a drink there before calling it a day. He obviously wanted his son to have as much exposure as possible to Lorne who was now a leading figure in the judicial world.

They all sat down for drinks but within minutes they got up to shake a leg to the tunes of the excellent band.

Lorne and Josh danced with their wives and David asked Peggy for the favour of a dance.

While the two married couples sat down after some time, the youngsters kept returning to the floor for encores. They obviously enjoyed what they were doing.

When Lorne said after about an hour "How about calling it a day. It's been a long day for all". Josh agreed, but Peggy and David begged their parents if they could stay a little longer. They were evidently having a good time.

Well, that night at the bar turned out to be a memorable setting for both David and Peg. They discovered that they liked each other and that they had a lot to talk about, their lives, their professions and their views of the world they lived in.

When they finally said goodbye to each other, they both knew that it was not an "adieu" but an "aurevoir". In fact, after their return home, they kept in touch by texting and the phone. What started as an after dinner dance eventually grew into a full-bodied love affair.

The crowning came a few months later when David proposed to Peggy and she laughingly accepted.

The two were married in Montreal in a beautiful ceremony followed by a reception in a downtown hotel, which was followed a week later by a similar event in Vancouver, where Dr. Cooper and his wife hosted a lovely dinner and dance in honour of their beloved son David's marriage to Peggy Bowman.

The young couple decided to make Vancouver their home. In fact, they had no choice because Lorne had offered his son-in-law a position in his firm's Vancouver office.

It was the start of David's career in one of the country's most prestigious law firms.
It was also the start of a successful marriage. Both David and Peggy seemed to have been made or destined for each other.

*   *   *

Needless to say, the three families, now united by the marriage of their children, kept in close contact not only by communicating with each other but also by frequent transcontinental visits which they all enjoyed immensely.

*   *   *

I think this story deserves an epilogue or a post mortem, if for no other reason than the relationships it conjured up.

Take Lorne Bowman, who never knew that his son-in-law was actually his very own son. Or his daughter Peggy who never knew that her husband was also her half-brother, albeit by adoption. Or David Cooper who never knew that his father-in-law was really his father. And how about Dr. Cooper who knew that his firstborn was sired by someone else without ever knowing that the "someone else" was his son's father-in-law as well as his father. Not to mention, of course, that David's two sisters never knew that their older brother was not really their dad's son.

And Jane, who never knew that her son-in-law was really the son of her husband, whose telephone call from his mother she accidently overheard in her husband's office, which really started this whole story coming to life.

Complicated relationships?

But in the end you may say: "Did it really matter in the lives of all these people, who was who?" After all, they all lived happy and fulfilled lives.

Remember the much maligned proverb: "What you don't know won't hurt you." Much maligned by those who maintain that many a driver, who did not know that his brakes were malfunctioning, did in fact get hurt and often very badly so.

Perhaps the real heroine of this story was Cathie Cooper who decided a long time ago that a secret is not a secret unless you never share it with anyone else. Period.

THE SECRET LIFE OF ARCHIE BENSON

Archie Benson had entered the services of a well-known and highly respected investment company for one reason and one reason only. He wanted to learn all the ins and outs of financial management in order to eventually set up his own business. But when he would do that, his real intention was not to provide honest to goodness asset management like he had learned but to actually defraud his unsuspecting investors. His reasoning was clear. If he associated his name with a top notch enterprise for a few years, he would have no problem in attracting clients to his own company later on.

Archie Benson was a person with a criminal mind whose plan was to steal a few million, making sure that he could get away with it, by erasing all traces of the theft and then disappear from view. He would set up residence in a comfortable place somewhere like Mexico and enjoy a carefree and pleasant life well into retirement. And he was determined to make all this happen.

After five years with Global Assets, one of the country's most respected financial institutions and an exemplary record which earned him not only a very attractive salary but also substantial appreciation from his employers, Archie, one day, told his supervisor that he wanted to set up his own shop, of course in a modest way, in order to further his ambition of one day being his own boss. His supervisor wished him well and a short time later a small downtown office in the financial district bore a sign outside the door that said "Archibald Benson Company - ABC Wealth Management You Can Trust!"

As he had predicted, he soon started to sign up a number of clients on account of his previous affiliation in the business. His policy was simple and straightforward. He guaranteed his clients an annual return of 6% on their investment, provided they could leave their deposits three years with him. He would either pay the 6% interest at the end of each year or add it to the invested money. Regular statements would be issued to reassure his clients that all was under control. Three years after the initial investment, ABC wold return the deposited amounts plus accrued interest of six percent per annum, unless clients preferred to cash their interests at the end of each year.

When one compared this guaranteed yield to what banks paid to savings accounts, Archie did indeed offer a very attractive investment opportunity.

This pledge to his customers was possible because Archie had actually contracted a secret agreement with the Mafia. Archie would funnel all the money he received from his investors to the Mafia's loan sharking business during a period of three years for a return of fifteen percent per year. In view of the sky high interest rates extorted by loan sharks from their unfortunate clientele, fifteen percent was a normal commission they paid to fundraisers like Archie Benson. Archie would keep nine percent and pay six to his own clients.

The Mafia also agreed to run this arrangement for three years and pay Archie his 15% every three months and then return the entire investment sum to Archie after three years had passed.

As is known to those familiar with the dealings of organized crime, they keep promises and pledges because otherwise they risk litigation and exposure that they certainly cannot afford.

Archie had discussed and negotiated this deal with local mafia bosses during several after hour meetings with them in designated bistros and pizza parlours and had been given the assurance that if he stuck to the deal sealed by handshakes and hugs, they would honour it to the last penny.

And so, ABC Investments began to attract clients who were told by Archie that he knew how to invest their money wisely in reliable valuables from all over the world and could therefore guarantee them the six percent return and then, after three years, the reimbursement, in full, of the originally invested amount.

Believe it or not, but this scheme worked perfectly well for three years. Archie received substantial amounts of money from all kinds of sources, including private people and companies.

He issued from time to time fictitious statements and paid periodically the six percent unless clients preferred to keep the return with the original investment. Archie, in turn, received every three months, his fifteen percent in thousand and hundred dollar bills, all neatly packed in ordinary boxes and cartons.

At the end of the third year the mafia asked Archie if he wanted to continue with the arrangement for another three years. Archie replied that he would consult his clientele before agreeing. He sent out letters and the overwhelming majority said: "Sure, why not?"

And so the fraudulent scheme went on for another three years during which all participants kept their promises. To all appearances the ABC financial operation was an aboveboard perfectly legal business.

When the sixth year came to an end, Archie informed all his clients of his impending retirement. True to their pledge, the mafia returned the capital in full, which Archie returned to all his investors to the last dollar, plus the accrued interest of six percent per annum.

And when all was settled and the books were closed, Archie Benson had amassed during these six years, an amount of over six million dollars. Not bad considering the limited time of operation.

In fact, Archie's decision to limit his activity to six years was a wise one, because prolonging it could have entailed all kinds of unforeseen risks.

*   *   *

It was a rainy late October day when Archie closed down ABC Investments and after having answered the many letters and phone messages from a satisfied clientele who praised him and his company for their honesty.

A few days later Archie drove to his vacation home in the Laurentians for a short rest and then for a trip to Mexico, where he intended to eventually take up residence for the foreseeable future. He was approaching his sixtieth birthday and he had every intention of spending the rest of his days in the peace and comfort he had set himself as an objective so many years ago.

The Laurentian home was actually more than a retreat. It was also the place where Archie kept his illegal loot of mafia generated profits.

Adjoining his house, like an extension was the garage in which he had dug a small square-like space in the floor. Into this space he had placed a steel box and this box now contained some five million dollars, all in large denominations, tightly packed and wrapped in sealed plastic bags.

Over this hole in the ground, Archie had placed a heavy iron plate to make it look like a covered drain or sump and to hide this innocent looking plate on the cement floor, Archie had parked an old car he had not driven for many years on top of it.

Thus, for all intents and purposes, the cache was neither visible, nor, even if it was, would not attract more attention than any iron plate on a garage floor would.

Before leaving for Mexico, Archie went back to his garage which he also used as a locker room or depository of discarded items packed in cartons, piled up against the garage wall.

He found everything in order and drove to Montreal from where he boarded a flight to Mexico City.

He checked into a downtown hotel and immediately started to contact a real estate agent who had been recommended by a friend. His intention was to buy a nice seaside property near one of the popular vacation spots and pay for it in cash which he was to bring to Mexico in a container hidden under the rear seat of his spacious car.

He had planned it all very carefully. One step would follow the next one in logical sequence.

He met the real estate man, who was used to transactions with people from both South and North America who paid for their property purchases in cash, no questions asked.

Archie looked at several homes and intended to continue doing so for the next week until he could make up his mind. He was excited about the prospect of having his own home near a beach and began to prepare himself mentally for a comfortable retirement.

*   *   *

Back in Canada, the month of April had been a real stinger as far as weather was concerned. Heavy winds and prolonged rainfalls alternated with below average temperatures, especially in the Laurentians, where some places had been flooded by overflowing lakes and streams.

But the heaviest storm came down on the weekend following Archie's departure for Mexico. That day it seemed as if nature had unleashed all its wildest fury. The dark sky was literally covered with lightning bolts followed by ear-shattering thunder to which there seemed to be no end.

It so happened, that one of these lightning bolts struck an old tree leaning against Archie's garage building. In fact, the lightning broke the tree and hurled the trunk on to the garage roof, crushing the flimsy structure and landing right over the parked car inside.

When the storm somewhat subsided, Archie's neighbor, who had witnessed the accident and knew that Archie had said goodbye to them before leaving for Mexico, phoned the local police station to report the accident. When the police arrived to inspect the damage, they noticed the broken tree trunk hanging over the parked car and moved it slightly away in order to protect the car. However, by doing so, they also exposed the metal plate covering the hole in the cement floor. As a precaution, they cordoned off the partially destroyed garage with yellow police tape. Then they contacted the neighbors and asked how they could get in touch with Archie. The neighbors gave them two phone numbers; one of Archie's Montreal home and the other of his son, a dentist. The next morning they got in touch with the son, reported the accident and asked him to inform his father, which he said he would do right away.

*   *   *

In the meantime, the news of Archie's garage damage began to circulate in the little Laurentian town and in so doing reached the ears of two burglars.

"Paul", said one of them to his pal. "How about we drive over to the broken garage during the night and see if the damage made it possible to access the adjacent house. Maybe we can find something of value, especially since the owners are apparently away." "Good idea", said the partner and that is exactly what they did during the night.

They drove to the place, crawled under the police tape, armed with powerful flashlights and inspected the garage and its door connecting it to the main residence.

As they looked around the garage, they noticed the exposed metal cover protruding from underneath the car.

"What do you think is under that metal plate?" said one of the burglars. "I don't know", he replied, "looks like a drain. Why don't we have a look? Give me a hand." Together they moved the cover, and to their amazement, they discovered a metal box lodged inside the hole. They immediately took it out, replaced the cover as it was before and decided to leave the place with the box, rather than continuing their search. Especially since one of the burglars had noticed a light in the window of the neighboring house.

It was precisely three-thirty in the morning when the two burglars left the scene, hurrying back to their car, carrying the metal container with them.

The neighbor who had been awakened by the noise of the burglar's car and had seen them search the garage, and shortly afterwards driving off with the box, phoned the police to report his observation.

Two constables arrived in due course, looked the place over and since they saw no forceful entry into the house and no apparent changes in the garage from the day before, they assumed that the burglars had stolen one of the boxes lining the garage wall, probably containing tools or clothing. They completed a report and intended to inform Archie on his return.

*   *   *

Archie was now in the third day of his exploration trip in Mexico. He had already seen several properties and had fallen in love with one particular villa on a hill overlooking a lovely bay not far from Acapulco. The price seemed right, the house was in excellent condition but above all, the previous owners were more than willing to accept in cash and could not care less about anything else.

When Archie reached his hotel in the evening, he found a message from his son. "Call me back, Dad", it said.

Archie called Montreal, and was told about the lightning accident and the severe damage to his garage. "I am sure the insurance will pay for the repairs," said his son. "No need to worry, Dad. Thank God, the tree did not fall over the house. You need not hurry back. The police have cordoned off your property. See you soon and have a safe trip home!"

Archie did not like this message from his son. In fact, he was scared that in the fracas and visits by curious neighbours, someone might discover his cache in the ground.

He took the first available flight back home and drove straight up North to look at his damaged garage, or more precisely at the metal cover on the ground. What he saw drained all blood from his face. The parked car had been moved, exposing the plate. He pushed the plate aside and looked with horror into a gaping emptiness, a hole. He was close to a massive heart attack. The box was gone.

With difficulty he sat down on a discarded chair, when he heard a voice from outside. It was his next door neighbour Emile. "Hello, Archie", he said with a vigorous voice that shattered Archie's stupor. "See what happens when you turn your back to Canada? Eh? First there was the deafening noise of the lightning splitting your tree, and then, a day later, during the night, at three o'clock I was awakened by a car noise and as I looked out the window, I noticed two burglars searching around your garage with flashlights and then shortly afterwards walking away, carrying a box. I assume they were scared off by the light in my window and grabbed the first box they found in your garage. I reported all of this to the police. Oh, by the way, when the police came to inspect the premises, a couple of hours after the lightning strike, I helped them move the parked car inside away from the broken tree which was dangling right above it. So, at least we saved your old car from any harm.

Oh, one final thing, the police came to inspect your garage after I had told them about the burglars and they found everything in place and no forced entry into your home. If you find some tools or other items missing you can always file a complaint with the police. You know, Archie, it could have been worse. The lightning could have broken a window or the falling tree could have damaged your house. Call your insurance tomorrow. Welcome home, Archie, tell me if you need anything." With that the friendly neighbor was gone.

More dead than alive, Archie limped into his house and like an empty sack, he fell into the sofa covering his face with his two hands. Gone were five million US dollars.

As he started thinking, after the initial numbness, he realized "gone for good!" There was nothing he could do to retrieve the money.

He could not reveal to anyone that he had lost this amount. The police and the RCMP would ask what five million dollars were doing buried in a garage. Where did this money come from? Perhaps from a crime or an affiliation with organized crime, which would certainly open a huge can of worms. He sat on the sofa and started to cry like a child who lost his favourite toy.

There was really nothing he could do to retrieve the loot. Even if the burglars were apprehended when trying to spend the money and would confirm that they stole it from him, he would have to deny any connection to it.

Six years of his life and a cleverly conceived scheme that had contained all elements of the perfect crime had gone kaput.

After a night survived with the help of tranquilizers and sleeping pills, he woke up the next day, saying to himself:

"Okay, Archie, you lost it all, but not really all. You still have your health but most of all you have an untarnished reputation of a trustworthy financial expert. All that you can do is to start afresh.

Barely two weeks had passed since Archie's utterly devastating and traumatic realization that he had indeed been deprived of his life's savings. He was still trying to come to grips with this unexpected turn in his life, when, one evening, he received a phone call from a person who said: "Is this Mr. Archibald Benson?" When Archie responded: "Yes, it is", the voice continued. "Archie, I would like to meet with you to discuss something. My name is Paul. You don't know me but we have something in common. You see, I know someone who was in your garage a couple of weeks ago." Silence followed.

Archie froze for a second. In fact, he did not know what to say to the stranger. His first impulse was to say "I don't know what you are referring to", but then he uttered: "Yes, what is it you want to discuss with me?"

The stranger must have sensed the apprehensive ring in Archie's voice and said: "Listen Archie, I am neither the police, nor anyone you should be afraid of, understand? I speak to you as a friend who wants to propose a deal to you. I just want to sit down and talk to you. Anywhere is okay with me. You pick the place and I'll be there. You come alone and I'll be alone. Okay?"

All kinds of thoughts raced through Archie's mind, but finally he said: "Do you know the boat station near the Restaurant du Lac right here?" "I do", said the man. "Behind the boat station is a small park with benches. How about the last bench closest to the restaurant?" "I'll be there" was the rapid answer. He hung up.

Archie's imagination was crammed with apprehension and curiosity, as he arrived the next day at the agreed upon place, still looking carefully around him. A tall man in a dark jacket and faded blue jeans was already sitting on the bench. He got up and shook hands with Archie and they both sat down. Archie was still looking around him but there was nothing that caught his attention other than some people in the distance and kids playing.

"So, what's on your mind?" Archie started. "Okay", said the man, "This is going to be a long conversation and I really don't know where to start."

Archie was somewhat reassured by the casual and even friendly tone in the man's voice.

"Well", the man started. "I'll come to the point and don't worry, I am just by myself. This is not a trap nor a trick. I want to propose a deal to you. You see, I and my partner who was with me when all this happened, are in possession of the box hidden in your garage. I suppose you guessed that much by now. You therefore also know that we found some five million dollars in that box. Now, I assume and believe that this is your money. I also assume that this is some kind of loot money you were hiding. I don't care where it came from, but it is certainly money you did not declare to the government and did not pay any taxes on. Otherwise why hide it? But all this is not my concern. My concern is what to do with this money. Like you, neither of us can go to a bank and deposit it into an account and draw from it without arousing attention. You know as well as I do that financial institutions make you fill out and sign a form for any transaction of more than a few thousand dollars.

So, I come back to my earlier question: What to do with the money? Well, I think my friend and I have an idea. How about the three of us become partners in a business?

Archie, who had not said a word since Paul had started his monologue, raised an eyebrow: "What kind of business?" he finally ventured to ask.

"Well, a business like opening a hotel and a restaurant right here in the Laurentians." He stopped and looked at Archie.

"Why do you need me to be a part of this business? You grabbed the money, so why don't you run with it?"

"Aha", retorted Paul. "That's a good question and I'll be perfectly honest with you. Because my partner and I would find it very difficult if not utterly impossible to start a business of our own for the simple reason that we both have criminal records. Mind you nothing terribly serious like murder or shoot-outs or even bank robberies, but several burglaries, credit card frauds, and forcible entries for which we both served time in jail on different occasions. We would find a brick wall in front of us if we approached any bank for a loan or the Liquor Commission for a license. We even lost our credit cards. You realize that if we build a hotel we would need more than the five million we laid our hands on.

On the other hand, from what we learned from our enquiries and checks during the past few days, you, Archie Benson, have an impeccable and indeed enviable reputation in the business world. So", continued Paul and the "so" was very long and drawn-out, "we need each other, if you know what I mean. You need us because not only are we sitting on the money, but because we know how to get a lot of construction and other work done for the hotel without receipts and taxable invoices. You just leave all of this to us. We will do all the work and there will be plenty of it.

And we need you because you will be the front man or the official President of the company we will create to sponsor the hotel project.

Do you follow my thinking?" he added, looking at Archie. "Let us simply say that not only do we need each other to create a good business, but neither of us can betray or cheat on the other without causing harm to himself.

Archie, I ask you, have you ever come across a safer venture than what I am proposing to you, not to mention the sound business reasoning for a first class hotel in a busy touristic and recreational area?" With that said, Paul moved slightly back and looked Archie straight in the eyes.

Archie was truly surprised about the man's proposal and definitely needed time to think about it. Also, it was getting dark in the little park and he preferred to end the meeting while people and children playing nearby were still around.

"Okay", Archie finally said. "Let me think about all this. Tell me how I can get in touch with you in a few days."

"Sure", replied Paul. He took out a piece of paper, scribbled a phone number on it and handed it to Archie

Needless to say, Archie had really no one to discuss this unusual proposal with except himself. And this he did at incredible length during the next couple of weeks. He consulted business and law manuals, reasoned about all the things that could go wrong, but in the end he phoned Paul with the curt sentence: "Let's meet some more. I have some questions and some ideas of my own." Archie had also drawn up a draft agreement to make the venture a perfectly legal business and to secure his part and position in the company.

They met a few more times, but in the end the three of them sat together in Archie's place for an ordered-in dinner and a few beers to celebrate their new enterprise.

*   *   *

Visitors to the "Auberge Des Trois Mousquetaires" who enjoy the hospitality and the many refinements of the cozy retreat up north have nothing but complimentary comments about the new hotel and restaurant. In fact, when leaving, they spontaneously promise the General Manager, Archie Benson, to recommend it to all their friends. "Merci et à la prochaine" is the joyful goodbye as they close the freshly painted doors behind them.

And yet just three people in the world know the real story behind this aptly named new Auberge in the Laurentians.

A LIFE IN COURT

Phil Harris had every reason to be proud of himself. He had graduated from law school with a summa cum laude, had been admitted to the Ontario Bar Association and, at twenty-eight years of age, was already beginning to make his mark in the Criminal Law department of a large Bloor Street law firm. He was tall and athletic-looking, with curly blond hair and a very determined gait. He clearly projected the image of a young man who knew where he was going and who definitely meant to get there.

During a party at one of his friend's home, he met Lisa, a twenty-two year old brunette who had just completed a three-year course as a social worker. Lisa was pretty, sexy and very intelligent, obviously the apple of her adoring parents' eyes.

What started as an invitation to dinner, followed by a prolonged dating period during which Lisa found in Phil a highly articulate and bright man with a razor-sharp mind, soon blossomed into a spirited love affair and eventually ended up in a proposal delivered by Phil during a champagne supper at a posh Toronto restaurant.

The two were married soon afterwards, embarked on a short honeymoon in Hawaii and returned home to set up digs in a rented apartment before moving into a small but comfortable house in one of Toronto's upper bourgeois neighborhoods. And the move came just in time to accommodate the now expanding family because Lisa discovered that she was pregnant. In due course a beautiful baby girl made her debut who was named Pamela or Pam for short. Needless to say Pam immediately became the focal point not only of her parents' but especially of her grandparent's lives.

Phil and Lisa were indeed a very good-looking couple which projected the image of the ideal young family about to start a long life of bliss and of making dreams come true, embracing traditional values, all bonded together by love and respect for each other.

This for all intents and purposes, was the premise under which Lisa had accepted Phil's marriage proposal and had then embarked on this long journey commonly referred to as *married life*.

To be sure she was prepared to give it all she possessed and could muster, and that was ample. She had beauty and grace, she was well educated, came from a well-to-do family and was brought up in an elegant style which also accounted for her sentimentality and romantic inclination to find beauty in life's daily perambulations.

But, soon, even in their first year of married life, it became apparent that Phil was a bird of a different feather. Was it that Lisa had not noticed his real character during their courtship or was it that she was too much in love with this virile hunk of a man who also happened to be a much talked-about lawyer, the fact remained that the couple did not see eye to eye on many issues and had indeed different values of life. In fact, they were different to the point of often being on opposing poles.

The main factor behind this difference was no doubt Phil's highly opinionated concept on many aspects of life which included his aversion to any view other than his own. Then there was also his very materialistic concept of everything and everyone around him. To Phil, money was the be-all and end-all. People without sizeable means were losers and insignificant fellow travellers, even if they happened to be erudite, honest and useful contributors to society.

This prominently voiced philosophy of life became even more assertive when clad in the professional mantle of the sharpest and most dreaded criminal defence lawyer in the business. In fact, Phil Harris was respected by any friend who appointed him to be extricated from criminal charges, or feared by any foe who had to face him on the opposite, and often losing side in a courtroom. And it was this professional obsession that Phil carried into his private and even into his family life.

This obviously led to lengthy and often acerbic conversations with Lisa in their living room or kitchen or even in their bedroom. He always knew better and was always right and that was it.

Naturally, Lisa tried to avoid such argumentative episodes as much as possible, but when Phil tried to discipline the growing child and left her running to cry in her mother's lap, Lisa began to realize that her marriage was on a collision course.

No wonder that as early as during the third year of their marriage Lisa was given to depressive episodes. Bridging the abyss between wanting to shield little Pam from Phil's frequent verbal outbursts, having to care for a demanding household and on top of that, having to cope with an overly assertive husband did not fail to have a very negative impact on her mood, and on her enjoyment of life.

To be sure, she often thought of calling the marriage quits. Just walking out on Phil. But she was always held back by her concern about the impact a separation and the ensuing changes would have on little Pam. That was the only reason why Lisa decided to soldier on for another year or so until the little girl had reached some degree of early maturity.

It was during the third year into their marriage when Lisa began consulting a psychiatrist and this on the advice of her family doctor who correctly diagnosed most, if not all, of her complaints as psychosomatic manifestations best brought to the attention of a qualified psychiatric specialist.

Lisa told Phil of her decision to see a "shrink" as he called the doctor. To him, her headaches, her insomnia and her stomach cramps were just due to "nerves" for which the doctor would surely give her some pills and that would be the end of it.

*   *   *

Five years had now passed since the beginning of this unpleasant family situation. Five years during which Lisa had seen several psychiatrists who did their best to help her deal with her problems by prescribing anti-depressant medications and counselling, but all treatments had not brought about any significant results for the simple reason that the cause of the problem, namely Phil, was still carrying on unabated.

For sure the couple had gone on trips together, had taken European and Caribbean vacations and had even been on a safari but their homecoming soon dispelled any temporary relief in their continuing tense relationship.

It was on the recommendation of her closest friend Betty that Lisa decided to see a new psychiatrist who was highly praised as being not much of a pill pusher but, instead practised the old-fashioned art of listening to his patients and helping them cope with their problems by building up their self-confidence and their morale, and then discussing with them viable alternatives.

Dr. Sam Goodwyn was in his early forties and was himself just emerging from the trauma of having lost his young wife to cancer.

Even on her first visit to Dr. Goodwyn, Lisa felt that this man could help her. He was soft-spoken, very well-mannered and preferred to talk to his patients as a friend trying to help them out of their problems rather than as a professional emitting diagnostic assessments while making notes on a pad.

Perhaps it was the treatment, even after a few visits, really helped her feel better and surer of herself, or was it that she had taken a liking to him or a combination of both but Lisa started looking forward to her weekly chats with Dr. Goodwyn.

At first, Lisa felt guilty about this sort of trespassing into uncharted emotional waters, but then she also realized that after years of an unpleasant and tense home life, her sessions with Dr. Goodwyn really made her feel like a normal woman again.

One early afternoon Lisa was at home in her bathroom and felt like phoning her doctor to ask him how she should handle an upcoming family situation. She followed her inclination and a lengthy conversation ensued during which Lisa, calling her doctor by his first name, Sam, used a rather intimate and personal form of repartee while discussing her problem. She even repeatedly referred to Phil as she had done during her visits in the doctor's office.

Unbeknownst to her, Phil had come home early that day because of a power failure in his office. As he climbed up the stairs, he overheard Lisa's phone conversation. Being used to investigative practices, he stopped short of entering the bedroom to listen in on his wife's repartee. And there was a lot to listen to, because he heard Lisa discussing him in a way that was far too intimate for what Phil considered to be normal dialogue between patient and doctor.

After Phil had had an earful of this cozy conversation, he burst into the bedroom with the anger of a furious husband apprehending a cheating wife.

"Aha!", he shouted. "Now I know what has been going on behind my back between you and that doctor. You are having an affair and you are going to face the consequences. You hear me? Shame on you!"

Lisa was shocked and frightened beyond words by this unexpected and sudden lightning bolt coming down on her. She hung up and went back into the bathroom, locking the door behind her. Her first reaction was to cry like a child caught with her fingers in the cookie jar. But after a few minutes, she started to think rationally. "Be strong", she said to herself. "Don't let that bully walk over you like a doormat. You have to stand up to him."

With that resolve in mind she came out of the bathroom. Phil had meanwhile gone down to the living room and shouted up at her "Come down. I want to have a word with you. Now!"

Still in her bathrobe, she came into the kitchen and before Phil could utter a word, she said, "No, I am not having an affair with Dr. Goodwyn but yes, I do discuss you with him. Of course I do. I have to. Don't you realize that you are the cause of my emotional problems? Did you listen to me when I told you time and time again that you must change your ways?"

"I'm not changing my ways!" he interrupted her. "My ways as you call them are just fine. That's the way I am. I am a good husband and a good father and I love you and my little girl, but I am not a weakling and not a liar. I just say it as it is. If people don't like hearing the truth, that's not my fault. By now, you should have gotten used to being married to a man who has his two feet on the ground and is respected for that. And you are fooling around with your doctor. Don't tell me 'no', I've heard enough today. It's all very clear to me."

"You are jumping to conclusions", retorted Lisa. "And I know you well enough that nothing I or anyone else will say will make any difference to you. All I can tell you is that I am very unhappy and I can't take it anymore. Correction, I don't want to take it anymore. Unless you make a serious effort to change your attitude as a husband and a father, I want out of this marriage."

As Lisa said these words, she burst into tears. Phil made no move to comfort her, but he said: "Calm down".

There was silence for a long time. Lisa was relieved because she finally said what had been on her mind for a long time and now that the traumatic effect of Phil's "aha" bursting into the bedroom had somewhat subsided, she thought that her reaction was the inevitable consequence of a mismatch that was allowed to continue far too long.

Like a boxer bouncing back into the ring, Phil said: "Well, that's not as easy as you think. Regardless of what you say, I am holding that Sam Goodwyn responsible for this situation and I am going to make him pay for it. I will report him to the Canadian Medical Association for having abused his relationship with a patient to the point of causing her to break up her marriage. And this may be the end of his medical career."

When Lisa heard this, she said: "Are you out of your mind? There is nothing between Dr. Goodwyn and myself other than the relationship that develops between a patient undergoing psychiatric treatment and her doctor. If anyone is responsible for breaking up this marriage, it is you not him. You, with your abusive attitude, your inhuman set of values and your lack of compassion and understanding. How can you say you love me? You have not said a kind word to me in ages. Listen, Phil, I've had it up to here, especially after that insane behaviour of yours tonight. I am taking Pamela and I am going to spend the night at my parents. I need a breather and I need to think it all over. One thing is sure I will not continue to live with you under one roof unless you change your ways completely and utterly. Goodbye."

With that Lisa went up the stairs and started packing. Within fifteen minutes she had thrown a few things into a small suitcase, had dressed Pam and had gotten behind the wheel of her car to drive to her parent's home which was less than ten minutes away.

Phil had watched all this in silence. In fact, he had his back turned to her and he kept looking out of the window.

At her parent's home, Lisa told them the entire story. They were shocked to hear about Phil's reaction to her telephone conversation, but then they had known Phil's aggressive ways for years and both her parents had repeatedly advised her to leave him before she suffered a nervous breakdown.

After having put Pamela to bed, Lisa had a bite with her parents and then went to sleep as it was getting late by now.

The next morning, the three of them met in the kitchen to talk about "where do we go from here?"

Lisa said she wanted to discuss the situation with Dr. Goodwyn. She did and told him about Phil's reaction to their conversation. The doctor listened in silence, but when she had finished he said very calmly: "Lisa, if you think that your marriage has reached a point of no return and you and Phil decide to break it up, I want to marry you right away, a minute after you hold divorce papers in your hand. We can discuss all the details later. I want you to be my wife, and I want to adopt Pam not as your but as our child, okay, Lisa?", he continued, "this is not a decision taken at the spur of the moment, it is something that has been going through my mind for months now. Because as I listened to your life story and you going through all of this, I developed a very strong liking for you. I felt like taking you into my arms many times. Now my thoughts have become realities and that's why I am proposing to you. Lisa, I promise to make you and your little girl very happy and fulfilled, I promise it."

Lisa had been listening to this long conversation with tears in her eyes, but now the tears turned to a sob. She was crying, like letting the tension built up for years and especially during the last twenty-four hours, break through a retention wall.

When she finally stopped crying, she mustered a smile and said: "You know Sam I never heard about a marriage proposal over the phone but it sounds good to me. You know what? I like you a lot and am sure we can make a success of it. I am sure we will love each other. You want an answer: Well, make it a 'yes'." With that the two broke out in laughter. "I have a great deal to go through until we stand at the altar", she said, "so bye for now. You will hear from me soon." "Make it sooner than soon", was Sam's answer. "Tell me if and when you need help, okay? Bye Lisa."

* * *

That same day, Lisa phoned Phil at the office and told him that she wanted to talk with him in the evening. Could he come home earlier than usual?

What followed that evening at the kitchen table of their home was a reasoned delivery by Lisa, who had by now regained her composure.

After a "So?", uttered sternly by Phil, Lisa started. "Look", she said. "You know it and I know it, we are not meant for each other. We went through it for five years. We both tried, but let's face it some people just don't change, in fact they cannot change because they believe their way is the right way. So, let's call it quits and let's go our own way from here on. Let's make the divorce procedure as fast and painless as possible. I guess you will take care of the formalities on your side and I will take a lawyer to help me get it all over with. For the sake of our little girl, I want it to be an amicable separation without the two of us hurting each other. Okay?"

Phil had listened silently, but Lisa realized that he was preparing his reply to her calmly uttered words, and she also knew that his reaction would not be matter of fact or measured.

"That's very nice what you are saying, but I have other words for it. First of all, I will consider you the causative party on account of your adultery. You are having an affair with your doctor. And, speaking of that man, I will beat the living daylights out of him for having ruined my marriage. I will see to it that he gets fired not only from the hospital, but that he gets kicked out of the medical association on account of professional misconduct. In other words, your good buddy Doctor Sam is finito, kaput, morto, do you hear me? Leave it to me, I will see to it that he will end up as a sales clerk in a shoe shop, if they will have him for that. That's all."

Phil's face had become red and full of hatred while he delivered his threats.

Lisa, still maintaining a measure of calm, replied: "If you do all this, it will not be   Dr. Goodwyn but Phil Harris who will be finito and kaput. I will tell all of our friends and the friends of our friends what kind of bully you are, how rudely you treated me and our daughter all these years and when I am finished with drawing this image of you amongst our and your circle of friends and neighbors, you go and try to find yourself another wife in this town. Perhaps in Zanzibar you may find a spouse or even a friend, but not in Toronto. You will be a social outcast. That's all I have to tell you. If you try to take any steps to damage the reputation or livelihood of a very honourable professional. And, if you sue me for adultery, I have plenty of neighbors who can confirm the shouts and outbursts they heard over the years from our garden and our terrace on summer evenings. Okay?"

When Lisa had finished, she had the impression as if Phil had met his match. At least, it looked like that to her, because he got up from the kitchen table and said: "I am going for a walk if you don't mind. I have heard enough."

But Lisa knew that the fact that he did not reply to her openly expressed threats, and preferred to leave the room was a sure sign that her words had sunk into him.

*   *   *

The divorce proceedings of Lisa Brown versus Phillip Harris on grounds of incompatibility of character were swift and thanks to Phil's expert handling, smooth to the point of a routine court case. They both signed a number of papers and statements about division of property, payments for childcare, Lisa's custody of the child and Phil's right to see Pamela at certain intervals as well as other matters. When it was all over Lisa Brown and Phil Harris were legally separated and free to go their different ways, wherever they took them.

An obvious mismatch had finally found its merciful ending.

*   *   *

Barely a month after the divorce, Lisa and Sam were married in a moving ceremony attended by family and friends, with little Pam standing at the altar between her mother and brand-new dad. It was a picture to behold.

The new family established its home in Sam's comfortable house and started to feather their nest with knickknacks and décor just like any new couple does, but it was not to remain their home for long. Leave it to good old Phil Harris. He could not keep his venom from spreading to some of his friends about Dr. Sam Goodwyn having broken up his marriage and, little wonder, these rumours did not fail to reach Sam's hospital. In fact, he was asked by the hospital director if there was substance to the rumour. When Sam explained the situation, the director appeared satisfied, but Sam was not. He sent out some feelers and, in a very short time heard from the Vancouver General Hospital. It was an offer to head their psychiatric clinic, a most welcome and prestigious position in a naturally beautiful surrounding.

Lisa was overjoyed and urged her husband to accept before they changed their mind. She had enough unpleasant memories attached to Toronto. Her only regret was to leave her parents, and that meant a great deal to both sides. But telling herself that you can't make an omelet without breaking some eggs, she started preparing for the move and within weeks, Dr. Sam Goodwyn, surrounded by a very relieved Lisa, not to mention, a happy Pam, left the city of their birth, of their good years and their bad years for the West Coast, where the family intended to start a new and promising life.

*   *   *

Phil Harris soon began to cope with a bachelor's life, which on account of his very independent ways and his financial means, was not too daunting a task. He hired a housekeeper who cooked and cleaned his home and started to look around for female company. To be sure, based on his past experience, he was now less inclined to enter into a new marriage, at least not for the time being. He was also aware of the fact that the rapidly expanding line of clients seeking his legal help would prevent him from devoting too much time to a brand-new wife. Under the circumstance he preferred to enter into non-binding relationships to fill his free evenings and weekends as well as his occasional vacations. And, he did not fail to find acceptable companionships. Toronto, like any big city, has no shortage of lonely ladies, especially when the suitor was one of the city's well-known legal wizards.

And a legal wizard Phil Harris was certainly shaping up to become. In fact, he had developed the well-earned reputation of being a master orator in court, often influencing judge, jury and prosecutor to the point of mesmerizing them and walking out of the court with a non-guilty verdict attained against all odds in front of a stunned audience.

His rapidly spreading reputation, often obtained through razor-sharp cross-examination and merciless interrogation of his opponents to the point of their complete mental and physical exhaustion and sometimes even collapse had eventually come to the attention of the mafia and other criminal syndicates that were frequent courtroom visitors.

When Phil, one day, was approached by one of these underworld dons and when he was told about the almost limitless financial resources of organized crime, his greed for money and more money immediately kicked in and he agreed to represent some of these delinquents in their battles in court. What started with one or two isolated cases, soon became an avalanche of clients and in a few short months Phil had become the most prominent lawyer of Canada's organized crime.

Phil was to hold this position for a number of years. He was both respected and feared by friend and foe, and as the years went by, he had accumulated a string of the latter variety. He had become used to the occasional threat, hurled openly or covertly at him, considering all this par for the course in a busy criminal lawyer's life.

But after many years of going through both a hectic and hazardous professional life, one day the inevitable happened. He received a phone call one evening in his home from someone telling him in a muffled voice that unless he ceased his defence tactics in the trial of one specific accused opponent, he would be killed. As was to be expected, Phil ignored this warning and continued his action in court.

Sure enough, a few days later as he stepped out of his car one evening to enter his home, a dark shadow suddenly emerged from hiding and fired two shots at his legs from a hand gun equipped with a silencer. Just as he had appeared from nowhere, the attacker also disappeared, leaving a bleeding and screaming Phil on his doorstep. Neighbors hearing the screams, rushed out of their homes and called an ambulance and Phil spent the next weeks undergoing two surgical procedures because the assailant's well-aimed bullet had broken the bones in both legs and both were complicated fractures.

A few weeks later Phil was back home, where he nursed his injuries before he could move properly again. But the accident had left him with a limp because one bullet had not only shattered the bone but also severed some nerves, all of which caused him pain while walking.

This attack was to have more profound effects on Phil than mere pain and scars. It caused Phil to stop and ponder about his life in court and the meaning of it all.

He came to realize that although the years of rushing from one case to another had left him with a sizeable fortune, for the underworld had paid him very handsomely for his services, he had also developed a number of stress-related ailments that were certainly destined not to go away, but on the contrary, only to get worse with advancing age.

He had suffered two mini-strokes, he tried to control high-blood pressure and he had developed an irregular heartbeat. His doctor constantly reminded him to "take it easy".

Phil had now gone through almost twenty-eight years since his break-up with Lisa. While he had never had any contact with her since then, he had maintained close relations with Pam, by now a happily married wife and mother of two children. Over the years, Pam had repeatedly urged her father to either leave his stressful day-to-day routine or choose a more sedate legal activity such as counsellor or advisor. Needless to say, Phil had always brushed this well-meant advice away with "Not yet, Pam, one of these days!"

Well, the armed attack on his doorstep appeared to herald "one of these days". Using his approaching sixty-fifth birthday as a pretext, he resigned from his law firm and announced his departure from practicing criminal law. He also told Pam that he would like to move to California and spend the rest of his life in a place near where she and her family lived, doing things he had always wanted to do but could not because of his all-consuming professional career.

Phil had not remarried but had maintained close ties with two succeeding ladies over the years.

When he informed Pam over the phone about his plans to retire she was delighted to hear that he wanted to live somewhere near her. In fact, she was moved to tears when she listened to his tired voice which was beginning to lose its vigour and stamina after years of haranguing, yells and shouts. She thought she was facing an aging lion seeking the shade of a tree or the calm of a den after a lifetime of hunting and fighting.

Within a few weeks, Phil had sold his Toronto home and most of its contents and he moved to Los Angeles where he bought a condo in a new development some ten minutes away from where Pam and her family lived.

Pam's husband was a very successful businessman who owned a clothing store in downtown Los Angeles, as well as other stores, located in shopping malls in and around the West Coast.

For the first time in his mature life, Phil was beginning to savour going to concerts, playing golf and enjoying dinners at his daughter's home. He was not a happy retiree, because retirement was not his cup of tea but he grudgingly accepted it as a necessary phase in anyone's life.

But Phil's imposed retirement was not to last for too long. After a mere four years he was beginning to complain about a number of aches and pains which his physician diagnosed as a badly bruised cardiovascular system due to a mild heart attack suffered years ago and his persistent high-blood pressure.

All this eventually made Pamela decide to place her father in a retirement home where he had access to constant supervision and other health services.

Barely a year after his move to this residence, Phil's heart took a sudden turn for the worse and he had to be hospitalized. That was to be the end. Two weeks later, Phil suffered another heart attack, this time a major one which claimed his life. The funeral took place in Los Angeles. Not too many people attended, since all of Phil's friends still lived in Toronto. Lisa and Sam came from Vancouver and Pam and her family all attended. In fact, Pam read the eulogy, in a moving and very emotional voice:

"Dear friends,

It is my sad duty to deliver the eulogy of my late father. Sad for a number of reasons, some of which are obvious, but some others may come as a surprise to you.

When I penned these words last night, I hesitated whether I should say what I am about to tell you, but then I asked myself: If not now, when?

So, here in a few concise sentences, is a partial review of Phillip Harris' passage through life, and believe me, it was anything but a smooth or pleasant one, neither for him, nor for the people he lived with.

As you all know, my father was a dedicated criminal lawyer, according to the Ontario Bar Association, one of the best if not the best in recent memory.

He defended his clients and accused his opponents with equal vehemence and a razor sharp legal mind that left judges, juries and everyone else in the courtroom not only speechless but also defenceless, His logic, his intimate knowledge of the case at hand but above all his familiarity with the law, were his impeccable and invaluable assets. He was prepared to deal conclusively with any objection, any denial hurled at him, often rendering prosecutors and opposition lawyers powerless. His was the mesmerizing oratory of a Caesar and when he sat down after his delivery there was inevitably complete silence in the courtroom, because his audience needed time to come to grips with what he had said before they could muster a reply, if any reply there was.

As you can easily imagine this dominance in the courtroom created many friends who owed him the successful conclusion of their trial but it also created many bitter enemies whose conviction and prison sentences he had brought about.

In short, my father's life in court was far from being a nine-to-five routine. It was a day to day battle, a struggle and an endless fight.

And, unfortunately for those destined to share their lives with him, he was incapable of hanging this fighting spirit, this abrasive behavior, on a hanger in his office before heading home in the evening. He brought it right with him into the kitchen, into the living room and sometimes even into his bedroom.

Sadly, this was the life of my mother and myself and it continued to be the life of all those who tried to recreate a family around him after the breakup of his marriage.

"My dear friends, what I have told you so far was the story of my late father's behaviour, of his comportment, perhaps even of his façade to the world but it was not his soul, not the reflection of his innermost feelings. It may be true that we are perceived by the way we come across to others but this perception is often far from the reality of our true persona. And that person, that real Phillip Harris was revealed to me when he retired from his life in court and decided to come and live near me and my family in California.

Perhaps it was the aging lion who had lost his bite, perhaps it was the wisdom that permeates our feelings and our endeavours the day there are no more battles to be fought, but throughout the few short years of his retirement I discovered in my father, a loving, a caring and a compassionate human being of the finest ilk. I had the impression of finally finding in him the lone stranger, the real Phillip Harris.

And it is to celebrate the memory of this very person that my mother and I, who inherited the sizeable estate of my late father, decided to create the Harris Foundation.

This institution to be known as the "HARRIS SHOP OF HOME REPAIRS" will be dedicated to just that. To repair broken or damaged homes because of the attitude or behaviour of one or both partners in a marriage. It will be staffed by psychologists, lawyers and social workers who will offer their combined services to families or individuals who have difficulties in living peacefully and mutually beneficial home lives together because of their incompatibilities, especially when their problems are compounded by children.

The services of "HARRIS HOME REPAIRS" will be offered free of charge to applicants who cannot afford to pay for them and for nominal fees to those who can.

They will not only consist of advice and counselling but of follow-ups, group therapies and social activities aimed at giving affected people the opportunity to interact by comparing and discussing their stories with others within the framework and under the umbrella of professional practice. Only in the event of complete failure of the repair process will the Harris Institution provide not only legal services for separation but also help in the social rehabilitation of family members, especially, the children affected by the separation.

The Harris Foundation will be staffed by both volunteers and paid professionals and it will be funded by endowments from the substantial estate left by my late father.

Dad, my mother and I believe that we could not have come up with a more fitting manner to not only honour but also perpetuate your memory. May you finally find, in death, the peace and satisfaction denied to you in life."

KARL

In the mid nineteen-fifties, I unexpectedly – out of the blue – became a player, perhaps even a key player in a family drama. It was a gripping and emotional event which shook my otherwise regular life, leaving behind memories that still haunt me.

Perhaps the time has come to share these memories with you, especially since most of the players have long since passed away.

*   *   *

My maternal grandmother had two brothers who had inherited their father's contracting business in Istanbul. Over many years they imported and sold to the Turkish government major items such as ships and turn-key factory installations. In the process, they amassed a sizeable fortune.

The older brother, Morris, was married and had three children, while Norbert, the younger one, was also married but had no children because of his wife's health problems.

Although the two brothers were very close in their personal relations, their lifestyles differed substantially. Morris led the life of a baron. He had an elaborate winter residence in Istanbul, a summer home on the French Riviera and a large flat in Paris for the opera and concert season. The family of five had servants galore and the children were brought up in an opulence fit for royalty. Nothing was denied to them, absolutely nothing. The son, Karl even had his own car at the age of fifteen, driven by a chauffeur until the day he would obtain his own license.

In time, the two girls married into similarly well-to-do families but their brother, Karl, grew up a drifter and eventually turned into a playboy. Shying away from any kind of education or professional training, he spent his days travelling, and, like a bumblebee sucking nectar from many flowers, he lavishly entertained a succession of beautiful girlfriends, taking them on trips and buying them expensive gifts.

In contrast to his older brother's extravagant lifestyle, Norbert lived elegantly but modestly and sensibly, like someone aware of the fact that times of plenty may sometimes be followed by lean years and it behooves responsible people to be prepared for that eventuality.

And indeed, as was to be expected in the turbulent days of the nineteen-forties, the contracting business of the two brothers came to a standstill on account of the war raging in Europe. Morris retired, spending the rest of his days with his wife in their accustomed style until their fortune, including their own home, was gone and the aging couple passed away. Their two daughters had moved to Europe with their families, leaving Karl to fend for himself in Istanbul. And Karl turned out to be a very poor fender indeed! Devoid of any professional training and lacking education, he tried to find employment in a variety of enterprises but the reality soon began to sink in that good-looking and jovial Karl was indeed charming and loveable but he was utterly unprepared to earn a living in a demanding commercial world.

It was at this point that his uncle Norbert came to the rescue by offering Karl a home in his own residence which included meals and everything else the generous uncle deemed he was obligated to, in memory of his late brother, Morris.

This situation lasted a number of years. It was now the mid-fifties and Karl was forty-five years old, still a drifter, still not gainfully employed but still loved by the rest of the family and this for two reasons. Firstly, Karl was the epitome of charm and joviality, just a nice guy, but more importantly the family blamed his inability to cope with the reality of daily life not on Karl, himself, but on his parents, who had brought him up completely unprepared to face it.

By late 1955, Uncle Norbert also passed away a few months after his sickly wife had died. Since he had left no will, the estate was subject to Turkish Succession Law, which deals with all aspects of an estate. We were soon informed by a court that Norbert had left twenty heirs, all children and grandchildren and that all twenty were entitled to equal parts of the estate. At a subsequent family gathering the family decided to appoint me as the executor with power of attorney to handle all formalities.

My first action was to take stock of the deceased's assets which turned out to be two small buildings in Istanbul. With the consent of the family I sold them and duly allocated one twentieth of the proceeds to all heirs including myself and, of course, Karl.

But then, during a later family meeting I was advised that like many other businessmen in Turkey, Norbert had a business branch in Switzerland and therefore must have had an account in a Swiss bank. I was also told that Norbert's best friend was the manager of an American bank in Geneva. Why not contact him to find out whether there was any money and where it might be. It so happened that this manager, a native of Istanbul, was also a friend of my late father. I had often met him before he moved to Switzerland.

The next day, I phoned this man, who told me to take the next plane to Geneva. "I will help you as much as I can. Bring with you all legal documents to prove your identity, as well as your power of attorney and come see me" he said.

Within days I had everything put together, taking care to have all documents authenticated by the Swiss Consulate in Istanbul.

It was a dull September morning when I entered the office of the bank manager in Geneva. After a brief discussion, he recommended the following course of action: "Look", he said. "I know that Norbert had money in Switzerland, but he never told me how much and in which bank he kept it. However, there are really just three possibilities. The Swiss Bank Corporation, the Union Bank of Switzerland and the Crédit Suisse, all have their head offices in Zürich. I know their managers very well, but I cannot ask them if Norbert had an account with them. This is against the law. However, I can phone them and tell them about the situation, adding that you will be calling on them shortly and asking them to help you. What they do is up to them but at least they will welcome you as a friend of mine. I am sorry I cannot do more but you should be able to access the accounts. Keep me informed."

I thanked him and headed back to Zürich where I stayed at the Alpenhof Hotel on a side street adjacent to the legendary Bahnhofstrasse, Switzerland's equivalent of New York's Fifth Avenue.

Tired from the day's travelling I slumped onto my bed before going down to the hotel's restaurant for dinner.

I was just getting dressed when someone knocked on my door. I opened it and faced the surprise of my life. There, in a light summer suit, stood Karl with a stern and determined look on his youthful face. "Karl", I exclaimed, "what are you doing here and how did you know where to find me?"

"Well", he said, sitting down, "It's a long story and prepare yourself for an interesting evening." His voice was grave and there was an ominous ring to it. "Go ahead Karl," I said, still in awe of his unexpected appearance.

"To answer your question, I found out that you are in Zürich and in what hotel from the bank manager in Geneva, when I phoned him earlier today. He told me that he had talked to you and suggested that I get in touch with you. Meanwhile, on my arrival yesterday from Istanbul, I went to see the manager of the bank in Zürich where our uncle had his account. I knew not only the bank but also the account manager because I had accompanied Uncle Norbert on one of his trips some time ago. The bank manager asked if I had brought with me all legal documents such as power of attorney and death certificate. When I said that I had no documents with me, he replied: 'Sorry but I cannot pay you. Bring me the papers and I will do the rest.'

So there you have it Ben. I know where the money is, I know the manager is ready to pay me but I don't have the documents required for the transaction. You, in turn have the documents but you don't know where the money is, and believe me, no manager will tell you if his bank is holding our uncle's account even if you have an introduction from our friend in Geneva.

Now Ben, do you understand what I mean if I tell you that we need each other to get the money?" "I do, Karl", I replied, adding: "Do you know how much there is in the account?" "Of course I do", he shot back. Three million American dollars. Three million", he repeated.

Needless to say, these emphatically pronounced words took my breath away. "Three million" I said in disbelief. "Yes, Ben", he replied.

"Okay then", I continued. "As you know we are twenty heirs. Tomorrow morning we go to the bank and I bring all the papers with me. We take the money and I begin doling out amounts of 150,000 dollars to each of the twenty legal heirs. What is more, I will transfer all amounts through official bank channels to enable the people in Istanbul to pay taxes as required by law. You, Karl, can take your share immediately and do what you want."

As I was saying these words I noticed that Karl's expression had changed into a grimace of anger or even fury. "What?" he shouted. "Are you crazy? You want to divide the three million into twenty parts? You don't know what you are talking about. You will do nothing of the sort. You and I will share this money. You get a million and a half and I get a million and a half. That's it."

I started to laugh. It was actually more of a bitter grin in reaction to Karl's forcefully ejected words.

"How can you say that?" I retorted. "I am representing the estate. We are twenty heirs and we each get one twentieth of the money."

"No…no…no" Karl interrupted, jumping up from his seat. "Nobody gets anything except you and me: fifty-fifty. All you have to do on your return to Istanbul is to tell them that you tried very hard but in compliance with Swiss laws no bank would reveal if Norbert had an account with them. That's all. Tell me Ben, can any of the twenty family members find out otherwise? Can they come to Zürich and talk to the banks? No. Nobody, and I mean nobody will ever know that we took the money and split it between us.

By now Karl had worked himself up into a fit. He was sweating, breathing heavily and his face was crimson with anger. He even made aggressive gestures waving a finger at me, like: you better do as I tell you or else!

I let Karl sit and calm down and after a few minutes of silence, I said: "Karl, relax and think rationally. Neither you nor I are thieves or robbers. We are members of an honourable family and I have a mandate to represent them. I will not and cannot be party to any scheme to defraud my next of kin. We will get the money and divide it up honestly. And that is final, Karl."

Realizing my very firm stance, Karl had now changed his demeanour. Rising from his seat he said: "Ben, I need this money. I must get it. My girlfriend's brother has a men's shirt store in London's Burlington Arcade and with this million and a half dollars I will become a partner in the business. I will get married and settle in England. This is the only way for me to make a living and have a family. Now, do you understand why I must have the money? I am lost without it", he shouted at me.

"I understand" I said, "but that does not mean that you can take something that does not belong to you."

Karl was just about to embark on another tirade, when the telephone rang. It was the concierge informing me that a letter had just been delivered for me. I guessed it may be from the manager in Geneva confirming that he had talked to his colleagues in Zürich. I told the front desk: "Thank you, I am coming down to get it." I hoped this would give Karl the opportunity to calm down. "I'll be back in a few minutes" I told Karl. "Try and calm down. Why don't you order a drink for both of us from room service while I'm gone." "I don't want any drinks", he said as I left the room.

I must have been gone ten minutes or so, but when I approached my room I heard loud shouts and shrieks coming from behind the door. As I opened it, I faced a scene that I will not forget for as long as I live.

The window was open. Karl stood outside the window on a ledge, holding onto a rail that ran along the upper floor of the hotel building. Across the narrow street there was an electronics store with offices on the upper floor and an open terrace with a cafeteria facing my window. Some of the people on the terrace had seen Karl climbing out of my window, ready to jump down to his death, which caused them to shout and shriek for help.

It was precisely at this moment that I entered my room. I ran immediately to the window and grabbed Karl by his jacket, pulling or rather tearing him back into the room with all my strength. In the process, we both fell back onto the floor, he on top of me. As I lay there, I noticed I was bleeding from a cut on my head from having bumped it on the window frame. Karl was lying on the carpet but then he slowly tried to get up, falling back several times. When he finally staggered to his feet he sat down on the chair, covered his face with his hands and started to cry like a child. I had never heard anyone sob so violently before. He just cried his heart out. I put my arms around him, told him to get up and lie down on my bed. I kept talking to him but I really wanted him to cry in order to get all pent-up emotions out of his system.

Amid sobs, he said: "This was my only chance to provide for myself. What else do I have to make a living? I am lost. I want to die. I don't want to become a doorman or a waiter. Even those jobs I wouldn't know how to do. Better I die," he kept repeating.

At this point, I went to the bathroom and came back with a glass of water in which I had dissolved two sedative tablets. I always take some with me on trips when I cannot sleep because of the jetlag. I made Karl empty the glass and stretch out on the bed. He calmed down within a few minutes, his eyes still full of tears.

I phoned room service and ordered two soups and two omelets as well as some fruits for dinner. As we sat down at the table, I told Karl: "First of all, you will spend the night here. You can take the bed and I will sleep on the small sofa. Tomorrow morning I will phone our cousin Eva in Istanbul and ask her to contact some of the family members, asking them if they would cede their parts to you. I am sure she will find some among the eighteen willing to help you. Leave it to me, Karl" I said, putting my arm around his shoulder. "We will find a way to help you Karl, trust me," I repeated. "I do" he said meekly. "I do" he said again. "Thank you so much Ben."

The next morning I got up early, dressed and went down to the hotel lobby. I phoned my cousin Eva in Istanbul and told her the sad story of Karl's desperate state and his suicide attempt. I also asked her to appeal to some of the family members who were well-off, enquiring if they would agree to cede their parts to Karl. Eva said: "Leave it to me. I'll call you back in a couple of hours."

Well, Eva came through and brilliantly! Karl's two sisters immediately agreed, as did one aging cousin who lived in Bulgaria and another cousin who was a rich merchant in Istanbul. I thanked her and broke the news to Karl who was still in bed.

"Karl" I said, "I can give you seven hundred and fifty thousand dollars. It is not a million and a half, but I am sure your future brother-in-law will not refuse you as part owner in his shirt business. After all, three quarter of a million dollars is a sizeable amount, even for a shop on fashionable Burlington Arcade in London.

It is difficult to describe Karl's reaction to my words. He hugged and kissed me with tears running down his cheeks. But this time they were tears of relief and happiness. He kept shaking my hand and patting my back, thanking me over and over.

Within the hour we were at the bank. We met the manager, I produced all my legal documents, and after a lengthy procedure of signing receipts and other bank papers, I was told that the funds were now available to me. I immediately opened an account with the three million dollars, gave Karl a certified cheque for seven hundred and fifty thousand, and transferred a hundred and fifty thousand dollars to each of the fifteen legal heirs on the list, including myself. All of it through official channels to enable the recipients in Turkey to pay applicable taxes.

Two days later, I boarded a Swissair flight back to Istanbul, relieved beyond words, and my mind loaded with memories to last me a lifetime.

This had been the most dramatic and, at times scary, but ultimately the most rewarding trip of my life.

*   *   *

I visited Karl and his family often during the ensuing years, leaving his shop every time with a complimentary shirt fashioned of the finest English poplin. I also joined him for dinner in his home on Bayswater Road with the inevitable toast of "Here's to Ben, who many years ago saved my life in more ways than one."

But perhaps my most memorable reward came in 1983 when Karl and Jane celebrated not only their twenty-fifth wedding anniversary but also the birth of their first grandchild, a boy who they named Ben. In his speech at the dinner party in a London hotel, a graying but radiant Karl said, looking at me, "We unanimously agreed on this name so that there will always be a "Ben" around even when you and I are gone."

I wiped a few tears from my eyes, silently thanking God for having guided my path to the hotel room in Zürich not one split second too late.

THE TWINS

Some people marry because they love each other, others because they need each other, still others enter matrimony because it seems like the natural thing to do. But have you ever heard of two people who married because they feared each other?

This is their story.

Jim and Kenny Astor were identical twins. Such was their resemblance that not even their parents could tell them apart. When they were young boys, their mother would make Jim wear a silver bracelet to avoid mistaking him for Kenny. Not only were their physical appearances identical, but they also spoke with the same intonation. As they grew up, certain mannerisms and gestures were the only discerning characteristics that helped their parents and close friends tell one from the other. Physically, however, they continued to be undistinguishable, much to the consternation of the people they came into contact with, and often to their own amusement. They often deliberately encouraged the ensuing confusion.

While their physical appearance continued to be remarkably identical as they grew into adolescence, their characters soon differed considerably. During their college years, their parents routinely saw Kenny as the hardworking, dedicated student, intent on excelling at whatever he turned his attention to. Jim was clearly a more fun-seeking and even irresponsible individual. Kenny sailed through all exams with flying colors, while Jim had a hard time keeping up with the curriculum. On graduation day Kenny received his summa cum laude diploma with deserved pride; Jim finished almost at the bottom of the class.

Soon after college, the diametrically opposed personalities of the twins became unmistakably apparent. Kenny decided to go for a Masters in Business Administration, and Jim got a job as junior clerk in a newly established trading company on the West Coast. When asked what kind of trading, he would only say that the new company was specializing in importing electronic devices from the Far East.

From then on, the two brothers went their own way. Kenny received his Masters Degree and soon joined a company that owned a chain of sporting goods stores. Because of his dedication to the job and his intelligence, he kept gaining promotions, until at the age of thirty-four he became general manager of the company's flagship store in Chicago. He was respected by his employees and superiors alike, and most people in the company were convinced that he would one day run the whole show.

Although Kenny never married, he had a long-time relationship with a very attractive brunette he had met at an office party. Kathy Forester was an accountant in the company's finance division. She was very bright and knowledgeable and was being considered for the important position of controller. Everybody in the company knew of their relationship and some wondered why they weren't tying the knot. From time to time, Kathy confided to her closest colleagues at work that she was getting fed up with the situation and that Kenny had promised to marry her several times, but never kept his word, always citing one excuse or another. Once or twice, a very frustrated Kathy left Kenny, but he came calling at her flat a few days later, promising that this time he would make up his mind very shortly. Then, something seemed to hold him back again.

Kenny was acutely aware of his aversion to and fear of getting married. Unbeknownst to Kathy, he had consulted a psychologist. After several sessions, it was concluded that the main reason for Kenny's phobic behaviour could be traced to his childhood and his exposure to the constant and often violent discord between his parents.

As time went by, their friends stopped wondering. They accepted the couple as two people who loved each other and who wanted to live together without the encumbrance of legal or religious ties.

*****

Jim's was a completely different story. The company on the West Coast he had joined was indeed doing business with the Far East, but a very crooked business to be sure. From smuggling Asians into the United States on overcrowded vessels for astronomic fees, to importing inferior quality electronic equipment fraudulently labelled as top Japanese brands, to engaging in the drug and stolen car business. All of this and much more was routinely handled by the First Orient Trading Company. Jim was one of the four partners. Often running from the law until one of his super smart lawyers could get him off the hook, Jim had three bodyguards around him at all times. His real nemesis was not the FBI or the IRS, but rival gangs from the Far East who were constantly trying to eliminate him and his partners Valentine Day Massacre style.

Jim possessed a brilliant intellect, and he knew very well what he had gotten himself into. He continued with his work for two reasons. The first was money. He was raking it in like a crime boss. His lifestyle was necessarily secluded but nevertheless grandiose. He surrounded himself with the most beautiful women money could buy, and he truly enjoyed being feared and respected by his entourage. The second reason was that he was far too deeply involved in what he was doing to simply walk away. He had a team of very smart lawyers and accountants, who, so far, had managed to keep him one step ahead of hearing the dreaded words "You're under arrest. You have the right to remain silent" and the rest of the familiar litany. There were times, however, when Jim thought that enough is enough, wondering how long before the law or his rivals would pull down the curtain on him. Jim was well aware that he would not retire from the company at the customary age of sixty-five with a gold watch and a set of golf clubs.

Over the years, Kenny and Jim had had rare personal contacts. They phoned each other on their common birthday, at Christmas, and perhaps once or twice during the year, but that was all. They never met, and Jim never even visited his parents, except during the first few years after he had left home. He called them on the phone occasionally, asked about their health, and twice a year he sent them an amount of money, perhaps to atone for not coming to see them and for the kind of life he had chosen for himself.

Shortly after the twins' thirty-seventh birthday, Kenny phoned his brother with the sad news that their father was very ill. In fact, he had been diagnosed with incurable cancer. The doctors gave him just a few more weeks. Kenny told Jim that he was going home to be at his father's side and suggested that his brother do the same. Jim agreed and they decided to meet in a hotel on the outskirts of Chicago, from where the two would drive to their parents' home.

A couple of days after that conversation, the two brothers met for the first time in many years. It was a strange reunion. Both felt and looked uncomfortable, at a loss for suitable words, but finally, they hugged each other, even wiping a few tears from their eyes. When Kenny told his brother about his business and his recent promotion, Jim listened but volunteered very little about his own life, except to say that he was still single and that he was beginning to consider alternate ways to make a living. When Kenny probed more into his brother's professional activity, Jim refused to elaborate, saying, "You wouldn't want to know."

Jim also met Kenny's friend Kathy, who had driven the car to the hotel so that the brothers could use it for their onward drive. Kathy said she preferred not to go with them because she felt like an outsider in this sad family reunion. Kathy left them shortly after turning over the car keys to Kenny and returned home by bus and rental car.

While getting ready for the trip, the two brothers stood in front of a mirror and looked at each other. They were absolutely amazed to see that they still looked exactly alike. The color of their hair, their eyes, their facial features were still identical. They laughed because they could not believe that despite the passage of time and despite their very different lifestyles, they still could not be told apart.

After a quick lunch, they got into Kenny's car to drive the two-hour long winding road to their parents' home. Jim, who was tired from the long flight from California, curled up on the back seat to catch a nap before they arrived.

It was just getting dark when Kenny started on the winding country road that would take them through a couple of small towns before they reached their destination.

He had been driving for a while when he noticed something strange with the brakes. When negotiating the frequent curves, he felt that the brake pedal was looser and mushier than usual. He had to practically floor the pedal to slow the car down. Wondering what could have gone wrong he decided to stop at the next gas station for an inspection. Coming out of a sharp corner and starting to roll down a hill, Kenny pushed the brake pedal down, but it went straight to the floor and the car did not stop. Kenny didn't know what to do and kept to the right side of the road, hoping to reach an ascending hill or some soft bushes that could stop the car. The decline kept getting steeper and his acceleration increased. His shouts of "My God, my God, no brakes!" awakened Jim in the back just as the car hit one of the trees lining the road. The car came to a crunching halt, tilting to one side. The entire front section was a pile of mangled metal.

Jim, who was badly shaken but otherwise unhurt, except for some bleeding and bruises, climbed out of the back door. He rushed to the front to check on Kenny. His brother was crouched over the steering wheel, which had been broken by the impact. The shaft had impaled Kenny, penetrating deeply into his chest. There was blood all over his face and body. He was motionless. Jim tried to pull him out of the wreckage, but the body was trapped. He listened for signs of breathing or a heartbeat, he touched the jugular, he tried mouth-to-mouth respiration, but all life had gone out of the body. Kenny was dead.

With lightning speed, Jim realized the opportunity offered to him. Methodically, he went through Kenny's pockets, taking out all identifications: credit cards, social security and driver's license. Then, he put his own identity cards, personal papers, driver's license and whatever he could find on him into Kenny's pockets. He also quickly went through Kenny's tote bag, removed all other personal items and replaced them with his own.

Remembering Kenny's desperate cry, "My God, no brakes," he checked the brake fluid line and made an amazing discovery. The fluid hose had been partly slashed. Someone had cut the line, but not completely, allowing the driver to cover some distance before repeated use of the brake pedal would cause the hose to rupture and deprive the wheels of any braking power.

Jim quickly broke off the incriminating severed ends of the hose and stuffed them into his duffel bag. He grabbed a nearby stone, to smash the underbody of the car. It took him quite a while to destroy most lines and conduits, including the brake mechanism, making it appear as if the mangled mess was the result of the accident.

Completely exhausted, he sat down on the grass near the accident scene and dialled 911 on his cellular phone. It did not take long for a police car and an ambulance to arrive. Kenny was extricated from his position and pronounced dead by the paramedics. Jim gave a brief report to the police, how he was protected by the back seat and how his brother must have fallen asleep at the wheel. He did not say a word about his discovery of the severed hydraulic line. He identified himself to the state troopers as Kenneth Astor, manager of a sporting good store in Chicago. He and his twin brother were driving to their parents' home to visit their sick father. He added that his brother Jim had flown in from California for this family visit and was probably tired from the long flight. Asked about his dead brother's family and occupation, he said he was managing a trading company in San Francisco and was not married.

Kenny, alias Jim, was taken to the station for verification of the accident report. His brother, on the other hand, was taken to a nearby hospital, where his accidental death was confirmed. Nobody inspected the mangled car. Later that night, Kenny was driven to his parents' home, where he spent two days, mostly at his dying father's side. Kenny's mother was terribly shaken by her son's death, but she and Kenny decided not to inform the moribund father. Instead, they told him that Jim would come later to visit. The day following Kenny's arrival, the old man passed away, leaving a heart broken wife, who had to come to terms with not one but two deaths in her immediate family.

Kenny left the following day for Chicago, heading for his dead brother's house. He entered with the key he had found in his brother's pocket. He knew that before doing anything else, he had to get in touch with Kathy. She might shed some light on the apparent attempt on his brother's life by cutting the hydraulic brake line.

He was also aware that if he wanted to assume his brother's identity, switching from contraband operator to respectable company executive, he needed her full cooperation. Only she could help him make the transition.

It did not take long to find Kathy's phone number and ask her over to the house. Realizing that there was no point in hiding his true identity from as intimate a companion as a lover, he immediately revealed himself to Kathy, told her of his scheme and asked her to help him. "I need you to tell me everything about the sporting goods business and about my brother's daily life and activities," he said, adding "since you were very close to Ken, it should not be too difficult for you to become my tutor and mentor. I will of course, remunerate you handsomely for your services." He would also ask the company for two week's leave which would help him go through his tuition.

Kathy listened attentively to Kenny's proposal. She did not commit herself in any way. He repeatedly asked for her approval of his plans, but she hedged. To change the subject, Kenny asked her about her relationship with his dead brother, and no sooner had he broached this subject, than she started pouring out her story.

Like a gushing waterfall bursting forth, she explained their initially beautiful relationship, which, over the years, had soured on account of his brother's repeated promises and subsequent refusals to marry her. And then, she came out with a bombshell. She was pregnant. His brother had known of her condition, but still refused to marry her. Instead, he suggested she have an abortion and nobody would be the wiser. When she refused to get rid of the baby, Kenny told her to send him the hospital bills for the childbirth, but that was all. He refused to be drawn into a shotgun wedding and kept repeating "No way, no way."

As Kathy was unfolding her story, Kenny noticed flashes of deep hatred in her eyes. In fact, her otherwise pretty face became distorted with passion and vengeance. She kept repeating that she gave his brother everything she could, and he compensated her with unkept promises. She hated him with all her heart and soul. Quietly, Kenny went to the adjoining room where his bag was and took out the slashed hydraulic hose. He held it in front of Kathy.

She started to get up from her seat, but then she fainted and fell to the floor. Kenny rushed over and lifted her onto the couch. She broke out in intense crying and sobbing. Her whole body was shaking. Kenny brought her some water, but otherwise let the outburst run its course. She kept sobbing for a long time, until she finally quieted down and regained her composure.

She told Kenny that she had not known that he was to join his brother. She admitted to slashing the hydraulic hose just before she left the car in the parking lot of the motel. When she met the twin brother, it was too late for her to do or say anything. She hated Kenny so much, she said, that she was prepared to kill him come what may.

The two sat in silence for a long time. Kenny produced a bottle of Scotch he had found in one of the kitchen cabinets. He poured generous portions for both of them. A plan had started to develop in his mind: Kathy would not only instruct and guide Kenny through all aspects of his brother's business, but she would also take the secret of the switched personalities to her grave. In return, Kenny would keep her secret as well. To Kenny, the plan seemed perfect, a sort of "gentleman's agreement," or better still "a conspiracy of silence."

Kathy had listened intently to "Kenny's" proposal. She did not interrupt him once. She continued to sip the Scotch, barely registering the taste.

Since no objection was forthcoming from Kathy, Kenny looked at her with a slight smile on his face. He expected a nod of agreement or even a handshake from his partner, but she said nothing. He finally said, "Well, what do you say? We don't seem to have much choice in this matter, do we?"

Kathy looked her partner straight in the eyes. "Not so fast, my friend. I'll say yes to your proposal and play the role you just described, but on one condition: You'll do what your brother failed to do. You'll marry me, baby and all. And now, I guess it's my turn to say we don't seem to have much choice in this matter, do we?"

Kenny had obviously met his match.

Kenny and Kathy got married a few days later in a simple church ceremony.

* * * * *

The First Orient Trading Company picked up the news about their partner's premature death from the newspapers. Not interested in publicity of any kind, the remaining partners lost no time in dividing among themselves the shares of their dead companion, especially since he had never mentioned to them any family ties or dependents.

* * * * *

For a while, Kenny, missed the excitement and sheer power that was part of his previous exposure to organized crime. He quickly realized that he had been living all these years on borrowed time, dodging the bullets or the prison cot that could have put an abrupt end to his "glamorous" lifestyle. And since his yearning to get out of the mob at the first opportunity had been so unexpectedly fulfilled, he was very happy indeed.

Kenny and Kathy lived an uneventful life, carrying their mutual secrets to their graves.

THE FAMILY SECRET

A smile briefly lit up his face as he glanced at the panelled doors of his company. The staff had gone home hours before. As usual he had stayed on to prepare next day's work, leaving instructions and memos on some of the desks.

Turning the key, his eyes fell on the shiny brass plate near the entrance:

> Louis Modiano
> Architect and Interior Decorator

He always enjoyed looking at his name before heading for home.

It had been a long way from the day he graduated from college, third from the top, to his years at the Technical University of Istanbul. He had sailed through all his studies with ease. The reasons were obvious.

First, he loved the concepts of building and decorating which seemed like natural extensions of his affinity for things beautiful, elegant and functional. He had a keen sense of comfortable and pleasant living which was not surprising since he was brought up in a beautiful home by wealthy parents who had travelled the world, not as camera-wielding tourists hurrying from one city to another, but who had taken the time to absorb and understand what they saw in the galleries and museums they visited.

Secondly, Louis' parents had seen to it that his years of tuition and training were not only amply funded, but also interspersed with exposure to books, lectures and art exhibits, all aimed at grooming as accomplished an architect as imaginable. Thus, when Louis proudly received his diploma from the dean, he was fully, if not overly qualified to embark on a career of building and decorating to the highest standards of the profession. No wonder therefore that at the relatively young age of thirty, Louis had built up a very successful company with some twelve young and motivated employees, all trying to embellish the urban landscape around them.

Louis Modiano was handsome, suave, an impeccable dresser, and as can be expected, one of Istanbul's most eligible bachelors. Which brings us to the more intimate side of Louis' life.

Like many others of his age, Louis belonged to a lively group of close friends who knew how to fill their leisure time with outings and trips, parties and events they all thoroughly enjoyed. Most members of the group were unmarried couples, and Louis and his girlfriend Rita were no exception. The two had met at a party some three years ago and had since become inseparable to the point that their names were always mentioned in the same breath. And yet, "Louis and Rita" were as different as human beings can possibly be.

While Louis was a sophisticated and mundane intellectual, at ease and even leading the way in any social setting or company, Rita was nothing of the sort. Endowed by nature with a truly spectacular beauty which extended to every part of her eye-catching appearance, these features were unfortunately far from being matched by her intellectual make-up. In other words, Rita was the traditional dumb blonde, and then some.

She knew little about and cared even less for events of the day. She spoke only one language and this with an inelegant accent. She lacked any appreciation for the arts and of necessity kept generally silent whenever the group engaged in any of their frequent thought-provoking discussions.

For three years now, Louis and Rita had forged a liaison based on three realities: Rita's passionate love for Louis, Louis' pride in being in the company of an extraordinarily beautiful girl, and, of course, the immense sexual pleasure both derived from their frequent get-togethers.

Unfortunately absent from this emotional triangle, however, was Louis' reciprocal love for Rita. In fact, there was little of it.

Rita's sorry state of intellectual sophistication was easily explained by her family background and her upbringing. Her father was a box manufacturer who had amassed a sizeable fortune supplying the city's myriad of pastry shops with foldable carton containers which his workers were churning out in a dilapidated basement on the outskirts of town. He and his wife were simple people, firmly convinced that their beautiful daughter's happiness would not derive from her knowledge of geography and history, but from making a good catch, meaning marrying a good man who would raise with her a family in style and opulence.

To be sure, Louis was always a most attentive companion for Rita. He constantly brought her gifts, treated her with respect and gave the outward appearance of a devoted partner. But he never harboured the slightest intention of marrying her. He either skirted the subject of matrimony whenever Rita brought it up, or when confronted with it, he told her that he was not ready for it, or else he brushed it off by jokingly telling her that he was not the marrying type.

This was obviously a lie because he did think of eventually settling down, but what he had in mind was a girl he could consider his social and intellectual equal.

While Rita's repeatedly delivered reminders should have made it clear that Louis did not intend to walk down the aisle with her, she chose to either ignore them or to try and change his mind. She was deeply in love with him and thought that in time her feelings would be reciprocated. She also kept warding off her parent's nudges by telling them: "He needs time to make up his mind. I am as anxious as you are to give you the good news."

But, as fate, or rather carelessness would have it, the good news came from an unexpected and rather unwelcome source: the gynecologist to whom Rita had gone to check out some irregularities in her menstrual cycle.

"Congratuations, my dear," said the good doctor with a broad grin in obvious anticipation of adding another customer to his clientele. "You are pregnant. I am happy for you and your family."

* * * * *

Call it the lightning bolt from the blue sky or the rude awakening from the good times. One thing became very clear to Rita as the doctor showed her out of his clinic. A new phase had suddenly dawned on her life. A phase she was determined to deal with and master to the best of her ability.

Her first move was to call Louis and ask him to meet her immediately. When the two got together in his small bachelor's flat she told him the story, adding with a benign smile that destiny had now made up his mind for him about marrying her. "All we have to do is to plan and prepare for a wedding. I waited a long time for you to make up your mind. Let's give our parents the good news right now. I am happy beyond words. Aren't you?" she said in a naturally excited voice. She moved closer to him on the couch and reached for his hand.

Louis held her hand, and looking into her glowing face, said: "Sweetheart, I am sorry, but I think I told you many times that I don't want to get married. This was an accident, and let's treat it as such. These things happen and they are not the end of the world. We will go the best doctor we can find and you will have an abortion. That's all. You are not the first nor the last to whom this happened. After a few weeks you will have forgotten the whole thing. I will of course pay for everything. How about a few days rest in a resort after the intervention to let you come back to your routine life? Eh? What else can I say, sweetheart," he added. He started to caress her hand, but she withdrew it with a sudden jerk.

"What," she said, wiping a tear that had appeared in her shining eyes, "you don't want us to bring our baby into the world? You want me to kill our baby? Is this what you want? Did our years of being together, of sharing our lives, mean nothing to you? I got news for you, Louis. I am going to have our baby, and you will be the proud father for all the world to see. We are getting married, and the sooner the better."

By now, the two were getting agitated. Louis jumped up and said: "Please, Rita, don't get emotional. These things happen all the time between lovers, and they deal with them rationally. What's so dramatic about interrupting a pregnancy? It was an accident, OK?"

"No, never," Rita shouted back. "I will not put myself under a doctor's knife. I will have the baby, no, we will have the baby, you and me, like normal parents." With that, tears ran down her cheek, as she clutched her handkerchief.

Louis shot back: "Don't be silly. Calm down. Go home and sleep it over. You will see that I am right. I will help you clean up the mess. Stop crying. Call me if you need anything. I'm not running out on you!! OK!" With that, he left the apartment and a heartbroken Rita, shaking with tears. The poor girl was really desperate.

* * * * *

That evening turned into the worst night of her young life.

When she failed to come to the dinner table despite her mother's repeated calls, her mom went to her bedroom and one look at her crying daughter told her that something had gone terribly wrong in the girl's life.

It did not take long for Rita to tell her mother everything: from her pregnancy discovered earlier in the day to Louis's reaction. Her mother's first words after listening in disbelief were: "My poor girl. What a catastrophe that you fell into the hands of a monster, an animal. And I thought that he came from a good family. Wait until your father hears the story. He will kill him and I won't blame him if he does." Her mother then told Rita to wash up and come to the table. Once dinner was out of the way she should tell her father the whole sad story.

Needless to say, it turned into a very long evening and night.

Rita's father listened in disbelief, but his face turned redder and redder while his hands kept fidgeting from his head to his mouth to his hair. He was obviously working up a rage such as mother and daughter had never seen him have.

Finally he said: "I don't know what you intend to do, but I, for one, will not let him get away with it. That's for sure." After a few furious remarks such as: "I knew that nothing good would come out of this relationship. Why didn't you send him packing a long time ago?" he said: "OK now, let's all go to sleep and tomorrow I will have a word or two with this scoundrel!"

And that's exactly what he did the following morning. He picked up the phone and dialed Louis' office.

"This is Jack," he started what was to be a rather long conversation." I am Rita's father. My daughter told me everything. Am I right that after having spent three years with her and after having gotten her pregnant, you refuse to marry her as any man of honour would do?"

"Well, Sir," replied Louis. "Let me put it that way: in the first pace I never promised Rita marriage, in fact I repeatedly told her that I am not the marrying type. And she continued our relationship knowing full well that this was an affair, a liaison between us and nothing more."

"Nothing more?" interrupted Jack. "You made her pregnant which changed the 'liaison' you are talking about. She is now carrying your baby and that is no more a liaison. That is the start of a family."

"You may see it that way," replied Louis, "but I don't. For me the baby was an accident that can occur when consenting adults have sex, and as an accident it can be remedied and repaired. That's why I told Rita to have an abortion and I will pay for it. I will even pay for a vacation or a rest in a resort after the abortion to let her get back to normal life."

"My daughter does not need you to pay for her vacation. And she does not want an abortion. She loves you and she wants you to do the honourable thing and marry her. Do you understand what I am saying to you? My wife and I want you to accept the responsibility of your actions and behave like a father and a husband, not like an irresponsible playboy!"

"I am sorry, but I cannot do that, and I am not a playboy," Louis said.

By now the two were reaching an emotional boiling point. They were getting very angry at each other.

"You cannot do that?" shouted Rita's father into the phone. "Now listen: I know people who deal with scoundrels like you. They will find you and beat you up so badly that you will not be able to recognize yourself. They will send you to a hospital for months. And if this is not enough, I will make sure your friends know what a shameful thing you have done. Let's see how many people will come to seek your services as an architect!

You will regret bitterly your criminal actions, but it will be too late. Nobody dishonours my dear daughter and gets away with it. I am warning you better look over your shoulder who is following you from now on, you dirty bastard."

With that, he slammed the receiver down and was close to complete exhaustion. He had to catch his breath even before wiping the sweat from his face.

* * * * *

Louis was not prepared for that violent outburst. He was shaken and when he reached for a glass of water on his desk, his hands trembled. He felt sick and scared after the threats hurled at him. He decided to leave the office and discuss the situation with his father who was home with a cold.

His dad listened to the whole story and told his son to calm down and think rationally about what his next step should be.

"Are you sure you don't want to marry her?" asked his father. "From what our friends tell us, she is a very beautiful girl and she loves you!" After a few moments of silence, Louis replied. "Dad, I am not in love with her and I don't want to be forced into a marriage by threats or pity or obligation. I don't want to marry her. That's all."

"Then you better take her father's threats seriously and plan your next steps with a cool head. To begin with, stay with us here for a few days. Don't go back to your own flat, and don't drive your car since they may be following you. Take taxis where you have to go.

"Secondly, phone your office and tell them you have a cold and will stay home for a few days. Give them instructions what you want them to do. Let a few days pass to cool off tempers and you will decide where you want to go from here.

"But right now go to your old room, lie down and take it easy for a few days. You are shaking. I will call our good friend Tommy who, as you know, is not only a good lawyer but also has a good head for dealing with family problems and ask him to come here tomorrow morning. Together we will see what to do. Don't worry, Louis, we will find a way out."

Louis did as told and spent the rest of the day at his parent's home. He had dinner with them but his mind was racing while trying to look more or less normal. He went from one "what if" scenario to another and in the end he really failed to come up with a clear plan how to handle the situation. Only after his mother gave him a couple of her sleeping pills did he close his eyes and fall into a deep sleep.

It was about eight the following morning when his mother knocked at his door and woke him up with the words: "Pick up the phone, Louis. It's for you!"

Still somewhat drowsy, Louis listened to an unfamiliar voice telling him: "Hey, Louis, you see we know how to find you." "Who is this?" said Louis. "Never mind who this is. Certainly not one of your buddy-buddy friends. We know what kind of shit you are and we will teach you a lesson you will not forget. Never!! So, watch out, pretty face! We will wipe out your grin very soon. You can count on it, you piece of shit!"

They hung up.

This ominous call left an urgent, if not immediate mark on Louis' thinking. In fact, he was now scared and panicky.

He told his father about the call and when Tommy, the family friend and lawyer arrived, they sat down and mulled the situation over. The lawyer's advice was brief and practical:

"First," he said, "Louis gives his father a power of attorney then, he appoints his assistant as office manager, to run his company for the next little while.

Second, Louis disappears from Istanbul without telling anyone where he is heading. He stays out of town for a few weeks. When his pursuers will not find him for two weeks, Rita's father will most certainly call off the hunt. He is smart enough not to pay these guys their high fees indefinitely. Then in a few weeks we review the situation again. But now," he turned to Louis: "Disappear and don't tell us where to."

Louis followed the advice to a tee.

He gave his manager instructions about running the office in his absence for a month or so, pretending he had some urgent and unexpected business to attend to.

Then, he packed a small bag, embraced his parents, telling them that they would soon hear from him and took a taxi to Istanbul's Atatürk airport. Looking at the departures panel, he saw that the next flight scheduled to leave was Swissair, destination Zürich. There were several later flights leaving for other cities, but Zürich seemed acceptable. He went to the counter and, yes, there was a seat available and he bought it.

The sun had not yet set over the nearby Alps when Louis stepped out of Terminal B at Zürich International Airport. He headed for the Schweizerhof, a comfortable hotel he had stayed at before.

He checked in, went up to his room, stretched out on the lily-white sheets and closed his eyes.

This must have been the most agitated and eventful day of his life.

With a grin of relief on his face, he realized that nobody, but nobody knew where he was. He felt safe. At least temporarily safe.

After a short rest, he took a shower and went down to the hotel's elegant dining room. He ordered a half bottle of the best red wine on the list to go with a juicy steak.

The next day he intended to start thinking and planning where to go from here. One thing became abundantly clear to him: his life would take a different route, at least temporarily from where the daily routine had taken him during the last few years.

The next morning, Louis started the day by taking a sheet of hotel stationary to write down a number of things he intended to do.

First, taking advantage of his forced escape, he wanted to explore the possibilities of establishing an architecture office in Switzerland, perhaps branching out from Istanbul into new ventures. This, of course, implied obtaining residence and work permits.

Then, he had to make arrangements to transfer funds to Zürich, for it is a well-known fact that life in this picture perfect country is not exactly cheap.

An hour-long consulting session with an immigration lawyer the hotel manager had recommended convinced Louis to abandon the thought of seeking a residence permit in Switzerland. This required professional certifications which would take him through at least two years of study at a Swiss university. As for the alternative of seeking employment, this was also out of the question.

In short, the lawyer concluded, "forget about Switzerland as your next home, unless you are prepared to invest large amounts in establishing a Swiss business or else, you opt for early retirement near one of our picturesque lakes."

Left with these sobering thoughts to ponder, Louis suddenly had a brainstorm.

For the last two years he had imported from Canada and successfully sold in Turkey prefabricated houses. He and his senior architect had become very adept at putting these wooden structures together. They had gained popularity because they were an inexpensive and practical alternative to conventional constructions.

In the process, Louis had also grown friendly with Sam Gold, the owner of the Canadian company. On an impulse he picked up the phone and asked Sam if he could help him come to Canada, perhaps to set up a branch of his Turkish architectural business.

Sam listened to Louis' plan and intentions and then told him: "I like the idea of you wanting to come to Canada. This is a good country from every point of view. But I would like to make another suggestion. How about coming here to work in my company as a starter? I need an architect who is familiar with the assembly of our prefabricated homes and you are the perfect candidate. If you are serious in coming here, I advise you to go to the Canadian Embassy in Switzerland, apply for an entry visa, stating that you already have a job offer. I will send them a message that I indeed have a position for you in my company because you are a qualified expert in assembling our structures. I am sure it will work. Come over and start working as soon as you get the visa, and my company lawyer will do the rest once you are here. How about that? Who knows, if you like the country, and Montreal is certainly a good place to live, you may decide to make it your home and instead turn the Turkish company into a branch operation. Let me know which way you want to go."

* * * * *

Barely three weeks had gone by since Louis had set foot in Zürich. Three weeks of endless thinking, soul searching, weighing one alternative against the other and finally reaching a decision, albeit with the thought in the back of his mind: "If Canada does not work out, I can always return to Turkey, of course after all the dust from my personal problem has settled."

And so, on a bright mid-summer day of 1960, Louis Modiano settled comfortably into the window seat of Montreal-bound Trans Canada flight AC 470. He looked out of the window as the plane gently moved onto the runway in preparation of lift-off.

His thoughts went back to Rita. Of course he felt sorry for her. After all, he had enjoyed her company for three years and she had always been a welcome and very pleasant presence at his side, not to mention the great sexual pleasures he derived from the relationship. As for the pregnancy, he was sure that she would do, unless she had already done so, what many other girls had chosen in similar circumstances, namely to resort to an abortion. In fact, he had sent her a cheque for a sizeable amount the day he had left Istanbul, with a note wishing her well.

One thing he was absolutely sure of, and that kept returning to his mind, was that he could not marry a girl that was miles below his own intellectual level.

And yet, despite his self-absolving "what else can I do?" deep down, he had recently developed the instinctive urge to change the course his life had taken during the past months.

He truly felt the need to turn the page and to explore new horizons and perhaps a new life.

On the other hand, his heart was also heavy in anticipation of what might be awaiting him in far-off Canada. Still, he was excited about the attraction of the North American experience. He had confidence in his sponsor Sam Gold to help and guide him in his first steps on unfamiliar soil.

The flight was smooth and eventless. Food and service were above average. No doubt, the glass of red wine did its share in gently pushing Louis into a nap from which he only awoke when the voice from the speakers overhead announced the plane's impending landing in Montreal.

Louis fastened his seatbelt in a pleasantly receptive mood, bordering on contentment and perhaps even on great expectations.

* * * * *

A week had passed since the telephone-delivered threat had been hurled at Louis. A week during which his pursuers had left no stone unturned to get hold of him. They really searched high and low, but finally they had to report to Rita's father that Louis had for all intents and purposes disappeared from the face of the earth, at least their part of it.

An angry Jack gave Louis' manhunters another three days to find their prey. But when that failed too, he paid them off and, with a rather ugly expletive for Louis, terminated their services.

Now all of his attention turned to his daughter, the unfortunate victim of the deplorable affair. In fact, Jack had worked out a plan. Without revealing anything about it to Rita, he called Simon Nassi, one of his company's two salesmen, into his office. He had picked Simon because he was twenty-eight years old, unmarried, good-looking, honest and a very good worker who rarely came back to the office Friday evenings without a bulging order book.

"Sit down, Simon," he told the young man, "I have something to tell you, but before I do, I want you to swear to me on your life that you will not whisper a word of all this to anyone, unless I tell you that you can."

"I swear to you on our holy books that I will keep secret whatever you tell me, Sir," replied Simon.

"Alright, then," continued the boss. "My daughter Rita, whom you have seen a couple of times when she came to the office, is in trouble. I'll make it short: she went out with a young man for three years, hoping that he would marry her. Now she got pregnant, and, believe it or not, the man disappeared from view. I am not kidding, he vanished into thin air, of course after refusing to accept the responsibility for his actions. It is a catastrophe. My poor innocent daughter became the victim of an irresponsible scoundrel."

The young man had listened in silence, but when he saw his boss' very angry expression he shook his head in disbelief and said: "My God, this is terrible. Who is this disgraceful person?" "Never mind him. I told you he is on the run right now. But let's talk about my daughter."

Something was beginning to dawn in Simon's mind.

"I have an idea, Simon," continued the boss. "Of course, I have not told it to Rita and I don't know how you will react to it. So, here is what I propose to you, Simon."

The young man was listening very attentively.

"How about you marry my daughter. You accept the baby as your own child, not as an adopted orphan, but as your own child so that it will never know that you are not its real father. Of course, you will also raise children of your own, but this unfortunate child will be part of your family.

"I don't need to tell you that my daughter is not only a beautiful girl, but she has a heart of gold. She is a perfect housewife and has learned from her mother to keep everything and everyone in tip top shape. I am not exaggerating, but she is a jewel."

Simon's eyes were beginning to light up like lanterns as he listened to this totally unexpected overture.

"Now, of course, I love my daughter very much, and I want to do everything to make her happy and allow her to live in comfort. I have therefore decided to take you into the business as a partner. I will also give you a house to live in. A couple of years ago I bought two houses in Erenköy as an investment. One of them is now available. You and my daughter can move in as soon as both of you have made up your minds to accept my proposal."

Without letting Simon say anything, Jack went on: "I thought of you, because you worked here for five years now. I know you as an honest and hardworking man. I know your family. As a matter of fact, I used to belong to the same synagogue as your father and your uncles. So, I am satisfied that my daughter will be in good hands. Of course, all this, if she and you go along with my idea."

Jack stopped talking and wiped the perspiration from his forehead with a large handkerchief he pulled from his pocket.

Simon's face had changed expression, and even colour, several times as he sat listening to his boss' offer. To be sure, the change was from initial surprise, even disbelief to slowly growing elation. He had just listened to the best imaginable offer that had ever come his way.

A beautiful girl in her twenties, a wealthy father-in-law, a partnership in a prosperous business and a house to live in. What more could he ask for?

He jumped up, went over to Jack's desk and shook his hand. "Thank you," he said, "Thank you from the bottom of my heart. Of course I accept. Wait until I tell my mother. She will be the happiest woman on earth."

At one point, Simon got so carried away that he felt like embracing his future father-in-law, but Jack held him back with a raised hand.

"Wait," he said, with a smile. "I have only done one half of my job. Now let me talk to the other side, and, to tell you the truth, I am not at all sure about her reaction. Don't forget that she loved this man and that she spent three years with him. You don't change companions at the drop of a hat, not my daughter. But on the other hand, she may want to give her child both a father and a home. That thought alone may make her say 'yes'.

"In any case, I will discuss our conversation with my wife first, even before talking to Rita. You know women know more about such things than men.

So, remember your promise of secrecy. Not a word to anyone, not even to your mother. No one must know about this before I talk to Rita. OK?"

"You have my word. I swore on our holy books, didn't I? Count on me and, again, thank you very much."

With that, a radiant Simon grabbed his coat and left the office.

This had no doubt been the happiest day in his twenty-eight years. "Wow."

*****

"Leave everything you are doing and come to the living room. I want to discuss something with you!" was the first thing Jack said to his wife when he came home from work that evening. "I don't see Rita. Where is she?" he added. "Rita is having dinner at her friend Becky's home tonight," said Lucy. "You know she has been very depressed and nervous these last few days. It breaks my heart to see the poor child go through a very difficult time in her life. Did they find Louis?"

"No, they didn't and they looked everywhere for him. That scoundrel disappeared into thin air. He must have left town," Jack added. As soon as they sat down on the living room sofa, he told Lucy exactly what he had discussed earlier with his salesman Simon.

Lucy listened very intently and when he had finished, she said: "I like the idea but I don't like the way you want to go about it."

"What do you mean?" asked Jack.

"You seem to forget that our daughter belongs to a new generation. Gone are the days when parents told their daughter whom to marry. Simon seems to be a good choice, but we have to make him palatable and acceptable to her. How about you telling us tomorrow night that you have decided to promote Simon to Sales Manager and in order to celebrate the event you have invited him to come over for dinner. That will bring the two together. Then it will be up to Simon to invite her out to a movie or to a restaurant, bring her some flowers and start the task of winning her heart, of seducing her. Give it a little time, and if Simon plays his cards right, Rita may well go for him. Right now she is sad and depressed, but a fresh face, a caring and loving gesture and the proper behaviour may well convince her that there is life after Louis and most of all that she is carrying a child that needs a father and a home."

Jack tenderly reached for his wife's hand and had only three words for her: "You are right," he said. "Let's do it your way."

* * * * *

Lucy was indeed right. A suitably prepared and coached Simon acted his part admirably. After all, there was a great deal at stake for him in this cupid's plot.

The two went out several times and, true to her mother's prediction, Rita saw in Simon an honest, dedicated no-nonsense man who thanks to his smooth and polite comportment stood a good chance of making her happy and raise a family not unlike her other friends and cousins.

The decisive point came one evening when he proposed to her and she told him of the only boyfriend she had had, who dated her for three years and when he made her pregnant just disappeared instead of accepting his responsibility.

Simon took her hand into his and said: "These things happen. Don't worry. I love you, and your baby will be my baby. We will never tell the child. Let's get married as soon as possible. I promise to be the best father in the world."

Barely six weeks had passed since the ominous diagnosis from the gynecologist when Rita and Simon stood in front of a smiling rabbi and jubilant parents to exchange vows.

Everyone seemed to be genuinely happy. Simon's mother and Rita's parents who were privy to the cabal that had worked out so well, and of course, the guests who could not take their eyes off the resplendent bride and the radiant groom walking down the aisle while a couple of little girls were strewing rose petals in front of them as if to sweeten the path the couple were about to embark on.

* * * * *

Louis was pleasantly surprised when the officer at the Montreal airport asked him: "Avez-vous des marchandises à déclarer, Monsieur?" after he inspected his passport and the visa from the Canadian embassy in Switzerland, certifying that he was to be admitted into Canada as a technical specialist in the building industry. "Non," replied Louis. "Je n'ai que des effets personelles avec moi."

"C'est bien," said the officer. "Bienvenue au Canada!" as he stamped the Turkish passport before handing it back to Louis.

With that, he collected his belongings and took a taxi to the downtown hotel which was to be his temporary abode until he and Sam Gold could find a more permanent place for him to stay.

The next morning, Sam picked him up and drove him to his office. To be sure, Louis was favourably impressed by everything he had seen so far in Canada. Montreal looked like an orderly and clean city populated by friendly people. This very first impression soon found confirmation in the way everyone at the CANDOR prefab construction company greeted him.

After an hour-long meeting with Sam and other senior people, they all agreed on his responsibilities, his salary and the fringe benefits due to a technical executive.

Louis walked into his new office and sat down at the desk with a pleasant feeling that he had handled a very unpleasant and potentially catastrophic situation in Istanbul with good judgement, even wisdom, and that the whole episode with Rita may have actually opened new and exciting horizons for him. He thought of the old French adage: "A quelque chose malheur est bon."

Despite his rapid immersion into a new world of fresh experiences, he often sat up in bed at night and thought about his life in Turkey and about Rita. Sometimes he even toyed with the idea of writing or phoning her, but all these thoughts came to an end the day his mother phoned to tell him that Rita had gotten married to one of her father's employees.

Louis felt relief mixed with a very real sense of nostalgia for the good times he had spent with Rita. But then he said to himself that everything in life must come to an end in order to make place for new things, hopefully good things.

Rita had now found a husband while he had started a new life in new surroundings.

* * * * *

And thus began to unfold the story of two people, united for a short time in their lives, but torn apart by events destined to lead each of them through very different paths.

Unaware of each other, living on different continents and in different cultural milieus, they started lives that were poles apart from each other.

* * * * *

Rita and Simon returned from a short honeymoon spent in Bodrum, a delightful resort town on Turkey's Aegean coast facing some of the storied Greek islands.

Both were still getting used to each other's ways, likes and dislikes, but given their accommodating natures, they soon found out that with a little effort they could not only get along well, but build a lasting relationship based on love, respect and shared interests. Intellectually they more or less matched each other. Neither of them were fountains of knowledge, sophistication or wisdom, but they amply made up for it by being street smart, alert and practical in their respective approaches to everyday life.

They settled down in their new home, furnished in their own taste. And while he continued to spend long and busy hours at the carton box company, she, under her mother's watchful eye, learned how to keep a clean and efficient home where everything had a place and a purpose.

In addition to all of this Rita had to cope with her advancing pregnancy, a task in which she found ready and dedicated support from Simon. It was he who insisted that she regularly saw her obstetrician, that she took frequent rests and that they all ate nutritious and healthy food, not only for Rita's but more importantly, for the baby's sake.

It was a grey and rainy day when Simon rushed his moaning wife to the hospital. It all went almost according to the medical textbooks. No complications and no excessively painful episodes.

A healthy boy made his screaming entry into the world as if to make sure that no one missed this important event. While both parents were delighted, Rita was pleasantly surprised to see Simon's face really light up as she was handed the little bundle of joy by the attending nurse. That happy expression on Simon's face seemed like ample proof to Rita that the little boy would find in Simon not a stepfather, but a loving and caring Dad.

*****

The early nineteen-sixties were on all accounts important milestones in the progress of Canada on becoming a world-class power house. Fuelled by the arrival and rapid integration of hundreds of thousands of immigrants from all corners of the world on one hand, and the increasing demand from a rapidly expanding global postwar economy for both raw materials and finished goods on the other hand, Canada firmly embarked on the road of economic, social and political ascent, if not predominance.

Both European and American conglomerates vied with each other to open branches and subsidiaries all over Canada to the point that job offers advertised in the Montreal and Toronto papers often filled several pages.

No wonder, therefore, that Louis Modiano soon came to realise that Canada was not only a country of opportunity, but that there was a specific demand for skills in the building and decorating trades, his very own fields of expertise. Also, his boss, Sam Gold, soon discovered in Louis a dedicated, hardworking and most competent worker who rapidly gained the respect and friendship of both the company's clients and his co-workers.

After about a year on the job, Louis decided to sort of draw a line under his Turkish past by selling his Istanbul company to the two managing directors, but not before signing them up as exclusive Turkish distributors of Sam Gold's prefabricated homes and warehouses.

In time, Louis applied for Canadian citizenship and looked forward to a fulfilling life and business career in his adopted country. In fact, he looked forward to it with immense expectations and confidence.

He soon developed a circle of friends, mostly with the support of Sam, who was now his closest friend, and, after a few years, his partner when Louis was given enough shares to gain a seat on the Board as well as a directorship in the company.

Louis now owned a beautiful house in Hampstead, complete with a garden and an small outdoor swimming pool, not far from Sam's home. He furnished it with exquisite taste befitting his reputation as a talented interior decorator.

All he needed now was to turn one of his several girlfriends into a permanent companion for life. And this came even sooner than he could have imagined.

Dahlia, the pretty and very bright daughter of one of Montreal's most prominent lawyers fell head over heels in love with Louis after only a few dates and get-togethers at friend's parties. It so happened that Louis had also singled her out as the most desirable companion on account of her lively yet tempered nature, not to mention her beauty and graceful appearance.

Perhaps it was her obvious maturity that in Louis' mind set Dahlia apart from the other girls. She was actually a thirty year old widow who had lost her husband of three years in a horrible skiing accident. Although an experienced athlete, he hit a tree so hard during a high speed descent that he never recovered from the fractured skull and the internal injuries he suffered.

Barely a year had passed since the unfortunate event and Dahlia was just beginning to find her way back to normal life which included caring for a beautiful two-year-old girl she had been left with.

It did not take long for Louis to propose and to exchange vows with Dahlia Gordon at a picture perfect wedding ceremony and reception attended by la crème de la crème of Montreal as well as by his parents who flew in from Istanbul for the happy event.

After a two-week honeymoon spent island hopping in the Caribbean, the Modianos settled in his Hampstead residence. They started going about their daily lives with passionate love for each other, with joie de vivre, sprinkled with a certain sense of humour and in a lavish lifestyle, all made possible by Louis' above average income and Dahlia's very generous allowance from her doting parents.

In time, the Modianos raised a spirited family of three children, all of whom excelled at school and went on to higher studies which they successfully completed with well-deserved degrees. Following in his father's footsteps, one of the boys, Phillip proudly graduated from McGill's engineering school with honours.

Of course, the Modianos also bore their share of mishaps such as Dahlia's unexpected bout with breast cancer, which was successfully treated, restoring her to full health and Louis' early run-in with elevated blood pressure, followed by an equally unexpected diagnosis of diabetes.

Other than these relatively bearable problems, the Modiano family sailed through the years with financial ease, with many joyful celebrations and vacation trips, a few tears of sorrow and sadness, but all in all as the good life enjoyed by the upper class bourgeoisie.

*****

Simon's genuine affection for the baby boy his wife of seven months had brought into the world continued to amaze Rita and her parents. Perhaps it was his innate love of children or his awareness of having helped Rita out of a dire predicament. No matter what the motivation, Simon turned out to be a devoted father for little Robert and he steadfastly remained his guardian angel for life. Three children of his own eventually rounded out the Nassi family.

In time, Rita's father, who had been plagued by recurring severe arthritic pains, took retirement from his beloved paper box business and passed the reins on to Simon, who, as the years went by and much to the despair of his loving wife, had put on a lot of weight. Buying new suits every year because he did not fit into the ones hanging in the closet had become a regular and inevitable ritual.

By contrast, Rita, more or less maintained her slim appearance and as time went on she continued to be an attractive lady despite her graying hair and a few wrinkles in her pretty face.

True to their vow, neither Simon nor Rita ever told their four children that Robert was a half-brother. Not only did they grow up as true brothers and sisters, but even in later years they maintained a very close and even intimate relationship with each other that withstood the passing of time.

Robert, the oldest was an exceptionally gifted child. He easily excelled at school and consistently brought home good grades which stood him in good stead when he eventually applied for admission to university.

As the years went by, the Nassis easily became a respected family among the Jewish community of Istanbul. Although Simon and Rita never penetrated into the intellectual and academic elite of the local society, they managed to gain respect and admiration for being honest merchant people and generous supporters of the Jewish community.

While his younger brother had gravitated towards the family business, and, after graduation from college had joined the box manufacture which by now had grown into a factory employing some two hundred people, Robert pursued the study of medicine at the University of Istanbul, a venerable institution that had shaped the minds of young Turks for over five centuries. In fact, in recent years, many practicing physicians had acquired their skills in the university's halcyon years in the nineteen-thirties and forties when it provided a welcome lectern to hundreds of Jewish professors escaping the Nazi Holocaust.

Robert went through medical school with flying colours. That is to say in the top four or five of his class, year after year, until his final graduation with honours and with a government grant to be applied to his post-graduate studies.

The fact that his father not only paid for his education, but also provided him with generous stipends in order to make it easier for Robert to concentrate entirely on his training, was certainly a major factor in the successful termination of his studies.

Rita was not in the least surprised when Simon wiped tears of joy from his eyes as he hugged Robert when he stepped down from the dais after having received his doctor's diploma from a beaming dean and a smiling professor vigorously shaking his hand.

Within days following his graduation, Robert had been offered an internship in one of Turkey's most avant-garde hospitals. He accepted and embraced his profession with an ardour akin to passion. As was to be expected, he soon drew the attention of department heads who wanted him to be on their team.

Barely a year had gone by since he had taken up his position when he won second prize in a hospital-sponsored competition based on a number of criteria including patient's satisfaction, diagnostic skills, report writing and introduction of improvements. The prize was presented to Robert by the Physician-in-Chief in the form of a certificate and a letter announcing that he had won an all-expenses-paid two-year internship in one of the university hospitals of his choice. One of the options was the McGill University Health Centre in Montreal.

* * * * *

Louis' sixty-fifth birthday was celebrated with all the pomp and circumstance due an adored family man as well as a top executive who, in the course of some thirty years had taken his company from a mid-sized manufacturer and exporter of prefabricated structures to a world leader in the field. They had branches and subsidiaries in many key markets and had gained recognition for the reliability and design of their product line which included complete family homes, factory sheds, warehouses and hangars, all proudly bearing the trademark CANDOR, the "OR" being a subtle reminder of the company's founder Sam "Gold."

In a way, the birthday celebration which also included a garden party for family and friends in his beautiful Hampstead home was also a bittersweet reminder for Louis to take it easy and leave the running around to others.

In fact, Louis had suffered a heart attack three months prior to his sixty-fifth birthday and underwent complicated open-heart surgery to repair his damaged cardiovascular system.

It was the chief of surgery himself, assisted by two other cardiologists who performed the complicated and lengthy operation. When it was over, a smiling Dr. Rosen came out of the operation room, greeting the family with the words: "Congratulations. It all went very well. Your husband has a new heart. I am sure you will enjoy a long life together. I don't foresee any complications. Rest assured, we will give him the best possible care to nurse him back to an almost normal life. By 'almost' I mean moderation in everything he does. I have assigned one of my assistants to be in charge of the rehabilitation program. He will contact you shortly!"

With that, the doctor rushed away, having received repeated "thank-you's" and "we are so grateful to you" from Julia and her crying mother.

* * * * *

Louis' recovery was indeed uneventful, if somewhat slow on account of the scope and gravity of the operation. Dahlia had seen to it that any and all communications from the office were withheld from her husband "until later" so that he could recover in peace, far away from the brouhaha of the phones and computer screens. Even Sam, his life-long partner, was told to omit any mention of business when talking to Louis.

The recovery, partly in the hospital and partly at home, provided Louis with time to think, to ponder, but most of all to reminisce. And there was certainly plenty to reminisce about.

He thought of his earlier life in Istanbul, his childhood and his growing up in an affluent and sophisticated Levantine environment, among close friends from mostly Turkish and Jewish backgrounds, which helped shape his versatile personality, allowing him to adapt and blend so naturally into the very different milieu he encountered in Canada.

He came to realize that more than thirty years had gone by since his arrival in this country. Thirty years! A lifetime! Apart from a few visits and a couple of short vacations with his family he had not been back to his country of origin. Attending his parents' funerals he did not count as visits. They were painful but brief departures from his busy schedule.

His mind went back to Rita with whom he had spent so many happy and carefree days as if there was no tomorrow. He had not heard from her in all these years and was convinced that she had terminated the pregnancy when he had told her to do so. Otherwise, he figured, she would not have been able to get married in the rather conservative and prudish Jewish environment where the mere thought of single motherhood was akin to shameful heresy. But that was all so remote and half-forgotten.

Thinking back, Louis concluded that the day he decided to come to Canada was probably the most auspicious of his life, by far.

*****

True to his word, Dr. Rosen had assigned one of his assistants, a young intern to supervise Louis' recovery from the surgical trauma. The young doctor could not have been more professional and dedicated in the performance of his duties. Not only did he direct the entire program by constantly giving instructions to the nursing staff, but he also personally checked up on his patient several times during the day, and sometimes even on weekends and during the night. When Louis was discharged from the hospital, the young doctor continued to monitor his patient by phone and house calls.

Both Dahlia and the children were very impressed by the extraordinary care provided by the intern and decided to ask him over for dinner one evening. Up to then they knew him only by his first name, Robert. When they asked him for his full name, he told them Robert Nassi.

Well over two months had passed since the operation and Louis was able to engage in many social activities, including taking short walks around the block. When Dahlia asked Dr. Nassi to join the family for dinner on a forthcoming Friday night, he immediately accepted.

The formally dressed guest arrived with a bouquet of roses for Dahlia and an engaging smile which reflected his obvious pride in having played a major role in Louis' rehabilitation. Looking at his patient and his family, Dr. Nassi felt not like a health professional dispensing treatment and advice to his patients but very much like a healer restoring life to people who were about to forfeit it.

Following dinner the family gathered in the living room for coffee and conversation during the course of which they learned that Dr. Nassi was from Turkey and enrolled in an internship program aimed at preparing specialists for senior hospital posts.

When Louis heard this, he told Dr. Nassi that he too was originally from Turkey, which, to the delight of the others, immediately opened the flood gates to an animated conversation between the two in their native tongue.

When Dr. Nassi took leave close to midnight, both the doctor and the family felt that they had come very close to each other and that a bond had been created that certainly deserved to be maintained and, perhaps, even strengthened.

And strengthened it was, in a rather significant way. Dr. Nassi had developed a strong liking for Julia, the Modiano's older daughter which had actually started when she visited her recuperating father in the hospital and grew stronger during the numerous encounters with the patient's family.

A few days after the dinner invitation, Dr. Nassi phoned Julia and asked her to be his guest at a cocktail party in the McGill Auditorium in honour of some visiting professor. She accepted and greatly enjoyed meeting a number of Dr. Nassi's colleagues as well as the Dean of the Medical School.

This date was soon followed by other invitations to dinner during which the two not only developed a strong liking for each other, but soon fell deeply in love. Julia found in Robert a warm, articulate and sincere human being who was not only loved by his peers but also admired by the university's governing body which was actually trying to persuade him to pursue his career in Canada instead of returning to Turkey at the end of his internship.

* * * * *

Robert was the happiest man in the world when he came home to his bachelor flat one evening after having proposed to a delighted Julia. In fact, he was so excited that despite the late hour, he sat down at his computer to break the news to his mother.

"Dear Mom," he wrote. "I have some great news for you and Dad. I am in love with a wonderful girl who happens to be the daughter of one of my patients. Her name is Julia Modiano, and, believe it or not, although she was born in Canada, her father Simon is actually from Turkey. He came over some thirty years ago. I am sure you and Dad will be delighted to meet her when you come to Montreal for the wedding which is set for later in the year."

Rarely has there been such an abyss between the exuberance and happiness of someone sending a message, and the deadly consternation of its recipient.

Rita thought a lightning bolt had struck her when she read the letter on her screen. What an incredible coincidence. What an unbelievable coincidence. Who would have thought that her son, Louis' son, would end up being the doctor of his own father and without either of them knowing it!

Rita could not believe all this, and yet it was true.

However, the real catastrophy was that her son, unbeknownst to himself, was about to marry his own half-sister.

Impossible!

Rita had to catch her breath before reading the email again and again.

So this is where Louis had disappeared. Canada, of all places.

Many years ago, she had heard rumors that he went to live in Switzerland and she gave it no further thought. She didn't care where he lived. She had completely and utterly taken him out of her life. But Canada? With a family including a daughter who was now going to marry her son, his son?

Rita went to bed that night without telling Simon anything about the dramatic message. She hardly slept at all, constantly thinking about the unexpected news from Robert.

The next morning, without any comment, she gave Simon a printout of the letter.

"What," he exclaimed as he read the email. "I don't believe this. It can't be! This is unreal!" he kept saying. "It's like in the movies."

Rita looked at him. "What do we do now?" was their jointly expressed question. "It's not simple," Rita said. "First one of us has to tell Louis to prevent this marriage from ever happening and then, and I shudder at the thought, Robert has to be told the truth. The truth we all vowed to take to our graves." As she said this, Rita burst out in tears as Simon took her into his arms.

"Come come now," said Simon. "It's not the end of the world. Let's go about it rationally. I mean one thing at the time. First and foremost, one of us must talk to Louis and tell him who Dr. Robert Nassi is. OK? Then we will decide how to handle the rest in a way to cause as little pain as possible to our dear Robert. Don't you think?" "Yes," Rita said. "You are right, sparing Robert the pain is our most important objective. Let's call Louis."

Rita sat down. She was very upset. "My God, what a situation," she said. "Who would have thought that this could ever happen? Our poor Robert. He is being made the scapegoat for something he doesn't even know, something he had nothing to do with. My poor child," she kept repeating.

After a while, she turned to Simon: "How do I get Louis' phone number?" "Very simple," he said. "Send Robert an email, asking him for his future father-in-law's phone number, saying that we wanted to introduce ourselves." "Good idea," said Rita.

Within the hour she had the information on her screen. She thought long and hard before making the fateful call, perhaps, she thought, the most painful conversation of her life.

The phone rang several times, and then she heard a voice that seemed to come from another world. "Hello." "Hello," she replied. "Is this Louis Modiano?" she asked. "Yes, it is," was the reply. "Louis," she went on, "this is Rita." There was silence, followed by an almost shrieking: "Rita, how incredible to hear from you. Where are you calling from?" "From my house in Istanbul," she answered. "What a surprise, to hear from you after all these years. How are you?" "Oh, I'm fine,' said Rita. "And how are you?" "Well, I'm much better now, but I was very ill. In fact, I am just recovering from major heart surgery, but thank God, it all went very well."

There was a moment of silence. "I know," said Rita very calmly.

"You know? How do you know about my heart problem?" said Louis.

"I know about your heart because your doctor told me."

"My doctor told you?" said a clearly agitated Louis.

"Let me tell you how come your doctor told me, bur first: are you sitting comfortably?"

"I am," Louis shot back.

"Louis, your doctor Robert Nassi is your son!"

Rita immediately realized that perhaps she should not have spoken so bluntly to a recuperating and fragile patient, but it was too late now. There was a prolonged silence. "Louis, are you alright?" she asked. "Yes," he finally said. "I am alright. I don't believe this. Dr. Nassi is my son?" "Yes," she repeated, "your own flesh and blood, OK?"

"My God," said Louis. "Why didn't anybody tell me?" "Who did you want to tell you? Me? Did you expect me to tell you that I never had the abortion you tried to push me into?"

Rita could feel that Louis was trying to cope with this totally unexpected conversation. He was at a loss for words. To bridge the gap of silence and avoid any further stress for Louis, Rita went on: "Louis, relax. All this is now that much water under the bridge. I married a very good man who made me happy and gave me four beautiful children. We brought up Robert not as a stepson or an adopted one, but as a real one. What I mean is that Robert does not know that Simon is not his biological father. Therefore, he does not know anything about you. As far as Robert is concerned you are the father of the girl he wants to marry. And that, Louis, is the reason why I am calling you today. To make it short, Robert wants to marry his half-sister. I need not tell you that his is an impossible situation, and someone must undo this whole affair. Do you follow me?"

By now, Louis had somehow recovered from his initial shock and was listening intently to Rita's lengthy speech with occasional "hmmms." But when Rita repeated her "do you follow me?" Louis interrupted her with a loud and even blaring: "Hold it, Rita! Hold your horses as we say in Canada. I have got to ask if you are sitting down." "Of course I am," replied a bewildered Rita.

"OK, listen carefully: when I married Dahlia, she brought a two-year old baby with her. You see, she was a young widow, who had lost her husband in a terrible accident. In other words, Julia my oldest daughter is really my stepdaughter. I am not her real father, and she knows it. And her siblings know it, but for all intents and purposes, she is just one of our kids, you see what I mean?"

Rita could not wait for Louis to finish. She kept interrupting him with "What?" and "Really?" and "Oh, my God," until he had said the last word and then she burst out in laughter. "I don't believe this, Louis. I really don't," she said. "And here I am phoning you to ask you to throw cold water on their wedding plans. I don't believe this," she repeated.

"Well, you better believe it. It's God's own truth. There is nothing to prevent the two from getting married. "Of course not," shouted an elated Rita into the phone. "Mazeltov!" "Mazeltov, indeed," Louis shouted back, adding: "Now that we have gotten this problem out of the way, what next?" "Nothing next," retorted Rita. "We have a wedding, that's all. Of course, we don't tell the children anything. Not a word. Don't you agree?" "Of course," said Louis. "Not a word."

Now that both were in a more relaxed mood, Rita said: "You know, Louis, in the whole affair, you will be the only one to suffer punishment." "How come?" asked Louis.

"Well," she said. "Robert will continue to love Simon as his father. I will bask in the happiness of being the mother of the groom. You and Dahlia will be happy parents leading their daughter to the altar, but you will see someone else take your son to the Chuppa."

"What a sweet punishment," interrupted Louis. "You know? I love it."

"OK, then," he continued. Not a word to anyone in the whole wide world about our conversation. This is our secret." "Yes," replied Rita: "That's for sure."

"Oh, one more thing," she added. "Remember, when Simon and I will come to the wedding, you and I don't know each other. You have to role-play like an actor and so will Simon and I. We never met before and we don't know each other. It will take some doing, but we have to do it for the sake of our children."

"Count on me," said Louis. "I will make Laurence Olivier look like an amateur."That's the idea," replied a laughing Rita.

"See you in Montreal for the wedding," shouted Louis. "Thanks for the phone call. You know, I feel like waking up from a dream." "So do I," replied Rita.

With that, two exhausted but utterly happy people, thousands of miles from each other, fell back on their seats, both heaving long sighs of relief.

* * * * *

Life, in its wondrous ways, shuffles people around, sometimes pulling them apart, seemingly forever, only to bring them together again when they least expect it.

Stranger than fiction…that's what life can be.

* * * * *

YOLANDA

Dr. Barkley's Medical Clinic, on London's fashionable Sloane Street, was full of patients on this rainy Thursday. They were sitting in the waiting room, quietly anticipating the door to open and to hear the receptionist call out their name and say, "Dr. Barkley will see you now." The doctor saw his patients in his private clinic three days a week.

Dr. Phillip Barkley, an Internal Medicine specialist, was from all accounts a very good doctor. He was liked by his patients as well as by the nursing staff at Hammersmith Hospital, where he ran the Internal Medicine Unit twice a week. Not handsome, but endowed with a ready smile and a pleasant disposition, he was considered by many of his patients as the "good doctor" incarnate. At 52, he was financially well off and looking forward to many more years of dispensing advice and treatment to his ailing flock.

And yet, Dr. Barkley was a deeply saddened and distressed man. He had recently lost his beloved wife. Barely nine months had gone by since he and his only son had stood, dumbstruck, in front of Gwyneth's grave, unable to grasp or accept the sudden demise of this lively and bright woman, for whom death had been a thought farthest from her mind. Gwyn had been visiting her ailing mother in a senior's residence in South Woodford and was on her way home. She had missed a red light and in an attempt to avoid oncoming traffic, she had slammed her car into a wall. Gwyn was pronounced dead by the ambulance doctor as a result of head injuries, even before the police could inform her husband of the terrible accident.

Phillip and Gwyn had been married for twenty-two years. It was a marriage conceived in love which, if anything, only grew stronger as the two sailed through a very happy and fulfilling life. It had been a life replete with memorable family and social events, including the joy of bringing up a handsome and bright boy named Christopher, currently, in his second term at the Sorbonne's Faculty of History in Paris.

Nine long months had passed since Gwyneth's tragic death. Thanks to his busy and absorbing professional life, Phillip had managed to keep his act together, but barely so. At work he put up a front, pretending that all was under control, but as soon as he closed the door of his nearby flat in Knightsbridge, he felt the world coming down on him. He was depressed and helpless to the point of often ignoring the meals the long-time caretaker lady prepared for him. Phillip had lost not only a wife, but also a close friend…a part of himself with whom he had shared anything and everything. The loss seemed to become increasingly difficult to bear. Being a doctor, he knew better than to seek solace or compensation in alcohol or mood-altering medications and so, he came to the conclusion that what he needed was a vacation. Not just a brief escape to a familiar spot, but a two-week immersion into a completely different surrounding, among different people, in an unaccustomed setting. After some enquiries with his travel agent he opted for a Club Med in Southern Spain. The brochure promised beautiful beaches, nice bungalows, all sorts of outdoor activities and gourmet-food befitting a sophisticated establishment. He signed up for a two-week stay at the beginning of September and juggled his clinic and hospital appointments accordingly. To be sure, he was not looking forward to more than a jolting break with the past, a sort of emotional shock therapy that could help to lift him from his present depressed state and plant him on a more realistic path, if not to normalcy, then at least to the acceptance of and coping with a widower's lot.

Phillip arrived on a late afternoon at the truly beautiful Club Med compound in Malaga on the picturesque Mediterranean coast. He was assigned a room with sea view in a bungalow which he shared with another male vacationer. He had his own bedroom, bath and balcony, but there was also a common area in case the two occupants desired to socialize. Phillip found the accommodations impeccably clean and very much to his liking. He also met his co-occupant, a middle-aged bank manager from Germany. After freshening up and changing clothes, Phillip set out to explore the sprawling grounds which were partly set in a wooded area and partly followed the sea shore, where he could see cabanas, parasols and, of course, bathers frolicking in the azure-blue waters.

Phillip was very impressed with what he saw. There were hundreds of small bungalows, similar to the one he was staying at, all built around a central two-story reception or social area used for meals and all sorts of indoor activities. There were sport facilities of every kind including tennis courts and even a soccer field. There were secluded spots with lounge chairs for those who preferred to read or play a game of chess. There were walking trails everywhere. In short there seemed to be something to satisfy everybody's quest for leisure, relaxation and privacy.

The whole area very vividly reflected the spirit of the Club Med, a French enterprise which offered people from all walks of life the opportunity to leave their familiar milieu behind and immerse themselves, for a few weeks, in a completely different setting. Here, they could pursue the activities of their choice and, at the same time, meet other people with whom they could have brief and temporary encounters or start enduring friendships and relationships that far outlasted their banter at tennis courts or the nightly dinner tables.

Phillip had been walking the grounds for about two hours. He returned to his room, washed up, dressed for dinner and proceeded to the beautifully decorated dining room at the club center. He was hungry and looked forward to one of those gourmet meals insistently touted by the brochure. Upon entering the dining room, he was met by a few young Maître D's known as G.O.'s (or Gentil Organizateurs). One of them asked him where he would like to sit. "All our tables are for ten people," he was told. "You have the choice of sitting with married couples or singles, English-speaking, French-speaking or German-speaking guests, younger or older people. Please advise us of your preferences, Sir." Phillip was perplexed. Unprepared for the options offered, he said "I am a doctor from England. I don't mind whose table I share. I guess married couples would be alright as long as they speak English. My school French is rather rusty, you know," he added. "No problem, Sir," he was told by the G.O. holding an array of lists with guest names in his hand. "How about table 37, right near the column on your left? Unless you wish to change it, this will be your assigned seating for the next two weeks. Enjoy your dinner, Sir."

Phillip proceeded as told and sat down between two diners. He introduced himself and found out that, on his left, sat a friendly looking divorced lawyer from Switzerland while, on his right, a couple from Paris had already taken their seats. The woman who sat next to him seemed to know everyone, as she conversed partly in French and partly in accented English with several people around the table. Everyone appeared to be in a relaxed mood, healthy looking and eager to experience a tasty dinner, as befits an upper class resort.

Part of the Club Med philosophy lies in aiming to establish relationships between its guests. Thus, dinner is served according to a strict ritual. Waiters place salads and soups in front of each guest, but the main course is brought to the table in a large terrine and, each night, a different person serves everybody around the circle. This routine obviously promotes an often lively conversation at the table and it is not unusual to have the dining room resound with laughter and animated repartees each evening...an obvious proof of the Club's successful formula. After the plates are cleared, the waiters return to announce the opening of the sweet table, which usually signals a mad rush to the beautifully decorated displays of fresh fruit and scores of tempting desserts, thereby, blowing any dietary resolves into smithereens. Finally, after the sweet table is reduced to Saharan desolation by succeeding waves of sweets lovers, obliging waiters serve coffee or tea to a crowd that truly seems to be feeling no pain. People leave their tables, either in little groups or with promises to get together at the beach the following morning.

Dr. Barkley adapted quickly to the routine and thoroughly enjoyed the main course...a piping hot Osso Bucco Alla Romana...one of his all-time favourites. He carried on a lively conversation in English with his table partners and found them intelligent and well-read. In concert with everybody else he stood in line at the sweet table, but when he returned to his table with the delicious desserts, he noticed that his Swiss neighbour had disappeared and, instead, the seat was occupied by a good looking, smiling lady in her mid-forties. At first, Dr. Barkley thought he was at the wrong table, but the lady, who noticed his perplexed expression, motioned for him to sit down and said in accented English, "I am your new neighbour, I hope you don't mind," which she underscored with a hearty laugh. Phillip was amused by the woman's directness and provoked another burst of laughter from the lady when he responded to her and asked, "Are we playing musical chairs?"

"You did not answer my question," she said, "Do you mind?"

"Well…no," he said. "Why should I? I guess that you enjoy change."

"Yes, change for the better, of course." Phillip smiled and had the distinct feeling that the lady had changed tables in order to sit next to him.

Something sheepish in the way she looked at him confirmed this feeling, especially since she talked only to him, ignoring the rest of the diners. While both indulged in the delicious desserts in front of them, his new neighbour kept asking him questions of a general nature, at first, but then slowly moving into more personal domains, such as "Are you alone here?" and "Do you have a family?" Her conversation was bubbly and she seemed genuinely interested in Phillip's replies. By the time coffee was served, it seemed to him that the lady had already extracted an abbreviated version of his curriculum vitae. He, in turn, hardly managed to ask a few questions about her, most of which were answered partly, very briefly or sometimes with just a burst of laughter. Their dialogue dragged into the night and carried on well after they had left the dining room to take a seat on a bench, in a small garden overlooking the beach.

At midnight, Phillip got up and offered to take the lady back to her bungalow. He was tired after a long day and an even longer evening in the almost exclusive company of a complete stranger who, within the past few hours, had managed to build a bridge between them…a bridge which according to all appearances, she fully intended to uphold during their remaining stay at the Club. When he finally said "Good Night" to his companion, he had the distinct feeling that the evening had set the stage for more than a casual relationship

Phillip went to bed, but his thoughts kept hovering over the unexpected encounter. He tried to form an opinion about Yolanda Marelli. She was divorced after some twenty years of what she described as "a mismatch from day one." She suffered through the years, firstly, for the sake of her daughter whom she did not want to grow up in a broken home and, secondly, because she had free access to a nice bank account…no questions asked. Yolanda's ex-husband was an Italian industrialist, presiding over a large holding company. He never had any time for her since he constantly travelled to keep his business empire together, but that was all past and forgotten. She was now free and out to have a good time. She was, however, very close to her daughter who lived in Italy.

Yolanda, now in her late forties, was attractive and sexy. She was impeccably dressed and groomed, wore her hair combed back which made her look even younger, and possessed not only a keen sense of humour but also a pleasantly sincere personality. In short, during the few hours they were together, Phillip found her company stimulating and enjoyable. He was also somewhat flattered that she had gone to some length in approaching him during dinner. He went to sleep looking forward to resuming their banter the following day at the beach.

This first encounter started a relationship which Phillip glided into effortlessly, pleasantly and so naturally that after a few days he felt like part of a couple that belonged to each other. They did everything together and enjoyed it. From swimming to bridge to music sessions in the garden and from long walks during which they talked about themselves and a variety of other subjects and, yes, a few days into their relationship they made love. For both, the urge to meet in bed came naturally and they both enjoyed it very much. In fact, Yolanda had found out from the Club administration that Phillip's bungalow companion had checked out, so she moved in, even without telling him. Phillip was surprised to see her luggage in his house when he came in for a shower.

The next ten days turned into a sort of honeymoon for both of them. They were inseparable and enjoyed each other's company like newlyweds. They laughed a lot, bought each other souvenirs from the Club's beautiful gift shop, but most of all, they enjoyed their sexual relationship which turned out to be a giving and taking of pleasures, such as they both professed to have never experienced before. The two weeks went by like a whirlwind. Since his flight to London left earlier than hers to Milan, where she said she would go to join her daughter, she accompanied him to the airport. In the limo, she constantly wiped tears from her eyes. They kept kissing and hugging each other and promised not only to keep in touch but to meet again at the very first opportunity.

In fact, Phillip had fallen in love and like any mature and responsible person he gave a lot of thought to the future of the relationship. He was determined not to write off the encounter as a vacation caper, but fully intended to continue seeing Yolanda again before long. Too many emotional, intellectual and physical bonds had been created and too many areas of common interest and thought had surfaced during their long talks to allow this to remain an incidental meeting.

Phillip returned to his professional and social life, in London, with renewed vigour and renewed hope that his life was about to undergo a change for the better. He started thinking in terms of "life must go on" and "you cannot and must not die with your loved ones."

During the next weeks, Phillip devoted a great deal of thought to his future life and Yolanda's place in it. To be sure, they were both free to chart the course of their relationship...she, a divorced woman with a grown-up daughter...he, a widowed man with a young son. Nothing prevented him from asking Yolanda to become his permanent companion, even his wife. He thought he knew of no more suitable partner for life. Yolanda was sophisticated, elegant, beautiful, easy to get along with, witty to the point of adding humour to many otherwise dull aspects of daily life and, to top it all, she was a most inspiring and enjoyable sex partner. She had no family encumbrances or obligations except her daughter Leona, whom she called Loni. She appeared to be very close to her. Loni studied Art, in Padua, where she lived with her mother in a house on the outskirts of the old University town. Yolanda very rarely spoke of her ex-husband, except to say that he was a closed chapter in her life and that divorce was merely the official confirmation of a relationship that was simply not meant to be. She definitely never wanted to see him again.

*****

Hardly a week had passed since their heart-wrenching goodbye in Spain, when Yolanda made her first phone call in what was to become a frequent, often daily, exchange of greetings, chatter about their daily lives and avowals of love. Yolanda soon became a very real feature of his life. She even began to mother him, like when he mentioned London's raw weather to her and she interrupted to make him promise that he would be dressed warmly. She told him that she did not like his shirts and that she was sending him three shirts she wanted him to wear, on weekends. In short, during the ensuing weeks and months the two became as close as any couple separated by a few hundred miles could be.

When Christopher spent a few days with his father, in London, Phillip told him about his relationship and hinted at his intention to propose to Yolanda. Christopher was glad that his father had found happiness in his life and encouraged him to continue his liaison. "Nothing will bring Mom back." he said, adding, "She would be the first to have you go on with your life and, incidentally, so would I. Good luck to you, Dad. I look forward to meeting Yolanda before long."

Some six weeks after their parting, Phillip and Yolanda met for a four-day week-end in Geneva. They were happy like teen-age lovers. On the second day of their stay in a beautiful hotel overlooking the lake and its graceful swans, while having breakfast in the elegant restaurant, Phillip proposed to Yolanda. He told her of his love and of his desire to make her happy and of also opening up their home to her daughter, Loni. In fact, Phillip said all the right things at all the right moments. He held her hand and pressed it as if to underscore some of his words. At first, Yolanda looked lovingly into his eyes, but then she lowered them as she kept listening silently to his eloquent speech. Her only reaction came from her hand with which she held his fingers, sometimes stroking them.

Phillip had finished and looked at her intensely. She lifted her head and looking straight into his eyes, she said, "Thank you, darling, I didn't know that you are such a good speaker. Thank you, but the answer is "NO." Darling, I don't know if you can understand, but I was married once and when I divorced, I promised myself never to remarry. Not again. "Listen," she added, "Why do we have to sign a paper? Why can't we be happy as we are? I promise to be yours and yours alone. I love you and will do everything and anything to make you the happiest man in the world. Apart from the love and the time I must give to Loni, I belong to you…body and soul, Phillip." She freed her hand from his and said, "Look, we can be together as often as your profession allows you.

London and Padua are a short flight away. I can stay with you in your London flat or we can meet anywhere for vacations, on weekends, whenever your busy timetable permits. Please understand me, Phillip. You know, people can love each other and be happy together without tying the knot. I just don't want to remarry…at least, not now. Maybe I will change my mind in the future. I don't know. For now, let's live together and enjoy each other as best we can. I love you, Phillip. I hope that you understand."

Phillip had not expected this reaction. Yolanda's demeanour, her manifestations of love, her intense interest in him, had all led him to believe that she would welcome the opportunity to be married to him, especially since she was unattached. Phillip tried to insist, perhaps to dispel her aversion to a renewed marriage, but he immediately realized that her resolve was firm. In fact, she tried to defuse the tension her rejection had created between them by laughing and telling Phillip, "You English prude! You thought that you had to protect my reputation by a priestly blessing in a church. Nonsense! We love each other and will live for each other until death do us part," she ended theatrically. She took both his hands and held them tightly. "Come on, Phillip," she said, "Let's plan our next get-together. How about a few days in your flat? I may want to make some changes in your decor. Before my marriage, I was an interior decorator, you know."

Phillip began to recover from his disappointment. He put himself in her place and tried to accept the fact that not everybody shared the same concepts of tradition, customs and social ethics. Not everybody embraced marriage as the only sequel to mutual love. And, furthermore, Yolanda had emphasized: "Not now…maybe in the future." This remark greatly helped in restoring Phillip's mood and even put a smile back onto his face. He merely said: "All right, darling. You'll tell me when you are ready."

The rest of their stay in Switzerland was picture perfect, like the glorious Alps nearby. They enjoyed every moment, took a boat tour on the beautiful lake, ate well and made love, not only at night, but also whenever they sneaked up into their hotel room. When they finally left for the airport, there were no tears on her face, but laughter in expectation of their next meeting in London.

* * * * *

Yolanda and Phillip's romance went on and became part of their normal lives. They phoned each other frequently and met every month or so. She introduced him to the idea of "mini vacations", mostly long weekends which they spent in Paris, on Greek islands, in Spain or on the Dalmatian coast. Yolanda made all arrangements, from flights to hotels to rental cars. She seemed to be an inexhaustible source of good hotels and even better restaurants.

Phillip repeatedly asked Yolanda why she did not want to come and live with him in London, but she told him that she did not want to leave her daughter alone in Padua. "Loni needs me," she said, "She is growing up without a father and I have to be both parents to her. As long as she is studying I want to look after her. Once she graduates I will be free to do what I want and this is what I meant when I said "later" about getting married." Phillip accepted this and got used to the idea of living with Yolanda on a sort of "loose" basis. To be sure, Yolanda made up for Phillip's craving for a regular home life by substituting it with the excitement of surprise trysts:

"Guess where you will sip your next dry martini, darling?" When they met, she always had a little gift for him, and often surprised him with tickets she had bought for concerts or operas. Phillip often asked Yolanda: "Tell me what you do when we are not together," but he never received a clear-cut answer. "Oh, I spend my time either looking after Loni or thinking of you," was her usual reply.

* * * * *

Almost three years had passed since they had met. The bond between them had grown to the point that, despite their frequent separations or perhaps because of them, they enjoyed each other's company from the moment they met until they left each other. Yolanda had become a frequent visitor to Phillip's London flat which she had remodelled and partly re-furnished. Phillip's friends took to her very easily because of her pleasant and outgoing personality and they had all gotten used to the idea that Yolanda shared her life with Phillip on her own terms.

*****

It was a windy and wet night in London. Fall had come with a bang after a warm and pleasant summer, so much so, that within a few short days, streets and parks were filled with dead leaves in all shades of yellow and red, blown off by the gusty winds. Phillip was alone at home, preparing to turn in after a busy day at the hospital, followed by an unusually long telephone conversation with Yolanda. He looked out the window to see how the trees in Cadogan Gardens were bending and shaking under the strong winds and heavy rain when his telephone rang.

He had not received any night calls in quite a while and thought Yolanda had forgotten to tell him something, but it turned out to be a doctor's call after all. Jim Ashton, his friend and tennis partner on weekends and Assistant Manager of the Ritz Carlton Hotel during business hours, was on the line. "Phil, he said, I'm awfully sorry to bother you at this ungodly hour, but we have a problem in the hotel and I thought you might be able to help. For the past few days we have here Bruno Roessler, the famous conductor from Vienna. He is actually guest conducting the London Philharmonic. This afternoon he reported being sick with stomach cramps and high fever. We wanted to take him to a hospital, but he refused, obviously shunning the adverse publicity this may cause. A short while ago, I called his room and he said that he was feeling awful and thought he had stomach poisoning. In keeping with his wish to avoid exposure I thought of no other doctor than you to come over and have a look at the chap. Do you mind, Phil?"

Half an hour later, Dr. Barkley was at the bedside of Bruno Roessler. He immediately recognized the celebrated Maestro from his pictures in the media. Roessler was a good looking man in his early sixties. He had a large head topped with abundant wavy hair that had mostly turned grey. His eyes were sharp and very alert. Phillip could easily imagine him standing on his podium and watching over even the farthest bassoon player at the back of a sixty-piece orchestra.

After an examination and a brief conversation, he put the patient on an antibiotic he had brought along and ordered rest, liquids and a strict diet until he received the analysis of the sample that he took with him. As he had suspected, the test results next day revealed an E-coli-type infection.

Phillip phoned the patient, told him not to worry, to continue taking the antibiotic and to stay in bed. In the evening, after leaving his clinic, Phillip went back to the hotel and noticed a slight improvement. The conductor asked Phillip to sit down and have a drink. The two talked about the infection the conductor had contracted and then they started talking about their lives. The conductor apologized for having dragged Phillip away from his family and Phillip explained that as a widower, he lived alone since his son was studying abroad. Roessler then began to talk about his family and said he also had a daughter studying away from Vienna…his home. The two men spent the best part of an hour talking about different subjects, often focusing on music, a profession for one and a preferred pleasure for the other. Dr. Barkley left his patient, promising to come back just once more, the next day, before allowing him to resume a shortened work schedule.

For the third and final visit, the conductor had arranged for Phillip to be served some canapés and fruit accompanied by a glass or two of champagne. The patient was feeling much better and was clearly on the way to recovery. The two men had obviously developed a liking for each other. Roessler asked Phillip to tell him about his late wife, about his son and how he coped with the loss of a soul partner. Phillip was impressed with the open and frank demeanour of his patient and told him about his work and his travels, and just as he was about to expand on his liaison with a divorced woman, Roessler, taking advantage of a break in Phillip's talk, said, "You know, doctor, we seem to have something in common as far as our family life is concerned. You have obviously found the answer as to how to live alone without actually being alone and so have I, you know…in a way."

He went on to say, "I have been married for almost twenty-five years to a beautiful woman. Our first years together were glorious. We loved each other deeply and we still do. But, after a number of years of dragging her from concert tour to concert tour, from one end of the globe to the other, I realized that she was not happy and we both came to the conclusion that you can love and care for each other without constantly holding hands. So, one day we decided to continue our lives in a more accommodating way. I would pursue my career of guest conducting, while my wife would travel, take tours and look after our only daughter, who is studying in Italy. You may ask me why I agreed to these arrangements. I will tell you. Firstly, I wanted to preserve our marriage and, secondly, I have complete and unlimited confidence in my wife. I know as I talk to you that I can trust her. Ours is a mature love and I know that she will never betray me...not one iota. When she is travelling we keep in touch by cellular phone. She comes home when I need her or on special occasions such as birthdays and holidays and is generally in charge of the household, despite her occasional travels. The fact is I could not live my present life without the knowledge that, somewhere, either in our home in Vienna or somewhere on a vacation spot in Greece, there is a beautiful woman completely dedicated and devoted to me, just as I am devoted to her. Well, doctor, there you are. Needless to tell you, good and solid marriages come in different forms and shapes and ours is indeed of a different variety." With that the conductor got up, walked over to his bed, and picked up a silver-framed photograph from the night table. "This is her," he said, with a contented expression bordering on the pride with which parents flash graduation pictures of their children.

Phillip put on his glasses to look at the photograph and felt as though he had barely escaped a heart attack or, at least, being struck by a lightening bolt. There, dressed in an elegant evening gown, smiling benignly stood Yolanda, snuggling up to her tuxedo-clad husband, locked onto his arm. It was a beautiful family portrait and it was quite a shock for Phillip. He put the frame back on the table in front of him, but his hand was shaking. Of all the surprises in the world, he did not expect to be confronted with this one. Not in a million years.

Yolanda, his great love, his soul and bed partner for the past three years, the divorcee from Padua, was actually Frau Roessler, loving wife of Bruno who was now looking at him with a concentrated expression because he had noticed something strange in the way Phillip had placed the picture back on the table. "What's the matter, Dr. Barkley," said the conductor. Don't tell me you recognized a patient of yours in the photo?" "No, not exactly, Mr. Roessler," replied Phillip. He got up and said, "May I use your bathroom?" "Of course," the Maestro responded.

Phillip closed the door behind him. His mind was racing like a speeding bullet. There could be no doubt. His Yolanda was actually the conductor's wife and from all accounts, he was unaware of his wife's double life. He did not know what to do next. His first reaction, that dominated all other thoughts, was that he could not walk out of Bruno's room and close the door on the horrid secret he had just been exposed to.

He had to do something, but what? He considered the different aspects of the revelation; Yolanda had lied to him and she had not needed to. She should have told him the truth, leaving it up to him whether to have an affair with a married woman or not. Now, even if she eventually decided to leave her husband for him, he would be breaking up a marriage, which was something he did not want to be a part of. Therefore, he just could not continue his relationship with Yolanda, as regrettable as this was. As for the betrayed husband, Phillip had gained the very clear impression that he was sincere when he spoke of his love for his wife and his trust in the reciprocity of her love for him. As he reached for the towel to dry his hands, Phillip had made up his mind, painful as it was to him. He would tell Bruno the truth…nothing but the truth. As a doctor he had learned, long ago, how to break good or bad news to people. Here was another test case, only this time it involved his personal life.

Phillip came into the living room of the suite, sat down and reaching for his glass of champagne, started one of his most difficult explanations. "Mr Roessler," he said, only to be interrupted by the conductor: "Please call me Bruno and allow me to call you Phillip. OK?" "Sure," said Phillip. "I guess this may help me in telling you what I think must be told, right here and now." He looked at Bruno and suddenly had the feeling that his host was expecting to receive some unpleasant news, because he looked at him intensely and said, "All right, Phillip, let's have it." To soften the impact of his revelation, Phillip started by describing how he had met Yolanda at the Club Med almost three years ago, how she had told him that she was a divorcee, free and eager to start a new liaison after her painful separation. How they fell in love, how he had proposed to marry her and how she had refused, telling him that she would consider marriage only after her daughter's graduation from University.

He spoke about their intimate and often furtive encounters. "She would sometimes talk on her cell phone and then tell me that she had to leave unexpectedly to meet her daughter. But she never let me take her to the airport. She always stepped into or out of a taxi when we met or when she left. "Now, I know why," he added. "That, Bruno, is in a few words the story of my relationship with Yolanda. I must add that we are in love with each other and that I fully intended to marry her as soon as she would be ready. That was, of course, until I heard the truth about Yolanda, tonight." Bruno had listened silently to the story. The expression on his face kept changing as it unfolded. At first, he was surprised, even expressed disbelief, and then he let an occasional smile wash over his face as if he, at last, understood why his wife had covered up certain disturbing clues whenever they talked about her time away from home. Finally, Bruno's face turned to anger over his having been taken for a fool for so long.

There was silence for a few minutes in the room. Then Bruno said: "All right. Now we know the facts or at least what happened. The next question is obviously, "Where do we go from here?" I will ask for a divorce on the grounds of adultery. How can I continue to live with a woman who has cheated on me in such a blatant way? Had you and I not met, by pure chance, she would have continued doing so." "Yes," he added, "I will ask for a divorce. Needless to say, I will provide for her financially and let her get out of my life. Incidentally Phillip, Yolanda does not live in Padua, but in our house in Vienna. Our daughter studies in Italy, but she lives by herself and does not need her mother to tend to her."

Bruno slowly calmed down. "Doctor, may I have a drink, now? I need it like the air that we breathe."

"Of course you may," said Phil. "Pour yourself a good shot and while you are at it, make it a double for me, please," he added. Phil looked at Bruno, "Where do we go from here?" he repeated.

"Look," he said, "what you want to do is up to you, but I know what I have to do. Frankly, I have lost my appetite for an affair with a liar. By hiding the truth from me, she did not take me into her confidence which means she did not trust me. Tell me how I can carry on seeing a woman that does not trust me, lives a double life and cheats on her husband? I'm afraid I have answered my own question. You know, I think I'm too old for playing games. I am utterly disappointed in her. It was lovely while it lasted, but I will walk away from the relationship. And another thing, I am getting tired of these hide-and-seek rendezvous. I want a normal family life, a home with a wife and all the rest of it, if you know what I mean."

"Of course, I do," said Bruno, asking: "So, when will you tell her?"

"Well, the sooner the better, don't you think? Give me a few days to put my thoughts in order and I will meet her somewhere, unless we can talk over the phone. No, on second thought, this is not a matter to be discussed long distance. We have to face each other. I will tell you as soon as possible, all right?"

"Wait a minute!" said Bruno. "I did not tell you about our upcoming 25th wedding anniversary, did I?"

"No, when is that taking place?" asked Phillip.

"In three weeks," continued Bruno. "We are actually hosting a big celebration in our house exactly three weeks from now. She hired the best caterer and decorator in Vienna and the invitations have gone out to some one hundred of our closest friends, not to mention the Prime Minister of Austria and other dignitaries. Phillip, could you hold on for another three weeks and have your talk with her, right after the Wedding Party? Let's do things one at a time. In any case, I am pretty sure that you will not see Yolanda anytime until the party is over. She and my daughter have been working like busy bees for weeks to put it all together."

"All right," said Phillip. "Right after the party I will tell her."

Phillip got up and with a serious expression on his tired-looking face said, "Sorry, old chap...deeply sorry. I had no idea in whose field I had pitched my tent. Trespassing is definitely not my forte and neither is snatching other men's wives."

It was well after midnight when the two men shook hands, like conspirators, sealing a pact between them. Needless to mention, neither of them enjoyed a restful sleep that night.

* * * * *

For the next two weeks Yolanda phoned Phillip a few times to say that her daughter had the flu and that she was tending to her. Phillip wished Loni a speedy recovery, smiling to himself.

* * * * *

October 29th had always been a special date on the Roessler's calendar, but this year it was very special. It was their 25th wedding anniversary. Bruno, Yolanda and their daughter Loni had planned it for months. Their guests had received engraved invitations emblazoned with the Roessler family crest. Not too many people knew that Bruno Roessler's grandfather was an Austrian aristocrat, who had been elevated to the rank of baron by Emperor Franz Joseph II for outstanding services to crown and country. It was only after the end of World War I that the by-then impoverished Roesslers decided to drop their titles as vestiges of a past era.

For weeks, Yolanda, assisted by Loni, was busy choosing the menu for the buffet dinner, the canapés and the drinks to be served. Fine vintage champagne was to be the main lubricant of the evening in quantities designed to create good humour, laughter and a really festive atmosphere. The highlight of the evening was the performance of *"An evening with Vivaldi and Mozart"* by the Viennese Baroque Ensemble. Dressed in costumes of the era, the players, all of them well-known performers, had offered Maestro Roessler the evening's serenading as a special gift to a venerated master. Yolanda, with her extraordinary sense of planning, had left nothing to chance. Every corner in the home was decorated to reflect the Baroque times which had once rendered Vienna the musical and cultural capital of the world. Even the waiters would wear special costumes borrowed from the Vienna Opera House. It was to be the party of the year.

Bruno returned from his London tour some ten days before the party. Still under the shock of that fateful evening with Phillip at the Ritz Hotel, he began to develop a strange feeling for Yolanda. For the first time he thought of himself in terms of leading a double life. Yolanda, although very busy with the party preparations, had still found time to be as loving and caring for him as she had always been, or as she had pretended to be, as he now knew. He was amazed at her capacity to be his devoted wife while, at the same time, living a separate existence with a lover. Bruno thought that men would be far too clumsy to master the art of travesty…of leading such a secret, Mata Hari-like life.

Another thought that now entered his mind was Loni. Could he plan to divorce his wife in the imminent future without telling his daughter? He came to the conclusion that Loni would never forgive him for this cabal and after all was said and done, he might end up not only losing a wife, but also a daughter. He certainly did not want that to happen. So, after going over the whole scenario in his mind again and again, he came to the conclusion that he would have to take Loni into his confidence.

After lunch he asked Loni if he could have a word with her away from home without telling her mother because it was sort of a surprise he wanted to discuss with her. They met an hour later in the back room of one of Vienna's many "Konditoreien". Over cups of coffee, Bruno told his daughter the whole story. He spoke about his chance encounter with Phillip, with whom her mother had been having a passionate love affair for the past three years. Loni was speechless. She had no idea of her mother's secret life and only knew what her father knew; that Yolanda spent a lot of time travelling and sightseeing and vacationing and that's all.

Bruno then told his daughter that he intended to ask for a divorce on the grounds of blatant adultery. Bruno was quick to add that he would fully provide for both Yolanda and Loni. "No need to worry about the future, my dear, he said. I will leave it up to you to stay with me or to stay with your mother or both of us. You have now lived alone in Italy for some time and you are managing your own life very well. I am sorry at having to break up our home, but your mother has already done that a long time ago. I really have no choice in the matter, as you can clearly see. I want you to be sure, sweetheart, that I love you and that I will always be your Father."

Bruno had almost come to the end of his story as he noticed that Loni had taken out her handkerchief. She was quietly crying, especially when he mentioned the breaking up of the home. Bruno took his daughter's hand and pressed it. "I am sorry, darling, he said. I am very sorry."

"Do you think Mom will marry her English friend?" she asked.

"I don't know, he said, but I have a feeling that she will not. You see, he is as mad at your mother as I am because she lied to him, for three years, telling him that she was divorced and that she could marry him only after you finished your studies because she lived with you in Padua. She told him a pack of lies, which he, in turn, related to his friends and to his family. He now feels that she made a fool of him. That's why he also wants to end the relationship."

"So, Mom would get it from both sides? From you and her doctor friend?" asked Loni.
"I'm afraid so," nodded her dad.

"That is not fair," said Loni.

"Why?" said Bruno. "Was it fair for Mom to cheat on me? I never, ever betrayed her, you know, and God knows if I had opportunities to do so. I was always faithful to her and I gave her whatever she wanted. I loved her, perhaps in my own way, but I loved her."

"Come on, Dad," said Loni. "Forgive her and forget the whole thing. She made a mistake. OK! That's no reason to break up a marriage after 25 years. Please, Dad?" Loni begged, looking straight into his eyes.

"I can't, sweetheart," said Bruno. "I really can't. She hurt me too much. This was not a brief escapade, it was a serious affair going on for the past three years, and who knows if she did not have other affairs before the doctor. No, Loni. I have made up my mind."

Then, he took Loni's two hands into his and said, "Can you promise me not to say a word about all this to your Mother? I will tell her soon enough…after the party is over. You have both put too much effort into it to spoil it now. I am counting on you, Loni. It's between you and me for just a few more days, OK?" Loni, still holding her handkerchief, nodded. She was very upset and kept wiping tears from her eyes. She hugged her father and hurried away.

* * * * *

Preparations for the anniversary party were in full swing. Yolanda's little office next to the bedroom was a beehive of activities. She followed up on everything that had to be done in accordance with the plan she had prepared. Nothing was left to chance. With Loni at her side, she made sure that the Roessler's 25th Wedding Anniversary Party would be the crowning of Vienna's social season.

In the early morning hours of the 28th, the day before the event, the delivery vans started to unload not only food, drinks and furniture, but also the special staff hired and trained to take the guests into a make believe eighteenth century world, complete with powdered wigs, crinolines and white gloves. Flowers and decorations had transformed the house into a glittering scene of baroque and rococo opulence. By noon, everything was in place for a brief rehearsal. Yolanda had planned to make sure the reception and all services were just as she wanted them to be…perfect to a tee. She had made minor adjustments and corrections but was satisfied with most everything. All was set for the next day.

Bruno had spent the morning doing some administrative work at the Vienna Philharmonic Society and came home in the early afternoon. In the bedroom, he found a note from Yolanda on the pillow; "Darling, everything is set for tomorrow. Your tuxedo and freshly ironed shirt are hanging in the cupboard. I am at the beauty parlour in case you need me. Love, Yolanda."

It was shortly after four o'clock when the telephone rang. It was Yolanda. "Where are you?" he said, "The caterer has some questions for you." There was a moment's silence and then Yolanda's voice came calmly through the telephone. "You better sit down, Bruno," she said, "because I have a few things to tell you and I want you to listen carefully."

"OK," she continued, "the poor terrified child told me everything you said to her, so the theatrics and games are off. You made your decision and I made mine. I am calling you from a hotel downtown and Loni is with me. Neither she nor I will come home tonight or tomorrow night. You want a divorce? You can have it, not in two weeks but right now. Yes, I was unfaithful to you. Yes, I have a lover and do you know why? It is because you neglected me. You treated me as part of your staff. Not only were you constantly away on tours, but you hardly ever asked me about my life and my problems. It was always you and your success and your music, when you called me late at night after your concerts. You took me for granted…that's what you did…you still do! You let me run a house and a family and expected everything to be in perfect order. What did you do for the reception tonight, for instance? You did nothing, nothing at all! You went to your rehearsals and let me do all the work. For years and years, I was faithful to you and never even thought of other men. Three years ago, I looked in the mirror one morning and I saw wrinkles in my face. Suddenly it came to me. How long would I have to wait until we could live together, again, like husband and wife…loving each other and doing things…together? Will it only be when I am old and grey and you can no longer wield a baton because of arthritis? So, three years ago, at the Club Med, when I met another man who made me feel like a woman…like a wanted and desirable woman, once more…I lost my head and started an affair. Of course I could not tell him the truth about us, so I invented things about me to protect the three of us. Yes, Phillip gave me happiness and I bet you did not even notice that in the past couple of years, I started buying better dresses, I went more often to the beauty parlour and I began to regain assurance and joie de vivre. It was because I felt loved and wanted, but enough of all that. It's all water under the bridge, now. So, all I want to tell you before we meet at the lawyer's office is, celebrate our 25th anniversary tomorrow without Loni and me. You are so good with words, so go and explain to your guests why we are not there."

Yolanda had said most, if not all, she intended to tell Bruno over the phone but she had said enough to hit Bruno like a ton of bricks. He tried once or twice to interrupt and argue that she had never told him she was feeling unhappy and frustrated and neglected, that he had to follow engagement schedules set years ahead of time, but her words rambled over his interruptions like an unleashed stream.

So, he let her talk. Now, she was silent. "Are you there?" he finally asked.

"Yes, I'm here," she answered. "Where do you want me to be? I am here with my daughter. So, have fun with your guests tomorrow."

Bruno sensed that she was about to hang up, so he quickly said "In what hotel are you?"

"Never mind that," she said. "Why do you want to know?"

"Because I want to talk to you," he replied. "You have said what was on your mind, but I also have things to tell you. Do you know how it hurt me to hear that you had a lover? Do you know how I felt when I found out that you have been lying to me, for years? I always loved you…you know that…perhaps in my own way, but I always loved you and I never looked at any other woman."

"Yes," she interrupted; you had no time for me so how could you find time for another woman?"

"Why didn't you talk to me about your unhappiness?"

"I tried to," she said, "God knows how many times, but I know that whenever I asked you to spend a few weeks with me alone, somewhere, so that we could recharge and rekindle our intimate lives, together, you always said: "Not now, as soon as the concert season is over." But that season was never over. You were constantly immersed in your work and I was never part of it. Do you forget how many vacations and trips we had to cancel or interrupt because of changes in your schedules? Well, I have not forgotten them."

"OK, OK," interrupted Bruno.

By now he had heard an earful of what he had, over the years, asked Yolanda to accept…a lifestyle designed to fit into his worldwide appearances. He realised that he had, indeed, made his profession a priority in their life without considering that his life was also the life of his family. As Yolanda went on citing more reasons for her frustrations, he became very much aware of her unhappiness and began to understand how and why a 50 year old beautiful woman would drift into the arms and, even, into the bed of another man who made her feel like a woman, again. They had been on the phone for almost an hour, by now. Yolanda's resolve to stay away from the party was firm. Bruno said, "Give me ten minutes to come back to you. I have to think it over. Please, Yolanda…just ten to fifteen minutes, OK?" She said, "OK," and gave him her phone number.

Never in his life, had Bruno been forced to think so fast and to come up with a stand on a problem of such magnitude. The foremost thought on his mind was that he had no choice at this point in time. It was some twenty-four hours before the party. He could certainly not welcome his guests saying that his wife had suddenly developed a headache. If he cancelled the event, he could just imagine the headlines in the Viennese newspapers next day: "Scandal at Conductor's Reception!" or "The Event That Wasn't!" He would be ridiculed in all the cafés of Vienna: "Have you heard what happened at Bruno Roessler's Party?" No, he could not face this catastrophe. He was caught like a mouse in a trap. On the other hand, he also realized that Yolanda had told him the bare truth. Over the years, he had given his profession precedence over his family life. That was clear to him. He often thought that one day he would make up for it…perhaps when he retired from the baton. In the meantime, Yolanda saw her time passing by, saw that she was not getting any younger and wanted to partake in life before the fleeting years ushered in middle age.

Bruno looked at his watch. He quickly dialled the number. "Listen," he said. "I have thought it over. We both acted foolishly. Forget my plans for separation…I mean, divorce. Will you immediately drop any and all liaisons you had or have?" "Not unless you promise to stop taking me for granted. Can you be the Bruno I fell in love with 25 years ago, again? Can you?" "I can and I will, so help me God" shouted Bruno. "Where are you? I'll come to pick you up." "No!" she said. "Loni and I will jump into a cab. We will be home in half an hour." She hung up.

*****

Bruno was very excited. A great deal of serious events had taken place during the past hour. It was like a movie and he and Yolanda were the main actors. He slumped down on his chair, but then he picked himself up and dialled Phillip Barkley in London. He was lucky to find the doctor about to leave his clinic. "Hey, buddy," he said, "sit down and listen to the latest news." "What's that?" said Phillip. "Don't tell me you had it all out with Yolanda the day before your big bash?" "Yes and No," said Bruno. "Listen, we had a long conversation and when all was said and done, we made up and decided to start all over again."

"Oh," said Phillip. "What brought that change about?"

"Well," replied Bruno, "my daughter spilled the beans. She told her mother about you, our conversation in London and my intention to divorce her. So, Yolanda left the house and told me to go celebrate without her and Loni. She also told me that she cheated on me because I had neglected her. You know what, Phil...she was right! So, after a lot of talk, we decided to give it another go. She will give you up and I will be her beau and devoted husband, again. It's that simple. We sort of forgave each other."

Bruno stopped. "Have you any comments? You told me you intended to end the affair, didn't you?" he continued. "So, things seem to be falling into place, Phillip."

"Yes, they do, don't they? When did all this happen?" asked Phillip.

"Just now, my friend…minutes ago. As a matter of fact, she is presently on her way back home, but the news I gave you was only one reason why I called. The other reason is that I want you to jump onto the next flight to Vienna and be here, tomorrow, to celebrate with us and I am not taking no for an answer. If you can't get on a commercial flight, on such short notice, I will ask my manager to arrange for a private plane to get you here and back to London. Take a cab from the airport to the Vienna Hilton. I am booking you in right now. The concierge will give you our address."

When Phillip interjected the flow of words with, "Bruno, I really don't belong in this party of yours," Bruno almost shouted, "You don't belong? Let me tell you this…if it was not for your sitting down for dinner at the Spanish resort, at the right moment in the life of my gallivanting wife, and if I had not fallen sick in London, the two of us would have never met and I would have never had the chance to find out what went wrong with my marriage. Ergo, I would have never been able to repair the damage, especially if you had not been around to save me from death by food poisoning. These are once-in-a-lifetime events, each of them worth a celebration and you, my dear doctor, are saying: 'You don't belong?' Nonsense, pack your bags. It's black tie. You be here on time. Do you hear me? Besides, tell me where you can find today a Dom Perignon brut vintage 1992?" With that, and a burst of laughter, Bruno hung up.

* * * * *

The Roessler's 25th Wedding Reception turned out to be the most talked about event in Vienna. Among the hundred guests were politicians, including the Prime Minister, diplomats, musicians, business people and scientists from Austria and other parts of Europe. La Crème de la Crème crowded around the richly decorated and deliciously catered-for buffet, sipped vintage champagne from tall crystal glasses and, then, sat down to an hour long concert of Vivaldi and Mozart, superbly rendered by well-known soloists dressed in costumes of the baroque epoch. It was an absolutely delightful evening, in a beautiful setting, with Bruno and Yolanda being the most graceful hosts imaginable. Yolanda had even thought of a little gift for every guest as they reluctantly said goodbye.

No wonder that the Weekend Edition of the "Wiener Tageblatt", Austria's most important daily newspaper, featured a detailed report on the Roessler's party. Pictures taken during the evening showed some of the prominent guests and celebrities. In the center of the page was a photo of a radiant Yolanda, flanked on one side by her husband and on the other side by Dr. Phillip Barkley, the well-known London physician who had cured the conductor from a serious illness during a recent London engagement.

After naming some of the most important guests, the paper featured parts of the gala address delivered by Bruno Roessler. No doubt, the reporter must have been greatly impressed by the conductor's eloquence because he devoted a whole column to the speech, some of it reproduced verbatim:

"Perhaps the most impressive feature of a memorable evening were the words spoken by Maestro Roessler, following dinner. After thanking his guests for honouring the celebration with their presence, he delivered some words of wisdom, which, because of their depth and openness merit repeating here: 'Wedding anniversaries," he said, like other celebrations, are really of little value other than that of having a good time, unless they give us the opportunity to reflect and allow us to appreciate what we are really celebrating. I need not tell you that if professional achievements and honours were the sole criteria, I can safely say to you that I am satisfied and, in all modesty, even proud when looking back on the past twenty five years of my life. But that, my friends, is only part of it. A much more significant aspect of our reflection is did we also give happiness to those who share our lives? Have we made them feel part of our achievements, have we created a family not of participants in a quest for success, but of equal partners in sharing our aims and dreams as integral parts of them? Therein, lies the real meaning of life. Not only to be an achiever or a public figure, but to be an equally celebrated husband, an idolized father or a beloved son, as well. Permit me to ask all of you successful men, if, when subjecting your achievements to your own scrutiny, you can honestly say: "I have achieved it all with the full involvement of my family and without ever depriving them of quality time, of attention, of my love and devotion. Indeed, I am where I am today, because of them. Ladies and gentlemen, may this beautiful evening encourage all of us to delve into the past, learn from it, make amends and corrections when needed and, above all, make sure that we celebrate not only personal achievements, but also family bonds and values. May I ask you to please, raise your glasses in a toast to my beautiful wife, Yolanda, and my lovely daughter, Loni, for having made this party possible and for looking forward, with me, to the next twenty-five years!"

It took just a couple of minutes for the glasses to be raised and drained and then, the applause was loud and sincere and seemingly endless. After that, there was absolute silence in the room, for the Prime Minister of the Republic of Austria had stepped forward and, holding his champagne up to the radiant Roessler family, he said: "My dear Yolanda and Bruno. Need I tell you how happy my wife and I are, personally and on behalf of our government and the entire nation, to congratulate you? You, Bruno Roessler have brought honours and respect, admiration and pride to our country coming from all parts of the world. We all share in your success and wish you health and long life surrounded by your family, your friends and your adoring public. I have one more word about your address. I thought it was inspiring and very much to the point. I could not agree more with what you said, especially since we can all see just by looking at Yolanda and Loni how successful you have been in your life by achieving fame and admiration, while at the same time having raised a happy and fulfilled family. Bravo, Maestro! Bravissimo and Encore!"

A PERFECT CRIME?

Who among us has not been tempted to seduce lady luck by spending a few bucks on a lottery ticket? I guess it is a combination of trying to get something for nothing, of the excitement of gambling, perhaps even the desperation of a few to lay their hands on some badly needed cash, but above all the anticipatory thrill of "What if I win?" that drives us all to the brightly lit LOTO QUEBEC counter.

Wally Balinski was no exception. At eighty-five and widowed for the last seven years, he had settled, albeit by dire necessity into a simple and unexciting life mostly centered around the care and concern for his failing heart. In fact, a cardiac condition diagnosed many years ago as congestive heart failure had, over the years, deteriorated to a point where two major open heart surgeries had to re-establish some make-shift functioning of his circulatory system. He was fully aware that his survival depended on the judicious use of several medications, a more than austere and drastically restricted lifestyle as well as the constant supervision by Dr. Fred Connor, his long-time cardiologist.

And yet, despite his physical limitations and his constant awareness of treading the thin line between life and death, Wally had not lost hope that God in his infinite mercy would not only continue to grant him a reprieve from the final call but would even somehow restore him to better health and increased enjoyment of what time was left to him.

It is in this spirit of hope that Wally bought three chances of a 6-49 ticket for six dollars on his way home from some late grocery shopping.

Wally lived alone in a small one-bedroom flat in a building mostly occupied by senior residents. His only child, a son and his family of three grown children lived in another part of town.

On the morning after his purchase of the ticket, Wally had an early appointment with his cardiologist. On account of his increasingly fragile heart condition, Dr. Connor had insisted that Wally come in for a check-up every two months.

Needless to say, over the years the two men had developed if not an intimate, but certainly casual relationship, which Wally often used to enquire about the doctor's family or vacation plans and to chat about his own daily life.

On this particular morning the doctor put his patient through the paces of a meticulously detailed examination which included an electro-cardiogram and an X-Ray. Not surprisingly the findings served to confirm the standing diagnosis of a severely damaged heart that barely eked out survival thanks to a combination of powerful pharmaceuticals and restricted living. If anything, Dr. Connor had noticed a slight deterioration of some vital signs, but he decided against passing this information on to the patient lest it increased his apprehension which could only aggravate an already compromised condition.

"O.K., Wally", said the doctor after he had completed his check-up. "You can get dressed now. I am increasing the dosage of one of your pills from one to two a day just as a precaution". As he sat down at his desk to write the prescription Wally chose to utter a few words of banter and jokingly referred to the lottery ticket he had bought the night before. Adjusting his tie, he said: "For my next visit you may have to come down to Bermuda, where I will be sipping champagne on the balcony of my seaside mansion." To the doctor's "Oh?" Wally went on to tell him that he had just bought a 6-49 ticket which he was sure would win the jackpot. The two men laughed and joked about the countless tickets they had bought over the years with precious little to show for except the occasional five or ten dollars consolation prize. But then, the doctor looked at the morning paper that lay on his desk and said: "Hey, why don't you show me the ticket and we'll check the wining numbers of last night's draw." Wally took the ticket out of his pocket and handed it over to the doctor who was now flipping through the paper.

What Dr. Connor saw was enough to make his blood turn to ice. There, while Wally was standing with his back turned, were the six winning numbers matching exactly the numbers on Wally's ticket. The prize was a whopping Nine Million Dollars. The doctor looked again and again to make sure. There was no mistake. In his hands was the ticket that would collect Nine Million Dollars.

His thoughts raced like shooting stars on a summer sky. He looked at his patient who was now combing his hair in front of the mirror and suddenly a frightening thought entered his mind. A thought that terrified and repulsed him at first but then, by impulse rather then by reasoning he took a spontaneous decision. This was it and he would do it.

As the patient turned away from the mirror, he noisily hit the desk with his hand and shouted: "Wally, you won the jackpot. Come here and see for yourself". He jumped up, took Wally by the hand, vigorously pulling him to his desk. "Here, Mr. Balinski, you are a millionaire. Not just a millionaire, but nine times a millionaire!" He shouted these words to Wally and went on: "Now you can have your Bermuda and your Bahamas, and you know what, you can fly there in your own private jet. Ha ha!" In a frenzy, the doctor kept repeating: "You made it Wally, you are rich, rich, rich". Like performing a tribal ritual, the doctor circled around a speechless Wally, waving his hands and shouting into his ears: "Millionaire, Millionaire".

All through this vociferous demonstration, Dr. Connor kept watching his patient's face and his trained eyes were quick to notice the sudden pallor on his cheeks, the fixed glare in his eyes, the open mouth gasping for air, and, eventually the sagging posture, the stumbling, the clutching of his chest and finally the falling to the floor of his patient. He knew exactly what his exaggerated display had triggered in a vulnerable and extremely fragile heart. He knelt down, listened to Wally's chest, and then he flung the door open and yelled at his receptionist: "Quick, get an ambulance. We have an emergency" but not before putting the neatly folded winning ticket into his own pocket.

Walter Balinski was pronounced dead on arrival at the hospital despite the frantic efforts at cardiac resuscitation performed in the speeding ambulance. On the lifeless body lay his voluminous medical file Dr. Connor had given the paramedics as they rushed out of his office.

A cursory search through Wally's pockets by the hospital staff revealed the name and phone number of his son who was immediately summoned.

Gordon was devastated. He broke down crying like a child. Although he was fully aware of his father's very serious heart condition he just hoped that his dad would enjoy old age a few more years, especially since he led a calm and regulated life. After taking possession of his father's personal belongings he decided to drive to his dad's home to make the funeral arrangements by phone.

As he sat down at the desk, he noticed a photocopy of a 6-49 lottery ticket. By sheer curiosity he opened the newspaper which he had picked up at this father's door to the page of the lottery results. He did not believe what he saw. There, for all the world to see were the winning numbers of last nights' draw and they matched exactly the numbers of the photocopy in front of him. He found it hard to think straight. Was all this really happening to him or was it a dream?

He immediately began to search the small apartment for the original ticket. Starting with the clothes his dad had worn. He looked everywhere. Literally everywhere down to the garbage can. He lifted carpets and looked under the bed. He found nothing. No trace of the original ticket. All he had was the photocopy.

He tried to review his father's last whereabouts. The ticket could have been lost either at the doctor's office or anywhere his dad had been since he purchased it. "Let me try the doctor's office" he reasoned.

When he arrived at the clinic he found an empty waiting room and a receptionist who told him that they had an ambulance take away a patient earlier and the doctor was so shaken that he went home. She had to cancel all appointments for the day. Gordon identified himself as the son of the patient in the ambulance and told her that his father had lost a lottery ticket which he my have dropped during the medical examination.

Together they went into the doctor's office and Gordon started to look around, especially where patients hang up their clothes or wash up. He found nothing. But when he looked at the doctor's desk he made a surprising discovery. The day's newspaper was opened to the page of last night's lottery results. He took a photo with his cell phone camera and asked the receptionist: "Miss, did the doctor return to his office after my father was taken to the hospital?" "No", she replied, "In fact, Dr. Connor left at the same time as the paramedics. He actually ran after them with the patient's file. He never came back. "And no one entered his office since?" asked Gordon. "No one" she said.

Gordon was puzzled. His father's ticket had won in the lottery and either the doctor or both he and his patient must have known about it as evidenced by the newspaper on the desk. But where was the ticket?

Gordon thanked the receptionist who was now about to close the clinic. She hoped that Gordon would find the ticket and expressed sympathy and regret over Mr. Balinski's death. "He was such a nice and fine gentleman," she added.

Gordon had by now seen and heard enough to make him very leery about the events of the day. He decided there was no time to waste and drove straight to the office of the lottery administration. Simultaneously he called his lawyer from his cell phone and asked to meet him in the lobby of the lottery building.

On arrival at Loto Quebec he requested to speak to someone in authority. He was ushered into the legal department. After identifying himself he told the official what had happened during the past few hours. He showed him the photocopy of the winning ticket his dad had purchased and said: "I have reason to believe that Dr. Connor took the ticket from my father. My lawyer will immediately file a request for an injunction to halt payment, in the event that Dr. Connor comes to claim the money. Will you cooperate? I have a strong feeling that some foul play is involved."

The lottery official replied: "If we receive a court injunction to halt payment to the bearer of the ticket, we will of course comply and wait for further notice from the court."

"Thank you very much," was Gordon' reply as he rushed out of the room.

His best friend, Gerry Turner, who also happened to be a successful lawyer, was already waiting for him as he stepped out of the elevator into the cavernous lobby of the building. Gordon briefed him on the events of the day while driving to the courthouse to submit a request for an injunction. They saw a judge in his chambers and explained the reasons for their request. Within the hour the application was approved and the lottery administration was issued an order to halt payment of the proceeds of the jackpot to the bearer of the winning ticket pending further notice.

*****

A broadly smiling Dr. Connor came two days later to the lottery head office to claim his prize. But instead of receiving a cheque he met an official from the legal department who told him that he had to wait for payment until Loto Quebec received the go ahead from the court. "Please keep in touch with us for further developments" he was told. Dr. Connor was puzzled and very upset. "I have the winning numbers here and I insist on being paid" he exclaimed. He demanded to see the manager who showed him the official court injunction. He left, saying he would come back with his lawyer.

Within a week he was served a summons to appear in court for a preliminary hearing in the case of the winning ticket he held. When he came, accompanied by his lawyer, he was informed that his deceased patient's son was accusing him of having stolen the ticket from his father during the latter's visit to his clinic, shortly before his death. The doctor vehemently rejected the accusation and said he had bought the ticket himself. This turned out to be an incriminating mistake by the doctor who did not know that the judge he was talking to had, in a file in front of him a photocopy of the winning ticket found in Mr. Balinski's home. He told the judge: "Anyone can claim that I took the ticket from a dead man's pocket. Dead men cannot talk. My patient's son is inventing a story. This is my ticket and I am entitled to the prize, he asserted. But when the judge asked him: "Where did you buy the ticket?" the doctor was first evasive and then said he could not remember, reasoning that he could not lie since all tickets bear encoded identification of the selling agent.

At the end of the enquiry the judge decided that there were enough coinciding suspicions to warrant a court case. He informed Gordon's lawyer that they could bring a case against Dr. Connor. The object would be for his client to convince a jury that his father and not Dr. Connor was the legitimate and rightful owner of the winning ticket.

*****

The case of Gordon Balinski versus Dr. Edward Connor opened on a grey October day at Montreal's Palais de Justice. Apart from the presiding judge, the court officials and a panel of jurors, there was Dr. Connor and his attorney, Gordon Balinski and his lawyer-friend, Dr. Connor's receptionist and two officials from the Loto Quebec administration. There were also a dozen or so people sitting in the audience section.

The proceedings opened with the plaintiff's lawyer presenting his case against the defendant. He told the court that his client's father had bought the ticket the night before the draw and had made a photocopy of it which was found on the deceased man's desk. A photocopy no one except the owner of the original ticket could have made. He added that the said facsimile was presented to Loto Quebec two days before the accused showed the original to the administration.

This statement stunned the doctor as well as his lawyer. They obviously had no idea of the existence of a photocopy.

The attorney went on to accuse Dr. Connor of having taken the original ticket from his patient's pocket immediately after his collapse in his office. He then called Dr. Connor to the witness stand in order to ask him a few questions that could shed light on the case.

A somewhat shaken Ed Connor stepped up to the witness stand and after being sworn in, looked to the lawyer with an uneasy perhaps even apprehensive expression.

"Doctor Connor", started the lawyer, "Can you explain to the jury how it is possible that Mr. Balinski possessed a photocopy of the winning ticket before he came to see you on the morning after the draw and you pretended that you bought this ticket yourself."

The accused sat up straight and as if he had been expecting the question, answered: "of course I can explain it. The other day when I was asked where I had bought the ticket I said I could not remember. Well, there was a good reason for my not remembering where I bought it. You see, I did not buy the ticket. I received it as a gift."

"A gift?" interjected the lawyer. "A gift from whom?"

"From the patient", replied the doctor.

"You mean to say that your patient presented you with a ticket that won nine million dollars?" At this strong voiced question the whole court, including the jury broke out in laughter, causing the judge to bring down the gavel several times. "Order in the court," he said, "Please."

"No, No," asserted the doctor. "When Mr. Balinski gave me the ticket neither he nor I knew that it was a winner. You see, the way it happened was that as the patient got dressed after the examination a folded 6-49 ticket fell from one of his pockets. He looked at it and said to me: "Hey Ed, I have been buying these tickets for as long as I can remember and apart from an occasional five or ten dollar consolation prize I won nothing, zip, nada. Here, take it, perhaps you are luckier that I. In any case I owe you for keeping me alive all these years. Good luck!" And with a chuckle, he handed me the ticket. That's exactly what happened in my office that morning."

"And when did you find out that the ticket actually won the jackpot?" asked the lawyer. "Oh, two days later when I remembered the gift and checked the list."

The lawyer had been waiting for this answer. "If this is so, and I must remind you, Dr. Connor that you are giving evidence here under oath, if this is so, how come the newspaper on your desk which your receptionist gave you when you ushered Mr. Balinski into your office, was opened to the page of the wining numbers? Furthermore, since you left your office for the day at the same time as the ambulance it stands to reason that you became aware of the win during Mr. Balinski's presence in your office and not two days later as you just told us.

"These are facts, Dr. Connor," continued the lawyer. I therefore revert to my earlier question. Why would the owner of a ticket that won nine million dollars give it to you as a gift? Unless you took it and I repeat, took it from him before his removal from your office."

"Lies and fabrications!" exclaimed the doctor. "I did not know that the ticket won the jackpot until two days later when I went to Loto Quebec to collect the prize."

No sooner had the defendant finished his sentence that the lawyer advanced towards the judge, and, turning to the jury, he said: "Ladies and gentlemen. I have here a cell phone photo taken by my client in the presence of the receptionist shortly after Dr. Connor left for the day and I want to remind you that no one entered his room following the hasty departure. You will notice that the picture shows the page of the winning numbers as well as the time on the doctor's desk clock. Your Honour," continued the lawyer, "I want this photo to be part of the testimony as Exhibit 'A'."

Still facing the jury, the lawyer continued: "I suggest that Dr. Ted Connor sitting in the witness box has blatantly lied to us not once but several times during his testimony. First he said he bought the ticket but could not remember where. A lie he himself contradicted by telling us that he did not buy it but received it as a gift. And then he said that at the time he received the gift neither he nor his patient knew it had won nine million dollars. An obvious lie since the photo I just submitted for the record clearly proves that either he or both he and his patient knew about the win while Mr. Balinski was still in his office that morning.

"Your Honour", continued the lawyer, "We are here in the presence of a cunning impostor. His repeatedly contradicting testimony as well as his claim that the received the ticket as a gift cannot be substantiated and can only support the accusation that he appropriated the ticket or in plain words, just stole it, from his unconscious or perhaps even dead patient.

The lawyer went back to his table and said: "No further questions, Your Honour, " upon which the judge told Dr. Connor: "You may step down. Thank you."

The judge then addressed the court and said: "During the testimony, we just heard that mention was made of the doctor's receptionist, who, I understand is here in court today. I assume she was at her desk in the waiting room during the events that took place in the adjacent office of the doctor. I would also like to hear her side of the story. What exactly did she hear and see during Mr. Balinski's visit that day."

Francine Duprès was a pretty and very neatly dressed young woman in her late twenties who had been Dr. Connor's receptionist for the past four years. She was a graduate of Secretarial College in Montréal and not only looked but also acted very professionally.

She took her seat and was sworn in. "Miss Duprès", said the judge, "Please tell us what happened in the doctor's clinic on the day of Mr. Balinski's death. We are particularly interested in the events that took place say between eight and nine in the morning."

Francine spoke with a clear and businesslike voice:

"I arrived as usual at 7:30 a.m. and readied the waiting room and then the doctor's office for the load of patients expected that day. I had ten people scheduled between 8:00 and 13:30 starting with Mr. Balinski, who, like many others were patients with chronic or severe heart conditions the doctor had been treating for many years. Dr. Connor arrived at about ten to eight and went straight into his office. A few minutes later Mr. Balinski came in. I informed the doctor on my intercom and he promptly came out to ask the patient in. I gave the doctor the patient's file as well as the daily paper which had just been delivered. The doctor closed his door and I went about my secretarial chores. About 30 minutes later, Dr. Connor flung his door open and yelled at me: "Quick, Francine get the ambulance. We have an emergency. I am trying cardiac resuscitation." I did as told and I must say that the ambulance arrived in record time to take poor Mr. Balinski away."

At that point the judge interrupted the testimony and said: "Did you hear or see anything unusual during these 30 minutes or so while the patient was in the doctor's office?'

"Well, yes," said the receptionist. "In fact not 'unusual', but most unusual! There were loud shouts coming from the doctor's office.

"What kind of shouts?" asked the judge.

"Shouts like 'You are a millionaire!' which the doctor kept repeating over and over again. Then he shouted: 'You are lucky, you are rich, rich.' At first I thought the doctor was trying to overcome the patients' hearing problem, but then I wondered why he kept on yelling 'You are a millionaire'. It was very strange. Even the two next patients who had in the meantime arrived looked at each other and at me and asked: 'What is this shouting all about? Someone is a millionaire?' 'Not me, for sure.' I told the amused patients. But then, the shouting suddenly ceased and the next thing I knew was that the doctor flung open his door and asked me to call an ambulance."

"Thank you, Miss Duprès," said the judge. "You may step down."

The receptionist's testimony had created quite a stir in the courtroom, prompting the judge to again call the audience to order.

No sooner had the noise died down than the prosecutor rose to recall Dr. Connor to the witness stand.

"I remind you that you are still under oath" he said. "Could you please tell the court what this shouting 'You are a millionaire' was all about?"

"Yes, sir," the doctor replied. "There is a simple answer. When my patient presented me with the ticket I told him: I hope it is a winner and makes me a millionaire and since Mr. Balinski was hard of hearing I had to raise my voice to deliver the message. This is what my receptionist must have overheard."

"I'm afraid your explanation is not very convincing" retorted the prosecutor. "According to the receptionist you repeatedly exclaimed: 'You are a millionaire', not 'it may make ME a millionaire'. There is a big difference between the two versions." Turning to the judge, the prosecutor said: "I would like the court to summon the two patients who also overheard the shouting from the adjacent room to corroborate either Miss Duprès' or Dr. Connor's testimony.

Furthermore, I have another question bothering me, to wit: Why would a cardiologist, whose patient has such a fragile and vulnerable heart condition repeatedly shout at him, regardless what he said? No one and certainly not a doctor yells at his patients, especially if they should be spared exposure to violent and traumatic outbursts. I am asking myself, could this non-professional behaviour not have been a factor in the patient's cardiac arrest? On second thought, ladies and gentlemen, I am not asking, I am pointing a finger at the defendant.

If it pleases the court I want to hear testimony from the two patients in the waiting room as well as the expert opinion of a prominent cardiologist before formulating my opinion for the jury."

"Permission granted." replied the judge. "The court is adjourned to reconvene with the three additional witnesses."

When the court sat again a week later the two patients confirmed under oath that beyond the slightest doubt what they had heard was 'you are a millionaire' and they had heard it repeatedly. They also heard the words: 'You are rich, rich, rich' several times.

As for Dr. Yves Duclos, head of cardiology at one of Montréal's largest hospitals and an international authority on the links between the nervous system and the heart, he testified that while an aggressive and scary exposure could certainly cause a severely compromised heart to go into arrest, it was very difficult to conclude that Dr. Connor's frightening antics and shouting were the actual cause of Mr. Balinski's death. They certainly did not help and as a certified cardiologist, Dr. Connor should have known better than to upset his patient as the testimony from the three people who overheard the ruckus clearly indicated. It is not up to me to determine whether some sinister reasons motivated Dr. Connor to behave the way he did, but I would certainly recommend that a copy of the court minutes be sent to the Quebec Order of Cardiologists. They may want to have a word with Dr. Connor. I personally find his shouting at a patient unprofessional and, in this case, irresponsible."

With that, Dr. Duclos was thanked by the judge and asked to step down.

It took the jury two days to deliberate. When the foreman rose at the court's third session in the case of Balinski versus Connor, he proclaimed in a loud voice:

"We the jury find the accused guilty of having stolen the lottery ticket from his patient. We reached this conclusion on account of the many contradictory and untruthful statements made by he defendant and his inability to convince the jury that he is, in fact, the legitimate owner of the ticket.

In the matter of the accusation levelled by the prosecution that the defendant may have caused or contributed to the patient's death we could not establish guilt beyond the shadow of a doubt. However, we found his shouting at a severely ill patient totally unacceptable and unprofessional. If nothing else, his behaviour exposed the patient to a grave risk the consequences of which he was well aware of as a heart specialist."

The judge was the last to speak. He wound up the case by saying: "I agree with the verdict rendered by the jury and I thank them for their able and expeditious handling of the case." He then turned to Dr. Connor and asked him to stand up. There was absolute silence in the courtroom as the judge continued:

"Personally, I believe that you are not only a liar, but you lied under oath, which, I need not tell you, is a grave offence. Being a liar also made you a thief and an impostor. I am hereby instructing the lottery administration not to pay you the prize money. It is indeed very sad that the rightful owner of the ticket could not enjoy his good fortune even though it came to him late in life.

As for the suspicion raised by the prosecution that you may also have been a murderer, I will respect the jury's verdict but I want you to know, Dr. Connor that if you did indeed wilfully and wantonly cause your patient's death in order to gain access to the money he won, no jail term in the world can come close to the burden you will carry on your conscience for the rest of your life. Not an enviable prospect for a physician who once swore the oath of a healer.

I am sending you to jail for two years for theft and perjury. This court is adjourned."

A STORY OF ART

London's Crawley Museum of Art is known worldwide for its beautiful collection of rare oils, sculptures and jewellery. Started in the mid-eighteen hundreds by Lord Crawley, a banking magnate, it has over the years amassed a truly unique array of sixteenth century Flemish, Dutch and Italian paintings, some outstanding renaissance and baroque sculptures as well as some more recent exquisitely crafted Faberge jewellery, mostly acquired from impoverished Russian nobility in the early nineteen hundreds. What adds to the importance of the Crawley Gallery is that its curators periodically enrich their collection by adding rare works of art when they become available to them.

There is no doubt that "The Crawley" is a place not to be missed by anyone who likes to get lost in reverie and delight when standing in front of a Rembrandt or Rodin.

Visitors to the second floor of the Victorian building housing the gallery will be regaled by some beautiful sixteenth and seventeenth century paintings and by a recently acquired display of four exquisite drawings, two by Rembrandt and one each by Raphael and Tizian.

Each of these drawings is sketched on now yellowed paper and was made by the masters as they created their paintings. Each page contains several trial sketches of some of the features later appearing on the completed painting such as a hand, a horse's head, a sword, a garment or even a child or a dog. Originally drawn in black ink onto white sheets of paper, the sketches had now turned dark red and the paper had yellowed. And yet, despite the passing of time, every feature drawn by the artist had perfectly survived as if it was just completed. The four sheets, each similar in size but very different in content and style are encased in a well lit glass vitrine right next to some of the paintings themselves as if to complement them and underscore the personal element behind the masterpieces on display. In fact, the sketches add another dimension to the paintings, that of showing that the Rembrandts and Tizians were not only geniuses who created art by inspiration and God-given talent, but also hardworking perfectionists who put their heart and soul into every detail of their creations.

Beside each of these four drawings is a label with the name of the artist, the date and a reference to the paintings for which these trial sketches were used.

There is, however, also another notice inside the glass case, holding the drawings that says: "For the story behind these four sketches, please view the special display near the exit of this hall."

Visitors intrigued by this invitation will see an encased display of four forgeries of each of the original drawings with an explanation saying: "The recent acquisition of the four original drawings on display across this hall brought to light an attempt by some forgers, who a number of years ago tried to sell forged copies to unsuspecting collectors. When apprehended, the originals of these treasures were returned to their rightful owners. The forgeries on display bear witness to the long and often adventurous journey the originals traveled until their acquisition by this Gallery.

* * * * *

This is the story of the more recent "adventurous journey the originals traveled" until they came to rest at the Crawley.

* * * * *

The very successful Great Exhibition of 1851 ushered in an unprecedented era of urban development and ensuing prosperity for many landowners in the London area. Among them was Lord Wyndham whose clever and often daring real estate manipulations had managed to endow with him a tremendous fortune. In fact, in just a quarter-century, he was considered one of the most if not the most prosperous landowner in late Victorian London.

Lord Wyndham and his family lived in a style befitting their social and financial standing, but it was Lady Wyndham who constantly prodded her husband to acquire works of art in an obvious effort to build a collection which she fully expected to carry one day the Wyndham family name. To that end she commissioned several well known London art dealers to help her fulfill this ambition. It did not take long for one of those dealers to draw Lady Wyndham's attention to a rare and truly precious find. Four sheets, each about 10 x 15 inches in size containing ink drawings made by Rembrandt, Tizian and Raphael.

Lady Wyndham stood in awe and disbelief in front of these four sheets. The sight was indeed stunning and so was the price asked for by the art dealer. Fifty thousand pounds each. Lady Wyndham's mind was made up the very moment she had set eyes on the treasures. She paid the dealer and drove home, clutching the most precious folder she ever held in her gloved hands.

There was little Lord Wyndham could do when Lady Sarah told him over dinner how she had spent that afternoon, other than trying to contain his outburst and protest. "You must be out to ruin me", he repeatedly told her, but in the end, she carried the day by convincing him that what she had done was not a purchase, but an investment. "Nothing, not even your land and properties will appreciate as steadily as genuine art. Houses can be rebuilt but Rembrandt cannot be replicated", she crowed. After a few more vain attempts at objecting to the acquisition, Lord Wyndham finally grudgingly agreed.

The four drawings were catalogued, registered with the British Museum and deposited in a vault at the Midland Bank, their home for the foreseeable future. From time to time, Lady Wyndham had the vault opened and in the company of an art expert as well as an agent from her husband's insurance company, examined the drawings to ensure proper storage conditions.

This ritual continued uninterruptedly until 1906 when the oldest of the three Wyndham girls was married to Mr. Peter Sinclair, a young and handsome Foreign office official with a promising diplomatic career ahead of him. And, on the weekend before the wedding both parents presented the young couple with a certificate drawn up by the family solicitor transferring ownership of the famous four master drawings to Peter and Elizabeth Sinclair. A grandiose wedding gift indeed. Needless to say the solicitor saw to it that the bank, the insurance company as well as the Curator of the British Museum were informed of the treasure's new owners.

Periodic inspections by the Sinclairs continued to ensure the physical integrity of the drawings until the mid 1920's, when Peter Sinclair not only received his first assignment of importance, First Secretary at His Majesty's Embassy in Warsaw, but also a knighthood from his ultimate employer, King George V.

Before moving his family to Poland, Sir Peter had the four drawings re-appraised to ensure their updated insurance coverage. To everybody's surprise the former fifty thousand pound assessment was upgraded by two art experts to five hundred thousand for each of the drawings.

This was accepted by the insurance company and Sir Peter was required to pay larger annual premiums commensurate with the new assessment.

For many years the Midland Bank continued to be the depository. Inspections were now carried out by Sir Peter's London solicitors while he himself held increasingly important diplomatic posts in Asia and then South America.

By 1939, just two months following the outbreak of World War II, Sir Peter was appointed His Majesty's Ambassador to Brazil, the largest country in South America. During a brief visit to London before embarking on his new assignment, he called on the insurance company for a new assessment, which now valued the four drawings at a cool one million pounds each. The drawings continued to be safely ensconced in the steel vaults of the Midland Bank.

Nothing further was heard about the four drawings until about two years later, when on one dark night during a "Blitz", the German Luftwaffe managed to score a direct hit on the Midland Bank's Piccadilly branch. Two days later, Sir Peter received a telegram in Rio de Janeiro from the Bank's manager, informing him that although his famous drawings were completely "safe and sound", the banks' underground vault had been damaged to an extent, that, until repairs were made to the safes, the bank could not assure the safety of their contents. Consequently, Sir Peter was requested to remove them into his own custody until further notice. This, Sir Peter did forthwith by instructing his London solicitors to take the drawings and deposit them in a mural steel vault to be immediately installed in the library of his house on Hans Crescent in Knightsbridge. The five story red brick building was the home of the Sinclair family where Sir Peter, his sister and two brothers had grown up.

It was now vacant, except for an elderly couple of caretakers who lived in the basement and kept the building clean and in perfect condition. All in expectation of the day Sir Peter and Lady Elizabeth would retire from the diplomatic service and return home.

But, as it often happens, especially in wartime, nothing is certain nor predictable, for, two days after the drawings were temporarily deposited in the library's huge oak desk, pending the installation of the steel safe, the Sinclair home on Hans Crescent received a direct hit during one of London's most devastating air attacks. In fact, almost the whole row of houses on that street were either turned into rubble or into blazing pyres because the enemy had not only dropped detonators but also incendiaries. That night, in 1942 London was one blazing and crumbling inferno.

The Knightsbridge area seemed to have been targeted in particular. From Sloane Square to Brompton Road fires were raging everywhere. The noise of crumbling walls and exploding bombs was deafening. As soon as the sirens sounded the end of the raid in the early hours of the morning, fire engines were rushing in together with brigades of firemen, auxiliaries, ambulances, constables and homeguard members. A group of paramedics was assigned the task of looking for victims possibly trapped in the still smouldering debris.

Robert Fenwick was an auxiliary paramedic now standing in the rubble of what was No. 21 Hans Crescent, the Sinclair House. He had climbed onto a pile of bricks and broken wooden paneling to look for any traces of victims. There were books everywhere. He surmised that this must have been the library. In front of him was a large desk shattered by a beam that had fallen right over it. He noticed that one of the desk's drawers was open and in it laid a yellow envelope. There was nobody else around him. Instinctively he grabbed the envelope and slipped it into his first aid backpack. He thought that the envelope might contain something of importance which he fully intended to hand over to his superior at the end of his watch.

By the time several hours later Robert Fenwick went home for tea and a well deserved respite, he had completely forgotten about the yellow envelope. It was not until early next day that he remembered it and took it out from his back kit. It was more of a heavy manila folder than an envelope. He carefully lifted the flap and saw four individually wrapped packages inside the folder. He took out one of the packages and after carefully removing several layers of protective materials he looked at a sheet of paper with drawings in dark red ink. He opened the other three packages and they all contained different but similar ink drawings. He had never seen anything like that before, and he did not know what these drawings represented, but judging by their very elaborate protective packaging, he realized that what he was looking at were objects of value, perhaps great value.

The destruction of several venerable building on Hans Crescent was, of course prominently featured in the press, especially the home of the Sinclair family. Photos in the papers showed the beautiful mansion as it once was and the piles of rubble it had been reduced to by the air attack.

Sir Peter learned about the disaster from a phone call he received late at night from his London solicitor, who had just come back from an on-site inspection of the ruined building.

After listening to the eyewitness account for a few minutes, Sir Peter asked "What about the master drawings. Were they already deposited in the wall safe?"

"No, Sir Peter, said the solicitor, I was getting to this. As you know, I contracted a locksmith to install the safe in the library wall, but the man did not have a chance to finish the work because your house fell victim to the air attack in the meantime. So, I placed them temporarily in the big oak desk in the library, and locked the drawer.

"So, what happened to the drawings?" pressed Sir Peter.

"I am afraid to report to you, Sir that they could not be found anywhere. As a matter of fact, the oak desk was completely destroyed by one of the beams in the library, the drawers fell out and I as well as my assistant searched through the rubble for hours to no avail, Sir Peter. We could not find the drawings. I must say that the whole library is one immense pile-up of bricks, torn books, broken glass and wood splinters. Moreover, most of your books were either completely or partly destroyed by flames or heat. The dump truck I had ordered arrived at noon and started pushing through the rubble, but I am afraid there was no trace of the drawings. Given the fact that your house was not only hit by explosive but also by incendiary bombs and the fact that a large section of the library is now a blackened and charred pyre, I must conclude that together with so many other valuables, the drawings were lost."

"Did you check with the police and the fire brigade?" asked Sir Peter.

"I did indeed, Sir," came the reply, "nobody seems to have seen the yellow envelope. Nobody."

"That is very sad news." Sir Peter said. "In fact, I am heart broken. What a stupid coincidence. First the bank is bombed and then my house, before we could place the drawings in a safe place."

"Yes, indeed." Agreed the solicitor.

"So where do we go from here?"

"Well, Sir, I had a long telephone conversation with the insurance company a short while ago. In fact, I spoke to the Managing Director. His answer was 'we shall pay Sir Peter the insured amount of four million pounds on two conditions. One is that payment will not take place before the end of the war, just in case the drawings turn up somewhere, and the other is that upon payment to Sir Peter, the insurance company will become the legitimate owners of the drawings in case they are ever found. I thought both conditions were reasonable, don't you, Sir?" asked the solicitor.

"Yes, I guess they are." Was the hesitant reply. "You know," added Sir Peter, "the house can be rebuilt, but these drawings are irreplaceable and they were our wedding gift. I cannot tell you how saddened I am by your report. Thank you for your help and goodbye."

With that, Sir Peter hung up.

*****

Robert Fenwick had a good friend and bowling buddy who, like himself had been exempted from military service because of health problems. Alfie worked as an accountant at a well known antique dealer. Robert decided to take Alfie into his confidence to find out exactly what it was that he had salvaged from the rubble. When Alfie saw the drawings, he almost keeled over.

"Do you know what these drawings are?" He asked Robert. "Of course you don't. How could you? Well, my dear chap, these are very valuable drawings by sixteenth century masters and they are worth hundreds of thousands of pounds each. Perhaps even more. What do you want to do with them?" said Alfie.

"Well, you tell me. I don't know anything about this."

"OK," said Alfie, "I am going to propose something to you. I know we have been good friends for many years, but business is business. You cannot turn these drawings into ready cash on your own. Let us do it together and we split everything fifty-fifty. If it's alright with you, we draw up a short letter of agreement, just to be on the safe side. But first of all, forget about giving these drawings to your supervisor. We'll keep them and after I find out more by looking up some of the catalogues and manuals at the office, we will decide what to do with them. Do you agree, Robert?"

"Yes, I agree." Was the spontaneous answer.

Robert somehow sensed he needed help in disposing of this apparent treasure and what better partner than his long-time friend Alfie. The two shook hands. Robert said "Fifty-fifty. Draw up something in simple language and I'll sign it." With that, Robert replaced the drawings in their original protective covers and hid the whole thing in an old chest padlocked in his basement.

It took Alfie just three days including some late evening hours to find out everything he wanted to know about Robert's loot. When they met on the weekend, Alfie told his friend: "Well, Robert, I have good news and I have bad news for you. What do you want to hear first?'

"The good news, of course", said Robert.

"Ok, then. Don't fall off your chair. "What you found is worth one million pounds per sheet for total of four and I repeat, four million pounds."

Robert did indeed almost fall off his chair. "Four million? So, how do we get them or rather when do we get them?" he blared.

"Not so fast, my friend", said Alfie. "This was the good news. As for the bad news – you can't get them. You really can't."
"What do you mean?"

"Well, what I mean is that these are well-known works of art which are catalogued and registered in the name of a certain Sir Peter and Lady Sinclair – by the way, the owners of the house in which you found them. So, whoever you will offer them to will look up the catalogues or ask the British Museum which authenticated the drawings many years ago and they will report you for possession of stolen art. OK? Unless, of course, you return the drawings to this Peter Sinclair in the hope of receiving a finder's fee or some other recompense."

Robert was listening with an expression of utter disappointment. He was close to crying out loud. "What kind of a friend are you?" he uttered. "First you tell me that we are holding four million pounds in our hands and then you tell me we are lucky if we get tipped by a Mr. Sinclair for returning them to him? Are you for real?"

"Yes, I am." Replied Alfie with a whimsical smile on his face. "I have not finished yet. I have given this whole matter a lot of thought and I think I found another possibility."

"Let's hear it," said Robert.

"Look," Alfie continued, "we cannot sell these damn things officially, right? In other words we cannot go to a Museum or to a Gallery or put an ad in the paper, but we can sell the drawings unofficially or secretly, and much more importantly, we can sell them and keep them too!"

"Now you lost me", said Robert, who looked at his friend in bewilderment. "What the hell are you talking about?" he asked.

"Well, I have not been working in the antique business for almost thirty years for nothing. Listen to what I propose. I happen to know a very rich man in Burma. In fact he is a billionaire and he is also an avid art collector, with no questions asked. This man will buy anything of value. He will not ask where it comes from. If the curator of the Burmese State Museum tells him the stuff is genuine and valuable, he will buy it to add to his immense collection. And once he buys something, he destroys all paperwork about the transaction, keeping only a record of the artwork itself and the price he paid for it. This is the way he works.

I have met him once or twice during some of his previous trips to this country. And I am sure he will remember me. So, what I am going to do is to offer him a forgery, yes, you heard me, Robert – a forgery of our drawings and tell him: 'Look, I came across these drawings. I don't know whether they are genuine or not. Why don't you show them to your friend, the Burmese National Museum Curator. If he tells you they are genuine, you keep them and remit to me four million pounds. That's their value. OK? Four million pounds sterling. If your friend tells you they are false, please send them back to me and forget the whole thing. OK?'

Why am I doing this, Robert? Simple, I don't want to let go of the originals. We cannot sell them now, but maybe one day things may change. So, I want us to keep the real stuff. Secondly, if my Burmese prospect ever accuses me of having sold him fakes, I will tell him: 'I asked you to verify them. You said they are real, not me, OK? Now, Robert we are going to have the forgeries made by the greatest living expert right here in London. This man is so good that practically nobody can tell the difference once he is through with his work. Believe me, he is extremely clever. So what do you think of my plan, Robert?" said Alfie after his lengthy speech.

His friend had listened in a spellbound manner throughout Alfie's proposal. He was speechless.

"I can't believe all this," he finally managed to utter. "Are you sure it will work? What if your buyer in Burma does not return the drawings or does not pay the four million?"

"Don't you worry about that," Alfie said. "In this shady world of mystery or stolen art, honesty is the name of the game. It sounds strange, but it is absolutely true, Robert. No buyer of illegal antiques can afford to be exposed to the police or the Courts. I feel confident that the forgeries will be so good, that this Curator friend will fall for them, lock, stock and barrel."

After a few minutes of silence, looking intently at Alfie, Robert finally said: "Well, you are the expert, you know what you are doing and besides, if something happens, all we stand to lose is the money paid to the forger."

"Which is a lot", interrupted Robert.

"But a mere pittance compared to the cool four million pounds we are getting paid."

"Yes" said Robert. "I still cannot believe the whole thing, but let's hope you know what you are doing."

"Trust me" were Alfie's parting words.

The events of the next few months seemed to confirm Alfie's well-planned strategy. The forger completed his work which was promptly sent to the Burmese mystery buyer. He had the artwork verified by this expert friend and true to Alfie's prediction, the Curator pronounced them "real and genuine", an obvious tribute to the "greatest forger ever". In due course the payment arrived by some devious routes, all meticulously arranged by Alfie. One evening he brought Robert a white canvas shopping bag stuffed to the edges with bank notes. Robert spent the evening in the attic counting the loot. It was two million pounds sterling less the well deserved fee paid to the forger. Robert hid the cash in the old chest together with the yellow envelope. Needless to say he did not breathe a word to anybody about the entire matter, especially not to his wife. A strong believer in the "need-to-know" principle, he figured that when the time came for her to start spending it, he would tell her the whole story. In the meantime this was another "war secret" as far as he was concerned.

*****

Almost twenty years had passed since the conspirators had come into their illicit windfall fortune. Twenty years that were marked by both happiness and misfortune for both of them.

Soon after the end of the war, Robert told his wife the whole story. They decided to spend the money as inconspicuously as possible in order not to draw any attention whatsoever. Betty, Robert's wife told her family and friends that they had won some money in the lottery. As a result they sold their old and decrepit house and moved into a really nice and modern one in a much better neighbourhood on the outskirts of London. Robert retired and after giving their two children some money, they lived quietly and very comfortably until Robert was unexpectedly diagnosed with cancer and died. Shortly before his passing he called for Alfie, gave him the drawings which he was still keeping in the padlocked chest and they both signed a paper to the effect that should Alfie ever make any money from the drawings, he would give Betty or her heirs one half of the proceeds.

To explain the loot to his own family, Alfie also concocted some story about an unexpected inheritance and then enjoyed twenty years of traveling, comfortable living and prosperity with his wife and son. He continued to put in regular hours in his accounting office just so as to keep the low profile of a well-to-do professional.

*****

But then, one day all of this prolonged "honeymoon" came to an abrupt end. It all started thousands of miles away from London, in Burma. The billionaire mystery collector died at the age of ninety and his sizeable estate was being liquidated by his legitimate heirs led by his two sons. In the process, the executors of the will also hit upon the drawings. They found no accompanying documentation other than their price tag, four million pounds, as well as the certificate of "authenticity" from the State Museum Curator. Anxious to sell this valuable item, they packed the four drawings very carefully and sent them to Sotheby's in London to be auctioned off to the highest bidder. Needless to speculate on what happened next. When the venerable auctioneers had the drawings examined, they were found to be forgeries; causing Sotheby's to return them to the Burmese estate liquidators with a note of regrets to the effect that they do not handle forged items. "However," added the note, "even if these items were the originals, they could not be sold since they were now the registered property of an insurance company and had vanished from sight during the wartime bombings of London. The note ended with the cursory: "We thank you for considering Sotheby's and hope to be of service to you on a future occasion." However, before returning the items to Burma, Sotheby's duly informed the insurance company of the curious event, even letting them have a look at the forgeries.

* * * * *

When the news about the forgery reached the people in Burma, something akin to hell broke loose. "Obviously the first question was 'Who sold these forgeries to the deceased collector?' and the second question was 'How can we, as legitimate heirs, get our money back?' Well, neither of these queries went anywhere. In true fashion of a collector of art, no matter where it came from, the deceased had destroyed any evidence that could lead to the seller. Nothing but the forged drawings, their price and the "Certificate of Authenticity" could be found and even the Curator who had delivered that certificate had died a long time ago. The estate executors were furious, but despite consultations with their lawyers and several phone calls to Sotheby's, they finally decided to consider this a profit and loss item and placed it on the back burner, so to say.

*****

As for the insurance company, the sudden surfacing of a forgery of their long lost treasure hit top management like a lightning bolt. After all, they were still out on the millions they had paid to the Sinclair family at the end of World War II. Like a bushfire, the news of the copies went from one department to another, finally landing on the managing director's desk. He promptly called a meeting with his senior staff. It did not take them long to establish the obvious.

Given that the forgeries were so well executed, they must have been copied directly from the originals, which could be in existence somewhere. Someone may have been holding on to them during all these years, fully aware that he could not sell them. Perhaps some private collector, perhaps someone who did not even realize what he or she had stashed away in an attic. After all more than twenty years had passed since they "sat as models" for the forger. Perhaps they had even been destroyed in the meantime. The repartee around the conference table was animated to say the least. Some managers suggested calling in Scotland Yard, while others thought that some discreet enquiries with leading art and antique dealers could lead them to a trace or clue. It was the youngest member of the board who won the day by simply suggesting to place an ad in the London Times inviting the holders of the drawings to come forward.

"Gentlemen," he said, "We want to get our insurance payment back and we can only do so if we can put our hands on the originals. The people who we hope presently hold on to them cannot sell them and will therefore continue to hold on to them maybe forever. We have to break the status quo by making it both possible and worthwhile for the mystery owners to come into the open. We could, for instance offer them to sell the originals through us, and share in the proceeds. I know this may not be the proper thing to do, in other words for us to do business with thieves, because after all, this is what those who spirited them away from the burning ruins of the Sinclair residence a quarter of a century ago clearly are.

But, we can legitimize the deal, by saying in our ad: 'look, come forward and return the drawings to us, the legitimate owners. We, in turn will sell them in an auction and give you a finder's fee or compensation which in the occurrence will be 50% of the proceeds. I think that unless we make it really attractive for the mystery owners, they will never come forward. And by the way, my preliminary enquiry with some reliable sources tells me that the four originals might fetch up to ten – yes, Gentlemen, ten million pounds."

There was silence around the oval table. Everyone looked at the originator of the idea and at the Chairman of the Board. Like spectators at a tennis match following the ball being lobbed between the two players, all board members alternately observed the two men sitting at opposite ends of the table. Finally, the silence was broken by the Chairman. "Alright," he said, "let's do it." Turning to the originator of the idea," he added: "Can you have the proposed text of the ad on my desk by tomorrow afternoon? I suggest you have it cleared by the legal department. I don't want us to be exposed to any wrong-doing even if it means making money." With that the meeting was adjourned.

Several days later the ad appeared in the London Times. There was no reaction. It was decided to repeat it a few days later, a wise move as it turned out, for a caller asked to speak to the insurance company's management "in connection with the notice appearing in the Times."

It was none other than Alfie, now well into his seventies, who told the insurance company: "Yes, I have the originals and I am prepared to have you auction them off, splitting the proceeds with me. However, I want you to write a letter addressed "To Whom it May Concern" confirming everything you said in the ad, including that no legal action whatsoever will be taken against me, put it in a sealed envelope addressed to "Mr. Smith" and leave it with the Concierge of the Royal Court Hotel on Sloane Square. It will be promptly picked up from there. As soon as I have your signed assurance on company stationary you can expect me to visit your Managing Director within a matter of days."

Everything went as planned. About a week later, a frail but very astute Alfie entered the Director's office clutching a metal box which once served to hold tea biscuits.

He untied several strings, unwrapped several layers of plastic and paper sheets until he reached the core of the bulky package. There in front of the Manager, neatly aligned lay the four original drawings, two by Rembrandt, one by Raphael and one by Tizian. It was as if their presence illuminated the entire room. A long time went by while everybody around the table stared at the artwork in awe and disbelief. Then, still wearing rubber gloves, Alfie put them back in their original packing and finally into the metal box. "There you are", he said. "I did my part of the deal, now you do yours." He shook hands with the several top company people who had come to the manager's office, politely declined the offer of a cup of tea and left, telling the Board: "If asked by any outsiders, you can tell them that the drawings were returned to you by an "anonymous source".

He took out a business card and said: "My name and address is only for your eyes." He revealed his identity only to the Insurance company board on the advice of his lawyer friend who told him: "You now have an official statement from the owners that no legal action will be taken against you, you have their confirmation that they will pay you one half of the proceeds of the sale and you are not selling stolen goods, since you are returning them to their legitimate owners in exchange for a finder's fee or other compensation at their discretion. You can safely reveal your identity and take the money."

The auction took place at Sotheby's in front of a packed house. The auctioneers had alerted a wide variety of museums, art galleries and collectors, both in the UK and abroad to this exceptional event. Needless to say, the bidding was highly animated at times, even fierce. When asked how they had found the drawings, the insurance company said "they were offered to us by an anonymous source", in compliance with Alfie's request to shield himself from prying reporters, lusting for a "story".

When the dust had finally settled over the seemingly endless bidding, London's Crawley Gallery of Art walked away with the coveted treasure, having outbid the British Museum, the Louvre and several American Art collectors. The final price fetched a total of twelve million pounds sterling. Sotheby's took their fee and gave the Insurance Company a cheque for ten million. Within days, Alfie received his share of five million pounds which he promptly deposited in his bank, pending settlement of accounts with Robert and Betty's only son and heir, a young doctor practicing medicine in Birmingham

He had met him years ago while attending first Robert's and then Betty's funerals. They had passed away within a short period from each other. At Betty's death, Alfie received a letter from her attorney reminding him that in her probated will she had mentioned his name as the half owner of "an object of value', which after her death should be passed on to her only son.

*****

As was to be expected the Sotheby auction of the drawings attracted a good deal of attention, primarily because of the record sum of money the sale had fetched, but also because of the story behind the "lost treasure" involved in the event. Some of the daily newspapers reported that the drawings, once belonging to the Sinclair family, then owned by an insurance company had been saved from destruction during an air raid by an anonymous individual who had now returned them to their rightful owners. There were pictures in the papers of the famous Crawley Art Gallery in London and the beaming Curator holding his latest acquisition for everyone to see. It all seemed like a happy ending of a "lost and found" story and it could well have been one. However, a young and inquisitive reporter, perhaps inadvertently but sensing there may be a juicy bit of a story for his paper behind the "anonymous person" who had returned the drawings was to see to it that the last word was yet to be said in the case of the "lost treasure".

After a few days of talking to some people involved in the case, the reporter managed to reconstruct and uncover some of the details, including Alfie's identity. The next day, the "exclusive" report appeared in the paper's column "Behind the News". Unhappily for Alfie, among the readers of the column was also an attorney who was once employed by the liquidators of the Burmese art collector's estate. He was quick to phone his former retainers in Burma who could now put two and two together in their effort to tie a noose for Alfie. They figured correctly that since he had the originals, only he could have had the forgeries made and only he could have sold them to their father. They lost no time in contacting Alfie, threatening to sue him for fraud unless he paid back the money he had received from their unsuspecting and duped father. What followed was a prolonged out-of-court battle between the Burmese claimants and Alfie. The Burmese asked for punitive damages and repayment at contemporary rates of the object, while Alfie counselled by his old-time lawyer friend maintained that he never claimed the drawings he offered to be originals, placing the onus of authentification on the buyer. If the buyer was ill advised by the then Museum Curator, this person should bear the responsibility for the transaction not Alfie. The Burmese solicitors on the other hand maintained that Alfie had committed blatant fraud, by asking for authentification of an object he perfectly knew to be forged. The battle of words and messages went on for a while, but in the end, the two sides settled out of court. Alfie was to return to them the four million plus one million in damages for a total of five million pounds in exchange for the worthless forgeries. It was Alfie who had insisted on getting back his corpus delicti. He had a reason for this request.

As soon as the final agreement was signed between the Burmese and Alfie, he transferred the freshly acquired five million pounds to Burma against a letter from the Estate confirming that they had no further claims and considered the matter closed and settled.

* * * * *

EPILOGUE

There is obviously nothing new in the circuitous routes many art treasures travel before they securely end up on display in a museum or a gallery or a private collection. Not unlike the masters who created them, these treasures have a life of their own, often causing happiness and pride but sometimes also bitterness and even crimes amongst their respective owners. All this it of course hidden from the unsuspecting visitor who stands in front of a work of art, looks at it with interest or admiration and moves on to the next painting on display. After all, he came to enjoy works of art and not their history. Yet, sometimes the latter is as worthwhile knowing as is the former. Like in the case of the four Sixteenth Century drawings, which survived fire and robbery with nary a dent.

As for Robert and Alfie, two simple people, they managed to set into motion a complicated chain of events that allowed them to spend a comfortable lifetime with impunity, on the proceeds of their felony.

HAPPY BIRTHDAY

Most birthdays come and go – but not this one. It wasn't only Fred's thirty-fifth, but also, give or take a week or so, his and Ethel's fifth wedding anniversary.

What an occasion to pop open the bubbly!

To celebrate in style, Ethel had made reservations for dinner at Bongusto, the most elegant eatery in town, where people go to see and to be seen. And then, surprise, surprise, for the following day she had booked a five-day escapade to Las Vegas. One day to get there, one for the return, and three glorious days at the fabulous Bellagio.

Needless to say, Ethel, in cahoots with Fred's secretary, had made sure that he did not have any important business engagements during that particular week. She had secretly worked on this celebration for weeks, finding it difficult to conceal her excitement from Fred.

Yes, Ethel and Fred had been married for five busy years, and there was good reason for having been so busy.

First and foremost there was Ethel's family background. She was the only daughter of an immensely rich industrialist, who, together with his wife knew how to enjoy a sophisticated and multifaceted life which included parties, the performing arts, sports and frequent travels, all done with close friends and family members.

Secondly, Fred, who was sales manager of a large chemical company constantly shuttled between subsidiaries and branches, both within and outside the country.

Amazingly all this socializing did not interfere with the young couple's parental obligations because Ethel had given birth in the second year of their marriage to an adorable set of twin baby girls.

Both Ethel and Fred were well educated, outgoing and good looking although Ethel's attractiveness did not derive from her beauty but rather from her very elegant and impeccably groomed appearance. She knew how to choose her dresses. Even Fred became the beneficiary of her excellent taste. It was Ethel who selected everything he wore.

Fred's birthday and the pre-arranged dinner fell on a Monday and the surprise Vegas caper was to start with the midday flight on Tuesday, ending with the return scheduled for the weekend.

That Monday turned out to be one of the busiest days Fred had in a long time. He attended two meetings in the afternoon, the second one running into the late evening. Although he knew that the Bongusto reservation was for seven thirty he could not extricate himself from the discussions before seven. He ran out of the boardroom and called Ethel, asking her to pick him up at the office building's front door at seven fifteen.

After collecting a pile of mail his secretary had left on his desk, he dashed to the elevator and as he walked through the lobby, he could see Ethel's car pulling up in front of the entrance.

Still clutching the pile of mail he had picked up, he jumped into the car and they arrived at the restaurant ten minutes later.

As they were shown to their table, Fred said: "Honey, why don't you sit down and order drinks for the two of us while I go to the men's room and freshen up." I must look a mess. He placed the mail on the table and quickly made for the washroom.

Ethel sat down and ordered two very dry martinis, one on the rocks with an olive and the other straight up for herself.

Waiting for the drinks, her eyes fell casually on the small pile of papers Fred had dumped on the table. She saw several computer printouts and handwritten notes from the secretary, but sticking out from the pile she also noticed a small pink envelope. Curious, she pulled it out from the rest.

It was a small, square envelope addressed to Mr. Fred Miller, but on the bottom ran a line in bold letters "Strictly Personal." She smelled the letter and a faint but somewhat familiar perfume emanated from it.

The smile suddenly disappeared from her face. Who in the world would send her husband a perfume scented letter marked "Strictly Personal?"

She was intrigued. Who indeed? Instinctively she opened her purse and slid the small envelope into it. She needed time to think what to do next.

A few minutes later, a smiling Fred with his hair neatly combed returned to the table, just in time to lift the martini glass in a toast to Ethel, who replied warmly, wishing him a happy birthday. Fred jumped up, went over to Ethel and gave her a resounding kiss.

He sat down and they ordered dinner. Fred picked up the pile and placed it under the table with the words: "The usual stuff, I'll look at it at home or better still, tomorrow morning."

They both seemed to enjoy their seafood dinner as well as the half bottle of Dom Perignon Fred had ordered. But although she made an effort to appear completely normal, her mind kept creeping back to the little square envelope inside her purse.

During dinner the conversation went from his day at the office to hers at home. Nothing more than the usual repartee between husband and wife at the end of the day. When they had finished the main course and the waiter had cleared the table, Ethel said: "Now it's my turn to powder my nose, honey. See you in a few minutes."

Purse in hand, she quickly walked to the ladies' room, locked herself into one of the toilets and tore open the pink envelope.

This is what she read on the two hand-written pages:

Dear Fred,
This letter comes to you after long, very long reflection and soul searching. Believe me, it wasn't easy for me to put pen to paper and tell you what has been on my mind for some time now.

When we started our relationship six months ago, I soon fell in love with you and I believe you reciprocated my feelings to the point that made me realize that this was not meant to be a fleeting adventure, but a liaison for life. Your frequent descriptions of how unhappy you were because of Ethel's domineering and overly assertive behaviour relegating you to the role of a henpecked husband in tow or even worse, gave me the very clear impression that you definitely wanted out of your marriage. This was not only my impression but you confirmed it to me on numerous occasions, you made me believe that you intend to leave Ethel and take me as your wife, of course after I extricated myself from Lorne.

I was so happy, believing that soon you would be mine to have and to hold for good.

Can you remember how many times you told me you would inform Ethel it's all over and you are leaving her to marry me?

You promised again and again to talk to her but by all accounts you never did.

Fred, enough is enough.

I have decided to terminate our relationship. Better now than later. For one, Ethel is bound to find out about us and raise hell, and so will Lorne. You can't hide these things forever.

And speaking of Lorne, I came to the conclusion, bitter as it may be that there is worse than having to share your life with a bore and a cold fish. Fred, I am giving you until this coming weekend to come clean with me and live up to your promise to finally send Ethel packing.

If I don't hear from you by Sunday night, you can burn this letter together with all hopes of ever holding me in your arms again.

Who said that dreams must come true?

Betty

Never before had Ethel devoured the contents of a letter with such speed and growing anger. She was livid and shocked. Not in a million years would she have believed that her husband was carrying on an affair, and with whom? Betty, her best friend.

Like in a trance she quickly walked back to the table. As she sat down, Fred must have noticed a sudden change in her expression. "Are you alright, Honey?" he said. "Something wrong?" "Yes," she said, after a moment of hesitation. "Fred, while in the restroom it hit me out of the blue. One of my nasty migraines. I am sorry to spoil your evening, but please pay and let's go home. Okay?"

"Of course," Fred shot back. "Right away." He motioned the waiter, settled the bill and ten minutes later they were in the car on their way home. It was a silent ride as befits a "migrained" person holding her hand to her head, fighting back tears that were now starting to fill her eyes.

* * * * *

During the next few hours the usually peaceful Miller home became the scene of one of those bitter family disputes most people will remember long after the last word was said. It started almost immediately after Fred had turned the home door key. Ethel went straight into the kitchen and summoned Fred to join her. "What's up?" said Fred. "Sit down," replied Ethel, trying hard to keep her composure. She looked Fred straight into the eyes and, without any reference to the letter, she said point blank: "Are you having an affair with Betty?"

Obviously surprised and stunned by the blunt question, Fred mumbled: "How do you know?"

"Never mind how I know, just answer my question, Fred. Are you having an affair with Betty?"

Fred sat down and said: "Yes, I guess you could call it that!"

"And how long has this been going on?" she asked.

"Oh, I don't know, six, seven months I guess."

"For six months you have been cheating on me, you have been screwing around with Betty, supposed to be my best friend, behind my back and behind the back of your children. Is that it?"

Fred didn't answer.

"You dirty rotten bastard, you scum, how could you do a thing like that and why did you do that? Aren't you ashamed?"

By now Ethel was clearly beginning to lose her composure. Emotion had gotten the better of herself and she shouted at Fred: "Why? You bastard, why?"

"You want to know why? I'll tell you why, he shouted back. Because I was unhappy, because I couldn't stand it anymore being told by you what to do and how to do it and when to do it! I tried so many times to tell you to stop it, to change your ways, to respect me just as much as I respect you, but you never stopped. You went on and on ruining my life, ordering me about, criticizing me, humiliating me. Everything I said or did was wrong. You even contradicted me in the presence of others. Do you know how I felt when you did this in front of your parents and their friends, even our own friends. It made me feel rotten and humiliated. There's just so much I can take and I took a lot of it. But finally I couldn't anymore and that's when I started seeing Betty."

Ethel had listened to this tirade, but at this point she interrupted him. "OK, I have a strong personality and I may come across as somewhat bossy, but is this a reason to betray me and go to another woman? Why did you never bring this out into the open?

"I did, Ethel," he replied. "Oh God knows how many times I did, but all you said was: 'OK, OK.' You changed for a little while but as soon as the next opportunity came up, Bingo, you were right at it again with your domineering manners. And then came the party at your parents' home last year when my flight was delayed because of bad weather and I arrived late for dinner. Although I had phoned ahead asking you not to wait for me, you gave me hell right in front of all the guests. When I apologized to your parents, you said in a loud voice: 'Here is my late husband. He did it again. Business comes first' or something to that effect.' Everyone looked at me as if I was a criminal.

"That did it, Ethel. Right there and then I decided that I had all I could take of your shenanigans, Of your nasty manners. The rest is history."

"That's ridiculous," she countered. "You were late for my parents' fiftieth wedding party and I reacted as any other person would have!"

With that, Ethel walked out of the kitchen and went up to the bedroom where she sat down on the settee, exhausted and wiping tears from her eyes.

Fred had stayed in the kitchen, nursing a drink he had poured himself during the acrimonious repartee.

Ethel's thoughts went back to what Fred had just said. Was it really "ridiculous?" Of course she was assertive and she knew it. What was wrong with that? Somebody had to take decisions in a family and when Fred did not, she had to. But "domineering?"

She began to ponder and to her surprise, she had to admit to herself that she did criticize and admonish Fred from time to time. But he deserved it, didn't he? "Isn't marriage supposed to allow, even oblige the two sides to learn from each other, to correct each other? And yet, Fred very rarely corrected her. Was she not going too far in assuming she had all the answers and was therefore entitled to correct him?

After having sat thinking in the bedroom for a while, she went back to the kitchen. Fred had poured himself a second drink and had loosened his tie. He was deep in thought as Ethel entered.

After a long silence, Fred was the first to talk. "So where do you want to go from here," he said, looking at Ethel.

She said nothing but in her mind, thoughts were racing back and forth like speeding trains.

Where to go from here, indeed. Several ideas now began to crystallize in her mind.

Uppermost was Betty's treachery. She had known her since high school and they had maintained close ties ever since. They were on the phone at least two, three times a week, often sharing views on anything and everything going on around them. How could this assumed friend have taken advantage of Fred's marital discontent and lure him away into her life. Ethel was convinced that while it took two to tango, Fred would not have drifted into Betty's orbit unless she beckoned him with wide open arms. Besides, Betty who was a very attractive woman, had often complained to Ethel about her own unhappy marriage.

Ethel was furious. She was determined not to let Betty ruin her marriage. She wanted to save it at any cost.

And the children? Let them grow up in a broken home?

She looked at Fred for a while. She loved him. That's why she had married him.

Ethel got up and walked over where Fred was sitting, silently sipping his drink: "How serious is this affair?" she asked.

"As serious as the problem between you and me," he replied. "What do you mean?" said Ethel.

"What I mean," replied Fred "is that if our problem is so serious that it cannot be remedied and corrected. Then my affair is very serious indeed.

"I see," said Ethel.

At this point, Ethel's mind was pretty much made up to save her marriage and to forgive Fred, provided he was willing to put an immediate and clear cut end to his liaison with Betty and come back to the fold.

She in turn was prepared to seriously work on changing her ways by learning to refrain from anything akin to dominance, ordering or slighting her husband in private or in public. In other words, she would immediately start at eliminating any and all the reasons that drove him away from her. She was very serious in her resolve.

After a long silence and a good deal of heavy breathing, Ethel sat down near Fred. She gently placed her hand on his shoulder. A minute later she said: "Hey, big boy, let's make a deal. I change my ways to be the wife you want and you end your relationship with that woman as of now and forever. How about it?"

Fred put down the glass he was still holding and said: "You've got yourself a deal", reaching out to Ethel with both hands. They embraced for a long time.

Then Fred said: "Come on, let's go up to the babies' room and repeat our vows before the children.

"I'd love that," said Ethel.

They stood in the dark room of the sleeping twins, holding each other very tightly, whispering words of affection and love into each other's ears.

Closing the door to the babies' room gently, they walked over to their own bedroom and a short while later were fast asleep with Fred's arms wrapped around his smiling wife.

It had been a long and memorable day.

* * * * *

The next morning, Ethel woke up at six, a full hour before the alarm went off. She quietly went into the bathroom, locked the door and took out the iPad to text a message to Betty. It read:

Dearest Betty,

It took your letter to finally wake me up from lethargy and make me do what I promised you. Last night I told Ethel it's all over between us. I gave her the reasons and after an hour-long ugly discussion, she stormed out of the room. It's now up to the lawyers to file the divorce papers. Which means that in a short time we can get married, of course as soon as your own divorce materialises.

Needless to say, Ethel took it very badly, especially since she did not expect me to call it quits.

She bundled off the girls and left for her parents' home. My house is now empty and quiet, finally.

Please come to my home tonight at about seven. Bring things to spend the night and we will discuss, among other things, our future together. Glad it's all over.

See you this evening. I can't wait.

Love you,
Fred.

P.S. *Don't try to reach me during the day as I am in and out of meetings.*

* * * * *

That was the first item on her agenda.

She unlocked the bathroom door and sneaked back into bed, only to wait for the alarm to go off at seven. As Fred awoke, she asked him to meet her in the kitchen for an important announcement.

"Well, Good Morning, dear. Wake up to a truly busy day. Listen carefully," she intoned in a heralding voice.

"Surprise, surprise! We are going to Las Vegas because you and I have lots to celebrate. Haven't we? O.K., I made reservations for us to leave this afternoon, stay three days at the Bellagio and come back on the weekend. Yes, I know about your business schedule but I'll phone your secretary to say that you had a bad cold. Okay?"

"So, my dear husband, go upstairs, pack your bag and be ready to leave at two for the airport. On our way we will drop off the girls at my mother's who can't wait to cuddle them.

"Wow, I don't believe this," was Fred's reaction delivered with resounding laughter. You are terrific. No, you are super terrific." Fred jumped up and embraced Ethel.

The rest of the morning was a mad rush, but it all came together when the bags were stowed away in the car and the babies were safely bundled up in the back seat.

Just as Fred was about to start the engine, Ethel shouted from the back seat: "Hold it Fred. I almost forgot to leave a note for the milkman not to leave milk until the weekend. Give me a minute."

"Sure, go ahead," said Fred.

Ethel ran out of the car and taped a little note on the front door. It read:

Betty,

You didn't really think that I would stand by and let you wreck my marriage. You "bitch!" Fred and I made up and we are out West on our second honeymoon.
As for you, why not trot home and try to warm up the cold fish, unless you have already thrown out the baby with the bathwater.

Ethel

THE ROBBERY

Phil Molini, now in his early forties, sat in his small flat on Manhattan's Tenth Avenue, pondering what his life was all about. It was Saturday morning and he had just finished his self-prepared breakfast. In front of him, spread out, lay the New York Times featuring all the exciting activities the Big Apple has in store for the weekend. He folded the entertainment section and pushed it away. He wasn't interested.

Phil lived alone in the true sense of the word. He had been married to Brenda, an attractive brunette, who, after five years of a childless marriage had left him for another man.

After the divorce he had nibbled at several relationships but none of them had lead to a meaningful or lasting liaison.

The truth was that Phil didn't really possess any particular talents or special interests to drive his imagination or creativity, except an intense urge to be rich and to be able to enjoy a life of ease and comfort, to sit in the garden of his own home, sail the ocean in his boat and drive a late-model luxury car. That's what he wanted. The good life.

And there was ample reason for his craving. Phil came from a very poor family of Italian immigrants who surmounted immense difficulties to put their five children through school and college. It was only by holding not one but two jobs that Phil managed to pay for his education at the engineering institute. Although he never graduated with a degree he managed to obtain enough certification to find a job as a supervisor in a New Jersey construction company. That was the start of a number of more or less successful careers in two other building firms.

Now, at forty-two, he was team leader at one of New Jersey's largest contractors. He made enough money to live a medium-income professional's life, complete with summer and winter vacations, a few dollars in his savings account, but nothing even approaching his dream of care-free opulence.

But then, one day Phil went through a filing cabinet in the office, looking for some old building permits. As he leafed through the files his eyes fell on a bulging folder containing work sheets, accounting data and plans relating to a job his company had completed and delivered five years earlier. The customer was a New York bank and the job was the construction of a small savings and loan branch office in the Bronx. He looked again at the folder and saw the detailed building plan of the bank's underground vault. A sudden thought entered his mind: What if he tried to rob the small two-storey bank on the corner of Conway Avenue and Second Street?

He had the complete plans of the underground construction, he had all the information on its location, on the thickness and materials of the three cement walls and he knew what equipment to use to reach and then break into them, of course avoiding the fourth wall which housed the steel door with all its locks and alarm devices. All he needed was a basement next to or behind the bank building.

The more he thought of the relative ease of the operation the more he became obsessed with the excitement of entering the vault, taking what was there and disappearing from the scene of the crime in order to resurface with impunity in a different world.

He could do it, and what's more he could do it by himself without any help. All he had to do was to prepare a plan or a worksheet as it was known in the trade and follow through. That's all.

That evening he sat up in his armchair at home, looking at the copies of the contraction plans he had spirited away and pondered long and intensely.

He realised that if he wanted to elude the long arm of the law he had to prepare the robbery as well as it's aftermath very carefully.

Since his name, his photograph and even his fingerprints were on record in his employer's files he had to substitute all that evidence with a new name, new identity documents and a new face. All this, he figured could be done.

But before anything else he had to find out if there was a building adjacent to the Bronx bank from where he could launch his tunnelling operation.

Everything had to be planned and executed with perfection because Phil did not see himself as a future fugitive running and hiding from the law, but rather posing as a retired businessman, enjoying life in a quiet environment and without arousing any attention.

* * * * *

It was a sunny Saturday morning in October, just a few days after Phil's big decision to go ahead that his plan started to take shape.

He drove to the Bronx to look at the site and at it's surroundings. He easily found the Bank building, a small two storey structure with street-level access to counters and tellers, and offices on the floor above. He also knew that the vault was in the basement and could be reached through a staircase in the rear of the counters.

The bank building occupied a corner on a small block. Next to it were stores, two homes and at the other end of the block there was a dentist's clinic.

Phil walked around the corner to the rear of the bank building and saw similar small stores, some homes and, at the end of the block, a real estate agent's office, all abutting the buildings on the other side of the block.

As for the bank, it backed into a home facing the other side of the street, Phil looked into the windows of the home but there seemed to be no one inside, It was the perfect place he needed to dig from one basement to the one next to it,

Phil continued his walk and entered the real estate agency, where a man was busy talking on the phone. He motioned Phil to sit down.

A few minutes later he said "how can I help you, sir?" Phil answered "well, I am looking for a house to live in. I come from Manhattan and find it increasingly noisy, I like this neighbourhood. It looks clean and has a variety of convenient businesses around it." Whereupon the agent embarked on a glowing description of the area. "you have come to the right place." He said, "what exactly do you have in mind?"

Phil casually mentioned the house in back of the bank. "Well" said the agent "This is truly an excellent choice. The house is clean, all repairs were made, no taxes owed. in fact, it is in walk-in condition. It is owned by an elderly couple who moved to Arizona. Would you like me to show it to you? I have the keys right here." "why not!" answered Phil.

The house had a living room, dining area, kitchen and bath on the street level and three bedrooms and toilets on the upper floor. What interested Phil the most was, of course, the basement, which was empty and could not be too far away from the bank's vault.

Phil was thrilled. He asked for the price and was told. "They want one hundred sixty thousand, but you make me an offer." Phil did, and within three weeks the agent negotiated, obtained agreement, then completed all financing arrangements and with a big smile and a hand shake, handed the keys over to the new owner. Phil could not believe how lucky he had been to find the right place, in fact the ideal place for his undertaking.

His next move was to resign from the job in New Jersey, pretending fatigue and telling his boss that he wanted to take it easy for a few months before coming back to the job. He said he needed time to "recharge the batteries."

A few days later the boss gave him a letter of recommendation and a generous going away cheque. He also said: "you can come back whenever you feel up to it."

* * * * *

The next item on the to do list was a visit to a plastic surgeon, asking him to make his long Italian nose shorter and more stubby and to shorten his earlobes. The surgeon said: "no problem, that's what we do here all the time. By the way, while I'm at it how about removing the bags under your eyes to make you look younger?" "I'd like that!" said Phil.

The doctor was true to his words. When Phil finally removed all the bandages and dressings and the scars had healed his facial features had changed considerably. He looked more like a Swede than an Italian, and appeared a few years younger. After he had dyed his hair from dark brown to blonde and put on fake glasses it was indeed difficult, in fact it was almost impossible, to find any resemblance between Phil Molini's before and after appearance.

* * * * *

Phil was now ready to see one of those underworld characters who make a living by providing people with fake names and fake identity documents, all guaranteed to pass any scrutiny by the authorities.

* * * * *

During the next two weeks a reborn Phil moved from Manhattan to the Bronx. Among his furniture and personal belongings were quite a few boxes marked "Refrigerator" and "Washer/Dryer" which actually contained the digging and boring equipment he needed for his tunnelling activities during the weeks ahead.

When he finally spent the first night in his new home, Phil heaved a sigh of relief, for he had successfully completed the first phase of his project. Now he couldn't wait to begin tackling phase two or the actual digging, accessing and penetration of the vault.

* * * * *

There was actually nothing unusual in underground work for Phil. He had supervised and directed it hundreds of times during his years in the construction business. He started on a weekend when the bank and adjoining stores were closed. He knew exactly in what direction to dig in order to reach the weakest part of the vault. He piled up the earth he removed in his empty basement.

It was painstaking work, made more difficult by the need to dig only during the night, on Sundays or whenever he felt it was safe to continue. He avoided noisy equipment and often just used picks and shovels.

It took weeks and weeks and his basement was almost full of displaced earth, but finally, one evening, he had reached the cement wall of the vault. He was elated and very proud of himself. He touched the wall with his hands.

The real excitement came when he put his ear to the wall and could actually hear the voices of people inside the vault. He thought to himself: "If they only knew that on the other side of their safety boxes and shelves and money piles is a man who is listening to them and will soon adversely affect their treasured inventory.

Phil spent the next few days completing all the necessary get-away preparations, packing some personal belongings in the small panel truck which was to spirit him away from the crime scene.

And then finally, one night, after having deactivated the alarm system by cutting some of the wires, he drilled a hole into the wall enlarged it quickly, stepped inside the vault and in the dim light of his battery lamp looked around. There were safety deposit boxes everywhere, some piled to the ceiling and there were wads and packs of bills on the shelves. He opened his plastic bags and started piling in packs of one hundred dollar bills, filling as many bags as he could. Then he started carrying them out into his house and stashed them in several suitcases he had bought for that purpose.

When he thought he had filled enough bags and he saw piles of bills of lesser denominations on some other shelves, he thought he must have collected a few million dollars.

"Enough is enough." he said to himself "Don't be greedy. Get out of here while the going is good." And he did.

After stuffing all the big suitcases with the loot, he carried them into his van on the street. There was no one around. He looked at his watch. It was exactly a quarter past four. He closed the door to his house and drove off, heading for the entrance to Route I Ninety-Five South. Just before accessing the ramp he stopped to cover the white sides of his van with blue panels he had taken with him, just to avoid recognition on the road. He also placed fake license plates over the existing ones.

It was still dark all around him when he started driving south, destination Florida, the sunshine state.

Phil was now driving at a steady pace in order to reach his final destination of Hallandale, Florida as fast as he could.

He had taken food and fresh water with him, as well as a few canisters of gas in order to avoid stopping at stations, where an alerted police car may have been waiting for him. He only stopped in rest areas to use the facilities, and when he was too tired to move on he caught naps in the parking lots.

Physically exhausted but titillating with excitement bordering on euphoria he finally reached Hallandale, where he checked into one of the many small motels usually reserved for vacationing or frostbitten snow birds stretching out on lounge chairs around the pool.

He parked his car right in front of his room and kept a steady eye on it.

He still did not know exactly how much he had set the Bronx bank back. He intended to perform the count as soon as he was in a safe place.

A few days into his arrival at the small motel, Phil located a real estate agent whom he knew to be making a good living by buying and selling properties paid in cash. It is a well known fact that many South American and other immigrants have loose money which they spirited away from their countries of origin.

Phil told this man that he is in the market for a nice waterfront bungalow with a small garden, garage and all the rest. The agent showed him several properties and, within hours, Phil chose what was a really pretty two-storey house with all the amenities Phil wanted in.

True to his usual practice, the agent told Phil, that the owners wanted one million but, in addition he himself asked for fifty thousand from Phil in exchange for a one hundred percent legitimate, iron clad deed never to be questioned by any one. Phil agreed to all condition and used his recently acquired fake identity for all formalities and registrations.

Following a thorough cleaning of the house, Phil moved in one day becoming the official owner.

His very first action was to carry the heavy suitcases into the house. After having locked all the doors, he sat down at the kitchen table, drew all the blinds and started to count the loot. It took him a very long time. He repeatedly had to get up and stretch his legs before resuming the count. But when it was all over and the piles were neatly stacked all over the kitchen, Phil realised with a big grin on his new face, still sensitive to the touch after the recent surgery, that he was the owner of four million one hundred thousand and five hundred dollars, most of it in bills of one hundreds.

"Not bad." he said to himself. What do you mean: "not bad." He went on "fantastic, unbelievable." He was so excited, and proud, mainly at the thought that he had done it all by himself, without any help, just using his head and his hands and, of course, the good plans he stole from the construction company.

He went to the living room and slumped down on one of the sofas. He suddenly became emotional. He realised that a new life had started for him right there and then. A life that could be beautiful and fulfilling in every sense of the word but that could also entail his demise and ruin if he either made a mistake that could lead to his detection or if he was unlucky enough to be traced and apprehended by one of these super smart sleuths you see in the movies.

Right now he felt safe and smug that he had beaten the system and gotten away with it.

He was determined to make the rest of his life a pleasant, and very enjoyable experience just as he had dreamed about so often in his small one bedroom flat on Manhattan's Tenth Avenue.

* * * * *

All hell broke loose on 2015 Conway Avenue at seven o'clock on a cold Monday morning. As a crew of five cleaners entered the Bronx savings and loans branch and realised that there was no power to turn on the lights. When one of the cleaners went to the rear of the bank and walked down the stairs to the vault room he noticed, through the bars of the vault door, a faint lamp light coming from inside the safe and, of course, the gaping hole in the wall. He ran up to tell his friends who called the police.

Ten minutes later the first cruiser was at the scene and the officer immediately cordoned off the area.

It did not take long for two more police cars to arrive and in one of them was Detective Gus Symons, who took charge.

In short order, officials from the banks head office as well as more police officers arrived to record all the evidence, which included photographing, fingerprinting and all the other routine procedures. Other policemen knocked at the doors of neighbouring buildings to ask if anyone had heard or seen anything.

When detective Symons entered the vault he was amazed at the clean job the thieves had done. There was no litter or mess, the safety deposit boxes had not been broken into and some money packs were still stashed on the steel shelves. He walked through the hole in the wall and entered an adjacent basement stacked to the ceiling with dug up earth. When he climbed up the stairs of the basement he found an empty house which the thieves had obviously used as their operating base. There was no one around.

The inspector walked back to the vault and as he started to look around, he soon picked up some interesting clues.

Judging by the correct angle the robbers had used to access the wall and the precisely calibrated drilling equipment to fit the thickness of the cement wall as well as the professional way the removed earth had been piled up in the adjacent basement Detective Symons was convinced that this was an insiders job. Also, the robbers knew exactly what cable to cut in order to deactivate the alarm system. This was not the work of amateurs but of a professional team with a technical background who knew what they were doing.

When the detective mentioned this to one of the bank managers who were on the spot he said: "How about someone who was involved in the construction of the vault?" "good thinking." said Detective Symons. He obtained the address of the New Jersey company and was told by them that the four people who participated in that project are still with them and they can vouch for their honesty, but, another employee, a man by the name of Phil Molini had recently left them saying he needed a break and he could have easily stolen copies of the construction plans of the job in the Bronx. The company gave the police Phil's photograph, his address, and even his finger prints since he had been bonded, like most of the other company employees.

Within hours the detective compared the finger prints with those taken from the drilling equipment they found in the vault and, you better believe it, there was a perfect match.

That evening, Detective Symons had the photo, the name and the fingerprints of the bank robber. Circulated across the United States, a country of some three hundred million people including one who had just changed his identity as well as his physical appearance.

* * * * *

As the first days in his new Hallandale home ran into weeks and then into months, Phil began to get used to his new life. To be sure, he loved it and soon settled down to a routine of upper bourgeois living commonly enjoyed by thousands of retirees living the Florida way of life.

In time Phil bought a beautiful boat from one of his neighbours, learned how to use it and began to spend many a day cruising on some of the canals, even venturing out into the ocean.

He also enriched his life by more than a boat and a white Mercedes. He met an attractive blonde divorcée at one of his neighbour's parties and, the two decided to live together. She moved into Phil's house and took care of everything, kept a nice and clean home and played her part in a lively sexual relationship.

Apart from enjoying their cocktail parties, their social intercourse with their neighbours, their regular outings to restaurants and their attendance at concerts in Miami, Phil and Linda occasionally ventured to Las Vegas and Montreal.

But he did not confine all his time to the pursuit of leisure. Phil also used his money for some secure investments. In fact, he bought fifty percent of a well run real estate agency and a thirty percent share in an Italian restaurant in South Beach. Both investments proved to be very judicious and Phil began earning serious money all of which he declared in his tax returns.

This perfectly above board and normal life continued year in, year out for many a years. In fact, Phil had completely blended into a world of well-to-do neighbours and friends.

* * * * *

Some twenty years had passed since the dark and windy night of the robbery.

The New York Police Department had long ago relegated the file of the Bronx break-in to a section of their archives where unsolved crimes were waiting for a sign, any sign likely to trigger renewed attention. To be sure some of these files were waiting in vain.

* * * * *

It was shortly after Phil's sixty second birthday celebration that he woke up with a headache and the unpleasant feeling that something was wrong with him. He thought it might be an upset stomach or a cold, but when this unwell feeling continued he went to see his doctor who set a battery of tests into motion. Finally, after the last results were in, the doctor gave Phil the devastating news that the diagnosis was Non-Hodgkin's Lymphoma, a sort of blood cancer.

Phil was hit, like a cut tree coming crashing down. He, who thought that the good times would be going on forever and ever was suddenly told: "That's it buddy!"

The doctor also told him that while half of all lymphoma patients die within months, the other half survive and get into a remission which can last for years even decades. "Let's hope for the best. We will start with the treatment and let's see where it will take us." concluded the doctor.

Phil had a hard time adjusting to the fact that he was very ill and that he may not have much time left to live.

A few days after he had been given the diagnosis, Phil sat in his living room and started to think about the futility of life and about what it is all about. After a while he sat down at his desk and wrote a letter:

To the President of the Bronx Savings and Loan Bank,

Dear Sir,

I am sure you will be surprised when you will read this letter. For sure you did not expect anything of this kind to land on your desk.

I am the man who robbed your bank twenty years ago. I, the undersigned did it, by myself and without any help from anyone. It was not easy and took a great deal of planning but it worked. As you know and as the police know, I got away with it.

How did I manage to elude the law? Well, I changed my identity as well as my appearance. Not even my brother would be able to recognize me. And, you know what? It all paid off beautifully. For twenty years I lived like a prince, no, like a king. I had everything I always wanted and dreamt about. I had twenty absolutely beautiful years in Florida, God's Own Country.

Why am I coming forward now to confess my crime? Because I have just been told that I have terminal cancer. I am going to die and I decided that although I lived as a robber, I do not want to die as one. In fact, by the time you read this letter I may already be dead.

I am sure I do not need to tell you that I drove away from your bank with some four million dollars.

Four million. They not only made it possible for me to live a comfortable and most enjoyable life, but I also invested some of it in two businesses, a restaurant and a real estate agency that flourished over the years and yielded sizable profits for me. All of which I declared and paid taxes on.

My home which I bought for one million twenty years ago and is now worth at least five. One million still left in the kitty, all in cash and most of it still wrapped in your bank's paper bands. And some three million which my two businesses earned over the years, total about nine million.

Come and get it. It's all yours! No estate claims, no liens, no debts. Nothing. I have even prepaid my funeral expenses. How about that!

So, what else can I tell you, except, that all good things have to come to an end. It was a beautiful ride while it lasted. Now it is time to Pay the Piper.

Thanks for the memories.

Sincerely yours,

Phil Molini

Phil signed and sealed the letter. Then he sat down with Linda, poured two glasses of his best scotch and started what was to be a long monologue.

"Listen," he said "You heard the doctor's verdict. Cancer and it looks bad, like it'll kill me. It took me a few days to accept the inevitable truth, but now I think I am beginning to live with it. I really don't have much choice but to undergo treatment and hope to God that it will work. To be frank, judging from the doctor's bleak outlook, I am not sure.

So, my dear, let's do the right thing now, while there is still time.

I have written a letter, which I sealed and I am giving it to you. The day the doctor tells you that I am in a coma, in other words that it is the end, I want you to mail this letter. That's the first thing I want you to do.

The second thing is I want you to buy yourself a small apartment building, say four floors with eight nice flats. After I die. I want you to live in one of the flats, and the rent you will receive from the other three flats will pay for your living expenses as well as for maintenance and taxes. I want to be sure that you have a roof over your head and that you have enough to live on for the rest of your life. I am leaving you a substantial amount of cash which you can keep in the safety deposit boxes of a few banks."

Linda had listened intently to Phil, clutching her handkerchief. In fact she had not stopped wiping tears from her eyes throughout his speech.

When he had finished, She jumped up and embraced him passionately as if to hold on to him while she still could. They had been living together for the best part of twenty years. Although their relationship was not one of passionate love, it was certainly one of caring and affection for each other, amply spiced with sexual intercourse and romantic closeness.

Linda promised to fulfil the two requests faithfully.

She had never heard from Phil about his criminal past.

*****

The next few months were spent mostly with visits to the hospital and clinics for the intensive treatment of Phil's cancer. Although he often felt tired and ill he was free of pain. He and Linda continued to see their friends albeit on a reduced scale.

But then some eight months in to his illness, several blood tests indicated a pronounced turn for the worse and he had to be admitted to hospital for observation and some urgent procedures.

Linda never left his side and even spent some nights sleeping on a cot in his hospital room.

About a week following Phil's hospitalization Linda received a phone call in the middle of the night from one of the doctors saying that Phil was in a coma.

She immediately drove back to the hospital and on her way she dropped the sealed letter Phil had given her in the first mailbox she saw. Just as he had asked her to do.

A week went by since the doctor had told Linda about Phil entering a coma.

Linda was at home when the doorbell rang. she opened the door and saw two men there. One of them said: "Is this the house of Mr. Joseph Kowalski?" "It is" said Linda. Whereupon the man continued: "Has the funeral taken place?" "What funeral?" asked Linda. Even before receiving an answer, Linda realized the circumstance of this visit. When she noticed the envelope of the letter she had mailed in the man's hand. While still puzzled she tried to find some connection between the letter and the visit, when the other man said: "Madam, we are here in response to a letter we received from Mr. Kowalski telling us that he is dying, in fact, that he may be dead by now."

He went on: "This is Mr. Fred Bullock, vice president of our bank and I am Charles Bandiera, chief legal council of the corporation. We came down from New York."

Still confused Linda said: "Do come in, gentlemen, Mr. Kowalski is in the garden resting he has been through some very difficult times lately."

She led the men into the garden and said: "These two gentlemen are from a bank in New York and came to see you! Are you up to it dear?"

Phil put down his paper and said: "Pleased to meet you. I am sorry I am still too weak to stand up but I would like you to pull up chairs and that goes for you Linda as well. Please make yourselves comfortable. I am glad you came to see me even if your visit may be somewhat premature or ill timed, but what is done is done. So let us get down to business."

Looking at the two men, both dressed in business suits Phil said: "I hope you had a pleasant trip."

"Yes, thank you." replied one of the visitors "By the way this is Charles Bandiera, our chief legal council and I am . Fred Bullock, vice president of the Bronx bank."

"Welcome to Hallandale." said Phil. Then, turning to Linda he said: "You are now going to hear things that you never, not in your wildest dreams, thought possible yet it is all true my dear. You see, twenty years ago, I robbed a bank. I, with my own bare hands broke into a vault and stole millions and for twenty years I lived with the secret of my robbery, until you mailed the letter when the doctor told you that I was in a coma. But as you know, with the help of God Almighty and the good doctors at the hospital I came out of the coma and I am now in a remission for how long, nobody knows. But I am in a remission. So, now you know the truth, my dear Linda.

Forgive me for having kept the truth from you for so many years and I honestly hope that you will understand and forgive me."

During the entire speech he was looking at Linda while she was sitting motionless.

Then Phil turned to the two visitors from New York.

"And now gentlemen" he said "for you I have no other secrets to reveal. I said it all in my letter and what I didn't say, you just heard from me."

"Take it away! Its all yours. Prepare the papers and I will sign it all over to the bank. And when you have taken everything back you tell me what you intend to do next. As they say, the ball is now in your court."

The two bank officials had listened in silence to Phil's monologue, they were obviously surprised and bewildered by his revelation to Linda. And they certainly did not expect to find Phil sitting in his garden reading the paper.

They sat there, stone faced and somewhat uneasy. There were no smiles on their business-like faces.

Bullock was first to break the silence which followed Phil's last words.

"I think we got the picture." he said "I have no other questions, but Mr. Bandiera will certainly have some during the transfer formalities. The bank will immediately take possession of the estate and Charles will see to it that all is done smoothly."

"Do you have anything further to say before we leave?" He said to Phil. "Yes Mr. Bullock." replied Phil. "I want the whole operation to be done and completed in the strictest privacy. No statements to the media and no public announcements. Can you promise me that?"

Bullock thought for a moment then he got up and motioned his partner to follow him. They stood in a corner of the garden talking to each other and returned a few minutes later. "Yes" declared Bullock "No public announcements, we may however have to notify the district attorney's office when all is said and done. If we do, you will be informed by us, but I repeat, the bank will not issue any public statements about this matter."

Then, still standing, he said: "We are now going back to New York and I will brief the board on everything, it will be then up to the board to decide what further action we intend to take. Needless to say that we will promptly inform you of our decision, in the meantime we expect you to fully cooperate with our legal people to clean up this mess as soon as possible."

"Finally, on behalf of the bank and speaking for myself. I can tell you that we are glad this amazing crime has been solved albeit under very unusual circumstances. This is indeed a once in a lifetime experience for me and I am sure for many of my colleagues."

He grabbed his leather case and said "As I indicated you will hear from us shortly. Goodbye." Both men rose and left the house.

* * * * *

Two weeks later, Phil received a registered letter from the bank marked: "Special Delivery. Private and Confidential."

He was sitting comfortably in the living room after one of his check up sessions in the hospital at which the doctors confirmed to him that he was in a remission from his dreaded cancer.

The letter read:

Mr. Joseph Kowalski,

The board of directors of this bank under the chairmanship of Jonathan Flaherty Esquire met in an extraordinary session to hear, discuss and rule on the matter of the robbery which occurred in our Bronx Savings and Loan branch during the night of October twenty one, nineteen seventy seven.

In consideration and recognition of the facts mentioned hereunder, to wit:

1- The subject robbery occurred more than twenty years ago and eluded detection by the authorities.

2- No arms were used and no one was hurt during the act.

3- You have come forward voluntarily to confess to your crime.

4- Of the four million dollars taken during the robbery you have returned to the bank about nine million.

5- You are now seriously ill and your survival is dependant on specialized treatment and supervision, neither of which could be provided adequately by a penal institution.

We, the board of directors have therefore decided not to lay any charges against you and to consider the case of the above mentioned robbery as closed.

We would also inform you of our ruling not to make the above decision public since we consider it an internal matter.

It may also interest you to note that the subject robbery has served to revise the construction standards and norms of our bank buildings in order to improve their security. As a result of these improvements not a single infraction has been reported by any of out branches during the past twenty years.

Please note that a copy of our ruling regarding the robbery will be made available to the office of the district attorney, which will, in turn inform the New York Police Dept. to deactivate the file in question.

Signed on this tenth day of May 1997 in New York, N.Y. on behalf of the board.

Arthur Francis Donahew, Chairman.

* * * * *

Within days following the visit of the two bank officers all assets, including the cash left in the secret steel box in the attic, the beautiful home, the cars and the boat as well as the bank accounts were transferred to the bank and Phil together with Linda moved into her newly acquired, small but very comfortable flat.

Phil was left with the income from his two investments which provided the couple with enough money to lead a modest but perfectly adequate life.

He told all his friends and neighbours that as a result of his illness he had decided to give up most of his social activities in order to devote his attention to the on-going treatment. They all understood his need for a restricted life style and wished him well.

* * * * *

With Phil and Linda's move to her two bedroom flat, a new life started for both of them. Not only did they change houses but also lifestyles. In fact, much of what they were doing circled around Phil's treatment and Linda's maintaining a normal life. She drove Phil to the hospital and never left his side during his regular treatments, until the day the doctors told him that he was definitely in a remission and should report for regular checkups only. No more treatments.

This good news turned out to be the beginning of a string of years marked by the very close relationship that had developed over the years between the two. In fact, they seemed to live for each other.

Phil also started to work part time in the Italian restaurant in which he owned a share, and that kept him busy. They had an adequate income from the restaurant but the realty agency business dried up and closed.

This perfectly normal and happy family life went on for a long time. Phil's condition continued to be stable. Both he and Linda went through the usual ailments associated with the all too familiar aging process.

Phil had been cancer free for nearly eleven years now. Most of the time he even did not give it a second thought except when he had to go for periodic checkups.

But as he turned seventy five, he started complaining about vague aches and pains, which prompted some specific tests and analyses. After weeks of alternating hope and despair the verdict was finally out: his cancer had returned. And this time it came with a vengeance. None of the familiar therapies seemed to work and his general condition kept deteriorating. He was definitely on his last stretch, when he was admitted to the palliative care ward of the hospital.

Needless to say Linda was constantly by his bedside. One day Phil felt particularly bad and had difficulty breathing. Sensing the end approaching he looked at Linda and, holding her hand he said: "I feel the end coming. I guess it won't be long now. Please don't let them give me more needles and more medications. Let me go. I had a full life and don't regret anything, except perhaps the fact that for twenty years I kept my secret from you. You did not deserve this. You have been my best friend, my trusted companion and indeed my guardian angel for thirty years, a lifetime. I am ashamed and feel very guilty for not having told you who I really was. Will you forgive me, Linda?"

He looked at her waiting for an answer. It came with a warm glow on her face and with the best smile she could muster. She said: "No need to apologize, my one and only Phil. I knew all along who you were. Not even a week after I moved into your house, you left the attic one day to answer the phone in the bedroom and forgot to lock up. When I cleaned the house I saw the door slightly open and as I entered the attic I saw a steel cabinet with hundreds of dollar bills held together with a paper band clearly marked: "Bronx Savings and Loans." That is when I immediately knew that you were behind the robbery. So, why did I keep this secret to myself all these years? Because had I told you, you might have been afraid of my spilling the beans or of my walking out on you, not wanting to live with a bank robber. In either case, it would have tainted our relationship, which I did not want to happen because I was beginning to really enjoy our being together. More than that I was beginning to love you. There you are, Phil. That is the honest truth."

Phil had not taken his eyes off Linda during her talk, a faint smile hushed over his tired face as he clutched her hand with all the strength left in him.

* * * * *

Phil Molini, alias Joe Kowalski was laid to rest a few days later in a simple yet dignified ceremony attended by his friends, neighbours and business partners.

He had lived a full life that started in poverty, changed to relative ease and then suddenly bursting into opulence and riches such as he had always dreamt about. For twenty years he had it all and he enjoyed every moment of it. Then came another ten good years of carefree and comfortable living in tender and loving company, until, finally death took its toll.

A good and full life by any standard.

Who said that crime doesn't pay.

FATHER AND SON

The city of Zürich, on the shores of a picturesque lake bearing its very same name is known for a number of distinctly Swiss characteristics. It is meticulously clean and well managed. It is home to some of the most venerable financial institutions in the world and its many jewellery shops offer the finest in watches and gems to an ever-present clientele that seems to be blessed with an abundance of loose cash. In fact, some of the rare specimens on view in the shops on the Bahnhofstrasse, the city's very own Fifth Avenue, are so precious as to be removed every night for safekeeping in underground vaults, only to be ceremoniously replaced the next day for public display.

But Zürich boasts also another attraction: a disproportionately great number of highly qualified doctors whose patients include ailing white-robed sheiks from the oil-rich Middle East to immaculately dressed members of British aristocracy. Needless to say that Swiss health professionals charge high fees for their services, but this has never deterred the upper crust from seeking their counsel and treatment. After all, health carries no price tag, as it is often said.

Dr. Rudolf Brunner, a dental surgeon was one of the city's better known health professionals. The son of a successful family physician, he attended dental school in two Swiss universities and upon graduation spent five years at a famous dental clinic in Boston, Massachusetts. It is there that he learned more than even cutting-edge Swiss medical colleges could teach. Blessed with an open mind and a keen intellect, he absorbed not only new techniques, but also a comprehensive knowledge of anything and everything that can go wrong in the oral cavity. He even managed to garner an additional Ph.D. while in Boston. Shortly after his return to Switzerland he was appointed Associate Professor of Dentistry at the well-known Zürich Kantonspital, another milestone in his ascending career. All this at the relatively tender age of thirty-four.

It is only natural that during these hectic years of learning, Dr. Brunner found little time for serious dating or for nurturing relationships with marriage in mind. He knew several young ladies, was often invited to parties and on weekends asked girls out for dinner or an occasional few days of sailing, or in winter, skiing on nearby slopes.

All of this uncommitted meandering suddenly came to an end shortly after his thirty-fifth birthday, when he accompanied a young Italian girl home following a leisurely dinner at one of the better restaurants lining the Zürich Lake. Laura Bernini was a student at his dental faculty and she had drawn his attention during classes because of her good looks and her resounding laughter which lit up her entire personality. Her easy smile dominated her pretty face even when she asked questions during dental classes. It did not take long for the two to regularly meet at the Kantonspital lunchroom and later at movies and concerts. Laura seemed to have everything Rudolf was looking for. Judging by how quickly she fell in love with him, he also appeared to have fulfilled all her dreams of a knight in shining armour. They were certainly a very good looking couple. She with her rich dark hair, beautiful big eyes and very attractive figure and he with his ruddy complexion, curly blond hair and athletic build, the result of frequent workouts whenever his busy professional life permitted. Emotionally, however, they differed considerably.

He had inherited through his upbringing some typically Swiss attributes such as a cautionary approach to things, a practical, down-to-earth mind and a measure of reserved comportment often bordering on stiffness. She, on the other hand, was exuberant, light-hearted and radiating confidence not only in herself but in a world where nothing could really go wrong that could not somehow be fixed or remedied. Perhaps it was her contagious optimism that drew Rudolf Brunner more to her than even her obvious physical assets.

The two were married in a quaint seventeenth-century church in Lugano, an absolutely delightful town in the southern part of Switzerland. After a brief honeymoon they returned to Zürich, where Dr. Brunner continued to tend to his steadily growing clientele. He also found time to constantly improve his skills and techniques, all of which made him one of the city's busiest oral surgeons with a fee structure that was the envy of many of his colleagues.

The Brunners' family life always took second place after his dentistry. Rudi, as Laura affectionately called him was so absorbed by his work that there was only that much time left for amusement and relaxation. Everything, including vacations and social events somehow revolved around his profession. Laura soon adapted to this lifestyle, although it meant departing from the carefree and even frivolous life she had come to like during her adolescence. Only when Rudi became too pedantic and too much obsessed with details did she either admonish or tease him. Overall, though, Rudi was a correct, even devoted husband, always remembering his wife's birthday and even often sending her flowers for no special reason at all. Theirs was a marriage, not dominated by passion and the emotional ups and downs endured and even enjoyed by many couples, but marked by a somewhat reserved yet sincere love and respect for each other.

About two years into their married life, Laura became pregnant and in due course gave birth to a healthy baby boy. While both parents were obviously elated, Laura was particularly happy at the thought of motherhood because she saw in it an escape from routine family life, even more than a physical fulfilment. On the insistence of his mother the boy was christened Julius because she wanted him to go by the name of Yul Brunner in emulation of her all-time silver screen idol Yul Brynner.

Yul's arrival did not substantially change the Brunner's life. To be sure, the birth created a good amount of excitement but after Laura came home from the hospital, things seemed to settle back into the usual routine, especially as far as the baby's father was concerned. For Laura, Yul was obviously the focus of all her attention and love, but for Rudi, the initial excitement of being a father soon gave way to acceptance of the baby as a natural event and that's that. Rudi devoted little time to tending to the baby's natural needs such as carrying him around or putting him to sleep. He never changed diapers and hastily summoned Laura when it appeared that the baby needed attention. As weeks and months went by, Rudi turned into a dutiful yet somewhat distant father, leaving most if not all domestic duties to his wife. Perhaps he realized that Laura's all-encompassing care already fulfilled all of the baby's requirements.

And so it was that Yul slowly but surely matured to the utter delight of his mother and to the approving smiles and occasional pats of his dad.

Yul was a handsome boy, physically combining many of his parent's features. He had the aquiline nose of his mother as well as her rich dark hair and the fair colour of his dad's skin and his lanky athletic build.

Yul's childhood came and went without any major problems, except for certain indications that became evident to both of his parents. He did not share much of his experiences with them. When questioned about school or play he gave mostly laconic answers indicating that he preferred to be left alone and that his life, even as a child, was mainly of his own concern. This behaviour was much more pronounced towards his father than his mom, with whom he sometimes shared not all, but some of his problems and views, something he almost never did with his father.

In all fairness it must be said that he was a good child, not only as far as his performance at school was concerned, but also for keeping out of the trouble some youngsters seem to be dragged into when getting mixed up with undesirable or even unlawful activities. Perhaps this was due to his not having too many friends.

Yul went through elementary and high schools always ending up somewhere in the middle of the class, neither excelling nor failing in his exams. His teachers considered him an average student, but were aware of his secretiveness and his preference to be left alone rather than being a team player. Some comments Laura heard when talking to his tutors were: "you really never know with him" and "he seems to be a deeper water than it appears on the surface".

If Yul's life at school followed a more or less uneventful course, much of the same could be said about the Brunners' family life. Rudi had successfully built a lucrative dental practice. He was busy to the point that his receptionist routinely had to refer patients requiring minor procedures to other dentists, keeping only the more complicated and financially rewarding cases. Over the years, Rudi managed to amass a sizeable and conservatively invested fortune.

No doubt Rudi's professional success came at the expense of his family and even his social life. The Brunners continued to take short and often business-oriented vacations. Rudi continued to be a devoted and loving, yet emotionally aloof and at times even distant husband and father. He meticulously monitored Yul's progress in school, keeping tagged files of all reports and exam results and he often queried his son about school-related events. However he never talked to Yul about the boy's feelings or views or even needs, treating him more like a ward for whom he was responsible than a son he emotionally identified with. Although this relationship was certainly not a good one, it must be said that Rudi's attitude reflected his own character and values. He did not harbour any negative feelings towards his son. This is the way Rudi Brunner faced everybody else and his son was no exception. Yet, Yul did not see it that way. He considered his father's attitude towards him as negative, unfriendly and even debasing. As a result he began to first dislike his father and as he grew older and came to realize that his mother had really wasted a lively and warm personality on a cold, unimaginative and reserved professional, he felt not only very sorry for her but equally hateful of his father.

To a great extent, Yul's perception of his parents' marital life was correct. Laura had certainly not found emotional or sexual fulfilment in her marriage. She often thought about her dreams and visions when she had tied the knot with Rudi. Visions of an emotionally exciting life filled with cozy evenings at home, with warm embraces and tender kisses, with wild nights in bed and with all the beautiful experiences a young bride can foresee. All this came to naught, almost immediately after their short honeymoon. To be sure, Rudi was at all times a caring and respectful husband, sometimes even reminding her of the best friend she could wish for, but a lover, or even an emotional partner he was not.

In time Laura managed to put her expectations to rest and reasoned that first, you can't have everything in life, secondly, Rudi loved and respected her, thirdly she had full and unquestioned access to money and finally she had given birth to a beautiful child. "What more do you want?" she kept asking herself and she soon found the answer: "Accept it and make the best of it."

By the time Yul graduated from college with passing grades, he really did not know where life's often unpaved roads would take him. Of one thing he was sure though, he did not want to study dentistry or even medicine, although his father told him he would not only pay for his tuition until he obtained his degree, but would even give him a stipend for living expenses. This generosity soon turned out to be misplaced, because Yul took it for an invitation to freely milk the paternal cow. He immediately started to ask for the stipend and began drawing a fixed amount every month.

Months went by and he still could not decide what to do. He moved out of the family home in Küssnacht on the lake and found a room in a creaky building in the old city. There he shared accommodations with two young men and an immigrant girl who worked nights as a waitress and spent the day catching up on sleep.

Yul soon struck up a friendship with the two lodgers and that was probably the worst thing he could have done. Highly vulnerable because of his unhappy relationship with his father and his lack of professional orientation, his unsteady mood found solace in the chummy friendship with the two Swiss young men, both from broken homes and both addicted to whatever hallucinogenic drugs they could lay their hands on. One of them had a menial job as a cleaner in a department store and earned enough to keep him above water and the other lived on a small allocation from his mother, supplementing it with occasional forays into the pockets of unsuspecting tourists. It did not take long for the two to talk Yul into "just trying once". That fateful "once" turned to repeats in a matter of days. Drugs became part of Yul's daily routine.

Yul still roamed the admission offices of teaching institutions in and around the city, but he did it more out of curiosity than in the earnest determination to study. Yul was well on his way to become a drifter. He continued to use drugs and often sat for hours in seedy bars in the old city nursing a beer with his unholy neighbour friends.

At home, during dinner, Rudi regularly asked Laura: "What do you hear from Yul?" to which she could not reply anything else, than "He is still looking," adding "you know how these kids are nowadays. They have to find themselves, whatever is meant by that. By the way he says hello to you". Rudi's usual reaction to this was a "Hmm. Let's hope he doesn't take too long". Then, the conversation changed to other matters until a week or so later when the subject of Yul would come up again following more or less the same pattern.

While Rudi was completely unaware of Yul's drug problem, Laura was not. Like all mothers she sensed there was a reason for Yul's slurred and hesitant speech on the telephone. She confronted her son by insisting he tell her the truth and he soon did. After a few sleepless nights, she came up with a scheme to wean Yul off drugs. It was an ingenious idea, and it worked. She told Yul: "You used to tell me that when you grew up you wanted to become an airline pilot. Remember how your room was full of model planes? How about it?" She described the advantages and benefits and even the prestige of wearing a Swissair captain's uniform and after several conversations, Yul agreed with his mother.

It took a little while, but in the end he decided to apply for admission to the Swiss Aeronautical College in Bülach on the outskirts of Zürich. On a rainy afternoon, he sat in front of a panel of the school's faculty fielding a number of questions all aimed at establishing his emotional, educational as well as physical aptitude to study for a commercial pilot's license. This 3-year course would take him from Bülach to another flying school in Kloten, near the airport and finally to an advanced academy from where he would graduate with the shiny brass pilot wings pinned on his dark blue uniform and the two silver sleeve stripes of a co-pilot.

Yul came back for two more sessions with the school's admission board. Both he and the interrogators tried hard, but in the end he had to face rejection. The official reason was that some of the tests revealed an emotional instability underlined by his past bout with drug addiction. He was openly told that too little time had passed since his decision to kick the habit for the panel to accept him as a candidate for an airline pilot. He was told that he could re-apply in six months.

Yul was very disappointed with the school's decision, but not to the point of abandoning the idea of one day flying a plane. His childhood dream had apparently lain dormant, waiting for an opportunity to come to the fore and this was it. He moved out of the unsavoury environment in the old city into a student's hostel and abandoned drugs with the iron-clad determination never to return to them. He spent his time reading up on anything remotely associated with the world of flying and six months to the day later he re-applied to the Bülach College.

To his surprise he found that most of his previous examiners were still sitting in judgment over his request. Again they queried him for two long days and in the end they came up with what could be called a Solomonic Judgement. "The applicant Yul Brunner has satisfied the admission board to the extent that he will be admitted to Bülach College for the study and training to become a helicopter or small aircraft pilot. By "small" is meant a craft not carrying more than ten passengers including himself. Mr. Brunner will be allowed to apply for a full commercial airline pilot's license only after successfully completing three years of flying as a pilot of a helicopter or small aircraft as described above." After having read the boards' decision, the Dean of the College rose and looked Yul straight into the eyes: "Well, what do you say, Mr. Brunner, some things in life are hard to get but when you eventually reach them, they are much more precious than if they had fallen into your lap.

Do we have a new student or not?" Yul quickly reached out to the Dean with his two hands and clasping the one offered to him, he said: "I thank you and the Board for their confidence in me and I promise you that I'll one day be worthy of proudly wearing the four stripes of a Senior Airline Pilot. I promise you". To the sound of applause from the panel members, Yul left the room a very happy man indeed. When he met his Mother two days later for lunch, she presented him not only with a beautiful silver Caran d'Ache fountain pen but also with the best wishes of his father, who sent him a cheque of one thousand Swiss Francs together with regrets of not being able to join them because of an unexpected emergency at the hospital.

Yul, true to his form went through Aviation College, not as an exceptionally well qualified, but as an average student. In order to gain some additional pocket money he worked evenings in a local bookstore as a clerk. He did attend classes regularly and associated mostly with fellow students, both male and female. He never went back to drugs and, apart from the occasional beer or glass of wine, kept well away from alcohol fully aware that the school's disciplinary board kept a watchful eye on the extracurricular life of its aspiring pilot students. Yul kept in touch with his mother, although at times it seemed like the other way 'round: often she had to phone him to ask how he was coming along and if he needed anything outside the regular allocations from his father. Every now and then mother and son met for lunch or dinner and Yul was always invited home for Christmas and Easter as well as for his own birthday.

It took Yul a bit longer than the prescribed 3 years to sail through aviation school because one of his teachers requested an extension of his flying hours. He wanted to make sure that Yul was perfectly able to fly and navigate all the commercial helicopters in use at the time. But finally, a smiling Chief Instructor gave Yul the good news that he had passed all the tests.

In a brief ceremony attended by both his parents and followed by a luncheon offered by the school, Yul received his silver wings, qualifying him to pilot commercial as well as pleasure helicopters. During the graduation lunch, Rudi, holding a glass of wine in his hand said: "Congratulations, Yul. Your mother and I are proud of you. You will now be able to fly on your own wings". The latter pun was a well-placed reference to the impending cessation of Yul's monthly financial allowances. Yul was outwardly amused by this unexpected reminder and asked if he could continue to draw on his fathers' purse until he found a job. "How long will that take?" he asked. "I don't know for sure, but the school has already informed me of some job opportunities". "Well then," said Rudi, "shall we say another two months?" "Alright, Dad. Thank you", answered Yul, still thinking that bringing this up at his graduation was misplaced and an indication to him that his father's support over the years was a token of paternal duty and not of love.

It did not take long for Yul to land a piloting job at a major Swiss industrial company some 60 kilometres east of Zürich. International in scope, this engineering concern provided its executives as well as clients and important visitors with easy access to the Zürich airport by having a small fleet of three helicopters at the ready at all times. Yul joined a complement of seven pilots, most of them graduates of his own alma mater. The pay was good, the hours appeared reasonable and he had access to a string of fringe benefits offered by the company. Yul rented a small furnished flat not far from his workplace, bought himself a second-hand car and settled down to a routine job the outward signs of which were his navy-blue uniform with the company crest on his cap and his newly acquired silver wings over his left-side breast pocket. Yul was truly proud of himself, a feeling he shared with his ever attentive mother.

* * * * *

Life at the Brunners' continued to follow its predetermined and well-planned course. Laura had become a member of a benevolent society caring for young girls in trouble, of which there were plenty in Switzerland. She also played bridge three times a week and did a perfect job in house keeping, that now included a second home near St. Moritz to which they retreated on most weekends. Rudi continued to manage a busy dental practice as well as teaching at the University. He was now full professor of dental surgery and served as Chairman of the Dentists Association of the Zürich Kanton.

In addition to the several dental technicians he employed, he had found it necessary to hire another dentist as a fully qualified assistant. She was an attractive German girl of thirty-five with silky blond hair, an elegant gait and expressive blue eyes. Annelies soon became Rudi's indispensable second hand, often replacing him in pre- and post operative procedures leaving only the actual surgery for the boss to perform. She was divorced and had no children.

A week or so after her fifty-fifth birthday, Laura came home one evening from a bridge game with the signs and symptoms of a cold. Her cough was dry and prolonged. Rudi ordered her to lie down, brought her some aspirins and told her to stay in bed. The next day her condition worsened in as much as she coughed a great deal. When she phoned Rudi about feeling very weak, he immediately came home, bundled her up and drove her to the Kantonspital for a chest x-ray. While she was resting, the hospital's radiologist, a personal friend of Rudi's came out of the lab with two x-ray pictures in his hand. He motioned Rudi to follow him into his nearby office, asked him to sit down and proceeded to tell him the most devastating news Rudi had ever heard. "My dear friend", said Professor Hildbrand, "I have bad news for Laura and yourself. The diagnosis is crystal clear. She has a small but well-defined cancer in her left lobe. Sorry Rudi, I wish to God, I would not have to tell you this." Noticing the ashen-faced glare of Rudi, Dr. Hildbrand quickly added: "You know as well as I do, that this does not necessarily mean the immediate end of the road. There are several treatments from radiation to chemotherapy to surgery.

We will do everything to save her, Rudi. Right now, the main problem is first to break the news to her and secondly to comfort and reassure her that she can be put into remission, hopefully for some years to come. We will leave no stone unturned to save her, of this you can be sure, Rudi". With this, the doctor was gone, leaving Rudi alone to cope with the horrible situation. And horrible it was. The rest of the afternoon was a nightmare for both Laura and Rudi. They cried and clung to each other for comfort. But, at the end of the day, it was Laura who, with a brave smile, said: "Look, Darling, that's my destiny. If I die, I don't want you to die with me. I know I am in good hands in this hospital. Let's all put up a good fight, and who knows, maybe we can all talk about it some day. Miracles happen all the time, you know. And now go home, phone Yul but don't sound too pessimistic. There is a nice dinner in the oven. Try to carry on and take good care of yourself. I need *you* now more than all the medications in the world."

It took several days for Rudi to resume his usual composure but he eventually continued to run his practice as he had done for the past twenty-five years or so.

Laura survived Dr. Hildbrand's original diagnosis for slightly more than nine months. She underwent or rather endured chemotherapy, radiation as well as surgery. She was repeatedly released from hospital only to be summoned back a week or so later for more observation and more procedures. Nothing seemed to help. Like a flower deprived of fresh water, she withered and faded away. Rudi spent time with her every single day, trying his best to comfort her. Yul came on his day off, usually once a week or every other week, according to his schedule.

At times Laura was hopeful and acted normally, even making plans for the future. But then, when becoming aware of the gravity of her deteriorating condition, she became depressed and resentful for having to abandon a beautiful life in the middle of its course.

The call from the young intern on nightshift came at five o'clock on a rainy October morning. "Dr. Brunner? This is Dr. Duclos from the Kantonspital. I am terribly sorry to have to inform you that your wife passed away a short while ago. I went into her room to check on the sedative infusion and found that her vital signs had ceased. My colleague and I confirmed the death. She died in her sleep. Please accept our very sincere condolences, Dr. Brunner."

Two days later Laura Brunner was laid to rest in Zürich's Central Cemetery in the far north of the city. Hundreds of people attended. Rudi stood side by side with Yul, often hugging his shoulder or his arm in deadly silence. Everybody was truly saddened. Laura had left this world at the age of 56, a beautiful, intelligent and caring woman who had not hurt a fly or said a harsh word to anyone in her short life. "She had graced our world" as the priest said at the gravesite.

Laura's death at first turned out to be a turning point in the lives of both Rudi and Yul, in as much as it necessarily brought them closer together, not because Yul felt an increased emotional need for his father, but rather because Rudi thought he should now reach out to his son in a gesture of keeping the family together. Also in an effort to somehow replace the role Laura had played in Yul's life. Rudi told his son: "Listen, why don't you come to see me more often. This is your home, you know. We could also go out for dinner when our schedules permit. Let's keep in touch, Yul, OK?" Yul's reply was a smile and a brief "Sure".

Laura's death had indeed brought profound changes into Rudi's life. Not that he had to do anything in the way of keeping house. This was done by a faithful couple of Swiss villagers, who, over the years, had taken care of all of the Brunner's domestic needs. Gerda looked after cooking and keeping the two homes in tip top shape, while her husband Freddy, took care of the two cars, did all the grocery shopping, ran errands, repaired whatever broke down and often drove the Brunners to their respective destinations. He also had a part-time job as a security guard in a downtown bank. For years, mornings at the Brunner's Zürich home started with Gerda opening the front door at 6:30 a.m. with the day's paper in her hand.

The real change in Rudi's life came about a year after Laura's passing away, and it came subtly and almost naturally. Rudi began to realize that his assistant Annelies was not only a very good dentist, but also a very attractive young woman. He caught himself repeatedly looking at her very shapely legs when he should have looked at the cavity she had just filled. In fact, both of them were slowly gliding towards each other. It started with an occasional touch or body contact during work leading to a furtive kiss when leaving the clinic in the evening and ending in a full-fetched love affair. Neither of them knew how it happened, but it happened. They were in love and wanted each other's company more than anything else in the world. Both agreed to keep their relationship secret until a full year had passed after Laura's death. Only then did both go out in public together, inform all their friends and relatives and last, but not least Yul.

* * * * *

In a way the year following his mother's death was a sad one for Yul, and this because of two reasons: first he missed the warmth that radiated from her attention and care and secondly because he found his work depressing. He came to realize that despite the pilot's wings he proudly wore, he was really nothing more than a glorified chauffeur. Just like the limos that whisked visitors and executives from the company door to their destinations, he was also required to ferry loads, often at a minute's notice, from his landing pad behind the parking lot to the special place assigned to him at the Zürich airport. Occasionally he had to fly to Basel or Geneva, but most of the time his was an airport shuttle service and the monotony of it soon got to him. The bossy commands from his superior: "Take two passengers to the airport and fly back immediately for another load. They are all catching international flights so hurry up. You can have lunch later, OK? And by the way, somebody complained that your cabin smelled of tobacco. You know you are not allowed to smoke at work." As well, the tips some company guests slipped into his hands on stepping out of his craft started to get on his nerves. He began developing a dislike for his ho-hum job and in particular for his domineering boss.

Another reason contributing to Yul's unhappiness was his ruminating that while he was working so hard to make a living, his super-rich father was really raking it in. His mother had once told him that Rudi had named her as principal beneficiary in his will. What would happen now that she was gone? His father had never mentioned anything to him about an inheritance. To whom would the money go when his father died? To Annelies?

All these thoughts occupied much of Yul's mind. His father had become the single most negative personality in his thoughts. After some reflection he decided to confront him openly and ask him who would inherit his money. One evening he picked up the phone and told his father: "We have not seen each other in a while. How about dinner or something?" Rudi immediately said: "Sure, Yul. Why don't you come over for dinner on Saturday night? I even have a surprise for you." Yul accepted, wondering what the surprise would be. Well, the surprise turned out to be Annelies. Without too many words, Rudi introduced her to his son as "My Annelies". From her behaviour that evening, it became perfectly clear to Yul that she was indeed the next woman in his dad's life. She was in charge of whatever happened that evening, from serving drinks and dinner, to asking Yul very pertinent questions about his life, indicating that she was part of the family. After dinner, over an old French cognac, both opened up and as they had already informed him over the phone, told Yul that they had decided to live together as a couple. Obviously, the emphasis during the evening centered on Annelies and precluded Yul from broaching the inheritance subject.

Driving home that night, Yul's mind tried to digest all his observations and his interpretation of them. First and foremost, he was stunned by the extraordinary beauty of Annelies. From her silky blond hair to her exquisite legs she was a picture of perfection and sexuality. Yul could not take his eyes off her throughout the evening. Although considerably younger than his greying father, the couple seemed to be very much in love and at ease with each other. Yul also recalled that when he thanked and bid them goodnight at the door, Annelies repeatedly asked him to come back, not only for dinner but whenever he felt like relaxing from a busy day at the controls of his helicopter. Yul decided to take her up on this invitation.

He did so, just two weeks later. He phoned one evening to ask if he could come for dinner. "Of course, Yul" was Annelies' ready reply. This time they had also invited another couple for dinner. Again, Yul caught himself staring at Annelies. She wore a tight-fitting dress revealing all the details of her figure. During the next weeks and months, Yul became a sort of regular caller on his parental home, not at all to see his father but to see Annelies. Just looking at her seemed to fulfil his erotic and sexual fantasies. During all these encounters, most of them taking place in the presence of his father, Annelies acted her usual self which was friendly and even somewhat chummy, often engaging in personal repartees. It was all meant to put Yul at ease and make him feel at home, and not one iota more. But, as it often happens, her openness was misinterpreted by Yul as a sign of revealing some emerging feelings and emotions towards him. Misreading these signs, he thought he had found a willing partner in a relationship he was secretly trying to nurture. Yul had actually fallen in love with a woman for whom, reciprocating any emotional feelings or intentions were the farthest from her mind. When she felt that he was somewhat crossing the line, she immediately left the room under some excuse trusting that Yul would realize that he was stepping out of bounds. Yul was, of course, aware of this gentle "putting him in place", but he had no intention of letting up. Carefully avoiding any gesture or compromising remark in the presence of his father, he continued to send disguised yet unmistakable messages of his feelings to Annelies. This intolerable situation soon reached a critical point as far as Annelies was concerned.

One evening, when Rudi briefly left the house to put the car in the garage, she told Yul not to come to his father's house for a while. "Yul," she said, "I respect your feelings, but I'm afraid I cannot reciprocate them in any shape or form. I repeat not in any shape or form. I tried to tell you this many times, but you either ignore it or don't want to accept it. My relationship with your father is complete and sincere and I have no intention whatsoever to deviate from it. Not now and not ever. In order to avoid hurting the three of us, I must request you not to come here for the foreseeable future. If your father asks why you don't come anymore I will tell him that you are busy at work. Please Yul, no discussion or any more remarks on this subject. It is completely closed for me and I hope, for you too." Yul listened in silence to this monologue delivered with a somewhat emotional but very firm voice. When she had finished, he silently got up. Muttering a hardly audible "goodbye", he grabbed his jacket and left the house.

During the next weeks and months, Yul spent a good part of his spare time thinking about Annelies' words in the context of his life in general. In fact, ruminating became Yul's favourite occupation. He felt his life was in a mess and he really didn't know how to deal with it let alone solve it. His work did not provide any excitement, except that of receiving his weekly pay check. He had not really made friends, male or female since he started working as a pilot. And because of the need to be on stand by, he could not plan any long term vacations or travels. He was depressed and he blamed his woes in an indirect way on his father. The reasons were many:

He hardly kept in touch with his father and when he did talk to him, it was just a few words: "How are you? Enjoying your work? Any plans for vacations?" Yul was also very bitter about his mother having wasted a life with a cold and disciplinarian husband. Furthermore he was resentful and jealous of his father for having captivated Annelies for whom he was still harbouring very strong emotional and sexual feelings. Another thought that kept coming back to his mind was the considerable fortune his father was sitting on. How come his father had never mentioned to him that he had named him as an heir and what if he had left everything to Annelies and to charities? As time went by, Yul's aversion and even hatred for his father grew. It grew and became, in his mind, the single most important reason for his unhappiness.

Rudi was of course, not aware of his son's state of mind. He knew that Yul was not an outgoing, communicative and happy individual and therefore did not ascribe too much importance to Yul's curt and perfunctory replies when they talked with each other. He knew nothing at all about his son's approaches to Annelies. She had not told him a single word about it for fear that it would create serious discord between father and son.

Annelies had become a very important part of Rudi's life. She was his assistant in the clinic, she ran his homes with perfect timing and attention to detail. She was an extraordinary sex partner who managed to evoke feelings in Rudi, he himself did not know lay dormant in him and, above all she was a close friend with whom he could discuss anything and everything.

That he was almost twice her age did not seem to play any role in their relationship. After all, at slightly over sixty, Rudi still cut a very handsome and virile figure, enough to cause many younger women to turn their head twice when they saw him in his immaculate white smock at work.

December 16th was Rudi's birthday. When Laura was alive it used to be the occasion of beautiful parties to which she invited family and friends for dinner followed by spirited conversation generously laced with vintage brandies. Of course Yul was also present at these gatherings. However, since Annelies had entered Rudi's life, the crowded birthday parties had given place to one-on-one intimate candle-lit dinners at one of Zürich's most elegant restaurants followed by an even more intimate togetherness at home. It took a long time for the lights to go out in the couple's bedroom.

Annelies broached the subject one night over dinner. "Is it alright if I make reservations for this year's birthday dinner at the Hummer Bar?" She asked, "You love seafood and it is probably the best place in Zürich to enjoy it". "No", replied Rudi, "You know what I have in mind? Lets' all go skiing instead. You, Yul and myself. It will give us an opportunity to be together, besides we all need a few days of relaxation. Let's combine my birthday and Christmas. I am sure Yul can get time off for the holidays. I leave the choice of venue to you. We are a bit late in the season, so we may have to go to resorts having vacancies left. What do you think, darling?"

Annelies was taken aback. She welcomed the idea of spending a few days skiing but, at the same time she did not want to be in the company of Yul. She tried a: "How about just the two of us?", but Rudi insisted on a family reunion of sorts. Annelies had no choice but to say: "Of course. I am sure we will all have a great time. Let me see what I can find at this late date."

She was lucky. Perhaps they were cancellations but she found two rooms at the Alprösli Hotel in Zermatt. They would stay there from the twenty-second to the twenty-ninth of December. This was peak season offering all the usual Christmas parties and, of course, the prospect of glorious skiing on some of the best slopes in the world. Rudi was elated and immediately informed Yul. "Thanks a lot, Dad, I am sure we will all enjoy it. I will meet you at the hotel in the afternoon of the twenty-second. See you then." was his reply.

The three of them spent the few weeks before the vacation preparing mentally and physically for the impromptu event, albeit with different thoughts occupying their minds. Rudi was very happy at the idea of practicing his favourite outdoor sport in the company of his beautiful Annelies. He also felt satisfied to have done the right thing by inviting his son whom he had not seen in a long time. He even thought that he should repeat this every year from now on, making the winter vacation a family tradition to bring everyone together.

Annelies certainly did not look forward to the event for one reason that over-shadowed all the pleasures of being with Rudi in a relaxed setting away from their busy daily life. She simply dreaded the presence of Yul. His unsolicited and unwelcome advances were still fresh in her mind. She had actually developed a very negative opinion of Yul bordering on an aversion to being in his company. How could a son who had benefited so much from his parents betray his own father by trying to steal his woman? Yul was a good looking man with a steady job who had access to many girls in his world. Why did he have to improperly reach onto his father's turf? She came to the conclusion that Yul was an amoral opportunist for whom nothing was sacred when it came to satisfying his desires. What saddened her even more was the thought that Rudi was completely unaware of this blatant breach of trust. When thinking of the rapidly approaching confrontation she mulled over the fine line she would have to walk in Zermatt between being civil and nice to Yul and the risk of somewhat betraying her true feelings.

Yul was probably the most indifferent of the three in his expectations of the forthcoming reunion. He certainly did not look forward to Zermatt with feelings of love and warmth for his father. Over the years he had developed a coolness towards him to the point that he now considered the all-expenses-paid vacation as just that. An opportunity to make his father pay for a week of carousing, eating and drinking the most expensive goodies the Alprösli had to offer, acquiring a new pair of skis and a matching outfit at the hotel's Pro Shop with a mere: "Put it on my father's bill". As for his feelings towards Annelies, he firmly intended to try again. Women are fickle.

Someone had once told him that if a lady says "No", she really means "Maybe", if she says 'maybe', she means 'yes' and if she says 'yes', she is not really a lady." He even envisaged his father's reaction if Annelies would inform him that she decided to leave his dad. When he thought of that possibility he became so excited that he told himself: "This possibility alone is worth the stay in Zermatt." He saw the dejection and fury on his father's face and loved every moment of this contemplation.

The Alprösli is a sprawling old-style hotel, which was built at the turn of the century. Frequent redecorations and improvements had however kept pace with modern expectations of a very discriminating clientele which included princes and kings. The late Shah of Persia had a permanent suite on the upper floor and so did some other heads of state. It was not the most modern but it was certainly the most coveted place to stay for all those who wanted to enjoy their winter sports amid the rich and famous.

The hotel lobby was a vast wood-panelled hall decorated with exquisite bronze sculptures and beautiful paintings. The roof was one huge stained glass dome featuring multi-coloured flowers and plants arranged in art-deco style. From it hung a chandelier that seemed to reflect the grandeur of a French *palais*. Every corner of the reception hall exuded good taste and refined elegance. The staff in their impeccable uniforms attended to their guests with quiet, almost whispering deference. There was no running or shouting of any sorts.

Rudi and Annelies were first to arrive. They checked in, left a message for Yul and went up to their room to freshen up from the long drive from Zürich. Just as they prepared to go down to the hotel's famous "Oasis" bar, Yul phoned saying that he had arrived, and would meet them later on in the hotel's restaurant for dinner. They had just ordered their meal when Yul finally showed up. There was an unemotional shaking of hands and ensuing small talk throughout dinner.

When they had finished, Rudi motioned his two guests to a small room adjacent to the lobby and told them of his proposed agenda. Days one and two, skiing on the intermediate slopes to get everybody into the swing of things. Day three rest and relaxation and day four, Rudi wanted to go with Yul on a full-day skiing trip for advanced skiers on the Matterhorn. This would start early in the morning and end later that day. The trip described in a brochure Rudi had picked up in the lobby was organized by a local travel agency and featured a helicopter flight to the top of the mountain, skiing all day and transportation back to the hotel at the conclusion of this "once-in-a-lifetime skiing experience". When proposing it to Yul, he said: "I have not done a thing like that lately, but I know I will enjoy it very much. I don't expect Annelies to come with us, but how about you, Yul? It's a long trail and you really have to know what you are doing. How about it?"

"Of course I am up to it. I'll come with you."

"Great," said Rudi, "Annelies will go shopping. When Rudy told Amelie about the ski tour with Yul, she smiled and said: "Don't worry about me. I will find lots of things to do that day. But I do worry about you. Are you sure Rudi you can handle these slopes some of which are pretty steep?"

"Of course darling," replied Rudi. "My cousin Bernie did it last year and he is eight years older than I am. If he could do it, I can do it, besides, I have often taken similar day trips." With that everybody went up to their rooms for a good night's rest in what appeared to be the most comfortable beds one could imagine.

Rudi's plan was followed to a tee. They all spent the next two days getting their fill on the intermediate's slopes, having fun, enjoying their meals and good wines. Most of the time, Rudi and Annelies were together without Yul. Under different excuses he disappeared for most of the day, catching up with them at dinnertime. He told them that he had met some people he knew from work. The day before the big skiing event, Rudi reminded Yul of all the gear and equipment he had to take with him for the long downhill schussing and Yul said: "Don't worry, I am ready".

The third day of their vacation was a Thursday and the big skiing trip was planned for Friday. On Thursday, Rudi and Annelies had skied a bit in the morning and in the afternoon had gone to see a movie they had missed in Zürich.

Yul was in his hotel room checking the equipment he would need for the next day's trip. The telephone rang. It was Juventus, the travel agency organizing the ski trip.

"We are trying to contact Dr. Brunner but are unable to. We have an urgent message for him. Is this his son, Yul?"

"Yes, it is". Yul said.

"And you are booked for the trip together."

"Yes, indeed", said Yul.

"What is the message you have for my father? I will meet him a little later for dinner." "OK", said the agent, "This message is actually for both of you. We have left a note at the hotel for your father, but can we count on you to inform him?"

"Of course you can", replied Yul.

"Well", said the agent, "We have just received a late weather report from the Matterhorn meteorology station saying that there has been a change in forecast and that there is a system developing that will entail stronger than usual winds on the slopes. Your father mentioned to us that this is his sixty-fifth birthday. Given his age, we thought that the expected strong winds and the sharply increased efforts to cope with them on the descent may expose him to severe physical stress. We therefore request Dr. Brunner's confirmation to go ahead with the event as planned or cancel it. Please discuss this warning with your father before making a decision. You can call us until nine o'clock this evening. Is everything clear to you?"

"It is perfectly clear to me." Yul hung up and sat down on the bed.

The last ten minutes had brought to the fore an idea that was never too far from his mind. An idea that he was sure would change his life for the better in many ways and that would draw a final line in an unhappy relationship that had long ago deteriorated into hatred. He let the phone call from the travel agent go through his mind again and again and he realized that here was a never to be repeated opportunity for action and, if he played his cards right, he could easily get away with it.

* * * * *

A few hours later, he phoned his father to tell him that he had suddenly developed a strong abdominal pain accompanied by vomiting and diarrhoea. He could therefore not join them for dinner. He then phoned the agent and lied, telling him that he had discussed the warning with his father and that the trip was on for both. After dinner he phoned his father, again saying nothing at all about the weather warning but he told him that he hoped to make it for the trip. "Please wake me at 5:30 a.m."

In the morning, he told his father that he had had a very bad night with fever and strong abdominal pain and that he could not possibly envisage a day of strenuous skiing. "Dad, you looked forward to it. Go by yourself. I am sure there will be other skiers on the slopes. I hope I will feel better by the time you come back. Sorry about that. I cannot help it. Have a great day."

Rudi was concerned about his son's problem and wanted to cancel the outing in order to take Yul to a hospital. "Nonsense, Dad." said Yul, "I have had these upsets before. They last a couple of days but they knock you out completely, if you know what I mean. Please don't worry about me. I will be OK in a couple of days. You go and have fun, Dad". "Are you sure, Yul?' insisted Rudi. "Yes, I am a hundred percent sure. Go." With that he hung up.

Rudi kissed Annelies goodbye and lugging all the equipment he had prepared the day before, got into the waiting car the Travel Agency had provided. They drove a short distance to the heliport, where a gleaming red and white whirly bird with slowly turning rotor blades sat poised for take off. The pilot jumped out, greeted Rudi, helped him take the gear aboard and after a short check of all board controls and a very matter-of-fact conversation with air traffic control, gently lifted the craft into the cool morning air. It took them a good 45 minutes to reach the top of the mountain. The view all around the cabin was spectacular, if not breathtaking. The pilot guided his craft gracefully around little towns and resorts before gaining altitude. Rudi was delighted and enjoyed the flight like a kid on a school outing. He recognized many hotels and slopes, most of them already teeming with skiers at this early hour of the morning. When they finally landed, Rudi thanked the pilot, collected all his belongings and went into the nearby cabin to gulp down a hot cup of coffee. He got suited up. He was very excited about the day ahead. A short while later he was standing outside the cabin, on his skis, backpacked and ready to spend a dream day on one of Switzerland's most beautiful slopes. There were very few people around, no trees but the most gorgeous expanse of snow he had ever seen. Wonderful, soft, virgin snow. Apart from a few rapidly moving clouds nothing but blue skies like a giant dome all around him. Rudi had often skied at high altitudes but he had never felt so overwhelmed by the panorama surrounding him. Nothing could compare to the majestic sight of the Matterhorn, he thought. He looked at his watch. It was a few minutes past nine and with a vigorous push of his poles and a big smile on his suntan cream soaked face, he started his descent.

According to plan, he would ski for the next two and a half hours, following the trail set out by the travel agent. He would then arrive at the half-way station around noon. This was to be the first of two stops on the way down. Here he was to be served a hot meal, have a short rest, check all his gear, and, most important of all, phone Annelies that all was well and he was continuing the trek in the direction of the second stop, where he would arrive two hours later for another break. The last leg of the trip was just over an hour and would end up in the village where a limo would be waiting to take him back to the Alprösli, a hot shower and a well-deserved après ski with Annelies. This was the plan he had worked out and as a veteran skier who had taken many similar ski trips he intended to follow it. To keep him in the right direction, he had in his parka pocket a compass, a souvenir form his stint in the Swiss army many years ago. Rudi Brunner was determined to enjoy a beautiful day in the Swiss Alps, the world's paradise for ski enthusiasts.

*****

Shortly after 11:30 a.m. an operator from the travel agent phoned the halfway station to make sure Dr. Brunner had made it safely to the first stop. He was told that Dr. Brunner had not arrived yet. The operator was also told another bit of news. The weather station at the top of the mountain confirmed the earlier report of very strong winds on most areas between their station and lower slopes, that is to say at altitudes between 3000 and 1500 metres. "At some places we are talking about gale force winds."

At twelve noon, Annelies phoned the Travel Agency to tell them she had not heard from Dr. Brunner. He was supposed to call her from the first station between 11:30 and 12:00. She asked whether the Agency had any news from the skier. They said "no", and neither had the station where he was to stop for lunch. They added that they would immediately start a search. She asked them: "How are you going to search for him?"

"Well," was the reply, "the only way is by helicopter which is on standby, but we have a problem. The pilot, after having returned this morning from the trip with Dr. Brunner got into his car and drove away for the day. We are now trying to contact him, asking him to drive or fly back here immediately in order to start the search for Dr. Brunner. We have already advised two mountain guides who will accompany the pilot on his search."

"How long will it take the pilot to get back to Zermatt?" she asked.

"About two hours, plus half an hour to take the craft up to the slope."

"That is definitely too long." She said.

"We know" was the reply, "and we are trying to find another pilot from the local heliport."

Annelies had an idea: "Dr. Brunner's son Yul is a certified helicopter pilot. Could he fly the craft?" She asked.

"He certainly could. We didn't know that he was a pilot. We will pick him up immediately."

"He was not feeling well last night", she said. "Something like an upset stomach. That's why he did not go with his father. He is in room No. 412. I am sure you will find him there now."

She hung up, very worried about the situation, but confident that a search party would be out looking for Rudi very shortly.

Her confidence turned out to be misplaced. Yul, when requested to fly the search mission, refused on the grounds that he was sick, had a fever and was unable to walk properly let alone fly a helicopter. "I cannot risk my life, the lives of the two guides and the cost of an expensive helicopter in my present condition. I am sorry, but you will have to find someone else or wait for the regular pilot to return", he said. "But that may be too late and the evening may set in, making observation from above more difficult. You have to do it, Mr. Brunner", the Agency manager insisted. "We have to find your father. A life is at stake and you cannot abandon this rescue attempt because of indigestion," the manager practically cried on the phone. "Please, Mr. Brunner. We must find your father." The desperate plea fell on deaf ears. "I am sorry, Sir," Yul repeated, "I am unable to fly." He said "Goodbye" and hung up.

In desperation the Manager phoned Annelies and told her about the situation. She immediately phoned Yul and said: "I don't care what is ailing you. It's an upset stomach anyway. You must go out searching for your father, right now, before it's too late. He may be in trouble as we talk, please Yul, get dressed and get to the heliport right now!" Yul was unimpressed by Annelies' frantic plea. "I am sorry, but I am unfit to fly an aircraft. I am sick. I am sorry. Goodbye."

It took two hours before the rescue mission flew over the slopes of the mountain. The travel agency had moved heaven and earth, requesting help from other resorts and even the Swiss Army. In the end, the regular pilot as well as a volunteer from a nearby sport club arrived at the same time to fly the copter.

The craft circled the area following the charted trail, when one of the guides noticed a slight mound on an otherwise smooth snow surface. There were also traces of interrupted ski trails leading to the mound. It looked as if the skier had repeatedly stopped on his descent. When the helicopter landed a few meters away from the mound, everyone jumped out and, wading through the heavy snow started to shovel the drift off the mound. It did not take them long to find the lifeless body of Dr. Rudi Brunner. All helped to carry him back to the craft and just 20 minutes later the party landed on the roof of Saint Benedict Hospital, a welcome site for thousands of skiers with broken legs and sprained ankles. Rudi was immediately put on life support and cardiac resuscitation, but all to no avail. He was pronounced dead as a result of a heart attack he had suffered about four hours earlier. The cardiologist's words to Annelies who had just arrived at the hospital were: "I am very sorry, madam, we could not save him. He was brought to us about three hours too late. We could have saved him had he been brought in sooner."

* * * * *

Swiss law requires hospitals to immediately inform the Authorities of all deaths occurring on their premises. Annelies received a phone call from the local police station on her return to the Alprösli hotel. "We are very sorry about the death of Dr. Brunner. Please accept our condolences. Do you need any assistance? May we have a word with you in the hotel tonight or tomorrow during the day?" Annelies immediately agreed and asked the police to meet her in a quiet part of the hotel lobby the following morning.

Inspector Caselli and his assistant were already waiting for her when Annelies came down from her room. She was obviously shaken and her beautiful face showed lines and folds brought on by a sleepless night and the strain of coping with the catastrophe that had hit her so suddenly.

She was first to address the two police officers, even before they had time to start asking questions. "I know you are here to establish the circumstances surrounding Dr. Brunner's death and I assume that you will also talk to his son among other people involved in the tragedy. I have talked to our lawyer in Zürich this morning and he advised me to tell you everything I know. Of course you will have no difficulty in piecing together all the events that preceded his death, but there are some strange things that I became aware of this morning just prior to meeting you.

Dr. Brunner's son did not accompany his father on the ski trip as planned. He also refused to fly a rescue mission that could have saved his father's life although he is a fully qualified helicopter pilot. All this on the grounds that he was very sick in bed, vomiting and with high fever caused by severe food poisoning. This morning, when I asked the concierge if they had heard from Yul he said: "Yes, at midnight Mr. Brunner ordered from room service a full-course meal and a bottle of 'the best champagne in the house'." Also, yesterday throughout the day, Yul had repeatedly ordered food and drink to his room, according to the concierge. Now, I ask you, gentlemen does this not seem odd to you? Someone suffering from food poisoning, running a high fever, surely does not stuff himself with Chateaubriands and champagne. I think you should make a note of this, when Yul is asked to explain why he refused to join his Father on the trip and also why he refused to fly the rescue mission."

"Yes," said the inspector, "these are interesting details and may point to more than an accident. Thank you, Madam. We will speak to Mr. Brunner as soon as possible." They left Annelies. Back at the police station when they reported their conversation with Annelies to their superior, he told them that he had in the meantime received the hospital report stating that Dr. Brunner had died because he had been brought in three hours too late. "In view of all this, I will ask for an inquest to establish all the facts surrounding the death. "There may have been negligence or other circumstances involved."

Within the hour all those concerned were notified by the police not to leave Zermatt until further notice. On the list were Annelies, Yul Brunner, the manager of the Juventus Travel Agency, the helicopter pilot, the two guides of the rescue flight and a representative from the Alprösli Hotel as well as the doctor from St. Benedict Hospital who had confirmed the death of the victim. All involved were told that an inquest would be held two days later at the local courthouse, that they were requested to appear there and that they had the right to be represented by counsel if they so wished.

It was a cold day in the regional administrative center of Zermatt's Kanton. After several days of brilliant sunshine, the weather had turned grey, a sure sign of an impending snowfall, typical of the area's January forecast.

The courthouse was a simple, red-brick building which housed the Kantonal Administration offices as well as a small tribunal room, complete with seats for judges, seats and docks for witnesses and benches for an audience. On the wall behind the presiding judge was a painting of Justicia, goddess of justice holding an evened scale in her right hand and her left hand resting on a shield emblazoned with the Swiss Cross. This large allegory was flanked by flags of the Confederation and of the Kanton on either side.

Present, besides the Judge and his assistant, were three town officials and a stenographer. There was Annelies, accompanied by her late husband's lawyer who had hastily driven up from Zürich, Yul, who was unaccompanied, Udo Egli, General Manager of the Juventus Travel Agency, organizer of the fateful ski outing, the two guides as well as the regular helicopter pilot who had found and brought back the body. There were also two people from the Alprösli Hotel: a concierge and the assistant manager. A doctor from St. Benedict Hospital was present as well.

Apart from Annelies only Herr Egli had chosen to make use of a lawyer. There was no audience present, but one single uniformed policeman sat at a small table just outside the courtroom, a gentle reminder that the federal justice system was in action here.

After everybody had sat down, the Judge opened the proceedings.

His words were simple and to the point: "Death, on the ski slopes," the Judge said, "even of apparently natural causes merits an investigation and an explanation, as to what exactly caused it. This is our common mandate here. With everyone's cooperation and guidance, we will, I am sure establish a faultless record of events. If I am satisfied at the end of the inquest that we are dealing with a death caused by a heart attack and nothing else, this case will be closed as far as Swiss Federal Law is concerned and no further action will be taken. If, however, I have reason or reasons to believe that other elements such as neglect, mismanagement, misconduct or even foul play are involved in the death of Dr. Rudolph Brunner, I will refer the case to the Federal Court for further action, meaning the opening of proceedings against any suspect or suspects that may emerge from this hearing. I urge you therefore to tell the truth and nothing but the truth as your oath and Swiss law demands. I thank you all for your complete cooperation."

The Judge shuffled through some of the papers in front of him, and called the first witness. Udo Egli, general manager and co-owner of the Juventus Travel Agency.

After being sworn in and taking his seat in the witness box, the Judge said: "Mr. Egli, your agency offered and sold this one-day skiing excursion to Dr. Rudolph Brunner and to his son Yul. Can you tell us exactly what this excursion involved?"

Mr. Egli explained how Dr. Brunner had come to his office in the town center to ask if the one-day private skiing trips advertised at the Alprösli Hotel were available. I told him 'Indeed, we can offer you a one-day descent from one of the Matterhorn slopes to the valley with two downhill stops. The first for a light lunch and a brief rest and the second for coffee and another brief rest before the final descent. At destination our limo will take you back to your hotel.' We discussed all other details of the trip as well as the price and he told us that he would be accompanied by his son Yul. He also told us that this trip was a present to himself on his sixty-fifth birthday. We then talked about technical details regarding his gear, but he seemed to be a seasoned skier as there was little I could tell him he did not already know. He paid by credit card and left our office."

"Then what happened", said the Judge.

"Well, the next thing was that our driver picked up the client and phoned us to say that there was only one passenger. Apparently, Dr. Brunner's son was sick in bed. Our limo took the client to the airport where he boarded our helicopter and he flew to the Eiger Spitze, the trip's starting point at 3825 meters elevation. After making sure that he was ready for the descent, we left him and our helicopter flew back to its base at the airport."

Both the court's stenographer and the Judge were making notes as the witness spoke.

"And what were the weather conditions on that day, Mr. Egli?"

The witness took a deep breath and said: "They were not good, Your Honour."

"Not good? What do you mean?" said the Judge.

"Well, at 12 noon on the day before the scheduled trip, we heard that there was a change in the forecast for the next day in as much as stronger than usual winds were expected to develop around the mountain."

"And did you inform Dr. Brunner of this?" asked the Judge.

"Yes, we did, Your Honour." said Mr. Egli. "Well let me be precise." He added. "At about 12:30 p.m. we phoned Dr. Brunner at his hotel room. There was no answer. We left a message for him with the weather information and a request to call us back. We then contacted the second passenger. We found Mr. Yul Brunner in his hotel room. We told him about the expected strong winds and drew his attention to the risk this implied for his father. 'Mr. Brunner,' we said, 'you are a young man, but your father told us he is sixty-five. Strong winds require an extra effort during skiing. We would like you to ask your father to confirm the trip. If need be, we can re-schedule it, you know!' Mr. Brunner interrupted me repeatedly and said: 'Ok, Ok, I will talk to my father as soon as he returns from his shopping spree downtown and ask him if he still wants to go or postpone.'

'Can you then phone us or ask your Father to phone us?' I said. 'Certainly' was the reply."

"And did you receive this confirmation for the trip?" asked the Judge.

"Yes, I received a phone call from Mr. Yul Brunner, saying that he had just talked to his father, mentioning the stronger winds on the slopes and the risks involved. As expected, his father had laughed it off, asking him to call the travel agency to thank them and 'tell them that the trip was on as planned. So Your Honour, we had trip confirmation from the son who said he also spoke for his father. Since we did not hear from Dr. Brunner after he received the hotel message, we assumed that all was in order and we had the green light for the trip."

"Thank you, Mr. Egli," said the Judge, "You may step down now. I would like to establish the true record of the day in a sequential manner. That's why I would like to listen now to the testimony of Miss Annelies Steiger, Dr. Brunner's companion."

Annelies, still visibly shaken by the unexpected death of her friend, exchanged a few words with her lawyer and then entered the witness box. She was sworn in and the judge, in a gentle tone, asked her to tell the inquest everything that had happened on that day and the day before that could shed light on the events under review.

"Your Honour," she started, "There are many things that may shed light on the death of my beloved friend. Where do you want me to start?"

"Well, let's start with the question why Dr. Brunner did not return the phone call to the travel agent after receiving the message at the hotel."

"The answer, Your Honour," she said, "is that Dr. Brunner never received any messages from the travel agent. We checked in together in the late afternoon. The concierge gave me the room key and a couple of letters addressed to Dr. Brunner, but there was definitely no telephone message from the travel agent."

The judge was not the only one who looked up, bewildered by that last statement. The stenographer could be seen furiously taking notes. "I see," said the Judge, "But if Dr. Brunner did not hear about the strong winds from the Juventus people, he must have heard it from his son, as Mr. Egli just told us."

"No, Your Honour," said Annelies, "Dr. Brunner actually had three telephone conversations with his son, just prior to the trip. During the first, Yul told us that he would not show up for dinner on account of his stomach problem, the second was to ask his father to wake him at 5:30 on the morning of the trip and the third to tell his dad that he would not join him on account of his having had a terrible night and still being sick in bed. On all three occasions I happened to be very close to my friend and very close to the phone. In fact, I heard every single word that was said and there was never any mention of weather conditions."

"You are absolutely sure of that, Mrs. Steiger." said the Judge, "I need not remind you that you are under oath."

"Your Honour," said Annelies, accentuating every word, "I repeat that Dr. Brunner was definitely not told by Yul or by anybody else that he would have to face extra strong winds on his descent from the slopes."

"I hear you loud and clear." said the Judge. "Do you want to add anything to that testimony, Mrs. Steiger?"

"Only that during the last phone conversation, Dr. Brunner offered to take Yul to the hospital and cancel the trip, but Yul was adamant. He refused any medical care and insisted on his dad taking the trip alone."

"Thank you, Mrs. Steiger. You may step down." said the judge

After a brief recess for lunch, the hearing continued in the early afternoon. The first to be asked to the witness stand was Yul. He was duly sworn in. The Judge asked him to give a full description without omitting any details of the events leading up to the death of his Father. Yul realized that starting with the Judge, everybody in the courtroom was listening intently to his testimony. He was calm and spoke unemotionally.

"The whole story started with my Father inviting me to spend a day schussing down with him. I love skiing and accepted the invitation immediately.

I spent the day before the trip checking all my gear and equipment. In the early afternoon of that day I was in my hotel room when the manager of the Juventus Travel Agency called to tell me that they had tried to contact my father but could not reach him. Mr. Egli went on to say that since I was the other participant of the trip, he would request me to pass the information on to my father. 'What seems to be the problem?' I asked Mr. Egli. 'We just picked up a report from the weather station to the effect that they are expecting strong winds on the slopes tomorrow.' he said. 'I wanted to have your confirmation that you will proceed with the trip as planned.'

I told Mr. Egli that I would consult my father before giving the final OK for the trip. 'We must hear from him or you before five p.m. today to give us time to either cancel or go ahead.' That was the gist of my conversation with Mr. Egli," added Yul.

The Judge was listening very carefully, occasionally making notes or exchanging looks with the other officials flanking him. "Please continue, Mr. Brunner" he said. "What happened next?"

"Shortly after the telephone call from Mr. Egli, I began to feel pains in my abdominal area, like cramps accompanying an upset stomach. These pains became stronger and I had to run to the bathroom because in addition to the discomfort and shivers and headache, vomiting and diarrhoea started. I was suddenly very sick. I went to bed hoping to feel better soon. But I did not. I had a splitting headache and when I tried to go to the bathroom I felt dizzy to the point of falling to the floor. Still I hoped to feel better after a good night's rest and take the trip as planned.

At 4:30 p.m. I phoned my Father in his hotel room to inform him of the weather alert. I related to him exactly what Mr. Egli had told me earlier and warned him of the extra strain the strong winds would put on him. I asked him specifically if he did not prefer to cancel the outing. My father's reply was: 'You know that I have dealt with much more hazardous slope conditions. I will cope with the strong winds. Tell them that I thank them for the warning, but we will take the trip as planned.' Having received the Ok from my father, I phoned the travel agency to confirm the trip."

Yul took several sips of the water in front of him and after a few seconds, continued. "That night was one of the worst of my life. Not only could I not get any sleep, but I could not even rest. I felt awful. My stomach was aching like hell. My head was throbbing and I was shaking from the fever that had increased in intensity. At 5:30 a.m. when my father called to wake me I was still shivering. Naturally, I excused myself and told my father that I was in no condition to go downhill schussing. I also reminded him again of the strong winds he would have to cope with and wished him good skiing. I hung up and went back to my misery."

"Did your Father offer to take you to a hospital?" asked the Judge. "Yes, he did." replied the witness. "But I told him this was not necessary since I knew how to handle a stomach poisoning and all I needed was another day in bed. That's all."

"Thank you, Mr. Brunner." said the Judge. "You may step down. Since we are reconstructing the events in a chronological order, we will now retrace Dr. Brunner's day until his arrival at the hospital on the evening of the 27th of December.

I will now ask Mrs. Annelies Steiger to return to the witness stand and tell us what happened after the phone conversation at 5:30 in the morning. Mrs. Steiger, please."

"Before I relate to the court what happened on that day, I must point out again, Your Honour, that all the telephone conversations between father and son took place within centimetres of my ear. At no time did I hear his son tell him anything at all about the weather alert and about strong winds expected on the slopes. Nothing at all was said about that. Furthermore, no mention was made by Yul about any messages received from the travel agency. I wanted to get this off my chest, in the wake of Yul Brunner's testimony, Your Honour."

Most of the people present looked at Yul, who was sitting without any expression on his face.

Annelies continued, "Well, the day started as planned. Dr. Brunner had some coffee, showered and shaved, and after collecting all his alpine gear, he kissed me goodbye and left to take the waiting limo. Oh, no there was something else. He told me that around 11:30 he would call me from the first stop, halfway down the mountain to reassure me that everything was going according to plan."

"And did you receive that phone call, Mrs. Steiger?" asked the Judge.

"No, I did not." She replied. "In fact, I waited until 12 noon and since I did not hear from Dr. Brunner I phoned Mr. Egli at the Agency to report that fact. At that point I was beginning to worry that something was not right."

"Continue, Mrs. Steiger." pressed the Judge.

"Mr. Egli told me that he was actually on the verge of phoning me because he had received a phone call from the Station at 11:45 to the effect that the expected skier had not checked in. I then asked Mr. Egli to organize a search party immediately. Dr. Brunner could well have had an accident on his way down. Mr. Egli fully agreed, but told me that he had a problem. The helicopter pilot who had flown the skier to the top in the morning had in the meantime taken a few hours off and was not expected back in Zermatt before 4 p.m. 'We cannot wait that long,' I told him. 'How about another pilot to fly the craft?' I asked. 'I will try immediately to locate another pilot for this emergency mission', he said. But then, I had an idea. I knew that Yul was a fully qualified and licensed commercial helicopter pilot. So, I told Mr. Egli to contact him immediately. He said he would do so. About fifteen minutes later, Mr. Egli called to say that he had explained the situation to Mr. Brunner, who had refused to fly the craft on the grounds that he was very sick in bed, that he had a high fever and that he was in no condition to fly.

I could not believe this. I was furious, and asked Mr. Egli what he proposed to do now. He said he would first send a telephone message to the regular pilot, asking him to hurry back to Zermatt and also that he would try to find alternative pilots. 'I will keep in touch with you as soon as I know more' were Mr. Egli's last words."

"I also did something else." continued Annelies, "I picked up the phone and implored Yul to go to his father's rescue. I obviously talked to a brick wall. He said he could only repeat what he had already told the Agency. He was too sick to fly and hung up."

The Judge thanked Annelies and asked her to step down. "We have two more witnesses to hear from tonight." said the Judge, "Then, I will prepare my report and ask you all to come back tomorrow to hear my decision as to where we will go from here."

First I would like to call on Mr. Valenti, Head Concierge at the Alprösli Hotel. I have asked Mr. Valenti to discuss a number of points with his colleagues before coming here and to bring with him the log book of the night porter so as to be in a position to answer any questions regarding the whereabouts of his hotel guest, Mr. Yul Brunner. Will you please come forward, Mr. Valenti," he said.

The rotund, bald, middle-aged concierge moved to the front and flashing the smile he had honed for three decades when talking to hotel guests, he said to the Judge, "I am ready, Your Honour".

"That is very nice, Mr. Valenti", said the Judge. "Thank you. You have the records of some of the activities that involved room 412, the room occupied by Mr. Yul Brunner".

"Yes, Your Honour" said the concierge. "I have the records from room service, from housekeeping, from the front desk and from the switchboard, if that is what you mean, Sir."

"Yes, this and your own observations while you were on duty are of particular interest to this hearing. So, what can you tell us that can shed light on the events of these two days we are presently reviewing?"

Toni Valenti was obviously ready to tell everything he had found out or had observed while standing behind his desk under the concierge's traditional sign of the two crossed keys. "First of all, Your Honour, there is the incident of Mr. Brunner coming up to my desk at around 2:00 p.m. on the 26th of December asking me to give him a note with a telephone message that had been placed in his father's key box. He said to me, 'Somebody just left a message for me, but apparently it is marked "Dr. Brunner" my father, whereas it should be "Mr. Brunner". This message is actually for me. Could I have it?' I saw no problem in this request and handed the message over to Mr. Yul sitting right here." The Judge immediately made a note on his pad.

"Anything else, Mr. Valenti?" asked the Judge.

"Well, yes, I have the records of room service here and they show that during the period of December 26 to 27, room service delivered to Mr. Yul Brunner's room four complete meals, two bottles of Beaujolais Superieur, two bottles of Dom Perignon champagne as well as several orders of assorted brandies."

"Did the waiters delivering all these foods and drinks to room 412 report anything unusual?"

"No, Your Honour." said the concierge. "They did not report anything unusual and neither did the maids repeatedly making up the room. Apparently, Mr. Brunner was sitting alone at his desk reading or watching TV while they were cleaning up. They also reported that the bed had not been used at all during the day and evening. When they opened the bed for the night at 9:30 p.m., the two beds had not been touched. Furthermore, there were no indications whatsoever that someone in the room was sick or needed help."

"Thank you very much, Mr. Valenti." said the Judge. "You have been most helpful. I dare say, more helpful than you think. You may step down."

At this point the Judge said: "Ladies and Gentlemen, let us all stretch our legs for 15 minutes. I am calling a brief recess."

When they reconvened, it was Mr. Egli's sad task to describe how, where and when they had found Dr. Brunner.

Without any introductory remarks, Mr. Egli went straight to the point: "Following Pilot Brunner's refusal, I and two of my assistants phoned every possible place to recruit someone to fly the rescue mission. We even tried the military airbase in the neighbouring Kanton, but in the end it was the original pilot who came to the rescue. He took a small Cessna plane from Zürich to here and managed to climb into our helicopter together with the two guides I had summoned at about 2:00 p.m. By 2:30 p.m. the craft was scanning the slopes at close range, sometimes so close that the snow was blinding them. It did not take long for them to spot a snow covered small elevation. The pilot decided to put the craft down just beside the mound despite the very strong winds that were blowing around them. What they found indeed confirmed their worst fears. Dr. Brunner was lying on his side in a crouched position. The glove from his right hand was removed and his hand was clutching his chest. His face was distorted as if experiencing severe pain. The body was lifeless. He was immediately placed in the helicopter and given oxygen. About 20 minutes later he was brought to the St. Benedict Hospital in Zermatt. During the short flight he could not be revived. That is all I have to say, Your Honour. Like the rest of us, I am heartbroken and wish to express my condolences to his close relatives." Mr. Egli was obviously very shaken at the end of his testimony.

"Thank you, Mr. Egli, for a very vivid account of events. You may step down. And now," he continued, "we will hear from the final witness. It's just as well," he added, "I am sure we are all tired after a long day. We will now hear from Dr. Beat Stuckli, Cardiologist-in-Chief at St. Benedict Hospital. It was he who established the death of Dr. Brunner and I have the death certificate right in front of me. So, doctor, I read that you diagnosed the cause of death as being an acute coronary thrombosis, or in layman's terms a heart attack."

"That is correct." Said Dr. Stuckli, a handsome fiftyish man with greying wavy hair.

"Do you want to add something to that official diagnosis?" asked the Judge.

"Yes indeed, Your Honour," said the doctor. "Dr. Brunner did actually not die of the heart attack itself. He died of hypothermia, that is exposure to the cold and the wind. Had he been brought to us just two hours before the actual rescue, we could have definitely saved his life. The coronary thrombosis itself was neither a massive nor fatal one. There was plenty of muscle tissue in the myocardium left unaffected by the necrosis. What I mean to say is that what really killed Dr. Brunner was his being found and brought to the hospital too late for resuscitation. It is a great pity that the life of a 65 year old man in his most productive time was lost because of his delayed rescue. And there is another thing I would like to mention. It is actually referred to in an addendum to the death certificate, Doctor Bernier and I signed on behalf of the hospital.

During the autopsy we found an inordinate accumulation of lactic acid not only in the myocardium, that is the heart muscle, but in Dr. Brunner's legs, chest and arm muscles indicating extreme physical exertion just prior to his heart attack. Dr. Brunner must have spent a superhuman effort to cope with the strong winds that were practically blowing him off the trail. To summarize, Dr. Rudolf Brunner's death was the result of a heart attack caused by extreme physical exertion due to his having to fight against the strong winds. Also, by having been brought to our hospital too late, much too late. That is all I have to say, Your Honour." concluded the well-known cardiologist.

There was complete silence in the courtroom. As the last witness regained his seat, all eyes were on Yul Brunner. He sat there staring at nothing at all. His face was devoid of any emotional expression as if the whole matter had nothing to do with him.

The judge let the weight of the cardiologist's last words sink in for some minutes before addressing the audience. "Ladies and Gentlemen," he finally said: "I want to thank you all for a very revealing session. I believe we have heard most of what is relevant in the case of the death of Dr. Rudolf Brunner. I will now ask your indulgence for one more day to give me time to prepare my assessment and interpretation of the evidence presented today. As I told you this morning, my conclusions will entail two possible consequences. Either I find no evidence of any wrongdoing whatsoever in this matter and I will recommend to the State Prosecutor to consider it closed. In which case everybody present here today will be free to go home and deal with the passing of Dr. Rudolf Brunner in his or her own way, or, Ladies and Gentlemen, I will find reason beyond any doubt that something wrong, something wilfully wrong has taken place in the matter of the death of Dr. Brunner.

In this second instance I will, of course, recommend that the case be brought before a Court of Justice in which today's witnesses, guided by lawyers and other counsel will have to explain their involvement and, perhaps submit to cross examination. The proceedings will be submitted to a jury of twelve ordinary people, who, using only their common sense and judgement will decide whether anyone among you is guilty and of what. The final decision will then belong to the Judge, who will pronounce the verdict.

Ladies and Gentlemen, I need not tell you that I have a very busy day ahead of me. May I ask you to reconvene right here, in the same place on the day after tomorrow at 9:00 hours. I do not foresee a lengthy session. Unless I have some additional questions to ask, the whole meeting should be over by twelve noon. Again, thank you all for your cooperation."

It was almost six o'clock when everybody filed out of the courthouse into the cold and windy evening.

* * * * *

Annelies had a very busy day starting early next morning. She had to pay all the hotel bills, she had to make arrangements with the undertakers, pack, and most of all, brace herself for a new reality. That of a life without her beloved Rudi. He was gone for good and she had to prepare herself for a completely changed and, as far as she could foresee, very difficult life. Rudi had been the centre of her everyday existence. For many years professionally and for the last few years also emotionally. She loved him very much.

She asked the family lawyer to help her in dealing with the problems and tasks that lay ahead, many of which she was not even aware of at this point. As she expected, he immediately pledged complete support in every possible way. He too had to cope with the sudden loss of a very close friend. "You can count on my wife and myself to help you sail through these hard times. There will be a thousand details to take care of before your life will be somewhat back to normal. We will be there for you." he said to Annelies. She knew he meant every word of it.

The day after the inquest, Annelies received many phone calls from family and friends, all expressing grief and sympathy over the unexpected news. She did not hear a word from Yul. Although she could think of many explanations for his silence, she nevertheless had expected some communication from him.

The day of the Judge's announcement dawned under dark grey winter skies. Annelies and the family lawyer joined the other witnesses in taking their seats in the courtroom. The Judge was a few minutes late. He looked tired and drawn as he greeted the small audience. Without much ado he read the statement he had prepared for the occasion.

"This, Ladies and Gentlemen is the introduction to the report I have prepared for the Public Prosecutor of the Kanton. Attached to and part of the report is a more or less verbatim transcript of the proceedings of the day before yesterday. My decision and recommendations to the Federal Prosecutor are summarized in the text I will now read to you.

In the case of the death of Dr. Rudolf Albert Brunner of No. 22 Bundesstrasse, Zürich which occurred on the slopes of the Matterhorn on December 27, I recommend that the Public Prosecutor indict Mr. Yul Brunner, the son of the deceased on the grounds that he was wilfully negligent and a premeditated conspirator in the death of his father. I base my decision on conclusions from the testimony presented to me by the witnesses, whose names and addresses appear at the end of the report. I am referring in particular to the following discrepancies in the sworn statement of Mr. Yul Brunner:

No. 1: It is clear beyond reasonable doubt that Yul Brunner withheld from his Father the weather report about the strong winds expected on the day of the outing. Had Dr. Brunner known about this important weather change he might have cancelled the fateful trip.

No. 2: It is clear beyond any reasonable doubt that Mr. Yul Brunner's refusal to join his father on the trip on the grounds that he was sick in bed with a severe digestive ailment was not true because he drank and ate a number of heavy meals washed down with wines and champagnes ordered to his room throughout the day and night.

No. 3: It is clear beyond any reasonable doubt that Mr. Yul Brunner's refusal to pilot the helicopter on a rescue flight, which, according to reputable medical opinion could have saved the life of Dr. Brunner on the grounds that he was too sick to fly was questionable because of the same reasons mentioned under No. 2. Furthermore, we have testimony from two maids who came to Mr. Brunner's room during the day to the effect that he did not at all appear to be sick in bed. In fact, he never used the bed during that day.

No. 4: Based on the sworn statements deposited by Mrs. Steiger, Mr. Egli and Mr. Valenti I have reason to believe that Mr. Brunner repeatedly lied while testifying under oath.

The Judge removed his glasses as he finished reading from the papers in front of him.

"I regret to have come to these conclusions, Ladies and Gentlemen, but my mandate from the Police Magistrate was to establish the facts of the event and make recommendations. This I did to the best of my ability and with your help for which I am very grateful indeed.

And where do we go from here? Very simply, you all have to wait for a summons to appear in court. In the meantime, the Bailiff who is sitting right here will ask you all to sign affidavits to the effect that you will not travel outside Switzerland unless you notify your local police of your whereabouts. This applies to all of you, except for Mr. Yul Brunner who will be required to sign an affidavit to wit that he will not leave his present place of residence without notifying the police and that he will not leave the country until further notice. You are, of course, free to exercise your profession and go about your life as usual.

And now, as promised, you are out of here before lunch time. Thank you again for your cooperation. Goodbye."

Since the press and the media were not invited to the inquest nothing about what had gone on during the hearing reached the public. All that was known was that Dr. Rudolf Brunner, the prominent Zürich dentist and University Professor had suffered a fatal heart attack while skiing in Zermatt.

That is why the news that the Federal Court in Zürich had sent out summonses to all the witnesses participating in the inquest as well as to some additional people hit the media with fanfare and bold headlines. The reason for the opening of a court action was given as the public prosecutor's decision to indict Yul Brunner as a suspected party in the death of his father.

The first session of the Court was set for early May, barely five months after the event, a record turnaround for Swiss Courts, who usually take much longer to deal with criminal cases.

* * * * *

The proceedings of the Swiss Confederation versus Yul Brunner opened with the full complement of all witnesses as well as their lawyers in attendance. In addition to the original participants at the Inquest, the Court also had asked the two guides who found Dr. Brunner's body and carried him into the helicopter, the pilot of the Juventus Agency helicopter and the two maids who had been in Yul's room on the 25th and 26th of December.

The fact that the victim was none other than the well-known Dr. Rudolf Brunner attracted a crowd as well as representatives of the media who had to wait outside the courtroom for an opportunity to snap photos or fire questions at the witnesses.

Right from the start, Yul was read his indictment by the Prosecutor, most of it reflecting the findings of the Judge at the Inquest. Yul pleaded "not guilty" to all charges. He was seconded by a young and aggressive lawyer who had to be reprimanded repeatedly by the Judge for words and gestures not befitting an officer of a Swiss Federal court. Obviously Yul had made a bad choice, especially as far as impressing the jury was concerned. Instead of trying to gain their sympathy during his defence speeches, the lawyer managed to turn them against his client by belittling accusations or failing to address them properly.

As was to be expected, the entire chain of events from the visit of Rudi Brunner to the Juventus Travel Agency booking the trip to its catastrophic ending was reviewed.

During the three days of proceedings, the Judge followed essentially the same line and sequence of questioning as his colleague in Zermatt. He also read a great deal from the extensive statements that had been made during the inquest and asked the witnesses if they had anything to add.

Much, if not all, of what the witnesses said incriminated Yul. There was the statement from the concierge that Yul had appropriated the telephone message from the Juventus Travel Agency by lying to him. There were the reports from the two maids testifying that Yul was not sick in bed but devouring huge meals while listening to rock music when they entered his room on several occasions. Mr. Egli testified that Yul lied to him when he claimed that he had obtained his father's consent to proceed despite the worsening weather conditions. Perhaps the most damning statements were made by Annelies, who, under the prosecutor's cross examination revealed aspects of Yul's improper behaviour towards her as well as the disparaging and hateful remarks about his father he made during the unwanted courtship. All of this left little doubt about some of Yul's motives for wanting to eliminate his father from the face of the earth.

After all statements were heard, the prosecutor rose to accuse Yul of obviously lying, of withholding and destroying evidence and of cruelty, all of which clearly and undeniably led to his father's death.

After the recess, the prosecutor asked the cardiologist from St. Benedict hospital to take the stand. His report, presented with clear-cut precision impressed everyone especially the members of the jury when he emphasized that it was not the heart attack, a relatively minor one, but the delay in getting him to the hospital that caused the death of Dr. Brunner. As for the coronary itself, the extreme physical exertion by a sixty-five year old man battling against gale force winds could certainly be described as one, if not, the contributing factor.

Yul's testimony and replies during cross examination by the prosecutor were mostly defensive and weak. He kept on claiming that he was very sick at the time and that he did tell his father about the strong winds. When asked by the prosecutor how come he devoured huge meals while claiming severe food poisoning and vomiting, Yul said he could not remember what happened that night.

The deliberations had lasted for three full days. On the morning of the fourth day, the prosecutor recapped the case for the benefit of the jury. He described Yul as a spineless, bitter, revenge-seeking individual who came along on the fateful ski trip to enjoy making his father pay for extravagant meals and wines and for having another go at getting to his father's girlfriend. When he heard of the weather alert from the travel agency, he decided that this was the once-in-a-lifetime chance to get rid of this father. This was his chance to put his hands on his money and his girl.

"Ladies and gentlemen of the jury," intoned the prosecutor, "Yul Brunner thought he could get away with murder without actually pulling the trigger. But, ladies and gentlemen, Yul Brunner did not fool anybody, least not you and me. Lying, faking and cheating is one thing, but when it all ends up in the premeditated and wanted death of a person, punishment has to be meted out to the full extent of the law.

The concluding presentation by the defence tried to explain the death of Dr. Brunner as nothing else than a natural accident facing thousands of middle-aged people every day. Yul's lawyer said: "Perhaps you can accuse the defendant of forgetfulness or negligence for not warning this father about the unexpected weather hazards, you can accuse him of poor judgement in falling in love with the attractive lady friend of his father, you can even accuse him of cowardice and indifference in refusing to fly an aircraft when he did not feel up to it, but ladies and gentlemen, of the jury, you can not accuse my client of murder for Yul Brunner is not a murderer. My client may have hated his father, but that does not make him a murderer. He is the unfortunate victim of a chain of unfortunate circumstances that ended up in the death of an elderly man as a result of a heart attack while skiing. That's all. Yul Brunner is innocent of the charges brought against him by the prosecution."

The jury took two full days to deliberate. Their decision was reached unanimously.

In a strong voice the foreman said, looking at the Judge, "We, the jury, find the defendant guilty of being a contributor, a causative factor and therefore in part responsible for the death of his father, Dr. Rudolf Brunner."

It was all over for Yul. His lawyer slammed a pack of files on the table in front of him, causing the Judge to bring down his gavel several times.

Yul sat impassively in the dock, staring at nothing at all. If he felt any emotions he was hiding them very well behind a waxen face. Except for his answers during cross examination he had kept a very low profile throughout the proceedings. True to his character he confirmed his school teacher's opinion, when as a kid, he was described as "a still water that runs deep."

Annelies was visibly relieved that the whole episode was over. She was still struggling with her grief and looked tired and pale. During testimony she repeatedly cried and once she even had to leave the courtroom to get some fresh air.

Two days after the jury returned their verdict, the presiding Judge pronounced the sentence before a packed courtroom. He briefly recapped the case and when he came to the fact that the Juventus Agency did not have a pilot on standby while their client was still on the slopes, he reprimanded Mr. Egli by saying: "This court expects you to take the present case as a lesson and be better prepared for emergencies in the services you provide to the public." He then turned to Yul and asked him to stand up in anticipation of hearing the sentence.

"Based on the verdict returned by the panel of jurors, a verdict that I fully support, I herewith sentence you, Yul Brunner to three years in a federal penal institution. You will be permitted to apply for parole after two years of good behaviour in jail and on condition that the warden considers you no threat to society.

Yul Brunner, your father died for two reasons: first he suffered a heart attack most probably brought on by extreme physical exertion and secondly he was taken to hospital two hours after he could have been saved. In both of these causes, you, Mr. Brunner carry a heavy responsibility. Nobody can establish with a hundred percent accuracy the exact extent of your share in this responsibility. If we could, this sentence would have been much harsher, perhaps even prison for life. But of one thing we are all certain: you had several motives to eliminate your father. Therefore you did all you could, and I mean *all you could* to bring about his death and that, Mr. Brunner is the burden you will have to live with for the rest of your life. Compared to this curse, your three years in jail is a very light punishment indeed. *I do not envy you*, Mr. Brunner."

The judge brought down the gavel and declared the court now adjourned.

*****

Annelies Steiger, assisted by the trusted family lawyer, took several months to liquidate all the assets of the late Rudi Brunner. She also took possession of her inheritance which was the same as Laura had been allocated before her, namely seventy-five percent of the estate. After saying goodbye to all their friends in and around Zurich, she left for Tübingen, Germany, her family home. She opened a dental clinic and lived an intellectually and socially challenging life. She freely supported a number of charitable causes and had many friends, but never remarried.

Yul served his two years in jail and was then released on parole. He took possession of the twenty-five percent left to him by his father, a sizeable amount indeed. He never went back to flying, realizing that his criminal record would certainly be an obstacle in resuming a flying career. Instead he bought himself a house in a small community on the outskirts of Basel, adjacent to the border with Germany. In due course he landed a job as head of security in a large construction company. He married a simple, unsophisticated girl from a working class home and had two children. True to his form he never talked about his time in jail and the events leading up to it. He lived an orderly, uneventful life in sharp contrast to the somewhat overbearing professional and intellectual sophistication of his childhood home. It is often said that children either follow in their parent's footsteps or they go the very opposite way.

* * * * *

Dr. Rudolf Brunner rests in the Central Cemetery of Zurich, right next to Laura's gravesite. Two vibrant, yet widely different personalities finally in unison. What life could not accomplish, death did.

Visitors who pass their sites have been heard to say, pointing to his grave: "He was a well-known doctor whose son was sent to jail for causing his death. You know what Oscar Wilde said – children begin by loving their parents; after a time they judge them; rarely, if ever, do they forgive them."

THE EXECUTIVE

Most, if not all, weddings are graceful events. For one; bride and groom are attired in their finest and so are all those present. The prevailing mood is festive to say the least and the surroundings contribute solemnity and colour to make the day an unforgettable milestone in the lives of not only the two main players, but by association, in those of several others.

William and Elizabeth Benditch's marriage was no exception. Everything at the well-orchestrated ceremony reflected the dignity and decorum of a picture perfect wedding. Guests sitting in the pews kept whispering to each other: "This must be the most beautiful couple I have ever seen. Isn't the bride absolutely gorgeous?" And that, she no doubt was.

The religious ritual was followed by the usual reception accented by well-wisher's toasts and lots of laughter and light-hearted banter. The newlyweds took to the floor to the tune of Al Jolsen's immortal "OH, HOW WE DANCED ON THE NIGHT WE WERE WED" and, after a few rounds drowned by applause, quietly sneaked out through one of the side doors to change and embark on their honeymoon, leaving their guests to carry on until late into the night. Wow! It was a beautiful affair indeed.

And thus started Bill and Liz's family life.

They were an exceptional couple, to be sure. She, the daughter of a moderately successful accountant and his homemaking wife, was by all accounts a stunning beauty. Her dark hair surrounded a roundish face with the most regular and pleasing features one could imagine. She was truly a pleasure to look at because every one of her traits was in perfect harmony with the rest. Her light green eyes, her stubby nose, her full lips and her peachy skin combined to create an angelic face of classic and serene beauty. But it is by viewing all of her appearance that both men and women took a second and perhaps a third look. Liz had a truly stunning figure that complemented her facial features not unlike a Greek statue or a classical painting. No wonder Bill had fallen head over heels for her, like the proverbial ton of bricks, the very moment he set eyes on her at a friend's party.

Bill, twenty-eight at the time, was certainly what could be described as a good-looking and athletic young man. But, there was much more to him than his looks. He was smart, well-read and witty, and, on the wall of his office hung a SUMMA CUM LAUDE MBA diploma from a prestigious New England business college.

In fact, despite his relatively young age, Bill was sales manager of a pharmaceutical company with some sixty sales representatives spanning the whole of Canada. Bill was well-liked by both his salesmen and his superiors, who saw in him unmistakable senior and perhaps even top management material.

By contrast, however, Liz was by no means a match to her husband's intellect. She had made it through high school with relative ease but when she entered college, she came to realize that she was surrounded by so many much brainier classmates that she often felt like a babe in the woods or a country bumpkin when participating in discussions on subjects of even moderate sophistication. At first she thought that reading up on curricular material would provide the required background, but after immersing herself in books on history or literature, she soon discovered that she lacked the stamina to go all the way to the end of her reading material. She sensed that if she found it so difficult to cope with everyday geography, how would she cope with all the other subjects that could be thrown at her not only for intellectual absorption, but later on for writing complex exam papers.

And so, a few months after enrollment she decided to call it quits and perhaps opt for a less demanding education. After some thought she chose a course of "medical secretary", and, after a relatively easy training period, she started work at a busy dental clinic on the West Island.

She liked her job, and having no difficulty in surrounding herself with nice young men who knew a good thing when they saw one, she was regularly invited to parties and outings.

* * * * *

Liz & Bill Benditch had met at one of her boyfriend's parties. Introduced to her as: "Hey Liz, meet my tennis buddy, Bill. I don't know much about his other qualifications, but on the tennis court he beats the living daylights out of me, Haha!"

And so began a relationship that soon blossomed into intimacy and love. To be sure, most of the emotional involvement came from Liz, who saw in Bill not only a very virile and imaginative lover, but more importantly a man of substance and countenance she could look up to. Bill soon became her hero, her knight in shining armour as well as her mentor. Fully aware of the fact that in almost every field of knowledge he was so much ahead of her, she hoped he would raise her to his own level. She was very proud that a man like Bill had chosen her to be his friend and after-hours partner.

To live up to her role in this relationship, Liz thought she must try to render herself indispensable for Bill. Thus, she constantly planned weekends and all other social activities, taking care of reservations and all the rest. She also started selecting clothes for him, often meeting Bill with the words: "Oh, I saw a beautiful tie to go with your blue suit" or "I want you to look at some sports shirts to wear on the weekend. You keep using dress shirts which make you look older. How about some colour and short sleeves?"

Thus, within a year or so after they met, she had entered his life not only as a sex partner, but also as a lovingly concerned all-out companion. A combination very few men could resist. In fact, a cocktail that, in due course, went to Bill's head, leading him straight to the altar.

*****

Bill and Liz Benditch settled down to the customary lifestyle of their generation and social standing. They moved into a nice semi-detached duplex in Beaconsfield on the West Island. Together, they furnished and decorated the entire house, enjoying it immensely. Liz continued her receptionist's activities, albeit now reduced to three days a week.

Some three years into their marriage, Bill told Liz one day that he had decided to leave his company for another, better one, because they had offered him the position of sales and marketing manager, reporting directly to the company's vice president.

And so, days blended into weeks and weeks into months in what seemed like the life of an average upscale family. Until the day Liz phoned Bill from the doctor's office to give him the happy news that she was expecting a baby.

The next few months passed by under the impact of this announcement. Liz left her job not only to concentrate on her pregnancy, but also because she felt she had to compensate for her blemished physical appearance by increasingly occupying herself with Bill. She cooked his favourite meals, she kept his wardrobe in immaculate shape and she generally saw to it that her husband's wishes and needs were carried out to a tee.

Liz was convinced that she was fully living up to her role as the perfect wife.

The pregnancy was largely uneventful except for the couple's pre-occupation with any and all aspects of the forthcoming family addition. From selecting a fitting name, to clothes, to toys and to decorating the baby's room - every detail became the subject of after-dinner and weekend conversations mostly initiated by Liz who seemed to be captivated by her soon-to-be motherhood. Even her customary evening greeting of: "How was your day at the office?" now made way to: "Guess what I found today in a downtown baby shop?"

On a sunny day in early May, little Freddie arrived a day or so late, but in perfect health to the utter delight of his parents and to the rapture of his grandparents. Needless to say the speculation as to who the little boy resembled more ended in a draw since no agreement could be reached by the highly biased visitors. Suffice it to say that that at the end of the day, little Freddie was pronounced the most beautiful baby on earth by all sides. Liz's hospital room actually looked more like a flower shop than a room in the obstetrics wing of the Lakeshore General Hospital.

* * * * *

To say that Freddie soon became the epicenter of attention in the Benditch household would be a blatant understatement. Everything revolved around the baby, practically on a 24-hour schedule. While Liz seemed to delight in performing all the chores that come with tending to a newborn, Bill, although happily espousing fatherhood, soon distanced himself from the mundane tasks of changing diapers or getting out of bed in the middle of the night when the baby cried. Liz ascribed this behavior simply to her husband being less domesticated and more "manly" than other new fathers among their friends.

Freddie continued to dominate his mother's life for the first couple of years while Bill continued to assume the role of a caring, genuinely interested but not overly doting father. There was at least one good reason for that: Bill had started in earnest to climb the ladder of corporate ascendancy. In fact, his efficient, no-nonsense style of management and the clearly visible results he extracted from a motivated sales force did not fail to come to the attention of the Cincinnati head office.

He was increasingly asked not only to attend international company meetings but also to formulate business plans for new product introductions and marketing techniques that were applied to the company's global network.

Liz soon came to realize that she had not married an ordinary employee like most of her friends, but some kind of powerhouse, and if she knew what was good for her, she had better keep up with this dynamo, of course to the best of her ability.

Towards the end of the sixth year of their marriage, Bill sat down with Liz one evening after Freddie had been put to bed and started to talk about his job and his foreseeable future in the company. He told Liz that he had been informed by the president that he was earmarked for senior management. In preparation for this, he would receive rotating assignments in foreign, mostly third world countries, since some of the Company's new products were widely used in Africa and the Far East. He also told Liz that these travelling assignments could come on short notice and could last for days or even weeks.

Liz listened carefully to Bill's measured and carefully chosen words which often gave her the impression of an early warning of what was in store for her and their family life.

If this after dinner conversation was meant to be an advance notice it was certainly not wasted on Liz. Already beset by guilt feelings of neglect towards Bill on account of her preoccupation with the baby, she decided to do everything possible to resume her role of doting wife, passionate lover and close companion she had played so well in the early years of their marriage.

Taking advantage of Bill's steadily increasing income she bought herself dresses to accentuate her still impressive physical assets. She retained the services of a young girl to help with both housekeeping chores and looking after Freddie. She was often able to call Bill at the office: "Guess what? Darling, I reserved a table for dinner at your favourite seafood place. Don't be late!"

Bill seemed to respond to this accelerated lifestyle with tempered satisfaction expressed as: "Thank you, dear. You think of everything, you really do!" And yet, Liz increasingly felt that their wild, passionate relationship had run its course and that in its place a steadily growing distance was developing between them.

What really confirmed this awareness was when they came home one evening from an outing and Bill, instead of going to bed, went straight to the computer. He said to Liz: "Oh, I have to go over some points in my presentation to the board tomorrow morning. Why don't you go to bed and I'll join you later", to which Liz replied jokingly: "are you sure I can't help you?" rushing up to him for a kiss. Bill quickly turned to his desk and said: "Yes, I am sure, dear. Believe me; you wouldn't understand a single line in my presentation. Not if your life depended on it. You go to bed, Okay? I won't be long."

These few words, although spoken without any malice hurt Liz very much. To her, this was an obvious reference to her intellectual inability to keep up with his professional life and to be just good for bed and keeping a nice and orderly home. Not that she was not aware of her shortcomings. Bill rarely discussed any business aspects of his job with her except occasional references to office gossip or personnel changes. But Bill's words, delivered in a matter-of-fact, rather than a joking tone, hit her like a cold shower. To her this was a clear indication that she was definitely not part of his "inner circle".

Without another word, not even a "good night", Liz left the room.

This relationship went on for some time. Liz continued to divide her time between bringing up Freddie and tending to her home and to her husband. She never changed her attitude of giving Bill all the attention and love she was capable of and that was by all standards, a great deal. He, increasingly, assumed the role of a satisfied husband who takes his family life for granted. He acted out his part as father by taking Freddie to the playgrounds, teaching him the basics of hockey and baseball and whatever else fathers are supposed to do. Freddie dearly loved and perhaps even adored his dad.

Bill was fully aware of Liz's romantic advances but he never went overboard reciprocating them. Liz often felt as if they had been married too long and there was little left the two had to say to each other. This feeling greatly pained her, especially when she wore a new or sexy dress and Bill failed to take notice of it although she had bought it just to please him.

In time, Liz reached the conclusion that this must be the ultimate fate of all romantic marriages. Nothing is forever and even the wildest passion eventually ebbs and fades. This, she could somehow accept but what really gnawed at her pride and ego was Bill's refusal to share any part of his office life with her. She even started to ask herself: "Does this man not need to talk about his professional life with anyone outside his company? Is he really that self-sufficient?" And when she followed this train of thought a voice within her proffered a sinister answer: "Maybe there is another woman in his life with whom he does share some things, including his business life. This thought soon became her "idée fixe" which increasingly explained a number of aspects in his behavior. And yet, none of these forebodings were strong enough to confront her husband and demand an explanation for his growing aloofness.

Liz's doubts and apprehensions were soon to be answered and it started, not with a domestic confrontation but, of all things, with a small dinner party at Montreal's RITZ CARLTON HOTEL. Hosted by the president of Bill's company, the guests were to celebrate Bill's appointment as vice-president, one of six in the organization. He was now in charge of market development with responsibility for expanding the company's current range of products as well as their market penetration. A pivotal and, accordingly, well remunerated position indeed.

It was at this dinner party also attended by three other division heads and their spouses that Liz noticed a silent yet unmistakable affinity or closeness between her husband and Jennifer Brooks, the personnel manager. Jenny, as they all called her, was single, in her mid-thirties and attractive without being beautiful. Sexy enough to draw any man's attention, there was a certain self-assurance radiating from her assertive personality. Jenny was obviously very well versed in the company's affairs and repeatedly engaged in lively and witty repartees with the other managers including the president.

The dinner itself was lavish, the ambiance was bubbly and the president's speech was mercifully short, but explicit enough to laud Bill for his past achievements and to briefly describe his new responsibilities. The president was particularly proud of the decision by the U.S. head office to keep Bill in Montreal, given that his area of responsibility was now more of a global nature. The president considered this a clear indication of the Canadian subsidiary's leading role in the company's worldwide organization. As was to be expected, Bill's promotion entailed a dramatic change, not only in his work, but by extension, also in his family life. From now on, he was a world traveler, like he said in his acceptance speech at the RITZ dinner: "I am now joining the brigade of those who have breakfast in Hong Kong, dinner in Berlin and their luggage is in Bangkok."

Bill immediately immersed himself in his new duties and soon confirmed Liz's foreboding that he would now become a guest; a visitor in his own home. In fact, there were days when he left the house at dawn to catch an early morning flight, leaving behind notes and reminders for both Liz and Freddie. He attended to the duties and obligations that come with being a husband and a father but it was all done in a business-like manner, often with the help of his very efficient office secretary.

For all intents and purposes, the warmth and interactive closeness had gone out of the Benditch marriage.

* * * * *

Liz's apprehensions concerning Jennifer following her observations during the president's dinner party were, alas, correct.

From the faint perfume on Bill's clothes when she hung them up in the closet, to the practical impossibility to track down his whereabouts due to his frequent travels, Liz became increasingly convinced that Bill had an extra-marital life. He continued to observe the rules of civility and correctness expected of a family man but Liz could see through all of this and what she saw was a husband drifting away from her.

And the more this feeling took hold of her, the angrier she became. To be sure, she was not angry at herself, for as far as she was concerned, she had fully lived up to all the obligations and to all the vows she agreed to when she married Bill. She had given him everything, her youth, her unlimited love, her devotion and loyalty. She had even given him a handsome and bright boy, who was now in his second year of elementary school. When comparing her role as a wife to some of her friends, she felt confident that she had gone out of her way to make her husband the happiest man in the world.

It was perfectly clear to her that Bill had drifted because his professional success had gone to his head and because he was tempted by the many younger and attractive girls surrounding him. Liz thought of the old adage that "when a man becomes rich, his wife is not pretty anymore."

For a number of months, Liz acted out her role as the silent victim in the same way as Bill played his role as a titular husband. Both pretended that "business was as usual" yet both knew otherwise.

But then, something happened that abruptly and painfully put an end to this unreal state of affairs.

It was the night that Freddie was hospitalized because of an accident during a school outing. He had fallen from a cliff protruding into a lake in the Laurentians and had sustained two broken bones and some lacerations. Liz rushed to the hospital and, on the way, called Bill on his cell phone. He had left the day before for a company meeting in Boston. But when she spoke to him, he said: "What hospital? Okay, I'll be right over!" And so he was, half an hour later. Bill was obviously not in Boston.

Freddie underwent complicated emergency surgery and eventually recovered with no trace or consequences of the accident. But Bill and Liz's marriage did not.

After having spent most of the night at the hospital, Bill and Liz drove home when the doctor told them: "We fixed him up. He will be as good as new. No need to worry." They both fell into sofas to catch a few hours sleep but when Liz served breakfast around noon; she opened up on the moribund stage of their relationship, not with hysterical recriminations, but with an outwardly cool: "So, Bill, it's all over?"

Bill, slowly sipping his coffee, simply said after an endless silence: "Yes, if I understand you rightly, I'm afraid the marriage is over. I'm sure it doesn't come as a complete surprise to you. I tried not to hurt you and kept putting this conversation off for as long as I could, but that doesn't make any sense, does it? You can't make an omelet without breaking the eggs. I guess we have to face up to it. I am very sorry that this talk had to take place when Freddie is in the hospital, but perhaps it is just as well. It had to come out anyway."

Liz was now crying silently. Without saying a word she kept wiping the tears from her eyes.

After a long silence, Bill continued: "Listen, Liz, I hope we can go through this like two mature people without hurting each other too much. Some marriages work out, some others don't. It's as simple as that. I'm really sorry ours did not. I know how much you tried to make it go, and, believe me, so did I but I obviously failed. I don't want you to worry about living expenses. You and Freddie will be as comfortable as before at least for the time being. Of course, the lawyers will work out the details, but if you agree to let me go, I will see to it that you will not come to harm financially in any shape or form.

I need to tell you that I continue to respect you for all you have done and I am deeply concerned about Freddie and his future. I know how much he means to you and how much you two need each other. He will stay with you, and as I said, I will take care of all of your and his reasonable expenses until he completes his education and can stand on his own two feet."

Bill stopped talking and looked at Liz who was clutching her handkerchief, but was not crying any more. She suddenly looked years older and stared straight ahead, avoiding any eye contact with Bill. Taking advantage of the silence following Bill's last words, she now looked at him and said: "Do you think I didn't know what was going on behind my back? I sensed it a long time ago that you were having an affair with another woman. But I thought it might be a passing thing, that your new job went to your head and that, after a while, you would come back to us. But now I see I was a fool to expect this from you." "Bill" she continued, raising her voice. "I gave you everything I had because I loved you and because I wanted to make you happy, but, apparently all this was not good enough for you. You, nobody else, but you broke up a home and a family and neither I nor your son will ever forget that. And we will never forgive you, never. Get out of my life and go to your lover. Tell her about the hearts you have broken, tell her what you destroyed in exchange for her favours. I don't want to see you ever again. Now, pack your things and get out of this house. I am glad Freddie is not at home to witness all of this, but don't you worry. I will tell him what a fine man his daddy is".

Bill jumped up from his chair and shouted: "No, you will not do this. I love my son and will do everything to help him grow up as a decent man. You cannot vent your hatred for me on this innocent boy."

"You asked for it, didn't you" Liz shouted back. With that she left the kitchen and went upstairs, while Bill slowly walked out of the house which had been their home for close to ten years.

What had started as a beautiful dream and came to life as the perfect union of two people who seemed to have everything for living happily together, had come to a screeching halt, like a car at the end of a road.

The next few months were utterly painful for all participants in this drama.
Bill's lawyer, a close family friend almost immediately contacted Liz to tell her that if she consented to the divorce, she would receive the fully paid-up house and monthly alimony payments until she remarried and Freddie completed his education. Bill asked for regular time with his son and full consultation before any decisions were made about Freddie's studies and other important matters.

Liz agreed and signed the necessary papers, allowing the divorce to proceed smoothly and without the rancour and recriminations that often accompany separations. Liz was impressed with the speed with which the lawyer handled the case and wondered why Bill was so anxious to put the matter behind him.

She was soon to know the reason for the haste. Two days after the divorce had been officially finalized, the lawyer informed Liz that Bill was about to marry Jennifer Brooks, the mother of a three-year old boy fathered by none other than Bill Benditch.

This news came as a terrible shock to Liz. Not only had Bill abandoned her for another woman, but for years he had led a double life, had lied to both her and Freddie. Like a con artist, he had made a mockery of marriage, of fatherhood and of all the values embodied in family life. Liz felt betrayed by a man, who until recently had shared her bed, and indeed her whole life.

All she could say to the lawyer was: "Tell Bill that if I lived to be a hundred, I never want to see him again. I hate him. I really do!"

* * * * *

It took Liz a long time to get over the worst of the trauma caused by the separation. But several events helped her during the painful transition period. First, she went back to the dental clinic she had worked for years ago and found out that two of the original team of four dentists were still working there and they both told Liz that she was welcome to resume her former duties beginning next week. Liz was very happy, not only because of the regular income but also because the nine-to-five job would take her mind off the many unpleasant thoughts that kept ruminating in her mind.

Besides, her almost immediate employment went a long way in boosting her bruised ego and general morale.

Freddie was now almost nine years old and with a bit of planning and the help of her next-door neighbor, she could manage both the boy's daily activities as well as her job reasonably well. Millions of working mothers could do it, why shouldn't she?

Another event that helped Liz cope with the reality of her new life was the news from Freddie that his dad had told him about the company moving from Montreal to Toronto. Liz greatly welcomed this, since it meant that she would be spared running into Bill or Jenny at the local supermarket or the shopping mall.

And so, the two Benditch families slowly settled into their new lives. The sharp pain following the initial shock was subsiding and everyone adapted to the reality of their day to day routine.

But, as can be expected from people in their active midlife, it would not take long before events changed and redirected the course of their lives.

*****

Liz adapted reasonably well to her new role as a single mother. In fact, despite the disillusionment and pain brought on by the divorce and betrayal by the man she loved, she still held a number of assets in her hand. She now had an interesting and absorbing job, she owned a very nice house, she received monthly alimony payments and she was still young and attractive. But, most of all, she had a handsome and bright boy to care for. When she sat down on her bed after a long and busy day, she often said to herself: "Stop looking back, you came out pretty unscathed from this brouhaha. Count your blessings and rebuild your life." Positive thinking and confidence in herself now became her philosophy of life. And this attitude soon began to pay off.

One of the original dentists in her clinic, a handsome widower in his late fifties took her out for dinner repeatedly and eventually asked her to marry him. Despite the difference in age, she found Dr. Brian Gold to be very considerate and even romantic. He spoiled her with flowers and gifts and promised to do everything in his power to make her happy.

Brian had two married children, both living in Vancouver and he soon managed to gain the respect and admiration, if not outright love, of Freddie. He took the two of them on trips and was the perfect gentleman in the eyes of both Liz and her growing boy.

Freddie occasionally spoke to his father over the phone and sometimes went to Toronto for a one or two day get-together, usually before Christmas or during summer recess. He never gossiped or criticized his dad but it was very clear to Liz that the boy was fully aware of the harm he had inflicted on her.

Without much fanfare, Liz became Mrs. Gold in a discreet yet moving ceremony followed by an elegant reception in a downtown hotel.

As was to be expected, Liz and Freddie moved into Brian's very attractive home on the lakeshore and she sold her own home for a handsome sum. With the guidance of Brian, she invested the money wisely.

All in all, Liz was now a well-to-do middle-aged lady, with nary a worry, except that of running a typical upper bourgeois family.

*****

After his marriage to Jenny and their relocation to Toronto, Bill continued to climb the corporate ladder. After a few years in one or the other position, he finally made it to president and C.E.O. of the Canadian subsidiary. He now had some three hundred people reporting to him and carried the responsibilities of making Canada shine at international company meetings. There was no doubt in anyone's mind that Bill Benditch was indeed an inspired leader and manager of people.

Jenny and Bill and their young son, Harold, had settled into a beautiful home in one of Toronto's most exclusive neighborhoods. They soon became part of a closely-knit group of friends who shared their addiction to sports, travel, cultural sophistication and, most of all, professional prosperity. Attending the opening of the opera season at Covent Garden in London and combining it with a glittering night on the town in Paris before returning to Toronto was one of the many "guess what we decided to do next weekend" greetings, members of the group heard from their wives when coming home from a long day at the office.

Bill and Jenny truly enjoyed this life in the fast lane. It seemed as if they were made for it. Most of their friends had children, and, although they were all loving, and even doting parents, it was clear that they had opted for a lifestyle in which bringing up children did neither prevent nor interfere with living the exciting life of upscale couples.

*****

Liz continued to enjoy the comfortable life she had snuggled into years ago. Freddie now had a law degree from McGill to his credit and had managed to find employment in a large Toronto legal firm.

Dr. Brian Gold retired after a long and successful dental practice. He and Liz started to take prolonged vacations replete with Alaskan cruises and African safaris. It seemed as if Brian wanted to make up for his many years of facing gaping mouths day in and day out. No sooner had they come back from one trip that he started to plan the next one. At times Liz felt that her husband was burning the candle at both ends. And, alas, she was right. During one of the trips to St. Petersburg and an extensive tour of the Hermitage collection, Brian went to one of the washrooms. But when he failed to join Liz and the other tour members and she went to look for him, security guards found a locked toilet. Forcing it open, they saw Brian lying on the floor. He was rushed to a nearby hospital where the doctors pronounced him dead of cardiac arrest. He was just a few days short of his seventieth birthday. In fact, he and Liz had planned to celebrate the happy event aboard the cruise ship.

Two days later a truly heartbroken Liz returned to Montreal in a plane that also carried the remains of her deceased husband. It was a tragic end to a very happy life that Liz and also Freddie had enjoyed in the company of a remarkably kind and gentle man.

Brian was laid to rest at a funeral ceremony attended by his grieving two sons and their families who had flown in from Vancouver, and by a helplessly sobbing Liz. She had gotten attached to Brian even more than she realized.

Unbeknownst to her, Brian had not only willed their home on the lakeshore to her, but also one third of his entire estate.

*****

Bill heard about Liz's loss through Freddie. He immediately penned a "Dear Liz" note, expressing sympathy and condolences. A few days later, Liz sent him a simple "Thank you" card without the "Dear Bill" opening and without closing greetings, signed "Liz".

Apart from rare communications regarding Freddie, there was no link whatsoever between the former couple, not even on special occasions such as birthdays or Christmas. In fact, both were fully integrated and immersed in completely separate and unrelated lives.

* * * * *

The passing years had been very good for Bill. He consolidated his position as chief executive of the Canadian branch by surrounding himself with competent managers and assistants and continued to run the business skillfully in a stable economic environment. The company was one of the major players in the pharmaceutical market and maintained its ranking without running into unexpected losses or windfall successes. At corporate headquarters in Cincinnati, he was considered a steady and reliable country manager very much in line with what was expected of him and of the Canadian subsidiary.

Bill's personal lifestyle, however, was anything but conservative. Over the years, the company had seen to it that their chief executive lived in a manner befitting his position. Apart from a bungalow and a beautifully outfitted houseboat in Palm Beach, he had two company cars, one of which was a late-model Porsche. The company paid for all of his and Jenny's frequent travels as well as for their lavish entertaining in Toronto.

Jenny had kept her job, of course with periodic promotions and was now Vice-President of Human Relations and Public Affairs, a resounding title which she fully lived up to by her dedicated and highly competent work performance.

* * * * *

Bill and Jenny had now been married for some fifteen years. What had started out as a clandestine extramarital love affair had matured into a matter-of-fact union between two self-centered and assertive professionals who often glanced at balance sheets and business plans in bed before turning off the lights. This was the life of company executives and they enjoyed every moment of it, especially in view of the many perks that came with their exalted positions.

Harold was now a strapping eighteen year old, studying engineering at a technical college in upstate New York. He, himself, had opted for the opportunity to complete his education away from home, partly because his parents were so frequently away that he had gotten used to preparing his own breakfast and ordering dinner from a nearby restaurant.

* * * * *

Shortly before Bill reached his fifty-fifth birthday, he received a phone call from the president of the company in Cincinnati, informing him of their decision to offer him a seat on the international board and to make him an executive vice-president of the corporation, one step below the very top job. He was also told that the official announcement would be made in two week's time at the annual shareholders meeting. Until then, he was asked by the president to keep the news under wraps.

Bill was literally shaking as he kept thanking the president. In fact, he, the usually glib and eloquent speaker, was at a loss for words during the rest of the conversation.

This was it! He had made it. A flush of pride and joyous feeling swept over him like a rushing waterfall. He managed to keep the fantastic news for himself until the evening and then broke it to Jenny as she came home from the office. Without a word she sneaked out of the living room and came back a minute later with a chilled bottle of champagne. After uncorking it and filling their two glasses, they silently drained them and hugged each other for a long time. The only interruption was Jenny's repeated whispering into Bill's ear: "Darling, I'm so proud of you!" She was indeed, as the tears in her eyes amply proved. The rest of the evening was pure celebration over dinner and way into a night of lovemaking and sips of their favourite vintage wine. It was, by all accounts, a night to remember.

*****

Two days had passed since Bill was given the ultimate corporate nod, when he scanned the morning paper while having a quick breakfast before heading for the office. As usual he looked at the business section first, and there, on the front page he noticed a news item, announcing that one of the generic pharmaceutical companies had filed for bankruptcy. After describing the reasons that lead to the collapse of Ducopharma, the paper added that a court-appointed bankruptcy law firm had already started with the liquidation proceedings of the now defunct company.

Bill went over this item twice. He never thought that Ducopharma would fold after what everybody in the business took for a steadily growing company employing some two hundred people in Montreal.

Bill folded the newspaper and drove to the office for what he expected to be another busy day of meetings, telephone conversations and memo dictations. And so it was.

That is, until he left the company in the evening, and noticed two cars he had never seen before parked in spots reserved for senior company management. He looked up at the building and saw that the controller's office was brightly lit. That was unusual because Tim Chessky, the company's chief bean counter was known to be one of the first to leave after office hours.

Bill drove home and tried to put all this out of his mind, but when he noticed the same two cars parked in the lot the next day and saw the lights in Tim's office were still on, indicating that something was going on in the comptroller's department, he started to wonder. What, he asked himself, was happening in the company he was not being told about?

Well, Bill found out soon enough.

Hanging up his jacket after arriving in the office the next day, he noticed a slip on his desk. On it was scribbled: "Bill, please come to Tim's office right away." It was signed by Joe Preston, none other than the chairman of the company's board of directors. Joe was Bill's one and only superior in Canada.

When Bill opened the door to the comptroller's office, both Tim and Joe Preston rose. Joe said: "Good morning, Bill" and motioned him to sit down. Then, he picked up the phone and said: "Susan, be an angel and bring coffee for the three of us, and, please Susan, hold all calls. I mean 'all', okay? Thank you."

Then, after a few comments about the weather and after Susan had placed cups of coffee in front of them, Joe opened the conversation, which, for all intents and purposes, turned out to be more of a monologue. To be sure, one, that would ring in Bill's ears for a very long time.

"Well", started Joe, "believe me, Bill, I can think of a hundred different things I would rather do on this particular morning than sitting here and having to tell you what, if I am not mistaken, you may have been turning over in your mind ever since you heard that Ducopharma went belly up."

Continuing to look straight into Bill's eyes, Joe spoke with a certain unmistakable emotion in his usually measured voice: "Look, Bill", he said. "I don't want to make this into a showcase of an accusation, asking for answers, and, I want, by all means to minimize the impact and consequence of what I have to say to you. Believe me; this is very hard for me. I did spend a sleepless night. I hope you will believe me, Bill."

At the mention of the generic company's name, Bill perceptibly looked up and his facial expression changed from anticipatory to very serious.

"Okay," continued Joe, "enough of beating about the bush. Here are the bare facts: "The forensic accounting firm in charge of the liquidation of Ducopharma has discovered during their audit a box in the company's safe. In it there were documents showing that over a period of several years, while you were sales and marketing manager in Montreal, you have continuously given confidential company information to and were handsomely paid for this by Ducopharma.

First, let me be precise about what you have given them: Manufacturing data on eleven of our products, marketing and sales data, that is promotional information on practically all of our products, and, as if that was not enough, you have even disclosed to them weaknesses and contestable points in our patents, allowing Ducopharma to challenge some of them in court, which they actually did."

"In other words, Bill, although all this is, I believe more than fifteen years back, you have betrayed and spied on this company, a company that gave you every opportunity and every recognition it was capable of. I must say, Bill, I find it very hard to accept all this. It sounds unreal. Your treachery reminds me of some stories we see in the movies and I admire you for having led a double life for so long."

Bill was listening intently, but his face did not betray any emotion.

"Now, if you wonder how come your implication in all this came to light, and I am sure you do, here is the explanation: after the accounting firm discovered all these incriminating documents they realized that the products in question were ours. So they quickly contacted Tim here and when they showed him the evidence, he immediately recognized your handwritten explanations as well as your give-away; "B.B." on some of them. Also, a number of notes bear the words: "Paid to B.B." But the real straw that broke the camel's back actually came from your own hand, Bill. When the accounting firm told Tim about this incredible discovery, they also asked for a piece of paper or anything your hands had touched. Tim gave it to them and they had it checked out by a fingerprint laboratory. Needless to say, all the papers you had slipped to Ducopharma bore your own fingerprints.

Tim and I met several times over the past few days to discuss what to do. Of course, I also spoke to the people in the U.S. who were shocked beyond words, especially in view of your impending promotion. I was advised to solve the problem as discreetly as possible.

Okay, Bill, I am very sorry and I mean it from the bottom of my heart. I am very sorry it had to come to this but before I go on, let me ask you: "What do you have to say to all this, Bill?"

Bill sat in his chair, slumped like a lifeless body. His face was ashen and pearls of sweat were on his forehead. He lowered his hand which kept reaching for his face and his head like in a nervous twitch, and after a few seconds, he said: "What do you want me to say, Joe? You did all the talking. There is nothing left for me to say. All this was a very long time ago and I had hoped it would remain buried, as they had promised me many times. I was wrong, obviously. I have nothing to say. Go ahead, finish your gory job."

"Well, here is what the company is proposing to you: You have two choices, Bill: You can fight your way through the courts and with the help of a smart lawyer, contest the charges. But in the end, the facts and the evidence will speak for themselves. You may end up with mud all over your face on the pages of newspapers plus fines and even jail for all sorts of illegalities. You know that juries are not too kind on cheating executives these days.

So that's option one. Option two is much simpler: You leave this office now, your secretary brings you your jacket and sends you all your personal belongings in a box in a day or two. So, you don't have to go back to your office now. The Company takes back everything, and I mean everything we gave you. The house and the boat in Palm Beach, the house here in Toronto, your golf club and other memberships. Your company pension is revoked, meaning that you just get back from the pension fund all you, yourself, paid in over the years, of course plus interest accrued. And we also repossess your company cars, both of them.

Bottom line, Bill, as far as this Company is concerned, you never existed."

These last words were spoken with emotion and sadness that fell over Joe's face like a shadow. He even turned away to avoid facing Bill, but then, after a few seconds, he said: "Oh by the way, two more things before I forget. All this has nothing to do with Jennifer; she is and remains a valuable and trusted officer of this Company. Unless she decides otherwise, she will continue in her functions and nothing concerning you will rub off on her. That's official.

The other thing is that I will immediately issue a Company memo announcing your unexpected departure for health reasons, no more, no less. If asked, we will say that you wanted to keep your health issue private. That's all I guess. Joe looked sideways at Tim who nodded somberly in approval.

Bill was still sitting in front of his cold, untouched coffee. His body was bent forward with both his hands framing his face. He slowly got up. Without saying a word to Joe and without even looking at him, he picked up the phone on the desk, dialed his secretary and said: "Linda, please bring my jacket to the comptroller's office."

A minute later he walked out of the room without looking at either Joe or Tim. He closed the door behind him and rapidly headed for the exit.

* * * * *

It is difficult to describe the scenes unfolding at the Benditch's house on that day and on the immediate aftermath. Jenny had been away on company business and only came home late in the evening from the airport. When she opened the door and walked into the living room, she found Bill stretched out on the sofa with a drink in his hand. He got up, briefly hugged Jenny and, without much ado, started to tell her exactly what had happened in the office only hours before.

While he talked, Jenny was listening with a gaping mouth and wide open eyes, slowly unfastening her jacket and kicking off her shoes. She kept saying: "No, I don't believe this. How come you never told me about Ducopharma? I don't believe this."

But when Bill had finished and she saw his shaking hand reaching for the drink, she jumped up and hugged Bill, repeatedly saying: "Oh, my God, how dreadful, how dreadful!"

She sat down next to Bill and said: "what are you going to do about it?" "What can I do?" he answered, "Nothing. I can't fight the charges. All this happened ages ago. I was sure it was long buried. Not only buried, but made to disappear. That's what they solemnly promised. Not a trace of evidence was to remain. They obviously lied to me."

"I am finished, Jenny", he added after a pause. "Finished for good." "No, you are not", she shot back, clutching the handkerchief with which she was wiping away her tears. "You are not finished, Bill", she repeated. You are not the first to whom a disaster like this has happened. You will remake your life, you hear me! Give it a little time. In the meantime, I have my job. Harry's tuition at the Renselaer Institute is paid up. You know what I thought? We have thirty days to leave this house, so we are going to move in with my parents for the time being, until we put our lives together again. Mom keeps complaining that the house is too big for them anyways. Let the company repossess everything."

* * * * *

There can be no doubt that this one hour in Tim's office had broken Bill. It was the most fateful day in his life and it had marked him. Although Jenny kept telling him when she left for work the next day that his was a temporary situation and he would soon find another career to sink his teeth in, he simply smiled coolly and said: "Yeah, sure", but he felt otherwise.

For some time Bill stayed at home, reading, and scanning the want ads in the business section of the major papers. He also spoke to some executive employment agencies. He refused to take any calls from company people who were inquiring about his health.

Eventually he started to answer, explaining that he had suffered a nervous breakdown and had left the company to recover at home or take a prolonged sabbatical.

One day he had a call from his ex-regional manager in Edmonton, a close friend and sincere confidant over the years. He could not avoid hiding the truth from him. His friend listened carefully and then he said: "Bill, I know what you are going through. Stop feeling sorry for yourself. Get out of your present environment or it will ruin you. Leave Toronto and come, at least for a little while, to Edmonton. Jenny will manage without you temporarily. Listen, a friend of mine here runs a successful business college. How about asking him if he can offer you a job as an instructor or teacher? You have an MBA, don't you? Do you want me to talk to him?" Bill thought it was a good idea and after a minute of hesitation, said: "Yes, please talk to the principal and let me know. Thanks."

Within a few days an interview was arranged. Bill flew to Edmonton and got the job. He was to lecture five days a week from two to three hours a day on subjects ranging from marketing strategies and sales management to administrative policies, all fields he felt very comfortable with.

Jenny agreed with Bill's decision. Her parting words to her husband were: "We will be in daily contact. You are right to leave Toronto, at least for now. Don't worry about me or anything else. I am staying with my parents. Take good care of yourself. Keep your head up, there will be better days, okay?"

Bill moved into a modest, but very nicely furnished one-bedroom apartment within walking distance of his school, all arranged by his Edmonton friend.

Thus began a new and a very different life for Bill Benditch. He soon adapted to the academic requirements of his job, read up on teaching skills and started delivering interesting and scientifically sound presentations to his class of aspiring business professionals.

After a few months he was even asked by the principal to also teach evening classes.

Bill talked to Jenny every day, sometimes for just a few minutes, sometimes longer, especially when they discussed Harry or other family matters. Jenny never ever spoke about her job or the Company. It was as if she lived in two completely separate worlds: that of her pharmaceutical career and that of her relationship with Bill. It was a strange dichotomy and one that would eventually prove to be both insurmountable and irreconcilable.

* * * * *

As the months went by, Bill settled into his new career and the new lifestyle that came with it. He created a small but lively social circle around him and had no difficulty in alternating busy days with equally stimulating evenings and weekends.

To be sure, all this was a far cry from the scintillating life in the fast lane he and Jenny had led in Toronto, but Bill accepted it philosophically. "There is a time for one and a time for the other in anyone's life", he kept telling himself.

* * * * *

Some five years had passed since Bill's move to Edmonton. Bill was now in his early sixties, but with his youthful gait and assertive demeanor, he actually did not look his age.

Over the years, his relationship with his two sons had, if anything, intensified. Ignoring and even avoiding any reference to his professional cataclysm and what led to it, the boys kept not only phoning him regularly but also visiting him, sometimes with their families to make sure that the ties were never in jeopardy. Once, when Bill developed pneumonia, Freddie's wife even came to stay with her father-in-law for a week to help in nursing him back to health. To the boys and their wives, as well as to the grandchildren that started to enrich the family, he was simply "Dad".

But Bill's relationship with Jenny was, alas, a very different story.

Within a year of the forceful distancing, Jenny's phone calls started to come intermittently and eventually were relegated to weekends, when she finally "found a moment to relax." To be sure, her business life was all-encompassing. There certainly was no other man in her life, simply because she was married to her job. Commensurate with her increasing responsibilities she grew into the ultimate and consummate corporate animal, the pride and joy of any company. Needless to say, that Bill had no place whatsoever in this world of hers and, because of his ominous past, he was even an encumbrance or an undesirable appendage.

A few years after their physical separation, Harry, during a visit to his dad, told him that Mom thought that a divorce, quietly and speedily consummated by lawyers would be the most logical conclusion of a union that lingered on in name only.

Bill realistically agreed and shortly afterwards the mailing address of William and Jennifer Benditch was a thing of the past. Finished and done with as if it had never been. Both sides went on with their separate lives without shedding any tears over it.

* * * * *

During the course of a telephone conversation, sometime later, Bill told Freddie that he was beginning to feel his age, that he was often too tired to go out for dinner, preferring to order meals from a nearby restaurant.

Freddie had the distinct impression that his dad was going through a depression. He called Harry and told him about it. "Let's go and visit him", suggested Harry and Freddie agreed.

They had not seen their father for some time and were surprised to find him visibly aged and tired-looking. They went out to a nearby restaurant for dinner and did not believe their eyes when they saw their dad polish off an entire bottle of red wine while leaving his steak and potatoes mostly untouched. They took him home, where they sat in the small living room, asking: "What's the matter, dad? You must get a hold of yourself. Stop drinking so much!"

After listening to the boy's concerned advice for awhile, Bill made some comments which he seemed to have harboured for some time in his mind. While looking at Freddie, he said: "Do you think it is right that I live here in Edmonton eking out a living, making do with a one-bedroom flat while your mother, lives in a beautiful home on the lakeshore with lots of money in the bank? Did ten years of marriage amount to nothing? Do you think this is right? He repeated to Freddie."

The two boys looked at him and said: "What do you mean, Dad?" "I mean that I should get together again with your mother. That we should live together again. I am not insisting on a second marriage, but I believe very strongly that she should share her good fortune with me. After all, I am the father of her son, am I not?"

The two boys looked at each other. Then Freddie said: "Dad, with all due respect I don't think this is a good idea. Don't you think you caused Mom enough heartbreak, I mean enough to last a lifetime. She has now found well-deserved peace and quiet. Leave her alone, Dad. You can't bring back the past, especially a very painful one as far as she, and I must admit as far as Harry and I are also concerned. Forget it. Besides, you are earning enough to make a decent living right now. Aren't you?"

It was clear that the idea of Liz sharing her money with him had been a dominant thought in his mind. In fact, the boys had the strong impression that their father believed that Liz's good fortune was in part due to him because of their former marriage. Both Harry and Freddie disliked their dad's persistent attitude, but when they left him to fly back to Toronto, Freddie promised to raise the issue in one way or another with his mother.

And this he did a few days later in a phone conversation. Omitting any reference to his father's claims on her money, Freddie merely mentioned his desire to make up and live with her again.

Liz did not even listen to the end of her son's story. She laughed at the idea and said: "Please tell your father that there is no place, none whatsoever for him in my life. This is a closed chapter and will stay that way until the day I die. He is out of my life and that's it. Let him ask Jennifer to take him back."

A few days later Freddie told his dad about this reaction, only to hear a defiant: "I don't believe this. My ex-wife living in luxury and I must eat humble pie. Where is the justice? I won't take this lying down, let me tell you."

After that conversation, Freddie dropped the subject, when talking with his mother and never referred to it, until it was brought up again a few months later under a different set of circumstances.

* * * * *

It was early December and Montreal had just experienced its first and unexpected snow storm. Howling winds dumped a thick blanket of snow all over the city and overnight temperatures dropped to record lows. The strong winds were especially prevalent on the lakeshore, along the river, where some roads had to be closed because icy conditions had rendered them unsafe for both pedestrians and vehicles. Sanding and salting crews were out all night opening up lanes.

Liz, unaware of the severity of the road conditions left her house in the morning to walk to a nearby grocery store for some needed items. Not realizing that under the snow there lay a thick sheet of ice, she slipped and fell, hitting the ground hard with the lower part of her body. It was a really bad fall because she could not get up. Luckily other passersby saw the accident and helped her to her feet. But she immediately felt a pain so strong that she could hardly breathe. An ambulance was summoned and she ended up in the emergency of the Lakeshore hospital, where she was promptly diagnosed with a broken femur. The surgeon affirmed that while it was not a complicated fracture, the operation would require the insertion of a pin and screws and that, furthermore, the healing process would be long and painful, especially as far as the physiotherapy was concerned.

Within hours of hearing the news, Freddie had rushed to his mother's bedside and he stayed with her until, three days after successful surgery, Liz was transferred to a rehabilitation center for exercise and nursing her back to health sufficiently for going home.

Everything went according to plan and some six weeks after the fall, Liz, now in a wheelchair rejoined the comfort of her home, albeit with a prolonged rehabilitation period ahead of her. Needless to say she was not alone in the house. In addition to her regular daily help, she also hired an assistant nurse to supervise her recovery.

Bill heard about the accident from Freddie the day after it happened. His immediate reaction was: "Oh, I'm sorry to hear that!"

But the news about Liz's accident started a chain of thoughts in Bill's ever active mind. For a few evenings and nights he began to mull over a number of scenarios of how he might take advantage of Liz's mishap to further his own plans.

After some days of thinking and without whispering a word about his intentions to his sons, he approached the principal of his school and asked for a transfer to Montreal. To his surprise he was told: "Well this is a coincidence! I received a message from our Montreal Branch yesterday inquiring whether we could spare not one but two teachers in Economics. They had an unexpected vacancy and are desperately trying to fill it. Are you sure you want to return to Montreal asked the principal. "Yes, Tom", replied Bill, "I am sure."

"Okay", was the answer. "Let me get back to them. It may take a few days before we re-arrange the schedules both here and in Montreal. I'll be in touch with you as soon as we are ready. Thanks, Bill!"

And so, about three weeks after this conversation in the principal's office, Bill Benditch was on his way to Montreal. While he boarded an Air Canada flight, his personal effects were being shipped in one single container. Since the Montreal branch of his school was in Dorval, not too far from the airport, he had rented a small flat nearby in a new apartment building overlooking the waterfront. He liked it and immediately went about the task of settling in.

About a week had passed since his arrival. His belongings had been delivered and placed in the two rooms which now looked cozy and quite attractive. Taking advantage of a day off he drove a few kilometers up the lakeshore to an address he had obtained through the telephone directory. He knocked at the door which was opened by a young woman to whom he said: Can I speak to the lady of the house?"

He had hardly finished the sentence when a wheelchair came rolling towards the door and a voice shouted: "Who is it Peggy?" By the time she swung around, Bill and Liz were facing each other. Liz was sitting in the wheelchair, with curlers in her hair, holding a cup of coffee in her hand.

Sensing an impending conversation between the two, the young housemaid was about to leave the scene and said to Liz: "Please call me if you need me."

"No, no", Liz shot back, "Please don't go, stay right here. Then she turned to Bill, who was still standing inside the house with his back to the closed door. Liz's eyes were wide open in disbelief.

"Why did you come here?" She said. "I thought you are living in Edmonton."

"I was", Bill said, "But I just moved to Montreal to teach at our Dorval faculty."

Without letting him go on, Liz said with a firm voice "Look, I know you had some kind of reconciliation in mind but I think I made it clear to Freddie that I am not interested. Not at all, Bill. I just want to be left alone and I don't need any company. I just want to get my health back and go on with my life. Starting or resuming a relationship is the last thing on my mind. Sorry Bill, but you are no longer part of my life and that's okay with me."

As she said these words, she saw Bill slowly turning around and heading to the door in preparation of leaving the house. He had not said a word since she had started talking to him.

"Look", she said, I don't mean to be rude, but I don't want you to come back to this house. If it's alright with Freddie, I don't mind going for a cup of coffee or a sandwich with Freddie and yourself next time he is in Montreal. I just don't want him to think that his parents hate each other. At this point in time, there is no hatred left in me. I'm just indifferent and devoid of any feelings towards you, if you know what I mean."

"I do", said Bill and left the house.

Liz fully recovered from her accident and met together with Freddie and Bill some two or three times a year around Christmas or on Freddie's birthday. They met in coffee shops or bistros and much of the attention circled around Freddie who sometimes brought his family along. In all these sporadic encounters there was not a trace of intimacy between Bill and Liz. In fact, they completely avoided direct repartee on private matters.

* * * * *

One evening while Liz was sitting down for dinner in her home the phone rang. It was Freddie who told his mother that he had just been informed that his dad had been taken to the hospital after a sudden heart attack. Liz had hardly time to go back to the dinner table when Freddie phoned again with the sad news that Bill had just passed away while in the emergency room. Freddie added that he and Harry were taking the next flight to Montreal in order to take care of the funeral arrangements.

* * * * *

Bill's funeral in Montreal provided the most eloquent testimonial to his life. It was a simple and dignified event observed in the presence of a handful of people. But what was significant beyond what words, either spoken or written could convey, was the actual attendance at the ceremony.

Not a single colleague from his one-time employers, the pharmaceutical company that he had worked for and later managed for some fifteen years, was present. Not even a token delegate or a representative.

Neither was his second wife, Jennifer, who let it be known, through her son Harry, that she was down with a severe case of the flu and that her doctor had ordered her to avoid the trip to Montreal by all means. She sent a large wreath instead bearing the clichéd words "In Loving Memory, Jennifer."

Liz sat right in front of the half dozen mourners. She wore black and occasionally wiped a tear from her eyes. There was no trace of emotion or pain discernable in her frequent bits of conversation with Freddie, who, throughout the funeral, sat by her side, sometimes holding her hand.

Perhaps the only touch of affection during the service was expressed by Freddie, who, following the priest's traditional words and prayers accompanying the departed's journey into eternity, rose from the pew to deliver a brief eulogy that was as sincere as it was touching.

He briefly alluded to his father's often tumultuous journey through life, emphasized his business acumen and his inclination for savouring success with passion as if there was no tomorrow, which may well have been a premonition that all good things have to come to an end; sometimes even to an unexpected and tragic one.

Concluding his brief outline, Freddie said: "There can be no doubt that during his productive years, dad partook of life with both hands. He took as much as he could, alas often without realizing the need of also giving."

But what really made Freddie's oration an emotional farewell rather than a biographical sketch was his affirmation in unison with his half-brother Harry that they both always loved their father, no matter what. That theirs was not to sit in judgment over him nor to separate his virtues from his trespasses.

They loved him because he was their father, who together with their respective mothers had given them life. That is why they stood by him throughout his difficult times, when the rest of the world had practically written him off.

Freddie's last words were delivered slowly and with measured emphasis:

"The long journey is over, Dad. Harry and I will never forget you. We cannot.

For you have left us with a legacy only those who were made to pay for their mistakes can leave to their children It is our legacy of why and how not to follow in your path. The very path that ultimately denied you the peace and the happiness all men aspire and are entitled to after a long and arduous life such as yours.

For this legacy, we thank you. Rest in Peace, Dad.

Made in the USA
Middletown, DE
01 April 2019